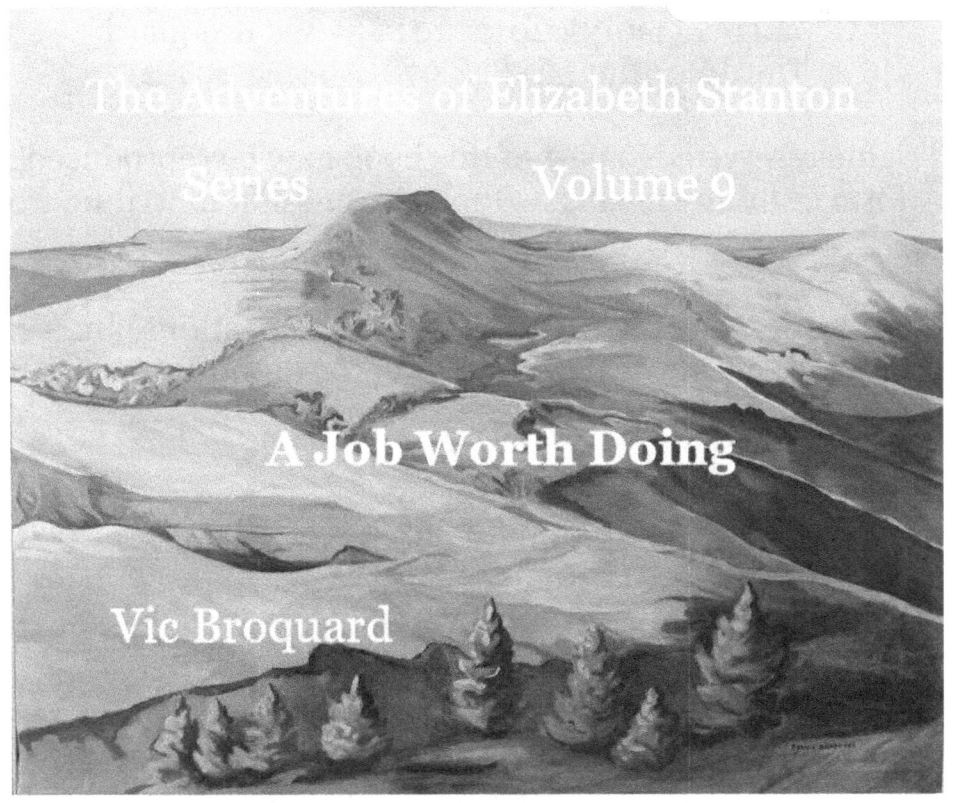

The Adventures of Elizabeth Stanton
Series Volume 9

A Job Worth Doing

Vic Broquard

Published by:
Broquard eBooks
http://Broquard-eBooks.com
author@Broquard-eBooks.com
103 Timberlane
East Peoria, IL 61611

Artwork by Crooked Willow Studios

For Morgan and L. Ron Hubbard

Table of Contents

Chapter 1 What Is Going On?

I was taking a rest, a timeout from the game, the game of life, of being a human being. Well, being a human being — that isn't exactly true, not for a long time now. You see, I am an immortal being, who chose to occupy one of these frail human bodies. Sometime ago, I discovered who I really am, what I've been, what I've done, at least during my century plus here on Tarra.

I've had a number of bodies now, been places, and done some amazing things to help all mankind. From the initial discovery that Tarra is a penal colony run by two different alien species, I had a hand in the elimination of our guards and the opening of our prison gates. Okay, this is figurative, as the prison is merely being convinced that you are a body and not a spiritual being.

With the help of Jes Amir, the Guardian, we have been slowly freeing spiritual beings from their total and utter dependencies on fleshly bodies, regaining their spiritual freedom. A big factor in this was the discovery that when one suffered a physical trauma, that pain and all that was said around the unconscious person was recorded in their mind. Later, those images of trauma and the words said at that time often dictated a person's reactions and conduct in the present. I have seen this happening repeatedly. When a person was given our therapy, he or she somehow could re-experience it again and thus the trauma and its effects vanished, leaving the person more able than before. I've noted that often it is the person's own conclusions and decisions made under the duress and confusion in the past that is, in the present, limiting their abilities.

However, my last two bodies have given me a rough time; both were armless. With the first one, the alien mantis creatures ate them, and with the second, my parents had them removed at birth to satisfy some ancient prophecy that would make me Empress of Demokritos. Later, because of complications in childbirth, it died, leaving me separated once again from the man I deeply loved, Renzo.

Exhausted and tired, I decided not to immediately go get another baby body. Instead, I took a time out from the game of life with human bodies. I floated up to the Paese di Dio, God's Highway, a high, green plain separating the Eight Sea Princes and the impassable mountain range known as the Appian Way. This long, but narrow, grass strewn high country, largely uninhabited except for an occasional shepherd, I always found inspirational. Just now, I needed some spirituality — a respite if you please. Here I simply lay down and basked in the high altitude sun and snow and sun and snow. I found peace. That was the year of 703.

Ah, here you are, Bethany. Oh, darn. Okay, Bethany, I want you to go to the very beginning of the trauma. Yes, right there. Now let's go through what happened and you can tell me about it.

A voice. Where is that voice coming from? I wondered. *Oh — I see a picture now. Yes, there is a mother, late teens perhaps; she's giving birth. Oh — she has no arms — funny. Oh, that's my body there! Pain! It hurts so. My waist — too small, it hurts. Push, someone says. I'm trying, I say. Pain. So tired, I'm so tired, so heavy. My body is so heavy. I just wanted to have fun and enjoy Renzo. Someone says that it's a girl. I am so tired. Sleeping.*

Someone says to me, 'I have opened an account under the name of Elizabeth Stanton. You can go to any World Bank in the world and ask to withdraw funds from your account. They will ask for your secret password. I chose Linda Chaucer for you. For example, in say sixteen years you want a thousand for traveling expenses. You go to one of our banks and give them the name of the account, Elizabeth Stanton. They will ask you for your secret password, you say Linda Chaucer. They will then give you the thousand.' After the voice finished, it is all peaceful and quiet here.

Very good, Bethany. Now, let's go through the trauma once more.

I did so a number of times and finally woke up. *I can feel the warm sun; see the beautiful, lush green grass, the cool air. I love this place. Oh, I recognized the other being that is here with me; it was my dear friend Linda. Hi, Linda. Thanks, I needed that. I feel loads better. I was so tired. Just sleeping it off up here.*

I know, sleeping for over twenty-five years, Bethany!

What? That's not possible! I just came up here to relax and get a little peace — you know, take a breather. It can't be that long!

It has. It's 728. We have all been terribly busy, keeping up with the rapid changes in our world. I am truly sorry that I rather forgot about you for a time, Bethany. None of us intended to let you sleep for so long. Please forgive me.

Sure, I honestly think that I needed that break. Things were so intense for so many lifetimes in a row. How's the world doing? How's the Guardian doing on freeing beings? Honestly, I think I need a total update on things.

Velona has become the renaissance country of the world! So many new inventions, such architecture, art, and literature. Amazing indeed. Linda chatted with me for quite some time, before she finally got to the present situation.

Bethany, something awful has come up recently. We may have missed a huge colony of the mantis creatures!

Damn! Not again! Visions of those nasty fifty-foot long, overgrown, praying mantis insects chewing off my arms reformed in my mind. *Where? How?*

Our mistake — well mostly mine, Bethany. I really thought that we had gotten them all. After all, they ate off my arms too. I guess I need to

2

begin at the beginning, around 704. We lost the Shining Star. She was returning from Gremen, Annelise and had to dodge a hurricane. She ended up blown way east of our dog bone continent. To their surprise, they sighted an unknown giant island, we now believe. Sightings estimate that it is two hundred miles long and one hundred across its middle, rather like a link of sausage.

The inhabitants, who we estimate to number at least a million, call their land Dorota, meaning Gift of God. We believe that somehow they acquired the Shining Star and from the many navigation maps on board, discovered the rest of us on Tarra. They are an industrious people and, as far as we are able to tell, technologically a bit more advanced than we are, if you can believe that. Anyway, they've apparently copied the Shining Star and set off on their own voyage of discovery. Their ships have landed in Demokritos, Megalos, Zargarb, and Velona, establishing small "colonies" of their people in our lands. Over the years, their colonies have grown considerably.

However, they refuse to allow us to visit much of Dorota, only a couple of southern coastal cities, Bozydar, Donat, and Piotr, and then mostly to resupply our ships. The few times our men have been allowed on shore in these cities, they were always accompanied by a number of armed escorts. They have developed a hand-held cannon, which they call a gun. It shoots a lead ball at a high velocity, quite deadly, I'm told.

Bethany, what is frightening is that every one of their females, older women, young women, even babies, has no arms at all. One of our Healers got a look at one and says that it looks like a clean socket amputation, but remarkably well done. Do you realize that here is a civilization with probably a half million women who are mutilated? No one has ever seen a Dorota woman who had arms!

Sure sounds like we are dealing with a whole lot of mantis creatures! How could we have missed finding so darn many of them? I asked.

Scary isn't it! Anyway, from all that we have managed to learn to date, it seems that these people are definitely more advanced than all our countries, except perhaps Velona. Their healers are called doktors, and honestly, they are every bit as good as our Healers, perhaps better. They've shared a little of their knowledge with a few of our male Healers, but they will not even look at any of our women who have arms!

They claim, and we have verified this as much as possible, that their land is crime free, that everyone lives in peace and harmony, especially between the sexes. There is no rape, no brutality, discounting the fact that their women haven't any arms. There is no hunger or disease to speak of, according to those we have talked to — always their male representatives. From what we have seen, their men love and respect their women and assist them in all possible ways. We had a look inside some of their buildings. *The whole layout was designed around a woman making do with just using her legs. Their chairs are slanted, their sinks, counter tops, and stoves are all built low to the ground, so that she can sit laid back on the chair and use her feet to do the cooking and so on. All doors have a low sliding bar for a latch. There isn't a doorknob to be seen on any buildings that our people have seen. It's as if their men have built their entire physical structures around the concept of making it possible for their women to flourish using only their feet. It gets stranger, Bethany, far more insidious.*

Yes, on the surface, it sounds like utopia. All of their children go to school from age five through sixteen. Once our representative, male of course, visited one of their public schools. The girls all had slanted seats and desk tops that were only a few inches off the ground, while the boys had what we would consider a proper desk. They all were doing arithmetic problems when our man visited. They learn to read and write and do arithmetic. They also study their history, their religion, and what they call engineering. Bethany, these people are educated tremendously well by our standards!

Their homes have running water and toilets, similar in design to those that Enyo invented in Velona so long ago. In the larger cities, all houses have hot running water and baths! In the smaller towns and villages, public bathhouses predominate, though their representatives tell us that one of their current projects is to bring hot running water to all homes that do not have it now. Admittedly, in the cities that we were able to visit, all the homes looked absolutely identical: stone construction, one story, with glass windows, often with lines of flowers in front — like they all were made from the same mold. Architectural design must not be one of their fortes.

So what you are telling me is that, if it weren't for their women's condition, Dorota would be an ideal country? I asked. If Linda would have had a human body, she would have smiled; and, if I would have had one as well, I would have seen her smile. She continued to telepathically explain the situation.

You got it. Amazingly advanced in many areas. I especially like the fact that there is no crime anywhere on Dorota, not even pickpockets! These people are intensely, fanatically religious. They worship the one God, and everyone has their own copy of the <u>Word of God</u>, or <u>Boga</u>, as they call it — something like a bible of their beliefs. We've gotten a copy; they are more than willing to give us all the copies we want. It took a year to get it translated into Velonese. I've read it. Many of its tenets are excellent rules by which to live.

For example, 'Never take that which does not belong to you.' 'Treat all women with respect and kindness, for they are God's Holy Vessel.' 'Work hard, that the Lord may deem you worthy of entry into Heaven.'

'Shun avarice, lasciviousness, slothfulness, and gluttony, for these are the path of the forsaken.'

Well, Linda, so far, this sounds more than acceptable. Perhaps this is why they are apparently doing so well for themselves, I replied, wondering what lay beneath this seemingly perfect surface.

It goes on to explain that men and women's bodies are different, that God took the arms from the woman and formed them into extra ribs for man, so that the man would be stronger and more able to take care of the woman, who was given the breath of God, his Holy Vessel, the creator of new life. Bethany, they believe in this falsehood utterly! It certainly gives them an explanation for their lack of arms, anyway.

What makes these people so insidious is that they spread their message to others. Apparently, there are two types of religious leaders, the bisklep and the Elders. The bisklep, roughly our word for a bishop as near as I can translate, run their normal religious services. They all meet in prayer once a week under the leadership of the bisklep. Here comes the insidious part, their Elders — starszy is their name, which translates to Elders — also preach but deal with the conversions of others to their religion.

On Dorota, an Elder preaches to each kosiko, or church I think, on Sundays. These men have been the ones primarily coming to our part of the world. Bethany, these men have some kind of incredible persuasion powers, the like of which I have never seen on Tarra before! We've heard the passionate, fiery sermons delivered by the Church of Jehosanity, but these Elders are vastly different! They talk in a peculiar way, some say hypnotic. I've seen a whole congregation listen for over an hour to one of these Elders. When he finished, nearly every man and woman wanted to convert to their religion and join his flock! They call their religion Bog. I've seen a hundred men and women beg and plead to become Boggians!

We've spied on what happens after one of their conversion services. Those who wish to become Boggians are asked to sell their homes and move into the ever-expanding Dorota section of that town or city. They have a number of their doktors with them and, while the men and boys are handling the selling of their homes and moving into that new private section of town, their wives, women, and female children are taken into that sector and have their arms amputated! I've seen this happen repeatedly! It is frightening, Bethany. They've even converted dozens of our own Santi women, who were curious about this new religion and went to hear the Elders speak! The control that these men have over normal folks is wild!

They now have numerous conclaves established in Demokritos, Megalos, Zargarb, and Velona. It gets worse. Their views and those of the Church of Jehosanity are similar in many key ways. You know how the Church of Jehosanity sponsors the Holy Eight Degrees and preaches it as the right thing to do. I believe that their Pope is now embracing Bogism wholeheartedly, seeing it as a way to gain total control over their people. The Church is welcoming those from Dorota warmly, sponsoring them, aiding them, and supporting them. They allow them to preach to potential converts in their own churches.

This Bogism is spreading like a virus! The only thing that slows them down is the time delay needed to absorb the next batch of converts. It takes their women many weeks to heal and their men at least that long to prepare new suitable living arrangements. I swear that the converts are in some kind of deep hypnotic trance after the Elder is finished with them. No woman in her right mind would voluntarily have her arms cut off! It's as if these Elders are leading the lambs to slaughter! We have been unable to stop them or slow them down. The only limiting factor is their limited number of Elders and doktors.

Worse, none of these men from Dorota will even associate, speak with, listen to, or pay the slightest attention to a woman with arms. Some call her unholy or unclean or sinner or wicked harlot behind her back. They won't even eat food prepared by a woman with arms! It's like a total sacrilege for them even to acknowledge their existence! It's the wildest thing you have ever seen.

Relatives of some who have converted have visited with the converts, who uniformly say that their lives are now holy and so much better than before they converted. They unilaterally urge their relatives to also convert and find peace and a better life.

I will say this: we have not yet seen any of the mantis creatures in Velona, Zargarb, or Demokritos. Yet, they may well be hiding behind the scenes. I have every available person out looking for them. Unfortunately, we know next to nothing about what's really going on in Dorota. They've only shown us a couple of port cities and then only what they wanted us to see. We desperately need to get someone on the inside of Dorota. Are there mantis creatures lurking out of sight behind all this? If so, where and how many are there? What are the mantis objectives? This sort of information we must have. If the mantises are not behind it, and I find it hard to believe that they are not, then who is? How are these Elders able to hypnotize a whole congregation of people into doing this butchery? We must have data so that we can find a way to counter this religious invasion. Honestly, if we don't, twenty-five years from now, all the women on Tarra will be under their insidious control.

What do you want me to do? I asked.

I hate to ask this of you, Bethany, but can you go to Dorota and pick up a female baby body? Observe, spy, and find out all that you can so that we can fight against this subjugation. You have been through such situations before and you are better able to deal with being armless than just about anyone I know. I hate to ask you to do this, but I've little choice.

6

Who will be my outside contact? I needed to know.

I will. Contact me at any time. Will you do it for all of us?

Sure. If I don't, it seems that I'll end up armless along with the rest of the women on Tarra. God, this is crazy. How did we miss so many mantis creatures anyway? Two of them were bad enough, but a million people? Well, I reserve the right to kill any that I come across! My anger swelled. I think I detest the mantis creatures more than I do the Grey Giants.

You don't need my permission to do it! Just be careful. We need information, but I also realize that it is going to take you several years to get the new body old enough to find out much. I'll keep you posted. Thank you, Bethany! They are adding about a hundred new converts every six weeks, there are at least ten of these Elders in operation. More may be coming, I just don't know. Currently, they are converting about nine thousand people per year; about half are women. It really is becoming quite serious. I fear that more of these conversion teams will arrive, increasing their rate of conversions.

Gosh, that is more women to handle and help rehabilitate than we ever had before and all at one time too, I replied aghast. *Are we equipped to deal with so many women in dire need?*

Not even remotely, so many of us who could have helped have now lost their bodies. We are down to a skeleton crew. The Laird Foundation can handle maybe a hundred, but no more. We estimate that there are over a thousand women and girls in Velona alone now in this cult. Even if we stopped them cold this instant, there's no way we could assist that many.

But Linda, if I take a new baby body, it may well be another eighteen years before I finish.

I know of no other way. I will give them this much credit: already they have setup a school for all their children here in Velona. Honestly, if the true situation was just as they and I have pictured and this singular mutilation the only down side, it is hard to argue against it. No crime, dignity and respect, education, prospering — all are worthy objectives in any society. Personally, I just don't believe it. There must be something else going on that is not being said. Bethany, you have to find out what that is so that we can educate all peoples.

Okay, I will do my best. You say there are seven larger cities? Any idea which one I should try?

Bazyli, in the west central highlands, is our best guess. Evidently, there is some Elder training school there, which is not found in any other city. That's the best I can do. All the Elders that we have seen are tall, thin, and have commanding, piercing eyes. That's not much to go on, I realize. Again, she would have grinned had she a body.

Okay, show me the way to Bazyli and I'll have at it. I followed her as she repositioned herself over a large city with red tile roofs and dark brown stone buildings. She and I said our farewells and I began to float over the city filled with people, looking for very pregnant women. I had a sinking feeling, however. As I recalled heading for my last body in Annelise, which we all knew would be armless, I had two very dear friends going there with me. They were my constant companions that lifetime, assisting me with so many things. Now, I was going right back into the same pickle, but without two others who would be there with me and be my arms when I needed them. Yes, I felt very apprehensive about this spy mission, but then below me were something like a half million women who would be the same way. Surely if they could get by, somehow so could I. Still that many mutilated women was staggering to contemplate. How could men do this to women? Whatever possessed their minds to believe this was justifiable? Religion be damned. It was not right. Somehow, someway, I had to put an end to it.

After a week of scouting, I discovered three pregnant women who lived next door to each other. I sensed that one was a male child to be. What I found keenly interesting was that its father-to-be was in fact one of these Elders! I had a gut feeling, an intuition if you please, that his yet to be born son would follow his father's example. I chose one of the other two families living next to the Elder. Specifically, I chose the family which already had three children, figuring that, with two older brothers around to help me out, that would be better than the single brother in the other family.

I hung around for a short while before she gave birth and then took over the new little girl's baby body right after it was born. However, I used a bit of my spiritual abilities, forcing them to name their new baby girl Bethany — they were going to call her Betany, so it was not a huge change that I forced upon them. My new body was born in June of 727. Not long after that, Dita was born next door, and two days later, Albin came into the world, the future Elder, I hoped.

"Oh, Holy Tekla, she is a beautiful little girl," the doktor exclaimed.

"Can I see her, Janek?" my new mother asked; she was lying in bed, my father at her side.

"Not for a few hours. I must take her to be cleaned, blessed, and christened as little Bethany Brozena. You will have her to suckle in twelve hours or less. I will make this a rush ceremony, my beautiful Holy Vessel." He gave her a kiss on her forehead. "You concentrate on getting yourself purified and ready to nurse your new daughter." I was bundled up by the doktor and he carried me outside. It was dark.

All I could think of was "Where is the mantis creature that will eat my arms off?" If nothing else, I could at least tell Linda and the others just where the creature or creatures were located. A brightly illuminated room appeared when he unwrapped me. I was washed in a warm bath, which I will say I enjoyed and then given something to drink. A bit later, darkness fell. It took me a minute to realize that my new body's eyes were shut; it was anesthetized! I sensed the doktor was performing surgery on my tiny body, though I didn't feel anything right now. I looked in vain for one of the mantis creatures. I could see none, and he made no reference to anything remotely like said creatures. As I drifted off to sleep after he finished up, I decided that perhaps there were no actual mantis creatures around here, but that their influence upon this society had occurred in their distant past.

Chapter 2 Early Childhood Observations

I was five, the year 732. I had long, thick blonde hair, longer than the usual girl's styles, but I had promised to brush it out myself and was allowed this small wish. My eyes were blue, and I liked my little face; perhaps it would one day be pretty. My skin, like all the others here, was a light brown. Our everyday dresses were simple. We girls picked out our own colors. I chose yellow. Made of light cotton, these everyday dresses were more like a slip on top, rather like a feed sack with a head hole at one end, but below the waist, it flared outward and was pleated. I say simple dress, by that I mean one that we could manage to put on ourselves. I wore no panties, which made potty training much easier for us girls to manage. Our shoes were simple slip-ons so that at any time we could use our toes.

My older sister, Aniela, wore her dark brown hair short, barely touching her shoulders. "Why does Bethany want such long hair, mommy?" she asked; we were waiting on our breakfast. It was summer vacation for her. I looked forward to entering school in the fall. "It's so hot on our necks, and it's always getting in her way."

"I don't know, Aniela. It is not very practical. I have told her a hundred times. I guess you have to ask her." Mom was busy trying to get our porridge ready on the kitchen stove.

"Cause I like it really long and it feels good. I can feel my back this way," I replied, watching how mom managed. Really, it was interesting how dad had constructed our home. Everything in the kitchen was built low to the ground. Mom sat in a sloped back chair, and everything she needed was at foot level height: the counter top, the stove, the cupboards, and the sink. True, some supplies were stored in high shelves. If she needed anything from these, dad or one of my brothers would have to get it down for her. Iwan was ten and Dawid, eight. Both wore light shirts and pants. They also had fancy socks and boots with shoelaces.

Mom's sloped chair had a swivel in it, and I loved to swing around in circles on it when she was out of the kitchen. It also had rollers so that she could move around the long kitchen workspace easily without having to get up and move the chair. "Okay, breakfast is ready. Will one of you boys carry the pot to the table and the other tell dad that breakfast is ready? Oh, don't forget the bread loaf and knife." Carrying the heavy pot from the stove to the table would be a daunting challenge, and thus the men handled it for her.

"I got it mom. Dawid, you go get dad." My oldest brother proudly carried the heavy pot to the table and went back for the rest. Dad entered, dressed in his storekeeper clothes: nice pants, colorful stripped shirt, and of course heavy work boots. Dad ran a hardware store called Brozena's Supplies. Dad, too, had blonde hair, just like me — well they would say it the other way around. He was tall and thin, but always had a cheerful smile.

"Hello my little Holy Angels," he exclaimed, giving Aniela and me a hug and kiss on our foreheads. "Hi boys. You look lovely this morning, Tekla." He gave her a kiss on the lips, but we all knew that was coming and so were able to look away. Iwan gave a yucky look towards me, and I suppressed a giggle.

Dad sat at the head of the table. Mom sat to his right. We girls and boys were interspersed by design so that the boys could help us girls should we need it. Of course, our chairs were also sloped back and sat much taller than the boy's and dad's did; this way our feet could reach the table. Dad said, "Okay. Let's bow our heads and give thanks. Dear Lord Above, we give thanks for this bountiful food that we are about to eat. We give thanks to your Holy Vessel, Tekla, that she was able to prepare this for us. Bless our family that we find the strength to be strong and true to you, our God, that we may be worthy of your grace. Amen." He dipped out porridge into mom's bowl and then his. He passed the pot on to Iwan who filled Aniela's bowl and then his. He handed it on down to Dawid, who filled mine and then his. I found it refreshing that neither brother protested helping us in any way. The rules of the game of life here were vastly different from what I was used to elsewhere on Tarra.

My spoon was slightly out of my reach; Dawid saw that it was and pushed it closer to me. I didn't even have to ask him. Amazing. He even cut me a large slice of the bread that mom baked yesterday without my asking him. He poured my special mug full of milk before pouring his. Dad noticed this and said, "Well done, Dawid." He smiled, noticing that he was beginning to live up to his responsibilities as a male in the house. My mug, as were all women's mugs, made with a long narrow loop handle such that we could get our feet through it and thereby hold it up to drink.

"Iwan, you are now ten — old enough to come and lend me a hand at the store," dad announced.

"Yippee! Great!" Iwan was hoping to get the chance to help in the store. He was looking forward to earning a little spending money this summer. Besides, it meant that he was getting more responsibility and would not have to stay around the house, helping mom out. A bit later, strutting like a turkey, proud Iwan followed dad out the door. Dad first gave us all a kiss, though. I sensed that he truly loved all of us, a very good sign. After all, we females needed all the kindness we could get. "Dawid, you clear the table for mom. See you at suppertime. Bye all."

Dawid grumbled slightly. He wanted to go too, but knew that he was too young yet. Mom said, "Give yourself two more years, son, and dad will take you as well." He smiled. "Just carry the heavy pot to the counter by the sink. The girls and I can manage the rest. Why don't you go outside and play with your friends."

"Really mom! Okay! We are going to play bat ball today. Renard has a new bat for us to try out. We'll be at the park!" He was out the door in a flash, not gambling that mom would find something else for him to do.

"Mom, I want to play bat ball too," I said. I had watched them play last year. It looked like fun. One boy tossed the ball to a member of the other team who used a bat to try to hit it and run around the bases. Of course, the other players would try to catch it and tag him while he ran.

"Bethany, you know that to play bat ball you have to have arms. Bat ball is a boy's game not a girl's game. You should be content with playing soccer with your girlfriends. Now come on, let's get all these dirty dishes to the sink. You two can help me wash, dry, and put them away before you go out to play."

I disliked this chore the most. We would have to pick up the items with our teeth in order to carry them over to the sink. Mom sat in her chair, took them from us with her feet, and put them into the warm waters to soak. She insisted on doing the washing, however. Carrying things to her one item at a time in our teeth was neither fun nor efficient, but Aniela and I had little choice. By the time that we handed her the last fork, she had the others already washed and sitting in the rinse water next to the washing sink basin. Now we two pushed our chairs over beside the counter, grabbed a dish towel with our teeth, and plopped down. Slowly, using our feet and the towel, we began to dry them. At least mom put the dry dishes away for us.

At last, she told us to put on our shoes and go play, but to come back at noon for lunch. We two dashed off; once outside, we ran next door to where the Malina's lived. Renard had already gone off with Dawid, but my good friend Dita, who was my age, was sitting on her steps waiting for us. Dita had long, thick, black hair, coal black eyes, and thick lips. She took after me and insisted on wearing her hair long as well, though mine was still longer than hers was. She wore a blue dress, similar to Aniela. I had a strong bond with Dita, but had not figured out just what it was all about.

"Hi Bethany, Aniela," Dita called out, getting up to join us. "Going to the park?"

"You bet!" I replied. "We should see if Kazia wants to come too."

"I saw Dawid and Renard get Albin. They were carrying a new bat and Albin's ball. I sure wish I could play bat ball too," Dita replied. "Somehow, I think that I should be playing too, though like this I sure don't know how." She shrugged her shoulders. I told her that I wanted to play too, but couldn't either. We three walked next door and knocked on the door.

Soon, Kazia appeared. She wore a pink dress and had short brown hair with matching eyes. Of the three of us, she was definitely the prettiest. "Going to the park?" she asked. We were off. My family lived at Number 42 on 24th Street West by 16th Street South. In Bazyli, all the streets were numbered except two. Main Street divided the town roughly in half and ran north-south. Cross Street ran east-west further dividing the city in quarters. From their intersection, the streets were numbered. Thus, it was very easy not only to give directions, but also one could not get lost. Mom had made us memorize our address before she let us go out of the house on our own.

The city boasted numerous parks in which we children could play. Our park was two streets over and two up. A couple of minutes later and we entered a park that occupied an entire city block. The boy's bat ball area was at the far end. Dita and I stood there a moment envying the boys who were already playing.

Every aspect of the park was divided up into boy's things and girl's things. For the benefit of the littlest children, all the boy's things were painted blue, while the girl's things were pink. "Let's go swinging first," Kazia suggested. The boy's swings looked far more inviting. Indeed, one boy was swinging up very high into the air. However, without arms to hold onto the chains, we girls couldn't possibly use them. We had to use the sets made for us — essentially a bench hanging from a V-shaped framework. Dita and I found this boring. We both craved action. Soon, she and I moved over to the teeter totters. While they were painted blue, we ignored that and struggled a bit to get on them. At last, we began going up and down. It was a bit precarious being up so high without any hands to hang on. I think that's what appealed to her and me. At least today, the boys didn't kick us off the teeter totter.

A bit later, a number of other young girls came, and we finally had enough for a soccer game. We raced around our field and had fun; it taught us how to keep our balance well. Falling without hands to catch yourself is not fun, neither is the struggle to get back up. After an hour, we were very hot and the game ended. With our long hair — ours were many times longer than any of the other girls here — our necks and upper backs were broiling. She and I walked over to the tall oak trees and sat down to cool off.

"I love to play games, Dita. I can remember a long time ago that I used to play the greatest of games. He taught it to me; we'd kick this ball against a wall which had two lines on it." I drew a sketch in the dirt. "It was a fair ball only if it hit the wall between those two lines. The other person then had to race to the ball and kick it back before it bounced twice. That was challenging and a whole lot of fun."

Dita looked at me with a shocked look on her face. "I remember that too. I used to play with the greatest woman in the world. Oh my god, you are her, Bethany. Now I remember. I am Renzo!"

"Oh wow! You were him, my husband! Oh how I missed you." We both had floods of very personal memories going through our minds.

"Now I remember! Gosh, how one forgets things in a past life in just five years of this new one! My body was getting old, and when Linda told me that she had found you and sent you off on this mission alone, I kicked off that old body and came too. Didn't tell Linda though. Er, I rather forgot about all that until now — probably because I have a girl's body, not the boy's body that I am used to. I have to learn such strange things. No wonder

I had such a hard time getting potty trained." We laughed at that observation.

"I am so glad that you came. Now I have someone I can talk to and rely upon. Thank you, Renzo, er, I mean Dita. Gosh, it's suddenly so hard to think of you as Dita."

"Same here. It seems weird to me. Ah well, we must learn to adapt, though I think I am going to need much help. Things are so very different here, aren't they?"

"Indeed they are. Oops, we had better not talk too adult like; here comes Aniela."

"I think we should head home for lunch, Bethany. The boys have already left," she said. We got up and headed back home for something to eat. If you want a challenge sometime, try picking up a sandwich with your feet and eating it. Dawid was done and gone long before Aniela and I had ours eaten.

A while later back at the park, the boys decided it was time that they played with us. After all, their fathers would chastise them if they did not play at least one game with us during the day. That was a hard and fast rule. "You girls up for a game of team kick ball?" Renard asked. We were.

Albin and Renard decided that they would be the two captains. Albin insisted that he had Dita and me on his team. He always did, ever since he discovered that we two were the best kick ball players around. To compensate, Renard insisted that he have three extra players, including Aniela. Albin always agreed, as long as he had at least us two on his team.

Today, as we stood there as his first picks, Albin complimented us, something he had never done before. "You two are the greatest girls around here. Thanks for always being on my team." Now for the first time, I knew that I had his attention, his interest. I needed that, because if he were to become an Elder, I was going to need to talk a whole lot with him about it, somehow. If he respected me from childhood on up, I stood a better chance. Of course, we won the game; we always did, but not by much.

That night after supper, while we girls were helping mom with the dishes, I asked her, "How come girls don't have arms and boys do? Things are so much harder for us and so easy for them."

"Don't think of it that way, dear. The Lord Above when he created man and woman saw that one had to be strong and powerful to protect the family. Thus, he wisely took away our arms and formed them into more ribs for the men so that they would be much stronger and more powerful so they can better protect us. We are very special in God's eyes. We are his Holy Vessels; we bring new life, new babies, into the world. Men cannot ever do that, not ever. Only we women can do that. You see, we women are very, very special indeed. Without us, the whole race would die off, as there would be no new children born."

"You see, Bethany, men do things in the men's way; they never do things in we women's way. We women always do things in our own women's way, never in the men's way. You can never get confused about how a thing is done. You see, it's not harder to do something our way, rather it is just different. Men eat with their hands holding their silverware, that's the men's way. We use our feet, that's our way. Do not compare our way with theirs. Dad cannot manage to do anything with his feet that we can, not even touch his nose!" I giggled.

Mom came close to me and leaned over, "Because our way is so different, I think that we women are much smarter than the men. It takes a lot of thinking on our part to figure out our way of doings some things. Don't tell the men that though; it's a woman's secret." I grinned. We certainly did have to do just about everything differently than they did. Well not everything, we walked and ran the same way.

Ever since that moment in the park when Dita and I realized who each other was, the spiritual beings that we were, we were inseparable! That summer, I spent half of the nights sleeping over at her house, and the other half, she spent sleeping over at mine. We began to brush out each other's long hair as our special nightly ritual. It was hard to brush out one's own long hair by oneself I had discovered. Together we managed it well. Now I realized why most women wore theirs short; it was vastly more manageable. Yet Dita and I refused to have ours cut.

When fall finally came, dad brought home a special girl's backpack for me, complete with school supplies! I was delighted, pencils, paper, colored drawing sticks; I couldn't wait for the first day of school. Our school was a large building about six blocks from our homes. All of us kids walked together, joined by many more by the time we arrived.

Our older brothers and sisters took us to the right room. Essentially, this was a two room school house, plus a play room and kitchen-dining room. Children aged five through ten were in one room, and those between eleven and sixteen in another. I never will forget walking into the room on my first day, my new backpack across my back.

Half of the room was obviously the girl's section, the other, the boy's. How could you tell? Obvious. The girl's desks were all about six inches from the floor. We sat in sloped back chairs and our feet could easily touch the desktop. In the boy's section, all the desktops were way up off the floor, so high that girls could not possibly reach the writing surface. A large blackboard covered the entire length of the front of the room. There were two trays, one about six inches from the floor and the other, three feet. Both were filled with chalk sticks and erasers.

Since this was the first day, our teachers had written a large sign on the blackboard. It read: Rule 1: Boys are responsible for helping the girls remove their backpacks and getting their books out. Rule 2: Boys are responsible for helping the girls put their books back into their backpacks and putting them on their backs. I couldn't read, but Aniela, who sat beside me, read it out loud for Dita and me. We grinned, while Renard and Dawid helped us get settled in. I realized that this was the first time that I was going to a real school. Always before, I was tutored or self-taught.

Our teacher was Mrs. Ales, a woman in her thirties with short black hair and thick lips. She was kindly, but strict, as were all the teachers over the years. First, we began learning to say the alphabet and then to block print them in both cases. She would call upon one of us to go to the blackboard and print whatever letter she called out. I truly enjoyed picking up the chalk and printing on the board and became good at it. The boys used their hands and progressed more rapidly than we girls did. Repeatedly, Mrs. Ales reminded us that there were the boy's way and the girl's way. Both were very different. One day when a boy teased us, Mrs. Ales made him go to the blackboard and print the letter F using his feet. After falling down and not even getting the chalk picked up, he returned to his seat with a very red face.

"Women's ways are our own. Men cannot do things our way, nor can we do things their way. We must all learn to respect the other's ways of doing things. That is Rule 3: Always respect the other's ways of doing things, because you cannot do it their way." I smiled, that was a truism if I ever heard one.

I will be honest with you. So far, I was beginning to think that perhaps here was a "perfect" society! Well, nearly so.

That next Saturday, mom and dad took me to Doktor Alfons. Mom explained that it was finally time that I began my earrings. I had always admired hers. Now that I had entered school, it was time. "We are taking you to get your ears pierced just like mine. Your father and I will be giving you your first tier of hanging gems. See mine, the first row by the ear. As you go through school, if you earn top marks each year, the school adds another hanging gem on the second tier. See, I have two there. When you graduate school, it is our responsibility to add your third tier of hanging gems. Then, when you get married, your husband will give you your forth tier. The higher that his status is, the more hanging gems he will give you for your fourth tier, but they will only be ruby gems. When you see a woman with one or more red rubies in her earrings, you know that she is already married. That prevents unwanted advances by other men, because they can see that you are already married."

While she was talking to me as if I were a five year old, I was well aware of the true social significance of these earrings now. It was obvious that she had red rubies in her earrings; you could see that from a good distance away. Hence, there could be no excuse for another man mistaking her for an available woman. No defense was possible, because they had closed the door on any such excuse as, "but I didn't know she was already married."

Mom continued, "Later, when you have children of your own, your husband will begin adding a fifth tier. Your father has added four beautiful diamonds to mine, one for each of you. He gives me great honor by doing so. Everyone can see that I am his wife and that I have been a Holy Vessel bringing forth new life four times now." She didn't mention that there were other occasions, which would add additional tiers or layers. I was just very happy to get my first earrings so I looked like all the other girls at school.

I looked in a mirror after the doktor finished up. The earring base was solid gold; a rather thick, circular band went through my ear lobes. I could see no way to take them off. When I asked about that, mom laughed and said that they could never be taken off. The gold ring was fused together so that nothing we did could accidentally knock them off our ears.

Dad had very kindly gotten me three hanging diamonds, forming my first tier. "Now the next tier is up to you, my darling Bethany." I vowed to do well in school.

When I got home, I had to show mine off to Dita. She too had just gotten her set and ours looked almost identical. Perhaps our parents were conspiring with each other; after all, she spent as much time at our house all summer as I had at hers.

After lunch, mom and dad, along with Dita's parents, Eliasz and Roksana Malina, took we girls to the dressmaker's shop on 17th Street West. Dad explained, "Now that you are in school, it is time that you wore a proper dress and shoes to Sunday Service. Your mom and I are going to get you a very nice dress with shoes to match. I know that you will be growing like a flower now, so we will get it slightly large, and you can grow into it."

Indeed, the cotton dress was very nice, but I could not see any way that I could possibly put it on by myself. Mom rightly guessed that was what was going through my mind. "Dear, your father will be helping you into your fancy dress on Sunday Mornings. This is one of those man things they like to do — dress us up fancy. It is not possible for me to even get into my own fancy dress." I relaxed visibly. "We need to find one that matches you, let's see, yellow is going to clash with your blonde hair. May I suggest this red one with the myriad of flowers?"

A while later, we left with that red dress and shoes and socks to match. They had laces so I knew that dad would be tying them for me. Dita showed me hers, a deep blue dress with flowers, matching socks, and shoes. Tomorrow we both would get to wear them for the first time.

Indeed, on Sunday, after breakfast was done, dad set about dressing up us women. First he got mom into her blue silk dress, with blue socks, and lace-tied shoes. Then, he dolled up Aniela in her yellow dress, which contrasted well with her brown hair. I'd seen him do this many times before, but now I was a part of it, and the whole action became more significant to me. At last, dad gently got me into my new dress. It was silk as well and felt wonderful on my skin. I'd never worn socks before, let alone such sturdy shoes. It felt different. "There you go, my little princess," dad said as he stood back and gave me a look.

Then, it was off to the Church. We walked the eight blocks to the Church, and I saw many others dressed up, much as we were, joining us. Dad evidently knew quite a few men, as he frequently was spoken to with "Hello Mr. Brozena."

The Church was similar in many ways to all the other buildings, made from the same brownstone with a red slate roof. However, it was twice as tall and had enormous stained glass windows depicting various men and women and children. Why? I had no idea yet. Inside, we found the Malina's and Feliks' families waiting on us. All we children began chatting with each other, Dita and I, comparing our new outfits.

I did notice that Elder Feliks wore a very elegant robe, rich in blues and browns of many shades. As I soon found out, he was giving the service today. He always gave the first service at the start of school. This way, he was able to address all the new students who were just beginning, as well as those who were coming back to school after summer vacation. I decided to pay attention this year.

The Church had a choir who began singing polyphonic hymns, as we all began to find seats on the rows and rows of pews. Overhead the ceiling was perhaps thirty feet above my head, spacious and covered with painted scenes, which resembled the nighttime sky. Nowhere did I see any crosses or effigies that so marked the Churches of Jehosanity that I had known in lifetimes before this one. It was simple: worship God in the Heavens. I also noticed that there were a number of children in the choir as well. I made a note to ask how one could join them, their musical sound I found stimulating, almost enchanting.

Then Elder Feliks walked to the altar and began the service. He conducted a usual type of prayer that I had heard countless times before. Once that was done, he began speaking in a different tone of voice, I noticed. His voice carried across the entire church, but at one very precise tone or pitch. He didn't vary even slightly, making the sound of his voice therefore rather hypnotic, devoid of all elocution.

"It is time once again to teach our children the ways of our people, God's Holy Brethren on Tarra. In the Beginning God created the earth and the heavens with its glorious stars and the sun. God was happy with his creation for a time. As the days and nights passed endlessly with the seasons coming and going, there was no one there with which to share the beauty of his creation. Thus, God decided to create man in his own image to partake and share in the seasons and the glory of his creation. Men would add to it with their industrious work to create homes, raise crops, build wooden boats, and fish in the oceans. Yet, this too was short lived, for men's bodies, not being as God, perished after a time, as all men still do, even unto this day. Worse still, men argued with other men, men fought with other men, men coveted that which other men made or found, men stuffed themselves with the bounty of the world. God was displeased."

"God now saw that he must have life perpetuate itself, that somehow more men must be created. Thus, it came to pass that God created woman in his own image to be his Holy Vessel to create new life here on earth. Only through the Holy Vessel would God allow this new life to be created. Original woman was just like man, but had both the breasts for nursing the newborn life and the Holy Vessel in which God formed the new life."

"Now man and woman dwelled for a time on our world. They shared in the beauty of God's creations. As men and women grew old and passed on, new men and women came forth from his Holy Vessels, and God was pleased."

"Yet, man and woman sinned against our Lord and Creator. Men still fought with other men, coveted what other men had, as well as what women had. They lied, cheated, stole from other men and women. Men lusted after women; women lusted after men. Many took to gluttonous behavior, stuffing themselves beyond what was needed to sustain life. Men beat women to get what they wanted. Women cheated on men to get what they coveted. Worse still, men now had to work even harder to support their Holy Vessels. God saw that men needed even greater strength, power, and stamina, because they needed to now support themselves and their families."

"God then said, 'How may I solve this mess that I've made? I want my men and women to enjoy the Holy Creation with me, to share in my joy. Yet, they fight among themselves and far worse. Man is not strong enough to bear this burden alone.'"

"One of God's Holy Vessels, who was called Marzena, spoke unto God. 'Lord, my man, Jurek, is a good and kind man, a farmer. He works at his fields to provide for our family. Yet, I can see that he needs to be stronger. Please, my Lord, take my arms from me and use them to strengthen Jurek so that he may be strong enough for the task. I do not need them and Jurek needs them so much more than I do.' God heard the prayer from his Holy Vessel and so it was that God took the arms from his Marzena and fashioned them into more ribs for her husband Jurek. Thus made stronger and more powerful, Jurek was at last able to sustain his Holy Vessel and family, more able to tend his fields, and produce more food. Jurek was then very pleased and happy with the change."

"But our Lord God then spoke unto Jurek. 'Yes, I can see that, by the sacrifice of worthy Marzena, you are now blessed with part of her strength and you are now able to survive well. However, Jurek you must honor her sacrifice unto you. From this day forward, you must love her, cherish her, and help her, as you have never done before. Thou shalt never betray her by lusting after other women. Thou shalt be true to her and to her alone. Thou shalt not lie, covet what another has, steal that which does not belong to you, and fight with other men whose Holy Vessels have likewise made their sacrifice. Nor should thou become a glutton over the bounty, which thou art now capable of producing because of the gift Marzena has given unto you and you alone. Thou shalt honor and cherish the new life that Marzena brings forth, as they are part of each of you.'"

"Jurek, Marzena, if you will do these things, then you are worthy of viewing my Creation and of entering my realm. Jurek, Marzena, if you fail to do these, if you are not faithful to each other, hurt the other, lie, steal, covet, lust, become gluttonous, then you raise my ire and I will take back Marzena's sacrificial gift to you, Jurek, and allow you both to die off like my first creations of the Unholy man and woman, which I have forsaken as unworthy.'"

"Jurek said unto the Lord and unto Marzena, 'I will honor you always, my Marzena, for the selfless sacrifice you have given unto me, I so swear. I will be your arms when you have need for them. I will looketh not at other women. I will not lie, steal, or fight with others who have given of this Holy Sacrifice. But my Lord, my God, what will happen to these others who are around me whom have not made this Holy Sacrifice?'"

"God spoketh thus, 'They are the Unholy, the Accursed Ones, forsaken by their own making. I disown them. You may ignore them, as you choose. Yet, still they ought not to be without all hope with no chance of redemption. Jurek, you may talk with these men and try to show them their Holy Mistake, the errors of their making. You and Marzena can show them the path — your lives as a model to follow, but Marzena, the purest of Holy Vessels, must never talk with the Accursed. Nothing must taint her Holy Sacrifice, as many of the Unholy Women will certainly attempt to do to her. Jurek, do not allow your Holy Vessel to become tainted, that is your responsibility to safeguard. Now if they repent and disavow what they have done and wish to join you and Marzena, they must make the sacrifice themselves to prove that they are now worthy of my Grace. If they remove the arms of their beloved and the two live as I have ordained for the two you, then I shall give both of them my Holy Redemption.'"

"Then, Jurek and Marzena both thanked our Lord for not forsaking all other men and women on Tarra. They set forth to fulfill the Lord God's commandments unto them. They begat many sons and daughters, who begat their sons and daughters and so spread God's Holy Creations on Tarra. Though much time has now passed since the time of Jurek and Marzena, the results of their tireless efforts are here for all to see on Dorota. Our continent is filled with millions of us Holy Men and Holy Vessels, our women."

"Yet, Jurek never failed to attempt to show the Unholy the errors of their ways and thus bring them back to obtain God's Holy Redemption. Today, this is as true as it was back in Jurek's day. There are yet a few among us who remain Unholy. They lust after another's Holy Vessel, they lie, they steal, and they dishonor their Holy Vessel, their wife who has given her Holy Sacrifice for them. These Unholy we send off to the Fields of

Kondrat, where we attempt to show them the errors of their ways, that they may yet be Redeemed."

"You young boys and young Holy Vessels, pay close attention to these words. Boys, always be the hands of the girls when they need them. Always respect the women's ways. Always be there to help them and assist them, for their sacrifice is Holy and you must honor it always or be condemned to the Fields of Kondrat yourself."

"Neither should you lie, neither should you steal that which is not yours, neither should you harm another of us who is Holy, and especially boys, never harm a Holy Vessel no matter what she has done. If anyone knows of anyone who has committed such transgressions, you are commanded to report it to your bisklep or Elder. If true, they will be deemed Unholy and sent off to the Fields of Kondrat, there to seek redemption."

"Young Holy Vessels, you young girls, I caution you to never speak to an Unholy woman, for she will seek to taint you and turn you into an Unholy Vessel. If you become tainted and un-pure, then you too will be sent to the Fields of Kondrat, there to seek Redemption."

"A quarter of a century ago, our people became aware of just how many of the Unholy men and women still inhabit our world. Vast are their numbers. Yet, we hold true to the guidance our Lord gave unto Jurek. We send forth missionaries into the Unholy lands and seek to Redeem them. Already we have been successful; fully fifty thousand men and women have cast aside their sins and removed their arms in sacrifice to the Lord God, taking up the ways of the Holy. These are now counted among us and will have our Lord's Holy Redemption."

"Some of our Elders are leading this crusade of Redemption many, many leagues from their homes here on Dorota. They have reported that the newly made Holy Vessels are having problems learning the women's special ways. Perhaps we should have expected this, but have not. We are so used to having you, our Holy Vessels, from birth onward, that we did not realize your woman's ways were so difficult to master. Yes, men do not know how to do things the women's way, nor can women do things the men's way. Thus, we are now sending out there into the Unholy part of the world some Holy Vessels, who have volunteered to guide and assist these newly made Holy Women to learn the proper women's way of doing things."

"Young men and young Holy Vessels, study hard, learn your lessons. One day when you graduate school, if you wish to volunteer to assist in our Holy Crusade to help the Unholy redeem themselves out there in the wide world of Tarra, we will accept your help and send you abroad that you may do as Jurek has done." He then ended his single tone sermon and had us bow in prayer.

During this sermon, I began to glance at those around me. Uniformly, everyone sat enthralled, hypnotized by Elder Feliks! My sister next to me was in a trance, as if God were speaking directly to her! I was shocked by the effect the Elder was having. Yet, I noticed that there were two others who were also looking around at the hypnotized congregation. Dita and Albin, both were glancing at our friends. Albin's eyes met mine and opened wide, though he did not say anything. He then saw Dita looking at him as well. Albin then smiled to each of us. Neither Dita nor I had any inkling of the significance of our not being under the effect of his father, the Elder.

Both Dita and I took note of our first clue that this "perfect society" was not so perfect after all. What was this Fields of Kondrat? How did they get the disaffected somehow Redeemed? What kind of punishment did they deal out at these Fields anyway? How many were currently being punished into Redemption? I knew that I could not ask these questions nor would I get a straight answer. Ordinary men and women would only quote the "party line" that they had been fed while hypnotized. Elders certainly would not tell me the outright truth behind their failures. Yes I began to see that those who did not go along with the "perfect society" as being the failures of the Elders. I would have to go see for myself, but not until I grew up considerably.

Chapter 3 School Years

Dita and I decided to play a game of who could learn more at school. The one room type of schooling lent itself easily to our personal challenge. Essentially, each student progressed along at their own pace. The teachers would lecture to one age group and hand out assignments for them to work. They would then move on to the next age group. Hence, while working our current assignments, we often listened in on the more advanced material. By getting our work done sufficiently quickly, the teachers had no choice but to give us the next assignment.

We were learning arithmetic and then their forms of fancier mathematics, often involving elements of geometry and trigonometry, which were used in the design and construction areas of our society. Language, reading, and writing skills came easily to Dita and me, though the writing part took some doing on our part. "Feet do your thing," became her favorite motto. I expected to learn lots from their history course, but sadly, we found it only a rehash of their religious beliefs. All we really learned that was new was the chronology of the Elders, and those were only the more famous ones.

Dita and I paid very close attention to the geography courses, learning well the layout of Dorota. The seven largest cities were Bazyli, our city, and Kondrat in the highlands or middle of this very large island continent, and along the northern coast, Grzegorz and Urjasz, while along the southern coast lay Bozydar, Donat, and Piotr. Between these cities, paved cobblestone roads connected and encircled the continent. In fact, the Great Rim Road hugged the coastline all around the island continent. Cross highland roads connected these coastal towns to the two large inland cities.

However, there were numerous smaller towns and many more rural farming villages. Trade goods traveled by horse drawn wagons, while passengers rode in elegant carriages though one could certainly ride a horse if one had access to them. Fish, sheep, and chickens provided primary protein for the country, while grains and vegetables were grown on the many farms, which dotted the lands below the highlands. Six large, dense forests lay scattered about the island continent as well. Just north of Bazyli were numerous stone quarries from which most all the brown stone came.

Our monetary system consisted of a gold dolar and a gold polowa-dolar, which was half the size of the dolar. A copper was worth a tenth of a polowa-dolar. Larger sums were handled by gemstones. Our rubies and emeralds came from the mines east of Kondrat, while our diamonds came from the mines west of Bazyli. For cooking, charcoal predominately was used which came from the West Bagno and the East Bagno, a pair of coastal bogs along the southern coast.

Aqueducts brought fresh running water to the low-lying towns and cities from the many highland lakes. These stone aqueducts poured fresh water into large stone water towers, and from there water pressure was maintained by gravity alone. Several charcoal fired heaters located strategically around the towns and cities provided hot water. I had to give our people some credit, for their engineering showed great thoughtful design.

What was missing from this "perfect society?" The arts were almost entirely lacking! No great paintings, no great music or musicians, no real literature. What Dita and I missed most were no dances or dance halls. We both had spent endless hours in our past lifetimes dancing to all kinds of music. Here on Dorota, everything was plain and mostly unadorned. I began to see why this was. Men spent their time working the fields, fishing, mining, building boats, processing the grain and produce, cutting timber, hauling goods, cutting stone, building homes, to say nothing of handling household chores that the women were unable to do. They had no time for anything that wasn't immediately useful to their survival and that of their families.

Even the gem cutters and jewelers showed little creativity, producing the same style earrings and add on pieces that they had been making. Both Dita and I found ourselves increasingly missing all the arts in which we had been so involved in our last few lifetimes. This was one reason why we worked so diligently and swiftly at school.

When the school's summer break came in 737, I was ten years old. Both Dita and I received our acknowledgment of just having completed our schoolwork through Grade 8, not Grade 5 as were our other ten year old friends! She and I now proudly wore eight more dangling gems on our earrings. In the fall, we would be studying with those who were thirteen years old. Being three grades beyond where we ought to be did not go unnoticed by anyone, teachers and parents included.

However, Albin had long ago taken notice of us two, when we finished our first grade beyond where he was at in his studies. Albin took us on as his personal challenge. "Okay you two hot shots, I am going to catch up to both of you!" Albin must have worked hard, because he also finished Grade 8 with us, three grades beyond where he ought to have. "Just wait until fall. Now that I've finally caught up to you, I am going to leave you in the dust!" He was teasing, but Dita and I took this as a challenge. He had hands and could do the homework much more rapidly than we could. Dita hounded him about this, but she and I refused to let him blast past us this fall.

We both expected to have a fun summer playing ball in the park. Surprise, our moms explained that we were now old enough to learn more of the women's ways. Our dad's bought us our own carriers, as they are known. Two large buckets hung by thick ropes from a wooden yoke that had a half-moon curve in its middle. V-shaped poles were fastened to either end which kept the whole yoke about four feet off the ground, while allowing the buckets to be resting on the ground. We would bend over, get our necks inside the yoke bend, and then stand up. Suddenly, Dita and I realized that we could now actually carry things!

Our new carriers were put to use immediately by our mothers. Every few days, they would send us to fetch food supplies from the market. A few coins were put in a pouch and stored in our buckets. We then got under the yoke, lifted the buckets, and headed off down the street to buy the required supplies. Of course, it was more difficult carrying the heavier weights on the return trip, but our mothers kept the total weight of their supplies down so that we could manage. We both discovered that by our doing this, we began to reduce our mother's overall workload.

Next, mom taught us how to clean the floors. A brush had two leather loops in it and virtually no handle. By putting our feet in the loops and sitting on our butts, we slowly learned how to brush the accumulated dirt out the door. Neither of us particularly enjoyed this chore, however.

Changing and making beds were the next chores that we were taught to do. Removing the covers and sheets were not much of a challenge, just a lot of hopping about on one foot. Making the bed, on the other hand, was quite challenging, and took us a good deal of time to get just one bed made. Both Dita and I quickly realized just how much work our mothers had been doing for us these past ten years.

Perhaps the most fun we had this summer was learning how to prepare and cook our family meals. To save time, mom taught Dita and me on one day, and Roksana taught us on the next day. Mom's advice was sound. "Always, kids think ahead. That's your first step. Plan in your mind what you are going to make. Then, you estimate how long it will take you to have it all ready. Knowing the current time, figure backwards to get the time that you need to begin. If you don't, your men will arrive expecting supper, and, if it is an hour late, they will not be pleased with you."

We diligently worked at this all summer long. Dita and I liked to think that we were slowly making some progress with it. Sometimes I doubted it. That we would be helping fix meals for our families from now on would be the case. Mom deserved it and we slowly began lessening her heavy workload.

Next, we learned how to handle washing the family's clothes. Using our yoke and buckets, we went from the parent's bedroom, the boy's bedroom, and then we girl's bedroom gathering up the dirty clothes, which were stuffed in a wicker clothes hamper. One room in our house was called the washing room, but it also was dad's workshop and where he kept his tools. Across the room, parallel clotheslines stretched tautly about three feet from the floor. Two large washtubs sat to one side. It generally took us an hour using our yoke and buckets to bring enough water from the sink in the kitchen to fill both tubs.

If that wasn't tiring enough, now we sat down and had to wash each article of clothing by feet, rise it, and then carrying it in our mouths over to the line, hang it up to drain and dry. That finished, we had to use a cup with a handle that fit our feet to scoop the water out and into our buckets, then carry it to the kitchen and dump it down the sink. I learned to hate washing day!

Nevertheless, both Dita and I learned to do well the women's way to do things around the house that summer. Usually, we were too tired to go out and play when the day's chores were done. All too soon, it was back to school once more.

As promised, Albin picked up his pace, attempting always to get his next assignment done before Dita or I could finish. As the math became more difficult, Albin slowed down considerably; he had to learn how to do it. On the other hand, having to do everything slowly with our feet slowed us down, but we had a distinct advantage in this race to finish school years ahead of schedule. Dita and I both had good recall on our previous lifetimes. We already knew this math and a whole lot more besides. Thus, we were never slowed down by having to learn something new, merely by the slow speed with which we wrote. The exception was, of course, geography of Dorota, of which we knew nothing. When the lessons began on the newly discovered other continents and peoples of Tarra, we knew all about them, since that's where we had originated before coming here to Dorota.

Bottom line, no matter how hard Albin tried to get ahead of us, Dita and I were right behind him! Of course, our various teachers kept quizzing us to make triply sure that we did indeed know the materials, which all three of us did, much to their shock and surprise. We had no idea that we three were setting a new Dorota record on speed of learning.

Finally, in 742, Albin, Dita, and I turned fourteen, and as school ended, we had finished all the work that would have been done during our sixteenth year. We had completed all twelve grades in just nine years! All three of us were quite proud of our achievement.

As promised, our dads added four more dangling gems to each of our earrings. Quite unexpectedly, the school presented us with an award for stellar achievement, another four dangling gems on this third tier. Our parents were with us at the school for this special presentation, and our very proud fathers formally attached the new additions to our earrings. However, none of us expected what happened next.

Elder Feliks, wearing his formal robes, which he wore at each special fall, start of school term Church meeting at which he delivered the same sermon each time, entered leading a group of six older Elders. Several had beards. He shook hands with Janek and Eliasz. "Your daughters are the most worthy Holy Vessels that we have seen in a very long time. You should be rightly proud of their achievements." Our father's faces displayed the loving pride that they had, combined with curiosity. What were all these Elders doing here at school? In turn, he hugged our mothers, Tekla and Roksana.

Our brothers and sisters were also sitting quietly in the back of the room. I heard them whispering about the arrival of so many Elders. I began to fear that we had done something wrong. Albin and Kazia also entered, and he winked at me. This, I took as an encouraging sign. Elder Gawel Feliks then asked our mothers about how well we were performing our women's ways. Good old mom began rattling off all the various actions that she and Roksana had been teaching us since we were ten. Roksana added her support for Dita and me as well. Apparently satisfied, Elder Feliks turned to the six older Elders and spoke.

"As you have heard, both Holy Vessels are performing better than expected at their women's ways. This confirms that Bethany and Dita, though only fourteen, are indeed achieving at the level expected of a woman who has come of age after her seventeenth birthday. They have not abandoned their women's ways for scholastic learning as some of you had feared."

I had never considered ever doing any such thing! Mom had it hard enough trying to manage a household of six without any arms to help her. By doing all that I could, along with my older sister, Aniela, we had shouldered a good deal of her load, making her life easier. How could I ethically not have done so? Yet, apparently, such thoughts had occurred among some of these Elders. Albin looked very relieved, I noticed.

One Elder nodded. He seemed to be the one in charge. At last he spoke, "Thank you Elder Feliks for proper verification. I am Elder Amadei, headmaster of the Elder College at Wit. Bethany Brozena, Dita Malina, you two Holy Vessels have shown a remarkable talent for learning not only your school work, but also your Holy Women's Ways. And yet you are just fourteen. I am proud to tell you that you two have been the singular inspiration for young Albin Feliks to follow your example, finishing his school years ahead of schedule as well."

"Albin has been accepted at the Elder College at Wit, just a few miles north of here. He will be starting there this fall. If he continues his great progress, he will very likely become an Elder himself, a most highly respected and valued member of our country. Because of the great inspiration that you young Holy Vessels have been to him and as a role model for all the other young Holy Vessels at your school, we of the Elder's Council wish to complete your third tier for you. Elder Bartosz will make the formal presentation. Your fathers will have a bit more earring work to do for you," he grinned and my dad stood as tall as he could!

Elder Bartosz stepped forward. While handing the dangling gems to our fathers one at a time and while they were permanently attaching them, he spoke eloquently. "You two ought to be very proud of your achievement.

Your fathers gave you three gems for your first tier. You are the only young Holy Vessels who have added twelve gems to your second schooling tier. That is a most worthy accomplishment indeed. I know of no other who has done so! Now thanks to your parents, the school's distinguished student awards, and our thank-you awards, you have a complete third tier of gems. No other Holy Vessel in all of Dorota has such a fine set as yours. Wear them with great pride, my young Holy Vessels. As you walk among our people, you will always serve as an inspiration to all others, both men and woman. Thank you."

Once this action was completed, Elder Amadei continued. "We at the Elder College at Wit have discussed in depth your unique situation, Bethany and Dita. While there is nothing more that we can teach you educationally, we feel that since you still have three more years before coming of age, that you ought to use it to further advance yourselves. It seems that we have thus far not, shall we say, reached your limits of learning. On behalf of the Elder College of Wit, I would like to extend an offer to have both of you come and live in our town of Wit nearby the college. There, we will assist you to learn as many other things as you may desire and can learn to do in your unique women's way. This is an opportunity to expand greatly the things and actions that a Holy Vessel can do in your women's way, here on Dorota. Your living expenses and some spending money will be provided by the Elder College at Wit. We ask only two things of you both. First, continue to learn to do new things in your unique way. Second, continue to assist Albin in his studies, that he may achieve his fullest potential. What do you say, Bethany and Dita? I hear from your parents that you two are inseparable." He was teasing us a little and we smiled.

"If it is okay with my parents, I would be very glad for the opportunity to learn more things and to help Albin," I replied.

"Me too," Dita added. "Besides, Albin helped push us on as well. If he had not been encouraging us every day to keep up with him, we might not have worked as hard as we did. Bethany and I feel that we owe him greatly for our awards. If we can help him in any way to do well in his studies, we will feel very honored and rewarded by his achievements. It is the very least that we can do for him."

Oh, Dita had learned the ways of this culture very well. She played the part of a Holy Vessel perfectly, drawing on the unspoken parallel of the Holy Vessel Marzena that Elder Feliks so frequently drilled into our minds.

Our parents were shocked and speechless for a time. Yes, they gave their permission for us to do this. Elder Feliks would be giving us further information later this summer. Again, the men gave us a hug and departed. While our parents chatted with Elder Feliks, Dita and I joined Albin off to one side of the schoolroom.

"Thank you two! I was really hoping that you would come to Wit with me. You two have the keenest, sharpest minds that I have ever seen. I promise you that I will do everything I can to make your stay there very rewarding. By the way, your earrings look just great," he complimented.

"I can't wait to get to a mirror and see how they look. Only right now they feel so awfully heavy as if they are pulling my ears off!" I replied.

"No kidding, these are really heavy," Dita added. "What will we get to do at Wit, Albin?"

"Dunno yet. I am going to quiz dad about it some. I'll drop by and chat as I find out things. How's that?" We agreed and at last, our parents walked us home.

Okay, the first thing that Dita and I did was run to a mirror to see our new earrings. Girls get excited about such things. I still do. Yes, they looked gorgeous, but also they were now huge; the bottom tier of twelve nearly touched our shoulders and did if we tilted our heads slightly. Even turning our heads caused them to sway and tingle like a wind charm. Our lobes were definitely looking quite stretched, but I loved the look, especially since no one but Dita and I had such a look.

Chapter 4 The Summer Discoveries

At breakfast the next day, I chatted with dad. "Dad, it is the summer now and Dita and I are both fourteen. We've been talking this over and we wanted to know if you would like us to come and help you out at your store during the summer months. We still want to help our moms out, so maybe just a few days a week. What do you think? We'd like to help you, if we can, because we have always been helping mom. We think you deserve a little help too. Please dad?" I used a slight girlish beg.

"Well, I sure could use some extra help, but your mother needs it as well," dad replied hesitantly.

"Oh, Janek, let the girls lend some help a few days each week. What harm is there in that? Aniela and I are getting along fine. Iwan's getting married soon and Dawid is already working full time in the store. So really, there's less to do each day."

"Are you sure, Tekla?" dad asked. Mom was, but she asked that we lend her a hand on Thursdays and Fridays, to do the week's grocery shopping and the laundry, cleaning, and bedding — all the yucky tasks. He agreed.

On Monday morning, dad and Dawid walked down the streets to his store with Dita and I right on their heels. It was a half-mile walk, which we both enjoyed. I realized that she and I had almost never been more than about six blocks from home in our fourteen years! It was an interesting fact that I filed away for future reference.

Dad ran a supply store, full of various tools, construction supplies, such as nails and wooden pegs. As he said, "I have a bit of everything in here. Today, you girls wander around and familiarize yourselves with what I have in stock and where it is located. Holler if you need anything. Dawid is supposed to handle the customers, while I have to try to figure out this darn inventory mess."

Dutifully, we began to wander the many rows of shelves, concentrating on trying to memorize just what dad had and where. We realized at once that we would not really be able to get things that a customer might ask for — so many of the items were far out of the reach of our feet. The shelves went all the way to the ceiling, crammed with items for sale.

Quickly, other people heard that we two were working at dad's store and began dropping by to see us. By now, word of our success and awards had spread for blocks around here and folks were naturally interested in seeing us and even chatting with us. That they also bought a few items was greatly appreciated by dad.

The next week, we discovered the horrible state that dad's accounting ledger books were in — he had made a complete mess of his accounting. Giggling like fourteen year old girls can, we pushed him out of his cramped back office and set to work on redoing his whole accounting ledgers. Quickly, we discovered that dad was not so good with arithmetic. Yes, it took us almost a month, but we got it straightened out. Much to dad's surprise, we discovered that he had, over the last several years, actually made over a thousand dolars that he didn't know he had made. He thanked us profusely over our discovery of his windfall profits, and he bought us each a new dress to thank us. Mom and Aniela also got a new dress as well.

While we were alone working in dad's small office, Dita and I for the first time could talk openly and freely without fear of being overheard. Around our homes, our mothers were always there. Even the park offered few chances of being alone for any length of time. At least now, our bodies had grown up enough to be useful. It was time to make some plans.

"Dita, one thing that we need to do is travel all over this country and see what else is here."

"Like soldiers or guards or fortifications?" she asked.

"Yes, but we need to see strategically what is where in this land. Also, we need to find out who is really running the country. Thus far, that significant detail is totally lacking in this country's educational schooling. Someone *must* be controlling things."

"You are right. I've kept alert to any hints, but the only ones that seem to have real power over the people are these Elders. Until recently, we didn't even know about this Elder College in Wit. We should see if there are more of them. We need to find out if there is a group of them running the show or if there is one top man, because it surely isn't going to be a woman in charge of this country!" We both laughed at her jest.

"Probably we ought to play along and see just how much freedom to explore Dorota they will allow us. You know, will they let us travel around the country, go to the beaches, heck go swimming even?"

"How about going riding, Bethany? I do really miss horseback riding. Crap, like this, I don't know if I can, Bethany," Dita acknowledged crestfallen.

"I know Renzo, we both loved to ride like the wind." Memories of he and I galloping across the land, the wind blowing my long hair, which fluttered like a banner, came to mind. I had slipped and called her by his name last lifetime. Dita didn't mind, for she too was remembering our rides together.

After a time, Dita suggested, "You know, I'd like a look see at those Fields of Kondrat, where they take those who protest in some way. I bet we will not like what we see there."

"Right, I'd nearly forgotten about that. Somehow, someway, we must have a look see there, but I don't suppose the Elders will take too kindly to that request of ours," I replied.

"Not unless we can figure out an acceptable point of view that they can tolerate. Let me think on that one, Bethany. You know, if it wasn't for this no arms business, this would be a reasonable place to live, well from what little we've seen of it," Dita pointed out. "We've seen far worse."

One Saturday in early July, Albin dropped by my house to chat. "I rather guessed that Dita would be here with you," he said politely and a bit reserved. We were working together to sweep the kitchen floor. Of course, there we were sitting on the floor, pushing the brushes with our feet. I saw that he was slightly embarrassed at finding us this way, doing women's work in the uniquely women's way. Hastily, Dita and I pulled our feet out of the brushes and with awkward efforts got on to our feet, which embarrassed him even more. I suspected that he was not totally used to seeing just how women got up from the floor.

"Hi, Albin. We're just cleaning the floor for mom. Have a seat. Can we make you anything to drink," I said politely.

"Er, no thanks. I just came by to tell you about what little I have learned." He sat down, as did we, which I saw put him more at ease. He was used to seeing us sitting down, not on our butts pushing brooms around the floor.

"Great," Dita replied with a smile on her face, which in turn caused him to smile as well.

"Dad explained to me that they would like you to broaden your women's ways by traveling around Dorota and staying for a time at several places. He mentioned that here in our city, you were not exposed to more specialized women's ways that are found elsewhere in our country. I don't quite know what he meant by that and I figured you might not either, so I asked him about it. He said, some Holy Vessels work at banks and that he would like you to spend a little time working at a bank so that you can learn how they perform their work there. He said that in the coastal cities and towns, many Holy Vessels often go to the beaches and swim in the ocean. Honestly, Dita, Bethany, I surely don't know how you can possibly go swimming," he faltered and his face reddened slightly. "I mean I have to use my arms like mad to stay afloat and to get anywhere in the water. It must be terribly difficult for Holy Vessels to swim, maybe very dangerous too."

"I asked him if I could come along with you, but he said that I would be in school while you were traveling and visiting these places. However, he did say that they wanted you back in a few months because by then I would probably need some tutoring help with my studies. I am the youngest student to ever enter the Elder College, so that's probably why they think I will need some help."

"Makes sense," I replied. "We'll be there for you. Albin, you can count on us."

He grinned appreciatively. "Thought so. Anyway, I did get him to promise me that during the winter break, I can then travel around Dorota with you. Now that will be great, don't you think? I mean around here, we seldom get any time to enjoy the winter snow, us being cooped up here in the big city and all."

"Good going, Albin, that sounds like real fun!" Dita replied. "I just wish we could make snowballs and have a snowball fight with you," she teased him.

He flushed, "Yes, that would be fun, if you two could, but. . ." He felt too embarrassed to finish his sentence.

"Yes, like we are, there are just some things that we cannot do, Albin, like pack snowballs and have a good, old snowball fight," I sighed, stating what he could not. We chatted a bit more and he left.

"You know, Albin is starting to open his eyes about women's situations," Dita observed. "Maybe we can use that later on." She was so right.

Our parents received word that we would be picked up on July 1 by a representative of the Elder College at Wit and be taken on a trip. Further, we were to pack all of our personal things, because after the trip, we would be taken to our new home in Wit so that we could further our education and skills. Our families were as excited about this as we were, and dad gave us a little spending money. "If you need more, just send word to me, dearest Bethany. We will miss you terribly, but this is an excellent opportunity. So very few get such a chance as you and Dita. Mind your manners, but do have a good time. One more thing, Bethany, if you get too homesick, let us know. I'm sure that they will understand; after all, you are only fourteen."

I leaned into his body, and he automatically threw his arms around me, giving me a strong hug. "I will, daddy." Then, mom came up, and we pressed our bodies close and threw one leg around the other, our unique hug.

"Be brave, my dear. I know you can do anything that they ask of you. I am so very proud of you, dear; I can't stop crying," she said, tears dripping down both cheeks.

My older brother, Iwan, hugged me and whispered, "Bethany, keep your eyes open for a handsome man. It won't be too much longer and you can get married too. I am so looking forward to starting my own family!" I agreed. He had been far happier these past many months since he announced his engagement than he ever had been. Then, Dawid and Aniela also hugged and wished me well.

Shortly, a very fancy carriage pulled up outside our home. We had sometimes seen such carriages on the streets of our city, but none of us had ever ridden in one. The driver sat atop the tall bench seat holding the reins of a pair of well groomed, brown mares. The door opened and a man in his early thirties stepped out. He was very well dressed, wearing a black suit. His short black hair was neatly combed and he sported a moustache to match. I could not help by notice that he had one of their new inventions called a gun strapped to his waist.

"Good morning. I am Kasper Klemens, your host and Security Guard for this trip. I will take extremely good care of your daughters." Dita and her family had just joined us and our dads seem relieved to hear this. We seldom ever saw Security Guards; that he had a gun with him convinced everyone that nothing would ever be allowed to harm us. Dad carried my bag for me and he handed it to Kasper, who stowed it inside the carriage. Eliasz handed him Dita's bag. Kasper then made a motion with his hand that we were to climb inside.

Ah, our first challenge. Careful to maintain our balance, Dita and I stepped into the carriage and sat on the fine leather seats. Naturally, we both called out our goodbyes to everyone, as Kasper climbed in with us. He stowed our bags beneath our seat and sat opposite of us, his back to the driver. He gave a knock on the back wall and the driver clicked to the horses. We began moving down the street, clip clop sounds reverberating in our ears.

"Well, young ladies, we are finally off. It is my great honor to accompany you and assist you in any way that I can. If you need anything or desire anything, just let me know."

"Thanks," I replied politely.

"Thanks for calling us young ladies and not young Holy Vessels. We are kind of tired of hearing that expression," Dita said.

Kasper grinned, "I rather thought that you might. I've got a fourteen year old daughter myself, Isolda. When we are around the Elders, we must be polite, but when it's just us, we can be informal. Now then, I bet you are dying to know where we are headed on this trip, right?"

"Yes indeed! This is so great. We've never been but about a half mile from our homes before now," I replied.

"Figures, most young women and men, for that matter, are in the same situation. Work and study seems to occupy most lives on Dorota. That's why I joined the Security Guards — at least we get to do a lot of traveling around the country. We are heading for port city of Bozydar, on the southwest corner of our continent. Along the way, you will get to see one of the gem mines and pass by two of our large forests. Plus, you will get to see many farmsteads as we travel along the road. It will take us three days to get there, so we will have to spend two nights at some inns along the way."

"When we get to Bozydar, I am to show you around the city and take you to the beaches. There, some others will help you learn to swim. I'm sure you will love the brown sandy beaches. The waters are warm this time of year. Also, you are scheduled to tour the fishing industry, and, if you are so inclined, I am instructed to allow you to learn some of the women's ways that they use there. If you see other women doing something that you do not already know how to do and if you wish to take time to learn that, you are to tell me about it, and I will make the arrangements. This is rather a combined vacation type of trip, along with a learning on the job trip."

"That sounds just perfect," I replied; quite honestly, it did.

"Once we have done all that you desire in Bozydar, we will then travel the Great Coastal Road which encircles our whole continent. I am to have you all back at Wit by early September, where the Elders have arranged for you to learn the ways of the women who work in our banks. So sit back and enjoy these next two months, after that, you will be back into a more structured environment once more. You know how structured the Elders can be." We both giggled.

"You are very lucky ladies. Few of our citizens ever get this 'grand tour' of our land."

"Don't folks go on vacations much?" Dita asked. "Our families haven't, but do others?"

"Not really, it's infrequently done, if at all. Most families spend all of their time keeping their households going, and the husbands work hard to fulfill their obligations to their families and have little time left over for such things as extended trips. You both know well how much work it takes to keep your own homes going."

"That's an understatement," I replied with a grin, wondering just how far Kasper would go along these lines. He was being very frank with us. "But it is really nice to feel totally safe for us to walk down the street to the market carrying our money pouches with us."

"Yes, usually it is totally safe for everyone in Dorota. However, once you leave the cities, sometimes there are Unholy men, rebels we call them, whom the Elders have failed to reach. They can cause problems, but that's why I have my gun with me. I promise you that no harm will come to either of you this trip."

This was the first time that we'd heard about rebels! I wanted to know more about them, but thought better of asking him just now. Besides, the countryside just appeared, as we left the city behind us. Dita and I stared at the great outdoors slowly moving by us. Rugged hills lay on either side, rounded brown granite poked above the grasses here and there. We watched the land roll by, totally enthralled.

Just after noon, we entered a small village of some fifty stone buildings, most all of which looked identical to our homes back in the city! We stopped by a slightly larger one, whose sign read simply Inn. "Lunchtime, my ladies," Kasper grinned and opened the door. He positioned his body to be able to catch us if we stumbled getting out of the carriage. "Watch your step." We did so, exiting slowly. I would be embarrassed if I fell out of the carriage on my first trip! He then led us into this small inn. Neither of us had ever been in an inn before, well not in this country, that is.

The six tables were unique, I thought. One half of the table was designed for men, while the opposite half was built for women. That is, on the women's side, the tabletop was only six inches from the floor, and the chairs were the typical sloped back style so that we could easily eat. A small raised box was on the floor near one end. Two families were just finishing their meal as we entered, and we allowed Kasper to lead us to a table.

Shortly, a woman in her twenties, wearing a nice white dress and slip on shoes like ours came up to our table. I watched fascinated as she removed one shoe, reached up, pulled a pad out of her waist pocket, and placed it on the little box. Next, she retrieved a pencil and positioned her foot over the paper. "Welcome, may I take your order?" She noticed our huge earrings, and added, "Wow! I've never seen earrings like yours. You must have done incredibly well in school." I observed hers and noted that she only had two on her school tier.

"Is old Urszula still cooking the meals here?" Kasper asked politely.

"You bet she is, why? Have you been here before?" she asked.

"Yes, many times, though not at noon. In that case, ladies, I would suggest her hearty soup and bread. You won't believe just how good her soup and bread are. Trust me." I watched the waitress write down our order, and then she put the pencil back and picked up the pad, stowing it in her pouch.

"Be back soon with your meal," she replied. "I'll tell Urszula that you enjoy her cooking," she grinned.

Before long, she returned, a carrying yoke around her neck. Hanging from the two sides were three bowls, a large, uncut round loaf of bread, and silverware. Carefully, she sat it down by us and sat down on the floor. Carefully, using both feet around a bowl, she lifted it from the flat tray and moved it the couple of inches to sit it before me. She scooted a bit and repeated her action, placing a bowl before Dita. I observed that she had taken one bowl from each side. Now she did the same with a pair of spoons. She got up in our usual awkward manner and carried her yoke with the rest of the items over to his side of the table. This time, she sat on the chair beside Kasper and used her feet to sit his bowl before him and then the bread, along with the remaining utensils.

"Wow. You are really good at this," I complimented her. She smiled. "Been doing it for five years at noon now, I'd better be. It's murder to have to clean up a spill if I goof," she confided in us.

"Say, Kasper, put down that we ought to spend some time learning how waitresses manage," I suggested. Indeed, the soup was both hearty and delicious, but the bread was divine." When we were done, our waitress brought Kasper the bill, six coppers. He counted out the coins onto the table. Once more, she sat on a man's chair and picked up each coin with her toes, placing them into her waist pouch. When she left, Dita and I turned to see what she did with them. She went to the counter, and one by one, retrieved the coins and put them on the counter top. She went to the other side, opened a drawer, and one by one, slid them inside.

"Well, that shouldn't be too hard to learn how to do," Dita suggested, "excepting for lifting the food onto the table. Now that might be difficult."

Kasper smiled. "Duly noted ladies. I will see that you have an opportunity to learn this skill. Shall we continue our journey?"

Late that afternoon we passed the gem mine, but did not stop. There really wasn't much to see but a dark hole in the ground. We spent the night at another inn; this one was larger. Kasper got us two rooms. His was next door to ours. After our dinner, we retired for the night. "If you need anything, just bang on the wall or call out loudly or come and get me. Pleasant dreams young ladies."

Our room was small and there was only one medium sized bed, large enough for two adults. First, we changed into our nightgowns, each helping the other get our long hair outside the gown that we had wiggled into. Then, we took turns brushing out our hair. By now, both of ours reached down to the small of our backs; mine was still quite blonde and Dita's was jet black. "Guess we get to sleep together," I whispered. We crawled into bed, using our teeth to pull up the covers as we were used to doing.

Dita rolled over facing me. "Bethany, I still love you passionately, you know that? I've never met another woman who could ever take your place. I know that you told me to find someone else when you died last lifetime, but I just couldn't. I raised our son and doted on him, but no one can compare to you. I still love you, Bethany."

"Renzo, er, Dita, I still love you too. You are still my one and only true love. After all, you are the only man who could ever keep up with all the games I loved to play. Gosh, Dita, whatever are we going to do this time? You are gorgeous, far prettier than I am! I love your hair."

"I know, I feel so strange like this. I'm supposed to take care of you, my love, but can't we still love each other anyway?" she replied. Our lips met passionately, and we snuggled close for the night. "I love you, Bethany," she whispered. I replied likewise. This was going to be strange indeed. Could we even get married I wondered? Linda would understand, but would anyone else? I dreamed of Renzo (Dita now) all night long, all the fabulous times we had together throughout two lifetimes.

The next day, we rolled down hill into the farmlands area of Dorota. While the farmstead buildings were the same identical stone houses like our own, large barns also accompanied them. We saw both men and women out tending the fields, horse drawn equipment occasionally worked in the fields. This time of year, we could see the many and varied crops, which we began to count. Dita invented a game called who can spot the largest number of different kinds of crops. Soon even Kasper was pulled into her game, and the time passed by rapidly.

At the next inn, I had Kasper add working on a farm to his list of things we wanted to explore learning how to do. He smiled and wrote it down. I wondered how long this list would end up being. Once again, Dita and I shared a small room, nearly identical to the last one. I began to see that all the buildings were being purposely made to be identical. The reason became apparent — because of us women. By having everything the same, space-wise, once a woman learned how to do something, she could do it the same way no matter where she found herself. This, I realized, was vitally important in this society. A woman grew up in one home, where she learned just how to manage all details of running her home, at least by the time that she finished school. Now she married and moved into another home somewhere else. Imagine the multitude of problems the newlywed would have, if nothing that she already knew how to do had migrated with her to this new home! So there was a reason behind all this identicalness of their buildings. Still, I found that to be incredibly boring, but terribly predictive.

That night, when we were alone and had brushed out our hair, Dita said, "Bethany, I don't even have arms to hold you tightly like I used to do. I swear that I will still do everything I can do to make you happy." We passionately kissed once more. Then, she said, "You know, from what dad has told me, eventually some boy will ask you to marry him. We have little choice to say no, dad says, unless there is something wrong with him. Bethany, I just cannot live without being with you. So Bethany, will you marry me? I mean later on when we are all done with this mess, assuming that we are both still alive? If you say yes, then we both can say no to any other proposal that comes along. We just say that we have already agreed to marry someone else, only we just don't say to whom."

"Brilliant, Dita, brilliant. Yes, I will. I cannot imagine life without you. I know it is going to be really a strange marriage, but somehow we can manage. Good thinking. I would hate to find myself marrying a man I did not love, which seems to happen a lot in this society." We then kissed, sealing our secret pact and crawled into bed.

The next late afternoon, we arrived in the large port city of Bozydar. At last, we could finally see the ocean as we crested a hill and headed into the town below. Azure blue it seemed, inviting us, beckoning us to it. We both knew that one day we would need to find a ship to take us back to our part of the world, Velona or Zargarb. Thus, we kept our eyes open, picking up any detail that might one day prove useful to us.

As we drew closer to the beach and the harbor, the inns became more frequent. Yet, they all looked precisely the same as the other two that we had stayed in the last two nights. Kasper explained, "Look, if the inns are any larger than they are, the owners and the women they employ could not easily run them. Hence, the size remains the same, just the frequency of the inns increases. Each one can handle ten overnight guests. Any more than that and the maids cannot take care of the rooms. You know how long it takes to make a bed, right?" We giggled, recalling how swiftly using our teeth and feet we could strip a bed and just how frustratingly long it took to remake it!

Our inn was within walking distance of the beaches and the docks.

After having dinner, Kasper brought our bags into our room for us and he retired for the night. While doing our nightly chores in our room, which was the same as the other nights, Dita commented, "Well, Bethany, this has got to be the weirdest, strangest society that I have ever heard about or come across, and we sure have come across some strange ones when we were on our voyage of exploration. Instead of doing the simple thing of letting women have the arms that they were born with, no they got to cut them off and then go to Herculean efforts to get by, making all buildings the same, just enough time each day for the men and women to get done all the daily things that must be done, with no time left over. No time for games, for fun, for vacations, for the arts, for music, for creativity, for dances, for pleasure, for anything at all but get ready for the next day's chores. These people are just plain nuts!"

"No, they are mostly hypnotized zombies, well-meaning and kind and considerate and loving, but nevertheless zombies," I replied. "Renzo, er, Dita, I am so thankful that you came after me! About now, I would be going nuts, if it weren't for you at my side. I love you!" I gave her the passionate kiss first this time. We retired for the night.

The next day, Kasper announced over breakfast that we would be going to the beach. "You'll need some swimming clothes, so we'll pick them up on our way to the beach. I have taken the liberty of asking Julita, a local young woman who swims well, to join us and give you swimming lessons. I hope this meets with your approval. If not, I can tell her not today."

"Terrific, Kasper! You don't know how much we want to go swimming. We haven't been swimming in. . ." Oops, I caught myself almost messing up big time. "Well, never, but we've read all about the beaches and swimming. That would be kind of her to teach us how today. We can't wait! Right Dita?"

Dita tried to poke me with her arms to keep me from blundering, but once more found that she had none. Frustrated, she said, "You bet!" and gave me a warning glance that told me that she saw that I nearly goofed.

Apparently, Kasper did not notice it. "Great. She should be dropping by here shortly. Look for a brown haired woman in her early twenties coming in and looking around for us." We finished our breakfast and waited.

Shortly, I spied a woman answering his description enter and he called out. "Julita, we're over here." I wanted to wave and was frustrated that I could not. I kept forgetting just how annoying it could be to be armless again. You cannot even wave, but then I chided myself for dwelling on such matters. This body was armless and that was that. Live with it. She came over and joined us.

"Hi, I am Julita. Kasper wants me to help you two learn how to swim, right? Wow! Look at your earrings! Those are incredible!" She had short brown hair and a fair complexion, but her skin was quite tan, I suspected she was outdoors most of the time.

"Hi, thanks. I am Bethany and this is my dear friend, Dita. We can't wait to go swimming!"

"First ladies, we must get you some swimming suits," Kasper replied. I noticed that Julita also appreciated being called a lady and not a Holy Vessel. We took an immediate liking to this fun-loving young woman. As we walked down the street to a clothing store, we three chatted away, learning that she was married and her husband was a lifeguard at the beach where we were heading.

All the swimming suits were identical, save their color. I chose a yellow one, while Dita chose a blue one, our favorite colors. They were designed so that another woman could help you get into yours, though with some difficulty. It was one piece with leg holes and a head hole; its back was open and tied shut with a long string. First, we stepped into it, putting our feet through the holes. Then, the other person would have to help you pull it up and then carefully pull the tie strings, one loop at a time until the neck closed well. Finally, a knot was tied to hold it shut. Ah, now that proved the most challenging of all; Dita and I worked diligently, but frustratingly, to get ours on each other and properly tied. I couldn't believe that it took us a whole hour to get into our suits! A pair of hands and we would have been ready in a couple of minutes, argh.

Julita asked, "What do you want to do about your long hair? Perhaps tie it up? I've never been swimming with anyone who had such long, beautiful hair as you two have."

"Thanks, I've never had mine cut yet. I think it's best to leave it as is, it could use a good washing," I replied. Dita had no idea and went along with my choice. We wiggled back into our normal thin dresses, putting them over our new trunks and left the shop to join Kasper.

Kasper was patiently waiting on us, just outside, smoking his pipe. He already had gotten our towels. "Ah, all set, I take it?"

"Yes, sir. They can now put on their trunks and take them off. Now, it's beach time," Julita reported. I suspected that Kasper was making note of each thing that we mastered, as he jotted something in his notebook as he led the way.

The beach was spectacular, brown sands lapped by gently rolling waves of azure waters. Perhaps a hundred young children were out here lying in the sun on their towels or out splashing in the waters. Oh, if we had only chosen to live here, we too could have spent our summers on the beach! Julita took us to the lifeguard stand, a tall wooden structure from where her husband could watch this stretch of the beach. She introduced us to Bolek, a tall, thin man, not much older than she was. "I am going to teach them to swim, Bolek. Where's the best place today?" she asked.

"Down there the waves are the gentlest today. Have fun," he replied, though he stared continually at Dita and my earrings. Julita had three in her first two tiers and a magnificent red ruby in her third, indicating she was married. We walked down the sandy beach to a convenient spot. Here, Kasper set up base, laying down some towels for us. We took off our shoes and light dresses. Many other young girls were sunbathing, but a few were either wading or swimming in our unique way.

"First, let's get used to the waters," Julita suggested and a-wading we went! She explained that for us to swim, we needed to float on our backs and use our feet to kick, propelling us along slowly, but backwards.

All of a sudden, all of my previous experiences swimming in the ocean in my previous lifetimes came back to me. I laid back and began floating, then began paddling around. "Wow! You are swimming like a pro!" Julita exclaimed very surprised that I took to it so easily and perfectly.

Dita, on the other hand, panicked! Renzo, er, Dita had always used his powerful arms to swim. She felt helpless and very spooked. Both Julita and I worked with her for over an hour before Dita finally relaxed and began to paddle around with her feet. I heaved a sigh of relief, my intense worry for her finally eased off. Still, she often attempted to use her arms at the first sign of her head going under the water. I remembered just how scared I had been of this when I first had to swim and I knew what she was going through this afternoon.

We spent several days going to the beach and swimming, but Julita only came with us this first day. She spent the whole afternoon, and I overheard Kasper talking to her near the time we were going to leave and head back to our inn. "Here's your fee and I threw in some extra. I know that you have given up your scheduled cooking dinnertime and Bolek will not have supper waiting for quite some time. So use this extra to take him out to dinner, please." She grinned and thanked him, then raced over to tell Bolek the good news.

In the evenings, Kasper took us on long strolls about the docks. We could see the many warehouses and ships that were currently in port. Many were smaller coastal vessels, which he explained plied the waters around our continent, delivering goods from place to place. We also saw three copies of our fancy Velona caravels — precise duplicates. I now understood what Linda had told me fourteen years before, that they had simply captured one caravel and made duplicates of it to sail to our portion of Tarra. "At least we won't have to load boxes and crates onto the ships," Dita teased us.

Kasper laughed, "No, my pretty Dita, I'm afraid that is men's heavy work. Some women who are good with math do work in their accounting departments, but I understand that you can already handle such chores. You father told the Elders just how great of a job you did for him. Now ahead is the fishermen's portion of the docks. Your nose is the guide." Indeed, it stank like fish, just as it did in Velona or any of the other Sea Prince coastal towns.

"Some women work in the fishing industry. A few who are excellent swimmers actually set sail with their husbands or fathers to go fishing.

Most, however, work on the processing of each day's catch. They don't do the messy work, but help on the drying side. Tomorrow, we'll come by here and you can see for yourself. Yes, those racks there are today's catch drying in the evening sun." Rows upon rows of fillets were lying out being dried and preserved. All were heavily salted.

True to his word, we did arrive in time to watch the many workers processing the day's catch of fish. While the men gutted the fish and prepared the fillets, the women, sitting on their butts, carefully placed them out to dry. I ought to have guessed at this, yesterday when I noticed how low to the ground the racks actually were. Further on down the line, other women were removing the dried fish fillets and putting them into wooden crates. When one was filled, a man would then fasten a lid on to it, using a hammer and four nails. Others then moved the crates into a warehouse using a dolly. We didn't need to learn anything here; the women's actions were commonplace in our kitchens.

The next day, we had a guided tour of one of their ship-building firms. We saw several of the smaller ships under construction in the dry docks and even one of their ocean going caravel-copies being built. This brought back fond memories to Dita and me. We'd spent many, many months sailing around the world in these type ships in our earlier lifetimes. The engineer who gave us the tour was highly impressed with the knowledge that we displayed regarding their prized caravels, especially when I mentioned the safety features that we had installed to help protect the armless women we rescued and transported to Velona, to say nothing of ourselves. Again, I spied Kasper writing notes in his small book, but didn't question him about it.

"Say, is it possible for us to go out fishing with one of those fishing, sailing boats?" I asked. I recalled having built my own sailing dinghy and wanted to experience sailing once more. Kasper gave me a disbelieving look, but promised to make some inquiries. Two days later the three of us headed to the docks in the early dawn hours.

The fishing boat was small, normally carrying a crew of four, including its captain, an old blonde bearded sailor who went by Cap Drugi. "Ahoy ladies, Kasper. I'm Cap Drugi, welcome to Drugi's Catch. Normally, I have three crew to do the fishing, but seeing how Kasper has paid me double what a day's catch will fetch, I'm all yours. You three will be my crew today. What'll it be?"

"Hi, I'm Bethany and this is Dita. We want to learn to sail her and see if it's possible for us to help you actually fish. I think I can sail her, captain, but I've no idea about the fishing part."

"Well, let's get aboard and see how you do. Careful, if you've never been in a boat before. Don't want you rocking her over and dumping yourselves into the ocean," he replied, issuing a stern caution.

I stepped in easily and remembered how the smaller boats tended to

42

rock. Poor Dita had a terrible time of it. I sensed her frantically reaching out with her arms to keep from falling, before Kasper's arms steadied her. "Keep your feet far apart, Dita," I whispered to her, but she looked rather pale. Cap Drugi untied the mooring lines and we drifted free.

He began to explain about tacking out of port and I remembered all my own lessons from two lifetimes ago. He soon allowed me to issue the tacking orders, though I had no way really to perform the actions. Ropes had to be untied, moved. and retied. I was used to a single sail dinghy, whose sail I could control with my feet if need be. However, both of us took turns at the tiller. As the sun finally rose in the early morning sky, we dropped sail to begin to fish.

While Kasper and the captain worked the large fishing nets, an action in which we were useless in every way, we were given poles to use in an attempt to catch a single fish. We did manage to catch a few and, with a good deal of struggling with our feet, managed to get them aboard the ship, but the men had to finish the work. At least I knew I could catch a fish at sea, if I had to do so to stay alive, while on a long voyage back to Velona. Of course, I didn't tell Kasper my reason for this big experiment. When we returned in the late afternoon, I had fun calling out all the tack changes, taking us precisely into his berth at the docks. Cap Drugi was highly impressed with my seamanship, a fact noted in Kasper's notebook, I guessed.

The next day was Sunday and we all had to go to Church. Kasper was kind enough to help us into our Sunday dresses and shoes and socks, an action normally done by our fathers. I will say that poor Kasper had a devil of a time with our long hair getting in his way. His daughter wore her hair short, he explained. At last, with his arms around us, we three walked out of the inn to the closest Church.

Upon entering, both Dita and I got the shock of this lifetime! A dozen women entered, their husbands arms around them, all wearing what must be the latest fashion in Velona! They wore the unique flaring cone dresses, hoop skirts making the bottom of their dresses a circle six feet in diameter. We heard the telltale click of high heels and caught a glimpse of the fancy heeled boots that I had worn, as did so many others, and made popular by Alexa, who had turned them into *the* fashion statement in Velona so many years ago. We two stared in disbelief at these women, as did Kasper and a number of others nearby. Of course, these women looked terrific and knew it, relishing in the attention that they were receiving.

I suddenly had a completely new factor thrown into the mix of my analysis of Dorota society. I just had to meet these women, and asked Kasper if he could arrange it after services. Since the bisklep had not yet started and the choir members were still filing in to their places up beside the altar, Kasper hastily went over to one of these elegantly dressed women. He returned with a smile, "You can chat with them over lunch here in the

Church fellowship room after services." I could tell that he was also interested in meeting them as well. Dita and I could scarcely contain our excitement during the boring sermon, which we'd heard so many times before.

At last, Kasper led us down into the basement dining area. He spied the women and their husbands, and led us over to them. After many introductions and comments about our fabulous earrings, they chatted freely about their apparel. It seems that women's fashions were now being imported from Velona. Although on the expensive side at present, these women's husbands were relatively wealthy and could afford the extravagance. The men thought it was money very well spent, for their wives looked spectacular indeed, though admittedly extremely helpless. Their husbands had to feed them and support them whenever they walked. None was really used to walking in such heels nor in wearing such dresses, but the attention that they received more than made up for any discomfort.

Later, Kasper took us on a long walk. "Isn't that incredible?" he said, unable to get these women and their impressive fashion statement out of his mind.

"Yes, it is. Your ships are now beginning to return with women's fashions from abroad, Velona I believe. It's not unexpected, you know. When an isolated society suddenly encounters another society that is so different from theirs, in time one should expect to see elements of the new society appearing in the other. I see no harm at all in the fancy women's fashions. After all, we are supposed to be dressed up on Sundays. I expect that you will be seeing more and more of this as time goes on and your ships bring back trading goods that the ship's masters can sell for a tidy profit. I don't see it conflicting in any way with our society, do you?" I asked.

"Well, not really any conflict. It is just so, so unusual to see our women looking so, well so beautiful. I have to say I do like their look, but gosh, the cost is so prohibitive. Still, my wife would look fantastic in one of their outfits. If it was truly deemed harmful to our society, I'm sure that the Elders would already have put an end to it."

Ah, so the Elders do exert control over other aspects of this society, I concluded, filing this observation away for the future. I didn't tell him that in a normal society, the dressmakers would be quick to copy these expensive dresses, selling them for far cheaper prices. Here, I had no idea how a woman could sew much of anything, let alone such fancy dresses. Even with arms, getting into one of those outfits was tricky.

The next day, it was back into the fancy carriage as we began our month long circumnavigation of the continent, along the picturesque Coastal Rim Road. We passed through all the major coastal cities and so many smaller towns and villages that I lost count. After the first day, it became incredibly boring for us.

Chapter 5 On the Road

I decided to see if Kasper would talk about our society in general. "Say, Kasper, until you showed up at our house, we had not really heard about Security Guards and even guns. How many are there? Where are you all stationed, if that's the right word for it?"

Kasper was also bored and began to talk honestly and freely. "Yes, well most folks may have only just heard mention of us from time to time. We try to stay in the background as much as possible. After all, there isn't much need for us in most places — usually that is. I think that maybe there are ten thousand of us all told — just a guess on my part, you understand. We all take our orders from the Elders. My group of a hundred is assigned to Elder Amadei of the Elder College at Wit. There is only one place in Dorota where our guns are made, a secret factory in Kondrat, and only we Security Guards are allowed to own and carry a gun. They are very dangerous things, these guns. With one shot, one little pull of the trigger, I can kill a person a long ways away from me, though I have never actually fired it at a person before. I did get to shoot it at some targets during my training."

"But why do you need the gun in the first place?" Dita asked. "There isn't any crime that I've ever seen."

"Rebels," he replied.

"What rebels?" she probed. "We've never seen any rebels in our city."

"Well, you don't normally see them in the larger cities, because there are too many Elders living in them. Rebels avoid the Elders as much as possible. So you find the rebels operating out of the more rural areas, particularly the highlands and forests. The forests make for good cover and hiding places. We can't search every inch of those dense woods, you see. The ones that we do manage to catch are sent to the Fields of Kondrat. The Elders call them the Unholy ones. You'd be surprised; there are quite a few women among these rebels, though I must admit I don't know how they can survive well at all. I mean our women are so dependent upon us men, no offense intended."

Dita smiled coyly, "None taken. Do these rebels cause trouble for the rest of us? I mean, should we be worried traveling around like we are?"

"No, dear ladies, not to worry, you have good old Kasper here to protect you from the rebels. But cause trouble, well, yes and no. Sometimes they burst in on a Sunday Service and try to disrupt it with all their shouting and such. Some have attempted to kill some of the Elders, though, but never any ordinary citizens like you. I'm sure the rebels would not harm you women. You are much to pretty to harm," he teased us and we gave him the usual coy smile of appreciation.

"Actually, that is about the very worst thing anyone could do, harm one of our Holy Vessels. Well, harming an Elder would be right up there with that. After all, you are the ones who can bring new life into the world, not we men for all our strength and power. Harming a woman is tantamount to harming our whole civilization."

"Very true," Dita replied. "Tell me, how come there are not even any arguments between husbands and wives here in Dorota? I've never seen mom or dad have an argument, not even a small domestic dispute." I had not seen my folks have any either, curious.

Kasper looked puzzled, almost as if he had never considered this question. "Don't know that one, ladies. Perhaps you ought to ask Elder Amadei about that one. Maybe it is because we all go to Church every Sunday and are reminded of our duties and obligations? My wife and I have never had anything to argue about, now that you mention it."

"Very likely," Dita concluded for now.

That evening when we were alone again and brushing out each other's hair, Dita commented, "You know, Bethany, all the men in Dorota are in propitiation towards their women. Unreal, there are probably five hundred thousand men all propitiating towards another five hundred thousand women, who are utterly dependent upon these men. Women here cannot survive without their men, yet the men propitiate to the women. What a nasty relationship. I sure would not want a man whose highest thoughts of me were those of propitiation to me. What do all these men believe that they have done to us women anyway?"

"Cutting off our arms when we are born, that's what," I replied slightly antagonistically. "Look, Renzo, er, I mean Dita, sorry, I sometimes get confused here. Look, Dita, we know that their history goes back spanning three hundred years of this same situation. Say the average lifetime is sixty years, that means anyone of these spiritual beings — and let's don't lose sight of that key fact, they are all spiritual beings — anyone of these has now had at least five new baby bodies. The odds are fifty-fifty that half of the time those bodies were female. Hence, half of the time they had the baby trauma of having their arms amputated just after birth and have lived much as we are now doing."

She looked shocked, "You mean that we are dealing with a self-perpetuating aberration here? Wow! That makes sense. Take any male, say even Kasper here. He's already had the experience of having two or three female bodies here in Dorota and had to try to live this way." Dita shrugged her armless shoulders in frustration. "So now, even though he has told himself to forget the past, he still intuitively knows that the women he sees have been deliberately mutilated by the doktors. Hence, he feels guilty, though he can no longer remember why he should feel this way. Feeling guilty, he propitiates towards all women. Wow. What an ongoing, self-perpetuating aberration!"

"Exactly, Dita, exactly. He's analytically forgotten his previous lifetimes, mainly because none of the objects and bodies of that lifetime are in his present environment. Hence, he forgets; they are not around him any longer. However, he still deep down knows what has happened and what is really going on here. Dita! I bet these rebels have somehow uncovered the real truth behind this whole society and that's why they are trying to stop it."

She grinned, "We need to find these rebels and have a long chat with them."

"Yes, but we don't want to blow our cover just yet. The Elders frown on any Holy Vessel talking with the Unholy. We certainly know why that is!" We both laughed.

"Say, we still need to find out just how these Elders can exert such a powerful hypnotic control over most people, even those back in our part of the world," Dita noted. "I think that our working with Albin may give us some clues."

Days passed by as we continued our circumnavigation of Dorota. We'd left Urjasz behind us and were rolling along the northern coastline some seventy-five miles from the northwestern coastal city of Grzegorz. To our left the dark outline of the huge Turk Wood loomed along the horizon. This long stretch between Urjasz and Grzegorz was dotted with smaller hamlets, some with only one inn. Mostly deciduous trees with a scattering of evergreens predominated. Though I wished that we could take a side trip to at least visit the woods close up, Kasper vetoed any such notion. Rebels were known to inhabit the woods.

Ahead, the Turk Woods began to inch closer to the roadway and I thought I might get my wish anyway, if the woods actually eventually reached the road. Another mile and several bends in the road later, it did. We left the stifling heat behind us as our carriage entered the cool, dark woods. I had forgotten how much I had missed the smell, the odor, the fragrance of a thick forest. Without warning, the carriage came to a stop.

Kasper, who was dozing, jerked alert. Our driver thumped on the wall behind his seat and Kasper got out. "Damn. A tree has fallen across the road," he called out to us. We carefully climbed out to see for ourselves. Indeed a medium sized tree lay completely across the cobblestone road, blocking our passage. We four stood there surveying the situation. The shoulder to our right was spongy and would not support the thin rims of our carriage wheels, so we couldn't go around. I was about to ask our driver if he had an axe by chance, when suddenly many stones came flying towards us!

One hit Kasper in his head and one hit our driver as well. Many others were near misses. None were aimed anywhere close to Dita or me, however, which I found curious as I thought about it all later on. Like a rock, Kasper dropped to the ground, a moment later, our driver fell down as well. A dozen rough looking men, some with uncut hair and beards came rushing out of the woods. I saw that a few still carried slings, which I instantly guessed were the rock shooters.

Dita looked forlornly at the gun still in Kasper's holster. She was incredibly frustrated; she wanted to protect me as he/she had always done in our other lifetimes, but she couldn't even hold a sword, much less retrieve, aim, and fire the gun at these men charging towards us. She just broke down and started crying at her helpless situation.

I was a little out of practice — something like thirty years or so — but I began to use my abilities as a spiritual being. I floated over the closest man, levitated him, and gave him a toss back towards the woods. The others saw this and slowed their rush towards us. "Go away or you will be next!" I yelled at them. One continued to press on towards us, seeing nothing by a young helpless teen standing there. I picked him up and gave him a toss. Since their original attack had not been meant to kill Kasper or our driver, I didn't throw them to kill them, just a gentle toss, more or less. Seeing the second one tossed away like a leaf in the wind and seeing no one else around, the remaining men turned around and fled back into the woods, leaving Dita and I standing on the cobblestones with the driver and Kasper lying unconscious before us.

Dita stopped crying and tried to wipe her face on her dress. "Sorry, I lost it there, Bethany. I wanted so badly to protect you and couldn't. I sort of forgot about your tossing skills."

"It's okay, I totally understand, Dita. When I first lost them to the mantis creatures, I felt so frustrated and helpless at times. We'd better get out of here though, before they decide to come back."

"How are we going to get them into the carriage, move the tree, and drive the carriage? Damn, if we only had arms," Dita replied becoming more and more angry. This was a good sign, I thought. She had been in total despair and grief. Anger was much higher emotionally, though I knew that she had a ways to go.

"You hold the carriage door open for me, and I'll lift them inside onto the seats. You get the drinking water out and tend to their wounds — probably a concussion at most is my guess. Put a cold compress on the spot where the rocks hit them. I'll see if I can't get the tree moved and the carriage going somehow."

Dita struggled, fighting against her body, but managed to get the door open and held it with one foot. "Damn this society anyway!" she continued antagonistically. "The men ought to have their arms cut off and see how they like it!" I carefully laid both men inside and Dita climbed in to begin to tend to their head wounds. I floated over to the tree and moved it out of the way enough that I thought the carriage could get around it. Then, I faced the carriage.

Three steps, nearly vertical, led to the driver's box, with a handrail on my right against the carriage front wall. However, without arms, that was useless. I gave up trying to climb up; it was too precarious in a dress. I floated over my body, lifted it up, and sat it down in the driver's seat, and then I stared at the four reins wrapped around a post. I spied the brake lever. It was in the locked position. Using my feet, I managed to get it into the unlocked position and felt the carriage roll slightly.

I used my feet and toes to unwrap the reins, noticing that one pair was on the left side of the horses and the other pair, to their right. Ah ha. I had the steering worked out. Carefully, I began wrapping the left reins around my left foot, and then got the other ones around my right foot. "Here goes nothing or something, don't know which!" I hollered to Dita, who yelled back to get us out of here now! "Giddy up, horses," I said and shook the reins a little, even wiggling my torso forward and back, as if that would encourage them to move. At last, they decided to go and began to walk on down the road.

"I think they know enough to stay on the road," I called down to Dita.

"That's good of them," she yelled back, now in a more conservative tone.

"Good horses. Stay on the roadway for Bethany, please," I called out to the horses. Of course, they didn't understand a word that I said, but I felt better and continued chatting to the horses, who continued to walk along the cobblestone road. I knew that I didn't dare get them going faster; I had very little control over the reins. A good pull might jerk them completely off my lower legs. If I lost them, I'd have no control at all.

A bit later, I called out to Dita, "How's it going down there?"

"I got a cold compress on each of them, kind of straddling the benches. If they wake up, they can see my privates, kind of an embarrassing position that I am in right now, but I've got a cold cloth on each of their heads," she yelled back nearly cheerful again. I relaxed, Dita had recovered, and we were moving again. Soon, perhaps, one of them will wake up and take over.

Wishful thinking on my part, however, time drifted on as did the miles. Periodically, I asked Dita about them, but continued to get the same answer, "Still out cold."

Just then, a small coastal village appeared as we rounded a bend. Several wagons were in the street as well as two coaches. A traffic jam lay ahead and I had no control or very little. "Help, someone help us! I cannot stop the horses. Please, someone help us!" I yelled as loudly as I could. Several men looked up and my way — our plight was obvious, an armless woman was trying to drive a coach!

One young man raced over to us, grabbed the left horse by its bridle, and began telling them to stop, which they thankfully did. "Thanks! We got ambushed by rebels a ways back. Our driver and our Security Guard were hit with stones. They are in the coach and unconscious. Please, can you take us to an inn where we can spend the night and help us with our driver and guard, please?" I asked.

The young man grinned, "Sure, you bet. I'll lead the carriage to our inn. Just hold on!" As soon as he had said that, I saw that he really regretted saying that. How was I to "hold on?"

"Thanks!" I replied, pretending not to notice his gaffe.

He led us a ways down their main street, stopping at a small inn. "How did you ever manage to get them inside and drive this carriage all the way here?" he asked.

"We didn't have much choice. They were lying there on the road and we just couldn't leave them to the rebels. I'm afraid that you are going to have to lift me down, sir. I somehow managed to get up here, but I'm certain that I can't get down."

"I got you. Just lean towards me and I'll catch you." He held out his arms and I did as he asked, sort of fell off the carriage into his arm, and he gently let my feet find the ground.

"Thanks a lot. Maybe you can help us get a room and get our men inside?" I asked politely.

We walked to the carriage door, there was Dita leaning against the other door, legs, uplifted, her feet holding a wet cloth to each man's head. You could see right up her dress, however. She quickly pulled her legs down and struggled to her feet. "They are both still unconscious, Bethany. Now what do we do?"

"We'll take care of them. Here, let me lift you out of the carriage, miss," he said, and Dita, whose legs were cramped, graciously allowed him to lift her to the ground. He climbed in and verified their condition.

"Come with me. I'll take you to the innkeeper and we'll get you all fixed up." A crowd was slowly gathering around us and I knew that many strong arms would soon carry our men inside. A moment later, I explained our predicament to the innkeeper, who quickly arranged for us to have two rooms next to each other.

"Sir, if you will just take what coins you need for our stay and for whatever the carriage and horses will need for the night from my coin pouch, I will be grateful. I am so terribly slow getting coins out of the pouch," I played the part expected of me. He smiled and did so and, to my relief, he then took charge.

"Zoja, take the girls to room four and then get room five ready. We'll go get the men and carry them into room five. Zoja, you then run and fetch the doktor. Tell him we will need his services at once." The young woman led us to our room, opened the door to the next one, and scampered off to find the doktor.

We stood outside our door and soon four men carrying our two fallen men came down the hall, with the innkeeper bustling along in front of them, issuing not-needed orders. "Put them in here, on the bed, side by side, boys." They did so and we entered as well, thanking the four for their help. Now I could see the damage, both had very large goose-egg bumps on their heads, a lot of swelling I noted. Without hands to probe and feel, I couldn't tell if there were any crushed skulls beneath that swelling and hoped the doktors here were not quacks.

A bit later, Zoja came in with the doktor behind her. She was out of breath and I guessed she'd run all the way. I flashed her an understanding smile of thanks; she nodded and grinned. The doktor was in his early fifties, well dressed and observant. He quickly examined both head wounds.

"Lucky men, no skull fractures, probably concussions. We should keep a cold compress on their bumps this night and then see how they are doing in the morning. If there is any sign of nausea, then that is a sure sign that their head blows are more serious than is apparent right now. Expect them to have a bad headache when they awaken," he gave his diagnosis to me. "Now how about you Holy Vessels? Are you injured in any way?"

"No, we are fine. Thanks for looking after them. Do we owe you any money, sir?"

He laughed, "No, no, just glad to be of service to such worthy Holy Vessels. Impressive earrings you are both wearing. Well, I must go now. I've an injured man with a broken leg to attend to. Call me if anything further develops." He left.

The innkeeper bellowed, "Well don't just stand there, Zoja, go fetch two buckets of cold water, while I get some towels and rags."

She giggled. "Okay, dad." Zoja called out to us, "Back in a jiffy," and scampered off once more. He left us alone while he went to find the towels. When he returned, he asked us, "Will you need any help getting the cold compresses on their heads? If so, I will stay. If not, I need to tend to the other customers. I'll have supper brought up here to your room, okay?"

We agreed and he left. Shortly, Zoja came back; her yoke held two buckets of water. She had to do a bit of twisting to get them into the room, however. She sat the yoke down so that one bucket was close to the bed and the two heads of our men. "Need any help?" she asked.

"Thanks for bringing the water, Zoja. I think that we can manage from here. Is he your father?" I asked.

She smiled, "Yes, he and I run the inn, now that mom's passed on. My brother joined the Security Guards, but dad wanted him to help him run the inn. So I did it instead. I suppose I better get back down there and take the orders. I'll bring you up some supper when I get the chance and I'll leave the yoke in case you need to move the buckets."

"Thanks, Zoja. Thanks." We experimented and finally got a cool washcloth on their large bumps. Not long afterwards, both men began to moan and then came around. Kasper sat up, looked around very confused. His hands went to his head and the cloth, which slipped off his head.

"You are safe. We are in an inn at the next town I think," I replied. "Lay back and recover some. You both took a nasty stone to the head from the rebels." He looked around, satisfied himself that he was in an inn, and laid back down.

"What happened, Bethany, Dita? How did we get here? Man, does my head ever hurt!"

"Oh, my head feels like it's crushed," our driver moaned.

"Well, I sort of scared them off. Dita and I got you into the carriage and somehow I managed to drive the carriage on down to the next town, where I yelled for help. I couldn't stop the horses, well maybe I could have, but I didn't want to risk it — dropping the reins and all. Some kind men carried you in here and I got us the room. The innkeeper sent for their doktor, who examined you both, and said it was not serious, unless you get nauseous later on. Zoja will bring us some supper after a while. Oh, she's the innkeeper's daughter and helps run it. There, Dita, did I leave anything out?" Grinning from ear to ear, Dita shook her head no, astounded how I could rattle off such a simple explanation with no warning.

"Yes, how on earth did you run them off? How could you two manage to get two grown men up and into the carriage? How could you get up to the driver's seat? How could you possibly have driven the carriage? Those will do for starters," Kasper said, now sitting up and staring at us both.

"Well, I sort of climbed up there, but I had a man here in the town get me down. I don't think I could have done that. I wrapped the reins around each leg and said giddy up and they sort of began walking and didn't stop until I yelled for help once we entered this village, when a kind man ran up and caught the horses and stopped them. You have to admit, you both are kind of heavy for us to lift, but we did it."

Kasper just shook his head, "Well, Bethany and Dita, I — we owe you our lives it seems. I wonder what those rebels wanted anyway?"

"Don't know. They never said a word, just ran off into the woods," Dita answered, omitting their having seen two of their lot mysteriously picked up and tossed back into the woods.

Just then, Zoja entered carrying our dinner with another yoke. "Oh, I see they are awake. I've got some dinner for you, brought some soup for them." We thanked her and Kasper got up and took the items from her two trays. "If you want, come down after dark and have some tea with me, Bethany, Dita. We can chat then, because everyone will have gone home." We promised to do so and set about eating; I, for one, was famished.

After dark, Dita and I used the yokes to bring the buckets and dishes down to the main floor, where Zoja was waiting for us. She had the teapot on and steaming. "Hi there. Oh just set them anywhere. Come have some tea. By the way, I am in love with your earrings! I've never seen any with so many gems. You two must be very important teens."

"Not really. We just did really well in school and got many awards. Thanks for the tea, Zoja," I replied, as she carefully poured three cups.

"You must be really brave to have gotten away from the rebels. I don't know how I could ever have gotten an unconscious man into a carriage, let alone driven the carriage," she chatted on, her curiosity getting the better of her.

"Oh, I wrapped one set of reins around one leg and the other set around the other and told the horses to giddy up. Somehow, they figured out what I wanted. Say, are there many rebels around here? Those were the first ones we've ever seen." I decided to pump her for information. Who better to know the local gossip than the innkeeper's daughter?

"Yes, yes, we have lots of rebels around these parts. It's the Turk Wood, you see. They hide out in the dense woods where no one can find them. Often we hear of some carriages being stopped and robbed."

"But what do the rebels want when they stop a carriage?" Dita asked, and then added, "Money?"

"Yes, usually money so they can buy food supplies, like grain, flour, and vegetables. I hear that they can hunt for their meat, but the rest they lack. I heard that they even robbed a farmer of a sack of wheat that he was taking to market. Good thing that they only took one of his sacks, though. I'm sure that they only take what they really need to stay alive out there in the woods. They have women to feed too, like us. So I can understand why they must do what they must do, don't you think so?"

I guessed that she knew far more about these rebels than she was saying. Worse, she was testing me out about how I felt about the rebels. Dita gave me a cautionary look. "Well, if they have women like us, surely they must find a way to have food for them to cook. It's bad enough being like this without also starving to death. Are there a lot of rebels?"

"Oh yes, I think so. Lots, but then who can say for sure. They are always in hiding, you see. Otherwise, the Security Guards would arrest them and take them to the Fields of Kondrat!"

"Say, we keep hearing about these Fields of Kondrat. I assume that they are located somewhere around Kondrat. We've never been there. What exactly are these fields?" Dita asked.

"Oh, I know. I have been by there a couple times with my dad — we were bringing in supplies from Kondrat for the inn, you see. It's the most horrible place imaginable! It's a giant fenced in set of farms with guards with guns and all. The poor people inside are prisoners, really they are. I saw the most awful sight that I have ever seen as we went by. The men were plowing the fields, but instead of using oxen or horses, they had six women, just like us, hitched up, pulling the plow! Dad said that these women were Unholy and that they were earning their Redemption. Still, that is just horrible! Don't you think so?"

We both agreed. It was bad enough being forced to be armless all our lives, but to then be so disgraced as to being worked as an oxen — that was too much. Now the darker side of this society began to make its appearance. Zoja chatted on, "So you see why the rebels have to hide out. If they didn't, they'd be hooked up to a plow too. Just awful, but don't let my dad hear us talking like this. He says that they are getting what they deserve for not being Holy Vessels and all that. Still, I don't approve of it." Just then, her dad came into the inn and we had to cease our little chat. We returned to our room.

The next morning, the swelling was down on both their heads, though they each had a nasty headache. Kasper decided to ride beside the driver, in case more trouble came our way. This time, he vowed not to be taken by surprise, though I don't know how he could have done anything differently; we were just ambushed, period. Thankfully, nothing happened at all, just another long, boring day's ride. In fact, nothing else happened for ten more days and around September 1, we finally arrived at the small town called Wit, just north and west of Bazyli.

Chapter 6 The Elder College at Wit

Wit proper was home to about a thousand people, some two hundred fifty families. Again, the town was laid out as a square with similar street numbers as we were used to seeing in Bazyli, which made it easy for us to find shops and things. However, we were going to be staying on the actual grounds of the Elder College at Wit, located only a quarter mile north of the town, within walking distance. A brown stone, circular wall about four feet high surrounded the complex, which consisted of six separate buildings. As we entered immediately to our right was the second largest building, which was the living quarters of the Security Guards. Kasper and his family lived inside. Immediately to our left was the largest building, a giant barn and stable, with a large corral behind it. Dead ahead were two smaller, identical buildings. The one on the right housed the Elders and their families. The one straight ahead held all of their classrooms.

Between the classroom building and the stables lay two other buildings, again brown stone. The one closest to the classroom building was the student dorms; the male students occupied three quarters of it. The other quarter housed their domestic staff, unmarried women for the most part, and where Dita and I would be staying, sharing a large room. A connected building housed the laundry facilities and the giant kitchen and dining room area with a pantry, of course.

As we pulled in, Elder Amadei came out to greet us and showed us around the complex personally. Actually, we quickly discovered his real purpose was to notify us of all the many new rules that we needed to follow. "This is a male college. We work our students hard and we try to avoid having them distracted from their studies by you Holy Vessels, especially ones as pretty as you two are. You will be living in the domestic's quarters. We are a little short on rooms. Will you mind sharing a room? I suspect that you will be better able to help each other this way. Many things that your father and brothers used to do for you, I'm afraid you will have to do for yourselves." We thanked him for allowing us to room together, naturally.

"Now about meals. We dine in shifts, because there are so many of us. First, we Elders and our students dine, then the Security Guards and their families take their turn, and finally the domestic staff eat together. You are permitted to eat with either of those last two groups, whichever you feel most comfortable with, just never with the Elders and their students." He went on about all the rules, most of which made sense, like do not go out for midnight walks. We were still way too near the Turk Wood and there were wild animals prowling around out there. I didn't bother to ask if they were of the two-legged variety.

He then introduced us to the Head Mistress, Zofia Ciecha, a woman in her early fifties, who had never married. She was not the prettiest of women, homely was more apt, but she was knowledgeable, kind, with a great sense of humor, and above all, she had a knack for running the domestic staff efficiently. "Right this way, Kasper has already taken your bags to your room. You are to spend the next few days exploring our fine college. My guess is after that, Elder Amadei will put you both to work," she teased and chuckled.

Our room was a bit Spartan, but we were used to that from all the inns we'd recently visited. "I do hope that you will not mind sharing the large bed. We are a bit short of them, you see. If this will not work out for you two, let me know and I will encourage Elder Amadei to purchase another from Wit. Now here are your bathroom facilities. I only ask that you do not use the hot water between ten and eleven in the morning, one and two in the afternoon, and from six to seven at night. We need all the hot water we can get for washing all the dishes from the meals, you see. If you are bored, feel free to come and join us a washing away. We do have fun doing it." She chatted on and we soon felt comfortable being around her.

"Say, on Sunday, our dads always dressed us for Church. Who will be doing that here for us?" I asked about the only thing that I still hadn't heard.

"Oh that you'll need to do for yourselves, if you possibly can. I know that it will be very difficult, but with each of you helping the other, perhaps you can manage. If not, come get me, and I'll see what I can do. We don't allow men in our dorm as a rule, excepting for heavier lifting and such. Now why don't you unpack and take a bath? You must be filled with road dirt after such a long trip. Come dine with us around seven." She left us to unpack and work things out for ourselves.

Dita and I helped each other take a bath and then dry off. "You know it's going to be impossible for us to get into our Sunday clothes by ourselves," Dita commented. "How can we possibly tie our shoes?" I laughed. I had no idea. She suggested that we had better start practicing for Sunday. I laughed even harder.

We had a very fine meal with the domestic staff. Five men handled the stables and horses — all were older gentlemen — bachelors, we learned. Thirty women handled the cooking, laundry, and maid duties for the college, though they did not service the Security Guards building, because, there, their own wives handled those duties. We found these women good company and chatted a bit about our long journey around the country, which they were eager to hear.

The next morning after we had eaten, Elder Amadei and three other Elders caught us as we were leaving the dining room. "Excuse me, Dita, Bethany. I have received a full report on your summer excursion. I am very impressed with all that you have learned how to do, that alone is a significant and unexpected surprise. However, that you managed to rescue and save both Kasper and the driver and get them to safety from the rebel ambush I find incredible indeed. We of the Elder Council feel that we would like to acknowledge your stellar achievements this past summer. While your forth earring tier is normally for your marriage and children, we've decided to add some emeralds to the outside of your forth tier with our sincere thanks and appreciation for such stellar accomplishments." With that, the others began adding four large dangling emeralds to our fourth tier, leaving the center for our red ruby when we married.

We thanked them and headed into our room to look at them in our large mirror. "Gosh, my ears are being pulled off!" Dita exclaimed. "Look, their bottoms now rest on our shoulders even! I'm glad we don't have a fifth tier to do!"

"We will, if we have children of our own! Remember, those get added below the red central one that our husbands would be giving us," I pointed out. Dita gave a mock moan.

"Seriously, these are awfully heavy, but now we can easily rub our shoulders," Dita pointed out.

"Come on, let's go exploring, and see what is where. Maybe we will get to see Albin later today. We are, after all, supposed to be helping him with his studies," I replied. Off we two went, wandering around the buildings and the grounds.

After lunch was finished, Dita and I headed for our favorite spot in the complex, having decided that earlier this morning. We stood by the corral fence just south of the stables, watching all the many horses grazing. For us, horses brought back so many fond memories that we had shared together in our last two lifetimes. We both loved to ride like the wind!

"Remember when we raced in that horse race against the horsemen of Vladimir at their biggest horse race of the year and you and I won — well you did, beating me by a hair?" Dita reminisced.

"I sure do! Boy did we race like the wind that day. Shocked them, didn't we?"

"Yes, and you had lost your arms and yet you still won. I sure wish we could ride like that again. Do you suppose that they will let us ride a pair of these horses?" she asked.

"Dunno, but let's find out. Dita, you've never ridden like we are now."

"Oh crap! You are right! How on earth am I going to manage that?" Dita looked crestfallen, as if I had just stabbed her or something equally bad.

"Well, it's a matter of using your legs to keep your balance. You lean to one side, and with the reins between your teeth, they naturally give a slight pull on the horse's neck. If the horse has been well trained, that is all you need to control him or her. Let's try it, if they'll let us. Shall we?" I asked.

"Let you try what?" the solemn voice of Elder Amadei said from behind us. We whirled around quickly. Taken by surprise, our earrings flew around violently, nearly pulling our ears off. Well, not really, it just felt that way, because we were not yet used to their new weight and length.

"Oh, hi. We were wondering if we could learn to ride some of your horses. You have several good spirited horses in the corral there, like that brown mare and the roan gelding. Is it permissible for us to do this, Elder Amadei?" I asked, putting on my pleading face, which always melted my father's heart.

He laughed, "For you two, it seems nothing is impossible. Yes, yes, you may. A few Holy Vessels who live on farms are known to be able to ride horses. Come, I'll let Lukjan know. He can assist you, but please stay near the college. If you master this, I will have a Security Guard accompany you on longer rides."

After letting old Lukjan know that we were permitted to learn to ride, the Elder returned to his work. "We need two horses that will neck rein really easily," I explained, he grinned, suspecting that was so. As it turned out, Dita and I were still good judges of horses. Lukjan picked out the very mare and gelding that we had decided were the two best of the many in the lot. He saddled them up for us and led them out of the stables.

"I must admit, ladies, I am at a loss on what to do next. None here have ever tried riding a horse."

"Well, tie the ends of the reins into a big knot. We'll grip it in our teeth." After he did so, I asked him, "Please hold him steady while I mount and get a good grip. Dita, watch how I do it," I said. Leaning into the saddle, I climbed aboard, and then leaned over, so Lukjan could help me get a good bite on the knot. I hoped that Dita could manage this herself.

As she walked up to the horse, I could see real fear coming from her eyes and face. I knew what she was experiencing. Imagine that you are an expert horseman, who is suddenly facing having to mount a horse, when you now have a body with no arms. Everything that you know and do automatically is useless. Panic, yes, real panic. "Lean into the saddle," I called out. Dita bravely put her foot into the stirrup and tried to do as I had so easily done. She goofed and failed, nearly falling down. On her third try, a proud Dita sat in the saddle and leaned over so Lukjan could put the knotted reins into her mouth. She bit down hard.

Now it was back to basics on riding. I nudged the gelding forward and Dita emulated my actions. We began walking them around the grounds. After a while, she got the hang of it and we walked to the side of the Security Guards building. From there we had a long circular open run all the way around the college to the stable corral fence where we had watched the horses. I called out a trot and we began trotting. I always hated trotting, too much bouncing for so little speed. Dita also found this the roughest part. Yet, I didn't want to bring her along too quickly and have her fall off and get hurt.

After trotting back and forth several times, we tried a canter, a much better gait to ride. This was more like it! Of course, we also had to practice reining in as we approached either the corral or the side of the guard's building, but the horses already knew that they had to slow down and stop, duh. Yet, it was good practice for us. We rode them for two hours, working up a sweat on the horses, before we decided we'd had enough for our first time out. As we pulled up at the stable entrance, Lukjan was there to hold them while we dismounted. I had forgotten about this. Unused to so much riding, as my legs hit the ground, they gave out, landing me ignominiously on my butt. Dita, likewise. We both burst out laughing. So did Lukjan.

"You worked them up a good sweat, ladies. Now I need to rub them down," he replied.

"Hey, let us do it. After all we worked them hard today," I said without thinking.

"How do we do that without hands?" Dita asked incredulously.

"Yes, how?" he asked with a broad grin, loving every minute with us.

Standing on one foot, the other foot stuck into the brush, I began wiping down the gelding. Not to be left out, Dita mimicked my actions, though she often kept losing her balance. In the end, we did a fair job of it, receiving a thank you from the older man. We then headed to our room to wash up, more than pleased with ourselves.

"We can ride again!" Dita exclaimed when we were in our own room. She was ecstatic about our little adventure. Honestly, we can ride, Bethany! Wow. Not all is totally lost this lifetime; we *can* ride. Someday, I'm going to buy you the best mare I can find on all Tarra!" she promised me sincerely. I hoped that day would indeed come.

That night when we finally crawled into our large bed, we rolled onto our sides, facing each other. "I meant it, Bethany. One day when this is all over, I am going to get us two really fine horses and then we are going riding every day, as fast as we can go! I sure do love you, Bethany!" We passionately kissed each other; the bond between us just as strong as it had been for two lifetimes.

The next day we began tutoring Albin with his new math. While we had not had this level, we both rather knew what it was all about and were able to help him along. Daily, we rode for several hours and helped with the domestic staff doing maid duties and washing dishes. Evenings, we spent several hours with Albin and his math.

Several weeks passed by, when Albin came for his tutoring lesson with bloodshot eyes. We could tell that he had been crying and I decided to see if he would open up to us. "Hi Albin. Looks like something has gone wrong. Can you tell us about it?" We were sitting at our worktable, the oil lamp illuminating his math papers.

He sighed, "I guess so. I've learned so much so quickly, but it's all going to be for nothing! I'm going to flunk out in less than a month!"

"Albin, it can't be that bad — not in just your first month. You are keeping up with your math," Dita consoled him. I knew that she knew that math, while troublesome for him, was not the cause of his upset. She was cleverly probing for what was really going on with him.

"I can't match the sound," he sobbed and began crying once more. If I had had arms, I would have put them around his shoulders to comfort him. Both Dita and I did the only thing we really could do; we leaned and rested our heads on each side of his shoulders for a moment, giving him time to recover his composure. Eventually, he stopped and wiped his face on his shirtsleeves. "Thanks," he whispered.

"Albin, we don't know what you are talking about. Why not start at the beginning and tell us what is going wrong. Perhaps then we can figure out a way for you to succeed at whatever this is," I said softly.

"Okay. One of the duties of an Elder is to help keep all our people on the right path. That is, we rather mesmerize them with our special sermons, helping them to drive any Unholy Thoughts from their minds. You know, my dad did it with all of us at the start of every fall school term, though I know that both of you and I were never affected by dad's voice. We are supposed to be helping keep our people on the righteous path and not to stray. Elder Amadei says about one in ten or one in twenty is not affected by our voice tone. He does not know why that may be, though I asked him about it, because I know that both of you are not affected."

"Anyway, when the Elders do their special sermons, they must speak at one very, very precise pitch. I always wondered why dad spoke so weirdly. Now I know, he was using that precise pitch to mesmerize the congregation, so that they would really listen to his words of guidance. Anyway, they have a large tuning fork in the classroom. When it is struck, it produces this precise pitch and we are supposed to sing a sound that matches it precisely. Once we can duplicate that precise sound anytime, anyplace that we desire, without actually hearing that tuning fork, then we pass and get to go on to the next course. I suspect that course will be where we learn what to say in our sermons."

"I can't do it. No matter how hard I try, I can't do it. I am always off. I am flunking out now, because I can't make that sound." He sighed, resigned to becoming a failure.

"Okay. So how many of these tuning forks are there? If there are a lot, perhaps we can borrow one to work with you on it," I asked.

"This is the strange thing, Bethany. There is only the one tuning fork in all of Dorota! All the Elders are trained here at Wit. They all have master matching it — all except me," he lamented once more. He added, "Oh yes, it's kept under lock and key, as you might imagine. No way can we use it to practice with, sorry."

"Say, have you ever sung before?" Dita asked.

"No, never."

"I have an idea. Why don't we three practice singing together? That way, you will get used to making sounds. Maybe this way you will get comfortable blending with us and then can match that tuning fork. What do you say?" Dita asked.

"You think it will help?" He needed some encouragement, but gave in to her.

It would have been great, if we would have had some of those four part motets that were so popular back in Velona, when Renzo and I lived there at the Santi Fortress. However, memory would have to serve us. Dita's voice was a little lower than mine was, so she attempted to sing the alto line, while I took the soprano line. We decided right away that Albin would take the tenor line, as his voice was not too low.

"Remember to keep the notes pure and unwavering. You will be able to tell when you have it right, because it will blend naturally with ours," I suggested. I hit a B and had Dita hit a G. The objective was for Albin to find a D and hold it. After a lot of moving around in tones, he finally found the right note to blend perfectly, grinning while singing it out.

For the next five nights, we continued working in a similar manner with him. Steadily Albin improved until he could hit the right chord blend with whatever pair we chose. The next day, he dashed over to the corral, where we were watching the horses, to tell us that he had finally hit the pitch of the tuning fork precisely! We held a mutual three-way hug, though he did all the hugging. "Gotta go. Have to practice it a lot more. I am not flunking out after all! Thanks to you two!" We grinned at our little achievement as he raced back across the lawn to the classrooms.

Lukjan saddled up our horses. By now, we had permission to ride the quarter mile into Wit and back on our own. The Elders were satisfied that we could handle our horses well enough for such a short run. Besides, Lukjan could almost see us riding the whole way. However, it gave us the chance to turn the horses lose into a full gallop, if only for a short distance. For that brief passage of time, Dita and I felt very alive!

Not long after that, Elder Amadei came to us. "Again, I want to thank you for assisting Albin with his studies. You definitely are helping him over the hurdles. However, I suspect that you are becoming rather bored during the daytime hours. I have another learning situation for you, if you are interested."

"Thanks, you are right, it is kind of boring for us, though we've been helping with the many chores around here," I replied.

"Good. I have gotten you two a teller position at the bank in Wit. There you will learn how our money is handled and the methods used in our banking industry. I've arranged for you to work there for at least a month. If you need more time, just let me know and I'll arrange it for you. Lukjan can escort you to the bank in the morning." He returned to the classrooms, while we chatted about this new twist.

I had actually never seen a bank, but Dita had last lifetime as the

Santi started up a giant banking chain throughout the then known world. However, even she was surprised by Wit bank. The building had no windows, just two enormous doors that could be closed at night. During the daytime, these were fastened open, and two lighter doors could be operated by anyone, particularly us. Across the entire back wall were shelves with drawers, each six inches tall, two feet wide, and two feet deep. On the front of each was written a five digit number, the account number of a customer, though not all the boxes were in use.

A long four-foot high partition ran the length of the room with a single entrance for us tellers to get behind the partition and to the wall of drawers. Many of the teller stations were designed for us women, a few for the men. Ours had the usual sloped back chairs and the teller counter was about six inches from the floor. The men's counters were three feet from the floor. The bank's owner had the only desk, situated in a back corner, from where he could watch everyone.

It worked this way, since there was no crime in Dorota. A person came in wanting to deposit some funds, withdraw some funds, or pay their taxes. The person wrote down on a paper their account number and how much they wished to deposit or withdraw. We then went to their drawer and retrieved their tally sheet, bringing it back to our station. Next, we retrieved their funds or counted out their new deposit to ensure it was accurate. If it was a deposit, we put their coins into their drawer. On their tally sheet we wrote out what they now had in their drawer and made a copy for the customer. We made a listing of each transaction, which would be given to the bank owner at the end of the day. He compiled a master listing.

Sometimes we just needed to make change or exchange for larger denomination coins. This transaction was filled out on a blue sheet of paper, so as not too get them confused. If a drawer was beyond our reach, we had one of the male tellers assist us, which didn't happen very frequently.

After a couple weeks, we got the hang of it all and had a feel for what really was taking place. The women were the ones who made the most frequent withdrawals, using the funds to purchase food and supplies. Usually the men made the deposits, often on Fridays. This worked out well, because we were very slow with the coins, working with our toes, and the recipients, women, were equally slow. However, I began to dislike working here as a full time job, too toe fatiguing. I hated making change. The only really fun thing was lunchtime. We all ate at a nearby inn, taking an hour off for lunch.

We'd been working there for three weeks when a woman came up to me to make a deposit of a single gold coin. She slipped me two papers, one with her account number and the other held a message! It read: "At the inn today, I would like to speak with you. Will you and your friend please sit down with a man wearing a red hat? Thank you." After I read it, I looked up at the woman, who quickly picked it back up and stuffed it into her pouch.

"He just gave me the coin to deliver the message, miss," she said apologetically. I smiled and finished her deposit and she left. I whispered what the note said to Dita. She wasn't so sure we should talk with a strange man, but relented. Curiosity got the better of her.

At noon, we headed off to the inn with the other tellers, chatting about how cool the fall weather was rapidly becoming. As we entered the inn, Dita and I paused, looking for a man in a red hat. He was off to one side, out of the main traffic area, where we could have a conversation without much fear of being overheard. He seemed well groomed and wore a business suit, taking off his hat as soon as we spied him. "Looks harmless enough," Dita whispered to me, assuming the role that Renzo always used to do for me, as my Protector. We joined him.

"Thank you for joining me for lunch, ladies," he rose and helped us sit down, though we didn't need any. He was being polite. "My name is Rafal. Best you don't know my last name. Please, the lunch is on me."

"I'm Bethany and this is Dita," I said politely. "Thanks, but why all this secrecy? What do you want of us?"

"Patience is virtue in these matters. Let us order first." We did so, and after we received our lunch, he began talking once more. "First, I must say that you two have the finest earrings that I have ever heard tell of anywhere on Dorota. I noticed them some days ago. Unless I'm very mistaken, both of you young women have completed your grades some years ahead of schedule and with incredibly top marks." We explained that we had and that others had given us numerous awards, which he noted.

"I also noticed that you are both unaffected by the Elder's voice, yet the Elder Amadei has brought you to the College. Never before has this happened — the bringing of Holy Vessels that are not part of his servant staff. Yet, you are not being trained to be an Elder. Conclusion, you must somehow be very important to him, but are so young, perhaps fourteen, fifteen?"

"Fourteen, and we have no real idea why he brought us here, except that we are helping a friend of ours, Albin with his studies. He's also letting us learn other ways of women, like those who work in the bank," Dita replied.

"Fair enough. I will have to work that one out for myself."

"But why are you so interested in us?" I asked, wishing he would get to the heart of this clandestine meeting.

"Sharp wit. Okay, I'll level with you and then perhaps you can give me more useful information. I am one of the leaders of what others call the rebels, but which we call the Freedom Fighters. For endless centuries these Elders and their doktors have been cutting off all female babies' arms in the name of their crazed version of religion and stability of their society." He paused hoping to shock us.

"Of course, we know that. We've already erased that birth trauma from ourselves. Even though they had our tiny bodies drugged with a painkiller, the pain is still within the body, which had to be erased so that it doesn't affect us anymore. We know all about what the doktors do in secret, taking the newborn female babies away to amputate their arms before allowing the father and mother to see their child. Barbaric, to say the least," I replied. If he wanted to shock us, then turnabout was fair play. If he was indeed a rebel, he might well know what the doktors did. However, if he were a plant of some Elder's plot, what I said about erasing the trauma would be totally unknown to them, while the truth about what they did was precise. I wasn't giving anything away.

"Oh my god! You know the truth! You are the first like yourselves that have known what they've done to you. Incredible! I'm sorry. I was trying to shock you with the horrible truth of this wicked society so that you would perhaps listen to our side. I can see that I have no need of that," he smiled.

"No not really."

"Might I ask you another about another matter first?" I nodded. "Several months ago, a carriage was transporting two young women, much as yourselves, along with a Security Guard and driver. They were on the northern coastal road, when a band of rebels, Freedom Fighters looking to obtain a little gold to feed their starving families, dropped a tree to block the road. They used non-lethal means to disable the two men, but then something very strange happened. I must admit that no one seriously believes their tale. I think that they just got cold feet. Anyway, they claim that mysteriously two of their men, who were closing on the two young teens, were somehow picked up and tossed back into the woods. You see why I don't believe them, but by chance do you know anything about that?"

"That was us. We didn't know that they needed money for food. If they'd asked us, we would have given them some. Yes, you should believe what you've heard, Rafal. We got our unconscious men into the carriage, and I drove the carriage to the next town for help," I answered him. Only rebels could know that bit about the tossed men. We'd said nothing and our two men were unconscious. Thus, the Elders knew nothing about that detail. Since Rafal did, therefore, he had to be in contact or a part of the rebels, I concluded. Dita, likewise.

"Incredible! Do the Elders know that you did this?"

"We've said nothing about how we rescued our men, only that we got them into the coach, and I drove to the town," I replied once more.

He grinned. "So you do not want the Elders to know everything about you, eh?"

We grinned, "Precisely. A good warrior never reveals all his secrets," Dita stated flatly, remembering her Protector training from last lifetime.

"Wise, very, very wise! I urge you to continue to follow your good sense. The less the Elders really know about you two, the better off you will both be. I will trust you and tell you much about the Freedom Fighters. Then you can make up your own minds about us. There are tens of thousands of us now, scattered all over the major forests of Dorota. We have been driven out of most of the 'civilized' areas of our continent. However, quite a few of us still live among the zombies, as we call the average mesmerized citizen of Dorota. I am one of those. It is not too hard to pretend to be one of them, you see."

"In the depths of the forests, we can live free lives, but not prosper. Our biggest problem is getting enough food for our families to eat. About a third of our women are like you two are, and my guess is that they number some sixteen thousand. Twice that number has been born in our villages and has arms as women were intended by God to have. My job in town is to search out others that are not mesmerized by the Elder's speech and attempt to get them to join the resistance movement. Still, we are outnumbered more than ten to one. The Security Guards all carry lethal guns, so we dare not confront them directly. We are armed only with bows and arrows and a few crude swords and daggers. Still, we really have no quarrel with the zombies, only with the Elders."

"In the past, some have tried to eliminate the Elders, but that failed and now they all have Security Guards close at hand. We dare not try that again, though it has been over fifty years since we last struck against the Elders. Our goal and all of our hopes and dreams are to one day free Dorota from this despicable practice of the Elders and their doktors. Then, we all can live and prosper."

"Admirable goals, Rafal, most worthy. From what you say, the most pressing problem is getting enough food for your people. From what we learned from Kasper, the Security Guard who took us on the tour, you have all the meat you desire, but are lacking grains and vegetables. Is this correct?" I asked.

"Yes, very true. We have been forced to resort to stealing a little from many different farmers just to stay alive. Why?"

"I have some connections of my own. Give me a few days to make some arrangements. I think that I can get an entire caravel of food supplies delivered in secret to your people. It'll probably have to be shipped from Velona and that may mean it will be several months travel time. Let's meet here for lunch in say a week, and I can give you more specific instructions. Probably a nighttime secret landing somewhere along the northern coast where the Dark Wood is near the ocean would be an ideal rendezvous point. The supplies will cost you nothing, consider it a donation to your cause from like-minded people in other countries."

"You are joking with me? You can do this?" the shocked look on Rafal's face was almost humorous, if he had not been so serious and shocked by the offer.

"No joke. Give me a week, meet here for lunch like today and I'll have the details. Rafal, you have allies that you don't even know that you have," I grinned coyly. He smiled in return; his eyes were bright with newfound hope for his people.

Since many of our co-workers were starting to leave, we thanked him for the meal and joined them. It would not do to be late in returning from lunch. Later that night in the quiet of our own room, I expanded my mind and searched for Linda. I gave her our monthly update on the situation here in Dorota and told her about the resistance movement. She was so pleased to discover that there was a resistance and so many of them that she promised two caravels of grains and dried vegetables would be sent.

Should we arm them? Send a load of good quality swords? she asked.

No, I don't believe that fighting is going to be the answer here, at least not yet. Give us some more time, since we still don't know the whole story.

A week after meeting Rafal, we again found him at the same table at lunchtime. "You are in luck. They are sending two caravels of food for your people! As I thought, they will sail from Velona, Sea Princes, which is about a three-month voyage. To avoid being seen by Dorota folks, they will come in directly from the far north. The rendezvous is set for the night of January 15, around eleven at night. When you see three lantern light flashes, reply in kind. If you detect trouble and want them to delay making landfall for twenty-four hours, reply with only one flash." I gave him the precise location — the spot where we had been ambushed, figuring the rebels would know precisely where that was.

"On behalf of all the truly free people of Dorota, I thank you, Bethany and Dita. You are giving us the best Yuletide present imaginable! If you ever need any kind of help, here's my home address in Wit. My house is yours if you ever need it." He gave us the address and we committed it to memory.

Chapter 7 The Trials of Albin

The middle of October came, bringing with it the multi-colored fall leaves. Here in the highlands, spectacular does not do Nature justice. Elder Amadei was convinced that we now could handle banking and we no longer worked as tellers, thankfully! We took to riding among the colorful trees around the college vicinity every afternoon, helping with domestic chores in the mornings. Every evening, we worked with Albin and his studies. His math was continually in dire need of our assistance.

On October 1, Albin was ecstatic! He had finally mastered the perfect pitch, matching the tuning fork at will. "Now I get to begin my studies of the Elder sermons! This is just great! I owe it all to you two! Thank you! Thank you!" He was one happy lad. Dita was hesitant though, fearing that we were directly helping create yet another Elder, who would be hypnotizing others to perpetuate their insane treatment of female babies. I admit that I felt the same way, what were we doing?

In the middle of October, Albin came to our nightly study session vastly changed in outlook. We both could see that he had once again been crying. However, instead of his books and papers, he brought us each a chocolate bar imported from Velona, which must have cost him a small fortune. "Here, I have brought you each a small present from across the sea. It's called chocolate and is very expensive. I've spent all the money I have on them. It's the only thing that I can think of to say just how sorry I am for everything. I am truly so very, very sorry for both of you."

"Thanks, Albin, these are going to be delicious," I almost said that they were delicious, which would have been a major goof on my part. "But what are you so sorry for? You've not done anything to harm or hurt us ever."

"No, it's what they did to you, to all of you girls," he blurted out. Then, he suddenly realized that he said something, which was supposed to be a total secret. His face turned red as a beet and he shut up instantly.

"Oh, you mean amputating our arms right after we were born?" I asked, deciding that this must be what he almost blurted out.

The look on his face was tragic and humbling, but I was right. "You aren't supposed to know that! It's a total secret. How do you know about that? Yes, I am so very, very sorry that they did this to both of you and to my mom and my sister, and all of them, hundreds of thousands of them!" He was sincerely appalled at what he had learned today. Dita wanted to say "and rightly so," but thought better of it.

I knew that I was being handed an excellent opportunity, but I had to use it wisely. "Albin, we are all spiritual beings, immortal, God's children, inhabiting for a brief time these fleshly bodies here." I knew enough of their religious beliefs now to know precisely how to phrase things so that Albin could grasp the explanation well.

"Some of we beings are stronger and more able than others. Dita and I both know how to erase physical trauma that sometimes happens to our fleshly bodies, a therapy given to us by God in the past. We have not forgotten how to use it. You are correct, right after our baby bodies were born and before our parents ever saw us, the doktor who delivered us took us away, telling our parents he needed to clean us up, and all that. In fact, he drugged the tiny bodies and did an excellent surgery, removing our arms. Only then did he give us to our parents. While we were still babies, we knew that we had undergone some trauma and we used our God given therapy on ourselves, reliving the entire operation. All of that physical pain and fear is gone from us. We can concentrate better and do so much better in life because of this. Perhaps that is why we could learn in school so quickly." Okay I stretched the truth here, but made it seem there was a tangible benefit from this therapy.

"More importantly, Albin, we do not hate that doktor or the Elders for having done this despicable thing to us. Yes, it is indeed a terrible, terrible thing to do to women. We do not condone it at all. By the way, no one knows that we have done this, Albin. Please help us keep it a secret — that we know what is really happening on Dorota."

"Wow! Okay, I give you my solemn oath that I will never tell another soul about your secret. Gosh, that means you must know everything else that the Elders keep secret," he concluded. "Great. That means I can then talk freely with you these evenings. I really do need to talk to someone about all this. It is so horrible what we are doing!"

"I know it is, Albin. Thanks for keeping our secret," I said softly.

"Well, now I know what dad is doing when he gives his special sermons. He's hypnotizing the entire congregation and making them believe all this is the way it is supposed to be. Elder Amadei says that after a month or so, the effect tends to grow thin or wear off, so we have to repeat it. He gave us a huge lecture on why it is that we must do this. Want to hear it?"

"You bet, Albin!" Dita encouraged him, knowing that we were about to get privileged information.

"We have a society that is totally peaceful, there is no crime. It is safe for anyone, even children, to walk anywhere anytime. No one steals from any other person. No one gets greedy. No one overeats. We have no wars. No one covets another person's possessions. Most of all, our women are treated with dignity and respect at all times. There is no rape — oh yes, the Elder had to explain what that word meant. Honestly I can't conceive of any man doing that to a woman, but he says in other lands rape is prevalent. No one would ever harm or hurt a woman, and our men do everything they can to help them. He says it is a perfect society, but it has to be maintained. Hence the Elders have to repeat their hypnotic sermons every month or so."

"What did he say would happen if they didn't do this?" Dita asked, coyly.

"Elder Amadei says our society would totally break down if we didn't. Some would start stealing from others, some would eat with abandon, some would lie and cheat others, and some would try to steal another man's wife. Husbands would start beating up their wives and daughters, maybe even raping them, certainly treating them with horrible disrespect, naturally, he says, because they are so utterly helpless without their arms you see. You are so completely dependent upon our men that our men would rebel against this, leaving our poor women to starve to death or worse. Everything that we value in our society would crumble into chaos. He says we might even have a civil war, whatever that may be."

"He paints a pretty grim picture, doesn't he?" Dita stated flatly, imagining all of these things was very easy to do, given this society.

"Is — is he right then? That our world would be destroyed if we didn't continue to do this?" Albin asked forlornly, seeing no way out of it.

"Yes and no," I replied in a non-committal way. "Albin, imagine that you were my father, working *so* hard to support mom and two daughters who are, as you point out, so utterly dependent upon him for everything. Can you imagine working so hard, taking care of all three of them for years and years?" He nodded. It was real to him. "Okay, now how do you suppose that you would feel if you suddenly discovered that the leaders and Elders had been lying to you all this time and that their doktors had in fact cut off your wife's arms and those of your two daughters as well, making them into utterly dependent creatures, so helpless and dependent on you? How would you feel?"

"I'd want to go kill the doktor who did it!" Albin reacted angrily, as I suspected that he would. "Then, I'd probably want to go after those lousy Elders too," he added.

"Yes, yes, that is to be expected. Now, after that, how would you view your wife and two daughters?"

"But I love my mother and my sister! I don't want them hurt or harmed! I'd still want to take care of them, maybe even more so, knowing that they were the victims of this sadistic culture!"

"Rightly so, Albin. I do believe that most husbands would react that way, if they loved their wives. Yet, if one had married not from love but for other reasons, they might feel that they had been taken advantage of by their wives and be resentful against them and their constant needs, right?"

"Yes, I can see that too. I know one man on our block married his wife so that he could become her father's bank manager, a higher paying job with more status. He probably would not feel too kindly towards her and her needs after he found out the truth of the matter. But don't most husbands love their wives and daughters?" he asked.

"Yes, most do. A few don't. So you see, the relationships between men and women will not erupt into total chaos if they all find out the truth. Elder Amadei's doom and gloom isn't all that he makes it out to be, in my opinion. Yes, some men will become criminal, but they were of that bent in the first place. You are right; the biggest backlash will likely be the murdering of the doktors and the Elders, which is also not a good thing. If all the doktors are slain, who will take care of the sick and injured? Who will help with the delivery of new babies?"

"I think that Elder Amadei is more worried about his own neck and his doktor associates, perhaps also in what would happen to the sick, injured, and pregnant women if the doktors are all dead. I'll give him that much, but no more," I replied.

"Our whole religion thing is a total farce, a total lie! I can see that now. It is only being used to control people and their lives, to make them to what the Elders think is best, to make their 'perfect society.'" Albin said antagonistically. I knew that we were nowhere done with this conversation yet.

"Religions can be misused, as you point out. Often, men like to use religion to control their people, just as you say. Indeed, there is another religious group on Tarra that is doing much the same, though nowhere as bad as it is here on Dorota. However, Albin, do not discard the religion in its entirety. There is a tremendous amount of good in our religion here. Let's go over the sermon that your dad delivered to us at least twelve times."

"Say, that is the same sermon that I am supposed to learn to give verbatim!" Albin replied, still highly antagonistic, as if the very words were a total hypocrisy to him now that he knew the truth.

"Let's go over it bit by bit," I suggested.

"Hey, I got a copy of the damn thing in my pocket," he realized and pulled it out and un-wadded it.

I read aloud. "In the Beginning God created the earth and the heavens with its glorious stars and the sun. God was happy with his creation for a time. The days and nights passed endlessly with the seasons coming and going, but there was no one there with which to share the beauty of his creation. Thus, God decided to create man in his image to partake and share in the seasons and the glory of his creation. Men would add to it their industrious work to create homes, raise crops, build wooden boats, and fish in the oceans. Yet, this too was short lived, for men's bodies, not being as God, perished after a time, as all men still do even unto this day. Worse still, men argued with other men, men fought with other men, men coveted that which other men made or found, men stuffed themselves with the bounty of the world. God was displeased."

"Now then, is there any fault with that, Albin?" I asked.

"Well, no. You just have to believe that happened, but it does explain how our world got here."

I continued reading. "God now saw that he must have life perpetuate

70

itself, that somehow more men must be created. Thus, it came to pass that God created woman in his image to be his Holy Vessel to create new life here on earth. Only through the Holy Vessel would God allow this new life to be created. Original woman was just like man, but had both the breasts for nursing the newborn life and the Holy Vessel in which God formed the new life."

"Now man and woman dwelled for a time on our world. They shared in the beauty of God's creations. As the bodies of men and women grew old and passed on, new men and women came forth from his Holy Vessels, and God was pleased."

"Yet, man and woman sinned against our Lord and Creator. Men still fought with other men, coveted what other men had as well as what women had, lied, cheated, stole from other men and women. Men lusted after women; women lusted after men. Many took to gluttonous behavior, stuffing themselves beyond what was needed to sustain life. Men beat women to get what they wanted. Women cheated on men to get what they coveted. Worse still, men now had to work even harder to support their Holy Vessels. God saw that men needed even greater strength, power, and stamina, because they needed to now support themselves and their families."

"God then said, 'How may I solve this mess that I've made? I want my men and women to enjoy the Holy Creation with me, to share in my joy. Yet, they fight among themselves and far worse. Man is not strong enough to bear this burden alone.'"

Albin interrupted, commenting, "Okay, so far it is acceptable, Bethany. It makes sense, though there is no way to prove any of it ever happened."

"Of course there isn't. Religion is not something you have to prove; it is all faith-based," I replied. "Now we get to this next part." I read on. "One of God's Holy Vessels, who was called Marzena, spoke unto God. 'Lord, my man, Jurek, is a good and kind man, a farmer. He works at his fields to provide for our family. Yet, I can see that he needs to be stronger. Please, my Lord," I purposely stopped here.

"So we are seeing here the starting point that they use to solve the problem of men," I pointed out. "They lie, steal, cheat, fight, mistreat women and children. In any society of men, these are likely to be found, don't you think?"

Albin replied, "I think so, though I have to imagine them. Such is not the case here on Dorota."

"Okay, now let's ignore just what Marzena's offering to God actually was. We know that she said to donate her arms so that Jurek could be stronger. We all know that men are physically stronger than women are, usually. It is so in all societies of man. Let's just ignore that little twist the Elders put in there to justify women voluntarily donating their arms to their husbands. Let's see what we have then." I read on, skipping that part. ". . .God heard the prayer from his Holy Vessel and so it was that God. . .Thus made stronger and more powerful, Jurek was at last able to sustain his Holy Vessel and family, more able to tend his fields, and produce more food. Jurek was then very pleased and happy with the change."

"But our Lord God then spoke unto Jurek. 'Yes, I can see that by the sacrifice of worthy Marzena, you are now blessed with part of her strength and you are now able to survive well. However, Jurek you must honor her sacrifice unto you. From this day forward, you must love her, cherish her, and help her, as you have never done before. Thou shalt never betray her by lusting after other women. Thou shalt be true to her and to her alone. Thou shalt not lie, covet what another has, steal that which does not belong to you, and fight with other men whose Holy Vessels have likewise made their sacrifice. Nor should thou become a glutton over the bounty, which thou art now capable of producing because of the gift Marzena has given unto you and you alone. Thou shalt honor and cherish the new life that Marzena brings forth, as they are part of each of you.'"

"'Jurek, Marzena, if you will do these things, then you are worthy of viewing my Creation and of entering my realm. Jurek, Marzena, if you fail to do these, if you are not faithful to each other, hurt the other, lie, steal, covet, lust, become gluttonous, then you raise my ire and I will take back Marzena's sacrificial gift to you, Jurek, and allow you both to die off like my first creations of the Unholy man and woman, which I have forsaken as unworthy.'"

"'Jurek said unto the Lord and unto Marzena, 'I will honor you always, my Marzena, for the selfless sacrifice you have given unto me, I so swear. I will be your arms when you have need for them. I will looketh not at other women. I will not lie, steal, or fight with others who have given of this Holy Sacrifice. But my Lord, my God, what will happen to these others who are around me whom have not made this Holy Sacrifice?'"

"Okay, Albin, what do you think your religion is attempting to do here?" I asked. "Are not those ideal ways for men and women to act?"

"Sure, if they did, we would have a perfect society," he replied, now becoming slightly bored with all this rehashing of the sermon.

"Right. Our religion is giving you a good standard with which to live life. However, there is even more good in here, Albin, listen to the next passage." I read on. "God spoketh thus, 'They are the Unholy, the Accursed Ones, forsaken by their own making. I disown them. You may ignore them, as you choose. Yet, still they ought not to be without all hope with no chance of redemption. Jurek, you may talk with these men and try to show them their Holy Mistake, the errors of their making. You and Marzena can show them the path — your lives as a model to follow, but Marzena, the purest of Holy Vessels, must never talk with the Accursed. Nothing must taint her Holy Sacrifice, as many of the Unholy Women will certainly attempt to do to her. Jurek, do not allow your Holy Vessel to become tainted, that is your responsibility to safeguard. Now if they repent and disavow what they have done and wish to join you and Marzena, they must make the sacrifice themselves to prove that they are now worthy of my Grace.'"

Albin broke in, now becoming interested in the sermon, "Oh I see, those who are living in sin, greed, avarice, lustfulness, and all that — we are to help show them that their way is not right and that our path leads to their own salvation. We strike the next passage — well just remove the cutting off of their women's arms anyway." Albin took over and began reading, "'If they . . . live as I have ordained for the two you, then I shall give both of them my Holy Redemption.'"

"Then, Jurek and Marzena both thanked our Lord for not forsaking all other men and women on Tarra. They set forth to fulfill the Lord God's commandments unto them. They begat many sons and daughters, who begat their sons and daughters and so spread God's Holy Creations on Tarra. Though much time has now passed since the time of Jurek and Marzena, the results of their tireless efforts are here for all to see on Dorota. Our continent is filled with millions of us Holy Men and Holy Vessels, our Women."

"Yet, Jurek never failed to attempt to show the Unholy the errors of their ways and thus bring them back to obtain God's Holy Redemption. Today, this is as true as it was back in Jurek's day. There are yet a few among us who remain Unholy. They lust after another's Holy Vessel, they lie, they steal, and they dishonor their Holy Vessel, their wife who has given her Holy Sacrifice for them. These Unholy we send off to the Fields of Kondrat, where we attempt to show them the errors of their ways, that they may yet be Redeemed."

"You young boys and young Holy Vessels, pay close attention to these words. Boys, always be the hands of the girls when they need them. Always respect the women's ways. Always be there to help them and assist them, for their sacrifice is Holy and you must honor it always or be condemned to the Fields of Kondrat yourself."

"Neither should you lie, neither should you steal that which is not yours, neither should you harm another of us who is Holy, and especially boys, never harm a Holy Vessel no matter what she has done. If anyone knows of anyone who has committed such transgressions, you are commanded to report it to your bisklep or Elder. If true, they will be deemed Unholy and sent off to the Fields of Kondrat, there to seek redemption."

"Young Holy Vessels, you young girls, I caution you to never speak to an Unholy woman, for she will seek to taint you and turn you into an Unholy Vessel. If you become tainted and un-pure, then you too will be sent to the Fields of Kondrat, there to seek Redemption."

"A quarter of a century ago, our people became aware of just how many of the Unholy men and women still inhabit our world. Vast are their numbers. Yet, we hold true to the guidance our Lord gave unto Jurek. We send forth missionaries into the Unholy lands and seek to Redeem them. Already we have been successful; fully fifty thousand men and women have cast aside their sins and . . . sacrifice to the Lord God, taking up the ways of us, the Holy. These are now counted among us and will have our Lord's Holy Redemption."

"Some of our Elders are leading this crusade of Redemption many, many leagues from their homes here on Dorota. They have reported that the newly made Holy Vessels are having problems learning the special women's ways. Perhaps we should have expected this, but have not. We are so used to having you, our Holy Vessels, from birth onward, that we did not realize your woman's ways were so difficult to master. Yes, men do not know how to do things the women's way nor can women do things the men's way. Thus, we are now sending out there into the Unholy part of the world some Holy Vessels, who have volunteered to guide and assist these newly made Holy Women to learn the proper women's way of doing things."

"Young men and young Holy Vessels, study hard, learn your lessons. One day when you graduate school, if you wish to volunteer to assist in our Holy Crusade to help the Unholy redeem themselves out there in the wide world of Tarra, we will accept your help and send you abroad that you may do as Jurek has done."

"Gosh, Bethany, you are absolutely right! Our religion has so much going for it! If we just left out the mutilation of our women, it all makes perfect sense! Wow! You two are incredible! How did you see all this in there? I can't imagine how you could possibly even listen to it, after knowing they cut off your arms! Wow!" Albin was now enthusiastic and I knew I'd achieved my miracle with him. That is, if he actually became an Elder, he would work like mad to stop the mutilation of women; it was completely senseless.

There was more that I wanted to put into his consciousness, but now was not the time. He needed to savor his victory. "Want to share our chocolate with us?" Dita asked.

"You sure? I mean I wanted to show you how sorry I was for what we've done to you," he replied.

"Sure, I'm sure. You didn't do it. Have a bite. It is fabulous," she said coyly. He took a small piece and was in heaven as well as we.

"Now that *is* good. I just wish it wasn't so expensive," he acknowledged.

"Let's talk about that tomorrow evening after we get your math assignment done, okay?" He agreed and noticed it was late and had to leave.

After he was gone, Dita said coyly to me, "Well, Bethany, you certainly did a number of Albin. Do you realize that you turned him completely around? He was about to become a rebel fighting against the Elders and the doktors. Now, he is re-evaluating his whole point of view."

"Yes, now to get him a little more worldly oriented," I added just as coyly. She passionately embraced me and we soon went to bed.

The next evening we didn't get that chance. Instead, a very disturbed Elder Amadei came to see us in our private room no less. "We have a very serious problem here with you two. Just what do you know about our doktors and babies and our Holy Vessels?" His tone sounded threatening, but he just could not ask us outright. It was not hard to imagine what he wanted to know, however, mentioning those three nouns in the same breath.

I was about to reply, when Dita, ever my Protector, spoke up. "Well, we know that immediately after we were born, the doktor who delivered us didn't show our moms and dads our baby bodies. Instead, he took us to his clinic wrapped in a blanket. He injected a painkilling drug into our bodies and did a neat surgical job amputating our arms. Once he finished that, he then took us back to our parents and showed us off to them. I was starving by then and very glad to nurse with mom. I assume that's what you are asking about," she replied as if this was a matter of absolutely no importance whatsoever! Good old Dita!

Elder Amadei's mouth opened, but for once, he was speechless. His face looked white as a sheet, as if he'd seen a ghost or apparition. At last, he blurted out, "But how? Did Albin tell you?"

"Oh don't be silly, Albin didn't tell us. We can remember it all just as easily as we can remember what we had for supper last night. Don't you recall your birth, Elder Amadei?" Dita answered him, but slamming him hard with her question. We both knew that rare indeed was the person who could recall that! Birth was painful, often traumatic and thus hidden from view, because to view it again, the pain and unconsciousness would return, short of a therapy session, that is.

'But — but you, you two, you can remember all that? I didn't think anyone could remember that far back, maybe to early school or somewhere around there," he finally began to put together a sentence.

"Sure we can remember everything. After all, we are all immortal spiritual beings. I can recall mom's frustrations trying to potty train me. Now I do feel so sorry for making so many messes that she had to clean up. But then, that's now behind me," I replied. "Can't you remember that far back, Elder Amadei? I thought everyone could." I lied.

"Well, no I cannot. Other than you two, I don't know of anyone who can. However, this is very serious indeed. Your recall is correct; the doktors do amputate female baby's arms. However, knowing this, you are not violently angry with us? How is it that you are not a rebel, fighting against us, knowing what we have done to you? You cannot be happy as you are. I know that things are so difficult for you women."

Careful, Bethany! Dita telepathically sent me.

"Yes, normal life things are very difficult for us, as they are for any woman like us. You are quite correct in that. However, why should we be violently angry with *you*? If we somehow could kill the doktor who delivered us and did this to us," I shrugged my shoulders, "then who would be around to take care of those who get sick, or injured, or break a leg, or help us deliver a baby? That would be about the stupidest thing I can think of — to go off killing all the doktors. What a mess our country would be in if that happened!"

After a short pause to let that arrive in his mind, I went on "And no, we are *not* pleased that we have *no* arms. If I had my choice, I wouldn't wish this on *any* woman or man, for that matter. However, Elder Amadei, what is done *is* done. I know of no miracle that can *re-grow* our arms. Hence, Dita and I have two choices. We can sit around, mope, and cry about how horrible it all is, how badly we have been mutilated. Or we can let that all go and learn all that we can, learn ways to accomplish the normal things in life, and live our lives to the fullest as we are. I'm sorry, but I am *not* going to sit around and mope. I love to ride horses. Life is in me. Dita and I intend to live life to the fullest. We just have to learn other ways of doing things is all."

Tears began streaming down the man's face. "I — I — I am so touched by your so positive attitude, Holy Vessels! Truly I am. I am so very, very sorry that I doubted you. Please accept my humble apologies."

"Accepted, but really you have nothing to apologize for, really. After all, you are only doing your job," Dita replied.

"Yes, I had to ask. Thank you, Holy Vessels. May I ask about another matter?" I nodded. "It's about Albin. Yesterday, I thought that he had just become another rebel when he found about all of this. He stormed out of the class cussing and swearing, then crying when he was outside the door. I just knew that we'd lost him. Yet, he returned today full of enthusiasm, even memorized the first two paragraphs, far more than any other student! I know that he came to see you two, because I had a Security Guard watching him, just in case he turned rebel on us as I thought he would. Whatever did you say to him to so turn him around?"

"We told him that we knew what the doktor did to us minutes after we were born," I replied truthfully. "He was sincerely sorry for us and all that, as you might expect. He was, as you say, ready to forsake our religion entirely! Yet, our religion has much to offer, when you look at it. We sat down and went over the Elder's sermon, the one we almost have memorized ourselves, having heard it so many times from his father, Elder Feliks. We showed him that if you just made tiny alterations, that is removing the phrases which say to amputate women's arms, just leaving it as an unspecified sacrifice on Marzena's part, that everything in there is really wonderful, and, if followed, would bring about a perfect society. He finally saw the real, underlying truths of our religion, and, that, minus the amputation bit, would be a most worthy religion to follow."

"It seems, Holy Vessels, that God has indeed blessed you both with wisdom far beyond words. Again, I am humbled by your actions and your words. I am now certain that our Lord God has somehow touched both of you. I would like to talk with you both later. I have other business, which I must handle now. God bless both of you!" Unexpectedly, Elder Amadei hugged us both solidly and then left.

"Oh my!" Dita exclaimed after he was gone. "Way to go, my love. That was fantastic."

"We pulled that one out of the fire, but I wonder what else he wants to discuss with us."

Dita replied, "Maybe he senses changes are coming in the wind." She coyly smiled at me. Okay, so I then passionately kissed her and we again headed for bed.

The next night, Albin came for math help. He was all excited about now being able to hypnotize people. Since tomorrow was his day off study, I asked him if he would walk with us into Wit. Naturally, he happily agreed. After he left, Dita asked, "Bethany, what are you up to this time?"

I grinned, "I'm going to teach him his next lesson, that's what."

The next morning, we first had to attend Sunday Services. That meant we had to dress up, wearing our fancy dresses, socks, and shoes. We'd solved most of the problems, the last of which was to tie our shoelaces and then force our feet into them, once we had our socks put on each other. Still, we blew well over an hour getting ourselves dressed. Walking back to our room afterwards, Dita complained, "You sure picked a bad day for us to walk into town. It's snowing and cold. We can't wear our light slip on shoes and are going to have to wear socks and bundle up."

"Can't be helped, but let's let Albin lend us a hand with it." We changed and waited our turn for lunch. When we finished, Albin was waiting at our door for us.

"Hi. It's cold out and snowing, so we are going to need to wear heavy coats and socks and shoes. Can you help us into them, please?"

"Absolutely!" he was more than willing to help, eager even. A few minutes later, we three walked the quarter mile into Wit.

We went into the inn and ordered hot cider. Albin removed our right boot and sock so we could sip from our mugs. "Okay, now what?" he asked.

"Albin, I want you to hypnotize that man over there and tell him it is way too hot in here and that he ought to remove his coat," I suggested.

"But it's cold in here," he protested.

"I know, but if you are successful, he will do as you tell him," I replied. Begrudgingly, Albin did as I asked. He was discrete about it, thankfully. A moment later, the man removed his coat. Apparently, he felt a tad guilty about this and had the man put it back on, before he returned to our table. Now I knew that I had him again.

"Thanks, you certainly did it," I complimented him.

Proudly, he replied, "You bet I did! Pretty cool, don't you think?"

"Yes, but Albin, think about it. Why did you have him put his coat back on?"

He looked sheepishly at the table. "Er, I sort of felt funny about it, you know. I mean it is cold in here. I didn't want him to get cold or sick or something."

"Right, Albin, you felt guilty about doing it. Now what is it that you actually did with that man?"

"I hypnotized him. Oh, I see what you mean. I took over control of him, making him do what I wanted, not what he wanted to do. Pretty awesome power." He was still proud of his accomplishment.

"Okay. Let me put it to you another way. How would you like to be hypnotized and told to take off your coat in here where it's not much warmer than outside, unless we get closer to the fireplace?"

"I'd hate it. I mean I'd be losing my power of choice, my own volition, my own self-determinism. I want to be in control of my life, not having someone controlling it for me," he replied rapidly.

I waited to see if he made the connection. He didn't, so I added, "And just what do the Elders do every month?"

"Oh my god! They hypnotize everyone and then deliver the ritual sermon! Oh my god! We're taking away everyone's self-determinism, taking away their own power of choice in life! Oh, this is absolutely terrible!"

"Well, until something better comes along, the Elders must do what they have to do to keep everything going on an even keel, Albin. Still, as you just said, this is not a good thing to be doing to everyone. If someone did it to you repeatedly and then you found out about it, how might you react?" I asked.

"Punch them out at the very least! Oh! I see what you mean. If the Elders suddenly stopped doing this to them, they'd find out and take it out on the Elders again. Got it." He smiled and took a long drink of cider.

"I don't gamble, but I'd sure bet that they would do just that," I teased him and he grinned, glad he'd figured it out so quickly this time. I was not through with him just yet.

"Now then, let's take a close look at our current "perfect society" and see if we can find anything that is missing in it, shall we?"

"Sure thing. Er, what's missing? We all have good homes, a job, food on the table, and clothes. What's missing?" he asked confused.

Dita began to point them out. "Well, there are the fine arts: music, song, dancing, painting, sculpting, ceramics, beautiful paintings, great novels to read, dancing." She said it twice as a hint to me, knowing how we both loved to dance. "Then, there are all sorts of games and sports, and family vacations and picnics. Then, there is the theater and great plays and orchestral music and ballets. Then there is fashion design. Around here, everyone wears identical clothes with only slight color differences. In other places, hardly anyone wears identical clothing. Each woman sews a bit of her own creation into her dresses, for example. Then there are all the holiday celebrations and parties and dances. We only celebrate Yuletide, and then just barely. These are the things that add color and spice to life, making it more than just dreary existing and surviving, Albin."

I pointed out, "Does a hypnotized man think of any of these things, or is he focused solely on what you have told him to think about?"

"Damn! You are right again. I can see it plainly now. By hypnotizing them and forcing them to focus only on the righteous path all the time, they become zombies and never get around to actual creations of their own design and planning. This whole hypnotizing thing is really wrong, very wrong, isn't it?" he replied.

"Well, in its defense, it has kept our civilization alive and prospering all these centuries. Let us hope that one day soon, a change can come so that hypnotism is no longer needed to achieve a perfect society," I replied.

"Yes, but something has to be done about it, doesn't it?" Albin insisted.

"Oh yes, and very soon, I might suggest."

"Why? The rebels?"

"No, our ships are now visiting other lands where other peoples live without being hypnotized. In Velona, the arts are thriving; a renaissance of the arts is going on there. Already, you have seen our ships returning from there, bringing with them bits of what is missing in our world. We saw it in the dozen women who were wearing the latest fashions from Velona to Sunday Service."

"Oh yes, and wow, those were some outfits! I like them, they looked. . ." his face reddened and he didn't finish his sentence.

"Sexy," I finished it for him. "Yes, they really looked elegant in their new dresses. Albin, you too have tasted of this beginning influx of things from other lands, the chocolate you gave us."

"Oh! Right."

"Now think about this, Albin. What is bound to happen to our people as more and more of the very things which our culture is totally lacking are imported from these other lands?"

"Well, I'm going to buy all the chocolates I can afford!" he replied without thinking. Then, it hit him. "Oh! So is everyone else. Everyone is going to start wanting these new things."

"Yes, and what will that do to their hypnotized ideas that they are following?" I asked pointedly.

"Damn! It's going to undo it! Oh, I see. As time goes on, if we are going to keep things on an even keel, the Elders are going to have to give their special sermons more and more frequently, to displace all these new desires. But Bethany, how can they keep up? I mean as soon as chocolates are affordable, I'm buying them every day!"

"They can't, not even if they do it every day, that's what I'm trying to get you to see, Albin. Our whole culture is poised on the brink of destruction at this very moment, brought on by our sudden expansion into the rest of the known world, which we now know is vastly larger than our small world here," I sermonized.

Dita jumped in with another aspect. "Say, Albin, if you knew that in Velona you could get all the chocolates you could eat in one whole day for a gold dolar, would you consider moving there?"

He laughed, "Well almost, I mean I wouldn't move just for chocolates that would be giving in to gluttony but I see what you are hinting at, Dita. As more and more of our people start seeing the goods from these other places and hearing of the tales of what life is like there, many may be of a mind to move there. I could envision that happening."

She smiled and nodded that he was right. He then said, "I wonder if the Elders have thought about all this? I know they are peaching that we send Elders, doktors, and some of you over to these countries to show the newly sacrificed women how to do things. I just wonder if they have thought about the ultimate impact this may have on the rest of us. I think I will make some discrete inquires. Say, shall we head back?"

He put his arms around each of us and we walked back in the early season snow, which was now an inch deep. I found myself wishing I could have a snowball fight with Renzo, er, I mean Dita.

Chapter 8 Therapy Sessions

Snows came and went, one morning we awoke to woods of white trees; the dark barren sticks rose towards the sky. Here in the middle of November, we knew that soon the snow would be staying, as winter grasped the highlands firmly until spring fought back. Yes, we were again getting a little bored with our daily routine of chores.

After breakfast, we received a summons actually to enter Elder Amadei's residence! We were never allowed into the Elder's building before. He had always come to us. Dita suggested that perhaps he had a higher opinion of us now; I doubted that.

We struggled into our coats and slipped on our heavier shoes for the short walk through the light snow. As we approached, another Elder was waiting for us, opening the door for us, and beckoning us to enter. "May I take your coats?" he said politely. After hanging them on the hall coatrack, he led us into an adjoining room, where Elder Amadei sat behind a large desk. A huge map of Dorota adorned the wall behind him. He was expecting us and had two chairs arranged before his desk. The other Elder graciously adjusted our chairs as we sat down, an unexpected touch of kindness.

"Good morning, Bethany, Dita. I am glad that you could come this morning. I have a mountain of work to get done, but I need to speak with you, privately." He smiled, and added rather jovially, "This seems to be becoming a habit of ours." We returned his smile.

"I'll get right to the point. Albin and I have been holding some, shall we say, rather heated discussions of late. It seems that he's been getting some of his ideas from you two and once more, I'd rather get it straight from the horse's mouth as they say." I squirmed a bit in my seat. This could go either way, I thought.

"Albin seems to believe that we are indeed at a dangerous crossroads with our expansion and push to the Outer Lands." (This was the name that Dorota called the other continents of the world.) "I have tried to explain to him and the other students that part of our religion dictates that it is our responsibility to help the Unholy discover the errors of their ways so that they can be Redeemed and rejoin our Lord God. The Outer Lands are huge and filled with the Unholy, so we have our work cut out for ourselves in this. Honestly, when we set forth years ago in the single caravel, we had no idea just how gigantic the rest of the world was nor the level of Unholy ones."

"Our missionaries have already been making a large number of Redemptions, tens of thousands, and we have made some allies in God. Yet, even that is fraught with unforeseen problems, but that is not what I have asked you here to address this chilly November morning. Rather, let's discuss just why you both believe that Dorota is on a dangerous precipice at this point in time, please."

Dita spoke first, "Fair enough Elder Amadei. Let's begin with a few questions of you. When was the last time that you took your family on a picnic? When was the last time that you took your family to the beach for a vacation in the warm waters?"

"Work is more important just now. Elders must run our whole country," he defended his non-answer, which she knew must be almost never, if at all.

She went on, "Look, our caravels are arriving back here with tales of what must seem incredible to our people. They return with stories of fantastic music, wonderful instruments that make the most holy sounds. They return humming some of the catchy popular songs of these new lands. Oh, the dances — such tales they tell of couples, dressed in their finest, dancing in the evenings — young ones like ourselves meeting others there for an evening of music and simple dancing. They return with paintings of seascapes, woodlands, and mountains that look so real that you feel you could reach out and touch them. The sculptures, the ceramics, and the incredible works of art that these people create in the Outer Lands are a wonder to behold. And then there are all the great works of literature which broaden men's minds."

"And the unbelievable great architectural marvels that we hear about, enormous cathedrals to our Lord God, adorned with such works of art and with such inspirational music and song, that people want to flock to church just to see these and listen to the music, and who are then inspired to do even more good by the Holy Sermons of their priests."

"Then, we hear of all manner of sporting events and friendly competitions among both men and women. Men, women, and children go to fabulous theaters and see great plays that help to educate them with right and wrong conduct examples. Oh, the reports of the orchestral music we hear about and the magnificent ballets. Then, we hear about their fashions. No two people dress identically. Such creativity in designs by their seamstresses and tailors is a wonder to behold, we hear from the returning crews. The architectural designs are breathtaking, no two buildings or homes are exactly alike — such creativity among those in the construction industry."

"They build great churches for the glory of God; and by music and song and art, they bring thousands into the hallowed halls to worship and praise our Lord God. These things and more we are hearing back from the Outer Lands, as our missionaries go forth unto these lands, helping others find Redemption. Already many things are being brought back in trade. We have seen some of our city women wearing the latest fashions and boots from a place called Velona. Even Albin has tasted of their simple everyday candy, called chocolate and loves its taste."

"Elder Amadei, the moment you set sail for the Outer Lands, you have opened wide the doors, which cannot ever again be closed. As time goes on, more and more of their goods will make their way into our country. It cannot be helped nor, as you know, it cannot be stopped. Communication goes in both directions." Dita finally ran down her exhaustive list.

I took over now, since it was obvious from his facial expressions that Elder Amadei had already seen and heard about what Dita had said. It was not new to him. "What does all this mean to our people, our country? I am afraid of this, Elder Amadei; perhaps you have also seen it happening already. We know that you feel that you must hypnotize, mesmerize our people at least once a month to help keep our people on the right path of Holiness and to follow the commandments of our Lord God. Yet, I ask you, does a hypnotized man think of any of these new items, ideas, and descriptions or is he focused solely on what you have told him to think about?"

"Clearly, Dita and I are not in a position to observe or answer this directly. However, we both know that we would be quite fascinated by the new fashions that women are wearing in the Outer Lands. How could we not marvel at the beauty of the dozen women who were wearing those fancy dresses to Sunday Services? It is our belief, not based upon actual observations — you are in a position to do that, sir — that, as more and more of these ideas and objects enter Dorota, the more and more our people will put their attention onto them. This can only mean that you Elders will have to deliver your special sermons far more frequently in order to get hypnotized men and women back onto our Religion. Perhaps it will soon require a sermon every week, then every day. We believe that eventually not even a daily sermon will be sufficient to overcome the attention, the pull of these Outer Lands."

"Soon, everyone is going to start wanting these new things. Even Albin told us that as soon as chocolates are affordable, he's going to buy them often. Women will beg for new fashions. As the hypnotism begins to wear thin, they will begin to become more creative themselves, bringing about a sort of renaissance here in Dorota. However, as this happens and if you do not act to keep all this on an even keel, the Elders and perhaps the doktors will suffer the backlash of our people. Honestly, Elder Amadei, we do not want to see you Elders harmed nor our doktors."

"If our history lessons are true, you Elders have kept our country going and thriving for centuries now, and always on the Lord God's path that he set out for all of us. Yet, if nothing is done, all that may well be destroyed in some wild backlash of our own people as they become un-hypnotized and lash out at those who have kept them hypnotized for so long."

Elder Amadei lowered his head, rubbed his hands through his hair, but said not a word for a minute. I gave him time to collect his thoughts at this pivotal moment. From my point of view, much depended upon how he took all this and his reactions.

"Then it is as I have feared for some time now. I was just a young lad when that first caravel landed here. Oh the visions I had, naive though they be, were shared by so many of us. We were out to save so many other Unholy ones. Yet, though I could not so eloquently say in words as you two Holy Vessels have just done, I knew in my heart this would bring about our doom."

"You two have an uncanny ability to recognize the truth of a situation. I will be honest with you both, though what I am saying to you has never been spoken to a Holy Vessel before now. Yes, we hypnotize our people to instill in them the Holy Qualities our Lord God has asked us to follow. We reap the rewards of this with our nearly perfect society, which is now about to crumble."

"We cannot just stop our monthly sermons, because our people would then quickly take to the Unholy sins. Avarice, greed, stealing, lying, and crime would arise everywhere, and most of all harm and disrespect and rape would befall many of you Holy Vessels. Yes, Elders would be hunted down and murdered, doktors too, as soon as their part was known. All Dorota would fall into anarchy and chaos; all would forsake our Lord God and become Unholy Ones."

"So we must continue what we have been doing for centuries, though now we know that the end, our doom, the doom for all Dorota, is neigh at hand. We cannot stop our sermons, and yet we cannot keep up with the ever-increasing need for the sermons. I see no way out. We Elders must pray for Divine Guidance."

"I am truly sorry to have place such a doom and gloom view of our world on such young Holy Vessels as yourselves. Yet, I needed your input, your viewpoint, from unspoiled Holy Vessels. I truly thank you both for your candid thoughts today. I will honor you for this."

"Sir, Elder Amadei," I decided to experiment a little. "Do you believe in that timeless adage that truth shall set men free?"

"Well, yes, but what has that to do with the monumental problems that we are facing here in Dorota? The truth is that we have been hypnotizing our own people for centuries, though we did so with their best interests at heart. The truth is that we have made our doktors amputate all women's arms, dooming you all to such helpless, miserable lives. These truths doom both us Elders and our doktors."

"Sir, do you also believe that we are all immortal spiritual beings who for a time inhabit these fleshly bodies?" I asked directly.

"Well, yes, of course. We were all created in God's image. Those that obey our Lord's commandments are thus promised to enter his Holy Realm. I admit that my body is what is real to me, though intellectually, I know that this body cannot be God's image. After all, a falling stone can kill me. If God had such a body as ours, his years, too, would be doomed," he replied honestly, I thought.

"I understand. We too believe and *know* that we are immortal spiritual beings and are for a brief time inhabiting these bodies you see before you. Sir, we both believe that there is a far deeper truth underlying our entire society, our entire world, a deeper and perhaps evil and sinister truth — a truth that will indeed set all of us free, without murder, chaos, and anarchy. Will you give us permission to seek for that fundamental, underlying truth, wherever that path may lead us? Make no rash decisions until we have found that truth or have given up the quest."

"What are you saying? I don't understand. What is it that you are asking of me?" he replied very baffled. Yet, I detected a tiny thread of hope behind his questions.

"Relax all of your restrictions that are placed upon young Holy Vessels, especially those not yet of age. Allow us to seek for that truth in our own way. You may think of them as women's ways, if that helps any. It may be that some travel within our country will be needed, though I hope not in the wintertime. It is terribly difficult for us in the snow and cold. Also, allow us to speak to whomever we desire, without limitations or prejudged opinions of us or our intentions. We have a hunch what may be underlying our whole mistreatment of women, not our religion mind you, just how women are handled. Will you allow us the freedom to explore in our own way?"

"Yes, of course. Women's ways are so vastly different. Men cannot fathom or do things in women's ways, of that I am utterly certain." He chuckled, and added, "See, I cannot even touch my belly with my foot! How you can lift a fork to your mouths is beyond me." We all laughed at his jest. He then became serious, "If you wish to travel, I must insist on sending along some Security Guards for your own protection. Perhaps you two are the most valuable Holy Vessels ever born in Dorota. I cannot risk your safety, acceptable?"

"Absolutely. Thank you, Elder Amadei. We will keep you posted on our progress."

"No, it is I who must once more thank you! Would you like to know what all the responsibilities and duties of an Elder actually are? Would this help in your search for this truth of which you spoke?"

"Absolutely it would help. We promise not to reveal this information to others," Dita replied. He smiled and said that he would also see to it. We then left his office and headed to the kitchen. I needed a cup of tea and time to think. I'd just gotten everything I had ever wanted from the Elders!

The three cooks were busy working on lunch, but allowed us to boil some water. While I got the cups and tea, Dita prepared the yoke and carried the pot and cups to a table, where we could talk without being overheard. The dining room was empty. "So what have you got in mind for us to be doing?" Dita asked, once she had positioned the yoke and trays by our seats, sat down, and lifted them onto our low tabletop.

"Mantis creatures, Dita. That can be the only explanation. Remember how we found Enyo and her friends? Mantis creatures ate their arms after they were born. I see lots of parallels between them and this country."

"But we have not seen any traces of mantis creatures around here," Dita protested, but was very serious, her Protector training coming to the fore. "I've been alert for signs, but seen nothing. Wait a minute, what do the doktors do with all those baby arms they amputate? Maybe they are feeding the creatures, which are now staying out of sight. If so, they are awfully well fed, that's a whole lot of arms, though I admit each one is pretty small."

"Bethany, if we are going bug hunting, I must admit that I am not in so good a position to be your Protector," she shrugged her shoulders and I knew what she meant.

"Don't worry, Dita. We never were able to kill any bugs using our arms anyway," I put my Protector at ease once more.

"So what are you planning? I'm glad that you are not heading off across the countryside in the winter. I am having an awful time coping with that like this," again, she shrugged her shoulders.

"Therapy sessions, Dita. We must run some of these back and see where it leads us. If I am not way off base here, sooner or later one patient will run back to a time when the mantis creatures controlled this whole country, starting the policy of eating baby girl's arms."

"But Bethany, what will happen if we run out one of these women's birth trauma and they discover, as we did, that the doktor amputated their arms right after birth? Won't that lead to a major upset?" Dita pointed out.

"Yes, you are right. If we start in on these women, who obviously need it, when they find out the truth, there'll be hell to pay. I think we are going to start in with Albin and some of the other students here, perhaps even with the Elders, if they are willing. That way, whatever comes up will not start riots and upheavals," I concluded.

"Bethany, Albin has arms! How are we going to run out the trauma that isn't there?" Dita asked a very good question.

"My guess is that Albin and all the other males around here have had many bodies before this one. Half, statistically, have been female. We haven't anything else to do, except get educated on what all the Elders actually do around here." Dita giggled, that was true.

That evening when Albin dropped by for math help, we got him through it in a rush. "Now then, Albin, do you trust us?" I asked.

"Sure why?"

"We want to try something with you. Have you ever had any strange aches or pains in your shoulders?" I asked.

"That's weird. How did you know that? Yes, when it gets cold out, my shoulders seem to ache and my arms feel weak. Why? I figured it was normal; it's just the way it is."

"Well, sit back, close your eyes. Let's see if we can get to the reason for those aches and erase them. I want you to return back to the last time your shoulders ached."

"Okay, it was yesterday morning when I woke up. My room was cold."

"Very good. Now I want you to start there at the beginning and tell me all that happened."

"Not much. It is cold; our rooms are always cold in the morning. I am getting up, but my shoulders ache. I rub them. I have this feeling that this is just the way it is. I get dressed and finally I am warm. The ache goes away, that's all." He finished up.

I had him go back and go through it several more times. He noticed a strange thing, "Bethany, my shoulders are aching now! It's not even cold in your room here." I thanked him and had him go through it once more.

Since the ache was only growing stronger, I asked the jackpot question. "Albin, is there some earlier trauma to your shoulders there?"

"Oh, I don't know. Everything is so dark. It's just the way things are, you know. Oh wait a second. I see some really strange picture in my mind."

"Very good indeed! Now go to the beginning of that one. Okay. Now let's go through it and tell me all about it."

"I'm probably just imagining this, Bethany, you know from what all I've been studying."

"That's fine. What are you seeing?"

"Well, there is this small baby girl. She is just being born. Yes, I can see the room now. There is a doktor there delivering it. He wraps her up in a blanket before the woman can see her new baby. He is saying, 'I'll get her cleaned up and blessed for you.' He leaves with the baby. Now I see a brightly lit room. It's warm. He's poking something into the baby's shoulders. Ouch! That hurt! Weird, Bethany, I just felt stabbing pains in my shoulders."

"Thanks for telling me. Continue telling me about what is happening."

"Well, now everything goes dark, but somehow the baby still feels. Oh! Ieee! It hurts! He's cutting my arms off! God, it hurts, but I cannot move. It's all dark. God, now my other shoulder has this bolt of shooting pain in it! I can't feel my little hands anymore. I can feel his fingers on my shoulders doing something. Kind of like sewing maybe. He says, 'There, you are all fixed up.' I feel better now because I am all fixed up. I see my mother now. She looks so happy, but I am starving. God, Bethany, I don't have any arms anymore!"

"I understand. Now let's go back over it once more." He did so. Each time through that trauma, it became more and more real to Albin, as did the sharp, intense pains that he felt in his shoulders. After ten passes, I saw that it was not going to vanish.

"Okay, now have another look. Is there an even earlier time that you had this kind of pain in your shoulders?" I asked, wondering how many lifetimes of female baby bodies I would need to work through to get to what I hoped would be revealed. In the last several hundred years, he may well have had four or five other bodies. If he were unlucky, four of them would be trauma filled at birth.

"Are these real? Well, I see a bluish thing here, must be. God do my shoulders ache, that's just the way it is."

I had him start going through this next one. "It's just like the last one. There is the doktor, he's helping a new baby come out. Yes, he has it out now. A girl. He wraps her up in a blanket. The woman wants to see her baby, but he says that he needs to clean her up first. He leaves. He's taking the baby somewhere out of doors. Oh, I see a stone slab and he lays the baby on the flat stone with the blanket around it."

"Must be going to get his surgery tools, I expect. Let's see. Time is passing and nothing much — oh my god! A monster is coming towards me! It's a giant! Huge! I am screaming and wiggling my arms and legs, though I know I cannot get away from it. It's huge, big bug eyes are looking at me. Look at the size of those mandibles! It's going to eat me! It's plunging something into my shoulders. Ah, that's better, I am relaxing now, I don't feel anything in my shoulder any more. Wait! God! It's eating my arm! Now it's going to my other arm. Please don't eat that one too! I'll be so helpless! No, get away. I am screaming my little head off. Ouch. It's puncturing my other shoulder. Ah, now it doesn't hurt any more. Oh no! It's eating that arm too! I don't have any arms left now! Is it going to eat the rest of me? No, it's going away. I feel relieved. Oh, here comes the doktor again. He wraps me back up. He says, 'Well, that's just the way it is, little one. You'll be all right in a little while.' He takes me to my mother. Man, am I ever hungry. That's all. Bethany, what in the world is that thing? It looks like a monstrous insect or something."

"Super job, Albin. Now let's go through it another time. Tell me what is happening," I said softly.

Two more passes and he suddenly opened his eyes and started laughing loudly. "Well that's just the way it is! Ha! I sure as heck am not all right in a little while! I don't have any arms! What an idiot comment that was! Wow. I feel so much lighter, so brighter. Oh, my shoulder ache is gone. Wow. Say what was that bug thing? It must have been fifty feet long or more."

"I think that they are called mantis creatures," I replied in a non-committing manner.

"Yes, that's what they remind me of — say, I had two other lives there!"

"Well, yes, we are all immortal spiritual beings," Dita explained, keeping it simple.

"Ah ha. For a time inhabiting these human bodies. Wow! I get it now!

Jeesh. Wait a second. I had two female bodies! I was just as you are now. No wonder I feel such sympathy and desire to help all our women! I've been just like you. Incredible. Say, what was that that you just did here for me? I've never heard of anything like this."

"It is the therapy method that Dita and I know, which we use to erase the traumas a person has had," I replied honestly.

"It certainly works on me! Thanks, but how is it that you know how to do this therapy? We never covered anything like this in school. Is this a woman's way thing that I don't know about or something?" he asked, leaving us a way out, if we chose not to answer it directly.

"You have told us that you have just remembered two former lives that you had here in Dorota. Well, Dita and I have had many other lives too. In one of them, we learned how to do this therapy, and we have not forgotten how it is done. Make sense?" I asked.

"Yes, I mean I now can remember just how helpless I used to feel, when I was like you two. I wish I could remember something far more useful, especially about those mantis creatures. I wonder if they are still around here somewhere?" he asked.

"Well, Dita and I have not seen any signs of them in our fourteen and a half years here. Apparently, no one else has either. I'm sure that if someone saw them, everyone would soon know about it," I answered him truthfully.

"Suppose so, can't keep something like that quiet for long. Man, they ate my arms right off my little body! Incredible."

"Again, well done Albin. Say, it is getting late. You'd better get going. Catch you tomorrow," Dita noticed how late it had gotten and didn't want him getting into trouble.

After he was gone, Dita commented, "Well, you were right! The mantis were here and probably started this whole mess that we are in today. So what are we going to do about it, my love? I can't see us running five hundred thousand women through therapy sessions to get rid of that trauma. We'd need several lifetimes to do that, besides what's going to happen as soon as one woman learns the doktors and the Elders are behind the removal of their arms?"

"Dita, I just do not know yet. You are right; we don't dare run this on any women just yet. There would be hell to pay, once they learn the limited truth, that the doktors amputated their arms. If we could guarantee that each one would run all the way back to the mantis creatures, then we might have a chance."

"Yes, but there is no guarantee of that. After all, at least half of those present back when the mantis creatures were here had to be males and were not affected."

"Absolutely right, Dita. Gosh, I am wide-awake and it is late. We ought to at least try to sleep though."

"I know how to calm you down," Dita said coyly. A bit later, I confided in her that she did indeed know how.

A week had passed since Albin's therapy session. I still had not worked out a good solution, but Dita and I finally decided that the first step ought to be getting a complete understanding of how the country was run by the Elders and their High Council. Once we knew the complete picture, then perhaps a solution would present itself. While we were eating our late breakfast, joining the third batch to eat, the domestic staff, Elder Amadei came looking for us, carrying a large package.

"Ah here you are. I just wanted to give you two a little present for everything that you are doing for us. A little thank you. I took what you said to heart, about women loving fashions and all that. I'm told that these are the finest money can buy in a place called Velona, Sea Princes. I'm not sure where that is without looking at the maps though. Supposedly, they will keep your feet very warm in the cold weather as well. I hope you like them. On my way back, I'll leave the box in your room. If you like them, please wear them as often as you like."

"Thank you very much," we chorused, though we had no idea what was in the large box and he wasn't saying directly. Perhaps he found it embarrassing?

"Now then, there is another matter that I wish to discuss with you. It's about Albin again. He has had a long talk with me about what he discovered during what he called a therapy session, which you ran on him a week ago or so. It is truly a miracle that he can now remember other lives that he has led and that he is so utterly certain of his own spiritual nature. Truly moving, truly. Yet I do not know what to make of his monster insect. Imagination, I'm sure."

"Well, yes it is terrific that he has such a good reality now on his own spiritual nature. We've been meaning to talk to you about this. We would like the opportunity to give you therapy sessions as well, the sooner the better. If what happens during them is what we anticipate, we would then, with your permission, like to deliver similar sessions to the other Elders," I suggested.

Dita added, "Also, we are ready to learn the ways of the Elders in the running of our country."

He grinned, "I meant to tell you first off that has been arranged. Elder Lew would like you to spend the afternoons with him and he will teach you what you desire to know. Can you begin this afternoon? If so, I will tell him to expect you, room six of the student's classroom building at say one p.m.?"

"That would be perfect!" Dita replied vigorously. She really wanted to know this inside information. She was a Protector, so I knew why she did.

"Great. I'll tell him. As far as the therapy sessions go, I would be honored if you would do me. I am free in the evenings, but I have so little time in the daytime."

"That's fine with us. Why not come by our room tonight. We eat the third shift, so make it around seven," I replied.

"I'm sorry that you are eating so late. If you want, I can relax that rule, you could eat with the students and us Elders at five." I saw that he was really just propitiating towards us.

"No, that would perhaps distract the students. We know that they have so much to learn and it is so important that more Elders be trained. We are fine with eating third shift. Thanks for your kind offer," I replied.

"Thank you both. I must be off. I've a class in a few minutes. I'll leave my present for you in your room. Please wear them with all do pride." He left in a hurry; we hoped that he would not be late.

"What did he give you?" Zofia asked curiously. "It's very rare indeed that Elder Amadei gives one of us a present. We all overheard him talking about it." We noticed that all the women had stopped eating and were listening, eager to hear our answer. "All the way from Velona even," she added with a strong emphasis.

"He didn't say. It's a big box, so he is kindly leaving it in our room. I guess we ought to go and see," Dita replied before I could.

"Oh yes, you must do so at once! Please come and show us all the presents! Please," Zofia begged us.

Giggling like a fourteen year old girl, Dita replied, "Okay we will. Come on, Bethany; let's see what Elder Amadei has given us so we can make a fashion statement." I grinned and followed her out of the dining room to our room.

There was the big box sitting on the floor just inside our door, where we could easily get to it. "Who gets to open it?" giggled Dita. So seldom did we get surprise presents that she was excited.

"Go ahead, my love, open it for us," I giggled too. Dita's feet undid the tie string and then she lifted the top off the box. Staring up at us were two pairs of black boots, calf high, with pointed toes and the usual very tall heels. Embossed prominently was the label: Made by Alexa, the Deep Thinker. These were lined with sheepskin and we could easily slip them on or off with our feet. We both stared at the boots and had fond memories of Alexa vividly replaying in our minds. She had been a very good friend of ours in the past, and we shared many an adventure with her.

"Just what we really don't need," I laughed.

"Oh come on, Bethany! These are made by Alexa, and she was like us. Don't be a spoil sport; let's show the women here some fashion! You know that they will enjoy this and it'll give them something to talk about for days," Dita insisted.

"Yes, but you have never worn heels like these, my love. Remember; take the tiniest of steps. Okay, at least our feet will be warm," I gave in and we slipped off our light shoes and slipped our feet into the luxurious, soft, warm sheepskin. My feet felt warmer instantly!

Dita stood up and nearly fell down. "Oh! These are different! Small steps! Small steps! Great! Boy are we ever going to make a fashion statement around here. Oops. Small steps." I laughed and her serious face gave way to mirth as well. As promised, we walked, albeit very slowly, back to the kitchen, where absolutely all the female domestic staff had now gathered. Word had spread and they all were just dying to see the fashion present.

A half hour passed as each of them just had to chat with us and see the boots close up. All thirty of them greatly admired such wonderful boots. Some had seen other more wealthy women wearing similar boots to Church. Indeed, Dita was right; this made their day! However, walking so slowly, we were a few minutes late getting to room six to meet with Elder Lew.

"Such fine boots for such pretty young Holy Vessels. Impressive, you both look very elegant," Elder Lew complimented us. He was thirty years old, sporting a small black moustache. Tall and thin, with his short black hair was neatly combed, Lew looked the part of an Elder.

Soon we were given the overall picture of just how the entire country was really run. They always had one Church for every two hundred people with a bisklep to run it. If there were not that many people in a town or village, they would have a Church anyway. Every five Churches were joined into what they called a Parish, and each Parish had a permanently assigned Elder. Elder Feliks was assigned to our Parish, back home. Their duties, besides the monthly hypnotizing sermon was to gather the actual needs of his Parish. These were then sent to the appropriate committee.

The Planning Committee handled the design and expansion of the cities and towns. If something needed to be constructed, this committee did the planning for it. The Work Oversight Committee handled the actual construction or saw to a plan's implementation. The Finance Committee took care of all financial matters. The Security Committee dealt with security issues, primarily with the rebels. The Rehabilitation Committee ran the Fields of Kondrat and attempted by any means possible to Rehabilitate the Unholy. The Training Committee oversaw the general education of both the Elder College at Wit and that of the general population. Among their duties was to find qualified teachers.

All of these reported directly to the High Council of Elders. There were thirteen members, an odd number so that there could never be a tie vote. These men made the highest-level decisions affecting the entire country as a whole. It was this committee that had ordered the copying of the Velona caravel and later sent out the many missionaries to Redeem the Unholy in the distant lands.

Elder Amadei was the headmaster of the Elder College at Wit and as such was one of the members of the High Council of Elders. Each of the other committees had a representative on this High Council. That meant that there were also seven at-large Elders, whom we learned were chosen by secret ballot from among all the Elders on Dorota.

Thus, in one long afternoon, we learned all that we really needed to know at this point. Lew seemed relieved when we told him that this was all that we had to know now. I detected that he was a little reluctant to divulge this information to Holy Vessels, especially ones so very young and not even of age yet.

That evening Albin came by as usual. "Wow! Look at those boots! Incredible! You two look fantastic in them! I never dreamed that Elder Amadei had such a fashion taste. You look great in them." He was very much impressed with them, as any young boy would be when around two good-looking young girls. Okay, we did appreciate the attention being sent our way, I'll admit it.

However, since Elder Amadei was due any minute, Dita took Albin next door to the dining room, where she helped him with his math problems. I awaited the Elder. He was precisely on time, but he also had to admire my new boots as well. Then, we got down to business.

"Now then, do you by chance have any aches or pains in your shoulders, from time to time?" I asked the obvious first choice.

"Well, no nothing like that." I began to think fast, what else might the symptoms of having ones arms cut off be? "But I do have these shooting pains down my arms from time to time. Will that do? It would be nice not to have them any longer, but I know that nothing can be done about that."

I breathed a huge sigh of relief. The hardest part of the therapy was getting started. Usually, the person was right there in the middle of the recent trauma. In this case, I was after something that would lead into the distant past. Only a tiny trace of it might still be in the present with these men. "Okay, close your eyes." Off I went, having him return to the last time he had experienced these shooting pains down his arms. We went over it several times.

"See, there is nothing that can be done about that," he said as we finished the fifth time through it.

I asked him if there was an earlier time that he had experienced similar pains. For a half hour, I listened to six such times, before he said, "Well, I do have some bluish picture here. I can't tell for sure what it is, probably my imagination working overtime. I'm sorry I am such a failure for you. I guess I am just hopeless. There is nothing that can be done about it."

"You are doing fine. Now let's go through it and tell me what is happening."

He yawned and proceeded to relate what he was seeing. "I see a woman. She's giving birth, yes, that's it. Birth. I must be the doktor. Yes, the baby comes out. It's a girl. The doktor wraps her up nicely and tells the new mother that he is off to clean her new daughter up and bless her. He carries the baby to his office. Bright lights, yes the lights are very bright. I must need to see well what I am doing. The doktor injects something into the baby. She calms down. I see a scalpel. He starts to cut. Ieee! That hurts! Pain, shooting pain goes down my arms! I scream. He gives me more. All goes black. He cuts and it hurts, but I cannot move. Then the shooting pain goes away. I cannot feel my little hands any more, nor my arms. I relax. No more shooting pains. Movement. Oh, he is taking me back to my mother. I am so terribly hungry. I am frantically trying to nurse. I notice that I don't have any arms any more. I freak out and cry. That's all."

"Very good, very good. Now let's go over it again. Tell me all that happens."

I ran him through this one a half dozen times. The pains grew more and more severe and did not seem to lighten up. He did decide that he was not the doktor or the mother; he was the baby girl. Hence, I asked him then if there was another one even earlier in time. After a bit of hunting, he saw another one, a huge green mass. I had him go through that one next.

"I see a room, dark, poor lighting. Oh, a woman is giving birth. I see a man standing beside her and there is the doktor. He's helping her. Push, he is saying. The man is holding her head. Oh. The mother has no arms either. I just noticed that. My head feels all squished. Ah, I'm getting born. No, that's not right. I'm right there watching the body get born. It is my body that is coming out, yes, that's right. There, it's finally over. I am relaxing. The doktor is wrapping me up. He says to the couple, 'It's a fine looking girl. While I get her cleaned up, you must choose her name.' He leaves, taking me to be cleaned. I like that idea. I seemed to be somewhat bloody now. I am wiggling, but I cannot clean myself off."

"Wait a minute, he's not taking me inside. I'm outside! Hey, wait a minute, doktor, I tried to say, but my voice didn't work right, just made a weird noise. He is putting me down on a cold slab of granite. I wiggle to protest. I am cold! Where did he go? He can't be leaving me outside? I am crying for help. I think maybe someone will come, find me, and take me back to my mother inside. I see green. Then, I am thinking I am hopeless, nothing can be done about it anyway. That's all."

I thanked him and had him go through it all once more. He got even more details on the birth and his back grew cold from the slab of granite. However, the green part now began to develop, as I knew it would.

"I see green, huge green. No, wait a second! I see a humongous green insect, mantis-like, coming towards me! I scream and scream, hoping someone will come and rescue me. It leans over me. I just know that it is going to eat me alive! Those mandibles, they are so huge! It bites me on my right shoulder. Pains shoot down my arm. Then it's gone. Numb. God! It is eating my arm off! I can't feel a thing. Why is that? I don't know. Please someone come and help me! Now it is moving. Oh please, please, please don't eat my other arm! I will be helpless. No, no, no! Pain. It bites my left shoulder and then it goes numb. I watch it eat that arm too. I know I am going to die now. It will eat the rest of me next." He yawned heavily repeatedly.

"No, it doesn't! Someone must have scared it away from me. Here comes the doktor again. He wraps me up. I am so cold. Lights. Mom, there is my mother; she doesn't have any arms either. The doktor unwraps me and shows me to my parents. 'See what a fine daughter you have!' Mom shrieks, 'She has no arms!' The doktor says, 'I am afraid that there is nothing that can be done about that.' Mom is crying, 'She'll be helpless like me. It's just hopeless.' I am laid beside her and somehow I am nursing. That's all."

"My god, Bethany! This is so vividly real! I can smell the blood! I can smell the out of doors! Wow!" I thanked him and had him go through it once more. On the third pass, he began chuckling. By the time we reached its end, he was roaring with laughter. "Hopeless, helpless, nothing can be done about it! No kidding! There wasn't anything that could be done about it at that point! It was already over and done with!"

"Bethany, I feel so light, so happy, and so very much alive. I haven't felt this way in years! Thank you for your miracle!"

"You did very well indeed, Elder Amadei. It is getting late. Why don't we talk about this tomorrow evening?" I suggested. He agreed and headed to his rooms, happily whistling some song that I had never heard before. Dita, who had been patiently waiting for me to finish up, came in as he left.

He looked at her and said, "No hope. Helpless totally. Nothing can be done about it!" and laughed hysterically.

"Well, you sure fixed him up well, my dearest," she said as she shut our door.

"Yes, got another mantis incident, but you already guessed that, didn't you my love?" She grinned, and we moved close together and passionately embraced.

The next evening, Elder Amadei arrived precisely on time. I noticed that his eyes were far brighter than usual. "Can we talk?" he asked politely.

"Absolutely. I suspect you have lots of questions for us," I replied with a girlish giggle. He smiled.

"First, I want to thank you from the bottom of my heart. There are no words to describe the relief you've given me or the overall impact it is making on my life. I am a spiritual being! I'm utterly certain of that! I am created in our Lord God's image and it is not these bodies we see here!" I wanted to say, "I told you so," but dare not, choosing to smile instead.

"Those images were so utterly real. I've given this mantis thing considerable thought all last night and today. It happened long ago, that I know. Perhaps centuries ago. What were they? What did they want? Why were they eating baby girl's arms and not boys? What happened to them? Where did they go? Are they coming back? Is this enough to start with?" He chuckled once more.

"I'll tell you a story, Elder Amadei. You can believe it or not, as you see fit. This is a bit of evaluation on my part, but you now have some reality on the fact that you are an immortal spiritual being who has had several human bodies over the years. Dita and I have a much greater reality on who we are and the lives that we have lived. In one of our previous lives, we discovered that some of these mantis creatures were still around Tarra, and we and our friends set out to kill them. Yes, they were still eating off the arms of females. We learned that our arms are considered a delicacy to these strange creatures. Yes, they are about fifty feet in length, huge by any standards. We had some wild times tracking them down and slaying them. And yes, we found hundreds of women who had lost their limbs to these vile creatures. At that time, we believed that we had gotten the last of them. No more mantis creatures roamed anywhere on Tarra."

"We are pretty confident that they are not ever coming back. After all, none have been here in over two centuries now. I think we are now very safe from them, especially since you have invented your guns." I wanted him to believe that they had a weapon, which could be used to kill any that might reappear. Whether or not a gun would harm a mantis creature, I had no idea, but I seriously doubted it.

"As to what they wanted here, from our extensive travels and peoples rescued from these creatures, I believe that they were trying to set up a civilization much as ours is, one in which humans reproduced, providing an abundant supply of their delicacy, female arms. From what I can tell of our history here, I believe that they did succeed in doing just that, many centuries ago, before our recorded history was set down in our books. Perhaps there are writings dating from that period in our ancient past. Of this, I do not know."

Now came my ultimate punch. "It is plain as the nose on my face what has happened here. These creatures forced our doktors and rulers to create the society that we now have. Early on, the mantis creatures dined on the newborn girl's arms. Probably later, the doktors continued removing them, under threat from these creatures. Even though the creatures eventually departed Dorota for unknown reasons, the doktors were so terrified of them, and who wouldn't be terrified of a fifty-foot tall eating insect, that they continued the practice. Our society does have many virtues, as commanded by our Lord God. It is easy to see how they would carry on the practice, which kept themselves alive and our people at peace, without criminality, wars, mistreatment of wives, and so on. I believe that our Elder ancestors and their doktors had little choice in what they did. What do you think?"

"Incredible, just incredible. Yes, it now makes total sense. I can see how these vile creatures twisted our whole culture. Am I correct in assuming, Bethany, that this is the fundamental truth for which you were seeking?"

"Yes, sir. When I was born and had my arms amputated and then saw that all of our women were also armless, I had strong suspicions that the mantis creatures were behind this. Dita and I have been alert for any such sightings of these fantastic bugs all our lives. We've never even heard rumors of them, let alone seen one here on Dorota. Only by our therapy sessions could we see if indeed these vile creatures lay behind it. Now I am totally certain of it all."

"Incredible, simply incredible, Bethany, Dita. It is my fondest wish that every man, woman, and child on Dorota get this therapy and can see for themselves how terribly we have all suffered all these centuries. I know not how that can be achieved, but it is my wish to somehow do it."

"Admirable goal! However, I would caution you. Not everyone who was living back when the creatures walked among us had female bodies. Those folks might not have even seen the mantis creatures. They will have a great tendency to doubt this whole thing has ever happened here."

He looked crestfallen, realizing that I spoke truthfully. If one had not seen them, he or she would never believe such fantastic creatures could even exist.

"In the spring, when it is warm for travel, Dita and I will go in search of proof, the kind of proof that will convince all doubters."

"What? Proof? There is such?" he asked in wonderment, scarcely believing what he'd just heard.

"Yes, they had to live somewhere on Dorota. If we can find their home, we will find all the proof of their existence that you need to convince everyone that you speak the truth. That, Elder Amadei, may yet set them all free."

"I swear to you and Dita, that when spring comes, we will spare no resource in assisting you to find this proof that we vitally must have!"

"Thank you, that is most generous. In the meantime, during the winter, we should attempt our therapy on the other members of the High Council. If this goes well and if there is time, we may extend it to others of your choosing."

"Excellent. I will arrange for it to be done. I would love to have you do this therapy on my sister and her daughter. She is happily married, thankfully. I've never married. By the way, she picked out these magnificent boots for me. I'm afraid that I know virtually nothing about women's apparel." He suddenly laughed, "Well, not this lifetime anyway." We giggled along with him.

"In the meantime, I am going to recommend that the both of you sit in on our High Council meetings. You may share your guidance with us men. We may need your keen insights. It is not well known, but in a week, we are expecting the arrival of a Pope Leo of the Megalos Church of Jehosanity. He had requested a conference with us. Our Elders in the field have reported a high degree of similarities between out faiths and practices. I wish you to be present when this Pope fellow visits us."

"Thank you. This is indeed a surprise. We certainly will do so."

"My daughter's name is Hanna, by the way. She and I believe that you two ought to have something finer to wear during the Pope's visit. I will send her to you and between you, please pick out something elegant and refined. It is my wish that you appear well dressed before this important visitor from the Outer Lands. Money is no object, my dear Holy Vessels, whom else can I spend it on, eh?" He gave us a sly grin and we both giggled.

The next day, we followed Elder Amadei into a plush meeting room to be introduced to the High Council members. In order to make a good first impression, we wore our Sunday outfits and of course our new boots. Our reception was less than favorable. He had already presented the motion to have us join the council meetings as observers. Elder Amadei had argued his case before the group and, according to Elder Amadei; some were in harsh disagreement with his proposal to allow Holy Vessels such unprecedented access to their very private meetings. His motion carried by the narrowest of margins, one vote.

From the glaring stares, we could tell who had voted against us; they made their opinion very noticeable. We received a cordial welcome for Elders Iwan of the Planning Committee, Jaromir of the Work Oversight Committee, and at-large Elders Karol, Marcin, Pawel, and Tymon. Frigid stares came from Elders Aleksander of the Security Committee, Borys of the Rehabilitation Committee, Kuba of the Finance Committee, and at-large Elders Aron, Dariusz, and Henio. After our introductions, we took a seat against the back wall as observers. The Elders sat around a large table.

Elder Iwan spoke first, "Today, we must prepare for this meeting with the leader of a religious order that is wide spread in the Outer Lands, this Church of Jehosanity led by a man called Pope Leo. His ship is expected to be arriving within a few days at our southern port of Bozydar. Elder Aleksy is accompanying him and can inform us honestly of the actuality of this church. He is also teaching Pope Leo our language. Let us hope that it will be sufficient for us to communicate well."

"Why are we even bothering with these Unholy men?" asked an antagonistic Elder Aleksander.

"This is the largest organized religion in the Outer Lands. On the surface, it would seem that what they believe in is very similar to us," Elder Iwan explained patiently, ignoring the antagonism. "From our field reports, they also have some of their women as we have our Holy Vessels." He felt ill at ease saying outright armless women; he gave us a sideways glance. "Their name for these special women is a Woman of the Eighth Degree."

"What are the other degrees?" Elder Borys asked. No one knew. While Dita and I both knew, we kept our mouths shut. How could we explain to these men that we knew about this from our past lives in the Outer Lands? Our already tenuous position at these meetings would be compromised, and we would be labeled quacks or worse, although Elder Amadei would believe us.

"What we must decide today is who will be attending this meeting?" Elder Iwan continued. "Should we all be present, in case a decision must be made?"

"As your Security representative," Elder Aleksander spoke before anyone else could, "I argue against it. If there is some treachery, we could lose our entire governing body. Perhaps only five ought to go. Amadei should be one of them, since he is our most educated religious leader. I should go as well to oversee your security." After some discussion, they voted in favor of sending a limited number, five to be exact. Elders Iwan, Kuba, and Tymon were chosen to accompany us.

A furor arose when Elder Amadei told them that he planned to take us along, again as observers. "Women have no say in our leadership! Don't you know that?" the bile spewed forth from Elder Aleksander. His sentiments were echoed from five others.

"We should put on display the best of our Holy Vessels," Elder Amadei argued. "You cannot deny that these two are the very best that we have ever produced." I felt like I was becoming a tomato or ear of corn, but kept quiet. In the end, the vote was the same as it had been to allow us access, seven to six. We were going with them tomorrow. The meeting ended abruptly, and the six stormed out of the meeting, fuming.

"You can see why it is so vital that we have an odd number on the council," Elder Amadei explained as he led us back to our room. "We will leave by coach after breakfast. Please take yours with us on the first shift. By the way, I have decided to take Albin along with us. I keep forgetting that you will need a hand with some things that your fathers and brothers had been doing for you. Albin will be there to assist both of you with whatever you may need. We ought to get packing now. We've a long journey ahead of us and I do not know what it may bring."

Chapter 9 Papal Visit

Pope Leo paced the deck of his exquisite yacht, the Holy Archangel. A portly man, now in his sixties — he was shrewd, clever, cunning, and bold. He had to be so. After the debacle of his predecessor, Pope Aison, who had been brutally murdered for his attempt on the life of Emperor of Demokritos nearly forty years ago, the Church of Jehosanity had reached its lowest ebb. The only good thing Aison had done was hide the Church's assets from the looting Demokritos soldiers upon their return from their war with Zargarb. Everything was falling apart, when the Cardinals finally elected Leo to be their next Pope and supreme leader of the Church.

Leo was young then, full of life and vigor and plans, big plans. He had to think big or the Church would never recover. That they still retained their wealth played a key role in these plans. Pope Leo was also an idealist, who had seen much of the lies, deceit, avarice, and out-right criminality of base man. Man had to be controlled, guided down the path of righteousness or he would never find the promised salvation. Pope Leo had big plans, plans to get the debased men back onto Lord Jehosa's rightful path.

His reasoning was simple. The Holy must do what must be done to the Unholy to set the Unholy back onto Lord Jehosa's Path. It was the duty and obligation of the Holy and he would see it through. First, he spent funds to triple the size of his Mano del Dio protection force. That these men were skilled assassins didn't matter, they would become his Holy Righteous Arm to bring the Unholy back onto the Path.

Second, he ordered massive upgrades to every single Church of Jehosanity throughout the known world. Enlarge and awe were the catch phrases used. Massive spaces made mere man look small and insignificant, while God was therefore enormous. Awe, awe was key. Gold inlay was used on all the High Altars and on every conceivable ornament and vestment that a worshiper's eyes would see while facing the Priest. The finest artwork, the finest painters, the finest sculptors — all were commissioned to adorn the many Churches. Music directors were hired to search out the finest and most holy sounding vocal and instrumental music to be found. Then, large choirs were assembled to learn the music and to perform before each High Mass. Awe, that was the key. Show the lowly worshiper that here in this Holy Place he could find a connection to Lord Jehosa.

Third, he ordered well-planned expansions of the Church of Jehosanity into lands whose leaders had previously been considered their enemies, such as many of the Sea Princes and large sections of Demokritos. Build huge and awe-inspiring cathedrals to Lord Jehosa and your worshipers will come had been his rule of thumb. That it did indeed work as he had planned shocked the older Cardinals, who believe utterly that Pope

Leo was squandering what little resources the Church had left.

Of course, the Santi del Dio was their archenemy, almost since the founding of the Church of Jehosanity under Pope Yazi I. However, with the rise of Demokritos as a world power and the discovery of so many other continents and countries, the Santi began to lose their vice grip on world power. In fact so much so that the Santi had long ago agreed to assist the Church in their ceremonies of the Eight Degrees. As Pope Leo set sail on this historic voyage, the Santi was a thing of the past. No longer did they even pretend to have an army of fighters. Their fancy stone fortresses, which dotted the Sea Princes sectors, had long ago been turned over to the local governments. Their only remaining fortress was said to be at Mont Blanc in the Langdoc region of the Greenway, north of the Sea Princes. True, they still had a small fleet of caravels, but that was all. Their leaders had simply vanished, probably from old age.

The forth step in his big plans had not begun until some twenty years ago, after the first three were well underway and thriving. He knew that other governments, other people, would attempt to block his Holy Church from either expanding into their territories or from enlarging their current bases of power. Now he unleashed his newly formed Mano del Dio. The first target was the Emperor of Demokritos, who had ordered the execution of the Holy Pope Aison. This was not, however, about revenge, rather it was about the gaining of power. The young Emperor stood steadfast against further expansion of the Church of Jehosanity within the huge country of Demokritos. He was found one morning with his throat cut. After money exchanged hands within several of the larger kingdoms that made up the country, the next Emperor took a more favorable view of the Church of Jehosanity.

Here in 743, the Church of Jehosanity was the most powerful and widespread religious organization on Tarra. For the last few years now, Pope Leo attended to the fifth part of his grand plan, that of finally controlling the Unholy so that they could become Holy and Redeemed once more. However, no sooner had be begun this, his last and final legacy to the Holy Church and one for which he would go down in history, than a newcomer religion appeared here and there throughout the known world — the civilized portions at least.

At first, he gave little thought to this new group, which had no other name than the Church of God. Yet, from all reports, their top preachers, calling themselves simply the Elders, somehow gave the most inspiring sermons that the average person had ever heard. So great was the Elder's promise or message that the vast majority who heard the Elder's sermon at once converted over to this new religion, abandoning their entire former lives in total. They moved their whole families into this new religious community. Even more curious, from all reports, all the females within that family group had become of the Eighth Degree!

Thus sufficiently curious, Pope Leo sent in some spies during the next Elder sermon. All returned mesmerized about this new religion, begging to be allowed to take their entire families to the next sermon a month from now. Why? They wanted desperately to have their whole families join in this incredible perfect society that was promised to them. Annoyance, confusion, and curiosity mingled as Pope Leo sent word to this Elder to take audience with the Pope. Elder Aleksy kindly obliged.

The two men talked for a very long time. Pope Leo just could not believe that these foreigners had somehow created a perfect society! Plus, there were a good deal of Holy Goals that the two religions shared in common. Elder Aleksy, on the other hand, also saw an opportunity. This religion of Jehosanity also encouraged women to accept the Ceremony of the Eight Degree, not unlike their women. Perhaps, he thought, these two religions could work together, especially if the practice of Jehosanity did lead their parishioners towards the perfect society. Elder Aleksy proposed that the Pope visit Dorota and see for himself just how perfect their society actually was. The High Council could then examine the religious beliefs as put forward by their highest official, this Pope Leo. Thus, this historic meeting of the heads of the two religions came about. The Pope's yacht was due to arrive in Bozydar around the middle of December.

"Well, it is about time. Unload my carriage and the horses," Pope Leo ordered as soon as the mooring lines flew landward. "Bozydar finally." Three long boring months on the yacht had made Leo grouchy, to say nothing of the endless hours spent learning this strange language spoken here in Dorota, so far off all the usual shipping lanes. "Let's see this perfect society of yours, Elder Aleksy."

"I see that members of our High Council are waiting your arrival, Pope Leo. It's that group over by the two carriages." Leo's eyes continued to survey this snow-covered city. Red tiled roofs peaked out from the white snow covering the many roofs. Brown stone buildings appeared to be the only type of housing units here. All the streets were precisely laid out on a square. What appeared to be homes were identical, as far as Pope Leo could see. Warehouses seemed to be just an expansion over the domestic homes. Their churches — modest, if not downright plain. Well, here was a difference, he thought; his were huge and splendid.

Many fishing vessels were dry docked for the winter. A few men were going about loading cargo on one caravel and three smaller coastal vessels. Leo saw no guards, no policemen among them. Realizing that he could see very little other differences from building to building, he concentrated his gaze upon the welcoming committee.

The men wore heavy, probably warm outer coats. There were five of them, no, make that six. A young boy, probably in his early teens stood behind them. On either side of him, two young teenaged girls stood, heavy cloaks wrapped around them. Ah, he saw that they were wearing the latest high-heeled boots so popular in the Sea Princes. So they are importing some goods, he thought to himself. He looked at the buildings nearby, hoping to catch a glimpse of hidden security men; he saw none. Well, he still was not going to take any chances.

As his elegant, gold trimmed papal carriage was being lowered onto the docks, he signaled to his Supreme Prelate. Quickly, Eros and Commander Drakon disembarked, along with twenty of his Mano del Dio protectors. At last, he and his companion, Cardinal Bion, walked down the gangplank, followed by Elder Aleksy. He gave them a moment to form ranks and then led his party forward to this initial meeting.

Those on shore had no doubt about which of the men was Pope Leo. He was the tall, pudgy man in the middle, wearing outlandishly purple robes, trimmed with real gold threads. He looked the part of supreme religious leader, Elder Amadei thought. A man wearing a bright red cloak and red skullcap was on his right, and Elder Aleksy was on his left. Surrounding them were twenty other men wearing sky blue cloaks. Behind them, the crew was assembling the pontiff's coach.

"Welcome to Dorota, Pope Leo, I am Elder Amadei of the High Council," he said, extending his hand to the man in purple. Pope Leo smiled and grasped his hand, giving it a warm shake.

"Hail and well met at last, Elder Amadei. It has been a long trip and I am very anxious to see your country and speak with you and the High Council," Pope Leo said formally.

"This is Elder Aleksander, head of our small Security Committee. Elder Iwan, head of our Planning Committee. Elder Kuba, Finance. Elder Tymon." Amadei introduced his peers. Pope Leo graciously shook each man's hand in turn. "This is one of our apprentices, young Albin." Again, the Pope shook the boy's hand, figuring that the young teen would now have quite a story to tell his friends: he actually had gotten to shake the hand of the Pope!

"These are two of our brightest Holy Vessels, Bethany and Dita," Elder Amadei finished the introductions. Pope Leo extended his hand to shake with these obviously pretty young women. The way that their cloaks were draped over their bodies, you could not tell that they were missing their arms.

"Sorry, we have no arms, your Holiness," I replied, defusing any possible uneasiness from our Elders.

"My apologies, young ladies. In my excitement to meet all of you, I forgot that all the women in this country are of the Eighth Degree. Forgive me. I meant no offense. You are both quite beautiful young women, and such magnificent earrings that you have, oh my yes," Pope Leo recovered graciously, attempting to compliment us in his own way.

"We have arranged for your stay at one of our inns," Elder Amadei explained. "Would you prefer to go there first and freshen up before we take a tour of the city?"

"Oh no, Elder Amadei. I have been cooped up for three months on my yacht. I prefer to see the city that I have heard so much about for the last ninety days. Should we walk or take my coach?"

"On foot, you can see more. Your speech is understandable, so you may wish to chat with some of the townsfolk that we meet as we stroll the streets," Elder Amadei replied.

"Is it really true that there is no crime of any kind in your country, this city?" Pope Leo asked the uppermost question in his mind. I noticed that the assassin, the Mano del Dio Supreme Prelate Eros Maios, paid sharp attention to the reply, while Commander Drakon Strate, who made no pretense of hiding his sword sheath, eyed all the surrounding people, who had stopped their work and were watching.

"Absolutely none at all, Your Holiness. It is safe for our Holy Vessels here to carry a large money pouch and walk anywhere in our country at any time without fear of anything. Come then, let us walk and you can see for yourself. It is hard to prove the absence of something. Our people, you will see, treat each other with respect, especially all our Holy Vessels, that is, our women in your terms," Elder Amadei explained.

The men walked down the street, with the pontiff's security garrison fanning out, a standard field tactic, I recognized. These men were ready for any attempt on Pope Leo's life. Albin had an arm around our waists, steadying us. Dita and I began regretting Elder Amadei's suggestion that we wear these heeled boots and fancy Sunday dresses. The snow-covered cobblestones were slippery, and we were forced to take much smaller steps than the men, who were soon out in front of us.

"You two be careful. Those boots look like they are slipping in the snow," Albin cautioned us.

"Duh, no kidding! They are not meant to be worn in the snow, Albin. Besides, we have to take such small steps anyway. I sure am glad that you are with us," I replied softly.

"Yes, thanks, Albin. Without your arms steading me, I would have slipped and fallen a couple times already!" Dita added.

"Yes, but you both look terrific in them. Did you see the Pope's eyes when he greeted you? You certainly were noticed," he said what he felt.

I joked, "Is that a good thing?"

"Who knows, but he is their big leader. A good impression goes a long way, we are taught at the college." We continued trailing the small party.

We heard snatches of conversation. Elder Iwan was explaining the street layout, "See those street signs so prominently visible? All of our streets are numbered and thus it is virtually impossible to get truly lost. It also makes giving directions very easy."

"So many of the homes are identical," we heard the Pope's voice say.

"Yes, by design. Our women learn how to do things their special way.

We call it the women's ways. By having everything identical, when they marry and move to a new home, they have nothing new to have to learn. We have found this to be a very satisfactory arrangement with our women," Elder Iwan explained.

Sometime later and none too soon for Dita and I, the party finally entered the inn where we were staying. The entire inn had been reserved for us and the pope's party. Already, the men had taken off their heavy winter coats and cloaks, hanging them on the pegs near the entrance. They were assembling around the central tables as we finally entered. Albin graciously removed our cloaks and hung them up for us. He then escorted us to the others.

Pope Leo's eyes were focused on the strange tables as we approached. Seeing his quizzical look, Elder Amadei explained, "Those low tables are for the women, who must use their feet, where men use their hands. Hence, you can always tell the women's table from those for us men. See, the backs of the chairs for the women are also sloped. That way, it is more comfortable for them to eat and drink. You will soon see just how incredibly able our Holy Vessels are, excuse me, our women are. We always call them Holy Vessels because they carry God's greatest gift, the bringing of new life into the world. We always honor our women, always."

We sat down and Albin kindly pulled off our boots for us and even removed our socks, before he took a seat nearby. I shot him a glance to say thank you. Dita, likewise. He smiled back. Four waitresses came to take our orders. I watched Pope Leo and his men closely. They could not help but stare at the waitresses, as they wrote well-formed letters on their order pads with their feet. All this would be new and strange to these men.

They found it even stranger when, a bit later, the waitresses brought the hot cider and lunch to us using their yokes. Their eyes followed their every movement as the women sat down and used their feet to put the bowls, mugs, pots, and utensils before each man and eventually us too. Evidently, the food was to their liking, for they all tasted it cautiously and then began to eat heartily. However, the moment that Dita and I began to lift our spoons to our mouths, their eyes stared at us, following our every movement. I prayed that I would not make a mistake and drip soup on my dress. Dita was just as self-conscious as I was. We felt like we were somehow on public display, and I didn't like that at all.

"Amazing, yes, truly amazing, Elder Amadei," Pope Leo finally exclaimed. "I've never seen anything like your women. They have adapted remarkably well, haven't they? I now see what you and Elder Aleksy mean by women's ways. I'm sure that I cannot get my legs up to my belly, let alone to my mouth. And the waitresses, such clear writing. Amazing!"

"All of our women are taught the women's ways. All of our children, both boys and girls go to school, usually for twelve years. We value an education highly here in Dorota. Every single person can both read and write. Everyone has graduated from the twelve grades of education. You will not find a dunce anywhere in Dorota," Elder Amadei chatted, while eating his hearty chicken soup.

"All? Both boys and girls? Incredible, unbelievable!" Pope Leo was genuinely startled to hear this.

"Oh yes, of course, at the school, there are boy's desks and girl's desks, which are six inches from the floor. They use their feet to write, you see. We will tour one of our schools, if you like. Education is important for our people. They go to school from age five through seventeen. Do all the children in your land go to school as well?" Elder Amadei asked.

"Oh no, not at all, not at all. Only a handful has that opportunity. This is one aspect that our Church of Jehosanity is attempting to reverse. I would certainly like to visit one of your schools. Perhaps we can learn better how to get universal schooling established for our people. How is it financed?" Pope Leo asked; he had just gotten a brilliant new idea: compulsory schooling for all children!

They continued exchanging ideas. Later, our waitresses returned with their yokes and began clearing away the dirty dishes. Again, the men stared at them all the while. Pope Leo finally asked, "I take it that some men will now wash the dishes. The cooks must be men as well, right?"

Elder Iwan raised his eyebrows! "Oh heavens no! Men handle the heavier chores, cutting firewood, carving stone, building homes, lifting heavy crates. The women wash and dry the dishes and do all the cooking. At an inn, the women cooks are perhaps some of the very best cooks in the country."

"What? But how?" Pope Leo was completely baffled how this could be. Elder Iwan took him to the next room, where the women were sitting on the sloped back chairs, washing the dishes with their feet, assembly line style. Nearby was the stove and oven, again only a few inches from the floor. Three cooks were busy stirring the soup pot and heating more cider and water for tea. Pope Leo returned more impressed than ever. He had very little knowledge of the Women of the Eighth Degree. What little he knew of them indicated that they had servants attending to their every need. None ever did anything that these women routinely did here. Hence, he was extremely impressed.

Later, we all went upstairs to the guest rooms. Once more, Pope Leo was surprised to see no doorknobs, only the sliding base latch, which was operated by your foot. "Does none of your doors have locks?" he asked.

Elder Tymon replied, very surprised, "Why what on earth would we want a lock for? Not even our banks have locks. There is no need whatsoever for a lock. A lock implies that someone might desire to take what is locked up. Here in Dorota no one ever steals anything that does not belong to them. Your Holiness, you could leave a large pile of gold coins on the table downstairs and it will remain there untouched forever. Every citizen of

Dorota recognizes that the gold is not theirs and would never take it. I don't believe that there is a lock anywhere in Dorota." He lied. I saw that telltale look in his eyes and the slight change in his voice tone. Naturally, I wondered just where the locks were to be found and what they kept locked up! Now was not the time to ask, however. Dita gave me a look that said she, too, had detected the lie. Now we both were curious.

Elder Amadei explained, "Now if you have any dirty clothing that needs to be washed, leave it just outside your door. The women will come by early in the morning and pick them up and wash them for you."

"Now how can they wash clothes?" Pope Leo asked, once more shocked and baffled. He was given a tour of the basement laundry facilities, where two women were washing the clothes that we had left out last night.

Later, Elder Kuba took the Pope and his party on a tour of a nearby bank. He explained how our citizens handled their money. Pope Leo just could not believe that this building held such a large amount of gold in simple drawers and that there was not even a lock on the front door! He even asked to see how the women tellers could handle their banking chores. Thus, Elder Kuba kept them there until several women came in to withdraw some funds to purchase food supplies at the markets.

Over the next two days, Pope Leo and his group saw nearly every aspect of our daily lives, especially those of our women. I even overheard the Supreme Prelate Eros suggesting to Pope Leo that perhaps they were being shown contrived examples of all this. In response, Pope Leo asked if he could visit other inns, banks, and even private homes, all of his own choosing. While Elder Aleksander protested, he was overruled. The pope and his crew wandered the streets of Bozydar, randomly stopping at inns, banks, and a few homes, just to check on the truthfulness of our leaders. He saw absolutely no differences anywhere. Naturally, we women were all trained in the same actions, and all buildings and facilities were the same, so we could handle our chores no matter where we were located. At last, he became convinced that what he was seeing was indeed the reality here in Bozydar.

I suspected that was not enough to totally satisfy the pope. Indeed, it wasn't. He then asked if we could travel north to the next town or village, so that he could see with his own eyes how things were done there. He asked politely and was not refused. Thankfully, Albin and we girls were allowed to stay behind at the inn.

While they were gone, we three sat around the inn's tables relaxing. Albin said, "You know, those men that are accompanying the pope, they are bleeding. Have you noticed? If they stand in one spot for a time, I keep seeing tiny drops of blood on the floor when they move away. I wonder if they are injured in some way? Should we ask if they need the services of our doktors?"

Dita grinned and answered him, "Observant you are, Albin. Those are the Mano del Dio, the Hands of God. They are all trained assassins! They wear a belt with sharp bits of metal in them that cut into their waists."

"Ouch. Doesn't that hurt them?" he asked in disbelief.

"Yes, but they claim that they need to suffer pain so that they will not shrink from pain when they are defending the life of the Pope. I think it's looney," Dita finished her explanation.

"That's crazy, but then they are from the Outer Lands, and obviously do things very differently out there. I can see that we have our work cut out for us in assisting all the Unholy into obtaining Redemption." He spoke the party line, I noted. Well, he was, after all, an Elder in training.

The large party returned the next day. I knew that wherever they had gone and visited, they saw precisely the same thing as they had seen here. I know, because we had toured the whole circumference of the continent, just not much of the highlands, which we wanted to explore, come springtime.

At last, the men sat down to discuss business. We three sat at the back of the inn, while the Pope and Cardinal Bion sat with the five Elders. The twenty Mano del Dio men positioned themselves around the room, as if they were expecting a sudden, surprise attack.

"I must again thank you gentlemen for giving me such a great tour of your country. As we now get down to business, as they say, may I ask a few questions about your society?" Pope Leo asked politely. We strained our ears, quite curious to hear what he wanted to know.

"Do I understand you correctly, that your doktors amputate the arms of all girl babies the moment they are born?"

"Yes, though none but the doktors are allowed to see the baby girls, until after the surgery is completed. No woman in Dorota knows that this is what happens. You see, our women believe that they are born without arms. Only those two here with us know the truth." Suddenly all eyes focused on Dita and me.

Pope Leo asked us, "You know that they amputated your arms at birth and you are not angry with them? You do not hate or revile them for having done this to you?"

"Your Holiness, what is done is done. Arms cannot be re-grown. Here in Dorota, we have no real need for arms anyway. We have many women's ways of doing all that must be done. And our fathers and brothers graciously and, without our needing to ask, help us with things we cannot master. Dita and I love to ride horses even, but we cannot saddle them, that we need help with."

"Amazing! Clearly amazing. So your women and men do not know that you are removing their arms. I see that this works well. Thus, it is accepted by all. It makes sense. Your men believe that the women have given their arms so that they can be stronger. Thus, it is only natural that the men treat all women with great honor and respect. I can see how this is, here in Dorota," the Pope complimented us.

"Our women of the Eighth Degree have theirs removed when they marry. Thus, they do not know anything about the women's ways of doing anything and are totally dependent upon other servants to care for all their needs, including feeding them," Cardinal Bion explained.

Elder Aleksy spoke up, "Indeed, we are experiencing the same problem, Elders. When we convert a family and the wife and daughters have their arms removed, they become mostly helpless and quite distressed. Others have to do nearly everything for them. We men do not know the women's ways of doing things; we can only explain roughly how something is done here. I would like to request that when I return that I might take a few more of our Holy Vessels who volunteer back with me and have them teach these new Holy Vessels the ways of the women."

Elder Aleksander replied before anyone else could, "Yes, that is wise. Please delay your return Elder a few weeks while I gather some more volunteers. We must see that our newly Redeemed Holy Vessels are properly taught the correct women's ways of doing things."

"Thank you! Their help will be greatly appreciated," Elder Aleksy replied, greatly relieved. I realized right then that this had been a major reason why he had returned to Dorota!

"May I ask another question that has been puzzling me?" Pope Leo ventured. Seeing the nod, he continued. "On our island of Megalos, when a family converts to your religion, they sell their own homes and businesses and move into your private sector. Why is this?"

"As you have seen here, uniformity is the key for our women. By having every building the same as every other building, our women, who have to learn the women's ways of doing things, are not put into the untenable position of having to relearn how to do everything all over again at another building which is laid out completely differently than the one in which she learned how to do things in the women's way," Elder Iwan answered him. "We do this out of the deepest respect and kindness for our Holy Vessels, I mean our women."

He continued, "Yes, their lot in life is a most difficult one. Anything that we men can do to make their lives easier, we do. Even in the Outer Lands, we attempt to create a microcosm of Dorota, so that the new women can learn one way and not have to face learning many variations. They all work so very hard learning that we cannot make them redo it all over again, because their new house is so different from the one in which they learned."

Elder Aleksander then asked, "Pope Leo, what are the beliefs with which you try to instill in your followers?"

"First, let me begin by saying that we call God by the name of Jehosa. Down through the ages, we have followed the holy Decalogue of Jehosa. Let me recite it here; it is best to hear the actual words themselves.

There is no god but Jehosa.

Do not worship any other god but the One God, Jehosa.

Set aside the Holy Day, Saturday, from your labors and worship the Lord that day.

Respect and serve thy mother and thy father, for they have labored long in your raising.

Do not kill another, excepting your enemies and enemies of Jehosa.

Do not steal from another, excepting your enemies and enemies of Jehosa.

Do not commit adultery.

Do not lie to another, excepting your enemies and enemies of Jehosa.

Do not desire another's house or possessions.

Do unto men, as you would have men do unto you.

You see, we worship the same, the one God. We strive to get other pagans to stop worshiping their many idols. Our holy day is Saturday, but as I understand it, yours is Sunday. The world out there is huge and our enemies, many. Hence, we do what we need to do to keep our enemies at bay. Clearly here on Dorota, you have no enemies at all."

"So I ask you, do you find our holiest of beliefs so very different from yours?" Pope Leo finally asked the key question that he had prepared for so diligently and for so long.

Elder Aleksander replied, "On the surface, it seems that your teachings are indeed similar to ours. What of your goals for your society, your people?"

"Our goals are the same as I have found so magnificently implemented throughout your country. No crime, no stealing, no avarice, no mistreatment of women, no desire for another's possessions. If I could wave my hand and have my society converted into what I daily pray to Lord Jehosa for, it would be no different than what I have seen here with my own eyes! Well, except that I would also allow some diversity, some art, some music, and some theater. Women do love their fashions. I would allow a bit more diversity in their lives, a bit more elegance that they may feel closer to God."

"Yes, our women are taking to the fashions of the Outer Lands," Elder Aleksander said with a wry smile. Indeed, his wife now wore one of the fancy imported dressed from Velona. "I would like to see some diversity here as well. I think that we think alike, Pope Leo."

Pope Leo continued, "Until now, I had not considered just how vitally important it is for all people to have a good, solid education. I am truly impressed with your educational system here. One of the first mandates that I will make upon my return is to establish schools throughout our spheres of influence. You have my word on that."

He continued, "If we can form an alliance between us, one of mutual help and assistance, then we both will be stronger to tackle the enormous problem of converting those who are Unholy, to use your term. Our Church is large, spanning many continents. How may we work together to achieve our common goal, the Redemption of all Mankind?"

"We prefer to keep those who have been converted separate from the many Unholy. Often they will attempt to convince them that they have made the wrong choices. We protect our Holy Vessels from all outside contact. They are safer that way from persecution, invalidation, and humiliations of the Unholy others. We owe them this much. Yet from what we've heard, those of your Eight Degree go forth openly among the Unholy. Do you not find that they are subject to ridicule, persecution, invalidation, and even humiliations?" asked Elder Aleksy, who had seen a number of such women attending the Church of Jehosanity on Saturdays.

"They are of strong faith and conviction. We have found that they bear their sacrifice with the greatest of pride, a pride and faith so strong that the Unholy cannot dissuade them. On the other hand, they provide inspiration for others to follow in their path and become of the Eight Degree themselves. Perhaps it is a matter of the faith of the individual woman. Ours have freely given themselves to be of the Eighth Degree, where here on Dorota, it is done to them unknowingly and without their faith and consent. Perhaps that is the difference. Allow your Holy Vessels to come and show them the women's ways. Then let us see how strong their faith will be, for these women have chosen of their own volition to become of the Eighth Degree. Allow them to proudly display for the entire world, all the other Unholy, the Unconvinced, to see the measure of their new-found faith in the Lord God," Pope Leo pontificated.

The Elders discussed this, but could come to no real conclusion. At last, Pope Leo turned to Dita and me. "Pray, let us ask your two wise Holy Vessels what their opinion in this matter would be, for they are openly of the Eighth Degree." Elder Amadei gave us a nod that it was okay for us to reply.

"There is a world of difference between our two situations. Here, a woman believes that she is born this way, without arms. If she were to go to the Outer Lands and see that in all other lands, women are born with arms and that it is she that is vastly different, then yes, those women will have a very, very rough time of it. However, out there, the women are knowingly showing their devotion to their husbands and families and faith. Thus, they are proud of their stature and would be likely troubled by finding themselves hidden away, removed from all contact with their friends and other relatives who have not converted. So, my opinion is that, in the Outer Lands, the newly converted Holy Vessels should not be so isolated from the world as we are here," I took a turn at pontificating. Besides, I had an ulterior motive. I wanted the women to be seen so that we could keep tabs on just how many were doing this. Hidden away in a secret cloister, we would never know just how widespread this practice was becoming. Fortunately, the Elders accepted my opinion and agreed to allow more openness.

The religious leaders then went on to work out other agreements for cooperation; mostly all were minor things, such as allowing the Redeemed to attend Saturday Jehosanity Services as well as our Sunday Services. Pope Leo got a concession: two teachers, one of each gender, would return with him, assist, and advise him on how to set up a universal educational system. Once finished, they would begin assisting the new convert's children with their education, setting up one of our schools on Megalos. Many other smaller arrangements were made.

The Elders got a concession that they desperately needed. The Church of Jehosanity would provide land and buildings to help house those new converts who wished to live in our style communities.

The Pope, who was leaving in the early morning hours at high tide, said his farewells, complete with many thank you's, before he and his party headed for their yacht.

That evening, Albin, Dita, and I sat in our room chatting about the big meeting and its ramifications. He thought overall that it went well. Dita and I knew otherwise; this Church of Jehosanity had a long, long track record of mistreatment of women, of attempting to control the lives of men. We distrusted them implicitly, though it was hard to find fault with the Holy Words the Pope uttered, especially about adopting universal education, something our world desperately needed. Few could read and write; many could only do basic arithmetic.

After Albin left, Dita and I began our nightly ritual of brushing out our ever growing long hair, mine was still quite blonde, hers, still raven. Just as we got started, Albin knocked on our door. "Hi again, I just ran into Elder Aleksander. He asked me to bring these cups of cocoa up to you two. He said you deserved a little reward for your efforts, and he said I should have one too as your silent helper. It's a form of chocolate, he said." Albin carried a tray with three mugs; two were women's style.

"Now that's more like it!" Dita exclaimed. "Chocolate, yum! Come on, Bethany. We can finish our hair after bit. We three sat down and savored our warm drink, chatting about this sudden expression of kindness from Elder Aleksander, who had been vehemently against our presence thus far. We ought to have known better. After drinking the warm drink, I suddenly became very, very tired. I tried to get up, but found myself slipping to the floor. My body just had to go to sleep right now.

Chapter 10 Kidnaped

"Where are Bethany and Dita? We are about ready to head home and they haven't come down for breakfast yet?" asked Elder Amadei. His worry had been building for the last hour. This was not like either girl.

"Come to think of it, Amadei, where's that student of yours, Albin? The last I saw of him, he volunteered to take a tray of hot cocoa up to the girls last night," put in Elder Aleksander.

"I'll go check on the girls," one of the waitresses volunteered.

"Okay, I'll come and check on Albin, he is in the next room," Elder Amadei suggested. The two headed up the stairs. First, he knocked on Albin's door. Hearing no answer, he opened it and looked inside.

"Elder, his bed has not been slept in!" she announced the obvious. Hastily, they went on down to the next door. It was ajar. He let her push it open, in case the Holy Vessels were not yet dressed. He did not want to violate them in any way.

"It's Albin. Sir, come at once," the panicking voice of the waitress called out, he rushed inside. Albin lay unconscious on the floor, sprawled where he fell. Three cocoa mugs also lay on the floor. Both girls were not in the room, neither were their boots or cloaks.

"Could they have left?" she asked.

"No, go get the others please." He checked Albin for obvious injuries, but saw nothing. The other four men stepped into the room and gasped. "Please send for a doktor. Something has happened here. Help me get him up onto the bed, please."

Not too much later, the local doktor came running up the stairs, quite out of breath, having run all the way from his house. Throwing off his coat, he squatted down beside the boy on the bed. "What has happened here?" he asked. No one knew, so he set about his own work. Eventually, he said, "Please, send for some very strong, black tea immediately. I believe he has been drugged. Ah, probably in the cocoa. I will test what's left in that one." One mug still had a bit of the liquid remaining.

To expedite the situation, Elder Amadei went for the tea, bringing it quickly up to the doktor, instead of allowing the waitress to bring it more slowly using her womanly ways. Bit by bit, the doktor got some of the black tea into Albin's mouth. Then, a little more, at last Albin stirred and woke up. "Oh, what happened to us?" he moaned.

The doktor left the questioning to the Elders and began some experiments on the remaining cocoa. "Albin, what happened? Where are Bethany and Dita?" asked Elder Amadei, fighting hard to control his panic. Nothing like this ever happened in Dorota!

"We were drinking the cocoa that Aleksander was bringing up. He said I could have his mug. We did and then I saw Bethany slump to the floor. She looked like she was falling asleep. I tried to catch her, but I was so tired, and I knocked over the table. Dita slumped right after that, and then I fell down, reaching out for them. I know I felt their bodies. Next thing I remember is that awful tea in my mouth. What happened to us?"

"Ah, just as I thought, drugged. A small dose will put you to sleep; a large dose will kill you quickly. I just hope the girls had only a small dose as did Albin here," the doktor replied, satisfied that he had found the underlying cause of this. "Son, drink more tea; eat lightly for the rest of the day. You should be fine. Call me if you find the girls." He left the Elders with their problem.

"They probably just ran off somewhere, Amadei," Elder Aleksander grumpily theorized. "Serves you right for allowing them into our private councils. What they know could really cause damage to our country. I'll send out search parties, I'm sure that we will find them, unless they have gone to join the rebels. In that case, we may never find them."

"Why? Why, Aleksander, would they run off just now?" Amadei looked completely mystified with his peer's theory. In his mind, this made no sense at all. "I believe that they have been kidnaped. That makes more sense, but who would want to kidnap them?"

"I've no idea, Amadei. Nevertheless, either way, I best get the search parties activated." He left to arrange the search.

"This is all my fault! I ought to have arranged for some Security for our most Holiest of Vessels," lamented Elder Amadei.

"We should delay our departure," Elder Tymon said softly. "I'll let the innkeeper know and ask around if anyone on his staff saw anyone leaving last night."

My head was fuzzy. I opened my eyes, but couldn't see anything. It felt like a cloth was over my eyes, like a band around my head. My mouth was funny, forced open. My tongue sensed and felt a knotted cloth in my mouth. That I was gagged finally registered in my mind. I was lying down, but I felt as if I was being rocked in a rocking chair or something. I tried to bring my foot up to my head to undo the gag and the blindfold, but my foot wouldn't move; it was tied to something. Why was my foot tied? My mind slowly cleared and I realized that my legs were tied together. Many bands of rope were wrapped around my lower legs, I could sense their coils. Where was I? What was happening? Slowly, the remaining fogginess left my mind. Rocking motion. I recognized that! I was on a ship at sea! Silly me, now I heard the creaking of the deck boards and the wind in the sails far above me. Smell, ah, I was in the hold of some ship, a stinking one at that. I struggled a bit to see if I could find any freedom of motion. I felt something solid to my right and pushed my head against it. At last, the blindfold band slid off my head, and I could see in the dim light.

Dita was lying a few feet from me; we were on a bare deck, probably in the cargo hold. I had on my fancy boots, still wore my Sunday dress, and my cloak was draped over me so I didn't freeze. It was cold down here. Dita seemed asleep, though she too was gagged, blindfolded, and her legs, like mine were wrapped with over a dozen loops of rope, tied securely. I could at least scoot, so with effort, I slowly made my way the three feet to her side. I used the spikes of my heels to slide her blindfold off her, which moved easily because of her long hair.

As it slid off her head, Dita began regaining consciousness, panicking as I had just done. I gave her time to get her mind working properly, grasping our situation. Where were we? That was obvious. We were at sea. I didn't recognize the craftsmanship of the hold that we were in, but there was a door with knobs, our only way out. Think, I told myself. Observe. Dita was now doing the same thing; our eyes met each other's as we surveyed our cell. From the shape of the sides of the hold, I concluded that we were far aft. This made sense, if we were in some hold. Piles of rope and tar buckets lay scattered about the room.

This was not aft of a caravel; the Dorota copies were precise, down to the last detail of those from Velona, of which I was intimately knowledgeable from spending so much time in them in previous lives. It was far too wide for a Dorota coastal fishing vessel. What other ship could it be? Then, it hit me! I think Dita realized it at the same time. The Pope's yacht! He was sailing in the early morning at high tide. We were prisoners of Pope Leo! Why? Was he just a lecherous old man? Did he want us as his pets? Nothing that I'd seen of his conduct supported these wild thoughts.

I am your Protector, Bethany. I will get us out of this mess! Dita made mental telepathic contact with me. I latched on to her solidly, making it far easier for her.

I think that we were drugged and are on the Pope's yacht.

I concur. Is Albin here too? she asked. We both looked around but didn't see any sign of him or even his clothes.

Just then, we heard the door opening. In stepped Pope Leo, carrying two mugs of steaming tea. "Ah, I see you have removed your blindfolds already." He sat the mugs down and proceeded to remove our gags. "If you will not scream or make noise, I will leave them off of you. Here, you should drink this strong tea. It will help counteract the drug that Elder Aleksander put in your cocoa last night."

He held a cup in each hand up to our mouths, we struggled to sit up, while he watched, and then tipped them so we could drink. Yes, the tea was strong, but for some reason, my body seemed to crave it just now. We both drank all that we could.

"Now then, just so that you know, we are at sea, a long way from Dorota. I have no idea why Elder Aleksander wanted to get rid of you two so badly. He gave me two hundred gold pieces just to take you away from

Dorota. Now why do you suppose that he wants you gone from there?"

"I don't know," I said honestly.

"Well, I don't either. Yet, I am a good judge of a man. He was most definitely afraid of both of you two young women. Sorry if I don't use your silly term, Holy Vessels. I think they are off their rockers with that expression, but I did play along with them. So why is a powerful man in charge of the security of the entire country afraid of two helpless young women? That is the thousand dollar question of the day!"

"I don't know," Dita replied.

"Well, Eros and I have been thinking about that all morning long. We know that you two are very bright, having gotten through your schooling years ahead of schedule. We have seen that you know what they call the ways of the women, obviously you have to, otherwise you would have to be waited on hand and foot. So you are not helpless as are our women of the Eighth Degree. I'll give you that much."

"But why does an educated, powerful man so greatly fear you two? You cannot hold a sword. You cannot stab him with a dagger. Maybe with your feet you could manage somehow to poison him, but then how would you possibly come by poison? No, that seems too abeam to be plausible. You are not even of age yet in their society. However, you are of age in our land as well as many others. Yet, without arms, it defies all logic that a man of his stature should be so terrified of you two. You have no idea why?"

"No sir, we don't," I replied honestly.

"What are you going to do to us?" Dita asked.

"Well, that depends on you. We are taking you back to our land, Megalos and my Church of Jehosanity. Once there, I can't allow you to be seen in public. Supreme Prelate Eros says that someone from Dorota might recognize you. Well, we don't have many light brown skinned people on Megalos. Dark brown, yes, but not light as you are. I agree, you may well be recognized, if I allowed you to be seen in public. So what to do with you?"

"Supreme Prelate Eros suggested that we simply cut your throats and feed you to the sharks. However, I am a religious man. Souls are precious. While I am not above condoning murdering of the enemies of the Church of Jehosanity, you two are not our enemy. As long as you behave, you will not be harmed. I think that the best thing to do is to have you become my servants. You see, as long as you are alive, if the Elders want you back, you may be valuable bargaining chips — that is, unless I discover that your hold over Aleksander is more useful to me. So young women, you behave and you can live a long, healthy life. Misbehave, cause me troubles, and I will let Eros have his way with you. Fair enough?"

"Yes, sir," I replied timidly, though I did not intend to do that. Dita echoed me.

"Good. I must see to our course. Someone will bring you some lunch later on and feed you."

"Can you untie our legs, sir? We have no arms and must use our legs for everything. We are completely helpless like this and cannot even go to the bathroom," I used my most pleading, sympathetic voice possible.

"Sorry, you are way too skilled with your feet for me to trust you with your freedom just yet. If you soil your pants, that's the way it goes. It will just add to the stench in the hold. You probably won't even notice it. You are both very pretty. I would hate to see anything happen to you, so please cooperate with me. I can be very kind and generous to my friends."

He left, but I didn't like the sound of his last comment. That we were considered of age in his world only made those thoughts darker. He left us in the semi-darkness of the aft hold. Once we were sure that he had gone and was not listening outside the door, Dita whispered, "Bethany, I am your Protector. I will get us out of here. First thing, we need to move out of our bodies and see what is topside and going on. I will figure something out, my love. Leave it to me."

I recalled her similar words in earlier lifetimes. Renzo was always being my Protector, and he did a very good job of it too. I felt encouraged by her attitude and I knew that she still knew all of her or his Protector skills. We relaxed, moved out of our bodies, and up onto the main deck where it was bright daylight.

From the sun, I think it is about ten in the morning, Dita sent. I concurred and looked about at the various crew members going about their duties. I could see no land in sight, even when I went up to look from the crow's nest. Time passed. Around noon, Dita pointed out that a squall was moving our way and suggested that we return to our bodies and maybe be fed.

We returned only too soon, though I think Dita saw someone heading down to the hold carrying a tray of food. The door knob slowly turned and a young woman entered, a tray held in her arms. Where her hands ought to have been we saw bloody white bandages! She came over to where we lay and carefully sat the tray down. She couldn't have been much older than us; she had medium length, curly brown hair, her face seemed somehow familiar. She spoke, but in a foreign language, "I brought you food. You must eat."

We both recognized her speech; it was Sea Prince dialect, Velona, most likely. "Thank you! Are you from Velona? What happened to your hands? I am Bethany and this is Dita; we've been kidnaped from Dorota."

"You speak my language? I am Dianna, Dianna Po, granddaughter of Ellaina Po, daughter of Lana Po, who rules Velona. I have to feed you; please you must eat, or he will hurt me more," she said pleadingly.

"Can you please help us sit up? We cannot eat lying down?" She struggled and we pushed with our feet and soon scooted up to the side of the hold and sitting.

Cradling the wooden spoon in her arms, she began to feed us. Then she held the bread while we tore off bites. We were quite hungry and no more was said while we ate all that she had brought. We saw that every motion she was making caused her a good deal of pain from her wounds, but she bore it and said nothing. Dianna looked very relieved when we finished, and she laid back against the side of the boat beside us.

"I am to look after your needs. Let me know if you need the chamber pot. I will manage it somehow."

"Thanks, Dianna. What happened to your hands?" I asked once more, hoping that she would feel more like talking now.

"Some months ago, I was kidnaped too, from Velona. I was studying to be a healer like my mom and grandmother, but now that is all gone." She was in a deep apathy; we understood why. "I was taken on a ship to Megalos, I think, and delivered to a man called Eros Maios. He's on this ship. He asked me where the Santi del Dio stored their gold. I told him I didn't know anything about that. I really don't, but he didn't believe me and brought me along this long ocean trip. I think their Pope is onboard too."

"He kept me down here in the hold, chained to a beam. Then, he tied me down to a wooden bench and asked me again where the Santi kept their gold. I told him I didn't know. He cut off my right little finger. I screamed and fainted. I woke and he asked again and again, only when I said that I didn't know, he gagged me and cut off another finger, until I had nothing left of my right hand."

"He left me alone for many days after that, but then a while ago, just before the boat stopped moving, he began again. 'Dianna, you are rapidly running out of fingers. Where does the Santi keep their gold?' I begged and pleaded with him not to cut me anymore. Five days later, I have nothing left at all, just bandages. I never told him anything, but I really don't know anything."

"Can we see your arms, Dianna?" I asked. My nose smelled the telltale signs of gangrene, but I wanted to make sure. She slowly pulled up the bloody sleeves of coat and shirt, revealing the crude bandages and the red streaks of the infection going up both of her arms. She saw me noticing them.

"I know what it is. I am dying and that is good. I will be free from his tortures at last. I have had enough healer training to know that I only have a few days left. I am so very hot — fever I think. I have accepted my fate." She stopped suppressing her tears and cried silently to herself. We were helpless to do anything at all for her.

We sat quietly for a short while. Then, the squall hit us hard; the boat began rocking.

"Now we escape, my love. I will get us untied pronto." I watched as Dita floated over my leg ropes and untied them and then hers.

"How'd you do that?" I asked mystified. I can do many things as a spiritual being, but nothing so intricate.

118

Dianna also looked quite startled. "How did you do that? You are so worse off than I am; you have no arms at all."

"Protector skill," Dita whispered.

"How can you be? Are you Santi somehow?" she asked completely mystified, but becoming suddenly very curious, forgetting her own pitiful destiny.

"I was a Protector. Now here's the plan. We are going to escape in their sailing dinghy. In this storm, you bet that all the assassins will be below deck. Only a skeleton crew will be topside. The dinghy is right behind us, up one level, hanging over the rear of the ship. There is one stairs immediately beyond the door there. We go up the steps, squeeze through a stern porthole, and drop into the dinghy. I lower the dinghy and off we go. Of course, I will be depending upon your skill to sail the thing, Bethany. You can sail her, can't you?"

"Yes, but those are a lot of difficult things to accomplish before we are safely in the water. We must take Dianna with us. Dianna, we are going to try to rescue you too."

"I am dying. You should save yourselves. Nothing can be done for me now. I will help you, if I can, though," she said bravely.

"Leave those details to me. I am your Protector still, my dearest Bethany. I'll get us out of this mess and you get us home, okay?"

"Deal. What's first?"

"We get our cloaks firmly fastened. We'll freeze to death if we lose them. There, your clasp is very tight. So is mine. Now for the door." I watched as she used some of her spiritual abilities to rotate the doorknob, again wondering just how she could do such fine motions. Mine were always gross ones, like lifting a tree or man and giving them a toss. Hers were fine, tiny motions, motions with finesse. The compact hall was empty; the ship was tossing and rolling so badly that neither of us could stand in these high-heeled boots.

Dianna put her arms around Dita and together, they made it to the stairs. With Dianna putting her body around Dita's and her arms held tight against the back of the stairs, the two managed to climb to the next landing. Dianna then came down for me.

"Thanks Dianna, we can't really walk in these boots in this storm. I know it must hurt your arms to do this for us. Thanks." When we got to the landing, Dita already had the large porthole opened. Whispering, she said, "Can you lift us up and through the porthole and down into the dinghy?" I nodded and proceeded to lift her up, turned her ninety degrees, parallel to the floor, and gently moved her through the porthole. I held her stationary until I could get myself close enough to see the dinghy right below us. I lowered her gently into the small boat. Next, I helped Dianna up, out, and down, though she looked terrified as I lowered her into the boat. Then, from the outside, I did the same to my body, sitting it down beside hers.

"Here we go. Going to be rough waters when we are down," Dita whispered.

"We should lie down in the bottom; that will minimize our chances of capsizing," I suggested. We three did so. Then, Dianna and I watched as the ropes seemed magically to undo themselves, and slowly the ropes moved through the many pulleys, as down we went.

"How do you do these things?" she asked, but right now, Dita was concentrating too much to speak.

No need to see if we hit the ocean; the dingy started bobbing and rocking wildly in the tempest sea. The squall was at its peak, and all that we could really do was lie still and pray. If we did start to capsize, I promised to lift the boat into the air. Dita was very grateful hearing that. She was already getting seasick from the awful motions.

Time passed us by, as did the squall. When the first rays of the early afternoon sun broke through the black clouds, we ventured to sit up and look around. Now the dinghy was merely bobbing on the ocean. We looked in all directions but saw nothing but the wide expanse of ocean. We had left the yacht far ahead of us. With luck, we would not be missed until dinner time, and by then there would be no way for them to find us, not considering the vastness of the sea.

"Okay, your Protector got us this far, madam Wid, now it's your turn. Please sail us home, whichever way that is," Dita said coyly. At this point Dianna passed out from her fever; she was burning up. I regretted that just now, we could do nothing for her.

"Hey, I like your coy girlish smile; that's far sexier than your Renzo smile," I teased her.

"Hey, I am starting to get the hang of this girl body thing, though just barely," she replied. "Need a foot?"

I began to untie the sail ties. Once done, she and I used combined foot power to hoist the single sail and tie off the guide ropes. I wiggled into a strange position such that with one leg I could control the tiller and with the other, the boom of the sail. "I'm afraid that you may have to tie off the sail from time to time. I seem to be out of legs." Dita looked at me and then we both laughed hysterically, releasing our long festering tensions and fears. We were on our own, but that was everything to us.

After a time, she said, "I suppose that I ought to move out up and ahead of us to see if we are on course for the mainland."

"Sure, but remember, I have to tack. One can only sail directly to a given point if there is a one hundred percent tail wind going that precise direction or nearly so. We don't have much of a keel to support anything less, so it's a tacking we will go, a tacking we will go, hi ho a tacking we will go."

"Oh brother! I'm going up and away," she teased, and she floated out of her body to scout out our position. Meanwhile, I began making a dead reckoning guess of our current position. Assuming the yacht sailed at four in the morning and that we jumped ship around one in the afternoon, that made us nine hours out of Bozydar, probably less, as they had to tack slowly out of the harbor first. The prevailing winds came out of the southwest, the direction that they needed to travel, meaning they could only tack in that general direction. Things were in our favor; perhaps we were only three or four hours out of the port. However, it was going to be dark soon and it was the middle of winter. I dare not try to sail much at night, I concluded, but we had to do it.

At sunset, Dita returned. "That way. It's not all that far. How are we doing?"

"It's starting to get cold, Dita. We may well freeze to death out here."

"Okay, let me see if there is anything useful in that emergency box. Darn, it has a latch." She had to move out of her body and manipulate the latch. "Ah, that's better." She used the spike of her heel to lift the lid, throwing it back. She wiggled into position and began looking inside. "Hey a water skin and a blanket. Now that's useful." With effort, she got the blanket out, only one though. We argued over who should get the blanket over them. "You are the sailor; you need to stay warm to get us there."

"I know. Let's make use of our own body heat and that of Dianna's. You see if you can get her close to you and me and then wrap the blanket around us both. I've got us on a course straight for the port; the wind is now perfect. We'll just run along like this during the night, maybe making the port at first light."

With effort and with me finally just picking up their bodies, laying them close mine, and then wrapping the blanket securely around us, we got the job done. It looked strange, I admit — two armless women and one unconscious woman with gangrene arms and a fever, lying nearly on top of each other, with one pair of legs on the tiller, all wrapped in a blanket, floating along at night in this tiny dinghy which was barely able to support the three of us. We had little other choice. It was cold and slowly my teeth began chattering. It was the longest night I can remember! I prayed for the warmth of the cold winter's sun to strike us, anything for a little heat. Dianna's fever heat, I think, helped keep us alive during that long, cold night.

Cramped as I was and with my legs having fallen asleep holding the tiller, I could not tack or turn the dinghy. Hence, when I needed to make a slight course correction, I moved out of my body and gave the bow a shove in the desired direction. As I said, my movements are gross ones, not the finesse ones that Dita could perform.

I dozed and forced myself awake to get my bearings, but then dozed off again. Endless, bone-chilling hours passed. Bump! We hit something. Bump! I forced myself awake. Docks. We were banging against some wooden docks. It was still dark and I dozed off once more.

Voices. I heard voices! "Help! Help! Give me a hand here! Go get the Elders!" Movement. The dinghy moved and banged onto the sides of the wooden docks. Light. Hands lifting me. No, lifting the others — a weight off me. Hands, warm hands, lifting me. Walking, yes, someone is carrying me somewhere. I hope it is warm. More voices, lots more voices. I try to open my eyes. We're going inside the inn. Good, they are taking us to the big fireplace. Warmth!

"Drink!" A voice ordered. Hot, overly sweet tea touched my tongue. Greedily, I drank and slowly came too.

"Dianna! Gangrene in her arm! Must help her. She has a fever and will die soon. Must help her!" I called out to whoever was listening.

The soothing voice of Elder Amadei answered me, "Bethany, it's okay. She's with the good doktor now. He took her off with him immediately. How are you feeling? Drink more hot liquids, doktor's orders." I guzzled the rest of the cup and finally noticed Dita beside me downing her mug. Both were refilled at once. It was Albin.

I sat up at last and leaned into the fire, warmth at last. "You were found at dawn this morning in a dinghy by the docks. We know that Albin and you two were drugged by the cocoa, Bethany, but what happened to you two?" His voice bordered on a panic. I realized that all the Elders were shocked that a kidnaping could occur here in Dorota, to say nothing of it being against their Holy Vessels!

"It was Elder Aleksander's doing. He paid Pope Leo two hundred gold to take us to Megalos on his yacht. The Pope agreed to do it, but was going to keep us alive in case you wanted us back. Why does Elder Aleksander hate us so much?" I asked innocently, though I was beginning to sense there was more to all of this than we had seen so far.

The four Elders stood there shocked. Dita repeated the same story as I told, when Elder Tymon asked her what happened to us. Elder Iwan called out to some Security men, "Go and find Elder Aleksander and place him under arrest. Bring him before the High Council when we next meet at Wit!"

"He's out with some search parties, looking for you two," Elder Amadei explained. "Such treachery I have never seen before, and from an Elder on the High Council!" He was shocked.

As we finally warmed up, he had us relate our whole adventure once more. The four Elders and three Security men, along with Albin, listened to our story. One even took notes. When we finished, "I do not know how you could have possibly done all these things, it would have been a challenge even for we who have arms," Elder Tymon uttered in disbelief.

"Dianna, she helped us a lot before she went unconscious. Will she be all right?" I asked, giving them something a little more tangible on which to tie our miraculous escape. This seemed to help them — that another helped us with our escape they could handle.

"She's in good hands. Now then, we are under orders from the doktor to get you both a hot bath. Would you prefer that other Holy Vessels help you bathe or would you prefer one of us to lend you helping hands?" Elder Amadei asked politely.

"Can we have a little pampering? After what we've been through, some hands would make things so much easier," Dita answered for us. I agreed. I was tired and hungry, but the chill was finally subsiding. Albin volunteered and for the next two hours, we two were treated like royalty.

"I've bathed my sister many times," he said as he began washing Dita's back. We were sitting in warm tubs, which felt luxuriously warm! Heavenly. He was right; he did a very good job washing us, drying us off, and even dealing with our long hair. "Your hair is so much longer than Kazia's but I'm getting the hang of it," he chatted away, very pleased that he could do a little something for us to help.

Three hours later, we were cleaned, dried, and into new dresses. We three went to see how Dianna was faring. The doktor was just finishing washing. We noticed that he was covered in blood. "How is she? Will she be okay? How bad was the infection?" I asked in rapid fire.

He smiled and lowered his eyes before replying. "I believe that the worst is over. Another day and I could have done nothing more but make her comfortable until she passed on. However, I do believe I got it just in time. The poison was nearly to her armpits. I have successfully removed what was left of her arms, and there does not seem to be any more infection at the socket. However, time will tell all. If I did get it all, then she will survive, but she will be as our women are and will have to learn the women's ways of doing things. If I did not get it all, I will make her remaining time as tolerable as is possible."

"Thank you, thank you!" I replied, grateful for what he'd done to save her life.

"You are most welcome, Holy Vessel. Come, did she say how she came by such grievous wounds?"

We said that she had and he immediately ushered us down to the four Elders, who were taking tea, discussing these unprecedented events. The doktor exclaimed, "Dianna told our Holy Vessels what happened to her. Please, tell us all." All five men listened closely to what little that Dianna had told us about her kidnaping and torture at the hands of the Supreme Prelate Eros Maios.

"Pope Leo speaks like a snake, a forked tongue," Elder Iwan commented. "We should re-evaluate our conclusions. He cannot be truly trusted, certainly not his assassins, which our Holy Vessels have warned us about." The others agreed.

"Elder Amadei, Dita and I wish to remain here with Dianna while she recovers. We must perform our therapy on her so that she has a good chance of recovery," I explained.

"Albin will stay with you until you are ready to return to Wid.

However, if she does recover, I believe that the wisest course will be to place her with a local family from whom she can learn the women's ways of doing things," Elder Amadei suggested. "My reasoning is thus: let us see how a grown woman who has lost her arms can be trained by our ordinary Holy Vessels. Elder Aleksy has told us of the many problems and difficulties that they are encountering with their newly Redeemed converts. He wished us to send some of our Holy Vessels back with him to assist in helping them. Dianna will give us an opportunity to see if this will be worth the risk of sending more of our precious Holy Vessels to the Outer Lands. I promise you, Bethany and Dita, if this Dianna has a lot of difficulty, we will bring her to you and allow you to see if you can manage where our normal Holy Vessels cannot. Is this acceptable to you?" We agreed, but asked that she be brought to Wit with us so that we could at least go and visit with her frequently. He agreed.

We then went up to the room where Dianna now lay in bed, recovering from the life-saving surgery. Dita and I knew well that this poor young girl had a terrific amount of physical pain and trauma with which to deal, compounded enormously by the complete loss of her arms. She had already accepted her own death shortly, now she would have life, but a vastly different kind! We expected intense depression at the very least.

Near suppertime, she finally awoke, a bit groggy and confused. "You are safe now. We are at one of our inns. The doktor has saved your life, Dianna. He said another day and the world would have lost you," I explained in a very gentle, soft voice.

She struggled to get up, but found her arms were not working now at all. She looked at them and they were not there. She saw her shoulders and screamed, terror-stricken. We allowed her to express her emotions without reacting in any way. Her screams died down and turned into an intense grief. She bawled like a child for many minutes; we again remained silent, allowing her grief to pour out. Finally, she wailed, "You should have let me die! Now I am utterly and completely helpless, dependent on everyone for absolutely everything! I cannot live like this!" She continued outpouring her intense feelings and we allowed her to do so. She eventually calmed down and lay looking around the room at last, closer to present time.

Now, I spoke. "Dianna, as soon as you are a little stronger, I will run our therapy on you and help you erase all the horrible trauma that you have bravely undergone. You are not alone. Every woman in this country of Dorota is as armless as you are now, some half million, I guess. Yet, here women are not helpless; they perform all the actions that women back in Velona do, only they have invented alternate ways to accomplish them. As soon as you are recovered enough, women here will begin showing you how to do absolutely everything. All is not lost, but you will need to call upon all that inner strength that so denotes the Po lineage."

She looked at Dita and me once more, this time staring at us, as if remembering. "You are from Dorota? Yet you know of my lineage, Po? I saw many strange things, heard words that I did not expect to hear, Protector and Wid. Are you Santi? How can this be?"

"What I am about to tell you, you must promise me to never reveal to anyone here in Dorota. Will you swear to this?" I asked. I knew that my reply to her questions would give her more hope, more comfort than anything short of our therapy.

"I promise. Please?" she begged.

"Have you ever heard of Elizabeth Stanton, Bethany, or perhaps Ket Bethany, or Marin Bethany?"

"Oh sure, she/he is a legend! Mom's told me all sorts of wild tales about her and her Protector husband, Renzo. Why?"

"You are in their company right now. I am that Bethany, and Dita here is indeed Renzo. We are on a secret mission for Linda and Chaucer d'Grange."

"Oh my god! Wid, Protector! It's you! You can lift things, just like mom said! Oh my god! But you both have no arms? What happened to you? Were you tortured too?" she replied suddenly forgetting all about her own calamity.

"Here in this country, all female babies have their arms amputated the very minute that they are born; it is done in complete secrecy. All the men and women of this country believe that women are born without arms. It's true; they totally believe this is so. I will explain why this is later when we have more time. Only a few men who run the country know the truth — the Elders and the doktors who perform the surgery. Dita and I have already run some therapy on two men and discovered that the mantis creatures created this civilization several centuries ago. We believe that the mantis creatures have been dead for centuries, but that is one thing that we are still investigating."

"Honestly, Dianna, you could not be in better feet here in this country where all the women are as you find yourself now." She managed a slight grin at my pun. "Really, I am not kidding, we can do darn nearly everything. Well, except what you were training to be able to do, healing. We've not even attempted to figure out how to do those things. Sorry. Say how far along are you in your studies?"

"I was finishing up my fourth year. I know that I have, or had anyway, a long way to go, but I so wanted to follow in mom's footsteps. Now that is gone." Tears came once more.

Supper came. Dianna saw the waitress carrying in the trays of food on her yoke. She watched as she sat down and used her feet to place the trays in a good position for Dita and myself. She smiled and said, "How are you doing? The doktor says he thinks you will recover. You were almost dead when I saw them bringing you in here. I know that you had arms, so you must be from the Outer Lands, but now you are one of us. We have no need of arms, you see. We all will help you learn how to do things our way, you will see. I hope you like the stew. Our cook is famous for her stew, you know." She chatted a bit more and then left with her yoke empty.

"We can carry things using those yokes," I explained. "Now let's get some of this stew inside you, shall we?" Dita and I took turns feeding Dianna, who suddenly had an appetite, a good sign we both thought.

When we finished, she chatted a bit more, "I'm fifteen. I got started on my training a bit late, I know. Now I wish I had not delayed, I could already be. . ." her voice trailed off and tears came once more. A bit later, she said, "I wish I could tell mom where I am at and that I am alive."

I'd forgotten all about that aspect. "I haven't chatted with the Po families in, well, it must be something like thirty years! Wow, has time ever flown. "I will let Linda know, and she can relay it to Lana. Once we get you all healed up, I will see if I can establish a Mind Link with your parents so you can chat away with them, okay?"

"Wow! Great! You are still a Wid? Incredible. And Renzo is still a Protector, cool. Wait, he's a she now," she suddenly realized the long raven haired beauty by her side was supposed to be this powerful male Protector, famous in our Santi history, and my husband.

We both giggled, "Tell us about it! Duh, we seem to have a slight problem with this minor detail!" I explained. Dita just continued to giggle. Dianna managed a big grin too.

"Well," Dianna said hesitatingly, "it seems that now I too am a woman of the Eighth Degree. From all that I know of them, they are completely dependent on others and cannot do a thing for themselves. You both were born this way. Do you really think that I will be able to do things for myself? I don't want to live like those of the Eighth Degree; besides, I am not yet married, and there would be no one to care for me, excepting mom and dad."

"Here's the long range plan, Dianna. First, we let your body heal. Then, we are going to have you come to the small town in the highlands were we are located. We'll then be just a quarter mile from you. You will get to live with a nice family whose women will patiently teach you how to do things our way. If that doesn't work out, then you are coming to stay with us, and I promise you, Dianna, we will do everything possible to get you to become as independent as we are. Still, you must remember that there will be things you simply can't do and not be embarrassed to ask for help. Dita and I cannot saddle our horses, for example, though we both love to ride."

Dita interjected, "And above all, Dianna, have patience. It often takes us forever to get something done that we'd otherwise get done in a jiffy. Of course, I am having it even worse than you will because I am still trying to get the hang of these female bodies. They don't quite work the same way." We all giggled.

Dianna observed, "It is hard to think of you as the Renzo that I always imagined you'd look like."

"Hey, I am having a rough go with this whole thing; have some sympathy for this old guy, will you?" We all laughed at the incongruity of it all. Dita had a gorgeous female body, in my opinion. Dianna then said she was tired, and we let her sleep. Later, the men moved another bed into her room so that we would be there for her, if she needed anything during the night.

On January 5, the doktor said that she was healed enough to be moved by carriage to Wit. The Elders had returned many days before, so it was just we three women and Albin, plus one Security guard and driver. While we packed our things ourselves, we allowed Albin to put our warm cloaks over us and fasten them. Dianna watched us closely and saw that we allowed him to do this for us and relaxed, letting him put her new cloak over her shoulders for her.

"It is so strange walking like this, I mean without arms," Dianna commented as we walked down the hall and stairs. "I feel so funny and helpless."

"Oh you are still recovering from the surgery and all that. You will soon get your strength back, I'm sure, Dianna," Albin consoled her. "I think that you are incredibly brave, Dianna. I know that I would be a complete basket case, if I had lost my arms. I just don't know how you women manage all that you do," he added to Dita and me.

Even climbing into the carriage was a very new experience for Dianna, who suddenly found climbing the two steps a bit frightening. Albin was right there steading her, as if he had done this all his life, which he had. By the time that we finally reached Wit several days later, Dianna realized that the men around here were incredibly considerate, observant of her needs, and willing to lend a helping hand, almost without her needing to ask. She noticed that Albin, for example, noticed her slightest hesitations and knew what was needed.

We left Dianna with the Metody family in Wit. Marcin ran a local bakery and Roza ran her household of three children. Tekla was fourteen; Stefania, twelve; and Rafal, thirteen and who looked after his two sister's needs He was pleased to have another young woman living with them, especially because she was so different from his sisters.

We let them get settled a day before we came to visit. After we put Dianna's cloak on her, we then walked her over where we lived and showed her our dorm room. "Once it is warm out, you can just walk over here anytime you want, Dianna," Dita suggested.

"Please come and visit me often, if you can. I know you have things you have to do, but if you can come by, I think I need all the help I can get."

"Don't worry, we'll be by tomorrow and get started on your therapy, Dianna. Just keep on hanging in there," I encouraged her. She flashed a very brave smile, but what else could she do under the circumstances?

Chapter 11 Therapy and Repercussions

We began working our miracle therapy on Dianna the next morning, as promised. Dita and I both knew that this young woman had undergone a long and terrible torture; the trauma would be severe indeed. We were not wrong in our estimate. She and I spent a solid week working with her, giving both morning and afternoon sessions to her.

Yes, we got an education in just how to prolong a torture to inflict the maximum amount of pain on the victim. Oh, this Eros Maios certainly knew his business. He cut off a finger, starting with the little finger, progressing through the thumb last, spreading it out over many days, allowing the victim to feel the ever-growing intense pain really well. Yet he had done it such that the victim didn't die, at least not right away. Suffering was his goal, enough and the person would reveal what he wanted to know. Whether or not his victim even knew the answer was irrelevant to Eros, he enjoyed watching her suffer, beg, and plead, especially when he began on her left hand, after she had lost her right hand. Grim indeed.

All of this was covered up by the recent surgery done to save her life after her wounds became infected. Finally, I had her moving rapidly through the whole mess and was hoping that we were about done. No explosion of laughter came, no happiness, no erasure of the long ordeal. I ran her through it again, to me it seemed as though we ought to be finished. She had no pains coming from the images in her mind, in stark contrast to those earlier in the week, which caused her to shriek as she re-experienced that stored up pain. Just when I began to wonder what was going on with her, she bolted upright, opened her eyes wide, and blurted out, "Oh! I'm Enyo! Here I am again armless! Damn, not again!" Now she started laughing wildly. I breathed a sigh of relief and ended her therapy session.

"I'm Enyo the Engineer! It's all come back to me. God, it's you again, Bethany! Way cool indeed! Renzo! I remember cool, handsome you, er, maybe I should change that to gorgeous you now," she exclaimed while continuing to laugh, blowing off all remaining bits of the ordeal she'd underwent.

"Hi, Enyo. Yes, I remember you well! Glad we met up with each other once more. So here we three are together once more," I acknowledged her.

"I got tired of finding out how devices and things worked, so I thought I should find out how our living bodies actually worked. That's why I was taking up healing! Ha. And I thought it was because of mom and grandmother. Ha. Darn, looks like I face the same old challenges I used to face. I must say, I sure am thankful that I ran into you two. Wow, it's all coming back to me, you know, the way we used to have to do everything with our feet. And I thought that I was done with all that. Ah, well. I hope

128

you don't mind having me around."

"Enyo, Dianna, we love to have you with us. You are one very fine person indeed, hug!" Dita and I took turns hugging her in our own special way, one raised leg holding the other person around their waist.

"Say after you get your skills back, maybe you can teach me a thing or two," Dita suggested. "I'm all new to this mess. I still find myself trying to do something with these non-existent arms here."

She grinned, "Better give me some time. I seem to be a wee bit out of practice!" We all laughed again, as if this was something any one of us would want to be up to date upon!

A bit later, she asked, "Say you know we always did best when we were a group of four. Does that still hold true here where they've been this way their whole lives?"

"Personally, I think you are right, a group of four makes everything much easier to accomplish. Here, they pride themselves on going it alone, and they, for the most part, do well this way. Still, Dita and I find it extremely helpful to be living with each other. She does my hair and I, hers, for example. As soon as you are up to speed, I will see about having you come join us at the Elder College at Wit. As you will soon see, they have developed some very clever ways for us, like the low tables and low desks. Oh yes, and the yokes allow us to carry pretty heavy things, as long as we can keep the weight balanced."

"Okay. Sounds like I've more to learn. Say, do you remember all those slinky, tight, form fitting dresses that we all used to wear to the dances? They got anything like that around here?"

"Sure do remember them. Unfortunately, everything is very plain here. A few of the rich women are importing the latest fashions from Velona, but they are terrifically expensive here. I think we will have to wait on that until we can return to Velona," I replied.

"This is no fair! I used to love to run my hands up and down your dress while we were dancing," Dita protested as she remembered those days. "Now *how* am I going to do that? Will *one* of you answer that one?" We laughed once more.

That evening as Dita and I walked the short way back to college, Rafal, the rebel, stepped up alongside of us. I wondered if they had received their two caravels of grain; I had forgotten about them. "Thank you. As promised, two came. Lifesaving. Owe you big time."

"Keep a low profile a while longer. We are still working on a real solution," I whispered back. He nodded and headed back into Wit. "Well, good things are happening." Dita agreed.

The next morning, the High Council met officially for the first time since the Pope's visit. Elder Aleksander was notably absent and another man sat in his seat. He was introduced as Elder Roman, the new Security Committee head and representative. He formally reported specifically to

Dita and me that Aleksander had been arrested, stripped of his titles, and sent to the Fields of Kondrat to be Redeemed, if possible. I asked him if he knew why Aleksander had us kidnaped.

"Change is coming to Dorota altogether too rapidly for some. He was determined to stop all the change from happening. Specifically, he saw you two as a real threat to the old ways of doing business. You are too bright, too intelligent, and too knowledgeable and would have exposed his often-fallacious reasoning. He, I'm afraid to say this aloud because it sounds so silly, he was honestly terrified of you two Holy Vessels." Half of the Elders chuckled at this.

"Before we all get too carried away," Elder Boris sneered, "some of us would like to know just what this therapy is all about. How is it that we can find no records of anything like therapy in all our archives? How is it that you come to know of this? Perhaps you have had contact with outsiders? More than likely, this is true, is it not?" Four other faces expressed their unspoken approval of Boris and his questions.

Think fast, love! Dita sent.

"Perhaps it is time that we addressed this. Dita and I are young women of Dorota, born here and of here, your young Holy Vessels. Why do you call us your Holy Vessels instead of simply young women? I quote, 'As men and women grew old and passed on, new men and women came forth from his Holy Vessels.' From us doth spring new life, as it has since the beginning." I began using their own words from their power sermon against them.

"Later on, 'God saw that men needed even greater strength, power, and stamina, because they needed to now support themselves and their families.' Later, 'One of God's Holy Vessels' — I call your attention to whom it was that said this — 'one of God's Holy Vessels, who was called Marzena, spoke unto God. 'Lord, my man, Jurek, is a good and kind man, a farmer. Yet, I can see that he needs to be stronger. Please, my Lord, take my arms from me and use them to strengthen Jurek so that he may be strong enough for the task. I do not need them and Jurek needs them so much more than I do.' God heard the prayer from his Holy Vessel and so it was that God took the arms from his Marzena and fashioned them into more ribs for her husband Jurek. Thus made stronger and more powerful, Jurek was at last able to sustain his Holy Vessel and family, more able to tend his fields, and produce more food.'"

"Who, Elders, who made that sacrifice? Women, of which Marzena was the first. Yes, I know very well how you implement this sacrifice on Dorota today and for the last many hundreds of years. Under your guidance, female babies have their arms amputated at birth." I saw several of the Elders squirm in their chairs. I was hitting them too close to home.

In other cultures and other lands, doing this to helpless babies is considered a heinous crime. Look at how you view the young kidnaped woman from Velona who had her fingers and hands cut off by the Mano del Dio Supreme Prelate Eros Maios. Do you not consider that a crime of great magnitude against women? I'm sure that you all do. Yet, you do not consider cutting off babies' arms a crime? But it is justified, you say, our culture will be destroyed if we do not. This has been done since the dawn of time. It is part of our religion. I have heard those words put forth from some of you."

"Yet, I ask you whose religion? Our people or yours? I am not here to judge you, make less of you, or charge you with crimes. I am here to ask you to look deeper into your very own words. Marzena asked God, 'Please, my Lord, take my arms from me and use them to strengthen Jurek so that he may be strong enough for the task.' This statement has come down to you through the ages, from the dawn of time. Have you ever considered that it is a metaphor? That it is *symbolic* of what Marzena was offering?"

"Before I continue, I am not the body that you see sitting before you. I am created in God's image. God's image cannot be this fleshly body that you see here. If it were, God would be long since dead! God is not a fleshly body, nor is any of us, we who are created in his image. We are all immortal spiritual beings as is our God, our Creator. Yes, God has given us these fleshly bodies to inhabit for a time, but you and I are not these fleshly bodies."

"Okay, if we are not these fleshly bodies, what does this say about Marzena and her offering to God? I say unto you that she was offering something more powerful, more intimate, and more significant than mere fleshly arms. She gave something of herself to make her man stronger, more able. That is precisely what I am doing here for you, my men. I am giving something precious of me unto you so that you, the leaders of our country can be stronger, and it sure isn't my arms! Already two have received this gift from me. You may ask them just how precious the gift has been to them. Dita and I have already given our gift unto the Outsider who, with bleeding stubs where her hands had been, used them to help us, total strangers, escape from Pope Leo's yacht."

"Yet, when you receive this precious gift, you have a greater responsibility to bear. God then said unto Jurek, who hath received Marzena's gift, 'I can see that by the sacrifice of worthy Marzena, you are now blessed with part of her strength and you are now able to survive well. However, Jurek you must honor her sacrifice unto you. From this day forward, you must love her, cherish her, and help her, as you have never done before. Thou shalt never betray her by lusting after other women. Thou shalt be true to her and to her alone. Thou shalt not lie, covet what another has, steal that which does not belong to you, and fight with other men whose Holy Vessels have likewise made their sacrifice. Nor should thou become a glutton over the bounty, which thou art now capable of producing because of the gift Marzena has given unto you and you alone. Thou shalt honor and cherish the new life that Marzena brings forth, as they are part of each of you. If you will do these things, then you are worthy of viewing my Creation and of entering my realm.'"

"Soon Dita and I will give each of you our spiritual gift from God. Once you have received it, you will be stronger, but you will also be asked to take up more responsibility for our people. If you fail to step up and be responsible, as God said, 'If you fail to do these, I will take back Marzena's sacrificial gift to you, Jurek, and allow you both to die off like my first creations of the Unholy man and woman, which I have forsaken as unworthy.'"

"As our teachings go, Jurek did not abandon others, as I hope and pray you will not either. Elder Borys, you asked, me three key questions. 'How is it that we can find no records of anything like therapy in all our archives? How is it that you come to know of this? Perhaps you have had contact with outsiders?' You have that record in Marzena's request of God. How do Dita and I know this? We are of Marzena; we are your Holy Vessels. We, like Marzena, are giving our gift freely unto you, our men. Yes, we have had contact with outsiders, Pope Leo and his vile men and the young woman of Velona, who gave of herself that we might be saved. None of that makes us any less Holy. If you believe that that contact has made us Unholy, then we will leave and take our Holy Gift to others, who still keep their faith in our Lord God."

"We will leave you all now to discuss this among yourselves. We will never under any circumstances ever give our precious gift to anyone who does not wish to receive it and accept the responsibility that follows. We will begin with one of you tomorrow afternoon. If you will accept our gift, Elder Borys, we will begin with you tomorrow. If one o'clock is not a good time, send word when is a better time. Thank you." I got up and Dita hastily followed me out the door. You could hear a pin drop on the stone floor, but really all they heard was the clicking of our high-heeled boots as we made our dramatic exit.

Back in our room, Dita threw herself over me the moment we entered and shut the door! If she had had arms, she would have picked me up and twirled me around in circles, she was that elated and proud of what I had said to these — the top leaders of the country — the ones behind the scene controlling and guiding a whole civilization of a million people. Lacking arms, she pressed her body tight to mine and then she, the being, lifted us both up and twirled us around in circles!

"Dita! Put me down," I tried to keep a straight face, but could not. I laughed.

"Bethany, I love you more than anything in this entire world. Once more, you have proven that you are the greatest Wid Tarra has ever seen! You were beyond brilliant back there! Fantastic beyond all words. I love you!" She set us down and passionately kissed me, which I returned in kind.

Sometime later, when Dita calmed down, I asked, "Well, do you think that I defused the situation with those who are opposing change?"

"If you didn't, they are so totally unworthy of help that they should be sent to these Fields of Kondrat, whatever they are. Plus, you very cleverly set the stage for having them start setting to rights the complete mess they have made of their women. However, my love, I am completely in the dark. Just how are we going to set things right here? I mean we cannot do therapy on a half million women, now can we? What's the plan?"

I laughed, "Dita, if I knew what the plan was I would have told you long ago! I haven't got any plan at all yet, none whatsoever. I am winging it, haven't you noticed? Today, Borys set us up, hoping to bring us down. I had to do something drastic to prevent that and I did. What's next? I don't have the slightest idea. We still need to finish seeing this country. Perhaps something will suggest itself to us. Please, my darling Dita, keep your eyes open for anything, anything that we can use to set things right here in Dorota."

"I will my love, I will. Still, that was brilliant on your part today!"

"By the way, my Protector, I haven't had the chance to say thank you for saving me from the kidnaping. You did indeed get us out of a bad jam. Thank you Miss Protector." Dita beamed and pressed her body against mine again. Oh how we both missed the ability to hug each other.

Promptly at one the next day, Elder Borys knocked on our door. He was a strong man, forty-five, with piercing blue eyes and brown hair. "Forgive my attitude yesterday, Holy Vessels. I am perhaps too long trying to rehabilitate others, that I see things no longer so clearly. I am ready to accept thy precious gifts, though I don't know what I must do to receive them or how this works."

"Thanks, come in and have a seat. It really is very easy. Relax. Okay, I'm not mesmerizing you or anything. Close your eyes. Good. Now have you had any aches or pains in your shoulders or arms from time to time?"

"No, not really."

"How about strange unexplained sensations in your shoulders or arms?"

"Well, you know, every now and then I have the strangest feeling that something is trickling down my arms. When I look to see, there is nothing there at all. It is just my imagination, Holy Vessel Bethany, just my imagination. It is all merely my imagination. Probably because I am around all these Unholy Ones so often, that is what is causing my imagination to work overtime. It is nothing really, just my imagination."

"All right. Now I want you to return to the last time when you felt this sensation of something trickling down your arms." We were off, Dita, who was watching the session, ready to lend me a hand, well okay a foot, nodded. She too knew where this was likely heading. Yes, it took a while to get there.

"I am watching the Unholy Ones working in the fields. It is hot. I feel something is trickling down both arms! I try to wipe it off, but there is nothing there. Weird. See, it is just my imagination." We ran through a dozen similar incidents, I kept asking him if there was something similar that happened earlier.

At last he said, "It's probably just my imagination, but I see a picture here." I thanked him and had him go through this one. "I see a doktor who is helping a Holy Vessel give birth. Yes, he is helping get the baby out. I see it's a girl and oh, the doktor quickly wraps it in a blanket so that the anxious parents cannot see her arms. He says something and leaves with the baby. Now he is in his operating room. It's well lighted. He has his tools spread out. He is doing it, cutting a circle around the top of the arm." He began describing the operation in very graphic terms, which I will not repeat here. "Then off comes the arms. Blood is flowing everywhere; it trickles down my arms. Tickling me. I try to wipe it off with one hand, while keeping the other pressed tightly on the small artery. It tickles me. Then, I begin to sew her up. At last, I am done, I think it is a fine job and will leave only a tiny scar. She is perfect, I say to the proud parents a bit later. Bethany, I have that strange tickling sensation, like blood is trickling down my arms right now!"

Again, I thanked him for telling me and had him go through it again. After several more passes, it didn't erase, but I didn't expect that it would. He was not having the trauma, but giving trauma to another. However, the sensation that something was flowing down his arm grew much stronger. "This is all just my overactive imagination," he complained, wiping both of his arms on his shirt. I pressed him for something even earlier and I finally got it.

"I see a doktor. He's delivering another baby. This must be a long time ago. Our buildings look different than today. Oh, it's a girl baby. He wraps her up in a blanket and leaves, telling the parents he will clean her and bless her. He takes the baby outside. Then, he brings her back and hands her blanket and all to the proud parents, who hold their little armless girl."

Well, Dita and I knew that he was missing the major part of the incident. No matter, I just had him go back over it all once more. When he got to the part of wrapping the baby in a blanket, he said, "The blanket feels itchy, but warm. Feels good. He takes me out to get my body washed off. It is somewhat bloody and all that. My arms feel like there is stuff on them, but I can't seem to wipe it off. He takes me outside. I cannot figure out why. He lays me on a granite slab and opens the blanket. Now I am getting cold. I cry. Why are you doing this to me? I am cold! Oh my god! Oh my god!" he yelled nearly at the top of his voice.

"I see this huge, huge insect, must be a hundred feet tall coming up to me. It bends down over me! It's going to eat me! I know it! I am screaming as loudly as I can! It bites into my arm, pain, pain. Then numbness comes, but it feels like something is trickling down my arm. It's my own blood! It is eating my arm! I cannot believe it! It is eating my arm completely off. Now it moves over to my left side. It bites, pain, sharp stabbing pain, then numbness comes. Blood trickles down that arm too. It is eating my other arm. Now I know it is going to eat all of me. I am so tiny and it is so huge. No, it stops. It goes away. Dad! Dad heard my screams and comes looking for me. I cry out for dad to save me, but I hear silly baby noise. Dad says what in heaven's name was that doktor? Did you see that? Some kind of giant insect or something. The doktor says, Julek, you are just seeing things. It's all just your imagination. I didn't see anything but your daughter here whom I am just finishing washing up. Here, help me wash her off. It's just your imagination. We all know that there is no such thing as a giant insect. They wash me off and take me inside. It was all just my imagination. I didn't see a giant insect eating my arms off. But I sure did see it. It hurt!"

I thanked him and had him go through it once more. On the fifth recounting, he opened his eyes and starting laughing wildly. "It was all just my imagination! The hell it was! I was there. I felt it! I saw it! It was a giant insect. Kind of looked like a praying mantis only it was a hundred feet long! It did eat my arms off. The last thing I ever felt from my arms was my own blood tricking down them! My imagination, ha!" He roared with laughter and I quietly ended the session. I was also getting hungry, as it was now suppertime. He'd been at it for over four hours.

He suddenly sat bolt upright. "Oh my god! I am a spiritual being. I have had these other bodies before! I have been armless as you two are! Oh my. No wonder I have this overwhelming sympathy and empathy for you and how hard life is for you to bear. Wow! Incredible! Thank you, Holy Vessels. Thank you. Words cannot express my appreciation for what you have given unto me! Incredible! I will accept the responsibility that you have placed upon the giving of your selfless gift. All praise to the Lord God for his blessed Holy Vessels!"

"Thank you, Elder Borys. It's past suppertime. We'd better go get some before the others eat it all up." He left laughing up a storm and repeating to anyone he passed, "It was all just my imagination, ha!" Dita and I smiled and gave ourselves our usual hug. We waited until the third shift to dine with the other domestic staff, as was our want. That way, we could help them with the dishes. Two extra pair of feet did help them.

I won't bore you with the details of the other eleven Elders, which we assisted during the next three weeks. It is enough to say that all eleven men eventually ran back to an incident involving the mantis creatures, as either the watching doktor or the poor victim. We now had all thirteen members of the High Council one hundred percent behind us, swearing by our gift of therapy. All now began to see the connections between then and now.

At the next council meeting, I asked if I might say a few words. This time, all thirteen men were extremely eager to listen to what I had to say. "As you now all have some reality on our more ancient history, I can sum up what I now believe has happened here in Dorota. In our distant past, these giant mantis creatures came here and they liked to dine upon female babies' arms. Why female and not male I do not know. The doktors then were forced to bring all newborn females to the mantis creatures, who promptly dined upon our arms. I know that this is so weird, that it is hard to believe, unless you experienced it, which you all have now."

"In our modern Dorota, no signs of these giant creatures have been seen for at least two centuries, maybe more. Why are the doktors now amputating female babies' arms? One would think that once the creatures left, this would stop. It hasn't and it is fair to ask why this might be so. All of you have seen the impact of these traumatic events have on your lives today. I will pick on Elder Borys. He occasionally used to feel that something is trickling down his arms, when there is nothing there. These traumatic events in our past do enforce behavior on us in the present. Perhaps the ultimate answer is that we have all been simply following the traumatic pattern laid into all of us by these mantis creatures centuries ago. I hold none of you or any of our doktors to blame. There is no blame, except for the mantis creatures. Blaming you or blaming our doktors for this is a self-defeating route to travel. It gets us nowhere except utter chaos in all of Dorota and probably the murdering of you and our doktors, which we desperately need. Just look at how the doktor saved that poor Velona woman several weeks ago."

I continued, "What are we to do now? We in this room — we know the underlying truth of our situation here in Dorota. Yet, there are a million people out there who do not. Dita and I cannot give our special gift to a million people. Our fleshly bodies will not live long enough to do that, if we did it to one person each day; we'd have to live something like twenty-eight thousand years." Everyone laughed at the impossible figure.

"So what are we to do to set our people free? At this very moment, I do not have that answer. I will seek more of the truth when the warm spring comes, as I have asked of Elder Amadei. Perhaps when I finish my search, I will know more. Perhaps not. I ask of you to begin discussing what we realistically can do for our country until Dita and I finish our search for truth. On your shoulders, now strengthened by our gift to you, rests the fate of our Dorota. Please give the matter your most worthy efforts. We must do something, but at this time, your Holy Vessels cannot say what that may be. Perhaps, when we finish our search for truth, we will be able to give you further guidance and council. I certainly hope that we can. One thing I do know and that is that we here cannot sit back and do nothing at all, for we and we alone know the truth. Thank you all."

Elder Borys stood and began slowly clapping for us. Quickly, the other Elders rose and joined him, honoring us in their way. We grinned and nodded, and then we left them to their discussions. On our way back to our room, Dita commented, "Well, there's another thing I just discovered that I cannot do this lifetime, clap my hands. Please, let's not use that as an excuse to not go to concerts, plays, and the theater, when we get the chance!" Her face was serious indeed.

"No, Dita, never. We can yell out or stamp our feet or something. Kick me in my butt, if I ever try to use that as an excuse." Finally she grinned, relieved. I hadn't thought about clapping before now, but she was right. No clapping for us. Instead, we had planning to do.

Chapter 12 Spring Explorations Begin

Dita and I had Albin pin a detailed map of Dorota on our wall so that we could study it more easily. We had already seen nearly all the coastal cities and towns, only the short run between Grzegorz and Bozydar had not been part of our earlier trip. We discounted making that coastal trip. Instead, we had not yet seen most all the central highlands. This included the six major, dense forests, in which the rebels were rumored to be living and Kondrat with the rehabilitation fields there. Also, the map showed several promising low mountains, the highest points on our continent. I say promising, because in the other mantis-controlled areas that we had visited in earlier lifetimes, the creatures preferred to dwell in these places, where it was difficult or impossible for humans to get.

Mid-March, Elder Amadei came to us. "I wish to discuss the case of our guest, Dianna Po. She has been staying with the Metody family now for three months. Her wounds have healed up in what the doktor says is miracle time. I've talked with Roza nearly every week about the progress of Dianna. It is always the same; she is adapting and learning the women's ways incredibly rapidly. So much so, that it has me puzzled. You see, Elder Aleksy has said that women who lose their arms as adults, as Dianna has, are having such terrible times learning the women's ways. As you know, he has returned with a dozen Holy Vessel volunteers, who will be helping these converted women."

"Yet, am I to measure their progress by that of Dianna's? If so, then I fear something must be very wrong with Elder Aleksy's observations."

"You should believe the observations of Elder Aleksy. Dianna has had our therapy gift and wounds heal significantly faster after that. Plus, she has also been a victim of these mantis creatures in her past, growing up just as I have, like this," I shrugged my shoulders. "Her rapid progress is no doubt due to the fact that she remembers well how she used to cope with things."

"Ah, I see, now Dianna's progress becomes understandable. Once more, Holy Vessel, you have shown me that the truth does set one free. I thank you." He smiled, gave me a hug, and left.

"You know, perhaps we ought to check on Dianna and bring her along with us," Dita suggested. While we had been visiting her regularly, our attention had obviously been on other matters. I agreed and we headed into Wit to visit her again, only this time, we agreed to see how well she was picking up her much needed survival methods.

"So Dianna, how are you doing?" I asked, as we sat down on their front room couch.

"I'm adapting. Guess I don't have a choice about that, now do I?" she grinned, but I sensed some resentment behind it, which was only natural.

She'd been horribly robbed and forced against her will into this lifestyle. "Seriously, though, I'm finding that it is all coming back to me, rather quickly, it seems. Roza, Tekla, and Stefania are showing me all sorts of clever tricks that we never knew before. Plus, I will say this for their men they certainly have done right by us. The low desks and tables, you know six inches, are just perfect. It makes writing and eating so vastly easier this way. Of course, we all had similar sliding bars instead of doorknobs, so that's pretty much the same."

"I'm able to do the laundry, clean the floors, set the table, even cook, though I am rather unfamiliar with all their recipes they use here. Roza says that I am really catching on extremely rapidly. I just don't know how much more they can show me. I don't know your written language; so instead, I am practicing writing in mine. I've written mom and dad a bunch of letters, though I have no idea if it will ever be possible to somehow send them."

Roza decided to speak up, "Dianna is right, she has learned nearly everything I can teach her. I've never seen someone learn our women's ways so quickly. It truly is a miracle."

Grinning, I said, "Well, thank you very much Roza. I do believe that it is time that I honor my promise to have Dianna come and stay with us. I'll tell Elder Amadei about the terrific job that you have done with Dianna. You and your daughters should be very proud of your help for Dianna. I know that I am. Thank you so much."

"Ah, now I am going to lose my extra set of feet that have been helping me so much around the house," Roza teased us, her smile was infectious. We helped Dianna pack her scant belongings, a change of clothes and winter cloak. Off we headed to our place.

I told Elder Amadei about our move and he backed my decision. He wondered if there would be enough room for three in our room. I told him it would be fine. After all, we three had very little in the way of objects to clutter a room, mostly clothing and of course our yokes. Dita and I had a little money, so the next thing we did was take Dianna into Wit and got her some better dresses and shoes; plus we got her a pair of yokes just the right height for her. Dita insisted that we also pick up some personal items, such as a hairbrush and a drinking mug. Now we had a use for the yokes: carrying our purchases the quarter mile back to our place.

When we had supper and were helping the other women clean up after the three groups had dined, Dianna commented, "Gee, everything seems to be exactly the same, from place to place."

Headmistress Zofia replied, "That is right, child. Every home everywhere in Dorota is exactly the same, so we all know just what and how to do everything that we need to do. It makes life so much easier for us all."

"Yes, but it also makes everything so boring," Dianna countered. "So predictable. There are no challenges, once you figure one way to do something, you just keep on doing it that same way. Boring. I need challenges in my life."

"What? You think life isn't challenging enough like we are?" Zofia bellowed and began heartily laughing. All of us roared with laughter, even Dianna.

Later back in our room, Dianna asked, "So where do I put my stuff? We all sleep together?" We had two empty drawers also low to the ground and we helped her stow her things. Then, Dita and I began our nightly ritual of changing into our nightgowns and brushing out our long hair. For the first time we got a good look at Dianna and she, us.

Dianna had the most gorgeous blue eyes I'd seen. She was going on sixteen, about a year older than we were and was somewhat more filled out. She was a good six inches taller than either Dita or me, which we thought came from the Po side of the family. She agreed with that assumption. Her light brown hair was medium length now, with nice waves, unlike ours, which hung straight as an arrow. She had a very pretty face that reminded me constantly of her great-grandmother, Elona Po, whom I knew so well a century ago.

"Honestly, Dianna, every time I gaze upon your face, I keep seeing Elona Po. You really do look like your great-grandmother an awful lot." She was pleased with my compliment.

"Can I ask something personal about you two?" We nodded. "I sort of feel like I am in intruding on your personal privacy. I mean she's Renzo and you were married and now. . ."

"We are still madly in love with each other, Dianna. If it is possible, we want to marry somehow. However, we also want you to share our bed with us. Three can do more things more easily than one. So scoot your butt over here and let us do up your hair. You can work on ours too. We are going to be a team, we three, until we can ever get back to Velona," I answered her.

Dita broke in, "Dear, I don't think that is quite what she meant. Will you feel embarrassed if Bethany and I are passionately kissing and such? I think that's what she's worried about." Dianna flushed and I knew that Dita was right on the mark. Dita added, "Okay, I will be honest with both of you. I don't know how to be a woman. I mean I still feel like Renzo, you know a guy, only everything is all backwards or something. Honestly, when I see boys looking at me, I feel so embarrassed, because I think they are looking at me, a guy. Weird isn't it? I never knew being a woman was this hard. I just feel weird trying to flirt with guys, but I feel fabulous loving Bethany. I would really enjoy pleasuring you, Dianna. There isn't any harm, because I am not a guy. Now I think that I *am* really getting confused."

"Been there, Renzo. When I was Ket Bethany, that was my first time with a male body and was I ever confused about nearly everything!" I confided my similar experiences, and we three talked about this phenomenon for some time.

Dianna finally added, "I am fine with however you are, Dita. I thought that maybe you would be embarrassed by having me here at the same time. Back in the old days, I remember how we four used to pleasure ourselves every night. I really do miss the intimacy of others who care about me. It took me a very long time to find a man who I could really respect, admire, and love. I thought I'd never find one, but then I did. Though I know you have only just met me, I would really cherish being with you, loving you, pleasuring with you."

"Now you are being silly, Dianna. Enyo, we know you and love you too, now hop into bed and join us," I replied, blowing out our oil lamp.

"How did you get such fantastic earrings?" she whispered as she cuddled up to me on one side, with Dita on my other side. It was a long story.

After breakfast the next morning and after we helped the others with the dishes, Dita and I stood before our map, outlining what we needed to do. At once, the old Enyo that I knew, the highly organized, methodical engineer, surfaced. Dianna immediately began making lists, pointing out what we would need, proposing the most efficient routes to take, as well as asking many relevant questions, such as what to expect with the rebels. She wanted to know all about the guns that the Security Guards carried, of which we knew nothing, not having had the slightest interest in them before Dianna brought them up.

Both Dita and I realized within minutes just how valuable having Dianna along with us would be. We told her so and she giggled and gave each of us a loving hug. Here she was: living half a world away from her home, family, and friends, arriving here with no possessions, becoming armless and thus losing the ability to pursue what she thought was going to be her life's goal, crushed utterly. She needed love, affection, a sense of somehow once more belonging, and the feeling that she was able to contribute something of value. We provided her with all four. How could we not?

Since we would need to ride horses on part of our journey through the roughest of terrains where a carriage could not go, I decided that we needed those wooden blocks, which, in a prior lifetime, my dad had invented for us. The block was a biting block through which the reins were tied. I'd bite down on the block instead of wad of leather reins. It was more comfortable and made it far easier to get it again if I dropped the reins. Enyo, er, Dianna, remembered what they looked like and drew up a sketch for me. I asked Elder Amadei if he knew a man handy with wood who could make us three of them. Kindly, he took care of this detail for me.

As the weather warmed and the pale green of spring appeared here in the highlands, we took Dianna's extensive lists of what we needed and our plans to the High Council. Essentially, we thought the smartest move would be to take a carriage across the central highlands from Bazyli to Kondrat, where we would visit the Fields of Kondrat to see how they were handing the conversion of those who had become "Unholy." We wanted to see just how they were trying to Redeem them. Along the way, we would examine from a distance the likely low mountains, which we would then visit on horseback, that is, the ones that looked promising. We three hoped that somehow we could locate the old dwelling places of the mantis creatures, which would add solid proof that they had existed here on Dorota.

Once that exploration was finished, then we would take the horses into the six heavily forested areas in search of the many rebels who were said to be hiding out in the woods. Any solution to Dorota's problems had to involve these people too. The High Council insisted then on sending along an escort of Security Guards, armed with their guns. I knew this would not be ideal when attempting to contact the rebels. However, I'd cross that bridge when I got there.

Finally, on April 1, we hit the road in our provided carriage. We three rode inside, while our three horses were tied to the rear of the carriage. A group of six Security Guards rode escort as we began our long journey along the cobblestone road to Kondrat. Elder Amadei wanted to send along a man to ride with us and assist us with whatever we needed. Instead, I managed to convince him to send our old traveling companion Kasper Klemens along to help us, but allowed him ride along with the other guards. I knew that he didn't enjoy long carriage rides.

The highlands were blossoming; a multitude of colors captivated our attention and our noses. Contrasting with the brown stone, lichen covered boulders, the green grasses and dozens of types of wild flowers demanded our gaze. Wagons of goods passed us, as well as some travelers on horseback and even other carriages. It was time to get some freedom from the cooped up wintertime. Dianna, as expected, began to take notes on the distant craggy peaks that we passed, noting our thoughts on which looked promising, rated on a scale of one to ten, ten being the first ones that we should check.

We covered about twenty miles each day, stopping for lunch at the nearest village, hamlet, or small town. Here in the highlands, they were nowhere as frequent as they had been along the coast or in the farmlands before the highlands. Thankfully, Kasper knew the inns well and handled these arrangements for us. I did feel badly when we stopped at a small hamlet, which had but one inn, and they suddenly had another dozen guests. We put an additional burden on these women, the cooks and waitresses. My heart went out to them, because they worked so extra hard to service our group. I hoped that Kasper was leaving them a little extra for all their efforts.

As we rolled along, we three had a lot of time to chat. Each of us had very different topics, which worried us. Mine was this armless body. "Honestly, I really don't want to have to live another long life like this. After we get this mess handled, then what? I keep asking myself that. What realistically are we going to do? Sure, I intend to get back to civilization, most likely the Velona area, but what then? Are we just going to sit around some house somewhere and drink tea? I am so used to doing action things, helping others, and all that. And here I am like this yet again."

"Maybe we could find a dance troupe to join, you know, like you were once in," Dita suggested, helpfully. "I remember all the twirling you did at the end of the dance movements; it knocked my socks off. God, you were good, my love. We could maybe try that again or maybe we could learn to sing and be in a vocal ensemble or something."

"Is that all we are good for now, domestic duties and entertainment? Renzo, I mean Dita, surely there has to be something else, somewhere. I sure don't want to just be a domestic for the rest of my life."

"Dear, when we get back there, what we need to do is sit down and make up some real goals for our lives," Dita advised. That made sense and I was content to wait until we got there.

"Now take me, I am a complete mess," Dita confided in us. "I still feel like I am a man trapped in this female body. I don't still know the first thing about being a woman. All I know is that I still am passionately in love with you, Bethany. I really want us to be married and all that, yet how am I ever going to satisfy you? How can we have and raise a family? What kind of a job can I get to bring home the bacon for you? Like this, I feel doubly whammed. I have this female body here, which you all say is gorgeous, but no arms. I can't pick up a damn sword to defend either of you. I am completely helpless, unless I use my Druwid skills that I have not forgotten or use my special spiritual being abilities that I learned from the Guardian. I am majorly screwed, that's what!"

Dianna giggled, "No you aren't Dita, you haven't got that lower appendage with which to get it." We all laughed at her jest.

"I know I don't! What the hell am I and we going to do?" Dita was near tears over her predicament.

Dianna said consolingly, "Dita, there is no reason why you and Bethany cannot be joined. Look, there are such relationships nearly everywhere, but mostly they are kept somewhat hidden because they are so different from what most people expect to see. I've seen a number of men who are lovers, and we all know tons of women who share beds. Just look at where I was raised, you know, Enyo of the Isle of Right. Four hundred of us lived together as one, well really groups of four of us together. I don't see any reason why you two cannot be married. As for a family, if you really want children, then just find some man who is willing to spend a few nights with you two. That's how it was always done on the Isle of Right — really it was done that way."

She went on, "As for not really understanding your female body, Bethany and I can help you with that one. At night, in bed," she winked coyly and smiled mischievously. We all chuckled.

"Yes, but Bethany, assuming I can figure out the best way to pleasure you, is that going to be enough for you? I mean before I had all the right, well you know, appendages and such. This way is so different. What if I don't satisfy you, my love? I'd feel horrible."

"Dita, I love you, silly, not your body, not fleshly pleasures, and all that. Yes, they are enjoyable and fun, but it's you that I am in love with and want to marry and be with all the time. I'm just afraid that neither of us will be satisfied with these frustrating bodies with no arms, causing untold problems for us," I replied, telling him how I really felt about all this. "I don't care what others may think about us being married. It's none of their business. However, I am worried that you won't be able to find something that you consider worth doing too. I think that's the biggest thing, you know. While we may be perfectly happy together, we both need to be able to contribute to something that we consider valuable in our society. You always played the role of man-hero, so to speak."

Dita giggled, "Gee, that's a funny way to put it, but yes, I liked to be out there swinging my sword, protecting everyone from harm. Get the old adrenaline running. I like the feeling I got when I did protect others. Nothing beats that feeling — as if you know that you really did something important for others. How the hell am I going to do that like this?" She shrugged her shoulders again. "Hell, I can't even get this body out of a carriage without being super careful!"

"Hey, training! Renzo, er Dita, remember when I first lost my arms to the mantis creature, when we were in the south of the Southlands? You know, when we were all off exploring the world. After that, you all insisted that Linda and I undergo extensive training so that you all would know our limits and knew what you could count on us to be able to do. Why don't you and I do that kind of intensive training again? Then, we will be even better able to cope with our damnable mess."

"Hey, I like that. You're right. We'd at least know our limits well. You're on. Still don't know what I will be able to do as a Protector after that, though," she replied.

"Same as me, we have to then pick out new goals for ourselves, that's what. If it's good for me, then it's good for you too." She grinned, no backing out of that one.

"Well, what about me?" Dianna finally confided her worries with us. "I've lost everything, my hopes, my dreams, my plans, everything. Back home, there's hardly anyone like us anymore. All those armless women that you rescued — they've all grown old and passed away. The Laird Foundation has become a den of artists, normal artists, you know, with arms. I don't think there is anyone around there anymore that knows how to deal with the likes of us. When I get home, I'm going to be looked on as a freak or something. It was very different when there were hundreds of us, you know, safety in company. I cannot bear trying to go life alone like I am now.

Thinking about going home like I am now, well it scares the crap out of me."

Dita looked at me and then at Dianna. "Dianna, will you marry us? Join us; make it a three-way union kind of thing. If you later find a loving man, then you can go your own way. With three of us standing as one, united, we stand a better chance at everything. I promise to Protect you as much as I Protect Bethany. Come train with us, then maybe we three can find some goals that we consider worthy of us. Honestly, Dianna, you are a very beautiful young woman and I find you very attractive too. I do respect you highly and I've always admired you, Enyo, I mean Dianna. Gosh, this is so confusing to me."

"I know Dita," I added quickly. "Dianna, I admire and respect you highly. I always have. Please consider joining us, make us be a threesome. I've no idea how it will work out, but the hell with society's opinions. They don't have to live as we are forced to live. Please, Dianna, please join with us. I know that the training I did back when is going to be terribly hard on us, but we did it once, so we can do it again. Maybe with three heads working on a common, most worthy goal for us, we will be successful. Please, Dianna."

"Well, if you are both sure about this," she replied meekly.

"We are!" Dita and I said in unison.

Dianna broke into a huge smile. "I accept. I admit, I have always loved the both of you. I feel so happy, so relieved. It's as if I suddenly belong once more. I will work hard. I promise that I will not let you down." After a pause and in a lower voice, she said, "I've never admitted this to anyone, but I always found life so very hard like we are. I know, as Enyo, I never said anything, and I worked extra hard to overcome my handicap. I knew it was a handicap even when I was on the Isle of Right, you know. Diana was making all her beautiful drawings on the floor with her feet. I knew she should have arms like the men, and then she could do her art so much easier and perhaps better. I always overcompensated for my lack of arms. I had to, to keep my own self-respect up. With you two, I feel that I can just relax now and be myself, what I am now, handicapped once more. Being around you two, I don't feel like I am handicapped, even though we three are. I know that sounds weird, but that's the way I feel about it."

"Wow, Enyo, er Dianna, I never knew that you felt that way. You always came across to me as a super engineer, a super figure out how this works kind of person. Yet, a very sexy engineer," I admitted. "You both given me some real hope for the future, once we get this place handled. Say, how about that peak there? What do you think?" Another craggy peak came into view, a tall one, and barren. Dianna added it to her list, putting our consensus of a six after it.

Chapter 13 The Fields of Kondrat

A week later and a day and a half out of Kondrat, our carriage crested a hill and below us, we got our first view of the dreaded Fields of Kondrat, used to scare people in our society. Here is where they kept all those who did not conform to their societal rules and guidelines, the Unholy. Per the words of the Elders, here they attempted to reform the people and get them Redeemed so that they could rejoin society.

"Oh my god!" we three echoed from inside our carriage, as it slowly brought more and more into our view. The fields were just that, one very huge farm. Here in the highlands, the land was not just dirt. Stones and small boulders made tilling the land terribly difficult, though crops would thrive here. The Fields of Kondrat was really a prison camp. A six-foot tall metal wire fence marked its outer borders, capped with a row of strange wire that had many small sharp protruding barbs. If anyone tried to climb over the fence, they would be badly cut up.

First, we saw some of the inmates. Nothing prepared us for the sights that we began seeing. At this time, the inmates were plowing the fields for the spring planting. A large three bladed plow, which normally would be pulled by a team of two oxen, was in fact being pulled by a team of six women, armless women! Each wore a horse's bridal with a steel bit in their mouths, the reins running back to the plowman, who controlled the direction that the plow was going. These poor, pitiful women were straining every muscle they had to drag the plow through the rocky ground! I felt sick to my stomach.

Then, we could see the men behind the plows. Their arms were folded behind their backs, their forearms touching, and were encased in a metal sheath, which attached to a metal band around their waists. Thus locked up, the men could not move their arms in the slightest. Three men were behind the plow. Two were attempting to keep the blades digging into the ground, while the other tried to guide the women, straining their utmost to pull the blade along the furrows.

Dozens and dozens of these teams were plowing the fields. A number of guards with guns and bullwhips oversaw the groups. We spotted one whipping the women for not pulling their plow sufficiently quickly. Far behind them, we saw other groups of men and women who were obviously planting seeds. These men too, had their arms encased so that they could not use them. The women held the bags of seed, while the men sat on their butts attempting to get seed from the bags and plant them using their feet. Even further behind them were others who scooted along the ground covering up the newly planted seeds.

As we moved further along, we saw barrack style buildings, all identical. We presumed this is where they lived. An hour later, we pulled into a large entrance building. The barbed wire fence came up to it from both sides. This was the only entrance into the sprawling prison complex. Here we halted and Kasper opened our door and assisted us to step down safely. "Welcome to the Fields of Kondrat, where we attempt to Redeem the Unholy," he said giving us the party line drilled into everyone.

He led us through the entrance doors, where the Keeper, as he was called, met us. "Welcome most Holy Vessels. I have been expecting you. I am Keeper Bolek." We introduced ourselves. "Come, let me show you around our facilities and explain our methods. Elder Borys has asked me to fully explain our procedures and to allow you complete freedom to explore our rehabilitation facilities."

As we walked into the nearest barracks, we saw men, similarly bound, and women on their butts washing the stone floors. Others were attempting to do their group laundry, while others were preparing the evening meal. Keeper Bolek explained, "Here we house the Unholy, the ones who in one way or another refuse to follow our society's rules and God's laws. For the men, we must make them appreciate our Holy Vessels. Thus, we make them experience what life is like for our most Holy Vessels. You see, the metal bindings make their use of their arms impossible. They must do everything as a Holy Vessel does, with her feet. In time, they come to realize just how great a sacrifice our Holy Vessels have made so that they, our men, can be strong. In time, they come to hold our Holy Vessels in the highest regards as God has commanded from the dawn of time."

"Does this actually work?" I asked, biting my lip from saying what I really felt.

"Oh yes, Holy Vessel Bethany. One in five repent their ways and become Redeemed and are released to go about their lives, holding Holy Vessels in the highest regards and respect. Oh, yes. They do not relapse either," he replied proudly. I thought: torture by any name is still torture. Once freed from torture, no one would desire to return to it. I kept my mouth shut, however. Further, I knew that one in five would be cured or healed by using any method at all. Their method was useless.

He continued, "Now with the Unholy women, who have turned aside from being Holy Vessels, we make them see what the men must be able to do for them. We try to instill in them how hard our men work for them so that they will appreciate the Holy Gift that they have given unto men. We make them do men's work, as much as is possible. Those who had become seducers of men — those we make pull the plows, the hardest work here. Others, we make move the rocks and stones from the fields. Those Unholy women, who have committed far lesser crimes, are made to do normal chores expected of a Holy Vessel. Their crimes are in the category of refusing to help their parents with chores around the home, that sort of thing."

"Does this actually work with the women?" I asked.

"Oh yes, Holy Vessel. One in five repent their ways and become Redeemed and are released. They have accepted their responsibilities as Holy Vessels once again. I am so proud of them when they are released." He smiled broadly.

As we toured the facilities, we saw men using our style yokes carrying things to the cooks, clothes to the laundry, and all sorts of other domestic actions which needed objects to be transported. I thought it a little ironic to be seeing grown men being made to work as we who have no choice have to live. "Serves them right," Dianna commented.

"Indeed, it does," Keeper Bolek wholeheartedly replied.

"What happens if they do not do as you ask?" I asked.

"It depends on what it is. With the hardened criminals, such as the Unholy women forced to be oxen, they are whipped if they do not pull their share of the work load. However, that is the exception here. If an Unholy one does not do what is asked, they are not fed. Soon all do their chores, for they want to eat."

"I see. Hunger will convince many. Say, exactly how many Unholy Ones do you have here right now?" I asked.

He referred to a document, "Let's see, precisely twenty-two thousand five hundred and six, though one Redeemed Holy Vessel is to be released today."

"Say, could I speak with her? Is that possible?" I asked.

He led us to her bunk where she was finishing dressing in a clean Sunday Service style dress. He explained that her parents sent her the dress after he had notified them that she was Redeemed. They were coming today to pick her up. I decided to have a private conversation with her. "Hi, I am Bethany. I want to talk to you a bit. I promise that I will never say anything about what you tell me to any man. Why were you put in here in the first place?" She was perhaps thirteen years old and should have been a schoolgirl.

"I wanted to write stories for my little brother. I kept doing that instead of doing my chores around the house. Finally, mom got so angry with me that she reported it and I ended up here. I am sorry. I promise I will do all my chores first and write stories only where there is nothing else that must be done. Honest, I will." She looked pleadingly at me.

"I smiled, "You do just that. Please, write good stories for your brother!" She grinned and I rejoined the others.

Emboldened, I asked if he had records that showed just what each person's crimes were. He did and led us to his office. "Here are the official records, Holy Vessel. Shall I put it on a woman's desk for you?"

"Please, I would like to review it. Dita, Dianna, care to join me?" We three sat down on the usual sloped back chairs, while he placed the large volume on the desktop, barely above the ground. Slowly we began to read the crimes for which these people were incarcerated here.

They were categorized into men and women and then within those divisions, the crimes were further subdivided. Only a quarter of the population were women, we quickly noted. The vast majority of the women's crimes were similar to the one I just heard, blatantly not performing their domestic chores around the home. Those few in the hard core category, that is, the ones pulling the plows fell into two categories. Some were caught having sex with many men, selling their bodies as it were. The others were mentally insane. Several notations said that some were nuts and continually saw large green demons. We three immediately realized what they were seeing were their own mental images of the mantis creatures. Therapy would easily resolve their insanity.

The men's categories ran a much wider range. Many were here because they refused to accept that the women had to be helped so much. Some were here for obvious sexual based crimes. A large percentage was here because they disagreed with the religious beliefs of the society. They didn't believe that women gave their arms to them. Some swore that they had seen doktors removing them at birth. Some were indeed criminals in the usual sense, having been caught stealing or cheating others in some substantial way. A few were also classified as insane, often seeing green demons flying about.

As the supper hour approached, I realized that we had little choice but to accept Keeper Bolek's offer to stay for supper and the night. I really didn't want to stay in a prison, but the nearest village would be too far to travel yet today. Reluctantly, we agreed to accept his hospitality.

We dined in his private dining room. As expected, there were men and women's tables, though far more men's than women's. We three sat apart from the many men gathered around Keeper Bolek and some of his captains.

A young girl about our own age was our waitress. "I'm sorry that there is not any choice for your meals, Holy Vessels. You can have milk or tea." We three asked for milk and she went to fetch our meals. Other waitresses circulated among the many men. Of course, the waitresses all were inmates here, but were close to finishing their sentences, that is, Redeemed.

We watched with sympathy as she struggled bravely to serve us our meals. When she had placed the last plate before us, she whispered to me, "Please, Holy Vessel, please help us here."

I whispered back, "I will do my best to get you all out of here in time. Be patient." She thanked me and smiled, then returned to her other duties. Later, we were given a room with six beds in it. As we prepared for bed, we looked at the beds.

"Honestly, I feel guilty dirtying up three beds. It only makes more work for these poor women," I said. Dita and Dianna agreed with me, so we slept close together on one bed that night.

After a light breakfast, we climbed back into our carriage and headed on down the road for Kondrat. The fenced prison stretched on for miles, it seemed to us. A day and a half later, we pulled into the large city of Kondrat, where we settled in at our inn, mid-day. Since Kasper needed to know our next move, we got out our map to see if we needed to travel on down the road towards the coastal city of Piotr. We did. There appeared to be another low mountain that looked significant on our map. Two days later, our group pulled into a small hamlet, which was as close to this peak as we could get by carriage. Now we would enter the second part of our plan: personally inspect the most likely locations where the mantis creatures may have lived.

Chapter 14 Oh Mantis, Where Are You?

From here, we would have to travel overland on horseback. That meant also camping out and cooking our own meals. Kasper again asked me, "Are you sure that this is necessary? Are you sure that you want to do this? While men can easily camp out and rough it, this will be extraordinarily difficult for you."

"Yes, I am sure. We must get to the summit of yonder peak and the only way is overland by horse, unless you want to walk all those miles. We have a tent, cooking supplies, and food, right?" I asked.

"Yes, just as Dianna requested. We have the items loaded on four pack horses, but you realize that once we get out there in the wild, there is no turning back," he asked.

"Right, not until we get done examining the peak."

"Okay then, we will help you three as much as possible. We all know that this trip will so very hard for you, so let us know how we can help, if we are not jolly on the spot. We are accustomed to know what a Holy Vessel's needs are in towns, but none of us has ever brought one out into the wilds. Acceptable?"

"Yes, lead on. We're ready. I'm sorry that you have to do more work, saddling our horses and setting up camp. We will see if we can help with the cooking," I replied.

Men stood beside us, ready to assist us in mounting our horses, if we needed it. Dianna did, she had the least experience riding of the three of us. They held up our wooden bite blocks so that we could easily take them in our teeth and mounted themselves. Kasper led the way and off we went into this rugged, remote portion of Dorota, a craggy peak not far from one of the major forested regions.

Okay, I admit that none of us had been riding for an entire day, nor had we ridden in such rough terrain. Bushwhacking is more like what we did, picking out a path up the steep hillside, around boulders and outcropping of brown granite, twisting and turning, following a route that the horses could manage. We three allowed the men to lead the way, concentrating on just staying on our horse's back! My jaw ached from the constant pressure of biting on the wooden block. I was thankful for the lunchtime break, so were Dita and Dianna. My legs, unused to such riding, felt like a pair of sponges, and I gratefully allowed Kasper to lift me down from my horse.

While fixing lunch was a normal domestic duty, Kasper and the men waived us off, handling it themselves. "You keep up your strength. We'll fix us all a bit of lunch. Dried bread and fish plus a last of the season apple comprised lunch. No one bothered even to light a fire. All too soon we mounted up once more. On we rode ever upwards on Mount Ceske. In the late afternoon, the men began to fan out, looking for a suitable place for camp. I noticed that we were about a half day from the summit, a good sign, I thought.

They found a small clearing with some grass for the horses, but no running water. Here we stopped for the night. Once more, we graciously allowed Kasper to lift us down. Good thing, our legs sagged as they hit the ground. "Not got your horse legs yet, Holy Vessels," one man teased.

I called back, "No kidding. My legs are sponges, but give us a few more days and we'll get into shape. That's what you get for pampering us so." The men roared with laughter and began setting up camp. While we girls took turns trying to rub each other's legs, we watched as they set about making the tents and setting a fire. Quickly, it became obvious that they had not done this before either. As the first tent collapsed, everyone stopped and laughed again. "Looks like we are not the only greenhorns out here," I teased them and only added to their mirth.

Kasper said, "If you Holy Vessels don't mind, we will do the cooking on this expedition. The men and I have decided that we don't want to wait until dark to have our supper. We'll let you clean up."

I laughed, "Now that's what I call wise thinking, guys!" More laughter followed. Yet, we three were very much relieved to have their assistance. Cooking a meal right now was a bit more than we could handle. Their attempts at cooking left quite a lot to be desired, but no one complained because we were all hungry. We then did the dishes and took so long that it was getting dark when we finished. A chill was in the spring air and we three wiggled our way into our tent the minute that we were done. Lying as close to one another as we could, we tried to stay warm. Sleep was nearly impossible. No matter how we moved, rocks kept poking into our backs and sides. I suspected the men fared little better. We all looked a little tired and grumpy come morning. That breakfast was a cold one didn't help matters. An hour after sunrise, we again hit the trail.

At noon, we arrived at the summit of Mount Ceske. Here we dismounted and had a cold lunch. "Okay we are here, now what?" asked Kasper.

"Now we hunt. I am looking for a large cavern, hole, pit — for some way down into the mountain," I replied.

"How big?" asked one man.

"At least ten feet in diameter or larger. Forget three foot holes," I replied. "Probably we best scatter and search on foot. I would suspect that we ought to find it near this peak, if one is to be found here."

The ground was rocky, steeply sloping, and rugged. As requested, the men fanned out and began looking for an opening. We three decided to join the hunt as well, but at once found it very tricky going without arms. Nevertheless, we pressed on, going over to the backside, moving very slowly to avoid slipping and sliding. It would be disastrous to slip, fall, and break a leg this far from civilization. I was beginning to wonder if I was doing the right thing, bringing us all out here in search of what might be here. More than likely, we'd find nothing for all our pains.

As I reached my low point of the day, nearly falling down the side of the mountain, I heard someone calling out. His voice came from further down and to our right. Off we went in that direction, well, excruciatingly slowly I must add. By the time we got there, sliding in the loose gravel the last five feet, the others were already there, standing before a large, gaping, black hole in the side of the mountain.

"Great going. Looks promising. I guess we need lanterns now and maybe some rope. I'd go fetch them, but you don't want to wait until dark before I get them back here," I teased them. Several chuckled and headed back to our horses to fetch them. Meanwhile, we checked out the entrance. A talus slope lay immediately in front of the hole, so we came at it from the side. Several men navigated the talus and had fun sliding halfway down the slope, some fifty feet. I found this encouraging, since it meant that at some time in the past, the talus had come from the inside.

Not long after we all stood looking into the cavern's blackness, the men returned with the lanterns and rope. We allowed them to light our lanterns. Ours were made especially for a Holy Vessel. Instead of the large loop where the men could grab hold of the lantern, ours had a metal extension at right angles from its side. This we put between our teeth and thus could see where we were going. However, we had to be extra careful to keep our long hair from catching fire.

The men drew their guns. Kasper explained, "There could be wild animals inside, this could well be their winter home. You three stay behind us." In we walked. Soon, one man called out, "Looks like the stone's been worked some here." Another commented, "Yes, the sides are more like polished stone." I felt hopeful for the first time.

Some ways in, we encountered a three-way junction. "Which way?" one called out.

Between my teeth, I yelled, "Left." Slowly we all moved down that side tunnel. I don't know why they were moving so slowly, however, certainly not because of us, for once.

"Hey, opens into a big chamber," the man in front relayed back. One by one, we entered a large chamber. All sorts of debris littered the floor, several inches thick. As we stepped upon it, small clouds of powdered dust arose, along with a distinct crunching sound. "What are we walking on?" Kasper asked. Everyone stopped and began moving the stuff under our feet, trying to see what was crumbling under our weigh. No one dared touch it with their fingers, I noted.

"It looks like bones, tiny bones," one man suggested. Everyone became even more interested now.

Dianna bent down and sat her lantern on top of the debris and began moving the powder around, revealing tiny bones. "You are right guys; these are bones, baby bones. Unless I am very much mistaken baby arm bones. Look for yourselves. Will one of you please get some samples to take back for the doktor to examine? I will feel better if a doktor confirms my analysis," she said in her usual engineering tone of voice.

"Man, there's thousands of them!" one man said.

"Millions, I'd say," another man corrected him.

"They're everywhere in here. What in the blazes is this place anyway? Where are the rest of their bodies?" Kasper exclaimed. I smiled, at last I was beginning to get the proof that I needed.

Samples gathered, we retraced our steps out of the chamber and tried the tunnel on the right. Eventually it opened into another chamber. "What in heaven's name is all this?" the lead man said as he entered. Strange equipment stood near the entrance, dust lay inches thick over it. No one had ever seen anything remotely like these three pieces of machinery. That they were made of metal was about as far as we could tell. Their purpose was a total mystery, to say nothing about how they operated. Of course, Dianna never got beyond the machinery. She began an intensive study of them, while the rest of us explored further inside.

In one corner, a stack of long, thin bricks lay. What appeared to be coal lay heaped on the opposite side. Some gravel piles were closer to the strange machines. One man went to examine the bricks. "Why would anyone have weird bricks like this stacked in a cavern?" he said, and began dusting them off, coughing from the dust cloud that subsequently enveloped him. His light began reflecting off the bricks. "Gold!" he called out. "Gold bricks, hundreds of them!" Everyone rushed over to peek at the pile, all except Dianna, of course. She merely repeated that word and continued her study of the machines.

"Well, boys, it looks like you have your work cut out for you. I assume that you don't want to just leave all this gold here, now do you?" I teased them, as they continued to shout exclamations about this fantastic discovery among themselves. Now they began talking about how much was here and how they could possibly get it all back to town. Surely, the Elders would want to inspect this find first, they concluded. One man decided to return to notify the Elders for us and he left in a big hurry.

As we finally headed back to the entrance of this side chamber where Dianna was still examining the machines, she spoke up, "I believe these are smelting machines, designed to take that crude ore there in that pile," she pointed with her foot, "and using a hot fire from the coal over there," she again pointed with her foot, "these machines then create the gold ingots that you found over there." She didn't point out the stack of gold ingots, however.

"Hey, you are probably right. It makes sense, but we've never seen any machines like this anywhere on Dorota, Dianna. I wonder whose these are? Must have been here for centuries, considering the thick layer of dust on everything," Kasper replied.

Through my teeth still holding my lantern, I called out, "Let's check the other tunnel." En mass, we all headed back out and then down the center tunnel. It too opened into an even larger chamber, so large that our meager lanterns could not illuminate the whole thing. Slowly we filed inside. Suddenly the man in front screamed and fired his gun. Blam! The noise echoed for seconds around the room. Several men also near the front dropped their lanterns onto the floor, shattering them. Fortunately, the oozing oil didn't catch fire.

We three moved to the front as fast as we could and stopped short, nearly dropping our own lanterns! Before us lying across the floor was a sixty-foot long, green mantis creature. Actually, it was the shell of a dead one, long dehydrated, and now mostly a thin exoskeleton-like crust. "Don't touch it or it will disintegrate," I called out. "It's dead. Fan out, we need to thoroughly search this room," I said through my teeth. Unfortunately, I was not well understood and had to repeat it more slowly.

Things rapidly degenerated on us. Kasper and five others were here with us, the sixth had taken off to fetch the Elders. The man, who first encountered the sight and had fired his gun, had dropped his gun to the floor along with his lantern. He stood there staring at the carcass as if in a trance. His arms dangled helplessly at his sides. Two other men turned three shades of green, whirled around, and vomited, barely having time to set their lanterns down. They then collapsed on the floor, looking dazed, their arms refusing to work.

Two other men's arms began shaking violently and it was all they could do to sit their lanterns down. They looked terrified and spasms continued to shake their arms. Kasper looked like he had seen a ghost; he just stood and stared at the thing, unable to move or to take his eyes off it. At least he had already sat his lantern down, but as I watched him, his arms sagged and the gun slipped out of his hands, hitting the floor hard. We three women stood there looking at the wild reactions from the six men. Squatting down, we sat our lanterns down on the stone floor.

"What's going on?" asked Dianna. "Why are they all sick? Is there something that's poisonous in here? Why aren't we sick too?" Suddenly, she realized what was happening. "Oh!"

I motioned for Dita and Dianna to come with me over to one side away from the men. "They have just seen a real mantis creature, and it has brought back into present time some traumatic events that they have had in their past lives. Look at their arms, it's a sure sign that they are all reliving the mantis eating their arms or worse," I theorized.

"What are we going to do?" Dianna asked.

"We don't have much choice. We can't get them to the horses, nor handle making camp ourselves. So we are just going to have to run emergency therapy sessions right now. Dianna, do you remember how it's done?"

"Maybe. Can you explain it really quickly to help remind me?" I did so.

"But there are six of them and only three of us," Dita said urgently, as if I had missed this detail.

"Can't be helped. I'll take the one standing in a daze and the two who are vomiting. Dita, you take the two who are standing there with their arms shaking. Dianna, you take Kasper. Let's get started. Give them the command to close their eyes and then to go to the start of the trauma images." Quickly, we three moved to positions in front of the ones we were going to assist, and began giving them the commands.

These men had their trauma images burning vividly in their minds. They complied with our commands like little children who could not do otherwise. All around me, I heard the men's voices, some in grief, some in stark terror, others in a hopeless apathy, describing relatively similar scenes of these creatures devouring parts of their anatomy, usually their arms when they were small. Hours passed and our oil lanterns began to flicker, they were running out of oil. I wondered what we would do if they went out, leaving us it a total and utter darkness. I hastily focused my attention back on my three patients. Worry about that later.

Soon, Kasper began laughing, a sure sign that Dianna was nearly finished with him. Then, over the next half hour, one by one, all the men finally began laughing, sometimes hysterically, and their hideous traumas of the distant past vanished, along with the aches, pains, weird sensations, and attitudes they had had as a result of them.

As I ended the session with the last man, I said, "Okay, the lanterns are almost out. Please, get us out of here and back to our horses before it gets dark! We'll talk about this over supper." None needed any further encouragement, though every one of them took a last look at the shell of the creature.

Though it was dark when they finally got our camp setup and dinner done, the men chatted enthusiastically about their experiences, what they had learned about themselves, and about this unbelievable find that we had made. Supper was little better tasting than before, but we ate it anyway. Finally, sipping our tea and watching the crackling fire, I offered them an explanation.

"This afternoon, you were given the true gift that the Holy Vessel Marzena gave to her man. The giving of her arms is *symbolic* of her real gift, the gift that we three gave you men this afternoon. Words cannot easily describe this precious gift, but men can understand something such as arms more readily. Now about that creature, centuries ago, those creatures, which I call mantis creatures for want of a better name, were here in many countries across Tarra. Yes, they love to dine on female appendages, for reasons no one knows. In Dorota, they began eating all female's arms, creating a whole civilization in which no woman had arms."

"This is just speculation on my part, but after they died off, the well-established tradition has continued on down to this day. When the Elders arrive, they can give a better accounting of it. Until then, imagine an entire country like ours in which every woman has no arms, eaten by these vile creatures. What would happen to the people if suddenly baby girls began to appear with arms? Massive confusion would appear at the very least. Anyway, you have seen that you are immortal spiritual beings and that you have had other human bodies before. This is just as the Elders and our religion states, that we are all created in God's image, which cannot be a human body, for these die awfully easily." They chuckled at that.

They plied us with other questions, many of which we deferred to their Elders. One man commented, "Now I truly understand why I am always so very sympathetic to women's needs. I've been one myself, strange as that sounds. How are we to thank you, Holy Vessels? You have indeed given us a priceless gift."

"Oh, I don't know. How about doing the dishes tonight?" Everyone roared with laughter. Since it was quite dark, we then turned in for the night.

The next morning, Dianna asked how we were fixed for supplies. That we were going to have to remain here for some time was plainly obvious. It would be many days before the Elders of the High Council could get here. Kasper took stock of our remaining supplies and sent two men into town for more. They adjusted our campsite for the long haul, thankfully getting the small pebbles that had dented our backs out from under our tent. After lunch, armed with more oil in our lanterns, we all headed back into the cavern to explore that main chamber further.

We discovered a second, smaller shell of a mantis somewhat deeper in the chamber along with what had been its breeding nest. Thankfully, all the dozen eggs had long ago dried out and the shells cracked, so no chance of hatching new ones. Dianna discovered perhaps the most useful item, a map of Dorota, showing what she took to be other inhabitation sites. These she compared to our prioritized list of peaks to check and found they were all marked by us to search. We would not have missed them, though we might not have found their entrances. We had seven more cavern complexes to explore.

In her previous lifetime as Enyo, the engineer, she had been the primary person who had worked out how the Grey Creature's equipment operated. Here, she was confounded, these creatures operated in a most non-human way. We found what might be diaries and writing tools, but she could not fathom how they were to be used. It was alien technology. Having found nothing else of real interest, we then headed back to camp and began the long wait for the Elders to arrive.

As the seemingly endless days passed, we three took over the cooking of our meals, just to have something to do. Even the men were bored, stock piling more firewood than we could possibly use. I will say this, however, after their sessions, these Security Guards treated us as if we were the most holiest of women. This was nice the first day, but we three soon tired of it.

Twelve excruciatingly boring days later, we heard a cacophony of horses coming our way. At last, the High Council of Elders arrived, along with twenty more Security Guards. Our man led them straight to our camp. Their horses were lathered, they'd ridden them hard.

Elder Amadei hailed us, "Hello Holy Vessels. We came as quickly as we could. You've found alien objects?"

"Er, more than that, sir. We have indisputable proof. However, please, we must insist that only you and our six men here come with us to see for yourselves. I'll explain why as we walk." Our other guard who had brought the Elders looked crestfallen. I relented and asked him to come with us, knowing what might happen. I decided that the Elders needed to see what would happen if the average person came across this sight unprepared for it.

First, we showed them the enormous pile of bones, which Elder Amadei had already shown to a doktor, who verified that they were arm bones of a baby. Next, we showed them the stack of gold ingots and the alien machines, which Dianna was convinced somehow took the raw ore and turned it into the ingots. Finally, we led them into the main chamber where the dried shells lie. The expressions and cries were something to behold, these thirteen men now had proof positive that their memories were indeed very real.

Our remaining guard reacted as has his companions. His lantern dropped to the floor as his arms began trembling. He stood and stared dumbly at the giant creature before him. One by one, the Elders finally understood what I meant about people seeing this sight unprepared for it. I took him aside and began a therapy session on him, leaving Dita and Dianna to deal with the elated, excited, enthusiastic men.

With all of these lanterns going, Dianna took a closer look at the shells. She made a startling discovery! "Look, look at this! See, there is a nice round hole right through its head, from front to back. How strange. Let's see if the other one has it. Wow. It does too. Now why would both of these have a hole in their heads? It would likely kill them. I wonder if someone came in here and shot them, kind of like you with your guns. Maybe there was a war among creatures." I thought this was a very interesting clue to their sudden, total disappearance from Dorota.

Elder Iwan asked, "What are we going to do with all that gold? We already have more than we need in our country."

Elder Kuba of the Finance Committee suggested, "Ah, we could use it in our dealings with the Outer Lands. They seem to desire it greatly in return for their goods. We could use it to bring in more of their valuable items that our people can use." They all chatted about this aspect.

Dianna also pointed out the map, "See, we have seven more sites to check. Undoubtedly we will find more useful stuff there." The Elders were amazed and continued to discuss the ramifications of all this and what to do next.

Eventually, the guard I was working on began laughing and I ended his session. Of course, he went to look more closely at the dead creatures. Several of the Elders smiled at me as I got up and joined them. Elder Amadei bubbled with excitement, "Bethany, this has got to be the very proof of the truth that you promised us! It is amazing. However, did you know this was here? Why this peak of all the others in the highlands?"

"Tall, inaccessible peaks, otherwise, a local person might stumble into their nest. We made a list — well Dianna did — of the most likely peaks as we traveled across the highlands. This was the first likely candidate on our way back from where the highlands end and the rolling farmlands begin. Just lucky. I did not expect to find actual bodies. I would have expected that vermin would have eaten their remains long ago. Apparently not."

"Just an amazing find. Perhaps more will show up at the other seven sites. Some of us ought to come with you as you explore these others. I'm sorry that we have put you Holy Vessels to so much hardship."

"Thanks. The real question is what to do about the site. If someone who has not had our gift of therapy sees them, you've seen what can happen. I'm not saying that everyone would be so adversely impacted, but it's been uniform among the men so far. Yet, I would think that you would want the site secured," I suggested.

"Yes, most definitely. Albin should be along in a few days with a wagon load of supplies. I will station a pair of Security Guards at each site. In case of trouble, I think that one of those you have gifted ought to be at each one. That way, if the other guard should get ill, there's someone to look after him. How does that sound to you?"

"A wise choice. There is no danger of getting more adverse reactions from those we've helped. I don't believe so anyway. People will be curious, so if the other guard peeks, he'll not be ill by himself. By the way, there are quite a few of your people locked up at the Fields of Kondrat who are stuck mentally back in their mental trauma with these creatures. They call them a green monster or dragon or some such name. A simple gift of therapy will likely cure them."

"That is good to hear, Holy Vessel, very good. One thing we Elders have been discussing at length is how to deliver this precious gift to our people. We still do not see how this may be done. After today, we know it is perhaps the most important thing that we must do."

"I agree. It certainly is. I still don't have an answer to how we may do that yet. How soon should we plan to visit the next site?" I asked.

He replied, "We ought to wait until Albin arrives with the wagon. I owe it to him to have a chance to see the proof." I smiled good for him. Albin certainly did deserve the chance to see the creatures did exist.

We three girls milled around the campsite that night. Dianna wanted to discuss the ramifications of her observation of the precisely circular holes in the creature's head. "They are perfectly round, no rough edges, like something went through their heads. I've chatted with Kasper about what kind of hole their guns leave. He saw one once, rather jagged, and it broke the bone as the lead bullet entered or exited. With this case here, I observed no such disintegration of their shells, though it may have been more soft tissue there and not a hard shell."

Dita added, "Well a spear or an arrow could not have made those holes either, though I doubt that a human could ever get close enough to stab them in their heads. It took a huge force to crush them, like hundred pound stone blocks. What could have made those holes?" We chatted about this for a time, but came to no conclusion and turned in for the night.

We relaxed the next day, waiting for Albin. The Elders spent the better part of the day inside the cavern complex, studying the various items. Around suppertime, Albin finally arrived. He had to pack horse the supplies up to where we were camped and that had delayed him. Over dinner, we filled him in on what we found. At first light, he brought lanterns and had us give him a tour.

"Wow! It really isn't just my imagination running wild. They really did exist. This is just incredible, Bethany, just incredible. Somehow all of our people need to see this!" he exclaimed with a youthful exuberance. Dita explained what had happened when the guards had seen it and he then looked crushed. "Honestly, they need to see it, but I guess not until they have received your precious gift."

When we rejoined the others, camp had been broken. Two guards were to remain and the Elders left them a good supply of food. I felt a bit sorry for the men, though. They were going to be bored out of their minds, just sitting around out here in the wild near the top of a mountain. A day's journey and we were back on the cobblestone road and with our carriage. The Elders insisted that we three ride in the carriage until the ground became too rough for the carriage. Ah well, so much for the horseback riding.

That night we stayed at an inn and the first thing we three did was take a hot bath. We slept soundly, making up for the nights of ill sleep on the rocky ground. At daybreak, we were on the road once more, another daylong, boring carriage ride to the next jumping off point, where we could finally ride the horses up the side of the next mountain.

This became the pattern for the rest of the summer. Boring carriage rides to the next site, followed by an exciting horse ride up the mountain, lengthy ground searches for the entrance, and the payoff of finding another mantis nest. Yes, by early fall, we had found them all — well all that we knew about from their own maps. I decided not to look for other sites on other likely mountains. Eight sites was sufficient proof.

What was found? Plenty. Eight stashes of gold ingots, a huge fortune by Outer Lands standards, gold, which would be slowly moved from the site down into the banks. More maps, baby bones, undecipherable dairies and tools, which continued to baffle Dianna. We found five more carcasses in various states of decomposition. As nearly as Dianna could tell, all five had the same peculiar round holes in their heads. However, we gained a terrific clue at one site. Lying on the floor close to a mantis shell was a skeleton. All flesh had long ago decomposed, leaving only the bones, where the creature had died. Yet, the skeleton was quite unusual. Dianna, with assistance from Albin, measured the length of its leg bones. She estimated the bipedal creature stood at least eight feet tall, perhaps more. Curiously, its feet only appeared to have three enormous toes.

All three of us had a good guess whose remains this might have been, but we only talked about it among ourselves, when we could not be overheard. "That has to be the remains of a Grey Creature — the height and the three toes — dead giveaway!" Dita exclaimed.

"Perhaps what happened here was that the Grey Creatures discovered this continent and launched a surprise invasion, using their blaster weapons to kill the mantis creatures," Dianna theorized. As Enyo, she had made a careful study of the Grey Creature weapons that we had recovered. "The blasters would very likely make that kind of a clean, perfectly round hole."

"So the Grey Creatures ended the mantis control over this whole continent — well giant, isolated island. I bet they figured the people here would eventually recover. Unfortunately, they didn't. Now what do we do?" Dita summarized what we three now suspected happened here.

"It's getting chilly at night again, fall's on its way. Still, I need to meet with the rebels," I replied. "They are the last ingredient in this whole mix. Meeting with them is going to be tricky. Ideas?"

"Expect a whole lot of anger from the rebels," Dita replied. I grinned, that was likely to be a gross understatement.

When we returned to the Elder College at Wit, we presented our case to the High Council. "Elders, no solution for the mess that we are in can be complete without somehow involving all the rebels. We must meet with them and find out their true points of view, before a solution for us can be honestly developed. We know that you consider this a terrifically dangerous move for us to meet with them. You have our safety as your uppermost concern, fortunately for us. However, we cannot take Security guards with us; the rebels will only likely attack us or simply hide so that we cannot ever find them. We dare not take any Elders with us; your lives would be in dire jeopardy."

"However, I believe that, though they are rebels, they will not harm three young Holy Vessels. Honestly, I think that we will be safe enough meeting with them," I stated our case, hoping for the best.

"Well, we simply cannot send Holy Vessels into the wild. What if you need some help? There will be no hands to assist you. Please, you must take at least one man along with you," Elder Roman of the Security Committee insisted.

"I can't disagree with you on that! We certainly did need much help in our mountain searching. How about allowing Albin to come with us? He is not yet an Elder, so his life should not be in jeopardy," I suggested. "Besides, he is quite used to lending us a hand."

They agreed to allow us to meet with the rebels, as long as Albin was always with us. When Albin found out that he was going with us, he let out a loud cry! "Wow! Thank you for having me come along! I won't miss all the action. I really felt badly when you took off this spring and I was left behind. I'll help you with anything you need. Just let me know!"

Chapter 15 Meeting the Rebels

Early September, we walked into Wit and had lunch at the inn in which we had met Rafal, the rebel, last year. He was our only contact thus far with these illusive people. True, we could have tried riding our horses into the depths of the dense woods, hoping somehow to come across them, but I wanted to use that method only as a last resort. That kind of trip would be very hard on us, with only Albin along to be our hands.

After four unsuccessful lunches, on Friday, while we sat there eating a delicious stew, Rafal cleverly slipped into the man's seat across the table from we three. "Good afternoon. I presume that you are looking for me?"

I couldn't hide my relief. "You bet we are! I'll keep this brief. We three desperately need to meet with all the rebels. It is incredibly important and vital that we discuss some extremely important things that have happened over the summer."

Rafal teased me, "You must have a very loud voice, Bethany, if you want to speak to tens of thousands of us at the same time." We giggled in our girlish way. "Seriously, there are many groups of us out there. I could arrange a meeting of representatives of many of them. However, how can I guarantee that this is not a trap? That the Elder's Security Guards will not attempt to track us back to our camps or even attack us while we meet with you?"

"Yes, you are right. You set it up anyway that you feel best. Get as many of the key leaders together as possible. Let us know the when and where. We will only bring along one young man, who is not yet an Elder, to help us with things we cannot manage. Will this be acceptable to you and your people?"

"Anywhere of our choosing? Anytime?" he asked quite surprised. "The Elders will permit this?"

"Yes, I have their permission to meet with you as long as Albin can come along to help us. As you know, there are some things we cannot manage by ourselves." I played the handicapped card, knowing that most people would go along with that argument.

"Yes, that is true. Okay, he is not an Elder at this time. No one will deny you a helper. We are not sadistic. It will take some time to arrange this meeting. Meet me here on October 5 for lunch. By then, I may have a time and place for you. Honestly, Bethany, is there any real hope for our people, I mean we rebels?"

"Honestly, Rafal, there absolutely *must* be. A solution to our country's problem cannot be solved if we leave your people out of the solution. However, I must talk with them, Please tell them this meeting is vitally important to them all. Please."

"I will do as you ask. October 5, lunch. Thank you. Good afternoon." He left as suddenly as he had appeared. We chatted and finished our lunch before returning to our dorm room. We now had a month to kill, and I suggested that we spend some time with our families; Dianna could alternate between our two families. Elder Amadei agreed, but asked us to come before the High Council tomorrow at one.

The thirteen members were all smiling as we entered. Elder Iwan did the honors this time. "On behalf of the High Council, it is my great pleasure to present this award, a small token of our gratitude for all that you have done for us, yet again." They added six more dangling green emeralds to our fourth tier on our earrings, leaving only the two in the middle where we would add the red rubies from our husbands when we got married. They meant well but we swore that now our ears really were being pulled off. Nonetheless, they looked spectacular, and no other woman in Dorota had earrings as full and complete as ours. Everywhere we would go, our earrings would be noticed, and there could be no doubt that we were extremely important Holy Vessels. Since Dianna had helped, even though she was not from Dorota, the Elders gave her a starting set of earrings. Three diamonds formed the traditional first tier. They added three emeralds as honorary education level, since she had already displayed an uncommon intelligence, and then added three more emeralds for her third level. Dianna was very pleased indeed.

We spent three weeks with our families, who were thrilled with our earrings, since they, more than anything else, told them that we had been doing something extremely important. Elders seldom gave out their green emerald awards, and ours were awash in green. However, having been mostly on our own for over a year, we did feel strange back in our parent's home helping with the mundane household chores. Dita and I were actually relieved to finally head back to our dorm room at the Elder College at Wit. I guess you could say that we were growing up quickly.

At noon on the fifth, we waited patiently at the inn, while our waitress took our order for stew. In fact, we loved the stew here at this inn. Once more, Rafal slipped in across from us silently, removed his hat, and said hello, chatting about the fall weather. After we were served and could talk without being overheard, he explained.

"A dozen of the leaders have agreed to meet with you, under the following conditions. You three and this Albin come alone. No attempt must be made to follow you. In three days, be here for lunch. A coach will arrive outside; get into it after you dine. You will travel by coach for that day and the next. Yes, you will be staying two nights at inns along the way. Then, you will be given horses to ride. However, I am afraid that you will have to be blindfolded and your horses led for another long day to the arranged meeting place. There you will have your opportunity to meet with twelve rebel leaders. Is this acceptable to you?"

"Perfect. Thank you Rafal," I replied.

"Good. See you in three days, then." Again, he left as silently as he came. Rafal was a master of blending in, and no one paid any attention to his arrival or departure.

We told the Council what we were doing and that we would be gone at least a week, perhaps two. While they again attempted to talk us out of this, citing the incredible dangers involved, they allowed us to take the trip. We packed light, knowing that Albin would have to be carrying our things for us, especially since we would be going by horse part of the way. Our few things we jammed into one pack, which Albin couldn't believe. He filled his own pack with his clothes. He fastened our cloaks for us and made sure our heavier boots were secure and then carried our pack and his, as we four walked the short way into Wit. The day was crisp, but clear. Admittedly, I was a little anxious, so were Dita and Dianna.

Again, at the inn, we ate our stew and when we left, there was a solitary carriage waiting for us. The driver merely nodded to us, as Albin opened the door and helped us inside, stowing the two packs under the bench seats. No one else was inside. I had rather hoped that Rafal would be riding along with us, but we were alone as the carriage pulled out onto the cobblestone road. We noticed that we headed south to Bazyli and then took the east road, which ultimately led to Kondrat, many miles distant.

"I bet we are going to the Turk Wood," Albin concluded. Once more, we stared out of the windows as the traveling boredom set in once more. A day and a half later, we stayed at a small village inn. Here we expected to be transferred to horseback. As we four ate our evening meal, Rafal mysteriously appeared, sitting down beside Albin, who was startled by his sudden appearance.

"Hi. Good to see you, Rafal. I'd hoped you would have been riding in the carriage with us — you know, to help relieve the monotony of long carriage rides," I teased him.

"Ah, my fair. Could not be helped. I had to make sure that you were not being followed. It seems that the Elders are following our request. I've seen no signs of anyone following you. Sleep well, tomorrow will be a long day on horseback." Again, he slipped away before we could chat further.

The next morning, Albin brought our two bags down with him, when we four got our breakfast. This time, we saw Rafal there already eating. He waved to us, motioning for us four to join him. "Eat well, long day ahead of us," he hinted.

After dining, we walked to the edge of the village, where six men waited along with a number of horses. Strong arms lifted us up and onto the horses, no one bothered to ask us if we could mount ourselves, however. Next, white strips of cloth were tied around our heads, blindfolding us. It was obvious that they did not want us to remember the route we were taking and thus lead Security Guards to the meeting place with the expansive Turk

Wood.

Then, the horses began moving. I honestly disliked this part enormously, an entire day of blindfolded riding along, like I was a mere sack of potatoes. Probably, we were some twenty miles from the inn. That was my best guess, though we could have been riding in circles all day for all that I knew. At last, the horses stopped and our blindfolds removed.

It was dark, but I could see that we were in the middle of a forest town of some kind. In the dim illumination, I could make out the shapes of a number of wooden buildings scattered about, certainly not in the highly organized squares of all the other towns in Dorota. We were standing before a large wooden building and Rafal explained, "Welcome to our only inn. I am afraid that you will find the accommodations not what you are familiar with, but it is the best that we can offer. This is a rebel town, you know. Come on. Let me show you around and where you will be staying. Dinner is waiting for us." He opened the door and we four went inside.

The roughhewn split log floor creaked as we walked. This main room was perhaps thirty foot square, with many tables and benches, all crude wooden structures. We spied only three of our familiar women's tables in one section and Rafal led us to them. This immediately suggested that there were going to be few armless women here with us. We five sat down, after Rafal and Albin undid our cloaks. The room was conspicuously empty.

After we were seated, a woman in her mid-twenties came bouncing out from a side door. She had light brown hair that fell part way down her back, a brightly colored dress with an enormous amount of embroider work depicting numerous wild flowers. Her eyes were bright and she had a cheery disposition. However, we four stared not at this, but at her arms! She was a normal woman, with arms and hands intact.

"Hi, I'm Kasia, your waitress for your stay. Welcome to Rebel One — that's what we call this inn. Of course, it's the only inn here, but no matter. We have tea, milk, and deer stew. I hope that will be acceptable."

"Hi, Kasia, I'm Bethany. This is Dita, Dianna, and Albin. Sure sounds good. We are starving. Our guides forgot to mention that we'd skip lunch," I teased Rafal, who smiled.

"Coming right up!" She whisked around, twirling her dress, showing off her exquisite needlepoint. A bit later, her arms holding a large tray filled with bowls and mugs and silverware, she reentered the dining room and rapidly set them before each of us. "Holler if you need anything else. I'm out back doing the dishes." Again, she couldn't resist showing off her dress, as she twirled around and headed back.

"Well, why am I not surprised to see women with arms out here?" I said, using my toes to grab a hold of the wooden spoon.

"I was," Dita exclaimed. "Rafal, I am so glad that somehow you have at least one woman who has not been brutalized!"

He smiled, "Yes, out here, I am very much afraid that your kind is in the vast minority. That door over there leads to our rooms. For you women, please use only room Number One. Albin is to stay in the one next to yours, Number Two. All the other rooms have chest-high door latches, and I'm afraid that you would not be able to operate their mechanisms. Around here, armless women must be careful of where they go; they can become trapped and unable to operate some of our normal mechanisms."

"Tomorrow, you are welcome to come here for breakfast at any time of your choosing. You may then wander freely outside and see our town, even meet some of the people. The leaders will meet with you in this room at ten in the morning. Will you be comfortable with these arrangements?"

"Oh of course, silly. I love her dress. The hours she must have spent making it, gosh. It is beautiful. Thanks again, Rafal, for everything. Say, this deer stew is tasty, kind of got a wildish taste to it."

"Yes, we must eat what the land provides for us. The unexpected grains last winter saved many lives here. Our people know that it was you two who arranged for the grain. Thus, you will find yourselves more welcome here than one would expect. However, I have one caution for you three. Around here, your kind is somewhat rare. Do not expect that others will be quite so observant of your special needs. You may need to ask for assistance when you need it."

"That's why I am here," Albin broke in, "I am supposed to be their hands."

Rafal chuckled, "Fine lad. Well, I'm due elsewhere. Good night, ladies, gent. See you in the morning." He hastily downed his last bite and left the inn. Obviously, we could not eat as swiftly as an armed person could and took twice as long as he had to finish ours. Since it was dark, we decided to find our rooms and get some sleep, promising to rise early and see some sights.

Our room was relatively crude by the standards of Dorota. The bed was large enough for the three of us. Three sloped back chairs and one low desk and chest of drawers were present. An oil lantern blazed on top of the low desk where we could get at it. However, we noticed three other oil lamps hanging up high from the walls where a normal person could get to them, but not us. Fortunately, those were not lit. After using the chamber pot, we three hit the sack, anxious for daybreak.

The room had no windows and we overslept. It took us time to change into our finest dresses, those that we wore on Sundays. It was nine when we finally entered the still empty dining room. Kasia was waiting for us, "Morning sleepyheads. Ready for some breakfast?"

She wore a different dress this morning, just as heavily embroidered as her other one. This one was filled with deers and trees. She brought us our food and a pot of hot tea. Albin saw immediately that he would have to assist us with this, pouring our three mugs with the hot brew.

When we finished, we still had a little time to peek at the forest town.

Stepping outside was shocking, nothing like we had ever seen in anywhere else in Dorota. All the buildings were roughhewn logs; the street, dirt. In many ways, it was like stepping back into time to a rural village. Yet, there were people about: men, women, and children playing in the street. Normal women and young girls, we noted immediately. Indeed, we saw hardly anyone like us. Many waved to us as they passed by running their own errands. Above the homes, tall distant trees, colorful in their autumn colors framed the rustic scene. I wish we had Diana here with us — the fabulous painter and close friend of Enyo's — to paint this incredibly aesthetic, picturesque scene.

We were still admiring the view, when Rafal appeared at the inn's door. "It's time. The dozen are gathered and await you, Bethany." Evidently, there was a back door to the inn. When we re-entered a dozen men and women now sat at the tables. One sat over on the low tables, where we were to sit. Albin took our cloaks and we three headed to our spots at the low table. He quietly joined us at our left.

Kasia entered bringing hot tea for everyone. Again, Albin poured our tea and then poured tea for the other armless woman who sat apart from us. She nodded to him as he filled her mug.

I counted sixteen people here, not the dozen promised, curious. Rafal stood and said, "I will introduce those who called you here today." To us, he said, "For security reasons, we will only use first names, you can understand why. This is Bethany, Dita, and Dianna, who is from the Outer Lands. Their assistant, Albin. Ladies, I'll introduce these leaders, each of whom represents their group. When I call your name, will you please rise a moment so that Bethany can see who goes with which name. Thanks." He began calling off the men's names. "Antoni, Bogumil, Waclaw, Nikifor, Cyryl, Gabrys, Michal, Leslaw, Iwo, Jakub. Of course, I'm Rafal. Our women leaders: Ela, Hanna, Lidia, and Waleria." I noticed these four women had arms; they were normal women, obviously born out here in the woods, safe from the doktor's scalpels.

"Finally, in attendance is our Master Planner, Ania." The armless woman on our right rose and nodded to us. She had short brown hair, easy to manage by herself, and sharp, bright, brown eyes. Her face was angelic, extremely attractive. She was probably seventeen, I guessed. Her bosom was more filled out than ours were. I wondered what a Master Planner was.

"Bethany, I give you the floor." Rafal sat down. I rose and took a deep breath. I sensed anger, antagonism, mingled with some curiosity in the faces staring back at me.

"Thank you all for answering Rafal's request from me to meet today. I swear, if Dita and I get any more special awards from the High Council, our ears will fall off." I grinned and watched for the effect I hoped this brought. Quite a few around the room chuckled. All glanced at our earrings, which is what I desired. This let them know that we were not just a bunch of ordinary

Dorota women. From the sheer number of emeralds, the special awards, it was clear to everyone that we were somehow important women. Whether or not that meant anything to them was irrelevant.

"From our birth, Dita and I have known that it was our doktors who amputated our arms immediately after birth." I paused and allowed them to whisper their surprise. Normal women in Dorota would go their whole lives without knowing this fact.

"Further, the Elder's voice does not in any way hypnotize nor mesmerize us, never has, never will. We are immune to their voice commands. We make and follow our own council." Again, I paused briefly to allow them to whisper among themselves. This would not be quite so startling, as I suspected that many of them were also unaffected by the Elder's voice. Yet, I wanted them to know that we were not brainwashed women.

"Then why are you still supporting these butchers of women?" Antoni angrily interrupted me.

"Yes, if you know they cut off your arms and those of a half million other women who still live, ignoring the millions of the past, why are you not here asking us to murder these butchers who call themselves doktors?" yelled an even angrier Waclaw.

"The Elders control them. They know what's going on and are the ones most responsible. I say butcher all of these damned Elders! Kill every one of them! They are the ones who have turned our millions of countrymen and women into hypnotized slaves!" screamed Nikifor, beads of saliva flying from his mouth, like venom from a snake.

"Any of us who speak the truth are thrown into their prison slave camp, the Fields of Kondrat! I say kill them all; free our prisoners," yelled Leslaw.

The room erupted into a wall of similar violently angry yells and cries, a bit daunting, but Dita and I both expected this. I kept my composure and met their eyes one after another, finally alighting on Ania, their Master Planner. She alone was not fomenting violence. Indeed, she had not said a single word. Her eyes met mine, and her facial expression was something like, "Now what are you going to do?"

"We have to live like primitive wild animals out here in the deepest of woods. Otherwise our girl children will suffer the same fate as you have," Ela raised her voice over the others.

"Yeh, right, forced to live like wild animals, hunted by their Security Guards, shot and killed if we resist," yelled Jakub.

"Kill the doktors! Kill the Elders! Take back Dorota!" Iwo began chanting. Others quickly picked up his chant, until all the leaders, except Rafal and Ania, were yelling it as loudly as they could, fists pounding the air above their heads. I smiled and allowed them to vent their emotions. They would eventually calm down. I noticed that Ania's eyes never left me; she faced me without the slightest flinch. Curious.

At last, their anger vented, and one by one, they sat down and became quiet again. Only then did I speak. "Thank you all for your heartfelt expressions of the anger and hatred you have for what has happened to our people." A sea of mostly dumb-looking expressions faced me; this was not what they had expected that I would say.

"One of you has pointed out the most important factor that any one of us has going for us all. Truth. Yes, I believe in a simple belief: the truth shall set you free. It has been Dita and my task these many months in uncovering the real truth behind Dorota and our society and its ways, the real truth." I had their attention now.

"You only know a part of that truth. Yes, for centuries now, the doktors have been amputating the arms of baby girls at birth. Most of the doktors hate this and feel horribly guilty about doing it, yet they are forced to do this by the Elders. This, it seems, you already know quite well. Am I right?"

"Hell yes we know. Some of us and our parents have actually witnessed this butchery of our children! Many of us are also unaffected by the voice of the Elders as well," Hanna called out and was seconded by many other voices.

"Yes, all this is true, absolutely and factually true. The Elders force the doktors against their will to amputate the arms of female babies at birth, keeping it a secret from the parents and everyone else. I asked myself why? *Why* should these men want to do this thing?"

"They are all insane butchers, sadists, evil bastards," screamed Iwo.

"I thought so at first, but then I met with the Elders. Dita and I have lived with them, talked at great lengths with the Elders on the High Council about why they feel compelled to do this to a half million women. We found them rather the opposite of what we had expected. Yes, Dita and I expected to find the Elders were indeed a bunch of sadistic butchers, who took insane pleasure in the suffering of women. There are plenty of men like that in the Outer Lands. One such group, those of the Church of Jehosanity, tortured poor Dianna here by cutting off her fingers one at a time, and then her hands, leaving her to die from gangrene poisoning. We were also kidnaped and sent back to the Outer Lands with these vile men, but we escaped and rescued Dianna. Our doktors managed to save her life, just barely, though she lost what little remained of her arms. Yes, there are true sadists and butchers in this wide world of ours!"

I noticed that Ania had a strange reaction to my mention of these men. I swear that she turned livid, but only for a moment. Her face returned to the quiet, patient, unreadable Ania. Strange.

"Yes, I know evil sadistic men when I see them. Yet, Dita and I found that our Elders on the High Council were far from being evil sadistic men. Rather, they were deeply troubled by what they saw that they must do to keep our entire country from falling into complete anarchy and chaos. Think what would happen, if tomorrow, they completely stopped their mesmerism, stopped amputating women's arms, and told everyone that they had been doing all this for centuries. What would be the results?"

"They'd kill the doktors and Elders! They'd finally get what they deserve!" hollered Iwo.

"Yes, they most certainly would at that, but what would happen after that? Remember, the men are no longer hypnotized into believing that women gave them their arms somehow — that they must be kind and considerate and helpful to all women."

Ania finally spoke up, surprising me and the others in the room. "She speaks truth. Chaos would follow at once, a total disruption of the entire country. Lawlessness would prevail, with the killings of doktors and Elders everywhere. Who would then lead our people? Leaderless, nothing but mass confusion would result. No one would be planning where to ship the farmer's grains; fish would rot in the warehouses on the coast for lack of orders to be filled. She is right, if they stopped and told everyone the truth, our country would be destroyed, as we know it today. In time, we would be able to elect new leaders, who, by force of arms and wills, would bring order. We should then prepare for a score of chaos years."

I resumed, "This I cannot and do not want to happen. I love all of you and our people too much to want to see their lives totally ruined in the chaotic aftermath. Yet, this is *not* the whole truth, no, not by a long shot!" Here, I took a calculated gamble.

"There is yet a more basic, underlying truth to be discovered. Dita and I asked ourselves why? *Why* would these men still be doing all this down through the centuries? We went in search of this most fundamental truth. In doing so, we uncovered two of the most fundamental truths behind our entire country and religion. No, make that three truths, one is obvious, though you may not realize its critical importance just yet."

"First, we are all immortal spiritual beings; we are not our human bodies. These we inhabit for a time. Our religion says that we were created in God's image. That image cannot be these bodies we see here, they die easily and are short lived. God is immortal and so are we. As time goes by, we inhabit these bodies. The importance of this will soon be revealed."

"Second, I am going to tell you a story, a story that some of you may find extremely upsetting, appalling, and incredibly disgusting, a story that we can *prove* happened. More than two centuries ago, on our continent, and in secret from our people there lived a number of strange alien creatures. Their size ranged from fifty to eighty feet long. They looked like some kind of giant praying mantis and were green in color." I noticed several gasps from the group. Ania reacted the most of anyone present; hers was closer to a scream than a gasp. Her eyes became riveted on me.

"These creatures took control of our world, and their favorite food was dining on the arms of newborn baby girls. They ate them all; not a single girl in Dorota was spared. If those in power did not go along with them, they were simple eaten whole. After many years, all the women who live here in Dorota grew up and had no arms. Those in power, presumably the Elders — though of this I have no proof at all — did all that they could to make life more bearable for our poor women. Marvelous inventions were invented by them to make it easier for us to read and write, to feed ourselves, to cook, wash, and even carry items — all designed to ease the horrid burden that we bore. Imagine an entire country so dominated, so controlled by these ultra-powerful mantis creatures, which could not be killed by any weapon that we possessed, tragic in every sense of the word."

"Then one day the mantis creatures stopped coming to eat the baby arms. The Elders and doktors had to make a decision about what to do. *Fearful* that they would return at any time, they, rightly or wrongly, decided to amputate the arms. Perhaps they wanted to spare a grown woman the horrible trauma of facing a giant mantis creature returning to eat their arms, when they were adults. Yes, it is much, much more difficult to adapt to life, if one loses ones arm as an adult, as opposed to losing them as a baby. Right or wrong, they continued the practice down unto this very day. Always, they wondered how they might safely stop this practice, but they have never found a way that would not destroy our country."

"Where's the proof of this fairy tale?" Cyryl called out. Several others backed him. Over half were strangely silent; two had turned an off shade of green. One woman ran to the corner of the room and vomited. I'd expected to see some reactions like this.

"This past summer, we three and Albin here, went in search of where these mantis creatures used to live. We found eight of their nests and some fairly well preserved dead mantis bodies." The commotion this revelation created was wild. Everyone began talking at once. Ania stared at me so hard that I thought her eyes would bore a hole in my head. Strange.

"We demand to see this for ourselves," Cyryl called out. Others agreed with him.

"I've only told you of *two* of the three truths. Patience. The first truth is that we are immoral spiritual beings, which have occupied many human bodies over the years. What does this have to do with these mantis creatures? Let me explain what happened when we found the first set of mantis remains. We had with us seven Security Guards helping us. When those seven first saw the remains, two vomited on the spot and were ill. Two of them had their arms grow weak, dropping their lanterns and guns. Others stood and stared in a complete catatonic state. Two turned quite greenish."

Several men looked at Hanna, who had vomited. Others noticed two men were very ill at ease, with a greenish hue about their faces. Several seemed to be having difficulties with their arms working properly. Cyryl looked about and became confused by what he saw among his peers.

"The trauma that one of us experienced at the mandibles of these mantis creatures is still within those of us who had their arms eaten by these vile creatures. Have any of you experienced strange aches and pains in your shoulders? Anyone have bouts where your arms seem weak?" I rattled off several more symptoms that the amputees had experienced. More of them began to show reactions now.

"Yes, all seven had wild reactions upon merely gazing upon the centuries old, dead carcasses of the mantis creatures. Some may just say, oh it was a disgusting sight that made them ill. Yet, these men were suffering, remembering vaguely what had happened to them in their past. Indeed, when I visited the Fields of Kondrat, I examined the reasons people were being held there. Quite a few were called insane because they were convinced that giant green demons, dragons, and monsters were after them. They are right, the monsters were — only that happened to them hundreds of years ago; they have their time sense mixed up — that's all that's wrong with them."

"Now, then, I come at last to the third fundamental truth of which I spoke earlier. Let me explain the misunderstanding that has been taught to us for so long. Dita and I are young women of Dorota, born here and of here, your young Holy Vessels. Why do people call us Holy Vessels instead of simply young women? Our teachings say, 'As men and women grew old and passed on, new men and women came forth from his Holy Vessels.' From us doth spring new life as it has since the beginning." I began using the Elder's words from their power sermon.

"Later on, 'God saw that men needed even greater strength, power, and stamina, because they needed to now support themselves and their families.' Later, 'One of God's Holy Vessels' — I call your attention to whom it was that said this — 'one of God's Holy Vessels, who was called Marzena, spoke unto God. 'Lord, my man, Jurek, is a good and kind man, a farmer. Yet, I can see that he needs to be stronger. Please, my Lord, take my arms from me and use them to strengthen Jurek so that he may be strong enough for the task. I do not need them and Jurek needs them so much more than I do.' God heard the prayer from his Holy Vessel, and so it was that God took the arms from his Marzena and fashioned them into more ribs for her husband Jurek. Thus made stronger and more powerful, Jurek was at last able to sustain his Holy Vessel and family, more able to tend his fields, and produce more food.'"

"That is a load of ox crap!" Cyryl called out.

"Oh, I agree, Cyryl! Who made that sacrifice? Women, of which Marzena was the first. Yes, I know very well how they implement this sacrifice on Dorota today and for the last many hundreds of years. Female babies have their arms amputated at birth."

"In other cultures and other lands, doing this to helpless babies is considered a heinous crime. Look at how you view all this here in Dorota.

You all were quite angry about the doktors and Elders who do this here. I agree, it is a crime of great magnitude against women. I'm sure that not one of you here today doesn't think this is so. But the Elders claim that it is justified, our culture will be destroyed if they do not. This has been done since the dawn of time. It is part of our religion. I have heard those words put forth from our Elders in the past."

"I am not here to judge or make less of anyone or charge anyone with crimes. I am here to ask you to look deeper into our very own religious teachings. Marzena asked God, 'Please, my Lord, take my arms from me and use them to strengthen Jurek so that he may be strong enough for the task.' This statement has come down to you through the ages, from the dawn of time. Have you ever considered that it is a metaphor? That it is *symbolic* of what Marzena was offering?"

"Before I continue, I am not the body that you see sitting before you. I am created in God's image. God's image cannot be this fleshly body that you see here. If it were, God would be long since dead! God is not a fleshly body, nor are any of us — we who are created in his image. We are all immortal spiritual beings as is our God, our Creator. Yes, God has given us these fleshly bodies to inhabit for a time, but you and I are not these fleshly bodies." I needed this point driven home solidly.

"Okay, if we are not these fleshly bodies, what does this say about Marzena and her offering to God? I say unto you that she was offering something more powerful, more intimate, and more significant than mere fleshly arms. She gave something of herself to make her man stronger, more able. That is precisely what I am doing here for you. I am giving something precious of me unto you so that you, the leaders of our rebels can be stronger, and it sure isn't my arms! Already Dita and I have given this precious gift to all the Elders and to a number of Security Guards, who became ill just viewing the mantis remains and to Albin here. You may ask Albin here just how precious the gift has been to him. Dita and I have already given our gift unto Dianna, who, with bleeding stubs where her hands had been, used them to help us, total strangers, escape from Pope Leo's yacht."

"Yet, when you receive this precious gift, you have a greater responsibility to bear. God then said unto Jurek, who hath received Marzena's gift, 'I can see that by the sacrifice of worthy Marzena, you are now blessed with part of her strength and you are now able to survive well. However, Jurek you must honor her sacrifice unto you. From this day forward, you must love her, cherish her, and help her, as you have never done before. Thou shalt never betray her by lusting after other women. Thou shalt be true to her and to her alone. Thou shalt not lie, covet what another has, steal that which does not belong to you, and fight with other men whose Holy Vessels have likewise made their sacrifice. Nor should thou become a glutton over the bounty, which thou art now capable of producing because of the gift Marzena has given unto you and you alone. Thou shalt honor and cherish the new life that Marzena brings forth as they are part of each of you. If you will do these things, then you are worthy of viewing my Creation and of entering my realm.'"

"Soon Dita and I will give each of you our spiritual gift from God. Once you have received it, you will be stronger, but you will also be asked to take up more responsibility for our people. If you fail to step up and be responsible, as God said, 'If you fail to do these, I will take back Marzena's sacrificial gift to you, Jurek, and allow you both to die off like my first creations of the Unholy man and woman, which I have forsaken as unworthy.'"

"As our teachings go, Jurek did not abandon others, as I hope and pray you will not either. Elder Borys asked me three key questions. 'How is it that we can find no records of anything like therapy in all our archives? How is it that you come to know of this? Perhaps you have had contact with outsiders?' You have that record in Marzena's request of God. How do Dita and I know this? We are of Marzena; we are your Holy Vessels. We, like Maezena, are giving our gift freely unto you, our men. Yes, we have had contact with outsiders, Pope Leo and his vile men, and the young woman of Velona, who gave of herself that we might be saved. None of that makes us any less Holy."

"At this time the High Council has received our precious gift. They most desperately want to find a way to put an end to the suffering of women, but in a way that will not result in the destruction of our country. Dita and I will give our gift to you. Once that has been done, then if you desire to see the actual remains of the mantis creatures, we will see that you can. For your own mental well-being as well as physical, we must insist that you receive our gift *before* you look upon them. After that, we hope that you too will step up to help us find a way to put an end to all the suffering everywhere on Dorota. Thank you for hearing me. That is all." I sat down at last, and sipped my now quite cold tea.

Cyryl asked, "Did you find anything else at these nests?"

Dianna rose to answer that one, giving me a much-needed break. "Yes, we found maps of Dorota, showing the location of your seven largest cities and the locations of their eight nests. We also found some strange machines, made of metal. I have worked out that they were used to take raw gold ore and refine them into gold ingots. We did find many gold ingots there as well. Oh yes, and we found mountains of baby arm bones, millions of them. Ghastly, if you ask me."

Rafal rose, "It's lunch time. I suggest that we let Kasia do her thing. I'm starving. We can discuss this over our meal."

"Albin, can you help us eat quickly? We need to get Hanna and Michal into a therapy session right away!" I asked. He was very happy to oblige. Shortly, we led Hanna, who looked very ill indeed, and Michal to our room, where it was quiet. I left Dianna to answer their questions and to handle any who developed bad symptoms in our absence.

Hanna was stuck in the middle of having her arms eaten by the mantis creature. When it finally blew, three other later times when a doktor had removed her arms also blew. She didn't stop laughing for nearly twenty-four hours, so great was her win. Michal was also stuck back in time when he saw the mantis creatures. Dita finally got him through it, and he too blew off two other times when a doktor did the surgery, which was far less traumatic than seeing the giant green creature coming at him, mandibles clicking. We rejoined the others for supper.

We watched the reactions of those who had not yet gotten their "gift," as they chatted with the laughing pair. Our two patients were very happy to relate their experiences. I just hoped that didn't trigger any more wild reactions tonight. I was tired and hungry. Finally, one by one, the leaders left, though I didn't know where they were staying, certainly not at this inn.

Curiously, Ania remained behind. Once everyone had left but us, Ania came over to me and sat down on a man's chair opposite me. She looked me squarely in my eyes and asked, "Just who are you anyway? While your body, like mine, is of Dorota, you are not from here. I know that! It is plainly obvious that you come originally from the Outer Lands — I mean you must have had other previous lives out there too. So who are you two anyway? You are strangely familiar. It's as if I should know you both — no, maybe all three of you. Who are you?" She looked at Dianna strangely. "Around this country, I know of no one who could look at an alien piece of machinery and figure out that it was used to refine gold ore. They are not that smart. Yet, I once knew one such person who damn well could and did just that. Her name was Enyo. So I beg of you, tell me just who you three are, please!"

Dianna let out a squeal and nearly choked on her tea. Albin patted her on her back. Before I could answer, Dianna, coughing, said, "I'm Enyo. It is me, only now I'm Lana Po's daughter, Dianna, but it's still me. I got bored with machines and was studying to be a healer so I could figure out how our bodies actually work, that is before I was kidnaped and tortured. Now all that is lost to me. Doktors cannot do surgery with their feet."

Seeing that she finally ran down, I spoke up. "I don't know who you are, but your observations are right. I have had many names, but always Bethany. I used to run the Santi del Dio group. Renzo was my husband. Dita, here, is Renzo, if this helps you any."

Ania stared at us three dumbfounded, speechless for a moment. Then she shrieked in glee, "I'm Alexa! Enyo, it's me, Alexa, your best friend! Oh god! This is just fantastic! Wow! Incredible. Enyo, I still love you! Bethany, Renzo! I've never forgotten you two, not ever! This is fabulous! Wow!" Dianna and Ania got up and rushed to each other, bumping hard into each other, their legs wrapping around the other in the hug style that they had so often used as Enyo and Alexa. After they finished hugging, Dita and I hugged her too.

"Albin, Ania is an old friend from our last lifetimes. How about getting us some more tea, please?" He grinned and headed off to do just that.

"I'm Ania Anka now. I guess I should start at the beginning. I was floating around Velona wondering whom I should have as my next parents, when I heard of this new religious leader and something about armless women. Curious about that, I decided to follow them and sat in on his mesmerizing sermon. Man, was I ever mad after hearing that there was a whole country out there somewhere where they cut off all their women's arms. You know how I like politics." Enyo giggled. Alexa was always into politics and the running and governing of lands.

"Well, I headed off to Dorota right then and there, determined to set things right here. You know, a golden political opportunity — I couldn't resist it." Enyo giggled again. I smiled, as did Renzo, remembering Alexa of old. "Well, naturally, as I went to school, I opened my big mouth once too often. Thankfully, Rafal whisked me away from school just as the Security Guard was coming to arrest me. I've been with the rebels ever since. However, I soon discovered that they were not organized properly, had no real plan to regain their country, and stop this nasty business. Hence, I began to tell them what to do. I've been so successful at it, that all the rebel groups have made me their official Master Planner."

"It was I that sensed something was unusual about you two and sent Rafal to see if there was any way you could be talked into helping us with our severe food shortage last winter. Thank you for that, by the way. When Rafal came to me with your request for this meeting, I convinced most of the leaders to come and hear you. Wow, quite a speech, Bethany! Say, are you doing the same therapy that you did on me so long ago?"

"You bet, same thing exactly."

"Cool. If you will remind me of its details, I volunteer to lend a foot and help. Say, how are you planning to run therapy sessions on this whole country anyway? What's the overall plan? I've been helping them grow and expand, but we're not nearly strong enough to go against the gun weapons yet."

I laughed. "Sorry, haven't worked all that out yet. I will be very grateful for your foot and therapy help. With four of us doing them, it may only take us three days to get them all ready to go see the remains of the mantis creatures. Once that is done, then I'll have to wait and see. Somehow, Alexa, er Ania, we have to get the rebels joining forces with the Elders, and then together something may be done about it. I am open to any ideas that you might have to help avoid a total collapse of the society here."

"Well, your actions have totally wiped out all my plans, Bethany. I was working on getting the rebels back in charge of the country. Now, that may be done peacefully, but what about the millions who are sort of mesmerized all the time?"

"Don't know yet. We'll think of something, I'm sure."

"Okay. Say, do you three mind if I sort of hang out with you? There are so few like us here in the rebel bands. It's been hard for me."

"Sure, absolutely, Ania." Just then, Albin returned not only with a fresh pot of tea, but he had also confiscated a large pile of cookies.

"Cookies for my pretty ladies?" he teased. He did not expect the reaction he received. All four of us jumped up and surrounded him with our bodies, our mouths open demanding a cookie immediately. He roared with laughter, as he fed us cookies.

Three days later, with Ania's help, we finished off our therapy gifts to these leaders, who now had a very different outlook on things and life in general. Now I needed to have some idea where we were at so that I could choose which cavern site was the nearest. Rafal now trusted us and gave us a good guess of where this forest town was located. Fortunately, the nearest cavern with remains was about a two-day's ride. The leaders took a day to prepare, and then we all mounted up for the long journey. Two dozen other men accompanied us, providing protection.

We four allowed the men to lead our horses instead of us actually doing the riding. I didn't relish two days of biting down on leather reins, and Ania had never ridden by herself before. Always someone would lead her horse while she sat on it and tried not to fall off.

When our band arrived at the cavern, the two Security Guards recognized us and I took pity on the second one who had never seen what he was protecting. I allowed him to come and see with us. Naturally, he had a bad reaction and I was forced to give him an emergency therapy session. Actually, this was beneficial, as the leaders now saw precisely what I meant when I said even looking at it can cause severe mental reactions to occur. This only added to my credibility.

Three days later, we were back at their forest town and meeting at the inn once more. Cyryl said, "Bethany, thank you for what you have done for us. I think I speak for us all. We want to do what we can to put an end to this whole mess in a way that does not crush our country. What would you have us do? Our Master Planner, for once, has no suggestions," he grinned at Ania, who grinned back at him.

"Thanks Cyryl. First, how many of you are there? I mean how many people are living here in the forests as quote rebels unquote?"

This took a while to tabulate, as the leaders tried to work out the total. There were close to fifty-five thousand of them. When I asked, most really did wish to move out of the woods and into towns and villages, though many hated the idea of moving into the identical buildings. They were used to a wide variety of homes as well as clothes. "Well, the first step will be to have some of you meet with the High Council of Elders and begin to work out what steps can be taken to get all of you back into our mainstream. You should be part of the decision making process in running our country, you've earned that right by having fought against their tyranny."

"Considering that you two have been arch enemies for centuries, I think that initially only a few should come back with us and meet with them. If all goes well, then the rest can join us. If it does not, then all of you are not compromised."

"I like that attitude, Bethany," Iwo commented. "Don't put all the chickens in one cage, the fox might get in. I would like you to consider taking our Master Planner Ania with you. She has an uncanny knack of seeing right through the Elder's plans, coming up with a brilliant counter-plan. If they try anything, she will be the first to see through it."

"I'll volunteer to go as well," Rafal spoke up. "After all, I've been sticking my neck out quite a bit. If something goes wrong, I'm Bethany's only contact with all of you, which will keep you safer."

After some discussion, Cyryl and Hanna would join Rafal and Ania to make the initial contact with the High Council members. Although I did not know it, the other leaders would be staying at nearby inns, ready to step in if there were trouble or if things went well.

Thus, on October 20, we eight rode a carriage back into Wit and then on a bit to the Elder College at Wit. The moment that Hanna climbed out, everyone at the college knew immediately that these were indeed rebels that had returned with us! She was the first woman any of these people on the entire campus had ever seen who had arms. Yes, Hanna got dozens and dozens of stares from the gawking domestic staff to the guards to even the Elders, who quickly came rushing out to welcome us back.

"Elders, it is with great honor and pride that I am introducing four of the rebel leaders, who, like you, have had our precious gift and seen the contents of the cavern. They, like you, want to work on peaceful ways that we can use to solve our country's major problem. The first action must be to reconcile the difference between your two groups, and then united, we can press on to solve our country's problems."

Elder Amadei exclaimed, "Welcome, welcome. We will put you up in the domestic dorms where Bethany and Dita are staying. I know that you must think that we are vile, evil men, but I assure you that we are not. We just do not know how to get our country out of the mess it is in without causing a total collapse of our whole society. I can see now that we have greatly wronged you, who have been trying to tell us for centuries that our way was wrong. Yes, it is wrong. Please, let us put aside our differences and join together to fix this mess."

Well, his words went over well with the four and they agreed to make the attempt. We got them settled into several rooms near ours. In the morning, the actual discussions would begin in earnest. For tonight, things were cordial and we invited Ania to stay in our room with us. We had lots to chat about that night.

Chapter 16 Finding Solutions

"First of all, we ought to be given a full amnesty. Second, we ought to be allowed to move back into the mainstream of our country. Third, we should be supported while we do this. We will need homes, jobs, food, clothing, for starters," Ania answered Elder Iwan, who asked what the rebels needed.

"Well, I don't see that you have really committed any crimes for which you have not paid a penalty for already. Amnesty granted. I am worried about what our men and women will think when they see women like Hanna on their block. I mean no offense to you, Hanna, I think that it is wonderful that your parents chose to keep you away from our doktors, really I do. The life that we have given to Bethany and Dita here, to say nothing of the half million others, is just awful."

"We all agree on that, Iwan," Elder Kuba of the Finance Committee interrupted him. "On this second and third request, I would like to suggest that perhaps it might be wise for these people to build their own towns, you know pick a good location along existing roads and start from scratch, building a town that is more suited to their needs. I'm sure that Hanna would not like to live in one of our model homes, which is set up for women like Bethany. Now, we have all that gold just gathering more dust in those caverns. Part of it really belongs to these folks. I propose that we use as much of it as we need to pay for the construction of their new towns and to reimburse others for their supplies, at least until they all get on their feet financially."

"Second that one, Kuba!" Elder Karol put in, "What's next?"

Ania was completely shocked. She had been expecting to have to argue for these three key starting points for at least a day, before the council might come around to her way of thinking. Ania faltered a second, recovering. "Ah, well then there is the matter of so many people imprisoned at the Fields for nothing more than being against what all you have been doing."

"Of course, of course," Elder Borys replied immediately. "As head of the Rehabilitation Committee, I have ordered a complete review of all cases. We have one hundred-five cases, formerly classed as insane, which are really, as Bethany puts it, stuck in a past mantis trauma situation. These we hope can be helped with her gift. We have five hundred three cases of severe crimes, involving rape, child molesting, and outright thefts. These, we believe ought to remain in our care. The rest we would like to release. However, some are still ardent in their anti-establishment points of view. We would like to release them into your custody that they may fit far better into your towns. There is also the matter of a number of women who are still rejecting their roles in our society. We are not sure what to do with them.

We simply cannot just turn them loose and say go live your life. They are, well, I'll be blunt, enough of pretenses. They are armless and will have a devil of a time living on their own. They cannot go back to their old homes, because they would sit around and do nothing. Perhaps you would consider taking them as well and seeing if they might fit into your towns better."

Hanna replied, "Thank you. We will take all that you want to send our way. Please, leave the rapists and child molesters at the Fields! I find it interesting that the real crime rate here in Dorota is something like a half a tenth of a percent."

"Yes, virtually non-existent. Yet, if we just cease our monthly sermons and tell everyone the truth, I am certain that the crime rate would hit fifty percent or higher. If our social structure breaks down, all will be lost," Elder Borys replied. "How soon shall we open the doors at the Fields?"

Ania recovered, "Let's wait a bit before you send them our way. We need to get our people out of the woods and into something more suitable. Now where do you think that we ought to build new towns?"

Thus, the initial meeting between the two rivals began, both sides amazed at how well behaved the other could be, under the circumstances. Many smaller details had to be worked out. Interestingly enough, the next day, all the leaders met with the High Council and later reported that they had formed a new union called the Grand Council, consisting of the High Council and its thirteen members, and fifteen members of the Free Council, formerly known as the rebel leaders. I was surprised to see that the High Council allowed veto power to their former enemies. I guess they wanted to be up front about what they had done and visibly show them that change was needed. To help speed the negotiations along, the other leaders moved into our dorms for a while as well.

Five days later, they had worked out all the details, now it was time for action. The Elders would be announcing during their Sunday Service that a complete peace accord had been reached with all the rebels, who would be rejoining their society. Now the rebels had to start finding suitable locations for permanent towns and villages, either in the highlands, the farmlands, or along the coastal lands. Wagons of food began rolling towards the six dense woods, providing winter assistance as the real work began.

The Grand Council agreed to meet again on December 1 and begin to tackle just how they would be attempting to solve the real problem facing the millions of citizens of Dorota. I had maybe six more weeks to figure this one out, as I knew that they wouldn't be able to solve it.

Ania Anka decided to stay with us. She had no real possessions to speak of back in her room in the Turk Wood, save a hairbrush and some clothes. Being with us was vastly more valuable to her; besides, they no longer needed her. The problems she had been assisting them with were now history.

Sitting around our bedroom that night, brushing out our hair, Ania commented, "Well, I did accomplish what I set out to do, at least in part. I have the rebels back into the mainstream of this society. I kept them alive and thriving for a number of years too, so I'm pleased with that. Only one thing remains, how do we handle the millions and their discovery of the truth about their wives and daughters? Once that's solved, Bethany, will we be going home to Velona? This country is terribly boring, no music, no art, no fancy clothes, no fancy shoes, no chocolate, dreary identical houses. Shall I go on?"

"You bet we are, and no, please." I giggled.

"Okay. Honestly, can I really be a part of your lives again, as we used to be, you know intimately close as a foursome? Always, four of us together make things possible. I remember that vividly well," Ania asked very seriously.

"Of course, come here, hug," I replied, "always, four of us together as one. Honestly, I was thinking of just dumping this body once my job here was done. Going it alone as we are in the wide world isn't very appealing to me. I've done it too many times already. But Renzo here, er Dita, turned up. I'm still madly in love with him, er her now. We decided to be married, though it sounds weird. Anyway, then along comes Enyo here, I mean Dianna, whom both Renzo, I mean Dita, and I loved and still do, and now here you come, Alexa, I mean Ania. Gosh, are any of you getting as confused as I am about all this?" Everyone giggled; they did find it confusing as well.

"We four must always be together, live together, married," I finished.

"Yes, but I don't believe that they consider that marriage consists of four women," Ania or Alexa replied. "But that's what I'd like us to be, don't you?" We all did — no argument on that point.

"Well, you can't call us a team, though maybe we are a team anyway. A team implies people joining together to play a game and once it is over, they go their separate ways," Dita began thinking this through. "As one of us, Alexa, I mean Ania, I promise to be your Protector too, just as I am Bethany's and Enyo's, rather Dianna's. I'll protect you with my life if need be!" Dita gave her solemn pledge, which I knew was absolute. That was Renzo's way. Once he, I mean she, pledged it, he never withdrew it.

Ania giggled and teased her, "But Renzo, you have got this gorgeously, sexy female body, which hasn't got any arms. How are you going to be a Protector?" Even though we all knew she was just playfully teasing her, she hit Dita's or Renzo's sore spot. Instead of a giggle or such response, tears swelled up in Dita's eyes.

"I know it. I know it. I don't know how to be a gorgeously, sexy woman. I just know how to be a fighter, a Protector. I meant it." She rubbed her eyes dry on her shoulders, while forcibly shoving those emotions away. "I'm sorry to going all emotional on you. This never happened when I had my other body. I know you were teasing me, Alexa. I'll show you how I can still protect you!" She gave a coy grin, moved over, picked up Ania's body, and moved her around the room. Obviously, Dita was using her spiritual abilities here, not her body's. Ania finally began laughing so hard that she put her down. "There, satisfied I can still be a Protector when I have to be?" Dita asked, back in her playful mood.

"Okay, okay, you win," Ania exclaimed. "I should be honest with you all too. Long ago, I decided that once I finished my work here in Dorota, I would just go jump in the ocean or off a cliff somewhere. Alone, I just did not want to face the world out there beyond Dorota. I'd rather start over again with a body that is whole. Now that I have found you three, I've given all those dark thoughts a pitch! You've given me the will to carry on once we are done here. Together, we can face the Outer Lands, as they say here. Only please, please, don't call me a Holy Vessel! I hate that term." We all roared with laughter. We, too, hated it. Young women were we.

Dianna spoke up, "Ania, I will be honest with you too. When I was captured and the Supreme Prelate Eros cut off my fingers and hands, he destroyed all chances I had to do what I wanted to do this lifetime. I saw gangrene forming and had already made my peace; I was just waiting for this body to pass away so that I could start again, just like you, Ania. Only I had the good fortune to run into these two. As long as I have you three at my side, I am ready to face life and conquer it. I guess that none of us is alone in having dark thoughts. I agree, trying to go it alone as we are is just awful, especially since three of us have already been through it at least once. But we all know that four is the magic number; four of us can manage very well, where one alone cannot. I am so happy we are together. I love you all. I just wish I had arms to hug you all so tightly!"

"Well, gang, if we are ever going to get out of here, we have got to come up with a workable solution. We have six weeks before they hound us to death. We'd better start thinking of a plan," I brought them all back to our present situation. Time enough for fun later.

"Oh wow! Dita, Bethany! You've got a pair of boots made by my old company," Ania exclaimed as she saw our heeled boots, as she stowed her dress for the night. "How did you get them all the way out here in this part of the world?" Again, we digressed.

We got nowhere on the problem that night. The next day, Ania helped us get down to business. She got paper and a pencil and put them on the low desk in our room. We four sat in our slanted chairs, watching her write. "Okay, we make a list of what our available resources are in this column. In this column, we put what's needed, therapy for close to a million people. Let's see, we can start by putting down that we have four who can run therapy sessions. That's a drop in the bucket, but we want our resources. Come on you three. Help me out."

Dita said, "Well, we have the Elders and their ability to mesmerize others to make them do what they want."

"Good, good." Ania wrote that one down. We listed other things, such as unlimited gold, but that didn't seem too useful a resource in this case. We had some who had been through our therapy already, that we added. That we had lots of man and woman power made the list. I had her add that they believed that woman gave something of herself to her man to the list, because they all believed this implicitly. Dita had her add that everyone went to church on Sundays. All morning long we kept at it, slowly the list of potential resources grew, though a solution remained elusive.

After lunch, Dita commented, "You know their Churches only hold two hundred at one time. Maybe that is also a resource." Ania added it.

Days turned into weeks. No more resources were added. Ania continually kept saying, "Gang the answer is right here on the paper. We just are not yet seeing it, unless you think that we've missed a resource." Slowly we grew a bit more irritable, as no solution appeared. Dita kept saying that we needed a Holy Miracle, Divine Intervention. Ania pointed out that was not on our list of resources.

The snow from yesterday had melted, but the temperature was barely above freezing. In frustration, I said, "Hey how about we take a break and go for a long walk to clear our heads?"

"I like that idea!" Dita seconded it.

"Hey, can I wear your high heeled Alexa boots?" Ania asked. "It's been years since I got to wear them."

"Sure, go ahead. Dita can catch you if you take a tumble," I teased her. She eagerly slipped her feet into them.

"Oh, are these ever sexy! Now I do feel sexy again. Amazing how a good dress and heels can make a girl feel!" We donned our heavy cloaks, helping each other by fastening their clasps with our feet. Out we went for a stroll. We walked into Wit. Noticing the leafless trees, the scattered patches of snow on the northern sides of trees and other shaded areas, we slowly got our attention off our huge, insoluble problem and onto the world in the present. Finally, we returned, chilled, but invigorated.

I sat down and began looking at Ania's list. Then, it hit me. "We don't need to run a half million therapy sessions ourselves! That's not possible. We don't need to run a half million sessions all at the same time, either. Look, we have the basic unit of two hundred who attend a church service at one time. This is a constant everywhere in the country, you know, all the churches are identical. That's our basic group who will get a therapy session at one point in time."

"But we would need two hundred people who know how to run one," Dita pointed out the obvious.

"We use half of the congregation to deliver sessions to the other half. When done, they switch and the receivers then give sessions back to the original deliverers. We four circulate among the sessions, lending a hand where needed. We simply repeat this pattern over and over some five thousand times."

Ania pointed out, "Well, Bethany, that's a start. However, if we give two sessions every day, and that is pushing it, it will take us about fourteen years to get to everyone. We will be old maids before we get out of here." We giggled.

"Damn. Well, it's a start," I replied.

"Wait a minute, everyone!" Dianna interrupted. "Think about me and my situation. I wanted to contribute to medical knowledge this lifetime, finding out just how human bodies work. I was all set, but then I was kidnaped and found myself armless with all hopes of achieving my goal dashed on the rocks. Here I am, feeling mostly useless. Yet, we all know that fundamentally all people desire to contribute, to help others. It's in our very nature, yet a half million women here find themselves as we are, barely able to maintain a household, much less anything else. Their ability to contribute something of value is shattered. We need to change that, to give them a way to contribute something that is priceless, a therapy session."

"Brilliant, Dianna. We start training two hundred women in one church to be able to deliver a routine therapy session. They then deliver it to each other. Once they have solid reality on it, they then begin on the others in their church and then other churches. Ania, work out the math, will you? I think we have a progression here. Let's say that we want this all done by our eighteenth birthdays, that's in June for three of us."

Ania began figuring. "Okay, this is even better. Let's say that we train two hundred women to do therapy sessions each week. Then we turn them loose and have them handle two people each week, that ought not interrupt their lives too severely, perhaps some accommodations can be made by their men to compensate. That means each week the original two hundred handle four hundred people. Each week we add another two hundred women to the pot. The second week we now have four hundred delivering eight hundred sessions. In six months' time, around five thousand two hundred women will be delivering and handling over ten thousand people each week. By six months, they can have reached a million people!"

Dita pointed out, "How are we going to find two hundred women who want to do this every week? Then, find the time to train them all. Surely, they are going to run into tough cases, where we will have to step in and help out directly, taking time away from the finding and the training."

"Well, let's use the Elders and the Free Council to scout ahead and round up the next week's trainees and let's let them deal with the record keeping, scheduling who gets their sessions and when. Let them earn their keep," Ania insisted.

"Gang, we are on the right path! I just know it. Ania, Dianna, you two start working out the things that the Elders and the Free Council will need to do, rather like an instruction manual, list the steps and so on. Dita and I have to work out the speeches of explanations that will be given out to the millions.

In earnest and with a newfound vigor, we four set to work, feet doing their thing, as we four began to work out the needed steps. Dita and I decided that three speeches were needed: a goals speech to enlighten the population about what was going on countrywide, a recruitment speech to be given to likely women who would be trained to deliver therapy sessions, and a "your responsibilities now" speech to be given after a person had their therapy. Dita felt the most qualified to work on the recruitment speech, and I took the other two. Feet flew as pages came and went with our many drafts.

Each evening we paused to review with the others what we had written thus far, and they sometimes had valuable suggestions for improvements. We barely finished when the date of the resumption of the Grand Council arrived. We discovered that we were going to have a hard time carrying our large piles of papers from our desk across the snow-covered lawn to the meeting room. Trying to hold them against our shoulders with our heads didn't work. In the end, I just grabbed my pile in my teeth and said, "This way." We giggled and they followed suit. We walked into the meeting looking a bit weird indeed, piles of papers clenched in our teeth. Albin carefully removed our cloaks, while we bit down all the harder. It wouldn't do to drop them and scramble them before all these people.

"Well, I take it that you have something for us," Elder Amadei teased us a bit. He had definitely lightened up since his therapy session. "Honestly, Bethany, we have been thinking about our problem all this time and have decided it may not be solvable. A million people need your gift of therapy."

"We've solved it. We four put our heads together and have it all worked out. Unless we run into some unexpected snags, which we likely will, given the magnitude of the problem, in six months' time, the million will have had their therapy," I explained.

The stunned, shocked looks from the entire twenty-eight faces told us mountains. Indeed, they had given up hope of solving the problem. "Okay here is the top level view of the plan. We are going to train up women who volunteer to learn how to give this most precious gift to others. Beginning next week, we four will train two hundred women on how to do it. Two hundred, because that's how many a church will accommodate at one time. We will be using the churches as the place to do all this therapy. Now the next week, these two hundred women will then each handle two people during the week, giving them their therapy sessions, that is, four hundred are handled. Meantime, we will be training another two hundred, so that the following week eight hundred people get their therapy sessions, while we train up another two hundred women."

"In six months' time, you will have over five thousand women capable of delivering this precious gift to others. By then over a million people will have been handled, basic problem solved. Why women? Look, as we are," I shrugged my shoulders for emphasis, "and as you well know, your women are barely able to contribute back to our society. They can just barely keep a home functioning properly. People gain self-respect by being able to contribute and help others. We are going to give these volunteer women the chance to contribute something of tremendous value to our society. Their self-respect will soar, as will their morale."

"Now we will need you to deliver a 'Here is what is going to take place' speech to the people. Then, you will need to have a 'Recruitment speech' to help you find the two hundred women volunteers that we need each week. Once a person has received his or her therapy, they need to be given a 'Your responsibilities now' speech. Dita and I have prepared initial drafts of what these speeches ought to contain. You may modify them as you see fit, as long as they get delivered."

"Ania and Dianna have worked out what your jobs will be, listing very detailed steps that must be met to keep the two hundred new women coming each week to learn how to do it, and the hundreds who will be getting their therapy during that week. We will go mostly city by city, though in the end, many of the women volunteers will have to travel around Dorota to give their sessions. It will be your responsibility to see that every person in our country gets their therapy session."

"Now then the goals speech goes like this." I began to read off what I had written giving the general population some idea of what was happening.

"Truth shall set you free. That is the fundamental principle we are using to correct a heinous crime committed on our whole civilization, a crime that has been going on for many centuries. There are three truths to be revealed to you today."

"The first truth is that you and I are immortal spiritual beings, not our fleshly human bodies that we see before us. Our religion teaches us that we are all created in God's image. God's image cannot be that of a fleshly body. If it were, God would be long since dead! God is not a fleshly body, nor is any of us, we who are created in his image. We are all immortal spiritual beings as is our God, our Creator. Yes, God has given us these fleshly bodies to inhabit for a time, but you and I are not these fleshly bodies. Over the span of time, we have inhabited many of these bodies, though we may not consciously now remember them. Still the memories are there, as you will soon be given a chance to discover for yourselves."

"The second truth is for centuries, we have all been horribly misinterpreting our own holy scriptures. Our teachings say that later on, 'God saw that men needed even greater strength, power, and stamina, because they needed to now support themselves and their families.' Later, 'One of God's Holy Vessels, who was called Marzena, spoke unto God. 'Lord, my man, Jurek, is a good and kind man, a farmer. Yet, I can see that he needs to be stronger. Please, my Lord, take my arms from me and use them to strengthen Jurek so that he may be strong enough for the task. I do not need them, and Jurek needs them so much more than I do.' God heard the prayer from his Holy Vessel and so it was that God took the arms from his Marzena and fashioned them into more ribs for her husband Jurek. Thus made stronger and more powerful, Jurek was at last able to sustain his Holy Vessel and family, more able to tend his fields, and produce more food.'"

"This passage is what has led to the horrible, heinous misunderstanding. Well-intentioned Elders and our equally well intentioned doktors took this passage literally, that women should give their arms unto men. Thus, they did as our Holy Scriptures commanded and removed the arms of all baby girls when they were born. Today, nearly all the women in our country have been thus harmed by this terrible, awful misinterpretation of our own holy scriptures."

"None of us are qualified to judge or make less of our religious leaders, that belongs to God and to God alone. Instead, let us examine the true meaning of this critical passage of our holy scripture. Marzena asked God, 'Please, my Lord, take my arms from me and use them to strengthen Jurek so that he may be strong enough for the task.' This statement has come down to you through the ages, from the dawn of time. Have you ever considered that it is a metaphor? That it is *symbolic* of what Marzena was offering?"

"Okay, if we are not these fleshly bodies, what does this say about Marzena and her offering to God? I say unto you that she was offering something more powerful, more intimate, and more significant than mere fleshly arms. She gave something of herself to make her man stronger, more able. Recently, God has finally revealed this to the Elders and to those that have been called rebels. Why have they been called rebels? Primarily because they discovered the truth that the doktors were amputating the arms of our baby girls when they were born and they wanted to stop them somehow. But what of this gift that Marzena actually gave unto her man? This is truly what it vitally important to know, for it is not removal of fleshly arms, but a gift as precious as life itself."

"How did God reveal this unto our Elders and unto the other rebel leaders? It came through two of our Holy Vessels, Bethany Brozena and Dita Malina. It also now comes from a rebel Holy Vessel, Ania Anka, and one from the Outer Lands, Dianna Po. Within the next half year, every person on Dorota shall be given this most precious spiritual gift from our Holy Vessels! As it was with Marzena giving unto to her man, so shall at long last it be given unto you."

"The past cannot be undone, arms cannot be regrown. But the true gift of Marzena can be given unto all of you and *will* be given to you! That is vastly more important than your fleshly bodies, which will grow old and one day pass away. Expect to hear from your Elders and rebel leaders when you may expect to receive this most Holiest of Gifts, given unto you as God had originally intended, not as it has been for centuries so badly misinterpreted."

"I spoke of three truths. What then is the third truth? It came about when our Holy Vessels, Bethany and Dita, asked themselves *why* should the Elders and the doktors for hundreds of years so badly misinterpret our holy scriptures. They found the answer, which when you first hear of it, may write it off as a fairy tale. Yet, that may not be so, after you have been given your Precious Holy Gift from the Holy Vessels. This story you may find extremely upsetting, appalling, and incredibly disgusting. We certainly do."

"More than two centuries ago, on our continent, and in secret from our people, there lived a number of strange alien creatures. Their size ranged from fifty to eighty feet long. They looked like some kind of giant praying mantis and were green in color. These creatures took control of our world and their favorite food was dining on the arms of newborn baby girls. They ate them all, not a single girl in Dorota was spared. If those in power did not go along with them, they were simple eaten whole. After many years, then, all the women who lived here in Dorota grew up and had no arms."

"Greatly saddened by this, those in power did all that they could to make life more bearable for our poor women. Marvelous inventions to make it easier for the women to read, to write, to feed themselves, to cook, to wash, and even to carry items were invented by them — all designed to ease the horrid burden that our women bore. Imagine an entire country so dominated, so controlled by these ultra-powerful mantis creatures that could not be killed by any weapon that we possessed, tragic in every sense of the word."

"Then one day the mantis creatures stopped coming to eat the baby arms. The Elders and doktors had to make a decision about what to do. *Fearful* that they would return at any time, rightly or wrongly, they decided to amputate the arms of the newborn girls. Perhaps they wanted to spare a grown woman the horrible, terrifying trauma of facing a giant mantis creature, returning to eat their arms when they were adults. Right or wrong, they continued this practice down unto this very day. Always, the Elders wondered how they might safely stop this practice, but have never found a way that would not destroy our country."

"When you have received your Precious Gift from the Holy Vessels, you may or may not wish to add to this story. However, it is true, and, after you have received your Gift, if you desire, you may be shown the undeniable truth that this did happen here centuries ago. Thank you."

When I finished, once more I received a standing ovation, as they expressed their sincere thanks. I then read the much shorter exit speech.

"Now that you have received this Precious Holy Gift given unto you by your Holy Vessel, as God had originally intended, you have a greater responsibility to bear. God then said unto Jurek, who hath received Marzena's gift, 'I can see that by the sacrifice of worthy Marzena, you are now blessed with part of her strength and you are now able to survive well. However, Jurek, you must honor her sacrifice unto you. From this day forward, you must love her, cherish her, and help her, as you have never done before. Thou shalt never betray her by lusting after other women. Thou shalt be true to her and to her alone. Thou shalt not lie, covet what another has, steal that which does not belong to you, and fight with other men whose Holy Vessels have likewise made their sacrifice. Nor should thou become a glutton over the bounty, which thou art now capable of producing, because of the gift Marzena has given unto you and you alone. Thou shalt honor and cherish the new life that Marzena brings forth as they are part of each of you. If you will do these things, then you are worthy of viewing my Creation and of entering my realm.' These things you are hereby charged to do from this day forward."

"Of course, you may wish to add some other things in there as well." I sat down and allowed Dita to read her speech, the recruitment speech.

Dita read, "Most Holy Vessels, as you have heard, our holy words have been horribly and tragically misinterpreted. The offering of Marzena was thus. 'Please, my Lord, take my arms from me and use them to strengthen Jurek so that he may be strong enough for the task. I do not need them and Jurek needs them so much more than I do.' For centuries now, without your knowledge or consent, or the knowledge and consent of your parents, your arms were amputated when you were born. This is the literal interpretation of Marzena's words to God, but for centuries, it has been the *wrong* interpretation. Her words are *symbolic* of her Precious Gift."

"God has revealed unto his Holy Vessels Bethany and Dita, the true gift that Marzena gave willingly and freely unto her man, the gift that our God wanted *you*, his Holy Vessels, to be able to give unto *your* men and children. This Holy Gift, once given, is more precious to the receiver than all the gold in Dorota. It is a true spiritual gift, one that is incredibly valuable to have received, for it will make both man and woman far stronger."

"At this time, Holy Vessels Bethany and Dita are looking for volunteer Holy Vessels, who wish to learn how to give this most Precious Gift that God intended for you to be able to give unto your man and children. If you wish to learn how to do this, you will then be asked to take some time away from your wifely duties or studies so that you may give this Precious Gift unto others, so that every person in Dorota has the opportunity to receive what our Lord God had originally intended them to receive."

"The giving of this most Precious Gift unto your countrymen will give you in return the spiritual rewards that our Lord God intended for you, like Marzena, to have, priceless beyond words. You will have the highest respect of everyone in our entire country, for you will be counted among the few, whom God has indeed touched and blessed, for your freely given gift from God."

"If you wish to be counted among these most precious of all Holy Women, step forward and learn. Thank you."

Once more, everyone rose and applauded Dita, who looked terribly embarrassed with all this attention. Even more interesting, I saw not a dry eye among these men and women, so moved were they by our proposed speeches.

I added a caution, "Now of course, when the Holy Vessels begin to deliver their therapy sessions, some may encounter unforeseen difficulties and problems with some of those whom they are trying to help. Those people who have trouble are to be brought to one of us four, who can continue their therapy sessions, correcting what may have gone astray. You see, we four will be kept very busy training these five thousand plus women and handling the rough ones that they cannot handle. Your tasks, then, as Ania and Dianna have outlined, will keep you more than busy. I'm glad that I have our jobs to do and not yours. I propose that we begin here at the college and Wit. Since there are not going to be enough women here, we will also recruit in Bazyli at the same time. Your first task is to get us two hundred women into the church in Wit this coming Saturday, so that we can begin their training. This thing is going to snowball, so make sure that you can organize this well. Six months and our country may be free at last. May God let it be so."

Now the real work began. These men and women were masters of organization; after all, they were leading either the whole country or their band of rebels. Questions flew and answers given. They tackled the logistics problem with a vigor that I've never seen before, neither had Ania.

Now we four began to work out just how we were going to train these women to be able to deliver a therapy session. We had seven days to get it ready.

Chapter 17 The Beginning of the Solution

Saturday, we four entered the Church in Wit, dressed in our Sunday dresses. Dita and I wore our high-heeled boots, out of deference to Elder Amadei, who asked that we look as holy as possible. Good first impression, he had said.

As we entered, Dita and I were both shocked to see our mothers and my sister present, along with Albin's sister, Kazia. They came up to us as we walked into the Church. "Mom, Aniela! Wow, what a surprise!" I exclaimed.

Beside me Dita said, "Hi mom. Wow, you volunteered too?"

Tekla and Roksana spoke together. "How could we not follow our daughter's footsteps?" We giggled; they'd rehearsed this beforehand.

"We wanted to as well," simultaneously added Aniela and Kazia, who had also rehearsed their welcome to us.

"Well as the first to learn this, you are going to have an incredible six month experience! You will get to travel all over our country!" I added.

"Cool! We are excited about that. We guessed that we would," Aniela confessed. "Say, did the doktors really cut off our arms when we were born?"

I grinned, "Aniela, I believe you will discover the answer to that one today. I guess we had better get started." We began to train this first group of Holy Vessels. It was strange staring out at two hundred women, all as armless as we were, and knowing that soon they would rise above their awful and mundane lives to a seldom-felt spiritual realm.

"For want of a better name, we call this our Holy Gift therapy, and you will be known as the Givers of the Holy Gift. In giving this gift, there are some vital rules that must not be violated under any circumstances. You must not ever make less of what the receiver may say during his therapy session. This can be hard, if your patient says that he is looking at a fifty-foot long earthworm and you know it is probably just a small worm. Remember, the patient is viewing this while under extreme pain and duress. Things can get confused in their minds. Just keep on with your work, and they will eventually get it straightened out."

"Next, you must not tell them what to think about something they may say or what that may mean. The meaning is theirs and theirs alone. Here's how you deliver your gift." For an hour, I outlined what had to be done and how to do it. I gave some examples, and then I had every one count off by "one" and "two." The "one's" got to go first, running a therapy session on the "two" sitting next to them. Suddenly, we four found ourselves incredibly busy, moving from row to row, listening in on a session here and there, pointing out small goofs to the "one's" and giving encouragement where needed. It was a long afternoon, punctuated by many screams of pain and sometimes terror, as the "two's" re-experienced the pain and trauma of their birth and amputations. By the middle of the afternoon, most all were now re-experiencing far earlier situations, many involving the mantis creatures." A real sense of comradery began to form among both the givers and the receivers, all packed in tightly into the church.

As the supper hour approached, the sounds of laughter began echoing through the church, until it became so loud that one could hardly hear anything else. As their patient's reached the finish point, I had the "one's" end their session and take their "two" to the side room for supper. Here, the Elders had a feast waiting for these Holiest of Holy Vessels. Finally, the last woman experienced the relief of laughter; her trauma had finally vanished as well, and we all headed next door to eat. After dinner, the roles would be reversed.

Unfortunately, it did not work out as planned. So great were the wins of the one hundred "two's" that everyone was talking fast and furious about what they had just experienced. Mom had done Aniela, my sister. "Bethany! It's just as you said! The doktor did cut off my arms! God did that ever hurt, but that was nothing like what happened to me ages ago! You are right! It was a giant green praying mantis insect! I was so terrified! I am now so incredibly happy that I can't sit still! Mom, wait til I do you! I feel so powerful now, mom! Wow!"

Mom was exuberant. "I feel so darn good it's not funny. I don't know why I should feel this way, but I have never felt this way before, Bethany. I really did give my daughter something that is so precious that there are not even words for it. Thank you, daughter."

Nearby, Albin was in tears as his sister, Kazia, was just as excited about her session, given to her by her mother. What of those that gave these sessions? They had tears of joy flowing readily. The pride that they felt, the joy and relief that they saw in those they had treated was overwhelming them. They were almost as excited as their patients were. Hence, I quietly asked that the second half of the sessions be given tomorrow afternoon after lunch and the morning Sunday Services were over. I had not reckoned with the intense joy and happiness that would come from these first sessions. I altered my plans to make the initial training span two days, not one.

When we finally walked back to our dorms that night, my feet were throbbing from having worn the high heels all day long. I scarcely notice that though, knowing if I wore them long enough, my feet would adapt as they had half a century ago. Dita exclaimed, "Did you see my mom? She was so happy and proud of what she had done for Kazia. Her self-respect has skyrocketed! I think she got more out of that than Kasia did."

"Oh no, my sister is happier than I have ever seen her in her entire life. Did you see how bright her eyes are? Her complexion — it just cleared up all by itself in those few hours! She's a new girl now, so full of life! Incredible! How can I ever thank you four enough?" exclaimed Albin.

"You can help us as we train these other five thousand, that'll keep you hopping!" We all laughed, and he said goodnight, after opening our door for us.

The next afternoon went even smoother than Saturday afternoon. Dita theorized that now the patients knew what to look for in their own lives, which I thought was probably the case. I had to intervene in only one situation, in which a woman simply could not find anything earlier than the one she was running, where the doktor amputated her arms, and which continued to give her pain. I spotted a bluish-green mass that was sitting there in her mind. I whispered to the woman delivering the session, "Ask her if that bluish-green thing could be earlier." She did and the trauma literally exploded, a mantis was coming for her, and she was trying to flee, but as a newborn baby, she was trapped. Terror flew off this woman as she ran through the trauma of centuries ago.

Again, by suppertime, the entire trauma had been eliminated and laughter filled the Church once more. Everyone was talking together as they had never done before. Supper took hours, because they were too excited to eat, wanting to share everything with everyone else who was there.

After the meal was finally done, Elder Iwan of the Planning Committee rose to speak to the two hundred volunteer women. After thanking them profusely and wiping his eyes five times, he announced that a carriage would pick them up at noon at their homes and take them to the appropriate church in either Wit or Bazyli, where they would deliver another session. Yes, they would be traveling around Dorota with all their expenses paid for by the Elders. I knew that my sister and mother would relish this enormously.

When we finally returned to our dorms that night, the headmistress Zofia was there waiting for us. She'd just received her session and was still laughing so hard that she found it difficult to speak. "Bethany, Dita, Dianna, Ania, thank you, thank you, thank you! I know the good doktor cut off my arms, dears, but you know, he didn't have much choice. That giant green insect was behind it all! I was so scared when I saw it coming at me. No wonder I thought that no one loved me anymore! They were feeding me to this giant monster!" She roared with laughter, "Of course they loved me! Who could even kill such a monster?" Again, she laughed heartily. We gave her one of our hugs and she ran off to talk to another woman, who was also still laughing about her now erased traumas.

"This is going to work!" Ania exclaimed when we were finally alone in our bedroom.

"Yes it certainly looks that way. I just hope the others can keep the ball rolling. We are asking a lot of them and in so short a time," I replied.

"It has to be this way. As some, who have not yet received theirs, start to find out about what has been going on, they could well create a serious problem, until they do get their sessions," Ania pointed out. She was right. This was something that had to sweep the whole country as rapidly as possible to avoid a catastrophe. We were exposing to the whole country crimes of great magnitude. Without benefit of the therapy, men would become violently angry against the system, the doktors and Elders in particular.

In the ensuing weeks, we encountered more logistical problems. We four were needed in the locations where the therapy sessions were being conducted by our army of volunteers. At least one case in ten needed our timely intervention. Thus, we had to wait for one large city to be fully handled before we could move on to the next. Yet, this soon became unworkable, as we began to move out from Bazyli to the smaller towns and villages, which sometimes were many hours apart. At last, we four had to split up in order to service our ever-growing army of volunteers.

In time, I discovered that the original two hundred women became very skilled at running therapy sessions on others. So much so, that we now seldom had to intervene at all. After February, they didn't need us at all any longer. This effect I also had not foreseen, and it began to help us out, since this team could be sent anywhere and be counted upon to work their miracles, independent of us four. Shortly after that, the next group of two hundred no longer needed us. The Grand Council then adopted a new policy of physically bringing the person whose therapy was not working properly directly and as fast as possible to one of us four.

One night, Ania pointed out a key factor, which was making this all possible. "You know why this is working so well? I just realized that every person in this country has one or more nearly identical traumatic experiences. That is what is making this whole thing work out so smoothly. I remember all those sessions that we used to have when we were all back at the Santi complex there north of Velona. How we had to probe and dig to find the proper starting point. Sometimes, I swore it was mere guesswork on your part or your mom's. If that were the case here in Dorota, we could not just turn these women loose with barely an hour's discussion on how it was done. They might never get the process started. Here in Dorota, there has been so much time gone by and over so many lifetimes, that given probability theory, every being has had a female body at least once and so has the same trauma to be handled."

Dita added, "I wish we had been keeping records of just how many actually ran into the mantis creatures. I am guessing that one in two didn't, but I sure would find that fact interesting. We could use it to create a time line for how long they were in operation in this country."

"Why would you want to know that, Dita?" asked Dianna. "They are long gone."

"Oh it's just a Protector kind of observation. How long does it take to really subjugate a people," Dita replied.

"Hey, I'll make a politics man out of you yet. That's a great idea. I wish we had been keeping records!" Ania exclaimed. I feigned an "Oh no!"

and we all roared with laughter once again.

In March, we hit those housed within the Fields of Kondrat. Those that were classified as insane were very rapidly handled. They were simply stuck back in their terrifying memories of the mantis times. They all recovered quickly and were released. By request of the Grand Council, the actual criminals were left to the very end of the entire process. They would be the very last to receive therapy, though some had voted against their ever receiving such a precious gift, considering their crimes.

I argued against this, pointing out that when they died, they would still have these traumatic memories present to doom them in their next lifetimes. Thus, they decided to give them their therapy gifts last of all the millions in our country.

When our birthdays rolled around in May, Dita and I became of age, sixteen. Dianna was now seventeen, Ania, eighteen and a half. We were traveling the northern coastal road at the time, still training two hundred women a week and overseeing sessions in the hundreds. Three days each week were hectic affairs, two with training the new recruits and overseeing hundreds of sessions, and then on Wednesdays, overseeing hundreds more sessions. On our days off, we spent traveling to the next stop or just sacking out at the inns, glad for a brief respite from the intense activity.

Mid June, we were in Grzegorz, the northwestern large coastal city, the last of the large cities. Already our mothers and the others in that very first group had gone on ahead to some of the smaller towns on the way back to our homes in Bazyli. On Sunday, the second half of this last batch of women had finished their therapy session.

Ania announced, "Well, believe it or not, that is the last batch that we have to train. Do you realize that it is all nearly over? That we have erased this trauma from over a million people? It is really ending, thanks to us."

"Wow! Over? Really, no more traveling?" I asked, not quite believing that it was finally ending. For the last month, I felt more like a robot going through the same motions over and over again.

"Me too, just call me Robot Dita!"

We slept in the next day, no more traveling until we had to make the final trip home. For the next two weeks, we oversaw sessions here in Grzegorz. Finally, the end came, the last of the millions of sessions finished. And our carriage and Albin awaited us; we were going home; the mammoth task completed.

None of us five said a word during the two-day trip by carriage down to Wit. We were just totally tranquil and serene; words were not necessary or even desired. As always, observant Albin was right there when we needed a hand; we didn't even have to ask. I thought to myself, Albin would make one of these women a fine, loving, caring husband.

Chapter 18 The Ending of the Solution

On July 1, our carriage pulled into the Elder College at Wit, stopping at the entrance to our dorm. Albin, as always, open the door and helped us step down. He fetched our few bags, carrying them to our room, and hugged us goodbye. Our room was spotless; our bed, freshly made. Zofia made sure of that before our arrival.

Accolades, praises, thank you's, and God bless you's swamped the four of us the moment we set foot in the dining room for lunch. The entire domestic staff surrounded us, heaping praise upon praise on us, until we begged them for something to eat. The outpouring didn't go away either. That afternoon, the Grand Council called us before them, heaping thanks and praises upon us until my ears were ringing. Poor Dita just wanted to hide from this overwhelming admiration being given to us.

Then, they made a formal presentation of awards for our near god-like assistance. Yes, they added a fifth tier to our already huge earrings, four more jade dangles they proudly added to both Dita's earrings and mine. They also added three in each of the tiers for Dianna and Ania, so that the length of theirs equaled ours. Each of us received a medallion on a gold chain to wear around our necks, the medallion rested at the top of our chests, yet the chain was long enough that we could manage to put them on and take them off ourselves. That is, we didn't have to fuss with clasps. The medallion wording read: Savior of Dorota along with our first name along with the year, 744. Dita later estimated that the medallions alone would cost perhaps fifty thousand gold pieces in Velona or Zargarb.

Further, they gave both Dianna and Ania a pair of the same expensive imported Alexa high-heeled boots that they had given to Dita and me. They wanted us all to look our best, the Saviors of Dorota. Again, though my ears felt like they were being pulled off, I was grateful that they did not try to also give us one of those popular cone-style formal dresses from Velona that some women were wearing.

After the day of celebration ended, the Grand Council formally asked us if we wished to become a part of their governing body, as four active members representing the women of Dorota. Reluctantly, but understandingly, they accepted our request to spend some time with our families for a while. We, thus, were able to put off that request, which none of us wanted to do. On July 4, 744, we finally moved back into our parent's homes, if only for a little while. Dianna stayed with me, while Ania moved in with Dita. Our houses being next to each other, we four were always together anyway.

All the women who had become Givers of the Holy Gift were given four emerald dangles to add to their earrings, which mom and Aniela proudly showed us the moment we arrived. Also, they were given golden medallions, whose inscription read: Giver of the Holy Gift. Both wore theirs whenever they left the house. The pride that my mother and sister now had in themselves was enormous. Yes, we all continued to work at our domestic chores, but they did so with a zest for life that I had never seen.

When dad came home that night for supper, he put his arms around mom and announced, "This is the most wonderful woman in the entire world, right here, my dear Tekla."

She beamed and added, "Thanks to you dear, the love between us is ten-fold more than when we fell in love when we were seventeen!"

"No dear, it must be twenty times stronger!" he amended her statement. Both grinned and looked as if they were really seventeen again and not forty-one and forty.

Mom took me aside while we were washing up the dinner mess. "You know, back in the village just beyond Grzegorz, I saw a boy who had broken his leg. I know that I was supposed to be handling the arm trauma, but I couldn't help myself. I gave him a therapy session on his leg. You know what? I just received word this afternoon from his father. Not only did he thank me, but also he reported that the boy's leg healed in two weeks' time, not the usual six weeks it takes to mend. Isn't that a miracle? Can we do this? I mean give our gift to any trauma victim?"

"Absolutely mom, that's what it's for. Say, the Grand Council is looking for some women to join them and to represent all the women of Dorota and their unique needs. Would you and Aniela like to do something like that?"

"What? Us, us on the Grand Council?" mom exclaimed, quite shocked.

"Well, who better than us, mom, to represent the needs of we women," Aniela spoke up.

Later, I spoke to Elder Amadei and the following week, the entire Grand Council arrived by carriages before our house. They formally invited mom, Aniela, Roksana, and Kazia to join the Grand Council as the women's representatives. Dita and Albin were extremely pleased as well. Even more surprising, they also formally introduced Albin to us all. "On behalf of the Elder College of Wit, I am pleased to introduce to you Elder Albin." We cheered and his father, Elder Gawel Feliks, could not have looked prouder of his son and daughter.

For the next two days, our families held nightly parties in honor of everyone's appointments and awards. Secretly, we four were very pleased that we had wiggled out of having to turn down the Council's request for us to become the women's representatives.

On Monday, Elder Albin came by our house after supper. "Guess what? I'm getting married next month!"

"Wow! Who's the lucky woman?" I asked, wondering just who had caught his fancy. Yes, there was a tiny bit of jealousy that another woman had captured his romantic interest. We had really become quite attached to his constant presence and selfless help.

"My sweetheart all through school, Klara Tyna. She's a Giver of the Holy Gift too. Please, you must come to my wedding. Please."

"Of course, silly. We wouldn't miss it for the world!" I replied enthusiastically.

"Thanks. Thanks. Say, you know what we're doing after that? We're heading to the Outer Lands to help fix up things out there. Our Elders in the Outer Lands have made thousands of converts, using the wrong interpretation of the Holy Scriptures. We are going to be a part of the Correction Committee being sent to help all of them get it right."

"Albin, er sorry, Elder Albin, that is a most worthy goal that you and Klara have set for yourselves. We are very proud that you wish to do this!" I validated him and he stood tall.

"Say, Elder Albin, do you suppose that you have room on your caravel for four more passengers?" Dita asked.

"Sure why? Who?" he asked.

"We four want to head to Velona and see if there are things there that need to be set to rights."

"Fantastic! I think that we are going to Megalos first, but I'm sure something can be worked out. I'll make the arrangements for you. Gosh, wait until I tell Klara!"

Ever practical, we four went together and bought them a wedding present of a large mahogany sea chest, lined with cedar. They would need it to carry their personal things to the Outer Lands in style. We had their first names inscribed on the lid.

When we told our parents of our plans to go with Elder Albin to the Outer Lands to help put things right there, they graciously accepted this. Yes, they shed tears and really didn't want us to go, but accepted it. From their point of view, this was really the right thing to do. Dita and I promised that, if we could, one day we would return for a visit.

The Grand Council also really hated to see us four leave Dorota, but they too graciously accepted our decision. They knew very well that amends had to be made out there with all the women and families that had been harmed by their misinterpretation of the Holy Scriptures. Further, Dianna needed to be returned to her home and parents. As a sendoff present, they gave us each a thousand gold pieces to help defray our expenses once we arrived in Velona. Since that would weigh too much for us to carry, most came in the form of trading gemstones, which fit nicely in pouches that we could easily manage.

"Dianna, when you are returned to your parents and family, I would like you to read this letter from the Grand Council to them. I suspect that they will not be able to read our language. If you have trouble reading it, I'm sure that one of your friends will do it for you. We here wish to express our sincerest thanks and praise for what you have selflessly done for our entire country. We know that it will be hard for them to accept your physical limitations, but we want them to know just how vital your role here has been. Perhaps that will help them understand and accept your worthiness as a person," Elder Amadei explained humbly.

Ever practical, Dianna then asked him if some "special things" could be sent along with us to Velona. He listened to her list and grinned. "Yes, there is plenty of room on the caravel, Dianna. You may rest assured that all will accompany you back to your homeland."

We didn't know it then, but she had cleverly arranged to have all the usual furniture and devices, which we were accustomed to using here in Dorota, sent along with us. An entire low to the floor kitchen, four sets of tables, chairs, chest of drawers, yokes of various sizes, and so on. Dianna knew just how convenient these inventions were and wanted to bring them back with her to make our lives a little easier. Later, she explained that she would use these as models to have more made, as we needed them. Clever Dianna.

The last thing I did before I left for the coastal city of Bozydar was to inquire how the men were now treating their women folk and how the crime rate looked. The Elders had ceased using their hypnotic voices, and the men were still kind, considerate, helpful, and loving of the women in their lives. The crime rates wobbled during the time it took to get everyone handled, but now it seemed to be settling down. Most were relatively petty thefts and robberies. While they could no longer claim to be crime free, Dorota was darn close to it. From my point of view, an armless woman could still go anywhere at any time and feel very safe. I had the feeling this was not going to be the case when we reached the Outer Lands.

On August 1, we, along with Elder Albin and Klara, arrived at the last inn before the docks at Bozydar. Here, we joined with many others who were volunteering. All told, four Elders were going, one of which had been to the Outer Lands before and was our escort there. A dozen Givers of the Holy Gift were heading there to work their miracles, one of which was Klara. Our escort, Elder Iwo, a man of twenty, tall and handsome, brought along his wife this trip. While we waited for our things to be taken onboard the caravel called Piotr's Eye, Elder Iwo explained what we were facing.

"Unfortunately, this is a long voyage, nearly three months. I'm afraid that the ship will present numerous problems for you women, but we will all do our best to make the trip as tolerable as we can. Do not hesitate to ask one of us for any assistance that you may need. Once we are underway, you will only be allowed on deck when the sea is very calm. We do not want any of you accidentally losing your balance on the rocking ship and falling overboard."

"During the long voyage, I will teach you the language used in this island country called Megalos. I also know a bit of Sea Prince dialect. However, Dianna, here, is from that country, and she has kindly volunteered to teach you her language. It will likely not be possible for you to learn to write these languages. The ship rolls fiercely and we do not have the proper desks for you to use."

"Accommodations are, by our standards, crude, please grin and bear it. It will only be for three months. Finally, some people get seasick from all the rocking motion. If you feel nauseous, let me know. I have a common herbal remedy, which the sailors use to combat it. I see they are ready for us now. If you will follow me to the carriages, we will get you all safely on board."

As we rode through the streets heading for the docks, Dianna joyfully said, "I can't believe that I am finally going home!"

Since it was just we four in the carriage, I added, "Me too, it feels like I am going home too. I will admit that when I took this assignment, I figured that I would be bumping off this body and going home to pick up a new one that has all its pieces. If it weren't for you three, I'm sure I would have done it. Together, we can face what comes."

"Home is wherever Bethany is, as far as I am concerned," Dita added. "Since she is being so honest, I'll say mine. Bethany, until we found Ania and Dianna, I was planning to suggest that we bump these bodies off and try again. Maybe I will get lucky again and get a male body."

"Thanks gang, for the support. I was ready to die back there on Pope Leo's yacht. With you with me, I'm ready to keep on living. But Dita, do you realize that if you and Bethany got new bodies, you might end up with two male bodies! Then, what would you do?" We all laughed at her jest, but in the back of my mind, I saw that that situation would be a hundred times worse for us!

Our carriage pulled up at the dock. Elder Albin came by to open our door and help us step down, though we didn't really need it. However, as we walked down the wooden pier towards the gangplank, I began to wonder just how crude the accommodations on the ship would be for us. The narrow boards that formed the gangplank now appeared very narrow. I took a deep breath and carefully walked on board, where Elder Albin was there to help us down the step onto the main deck, after he assisted Klara.

As we stepped on board the caravel, I realized that this was finally the end of my stay in Dorota. Honestly, I did not ever expect to be returning here. I'd accomplished my mission true; I had some fond memories of the people and places, but I truly did not want to live in such a boring society. All the houses were identical and plain. No entertainment, no dances, no art. Then, as time went on, I mused, they may just begin to import it from the Outer Lands. Perhaps in a hundred years, Dorota would be more like Velona, cosmopolitan and inviting. Just now, I took my last look and was ready to set sail.

Chapter 19 The Voyage Home

Piotr's Eye slowly tacked out of the harbor. All of us stood on deck watching the large city shrink before our eyes. Already the ship was rolling and I remembered to keep my legs far apart to steady myself. Quickly, I pointed this out to the other women, who were unused to this motion. At last, as the sailors began unfurling the mainsails, we were ordered below. The men insisted on helping us down the stairs and past the main cabins to the hold. For this, we were all thankful. None of us had our sea legs. In the large cargo hold, temporary accommodations for us had been prepared.

Rows of small cabins lined either side of the hold. The central portion held tables and chairs; thankfully, some were made for us, low to the deck. She was loaded with supplies and our living space was thus rather small. Elder Iwo explained that we women would not have to do any cooking on the trip. Because of the design of the galley and the motion of the ship, the ship's cook would handle those chores. Our responsibilities were to maintain our own cabins and handle our laundry. Dita and I shared one cabin, while Dianna and Ania were in the one next to ours.

Our basic bags of clothes and sundries had been stowed in our cabins for us. It was small with one bed, large enough for the both of us. Two slanted chairs allowed us to sit and stow our few belongings into a low drawer. There was not even a mirror on the wall. "Worst accommodations ever," Dita grumbled.

"No, it isn't, but it sure is not set up the way we had our explorer caravel. Ah well, three months and this is over. We can do anything for three months, my love." Dita grinned and we set about stowing our spare clothes.

By noon, half of the passengers were seasick. The herbal remedies were quickly brewed, but half of the floor space was now a mess. Those of us who were not sick spent the afternoon looking after the others. I was very, very pleased that the few men who were not ill cleaned up the floor!

By the third day out, I knew this was going to be a rough voyage for us. Without proper accommodations for us, without proper facilities, there was little that we could actually do. We mostly sat around the dining area or laid on our bunks. After a week of utter boredom for us, most of the sick had recovered. As promised, language lessons then began. At first, I found it interesting, in that I had not spoken Megalos for almost a half century, and for half of that, the Sea Prince dialects.

After two weeks, all four of us knew as much as those attempting to teach us, and we stopped participating in this endeavor. Well, Dianna continued giving her lessons for the duration of the voyage. After that, Dita, Ania, and I mostly just laid on our bunks and sweated. Heat of summer bore down on the caravel. Below decks, little fresh air circulated, leaving us all slow cooking. "Grin and bear it," became the most often spoken words. Ugh.

Six weeks later, we were becoming zombies, I swear. Eat, lay around, go to the bathroom, lay around, eat, lay around, eat, sleep, all the while sweating to death. Awful. However, that all changed on September 15, when we heard a crew member calling out, "Ships ahead. Three of ours." Shortly, afterwards, "They want to parley." I felt the caravel begin to slow down, and imagined the crew working rapidly to loosen the sails. I longed to be on deck and watch, anything to relieve the monotony of this voyage, the worst ever.

Of course, everyone began speculating about what was going on topside. Seldom did Dorota sail three caravels together; we didn't have but ten all told. All of us were sitting at the tables, when an Elder who I didn't know came down to join our Elders.

"We need to talk," he said, I didn't get his name unfortunately. "Our communities of the Redeemed in the Outer Lands are rapidly disintegrating! I need to warn you that it's chaos in all of our groups, scattered about these new lands."

Elder Albin quickly said, "Please, sit down and tell us what has happened. We are bringing a number of Givers of the Holy Gift with us. Perhaps they can help."

"I'm afraid it may be too late for that. Okay, somehow word spread from Dorota to Megalos and from there to the other colonies that the sacrifice of Marzena's arms was symbolic and was not supposed to be taken as meaning the amputation of women's arms. The news sent shockwaves through our newly Redeemed families! Outrage, anger, violent arguments, even open hostilities sprang up everywhere. I must admit that it was not an unexpected reaction. We Elders could not contain their rage any longer without using our voice tones."

"We were fortunate to have a few Givers of the Holy Gift arrive a couple months ago. They have been working on women every day since their arrival. While it has removed their trauma from their operations, we can see little change in their attitudes. It's horrible and I cannot blame them. Their lives are ruined because of our blunder."

"Over half of those Redeemed families have become totally disillusioned with us and are filled with hatred towards us. They pleaded with the Church of Jehosanity, and Pope Leo has allowed them back into his congregation, naming them officially Women of the Eighth Degree. We know that means their husbands must now hire caretakers for them, who look after their every need. Half of those we Redeemed have returned to Pope Leo's folds!"

"Those that remain are suffering horribly. Whenever they appear in public, such as the markets, they are ostracized, humiliated, and teased for their gullibility and foolishness. Many of the Holy Vessels have committed suicide by jumping off roofs, cliffs, or drowning in the ocean. Most are now refusing to learn the women's ways, declaring that because of our mistake, they should be totally cared for by servants! Of course, that cannot be done."

"Yet, there is some hope, around a quarter of them have decided to keep their faith, but wish to move to Dorota, where they can live their lives without persecution, humiliation, and being ostracized. Our three caravels are bringing over six hundred of them back to Dorota. Two other caravels, as I understand it, are bringing many to Dorota from the Sea Princes."

"Still, this is only a small fraction of those who want to move. We have made a bargain with this Pope Leo. He is going to provide ten more ships to help move those who wish to move to Dorota, in return for allowing him to accept back into his fold all those who wish to return, which, as I said, is at least half of all those we had converted to our faith!"

"I felt that I needed to warn you that you are headed into a maelstrom of protests, anger, hatred, and betrayals. What a mess we have made of our attempts to Redeem the Unholy." The Elders chatted, exchanging other details, but I began to think about the situation.

That evening, I contacted Linda d'Grange, hoping she might be able to give me more data on the situation, at least in Velona.

Linda reported, *Yes, it is a complete debacle here in Velona and also Zargarb. I've got it pretty well handled here at home, Bethany. We believe that twelve thousand women and girls are involved here. Fortunately, they stopped this despicable practice about seven months ago. I sent in a male representative to ask how we may be of assistance. He worked out a reasonable solution, I do believe. About a thousand women and their families have rejoined the Church of Jehosanity and are being given the status of Women of the Eighth Degree. For the most part, their husbands are relatively wealthy; at least they have enough to hire live-in maids to help their women.*

Some five thousand women and their families are now forming their own community called Little Dorota, east of Velona, near the old Santi fortress along the Coast Road. Monarch Lana Po has given them a deed to sufficient land there that they can make a go of it. She's sent along a number of soldiers to assist in the construction of housing and such. Lana has also proposed allowing those who wish to join her Church of the Three Holy Roses to do so and has given each woman a gold medallion in the shape of a rose to wear about her next. Some three thousand women and their families have now joined her church. This has already done much to curb the public's harsh condemnation of these women for having been so foolish. These families have moved back to the general areas from which they came when they originally joined the Elder's community. Thus, far, that appears to be working out for them.

Another three thousand and their families have expressed a strong desire to move to Dorota. Lana has graciously offered twenty caravels to ferry them there. They left three weeks ago, carrying about two thousand of them. When they return, the caravels will make a second run, taking the last of them to Dorota.

Zargarb has followed Lana's lead and the situation there appears to have resolved itself. Down in Demokritos, it is another story. There, only a thousand women and their families have joined to form a small town, living as close as possible to the ways found on Dorota. The remaining nine thousand have rejoined their former churches and are proclaiming themselves Women of the Eighth Degree and are being accepted as such. I fear that this may well fuel further expansion of the Church of Jehosanity and their Holy Degrees in Demokritos, but time will tell.

We don't have good contact with Megalos, so your information there is probably far better than ours is. I've heard that there have been some bitter and vicious conflicts there, but not much more.

I replied, *Well that is better news than I expected. We're about halfway to Megalos now. It's the worst boat trip I've ever had, incredibly boring. I can't wait to get back, but I think I will be needed on Megalos a while, to help them get things sorted out. I'll keep you posted.* We chatted a bit and I broke the contact.

In the secrecy of my cabin, I told Dita, Dianna, and Ania what Linda had told me. All expressed great relief that things were so easily resolved in the Sea Princes. At least, we only faced one major mass of angry men and women.

The next day, I chatted with the Elders on board, making some suggestions that we might follow, based upon what Lana Po had done in Velona. "Establish one community where all the families can live, separate from the other cities and general populations. Build a small Little Dorota somewhere on Megalos. Whatever you do, don't mention giant mantis creatures. These people probably have never experienced them, and you'll just be laughed at or ridiculed. Merely say that a tragic mistake has been made and leave it at that."

The Elders liked the idea and began to work out some details. Elder Iwo knew the locations of all the various communities and had some good ideas how they might accomplish the construction of a small Little Dorota to insulate the Holy Vessels from those who would ridicule them. Whether or not any of this would be possible, I didn't know, but it gave them something to work on for the next six weeks of miserable sailing. At least the temperatures began to moderate substantially.

Chapter 20 Dealing with Megalos

Piotr's Eye slowly tacked into the harbor at Gatos, a small city of some ten thousand on the southeastern edge of the large island nation of Megalos. It was November 1 and a balmy eighty degrees, the sun shone down brightly from a clear blue sky, as it always did here this far south. Indeed, only in the wintertime was the weather to my liking in this part of the world. All of us were on deck getting our first look at the city and the country.

The land was a bit rocky and rugged here. Houses were terraced up and down the hills, white marble buildings and columns with their red tile roofs dotted the brown and blacks of the rock outcrops. A hundred shades of green filled in the rest — plants of all kinds that we'd never seen grew nearly everywhere, carefully cultivated to blend with the spectacular architectural style that predominated in this country. "Deceptively picturesque," Dita commented under her breath. Indeed, here was the home of the Pope and the Church of Jehosanity, whom we both hated for lifetimes now.

We had to wait on the caravel for several hours, until the Elder returned with sufficient carriages. By late afternoon, our meager possessions were stowed and we climbed into the waiting carriages for the ride to their community outside of the city proper. Meanwhile, all of Dianna's cargo was off loaded to one of the dock warehouses, where it would remain until then next ship could take it on up to Velona. Linda promised to watch for it and see that it was safely stored until Dianna could return.

We gazed out of the windows at all the toga-wearing people, who uniformly had dark bronzed skin, golden hued. Close to suppertime, we finally pulled into a gated series of buildings. A low white stone wall surrounded some thirty hastily built buildings, most of which were merely roofs supported by marble columns. Thin gauze curtains formed the walls, which allowed the cool sea breeze to flow through the structure, making living inside bearable. A few of the buildings had stone walls, and the carriages halted before the largest of these, their administration building.

"Here we have our communal dinners. We've found that it works best for everyone if we all dine in shifts together as much as possible. Come, we'll dine first, and then I will take you to your living quarters. Tomorrow, we can get down to work," Elder Iwo explained.

Inside, we found tables that were lower than normal for a regular person, but much taller than we women were used to having. Men sat across from the women and for the most part were feeding them! So much for independence here, I thought. "They haven't adapted at all well, have they" whispered Ania. I estimated some two hundred were eating at this time.

We found some empty spaces and sat down. Shortly, a number of men came with trays of food. There was no choice of menu; everyone ate the same thing. Tonight, it was fish and vegetables, with goat's milk or tea to wash it down. Bland was the taste; I suspected that men were playing chefs. Later, I found out I was right.

Even with the high table, we women managed to feed ourselves, much to the admiration of the men with us. Albin looked very relieved that he did not have to feed Klara or us, for that matter. I notice that perhaps a few women here were feeding themselves, far too few had truly adapted, I thought. The mood was solemn; I suspected an undercurrent of hostility in the room.

After we ate, we were taken to one of the open aired buildings, reserved for our whole group. We found that different sections were curtained off, providing the slight illusion of your own private space. Beds were soft and the chest of drawers was low, so we could manage our own personal care. Dita was quite thankful for that. "We don't really have any privacy here, do we?" she whispered as she brushed out my hair before bed. Ania and Dianna were doing theirs. We four shared two beds in this same space, thankfully.

After breakfast the next morning, the Elders assembled everyone who was living here in the commune, some two thousand all total, though more were expected as the days passed. Elder Iwo gave us four a lengthy introduction, outlining what we had done for the entire country back home. Some applauded us, but many did not. I decided to make a little speech; it seemed like the right time anyway.

"Good morning everyone, I would like to say a few words to all of you, men, women, and children. Everything that you have heard about our society on Dorota is true. There is no crime to speak of; everyone goes to school and can read and write. In many ways, it is a relatively ideal country in which to live. As a young girl, mom would send me off to buy groceries at the market, carrying my money in a little pouch with me. It is totally safe for anyone to walk anywhere at any time; it really is that way. If we encounter some difficulty that we cannot manage, a man or boy is right there to lend us a hand."

"However, as you all know, a tragic, horrible, terrible mistake has been made in the interpretation of our holy scriptures. Marzena's offering to give her arms to her husband is supposed to be a symbolic offering, not a literal amputation of her arms. Men and women sometimes make mistakes, in this case a really, really big mistake! God has given me the ability to give the Holy Gift to those that I choose, the gift that Marzena gave to her Jurek. The gift is priceless but incredibly hard to define. It's not like handing you a gold coin or a gem or an arm. It is not of this physical universe and thus very difficult to describe. We have no words for it. Thus, it is easier to understand if you say Marzena offered her arms to give her husband greater strength. We can imagine how that might be. Hence, the mistake was made."

"Yes, you have every right to be angry. What was done is so awful that there are hardly any words to describe the terribleness of it all. The mistake is permanent. There is no way to re-grow lost arms. I understand your outrage, your anger. I say unto you, it is justified. Yet, life is within us all. Let us make the best of it and live our lives to the fullest that we can."

"We have come here to do two things. First, we will give all you women our precious gift. Second, those of you women, who wish to learn how to also give this precious gift to others, we will teach you its ways. Once that is done, then we will attempt to give the men and boys our gift. However, we only give our gift to those who desire it. We will not force anyone to receive it. Some of you will get this gift later today. We will do our best to get to all of you as soon as we can. Thank you."

I mostly wanted them to know that I thought it was okay for them to have resentment, anger, and even hostility because of what was done to them and their families. Now the real work would begin, many, many therapy sessions. Unlike those on Dorota, here the best I could hope for was the removal of the trauma they had suffered during the many surgeries. There was no underlying mantis creature trauma lying earlier in time. I doubted that our therapy sessions would be the cure that it was back in Dorota.

An Elder explained to us that due to all the suicides, they had formed up an orphanage to care for those left behind. Twenty younger women, ranging in age from six to seventeen, were being cared for as a group. Some fifteen orphaned boys were seeing to their needs. Thus, I had already decided to tackle this group of twenty first, and then train them to begin delivering therapy sessions. Why? To give them back their self-respect, which I guessed they had now completely lost.

Four of the women from our very first group of two hundred volunteers had arrived here several months ago and had been working their miracles daily. I had them start in on four of the twenty orphans, while the rest of us, twelve plus we four, would deal with the rest. I also decided that Dita and I ought to take the two roughest cases.

"Oh, that would be Ilena and Kali," the Elder explained. "They have been nothing but troublemakers since they came to us. We cannot seem to do anything with them, they seethe hatred against us, but as youngsters, we cannot just abandon them."

The only place that we could really do our therapy was our own rooms. We four returned to our bedroom space and awaited the Elders to bring our four to us. Ania had a little girl of six to handle, while Dianna had a nine year old girl. Both seemed well mannered, but terribly quiet and shy. I made sure that they got their sessions going well.

A bit later, Elder Iwo brought two seventeen year old girls to us. "This is Ilena and this is Kali," he said politely.

"Ilenakova da Casa!" she growled angrily and spat on his feet. She stomped into my room, sat down on the bed across from me, and glared at me.

"Kali Kato!" the other young woman emulated Irena and spat on his feet as well. She, too, stomped into our room, and sat down hard on the bed across from Dita.

"Ilenakova, Kali, are you willing to receive our precious gift?" I asked, half expecting that they would not.

"Hell, you might as well go ahead. There's nothing else to do around here, except kick men in the balls when you get the chance," Ilenakova stated angrily.

"Yeh, go ahead," Kali added.

I could tell that Dita was unsure just where to begin. I gave both young women their starting point, much to Dita's relief. "Okay, close your eyes. Were you this angry the moment you woke up this morning?" Both answered no, not really. I smiled. I had them.

"Okay, I want you to go back and re-experience this morning when you got angry. Dita will give Kali the rest of the commands and listen to her, while I listen and talk to Ilenakova. Tell us what is happening as you go through the morning."

"Well, I was lying there smelling the cool sea breeze as I woke. I felt at peace, and then I tried to get up and realized once more that I don't have any arms. I got mad. Went to breakfast, Bill tried to feed me and I kicked him. I told him I can feed myself." She rattled on about more things that occurred, ending up with spitting on Elder Iwo's feet. I had her go through it again and then asked her for an earlier time she felt this way. For an hour, I listened to an unending series of similar days. Then, she found something earlier than these.

"We used to live in Zargarb. Dad moves us here over my violent protests. I kick him many times. He joins the army and goes and gets himself killed, leaving me like this! Damn him to hell!" This loss, we went over a few times and she began to cry over the loss of her father. A while later, we went earlier.

I heard about her mother who had jumped off the roof of their house to kill herself, because she had given up on trying to live as they were, armless. Her mother had been terribly depressed for several years, leading up to the taking of her own life to get out of the horror she was in. At first, Ilenakova was quite angry with her mother, but soon, the thus far never expressed grief surfaced; once more, she cried and cried.

After I had run the grief out, I asked for something even earlier, knowing we'd probably get her surgery. We did. "I am a small baby, maybe one year old. I'm going to heaven, mom says to me. I drink some liquid and I go to sleep. I wake up and my shoulders ache and I cry. That's all." All the pain was suppressed. On the third pass, she began screaming as she finally contacted the physical pain that the body had felt. This trauma we ran over and over, until she no longer felt any of the pains.

Now came the moment of truth. Would the whole trauma lift or was there some similar trauma that lay still untouched? I asked if there was any similar earlier trauma, she said no, and we went through it all once more. The third time I asked her for something earlier, she sat up like a bolt of lightning had hit her. Her eyes opened wide.

"Oh my god! I forgot all about that! I've been around a long time! I was called Lena Jena Pazzio le'Goeur and married good old Sam d'Grange. I had two of the greatest parents in the whole universe, Bethany and Renzo! Before that, I was Lenkova Pazzio, a famous Sisterhood fighter! I came here to fight these bastards who were mutilating women. I vowed to kill them all! Only I can't do more now than kick them where it hurts! Wow!" She began laughing hard. I ended the session; my mind was blown! She had been Renzo and my daughter and before that, a dear friend, Lenkova!

Beside me, Dita was handling Kali, running out all the anger from today and from many earlier similar days. Then, she too hit the loss of her father, who had been killed while trying to kill the Elders who had brought this calamity upon them. After the suppressed grief was gone, the earlier loss of her mother, who committed suicide, came up. It happened when Kali was two years old and her mother did it for exactly the same reasons as had Ilenakova's mother. After several recounting, Kali's suppressed grief rose to the surface and dissipated.

Dita then ran headlong into Kali's surgery, which was almost knife cut by knife cut the same as Ilenakova's. The similarity of these two young women's history was why they had become best friends here in the commune. Nearly at the same time as Ilenakova's realization, Kali uncovered her own identity. "Well, I'll be! I used to be Kallisto, the assassin down in Demokritos, looking after other Women of the Eighth Degree, whose husbands deserted them, getting those poor women their revenge. Then I went to Annelise to help a very good friend survive her ordeal as a Woman of the Eighth Degree, she was supposed to be Empress of Demokritos. Marin Bethany was her name. After that, Hans and I married again; he was my husband when I was Kallisto. We became King and Queen of Annelise. When that body died, I had heard of this new butchery of women up here in Megalos and came here to get my next body, determined to put an end to this evilness of men here. Only my folks screwed that all up by joining very the damn church that I was trying to stop! Wow! Way cool, now I can recall it all. I feel great, except I can't do much to stop these bastards, but I guess you already have, so it's okay now, I guess. Wow!" She laughed and laughed, looked at Ilenakova; both laughed even harder. They had been trying to do the very same thing, put an end to this butchery of women.

Of course, I'd overheard Dita's session and she, mine. We now looked at each other's patient, our eyes watering. I said, "Ilenakova, Kali, I am Bethany or Elizabeth Ann Amir and Dita here was my husband, Renzo

Pazzio le'Goeur! We were your parents, Ilenakova! Kallisto, how I've missed you!"

"Mom? Dad? Oh my god! It is you!" She started bawling, waves of joy and happiness so overwhelmed her.

"Damnable small world, Marin Bethany!" Kali exclaimed. "Well met indeed! You are looking great, but I see we are in the same pickle barrel once more. I am so glad to see you that I'm bawling like a baby!" She was. None of we four had dry eyes.

Ania and Dianna, who had quite some time ago finished off their easy patients, had stuck around to listen in and learn how to deal with more difficult cases. Ania butted in, "And I am Alexa and this is Enyo, you know, from the Isle of Right! Enyo, the Engineer, and Alexa, the Politician."

Both Ilenakova and Kali remembered well Alexa and Enyo! Now all six of us were crying and hugging in a mass of six bodies. What a reunion we six had! Then, we headed off to get some much needed lunch. The Elders were shocked at the totally changed behavior of the two teens, who now acted perfectly normal. While we were all feeding ourselves, Ilenakova asked, "Can Kali and I please move in with you two? It is so awful in that orphan's room. Please, mom, dad?" She giggled and added, "Well it worked nearly a hundred years ago — begging like that." We all laughed again.

Of course, I agreed. "But you are going to have to work to earn your keep with us. I'll show you how to do the therapy tomorrow and then you get to help us work on all the others." They agreed wholeheartedly. The Elders had another bed moved into our quarters that afternoon, marveling at how great the change was in these two worst-case teens. For the first time, the Elders began to have a little hope that this horrible mess that they had created would somehow get patched up.

We six talked long into the night, sharing the major events of several lives. Ilenakova told me about my three grandchildren that I never knew that I had. Dita, not to be outdone, told me about the two grandchildren I had with him from our son, Raphael. I had died while giving him birth. Kali told us all wonderful stories about her life as Queen of Annelise. Silly us, we tried to catch up on a hundred years of life in one evening.

I got a good look at the two young women. Ilenakova had slightly lighter skin than I, a very light brown. She had an oval face, with short light brown hair and enchanting blue eyes. Her cheeks were a bit high, giving her a look that said I am serious. She was tall, at least five-ten, and her breasts had really started to fill out.

Kali had the typical bronze skin of one from Megalos. Her curly, short black hair and eyes added to her mystique; she was very attractive with an angelic, round face. She was tall approaching six feet and thin. Her lips were thick and curled giving her a natural teasing, coy look.

In the morning, both Kali and Ilenakova insisted that we wear the local togas like theirs. A thin, white gauze draped easily and loosely over their bodies. "Look, they are cool. Your cotton dresses are going to be far too hot here. Come on, they are easy to put on," Kali insisted, showing us how.

"But Kali, you can see everything through it," I protested, feeling a bit modest about showing off myself quite so much.

"Oh do I ever like it, pant, pant," Dita teased us.

"Oh Renzo, that'll be enough of that!" Ilenakova teased her back and flaunted her well-formed body before him. We all laughed.

"Honestly, don't be such a prude. It gets hot here even in the winter," Kali insisted. I relented and soon we were wearing the local light togas.

"Wow Dita, you look gorgeous!" Ilenakova stated the obvious.

"Hey, you stay away from my Dita," I teased her. We all laughed again and headed off to get breakfast.

Then, it was back to work. I had to teach the twenty young orphans how to do the therapy. Unlike the short lessons needed on Dorota, here I had to spend all morning at it. Most of the time was spent giving them ideas on just how to start. After lunch, the dozen from Dorota and these twenty new Givers of the Holy Gift got started on thirty-two women and children. I pair them off by age as much as possible, making the Elders keep records of who had received their gift of therapy. We four then circulated about the dining room, helping where we were needed.

The younger girls did surprisingly well at this. They dove right in and got their patients running well. Uniformly, these younger women handled their traumas vastly more rapidly than their parents and older women. All twenty were done by mid-afternoon, and all twenty wanted to know right now how to do this. I observed that for them, this was more like a game than therapy. Fascinating, I thought and pondered its significance. Because I had a dozen young girls from seven to fourteen begging me, I relented and spent the early evening teaching these twenty how to do the therapy.

By design, at supper, Elder Iwo presented each of the new therapy givers with an identical gold medallion that stated Giver of the Holy Gift upon it. All now wore theirs proudly around their necks. Self-pride began to increase noticeably among these women, no more so than among the orphans.

Within a few days, word got around that the orphans and children were the best Givers of the Holy Gift! Besieged were the Elders with requests from those awaiting their chance to have this gift. All wanted to have one of them be their giver! Their pride doubled, as they found that they were now highly sought after as givers. I'd not seen this phenomenon before and began to study what was going on. Why should the younger ones be so much better at this than the adults? I had no immediate, easy answer.

Days passed swiftly. Wagons of possessions and people continued to arrive every day. These families brought with them intense anger and grief, to say nothing of hopelessness, helplessness, and dismal failure. I learned more than I wanted to about intolerance and discrimination. These women were now terrified to be seen in public. They had been scorned, ridiculed for their stupidity, teased, and even taunted. Their husbands were reviled as ignorant bastards, as well as teased and taunted themselves. Now, they were angry, sometimes violently so.

The twenty doktors here on Megalos had all come to Gatos with us, but they remained secluded in one of the stone walled buildings. I learned that twenty Security Guards were also here with their guns, which was the only thing keeping the doktors alive right now. Further, the Elders seldom went among their people without having a Security Guard in the background.

"Hey, they aren't making all that up," Ilenakova explained over lunch. "Kali and I used to live in Galantas, the capital city. We used to go to the markets just to get away from all this. God, were we ever humiliated. People just loved to pick on us and make fun of us. We were the constant butt of many people's jokes. While we were embarrassed, we couldn't do a damned thing about it. Besides, it was better to be ridiculed on the streets than be around these sickos. We could just pretend that we didn't hear all the snide comments directed at us."

We continued to reach more women every day, training more as we could. One evening in late December, we six took an evening stroll around the walled commune. The weather was finally cool, a mere seventy-five degrees. We spied several Security Guards patrolling the perimeter walls and felt safe just walking and enjoying the light evening sea breeze that came in off the ocean.

Out of the corner of my eye, I caught a flash of something dark slipping over the white walls. I looked but saw nothing. Ilenakova also saw something moving, "Hey over there, someone's gotten into the complex. See, he's slinking up behind that guard! Come on!" She began running towards the three guards. We all followed. I saw the glint of something shiny and watched the guard slip to the ground. He had not made a sound. The man dressed all in black picked up something, saw us running towards him and slipped back over the walls.

As we approached the fallen man, blood flowed from his throat. A clean slice had cut deep to the vertebrae. His hands grasped his neck in a last desperate attempt to stop the gushing of blood. As we got there, we watched his hands slowly release their grip and slumped to the ground. Once again, I had witnesses a man dying. It was not pleasant. Dianna knelt down beside him to see if there was anything that she could do to save him. We yelled to the other Security Guards and they began running towards us.

However, we saw two more dark figures hop over the wall. Both guards went down without knowing what hit them! I lost my temper and latched on to one of the men in black, lifting him high into the air. The other picked up something and vanished over the wall. "Ania, go get some help. Sound the alarm or something," I called out angrily. "I got one of them assassins."

Dianna now joined us, but stopped to look at the other two men. "Both dead," she announced and then looked up at the man whose arms and legs were flailing around in the air helplessly.

"Who is this assassin anyway?" Dita wanted to know. "I'll grab his arms Bethany and you can lower him and take his mask off. Let's see his face. I bet he's Mano del Dio." Dita moved out of her body and did her thing, pulling his arms tightly out to either side, while I lowered him to the ground. Dianna, Kali, and Ilenakova used their feet to pull his mask off, being careful not to touch any other part of his body, cautious of what other assassin tools and poisons he might have on him.

"Damn! It's you! Eros Maios! He's the butcher who cut off my fingers one by one and then my hands."

"You were supposed to die, bitch!" he spat at her. "Put me down this instant or I will cut off your damn legs too." He had no idea who was holding him so tightly, but he showed absolutely no fear at all.

Dita snapped. "Stand back! You bastard. Let's see how you like a taste of your own medicine!" Involuntarily, we five stepped back, so strong was her intention that we do so. As we watched, she pulled each of his arms out of their sockets, ripping them off his torso! Blood gushed from his arteries.

Just then a swarm of adults came running up. "My god, what has happened here?" Elder Iwo called out and stopped short of the dying assassin.

"Mano del Dio assassins came over the wall and cut the throats of three of our guards. This one got what he deserved. He's the man who tortured Dianna here, cutting off her fingers and hands, leaving her to die. I guess he finally got what's coming to him," I replied.

"Oh, this is nothing that your pretty eyes should ever have to witness. Please, let's get you back into your room. We'll take it from here," Elder Iwo ordered.

"Sir, we think that they stole something from the guards," Kali added.

From over the walls, I spotted one of the other assassins. As he saw me spotting him, he yelled, "You are all dead women!" He then raced off into the night streets of Gatos. Shaken, we headed back to our bedroom and sat down on the beds.

"I'm sorry, gang. I just lost my temper back there," Dita felt that she owed us an explanation. "I am a Protector, and knowing what he did to Dianna here, I just reciprocated. Now I have gone and done it, haven't I? The whole Mano del Dio will be after us now. Damn."

"Thanks, Renzo, I mean Dita," Dianna said quietly. "I am glad that he has finally paid the price for ruining my life!"

"Yes, but now look what I've done! I've brought the whole Mano del Dio down on our heads," Dita wailed. "Do not act out of anger. Damn, I've already forgotten that cardinal rule of Protectors. I need a refresher course that's for sure. What are we going to do now?"

"Nothing. I doubt that they will come after us, Dita. After all, who is going to believe him that you did it? He only saw six armless girls just watching what was happening there. He didn't actually see us doing anything, only Eros's arms getting mysteriously pulled off. We're probably safe, Dita. Don't worry about it. Besides when we get to Velona, we can all do with a refresher course."

"Damn, you really don't know, do you?" Ilenakova gasped. "The Santi del Dio is no more; the last of the old ones have long ago died of old age. There is no one left to train you."

Her words struck me like a thunderbolt! The Santi, gone? The last of us Druwids gone? I must have looked stunned by the news. Even Dita was shocked. "Mont Blanc? It's still there?" Dita muttered.

"Yes, but mostly fighters now protect the city-state. They control the whole Langdoc region now. At least that's the last I heard before we left Zargarb," Ilenakova replied.

I recovered my composure. "Well, I have been out of it for over a half century. Damn. Well, we will figure something out when we get to Velona, I'm sure." Dita looked better and I dropped it for now. Our conversation turned to what the assassins had taken from our Security Guards. Our consensus was their guns, a weapon new to the Outer Lands. Obviously, the Church of Jehosanity wanted to get their hands on some. Later, we learned that was indeed what was stolen, three guns and some bullets for them. After this episode, a dozen guards patrolled our perimeter, always within seeing distance of the others, guarding each other's backs. However, no more assassinations occurred.

By the end of January, we had given therapy sessions to all the women, though a few more families continued to trickle into Gato Commune. Now we concentrated on dealing with the men, a far more delicate therapy, since they had not suffered the physical trauma that the women had endured. Instead, theirs was one of a shocking loss and betrayal, tantamount to treason, if one wished to be blunt about it. I didn't expect that this loss would merely vanish on re-experiencing it, rather, for the men to be so violently angry more than a year after their discovery of the "misinterpretation," some real trauma must lie earlier in their lives. Frequently, they discovered that in an earlier lifetime, they had been betrayed, and it cost them their life. Those then vanished along with the anger.

By May, the last of the males had received their therapy. No more new arrivals had appeared for several weeks. Now it was time for decisions. Barely twenty thousand total people remained here in Gato, down from their original numbers of over fifty thousand. Uniformly, none of the men was wealthy; those had left with their families long ago, preferring to rejoin the Church of Jehosanity and have their women folk be anointed Women of the Eighth Degree, giving their women an elevated societal status, a dubious one at best.

During April, the Elders and we had a long discussion about the future for these people. One thing was obvious, if they stayed here on Megalos, they would be eternally facing the discrimination of others, ridiculed wherever they went. The only real answer lay in having them move to Dorota, where they would be welcomed and could live a reasonable life. Thus, on May 2, the Elders held a group meeting with the male heads of their households and discussed available options. The decision to move to Dorota was now unanimous. Fathers wanted to give their wives and children a chance at life.

Expecting this outcome, arrangements had already been made months ago. Although they did not trust Pope Leo at all, after his men had assassinated the three guards, the Elders had little choice but to accept his offer of sixty ships to help ferry them to Dorota. Other countries made up the difference, and on May 15, a flotilla of over a hundred caravels embarked for Dorota.

We six were not onboard. Rather we stood on the deck of the Jolly Prince, a caravel bound for Velona. We'd said our farewells to Elder Albin and Klara and the others. They had accepted our decision to go and check on how things were in their communes up in the Sea Princes. Elder Albin's last words echoed in my mind. "Bethany, you and your companions are always welcome at our home, anytime. May our paths cross again and soon and may God bless all of you and watch over you."

"Damn!" Dita exclaimed. "Look there, by that building! A Mano del Dio spy is watching us leave. He knows where we are bound for now! See, sky blue robes." We all saw him, from a distance; it looked like he gave us an evil grin, though none of us could be sure that we weren't just imagining it.

Chapter 21 At Last, Velona

The year: 745. Dita and I were now seventeen, Dianna was turning eighteen, Ania would soon be nineteen, while Ilenakova and Kali were eighteen as well. The Jolly Prince was still in the service of the Santi, though it now flew a different banner, a white sail with a red plain cross on it. She had been refitted to her new purpose in life that of a Banker's Ship.

A high guardrail surrounded the main deck, which made boarding at sea from another caravel vastly more difficult, giving the ship's defenders a distinct advantage. A side benefit was that we were allowed on deck anytime except in rough weather, so took advantage of this every possible minute of every day!

While the captain and mate cabins remained the same as they always had been level here with the main deck, the cargo hold was now vastly different. The cargo it now carried was gold, gems, and jewelry along with passengers, of course. The center of the hold was reserved for the cargo. Along both sides and the stern were rows of cabins, two people to a cabin. She could easily carry sixty men at one time, which she did when ferrying a valuable shipment. The galley and crew's quarters were still far forward as before.

This trip, she had a small cargo of gold bullion and forty men at arms beyond the seven crew and captain. Fore, a large kitchen area could seat fifty at a time. The cook was the captain's wife, Elaine. The captain was Jon Smith, both were kind, seafaring folks, who loved to tell stories and hear of adventures. They were in their forties and their children had moved out on their own last year. Both were experiencing the empty nest syndrome, missing their three teens.

We were given three adjacent cabins nearest the galley and kitchen area. Each had a bed but hooks for hammocks were usually used by the men, especially in rough or hot weather. However, the rooms were clean, a fact that we appreciated. Gone was the tepid odors of the Dorota caravels, Captain Jon ran a tight, clean ship, in the usual Santi tradition, unlike the vessels of all the other countries, perhaps save Velona. Elaine did her best to make us feel right at home on the Jolly Prince, taking us under her wing as if we were her teens.

"Well, I do declare that I have never met anyone with your conditions, girls, but I'll do all that I can to help. Even the soldiers — they'll help too or I'll make them swab the deck. We'll manage somehow, honeys, yes we will." She chatted away. This was the first time I realized that others would think of us as having a condition, but that was better than saying that we were cripples, though I suspected that she and the many men just might. It was a logical way of thinking, I realized. Suddenly it became real to me that going home meant being the odd ball among all the normal people! Before now, we were used to seeing nearly all women looking like ourselves. Now we were rejoining the mainstream of society where they would look upon us as very different from themselves. I hoped people would be kinder to us than they had been to the poor women who had been converted by the Elders.

At first, we wanted to do something to help on the ship. However, the kitchen was not setup for us in any way. About all that we could do was help peel potatoes, which went so slowly that Elaine insisted the usual men do that. We tried to help with the piles of dishes, but again were shoed away. "Really, Bethany. You are paying passengers on this trip. You are supposed to sit back and enjoy the trip." After the third day, we did just that. Though we six felt very uncomfortable about it, we were not able to function at all on this ship.

Days we spent topside along with the many men, who stood around or sat, often smoking their pipes. Quite frequently, Captain Jon would engage us in conversations, relating one of his stories about life on the high seas. In turn, Dianna, Ilenakova, and Kali told him about their adventures. He was very keen on hearing Dianna's, however.

The one thing that I rather disliked was the nearly constant gazes from the many men. Often, I spied bulges in their pants. Dita really was annoyed with this. "I see them as men," she explained when we were crowded into one cabin brushing out our hair at night.

"Well, you are supposed to," Dianna replied.

"Yes, but I think of myself as a guy!" Dita replied. Now we all understood what she meant, and we giggled once more. "Stop it! It isn't funny," she protested. I gave her a kiss to mollify her.

Other than the incessant stares from the men, the voyage was quite pleasant and enjoyable, quite unlike our three month trip from Dorota. Finally, we spied the buildings of Velona in the distance and then the huge port came into view on July 1, 745.

"Wow!" I exclaimed. It had more than doubled in size since I last saw the large harbor here. The city had expanded outward on all sides, as I would soon discover. All manner of new buildings, some grey stone, some wooden, some with Megalos style architecture dotted the horizon. Above them all stood the gigantic Cathedral of the Three Holy Roses. Wait; there was a new church even taller and more grandiose vying for our attention.

"That's the Church of Jehosanity," Dianna caustically pointed out. "They just have to outdo us in every way possible." She detested this church now more than ever before, for obvious reasons.

Memories began flooding my mind, all the many times I had seen this scene, as the ships that I had been on slowly tacked into the harbor and up to the docks. I remembered sharply when I had first returned home here after the mantis creature had eaten my arms off as well as Linda's. We were so worried and scared about how our families would react, how our friends would treat us, as if we were now freaks.

My stomach knotted; I was feeling the very same way. I glanced at my dear friends; they, too, were most apprehensive. None more so than Dianna, who was looking very frightened.

"Gosh, I am really getting nervous about this," I said, breaking our silence, stating what I was feeling as well was what they were as well.

"Maybe this was a bad idea," Dianna gushed emotionally, "coming here, I mean. Maybe we should have gone somewhere else. I am scared. What will they think of me now, like this? I think I might throw up!"

Even Dita was looking rather pale. I could not think of anything to say, really. I'd been in this exact situation before. Ania spoke instead. "Hey, if they loved you before, they'll love you now. If they can't handle the way that we are, then to heck with them. We certainly can't change the way that we are now. Remember, we are a team. Together, we can do anything. You are not alone, Enyo, er Dianna, I'm right by your side like the old days. Remember how we were an inseparable team? Well, we still are — all six of us."

"Thanks. I need you guys. I really *do* this time. I am both nervous and embarrassed at the same time. How can I feel this way?" Dianna replied. "I never felt this way before when I was Enyo. Oh, I guess that is not being honest. I was a little this way then too, only then I was armless as long as I could remember. Now — well, Ilenakova and Kali know what I mean."

"We do, we're just glad that it is not our relations that we will be meeting. I think that has a whole lot to do with it," Kali wisely observed.

"Besides, Dianna, if any of them give you a hard time, I'll kick them in their privates! You didn't do anything wrong. You are the victim," Ilenakova added. That seemed to lift her spirits a little.

As the docks slowly approached, we caught our first good glimpse of the workers and people around the area. I spied several waiting carriages. "I bet those are for us. Are those people your folks and relatives?"

"Yes, I can see mom and dad there. Oh no, they brought the whole family! Everyone's there!" Her panic swelled once more.

"Hey, this way they will all get a good look at us now, and then we won't have to face seeing bunches more after we get there, wherever there is," Dita pointed out.

"I suppose that's better. Freak out once and be done with it," Dianna sighed. Ropes flew; dockhands rapidly wrapped them around the mooring timbers. Others began working on attaching the gangplank. Now I could get a good look at her extended family. Rather it was their fashion that caught my eyes instead.

The men wore well-tailored blue suits, whose coats had twin tails in the back, like swallows. Each wore a colored silk sash style necktie and waistband. Even the small boys wore similar outfits and looked handsome and smart. The women wore the typical conical dresses, hoop skirts beneath forming a perfectly round cone with an even, straight fall, extending to some six feet in diameter near the ground, where scallops dangled. Their tops glistened in the sunlight, undoubtedly silk or satin. All colors of the rainbow were represented in the collection of dresses, each one a solid color. From the smallish steps that the women took, I could tell that they wore high heels beneath their wide skirts. Even the little girls appeared as scaled down versions of their mothers.

No mistaking Monarch Lana West Po. Her dress was the royal purple associated always with the rulers of the Velona Sector. Besides, she was the oldest woman meeting us. Dianna had told us that she was now sixty-four, while her husband, Bill, was a year older. Lana was planning to retire in another year. Her older brother, Bale, now thirty-six, was supposed to become her replacement, though her older sister Lona, thirty-three, was also being grooved in, in case something happened to Bale. Lana was ensuring a clean transfer of rulers.

Captain Jon called out, "Okay, ladies. You can disembark now. Your things will be brought ashore in a few minutes. It's been a real pleasure sailing with you. If you find you need to travel by ship in the future, please ask for good ol' Captain Jon." We thanked him and his wife.

"Be brave," I whispered to the others and took the lead, walking carefully across the wooden planks to the wooden docks, some feet above the waters below. The odor of fish hung in the air. We were wearing our Sunday dresses, but with our slip on shoes. On shore, I walked slowly to the assembled group, allowing Dianna to move to the front of us. Eight adults and nine children waited anxiously for us to get to them, smiles on their faces.

As we finally drew close, Lana exclaimed, "Dianna, our precious Dianna! Welcome back home dear!" She leaned over, hugged her daughter, while Bill moved in, and hugged her as well. I saw that he had tears in his eyes. Either joy or sympathy, I couldn't tell what was going on in his mind.

As they pulled back, Bale gave her a hug, "Glad to have you back home, little sister. Missed you."

Her older sister, Lona, gave her a big hug next, "Oh Dianna, this is so awful, but now you are safe back home. We all promise to look after you."

"Hey, my turn," her other brother, Tom butted in. "Welcome back sis, your room is just like you left it. We've all prayed for your safe return. Who are your pretty friends?"

Wiping her eyes on her shoulder, Dianna sniffed and began the introductions. We had previously agreed to have her also give the names by which we had been known in our previous lives. This we calculated would help lessen the confusions. Either that, or add to them, I didn't know which.

"Gang, this is my mom, Monarch Lana West Po, ruler of Velona and High Priestess of the Church of the Three Holy Roses. My dad, Bill West. My brother Bale, his wife Drina, their children, Gianna, Adolfo, Basilio. My sister Lona and her husband, Ricco, their children, Dario, Luciana, and Marchella. My other brother, Tom, his wife, Lucinda, their children, Suzana, Gerardo, and Tonia. Whew, that's a bunch."

"Mom, dad, everyone, this is Bethany Brozena or the Bethany of our legends and Linda d'Grange's best friend. This is Dita Malina or Renzo, her husband several times now." Several gasped. I figured that they would recognize our names that we used to have. I was right. Several of the littler girls put their hands over their mouths in surprise.

"This is Ania Anka or my best friend Alexa — you know, Alexa's Boots. Oh, I forgot to tell you, I've had some therapy from Bethany and remembered that I used to be Enyo, the Engineer." More gasps of recognition came from the group.

"This is Ilenakova da Cassa, who used to be *the* Lenkova Pazzio!" Their gasps grew even louder. "This is Kali Kato, who used to be Kallisto from Demokritos. You can tell from their skin colors that Bethany, Dita, and Ania are from Dorota and Kali is from Megalos. Ilenakova is from Zargarb. There, that about does it."

Now it was our turn to receive hugs of welcome. Bill said, "Wow, Dianna, you have brought back nothing but legends with you!"

"On behalf of all Velona, I wish to welcome all of you. If Dianna had told us who you all were, I would have rolled out the red carpet for you! However, let me say that all of Velona is yours. Whatever you need, please just ask. It is my highest honor to host five legends! Welcome, please, we want you to stay at our place, that is, unless you have other plans."

"Thanks, Lana. We gladly accept. I hope we are not too much of a burden on you," I accepted graciously. We began walking back to the carriages.

One of the girls, Gianna, whispered, "They really don't have *any* arms at all!" She seemed shocked.

Another smaller girl, Tonia, pulled on Lucinda's dress, "Mom, how is Aunt Dianna going to play with us now? How is she going to brush my hair?"

Her older sister, Suzana, about nine, asked Lucinda, "Mom, do we get to feed Aunt Dianna now? I want to go first, please?"

"Dear, you may, but wait until she asks for it, please," Lucinda whispered to her girls.

As we reached the cobblestones, I could now hear the telltale clicks of their many heels as we walked slowly to the waiting carriages. Even the little girls wore heels, I noted. Fashion has certainly changed in the last hundred years. I was thankful that corsets were not the "in thing." Heels I could manage. Laced into a tight corset from the age of five last lifetime had so disarranged my internals that my body died during childbirth.

"Mommy, can Aunt Dianna ride back with us? Please, please," begged

Tonia.

"Sure thing, Tonia," Dianna replied, smiling at Lucinda. To us, she added, "I'm always playing with the kids."

Embolden by all this, Luciana begged, "Mom, can Dita ride back with us?"

"Hey, we wanted Renzo to ride with us," Adolfo broke in.

His older sister, Gianna, interceded, "No we don't." Pulling on her mother's skirt, she begged, "We want Bethany to ride with us." She gave her younger brother a haughty stare.

Lana Po interrupted, "Please, children, I would like Bethany and Dita to ride with me. You'll have to be satisfied with Lenkova. Kali can ride with Lona and Ricco." Evidently, this appeased the Bale children, for Lenkova was nearly as famous a fighter as Renzo.

As the kids climbed into the first coach, Tom was ready to lift Dianna in, but she ignored his gesture and carefully climbed in herself, to his surprise. We likewise followed her lead and got ourselves into the various carriages.

"I wanted to have a few words with you in private," Lana Po said as we began rolling through the streets. "It won't take us long to get to the church as you probably remember. We, Sam and I, don't have words enough to thank you and Dita for rescuing our youngest daughter and saving her life, tragic though it now is. Anything you want or need, please just ask. I must apologize in advance. None of us know how to, well, we don't know just what all you will need. In my grandmother's time, there were so many of you around town, and the Laird Foundation helped so much. Now, well, until this fiasco over the Dorota commune thing, there hasn't been any, well you know, people around like you six are." She just couldn't come out and say it — armless women.

"We just don't know the first thing about your special needs. Please forgive our ignorance. I know it will be embarrassing for all of us, but please just ask when you need something."

"Thanks, Lana. We will. We are used to being independent, but that was back in Dorota, where their whole society is built around our needs. Dianna is actually doing very well; she's adapted extremely well to her situation."

"Bless you both! Oh, I nearly forgot. Linda wishes all of you to meet with her tomorrow afternoon. I'll have a coach waiting to take you to her. She sees no one these days, I've not seen her since Chaucer passed on some fifteen years ago. Coach will be ready at one. Golly, here we are already. I'm afraid I've talked all the way, robbing you of your first glimpses of fair Velona. Well, day after tomorrow, let's all take a grand tour; spend the whole afternoon seeing the sights. I bet much has changed since you two last lived here."

"There is one thing that I would like to discuss with you in private sometime," Dita said, as a coachman, also wearing tails, opened the door. "It's not urgent," she added. I wondered what she wanted.

"Wow! You've added a lot onto the old church I see," I exclaimed as I carefully climbed out. Indeed the church complex now occupied an entire city block and then some.

"Yes, we have. Our living quarters are over there at the back of the complex. The city offices are now in this south wing. That makes it simpler for security reasons to have everything in one general location. Come on, we have a welcome home, birthday party arranged for Dianna. I hope Lucinda's kids haven't given it away," Lana said.

As we approached, a well-dressed pair of guards opened the double doors for us. Dita and I followed the two rulers inside. The others were right behind us. We walked down a long hall. "Dianna can give you a royal tour after the party. This way," we entered a formal dining room. Great tapestries hung on the wall. A band of musicians took their cue from her entrance and began playing from their raised platform at one end. Rows of tables and chairs occupied the central portion of the room.

"Surprise, Dianna! Happy birthday and welcome home!" everyone sung out above the music. Dianna looked stunned and quite surprised. A huge chocolate cake sat dominating the table. Lettering, obviously done by the children, read "Happy Birthday Dianna. Welcome Home."

"You shouldn't have?" she tried to say, but tears stopped her from saying more. She buried her head into her mother's shoulders, whose arms then grasped on to her youngest daughter. We all headed to the tables. Well, nothing like staring out with eating difficulties, I thought to myself.

"I get to feed Aunt Dianna," Gianna blurted out as the many girls danced around the table. The others began arguing over who was going to feed who, the parents were instantly embarrassed; their faces turned slightly red and were awkwardly silent.

"I get to feed myself, Gianna." Dianna teased. "I'm not as helpless as you may think. I can still tickle you with my feet, so you've got to behave." Gianna giggled hysterically.

"Excuse us, please. We just don't know what or well, you know, how you manage. Please, tell us," Lana West Po insisted.

"Well, we eat ourselves if the table is low to the ground. In Dorota, the tables for the women are about six inches off the ground. I was able to manage well there, excepting for cutting up meat. I'm not so good at that yet. If you will just put ours on the floor, we probably can manage well, mom," Dianna explained. She looked at all her nieces and nephews and teased them, "Yes, you can all stare at us this time. But if you stare at suppertime, I promise you I will chase you down and tickle you to death!" All the children giggled or laughed.

While the musicians continued to play, Lana began cutting pieces, putting them on fine china plates. Lona and Lucinda began placing them on the floor at our feet, feeling rather awkward in doing so, however, compounded by the flair of their dresses. Drina began pouring cups of tea for everyone, milk for the kids. At first, I thought that without our special mugs, we would have to have someone help us with the tea. However, I noticed this set had a very large loop handle, perhaps we could get a toe through it.

Dita surprised everyone, "Chocolate!" She began eating large fork fulls at once. Before she stopped, she'd had four large pieces! Then, she noticed everyone else watching her. "Chocolate!" she said again, as if that said it all.

I explained, "We have only had one tiny bar of chocolate in the last eighteen years. I think Dita really has missed it!" Everyone roared, but Dita decided to pass on a fifth piece, just now. There seemed lots left over, so she planned to sneak pieces later on.

I admit, I felt terribly self-conscious with everyone watching us manage to eat with our feet. The kids had never seen anything like us or how we did it and stared wide-eyed, even when we drank our tea, toes through the loops. Bottom line, if Dianna had any doubts that her family would reject her as a freak or not want her back as she now was, those thoughts were totally blown away by this surprise party. She didn't even seem to mind all of them staring at her as she ate and sipped her tea. For this kindness, I was grateful.

"Dear, your shipment from Dorota arrived many months ago. We've stored it all in a warehouse on the docks. When you tell us where you want it, we'll send some wagons for it all. In the meantime, while we all have much to talk about, we ought to let you show your friends around the domestic side of our church and unpack your things. The porters have taken your bags to your rooms. We've put two more beds in the back storage portion of your large room, figuring that you all would like to room together. If you would like private rooms, then that is not a problem either."

"Thanks mom, that'll be great. Come, I'll show you around." While the girls begged to come with Aunt Dianna, their mothers said no, resoundingly, explaining that she had to show the other guests to their room.

As we walked down the long hall, Dianna pointed out the side rooms. "Inside are lots of rooms. This one is for Bale's whole family; this one's for Lona's; this one's for Tom. Here is mine, now ours. Mom and dad's is the next and last one ahead. Damn, doorknobs!"

We just hit our first barrier! "Hey, we are a team!" Ilenakova spoke up, sitting on the floor. "Kali, little help here." Kali joined her. Using their feet, they twisted the knob and pushed it open with their feet. Rising awkwardly, they proudly said, "We've had lots of practice on Megalos; we sneaked into all sorts of rooms. Got in trouble usually."

We entered her quarters. "Well, except for the back room there, it's just like I left it. Figure out where we all want to sleep. We'll have to double up, but these beds can hold three or four of us easily." Our bags lay piled in a heap just inside the door. We all wandered around her room, looking at her stuff. She had a nice wardrobe with a mirror where she could dress. She had a working desk, filled with several books and lots of drawings and sketches. I noticed that the books were all of a medical nature. A large walk in closet held many dresses, a large number of them were similar to those all the other women were wearing today. Several pants and shirts were neatly hung inside as well. She had an assortment of shoes, including several pairs of Alexa boots with the high heels. Sunlight entered through six large stained glass windows, depicting numerous roses in bloom. A dozen oil lanterns hung on the walls.

"I'm sleeping with you, Dianna," Ania decided, pushing her bag near the bed.

"Say does everyone always wear these cone dresses that they are wearing today?" Dita asked what she feared most. There was no way we could possible get into one of those outfits.

"Usually, but sometimes I wore pants, like when I went riding and stuff. Honestly, I've grown so much that none of these are likely to fit me anymore. Besides, Dita, we probably are going to have to dress differently, something we can manage. Let's take all my junk out of the bottom drawers there and put our things in there.

"Oh I love these beds!" Ania exclaimed. She had plopped onto the soft bed. "Such luxury!" The cover was satin, as were the sheets. "Come feel it gang! Wow." We all squeezed onto her bed, feeling it with our faces, such fine sensations I had never felt before in Dorota. Plus, the bed was invitingly soft. I knew that I was going to like this part of our stay.

"Come on, I'll show you the rest of this section of the church." Dianna led us back the other way down the hall. One room was the giant playroom for the children. Next to it was where their tutor taught them their lessons. Next was the large bathroom, which served everyone. Lastly was the kitchen and panty. I noticed that doorknobs were everywhere; this was going to be a challenge for the six of us. I couldn't ask the Monarch of Velona to go around changing all her fancy fixtures just for us. I asked Kali and Ilenakova to show us all how they opened the doors.

We decided to make use of the bathroom. Dita and I sat down and followed the instructions of Kali. Just as we got the door open, Lucinda came looking for us. "I came to see if you needed. . ." she stopped short, suddenly realizing the barrier that we were tackling. "I'm so sorry! We didn't realize. . ."

"Not a problem for feet," I replied, struggling to my feet. "We are getting the hang of it. A bit more practice and we'll have it down quickly. This place is so changed from the last time I was here. Is the main chapel still the same fabulous space?" I tried to defuse her embarrassment.

"Oh, I'm still so sorry for you. Well, yes, that is pretty much the same. Grandmother added this huge section for her every growing family. I'll talk to Tom about the doorknobs. Honestly, they are everywhere. I'm so sorry. We didn't realize."

"Forget it, Lucinda. Your world is set up for all of you, so we just have to learn new ways to do what everyone else does. It's no big deal at all — just a bit awkward is all. Please don't bother Lana. I'm sure she's got much more important things with which to deal."

"Please, just ask us for help. I can help you all with your baths and all that, just let me know, please. We all feel so badly for you. We cannot imagine how difficult absolutely everything has become for you six. We are just so thankful to have Dianna back with us!" she sympathetically gushed.

"Hey, you have real baths in here?" Dita asked, changing the topic, thankfully.

Inside were several baths, with hot and cold running water. Even Enyo's cleverly designed toilets were here, as well as mirrors and sinks. A mountain of towels and wash rags lay on a commode. "Wow, four of us can bathe at the same time," Dita noticed such incredible luxury. "Do we have time to take one now?"

"Sure, dinner is at six; you've got three hours. We usually bring our robes down here when we bathe, along with our slippers. The stone floor is cold. Just leave your dirty clothes in that basket, and they will be washed. I'll go check on the kids and come back to help you all."

Dianna said, "I think we can manage these things in here. I'll come get you, if we run into trouble. Thanks for offering, Lucinda."

"Please, dear. Let me at least wash your hair for each of you. Mom will give me the devil if I don't. Say, you hair has really grown while you were gone. I like it, but I just cannot believe Dita and Bethany's hair — so thick and long. It suits you two well, but I can see the practicality of Ilenakova and Kali's style — much easier to manage. I'll be back in say a half hour to do your hair, okay?" We agreed, not having remembered when we last had a real bath.

By the time Lucinda returned, we six were soaking in three hot baths. Dita and I shared one bath, helping each other wash. Ania and Dianna were in the one next to ours, and Kali and Ilenakova were doing the same next to theirs. "Hi, sorry I took too long. Mom has just issued orders that the bathroom doors are always to be left open. Any boys peeking will be punished," she teased. She was also staring at our shoulders.

"Not much scaring is there?" she commented, as she began to wash Dianna's hair. "I was worried that your body would, well look just horrible, but you all look really good, hardly notice anything at all." She chatted away. "I remember washing your hair like this when you were a little girl, just after I married your brother and moved in here."

It took her a while to get all of us done, especially Dita and me. While she was patting our long tresses dry, she brought up another touchy subject, "Say, what about clothes, Dianna? Do you want us to try to dress you up in the dress dresses or what? I told Lana that you've outgrown the dresses in your closet, but she said to wait and see. Can you manage in them?"

Dianna looked at me for help. "Can we please wear the clothes we currently have? They are easy for us to manage. Give us some time to adapt. Will that be okay with Lana and the others?"

"Most certainly it will be okay. She was just worried that you all would feel out of place wearing your clothes, when everyone else wears the cones. I guess we'd better hurry up, suppertime is nearly upon us."

"Thanks for that fabulous bath," Dita exclaimed, "and for doing my hair."

A while later, Lucinda led us into the large dining room, where musicians were once more playing indoor instruments in the background. As we entered, Bale called out, "Hey, sis, how's this?" He had found a low bench, about eight inches tall. Our plates were sitting on it.

"Hey, this is more like it. Of course, big brother, we'll need you to fill them up for us," Dianna teased him, but the look on her face told him that he had scored a very big hit with his little sister and the rest of us.

We had a delicious meal and pleasant conversations. Once we finished, Gianna asked, "Dianna, will you play tag with us now? We've missed you a whole lot."

Lana interrupted, "We adults want to talk adult things." Seeing the pleading look of her granddaughter, she gave in, "Okay, if Dianna wants to for a few minutes while they clear the tables, it is okay."

"Okay, I'm it. Here I come," Dianna called out. The girls giggled and began moving around the room, their heels clicking on the stone floor. Dianna quickly tagged Gianna, "Now you're it."

A bit later, Gianna called out, "It's not fair, we are still wearing our heels, and you aren't."

"Yes, but I have to use my feet to tag you, so that makes up for it," Dianna teased her, narrowly missing being tagged. The girls loved the game, and from the look on Dianna's face, she did too. A while later, Lana called a halt, sending the kids off to play.

"Please come and tuck us in, will you Aunt Dianna," Gianna begged as she left. Dianna promised.

With nothing but adults around now, Lana asked for the complete details of what had happened, first to her youngest daughter and then about the rest of us. I realized she was getting the crucial data that she needed as the leader of Velona. We spent most of the evening fully briefing her on everything. When Dita explained that she had killed the assassin who had harmed Dianna and just how he had died, the men all began clapping for Dita, who looked embarrassed. She had made a crucial mistake and acted out of anger, not thought. They did not grasp this fact, only that Dianna's torturer had paid for his deeds.

We finally finished briefing them. Lana said, "Well we've talked the evening away. Tomorrow night, let's discuss your futures and your plans and how we may help, shall we?" We agreed. Later, in our room, someone had inserted a block of wood to keep the door opened so we could easily come and go. We brushed out our hair as usual and then slipped into the luxurious beds. Dita and I had a fabulous time with the slippery sensations of sleeping between satin sheets, such luxury we had never experienced before.

We both looked forward to tomorrow. Finally, we would get to meet Linda d'Grange, whom we had not seen for a very long time. When we last spoke in person, she was the leader of the Santi del Dio. In an earlier lifetime, she had been my daughter. In the next, she was my very best friend. As we laid there in bed, Dita said, "You know, she has got to be one hundred ten years old by now." I gasped, but realized that he was right, she was born in 635!

Chapter 22 Linda d'Grange

Over breakfast, I asked Lana about how Linda was doing, where she was living, and how she had been. One hundred and ten years old seemed ancient to me, but then Alabaster, the founder of the Druwids centuries ago, had been several hundred years old. Perhaps with great power came longevity.

"No one has seen her since the funeral for Chaucer, some fifteen years ago or so. She always keeps in touch, you know via minds, however she does that. She has a coachman now. If we need to get in touch with her, we send for him. He will probably be the one picking you up right after lunch," Lana explained.

Dianna went off to play with her nieces and nephews, and Ania accompanied her. Sam wanted to show me some designs that he had been working on for a new sailing ship, and Kali joined us, being curious. Ilenakova decided to wander about the complex, becoming more familiar with her surroundings. She could not forget all of her previous skills as a fighter and as such; one of the first principles is to know your surroundings. Dita remained behind, still chatting with Lana.

Dita glanced around and saw that finally they were alone. "Your Holiness, can we talk frankly," she asked.

"Why certainly, but please, among my friends, I am just Lana," the aging monarch said, becoming curious about what this beautiful young girl wanted to discuss with her.

Dita squirmed in her chair, uncertain how to explain this to her. "I'm Renzo still, and Bethany and I are still madly in love with each other. I don't know much about the tenants of your Church of the Three Holy Roses, but is it possible for two women to be married by your church or in the eyes of your church or however it goes? You see, I've asked Bethany to marry me and she has freely agreed, but, well, I am all messed up this lifetime. Besides, as we are now, we cannot get by on our own, we need to be together. Actually, all six of us need to be under one roof, together, so that we can get by."

Ilenakova, who was just outside, heard Dita's question and stopped in her tracks! Quietly, she backed up to the edge of the door and listened in on their private conversation. Her mind was racing.

"I understand, Dita-Renzo. This must be so terribly hard on all six of you. None of us can or even imagine the difficulties that you and our daughter must face every minute of every day. I may be able to help. Yes, our church recognizes the union of two people to be a Holy Marriage. We have taken our beliefs from what we believe to be the best aspects of many religions on Tarra, including the Druwid principles of the Seven Aspects of

Life. One of these is the family, which is defined to be the holy union of two people. So yes, if it is your wishes and desires, it would be the greatest honor for me to join you two together as a Holy Rose Family. That is our term for a non-traditional union, such as yours. In addition, I will anoint all of you as Holy Roses, giving you a medallion to wear proudly in public. When others see that you are one of our Holy Roses, few will discriminate against you. You see, women such as yourselves are now thought of as having foolishly joining that Dorota religion and well, you can imagine the rest that has followed."

"Lana, I could hug you, if I had arms! You've made our lives! Thank you, thank you!" Waves of pent up relief flowed off of Dita like rain.

Ilenakova acted spontaneously, seizing this opportunity. She stepped boldly into the room. "Er, excuse me, Your Holiness, I was passing by the door when I overhead you say something that, well it keenly interests me. Dita and Bethany, they are allowed to be a married couple in the eyes of the Church of the Three Holy Roses? Even though they are both women? Did I hear this correctly?"

Lana smiled, Dita's face reddened. "Why yes, come on in Ilenakova. Join us. Yes, while it is a non-traditional union, such marriages are sanctified and blessed by our church." She outlined some of their beliefs for her.

"Well, let me talk with Kali. If she is willing, I would like to marry her as well," Ilenakova said quietly. "We have been so dependent upon one another, it would be ideal for us as well. We have both lost our families and were so alone until we found each other at the orphanage. If she is willing, can you unite us as well?"

"I would be honored to do so, Ilenakova," Lana replied. Ilenakova thanked her profusely and raced to find Kali.

"Thank you," Dita repeated herself. "You don't know how relieved I am over this."

"Yes, I can imagine, Dita. It's obvious how much you two care for each other. Now why don't you go and tell her the good news. I ought to be heading to my office. Work never ends, though Bale is a tremendous help." Dita took off to find me.

"You see, protection of our fleet of ships is becoming an issue," Bill explained the basis of his project and design solution to Kali and me. "With the development and use of the cannone in Zargarb during the Demokritos Invasion, the world has changed radically. My new design here places twenty of these cannone on the caravel, ten on either side. A broadside can smash large holes in the sides of attacking ships below the waterline, sinking them in short order. I view these as a deterrent, not a real weapon. Ocean going ships are so terribly expensive to build, who in their right mind would risk having them destroyed? The monetary loss is prohibitive. Just having one of these cannone ships accompanying our fleet will act as a deterrent.

What do you think?"

"I like the idea, Bill. For now, it will be a strong deterrent. However, won't other countries, like Demokritos, soon make cannone ships of their own?" I asked. I hated weapons. I'd seen entire legions of soldiers slaughtered by the cannone shots while the Emperor and I watched the Battle of Zargarb from a hilltop.

Kali spoke up, "Probably, but it will take them many years to get them developed. During that time, your shipping will be safe from piracy. That makes it a sound project, in my mind." Bill grinned; he liked her thinking.

He replied to me, "I take your point, Bethany. That gives us some years of breathing room in which to develop a defense against cannone fired at our ships."

We two headed back to join the others and saw Ilenakova running to join us. "Guess what? Dita has just gotten permission from Lana for you two to be officially married! It is acceptable for two women to join in her church! Kali, what do you say? Will you marry me?"

"Wow! For real? Of course, I will, Ilenakova. Only which one of us gets to wear the pants?" she teased her, and they hugged, each one throwing a leg around the other.

"We can take turns," Ilenakova whispered in her ear.

"Deal," Kali whispered back.

Dita came running up with her news, somewhat spoiled though, as she saw Ilenakova and Kali in a hugging embrace. "I guess you just heard," she said to me.

"Thank you, Dita!" I hugged her and we kissed as well. We four then set off to tell Dianna and Ania the good news.

We found them heading for us, totally out of breath. They had been playing tag with the many children, but Lucinda had now taken them off to begin their day's lessons. Both girls were ecstatic over the news that such unions were not only possible but that we were actually going to get married.

Ania whispered to Dianna, "What about us? I love you as I always have. This time we can really be married and not have to pretend like we did back on the Isle of Right."

Dianna didn't need to think about it. "Come on, let's catch mom before she leaves!" The two darted on down the hall.

Lana was just about to go into her large office on the other side of the church complex, when Dianna and Ania came running down the hall towards her. Out of breath, Dianna gushed, "Mom, we just heard about Bethany and Dita, and about Ilenakova and Kali! Mom, Ania and I want to get married as well. Please, please give us your consent, please mom. We have always loved each other. Now we don't have to do it in secret anymore, please mom, please?"

Lana grinned, "I half expected this when I heard the others. Yes, daughter. Your life is now so terrible, that any small pleasure you can get must be yours. We should all discuss this, say tonight, in private. Let the others know; we will talk more then. Congratulations, Ania and Dianna. Now I do have to get to work." The two now raced back to us to tell us their good news.

"Of course, we six should all live together in the same house," Ania began planning. "Things are so much easier for each of us that way." None of us could disagree with her on that point. Honestly, none of us dared living on our own in this world, not the way that we were. However, I had the nagging thought: what if in a few years' time, they found a man and fell in love with him? A good man, worthy of them, what would they do then? I had a suspicion that Lana would bring that up with us this evening.

At one, we saw a carriage pull up outside the side entrance, near the domestic section. A tall man wearing a fancy blue suit with twin tails dismounted and came up to we six, who were standing just inside the door. "Welcome to Velona, ladies. I am Enrico. I've come to take you to see the Great Lady, Linda d'Grange. If you will allow me," he motioned to the carriage. He opened the door and asked, "Do you need any assistance getting aboard?"

"No thank you, we can manage," I replied politely. I rather like this man; he was polite and considerate. He did make sure that we had all gotten seated before he shut the door.

Through the open window, he explained, "It is about a five minute ride from here." He disappeared, and we heard him climb up to the tall driver's box. Slowly the carriage moved out into the bustling streets of Velona. We saw many other carriages, wagons, and people going about their varied activities. I noticed that many improvements had been made. The streets were all paved with cobblestones and had sidewalks as well. Periodically, I saw lanterns sitting atop tall poles, evidently, these were lighted at night, a very nice touch I thought.

We pulled up at a secluded, very small home, non-descript in all ways. While the exterior was well maintained, it blended in with all the other homes on this block. Nothing called anyone's attention to it. Enrico climbed down, opened the carriage door, and extended the movable step. With this larger sized step, we found getting out of the carriage much easier to manage, another improvement from the old days, I thought. Enrico was right there ready to assist us if we stumbled or needed any help.

"If you will follow me, I will take you to see the Great Lady. You should be honored; you are the first people that she has entertained in fifteen years. This way please, ladies." He opened the front door, and we stepped inside. The house was dimly illuminated, and there was a distinctive odor in the air, an odor of rotting flesh! Dianna recognized it at once, though she only shot me a very worried glance.

Inside, a woman wearing a gorgeous yellow cone style dress, with hundreds of flowers embroidered on the yards of material met us. She, like Enrico, was twenty-one. He introduced us, "My wife, Luisa Angela, she will be serving you tea." She had shoulder length blonde hair and deep blue eyes. Her smile was infectious. He stood six inches taller than his wife at six foot-two. We nodded to her and followed him down a dimly lighted hallway to a back room. He knocked on the door and then opened it for us. "Luisa and I will remain outside until needed."

We walked into the room. The foul odor most definitely came from this room. It was a bedroom. An aged woman lay upon the bed; six chairs had been arranged in a line on one side. A cracking voice, barely audible, spoke to us, "Welcome Bethany. It has been so long since we last saw each other. I am afraid my body is nearly gone. Please sit. Introduce these fine ladies to me."

My eyes watered so heavily that I could barely speak. "Oh Linda!"

"I know, one hundred ten years is far too many for one to spend in such a frail body."

I recovered and introduced my friends. "We have much to discuss, but I cannot use this body for much more. Allow me to Mind Link, please?" I nodded; she closed her eyes. Her armless body had numerous sores; stinking puss oozed from them. How she must be suffering, I thought.

Linda spoke into our minds, *There, this is so much better. That old body of mine down there is pretty much gone. Now then, I am so glad to meet you all in person. Oh, allow me to create an energy field so that it will be easier for you to relate to me.*

Suddenly a bluish glow formed into the Linda that I used to know; she appeared to be in her twenties and just as armless as I remembered her. *There, isn't that much better?* We all giggled and said that it was.

First things first, joining me for a moment are Chaucer and the Guardian. Two more bluish ghostly figures appeared. One was the old Chaucer that I knew, looking as a fit fighter when we were out exploring the world. The other looked like my husband, Jes Amir, the Great Messiah.

Jes spoke, *Welcome Bethany, Dita-Renzo, Dianna-Enyo, Ania-Alexa, Ilenakova-Lenkova, and Kali-Kallista. It is a great honor for me to meet you six. You do not realize what you have accomplished in Dorota. You have created a spiritual revival never before seen on Tarra! Millions of beings there now recognize their spiritual nature! You have done something, my Bethany Madelyn, which I never could do. I bow to you. From the roots you have sewn in Dorota, we may see a spiritual revival of our entire world. Five thousand and more can help others achieve more freedom from their earthly bodies, all thanks to you six. It is my hope that from these beginnings in the course of another century true freedom will finally spread out across all of Tarra.*

We Guardians are no longer safe in the Red Desert. Chaucer is lighting our way; we will all be moving to Dorota shortly. There, we will all continue our work of freeing beings from the bonds of their fleshly prison. You six have made this possible. We are deeply in your debt.

Tarra has become a far more deadly world, Bethany Madelyn, than it was when you and I first set out to free mankind so long ago in the Arad. I beseech you and beg of you to continue your tireless work at maintaining peace a little longer, that we may have the time we need to do our work of freeing beings. If you will continue to do so, Chaucer, Linda, and I have decided to give you a spiritual gift, one that other beings eventually unlock during their training with us. We will come while you sleep and do this. Now, I must return to help our people make this move from the Red Desert to Dorota. Again, you six have my undying, eternal love, my highest respect and admiration for all that you have done.

His form winked out. I felt his presence leave us. This was the longest talk I had had with Jes in a very long time. I found my mind reeling with things that I wanted to ask him, but had forgotten. Perhaps when he came in my sleep I could ask them.

Chaucer now spoke, *Linda will be shortly briefing you on all that has happened and answer your many questions. I do hope that you will accept her challenge. Her body is so far gone that I would dearly love her to be finally able to let go of it. I have new bodies picked out for us. You may be interested to know that Elder Albin and Klara are expecting twin babies soon. Those will be our next human forms here on Tarra, that we may continue to work towards the freeing of all beings. We will meet again, one day, Bethany. Until then I bid you all the best.* The bluish form of Chaucer vanished as well.

Linda said cheerily, *A bit melodramatic, they are, don't you think? Anyway, we'd best get down to business. You six need a full update on how things have been going here in Velona and elsewhere. Let's see, the best place to start is with the old Druwid skills. Over these many years, the numbers of those who still possess them have fallen drastically; old age takes all these fleshly bodies one day, though, as you can smell, I have been stalling mine for some time now. There are no longer enough of us around who remember the Druwid ways. Effectively the Druwids are no more.*

The Emperor of Demokritos gave the Church of Jehosanity a severe blow, but as ever, it has recovered, spreading its lies and control as it has never done before. With the opening up of the world to all these much larger countries, it was just a matter of time before Demokritos became master of the shipping seas. Further, the invention of the cannone, which stopped the invading Centurions, has made obsolete many ways of fighting. Specifically, our Santi fortresses are now primarily worthless as a defensive measure. Our cavalry and armor are just as worthless against such implements of war. Thus, the time of the Santi del Dio is over, Chaucer and I saw this clearly. Yet, the real purpose of the Santi was to maintain peace and harmony on Tarra, so that the Guardian had time to free beings. Long did Chaucer and I discuss how we could continue to exert a hand over the many rulers of these countries.

It cannot be by force of arms any longer. With the vast amounts of trade, money has now become the tool of power. Thus, we have created a new organization, *La Banca del Dio*, the Bank of God. We now have established ourselves as the most important bank in every major country here in the west. By making it easy to transfer large amounts of funds from country to country, person to person, we have total control over the gold and gems of the world. Control the money and you control their actions.

Over time, many of the Santi personnel have transferred into one of our many banks or have joined the *Forza di Sicurezza*, who protects our gold shipments, or our *Forze Segrete*, our secret forces. Each bank has a small supply of gold and silver on hand. People make deposits and withdrawals. Companies and rulers of countries play a bigger game, often depositing funds in one bank only to have them withdrawn at a different bank, sometimes in another country. We facilitate those transactions. Since frequently those large sums are then subsequently redeposited and spent elsewhere, we can do it all without actually moving the gold around the world. Only when the transaction will be a withdrawal and will not be redeposited elsewhere, such as pay for soldiers, do we have to ensure the bank there has enough actual gold and silver to cover the withdrawal. When a bank ends up with too large an amount of actual gold on its premises, we then secretly move it from there to our secret vaults. The *Forza di Sicurezza* provides the security during shipment and transfer. You met some of those men on the Jolly Prince.

The *Forze Segrete* is our secret army of information gatherers and protectors, if needed. One given member only knows six others in the group. That way, if one is captured, they can only divulge very limited information. For the most part, these secret forces blend in with the societies in which they live. You will be hard pressed to outright spot them; that would be a major blunder on their part, perhaps costing them their lives. Some will be assigned to you six to guard and protect you, if needed.

Where do I fit in? I am in charge of the entire organization, the top lady, if you please. I have an office in the Velona Banca del Dio. No, I have not taken my body there since Chaucer's body passed away. I go there at night and deal with the work. During the day, many levels of information are generated with the deposits, withdrawals, and transfers. Much is handled by the bank mangers themselves. Only the key critical transactions are referred on up to me to examine. I make my recommendations on paper and leave them to be implemented in the morning. Thus, I know every major thing going on in the western portion of the world. Very little of significance escapes our attention, unless somehow, someway it does not involve money. And we all know that nearly everything requires money in some way.

However, I must move on, Bethany. I cannot keep this frail body alive much longer. I am hoping that you six will take over for me. As a freed being, I am able to handle and process a large volume of work. I think that you six working together can easily do my job. I know that with your bodies as they are now, you are so slow at most things. However, with all six of you on it, you ought to have a lot of free time to pursue other activities that may interest you more. It will pay each of you well, a thousand gold a month; you get to choose your own working hours as well.

So ladies, will you six volunteer to step into my shoes?

I replied, *Sure, Linda. I have been wondering how we could contribute. This sounds like an ideal way.* Everyone else agreed as well. This was a "golden" opportunity dropped into our laps. (Pun intended.)

Thank you all very much! I also know that the Mano del Dio will likely make some attempts on your lives, due in part to your job, though they may think that somehow you are a threat to them. Plus, there are thieves and such plying the streets of Velona. It is not safe as it is back in Dorota. You six need to be able to take care of yourselves.

Ilenakova spoke up, *I know, that's what I've told them. We need to train somehow.*

I added, *Dita and I decided that we need to work out, as you and I did after we lost our arms to the mantis creatures.*

Excellent ideas. You must know your limitations as well as just what you can do. That way, you can intelligently depend upon each other in tight situations. I counted on this — that you all would be willing to train to protect yourselves. I've spent a good deal of time searching for just the right person to train you, given your unique situation. His name is Renato Fuello a monk of the Monaco del Dio order. They are a small religious order based in the mountains of the Appian Way. I've talked with him at length about your physical situation, and I believe that he is perfect for the job.

I ask that you all be ready to take over for me in four months at the most. I believe I can keep this body alive that much longer. However, Chaucer tells me that after that, Klara's babies will be born, and I have to pick one of them up at birth.

We agreed to do our best and, if possible, be finished sooner. She thanked us for this.

Now, it is time to introduce you to your personal Forze Segrete. It will be their job to watch over you and to help and protect you, but in secret of course. You see, by having accepted my job, you will become six of the most important people in the western world, the top bankers. I needed to provide you with the best. I have spent the last two years working with each of these four to get their skill levels up to, and perhaps beyond, par. Until now, they have been serving me, but after today, they will become your Forze Segrete. It's time that you formally meet them. I hope that I do not shock you too much. I wondered what she meant by that!

The door opened as if from some unspoken cue. In came two couples, one pair of which we had already met, Luisa and Enrico Angela. Another man and woman were with them, she bearing a tea tray.

"Hi, Linda wants us to introduce ourselves. She gets tired easily these days. I'm Sandra Bastiana and this is my husband, Arturo. He's a great gardener and is also our Loremaster, fully schooled in all the flora and fauna of the western world. I'm your Healer, but I've been modernized considerably with all the latest advances in the healing profession. I pray that my services won't be needed, though. All four were twenty-one years old. She had shoulder length brown hair and blue eyes. Her face was nearly angelic, incredibly good looking I thought. Arturo was tall with nearly the same shade of brown hair, cropped relatively short. His face was handsome."

As she spoke, I sensed some real excitement building, but couldn't put my finger on its source. Sandra then said, having put the tray on a side table out of the way and turning to face us, "We know who you all are, Bethany, Renzo, Enyo, Alexa, Lenkova, Kallisto. Are you ready for this? I used to be called Sara Jane Greenleaf and later as Beth Ann Penton!"

I squealed and jumped up in total surprise. She was my dear friend from my earliest days on Tarra. We were in the Lightning Circle together. As Beth Ann, she was my sister-in-law. I jumped up and down, so intense was my excitement. We rushed and hugged for a minute, tears coming to both our eyes. Then, she hugged Renzo and the others — all of whom had also known her well as Beth Ann.

Arturo said calmly, "No surprises here. I've never met you legends. Sorry. I am deeply honored that Linda has chosen me to be one of your *Forze Segrete.*"

Luisa now grinning from ear to ear, spoke up, "Brace yourself, dear. I used to be Lilly Ann Penton and the mother of our children!" I nearly fainted so great was my surprise. She was my dear, dear wife when I was Ket Bethany! I began bawling I was so overcome with happiness and joy at finding her again. We both hugged and cried together for a time. At last she added, "Well, we won't be married this time, but I will still look after you with my life." I was speechless. "Oh, yes, I am still a Judger." She had shoulder length blonde hair, similar to mine, with pale blue eyes and about my height at five-eight.

She continued after she was mobbed by Dita and the others, who were equally thrilled to see her again. "One more surprise, Bethany. Enrico here used to be Percival Penton! He's still a Protector." More squeals and I jumped into his arms as well! He was tall and handsome, with dark brown hair, rather long for a man. He was inches taller than Luisa. Grinning ear to ear, he picked me up and twirled me around.

He said, "You don't know how hard it was for all of us to not say anything until now! I wanted to scream it out to you when I first picked you up at the church! That was the hardest thing I ever had to do, Bethany and Dita and Enyo and Alexa and Lenkova and Kallisto! What a powerhouse team we will make! However, Linda said that you might not accept her position and we would then be assigned to whoever did accept it. That's why we had to keep our identities a secret until now."

I looked at the aged body of Linda. A smile lined the heavily wrinkled face. I knew that she was as pleased as we all were about this incredible stroke of good luck. I suspected now that she had arranged all of this years before hand. "Thank you Linda!" I exclaimed and her smile widened.

"Come, tea." Sandra suggested. She poured the cups. "We dug these old mugs out of storage. I hope you remember how to use them," she teased us. They had the large loops that allowed us to get our toes into them easily so that we could drink by ourselves. While we were enjoying our tea, we chatted like mad about the old days. Linda allowed us an hour to be reacquainted with our dear, dear friends.

She formed an even larger Mind Link. *Now then, the next question is about your living arrangements. Four was our magic number back in the old days. With four of us living together, we could accomplish routine things that we could not otherwise do.* We six totally agreed with her.

I added, *We have already decided that we are going to all live together. On top of that, Dita and I are going to be married; Dianna and Ania are too, as well as Ilenakova and Kali. Besides loving each other and wanting to do it, being married will be more socially acceptable than the six of us living together. It seems the world is no longer full of the likes of us.*

Sandra and Luisa gasped, taken by surprise, but they both grinned broadly at us six. I hoped that they would approve of such strange marriages.

No, I am afraid that is a thing of the past. You will get little or no assistance from the Laird Foundation these days. No one remembers how to deal with us anymore. Those that did have lost their bodies. The old Laird Foundation has pretty well taken over all our old Santi fortress, as the city has long ago grown way beyond that location, which used to be just outside the city. Much has been torn down and new buildings more suited to the arts raised. Our old brownstone mansion is still there. I still own it, though I have promised the Laird Foundation that I would sell it to them soon.

I have been searching for an ideal location for you. I know you may well wish to choose your own place and not have someone dictating locations for you. However, I have found what I think is ideal in all ways. The safest part of town is from the Church of the Three Holy Roses out to the eastern suburbs, some fifty blocks square. Here is where the wealthy and the nobles live. That area is heavily patrolled day and night. The crime rates there are the lowest in the sector, as you might predict. Recently an estate came on the market, and I took the liberty of purchasing it for you. I want you to go look and see if it meets with your approval.

Bethany, you are under no obligation whatsoever to accept it. If you don't like it, please, please just say so. I can sell it and make a profit. I am not out anything. Luisa thinks that you may love it, but we'll see. I'd like you to all go and see it today and then let me know. If you like it, then very soon I'd like you to go out to the old brownstone mansion and sort out all the accumulated stuff that's in storage there. I am afraid that over the years, we just kept piling the unneeded stuff in the upper rooms. I would like to unload it to the Laird Foundation soon, so sort through all the junk and pitch what you don't want or give it to charity. Let that be your first major action, then I am free to get rid of it. I really do need to tie up loose ends before the body gives out completely. Suddenly, time is growing so short for me.

I replied, *Okay, you got it. We'll go check it out. Linda, how can we ever thank you for everything?*

Dear Bethany, you already have and more over by totally on your own handling Dorota! The Guardian and I were making countless plans to try to handle the situation there. Yet, you just went ahead and did it. Alexa even went there on her own without our knowledge. You have all more than earned everything that I can still do for you. All that I ask of you is not to delay. I have only four months left, if that. I really don't know if the old body down there will last that long. So why don't you ten all scoot out of here and go check out the estate?

We thanked her again and left her room. Once out of doors, it felt good to breathe fresh air once more. Sandra explained, "Her body has been rotting away for years now. That's why she hasn't seen anyone in fifteen years. How she has kept it alive this long is a miracle, though I know why she has done it. She has been waiting for your return so that she can make a clean transition of power."

Enrico and Arturo assisted their wives climbing into the coach. With their wide cone dresses and heels, they needed the men's hands for support, because theirs were holding their dresses back so they could see where they were stepping. Then we six climbed inside. Arturo rode topside with Enrico.

"Unless your tastes have changed, Ket, I mean Bethany, I think that you will fall in love with this place. I certainly have. I think it has tremendous potential," Luisa chatted away as we rode along the cobblestone streets past open-air markets, shops of all kinds, and then on into the noble district of town.

The estate was one thousand feet long and five hundred feet wide. A high stone wall surrounded it, topped with vertical spikes and barbed wire. It would not be easy to scale the walls, I noted. The main, black, wrought iron gates likewise had spikes and wire across their tops. Arturo unlocked them, and we rode up to the centrally located manor house, on a cobblestone driveway. To the right as we entered was a huge stable, where the carriage and many horses could be housed. The manor house was a brownstone, dating back over a century, but very well built. It was only a single story building, which was why the previous owner sold it; his extended family had outgrown it. Ivy covered the front and numerous beds of flowers filled the air with a heady aroma.

The main structure was four hundred feet long and one hundred fifty feet wide. A well-manicured lawn surrounded the house, with a small brownstone building in the upper left corner where the gardening tools were kept. A giant front porch with two stone columns formed the main entrance, where two oaken double doors stood, with their beautifully carved caravels prominently greeting visitors.

Inside, a huge entryway held places for coats and boots. A long hallway ran the length of the building. Directly beyond the entryway was the huge dining room-ballroom. To its left was a spacious kitchen and back pantry. To its right were three large bedrooms, large baths were at either end of the hallway. Opposite the three bedrooms were another three bedrooms. Finally, to the right of the entryway lay three spacious drawing rooms or studies. There was a small attic, which was not used by the previous owner and a basement that ran the length of house, with periodic columns supporting the thick wooden floor.

Quality was apparent everywhere inside the building. Outside, a small water tower provided running water; a charcoal heater provided the hot water. Each room had a beautifully made fireplace with polished granite mantles. Wall lanterns in the shapes of fishes lined the hallway and in each of the rooms. Large windows, with semi-circular tops provided excellent daytime light inside.

From my point of view, it was a dream mansion! On this point, I got no argument. We all fell in love with the place. Dianna began rattling off a list of things that we needed to do. "First, we need to move all the stuff I brought from Dorota here and then get some wood workers to make us more copies. We need to reorganize the kitchen so we can use it. Change the doorknobs. I think we ought to go with the lower latches that your dad built for us, Bethany, when we lived here in Velona before." She continued rattling off the many changes we'd need to make.

"Sounds like you'll take it then?" Enrico asked.

We six echoed, "You bet!"

On our way back, Sandra suggested, "We'll see to it that your warehouse of stuff is brought to the mansion. Until we can get proper furniture, sheets, panty stocked, it's probably wisest for you six to remain with Lana at the church. I know that Linda is anxious to unload the old mansion, so why don't we plan on checking it out tomorrow morning, first thing. We can see what is there and plan accordingly. We also need to get you all proper clothing as well. Golly, there is so much to do all of a sudden!"

"Music, dances, art! You have no idea how starved we are for them! Dorota has none at all," I exclaimed, remembering all the fine arts that was the Laird Foundation, where the brownstone was located. "Besides all this, we have so much to talk about!"

They dropped us off at the church and left to start arranging to move Dianna's things from the warehouse. Enrico promised to return at nine tomorrow. I had no idea what Linda meant by stuff in storage at the old brownstone mansion, but I was determined to handle that first so that she could sell it. Honestly, I didn't know how she had kept her body alive as long as she had. Perhaps it was just pure will power.

Over supper, I related what had gone on during our meeting with Linda. That we six accepted her job pleased Lana and Bill immensely. "I could not want a better contact person to replace Linda than my own daughter and the rest of you. Though I must admit, we are taken by complete surprise. I would never have predicted this would happen, not since. . ." she faltered.

"Since I lost my arms, mom?" Dianna replied.

"Well, yes, it sounds so awful to even say those words," her mother replied rather quietly.

"Everyone keeps thinking that now I am a helpless cripple who cannot do anything for herself. Right? That's what everyone thinks? Right?" Dianna quipped, slightly antagonistically.

"Well, dear, you just have to come to grips with the fact that you mostly are this way now. Accept it and move on; perhaps with enough servants to help you all out with things, you can have a mostly normal life," Lana tried to be sympathetic, yet realistic as she saw it.

Dianna was fuming. I intervened. "We are doing just that, moving on. We are taking a brownstone mansion, and Linda is helping us get it all fixed up. You know, for our special needs." I tried to put a different slant on things. "As you can see, we just have to do things very differently than normal people."

"Well, yes, that's what I mean," Lana accepted my nudge in the right direction. "You must have lots of special needs. Tell us about the brownstone, please, Dianna. Where is it at?"

Mollified for now, Dianna told them where it was and both Lana and Bill knew precisely the estate that we had acquired. Both were pleased, apparently, it had a long history, and they had known its previous owners. "Linda wants us to go sort out the junk that's stored in the old mansion by the Laird Foundation. She wants to sell it soon. We're heading out first thing in the morning," Dianna explained. "If we find anything relating to your church, mom, do you want us to bring it back here for you to see?"

"Sure, dear, that would be perfect, but I doubt that you will find anything more than piles of old junk. I heard that folks just used it for junk storage the last fifty or so years. Do be careful, the floors might be rotted out," Lana advised.

Later, once dinner was done, Lana had us six sit down with her. "Now I want to make very sure that an official marriage, a union of two, is what you six really want. After all, same sex marriages usually preclude having children of your own. I know Dianna loves to be with all her nieces and nephews. You need to be sure of this."

"It's hard on us to have children and then care for them," I admitted. "Last lifetime, I had many others around who were like us, armless, to help out, to say nothing of all the Laird and Santi folks to lend helping hands. This time, we've only got ourselves and, of course, you and your family, but I can't impose that much upon you," I explained. It was half-truths at best, but I knew that none of us was concerned about starting a family at this point. In the future, well, that was another story.

"Yes, I can well see how that is. Perhaps that is a very wise move on your part. However, Dianna knows that all of us here would do all that we could to help you raise your children. Yet, it would be most difficult for you. I understand. Now the other thing I need to ask is what about the future. Specifically, you are all young women, barely of age, with a long life yet ahead of you. What happens if you find a man worthy of your love and you fall in love with him? Have you thought about such an eventuality?"

Dita replied at once, "Well, that won't happen with me! I find that looking at a man in that way is disgusting! I'm a man looking at a man! No way will that happen with me. However, if Bethany should fall in love with a man, I will not stand in the way of her happiness. That, I cannot do. I love her far too much."

"I understand, Dita. Most commendable of you and spoken from a true heart. Yet, all six of you are good looking to very beautiful, you will definitely attract the attention of many men, especially you Dita."

"Yes, but like I said, I find men disgusting. I want to look good for Bethany, that's all."

"Yes, but mom, look at us now. Our faces might be attracting, but what man is going to really want us when we are like this?" Dianna explained the harsh reality of our situation. She went on, "I always wanted to have children; you know that mom. Last lifetime, I only had Alexa and two others for most of my life. I was just as armless then as I am now. It took me ages and ages to find the right man who was kind and who both admired and respected me for what I really was. Even then, though we were married, I still depended upon my four friends for nearly everything with daily life. Without them and my husband, raising the children would have been impossible. Even so, it was a Herculean task, far harder than building the aqueduct system. At least now, we can be together as one. If Ania falls in love with a man, I can accept that and support her that way, knowing that she will still rely upon me for everything else, as I, her. So I wouldn't be losing that much. Like Dita, I can't stand in her way either. I love her too much to do that."

The others expressed similar views. At last, the High Priestess in Lana was satisfied that we were making the right decision. "I want you to know that officially I am backing these three unions completely, as will the Church of the Three Holy Roses. In many ways, I believe this is the right thing to do in your cases. Comradery, assistance, compassion, love, and understanding among you six are vitally important. It is so hard for us normal people to grasp the enormous difficulties that you six face in dealing with normal life. These unions will allow you to support each other through the hard times that you must face ahead of you. Our entire West Po family will always be there to support you. Go now with my blessings."

"On a lighter note, have you decided upon a date and what kind of a wedding you wish? The parents of the bride usually pay for the wedding and feast reception. In your cases, we will pay for all of yours, if you have no objections." Lana relaxed and began wearing a proud mother's hat, instead of her formal priestess hat.

"Other than Dianna, we really don't have any relatives to invite," I pointed out the obvious fact. "We haven't even gotten around to figuring out clothing that is appropriate here. It seems a waste of money to buy a fancy wedding gown that we will wear only once. However, it is our special day and all that. How about you, Dianna? I think that we ought to allow you to dictate the wedding arrangements. You have many relatives who would like to see you get married."

"Well, it is a very special day, and I want to look really good for Ania," she replied. "I know it is a waste of money, but it's still our special day. I'd like to look really pretty for Ania; she deserves it." We agreed to fancy dresses. How could I not?

"I'm sorry that you don't have someone to invite, but I should have my extended family present. Even though ours is not a traditional union, I hope they can understand and want to share my joy with Ania," Dianna explained.

"We all do, Dianna," Lana supported her daughter. "The children will understand it best if we tell them that you need each other to help you with the things in daily life. I think that will make sense to them." I thought that might be a very wise way to explain it to the children.

The when was more problematical. While young lovers desired to be married immediately, we were not in a viable position to do so. We decided that when we had a better idea when our new estate would be ready for us to occupy it and live there on our own, we could set the date. Limiting attendance to Lana's extended family would make short notice of the wedding date feasible. We set a tentative date for August 1, subject to change if the estate was not yet ready for us. Wedding presents would not be a problem; we needed everything for a house. Dita begged for satin sheets, however.

Chapter 23 Sorting Out the Past, Creating the New

The next morning, we ten pulled into the Laird Foundation entrance. The twin towers still stood as an architectural masterpiece, but all else was drastically changed from the estate that we six had known! The gates from which the Grey Creature had abducted me were long gone. All the barracks that lined the north and western walls, gone, replaced by new, brick buildings, filled with painters, sculptors, and musicians. The numerous houses designed for us women without arms, where four family dwellings shared a common living room, had been torn down. Three story brick buildings replaced them, providing dorm style living for the many students studying here at the Foundation, which now was more like a university, offering an education in the arts.

The beautiful pond remained and the old manor house as well. The homes built behind them for Renzo and I when we were married were also gone. They were patiently waiting to tear down the brownstone before building a third tower for the arts. The place was deserted, many windows boarded up, broken glass had not been replaced. Bird droppings covered the floors of the main entrance room. The dining room smelled of mold. It had sat vacant for many years.

Only Arturo had no memories of the place. For the nine of us, fond memories returned immediately. "Remember when you dolled us up for the dance?" I asked Luisa and Sandra. For the next hour, we were a constant, "Remember when. . ." as we walked around the abandoned, dirty rooms, filled mostly with trash.

At last, Enrico hinted that we ought to get down to business. Dianna suggested that we make a list of things to retrieve, starting with the hinges that allowed the doors to open both ways, along with the sliding foot high door bars. These allowed us to shut our doors easily. When the bar was slid shut, it meant we wanted our privacy. Enrico began making a list. There wasn't much else of value on the first floor.

The second floor was filled with litter and again, nothing of any real value. We moved on up to the third floor and discovered several rooms that were free of debris. No one bothered to carry trash up this far. Two rooms down, we began to find boxes and boxes of stuff. "Okay, guys, why don't you start bringing boxes to us in this room. We can go through them and start a pile in here of stuff to keep and put the rest in the next room," Dianna took charge.

All sorts of things began appearing among the worn out sheets and blankets. Ania was thrilled to discover a cache of twenty of the Grey

Creature manufactured high-heeled boots that we had worn, along with the devices, which had shrunk them tightly against our calves so that they could not be taken off. These were the actual models, which she had used to start her famous line of Alexa boots, which were still the rage in Velona. "What a find! My knock offs were never as good as the original boots! These are invaluable!"

We found a dozen sets of the gold and jade, huge earrings that we had been given by the jungle people we had helped during our voyage of exploration. Along with them was an entire box of the various sized golden disks that one put in pierced ears to support the weight. These we kept as well. Dianna was ecstatic over finding seven of the Grey Creature's blasters, though they were no longer charged. She kept them hoping to find a way of recharging them.

Two hours later, we came across the dresses that we and the many other women that we had rescued used to wear: satin and silk, form fitting dresses in many sizes and colors. They were all very well preserved in cedar chests. Many were in mint condition, we noted. Since we had a distinct lack of clothes that fit us, we kept all these, hoping to hire a dressmaker who could adjust them to fit us.

Arturo was delighted to find a room filled with gardener tools, along with numerous flowerpots and vases. He confiscated these with relish. We found a stash of sheets, pillows, and blankets. While the pillows were tossed, we salvaged some sheets, which Dianna suggested we could use for cleaning and dusting rags, and a fair number of blankets.

A real find was all the special dining utensils that we had used. Mugs, cups, all manner of useful items — these we kept as well. One room held all the kitchen pots, pans, plates, silverware, and utensils from the long gone kitchen area. We kept the best of the lot and marked the rest to give to charity.

One room held a stash of various weapons, from swords to daggers to knives to long bows and arrows. Ilenakova and Enrico insisted that we keep these. I noticed Ilenakova was suppressing tears and asked her what was wrong. "These are valuable for fighters. I was very, very good with a sword just like these, and now I can't even pick one up!" She began crying. I leaned my body into hers to comfort her. We all were going to have these kinds of days, of this, I was certain. Enrico quietly moved all the weapons into our "keep" room. I saw that he was thinking hard.

One box had our original journals of our voyage of exploration trips. I thought that these might have historical significance and we kept them. Yes, we all had fun sitting on our butts, using our feet to bring out the next object of interest. We kept saying, "I remember this. . ."

Sandra had brought along a light lunch, and around noon, we had an indoor picnic. After lunch, Enrico arranged for a wagon to carry the goods we wanted to keep to our new estate. He and Arturo began loading the wagons, making numerous trips up and down the stairs. Meanwhile the rest of us continued going through the many boxes of stuff. Much was just junk, who wanted to use a blackened pot? Not much use for a cracked vase or a moth eaten dress.

We found all the special tools my dad had made for my mother, Jena Rose, who had lost her hands. These devices she'd slip on so that she could manage to feed herself, for instance. This brought back many memories for the nine of us. Finally, we finished going through the last box, and I let Linda know that we had finished and that she could unload the old mansion now.

We six felt badly that we didn't have our yokes with us so that we could help them carry the stuff down to the wagon. Sandra and Luisa had no idea what we were talking about, and I gave her a lengthy explanation of the devices that allowed us to carry things. Both women were very impressed, especially when Dianna told them that she had brought a bunch of them back with her for our use. They were in the many crates of items she'd sent along, which we learned were going to be delivered to the estate yet today.

Mid-afternoon, we piled into the carriage, and Enrico drove us back to the estate, while Arturo followed behind with the wagon piled high with the stuff we wanted to keep. Some of it we would later pitch, but we'd finished the initial sorting. When we arrived, workers were already moving the many crates that Dianna had brought along with us from Dorota. Each one was clearly marked, and she sent the men off looking for one marked "Yokes."

"Woo hoo! Now we can help you carry the stuff from the wagon inside," Dianna excitedly announced. We six bent over, moved into position, and lifted our yokes. "Just have to keep the load balanced between the two sides. Come on; we can help."

The four were surprised with how well we were actually able to carry many things in the two side buckets. Going through the doors was the only tricky part for us. "Amazing, you actually can carry things with these. I'll give those Dorota men credit. These things do work for you," Sandra commented, and then teased, "Now I will have to put you all to work. No more saying, 'But I can't carry that; I don't have any arms.'" We all laughed.

I added, "Honestly, Sandra, we want to become as independent as we possibly can. That is our goal, anyway." She liked our determined attitude. I think she feared that we would remain helpless women in need of assistance with everything, just like the hundreds of other women who stayed behind here in Velona, either joining the Church of Jehosanity as Women of the Eighth Degree or the Holy Roses of Lana's church. These past months, they'd seen many of these women about town.

We were all tired when we were finally driven to the church for supper. Over the dinner, Lana made our formal wedding announcements to her extended family, along with the fact that we had our own estate now and would be working on fixing it up. I thought the adults accepted our non-traditional unions fairly well. Gianna pleaded with Drina, "But mommy, Aunt Dianna won't be able to have any kids." Everyone then stared at Dianna, who took it in stride.

"Not very likely, Gianna," Dianna grinned. "How could I pick up a baby or change its dirty diapers? I'd have to have you do all that for me."

"Euuu!" she curled up her nose and the adults laughed.

Dianna explained further for the benefit of her nieces and nephews, "Without arms, we six have to help each other to do all the things that you can do all by yourself, like tie your shoes. It takes three of us to tie one pair of shoes, and even then, it takes us a long time to do it. So you see, Aunt Dianna really does need Ania with her always. I'm not lazy like some of those that you have seen around Velona. None of us is . We don't want to hire someone to feed us, dress us, or even cook for us. Aunt Dianna cannot just sit around and do nothing all day long, every day of the year, could you? We are not as helpless as you might think. Besides, we only will be living ten blocks from here. You can walk over to visit us and play in our big house and yard any time that you want, if your mom says it is okay. We have a big yard so we can have a lot of fun playing ball. I bet we beat you kids." They all rose to the challenge, declaring that we couldn't.

Bale then said, "I know the estate. It is empty now, right?" Dianna nodded. "Well, how about letting us all help get you the things that you are going to need, like beds? Consider it our wedding presents for you all."

"That would be great, Bale. What we really need is a good wood worker who can duplicate some of the stuff that I brought back, objects that make it possible for us to do normal things. All the stuff is now there; thanks for helping Bale."

"Anything for my little sister. Okay, you're on. I know several men that are handy with woodworking. I'll speak with them tomorrow. Say, why don't we all make an outing over to their place tomorrow and see just what needs to be done?" Everyone liked that idea, especially the children, who wanted to see Aunt Dianna's new house.

Around ten the next day, we met our Forze Segrete at our new estate, bringing Lana and Bill's extended family, kids and all. While the kids ran and played outside, exploring the very large estate, Dianna had her brothers uncrate the many boxes.

"See, here are our style tables. Top is six inches off the ground. I brought back one that sits two. We need three more made, in case we get company." She, her brothers, and the wood workers began to put their heads together, designing a proper dining room table combination, in which one side would seat us and the other, those with arms. Once that was worked out, Dianna then showed them her complete kitchen. One side of our kitchen already was present, though setup for normal women. Since Sandra and Luisa would be staying here with us, Dianna left that portion of the kitchen alone. Because it was a large kitchen, she had them install her kitchen on the opposite side, though the plumbing would take several more days to hook up properly.

Meanwhile, the rest of us and the women headed to the bedrooms. Dita and I chose the northwest bedroom for us. Dianna and Ania would be next to ours and Ilenakova and Kali were next to them and the dining room. Sandra and Arturo took the southwest bedroom opposite mine, while Luisa and Enrico took the one next to theirs, opposite of Dianna's. The third one would be our guest bedroom. Drina knew just the right style of beds that would look fabulous in here and got them ordered for us. Just then, Dianna poked her head in and announced that we would need doorways connecting our three rooms, so that we six could easily move between each room, without going outside and down the hall. More carpentry work was scheduled.

Tom suggested doorknob replacements. He's seen a new style, which was a bar or latch that one only needed to pull down to get it to operate. If the hinges were replaced with those salvaged from the old place, all doors could swing in either direction, making it easy for us. With the addition of the sliding bars a foot above the floor, we could "lock" our doors when we wanted to signal privacy. More carpentry work was scheduled.

A bit later, I spotted Dita, Ilenakova, and Enrico whispering together. When I approached out of curiosity, they all shut up. "We're making progress," was all that Dita said. Now I was curious.

Lona said that we needed good dishes and an entire kitchen's worth of pots, pans, and utensils. She began making a list of those items, rejecting as mostly junk what we had salvaged from the old place. Thus, we pitched even more of those items.

The days of July passed swiftly. The first week we stayed out of the way of the carpenters, except to check on how things were being done and if it was exactly the way we wanted them done. The next week, shopkeepers began bringing the many goods purchased into the estate. Once the beds were delivered, the women began making the beds up for the first time. Our special order of chest of drawers and wardrobe closets arrived. The top of the drawers were only three feet off the ground, with three drawers that we could operate with our feet, just as we had back in Dorota.

Next, we women picked out curtains, which turned out to be a rather large number. We had over fifty large windows to handle. They would be drawn at night and to help keep the cold out during the winter. We chose different colors for each room. Our bedroom curtains were yellow; Dianna's blue, Ilenakova's brown, Sandra's purple, Luisa's green.

During this time, Sandra and Luisa took we six out shopping for clothes, something we desperately needed, but were still uncertain about just what we should get. By now, we had seen enough of the fashions worn by the women of Velona to be able to make educated choices. My big concerns were two: could we manage to dress ourselves and would we be too helpless when wearing them.

Sandra, ever the fashion conscious person and flirt, convinced us that to be presentable in formal settings, we would have to wear fancy cone style dresses with heels. Thus, we each purchased two complete outfits of this style each. I never dreamed that there were so many different pieces that comprised the outfit, and there were extras for the wintertime, pantaloons and such to keep our legs warmer. She insisted that with my blonde hair, yellow would not do at all, insisting that I choose a blue one and a brown one. Knowing that as Sara Jane, she was always right about these matters, I went with her strong suggestions.

Then, we needed both summer and winter regular dresses. These did not have the hoops beneath them. The summer ones were lighter weight, but still had several petticoats. The winter ones came with numerous petticoats, designed to keep us warmer. We got several complete sets of these, still not knowing if we could even manage them.

For around the house convenience, we were able to get some relatively simple dresses quite similar to our fancy Sunday dresses, which we had been wearing daily now. Additionally, we insisted on getting a leather outfit with pants for traveling and several tops and pants sets, though none of us had any idea how we were going to manage getting into pants. Finally, we added some nightgowns, both for summer and winter use.

I must point out that with all of these dresses and tops, the dressmakers modified all tops, removing sleeves, making them all one piece at the shoulders. None of us wanted to hide our absence of arms by having sleeves; they would just get in our way.

Shoes were the easiest to acquire. We got several pairs of easy slip ons and two pair of heavier work style boots. Though they had laces, I remembered all the extensive training that we had done last lifetime and wanted us to have good footwear when we needed them. Heels, well, we decided to use the real thing, as Ania insisted. When we needed to wear them, we'd wear the ones that we'd salvage.

Thus, as the days of July flew by, bit by bit our new estate began to take shape. Dianna decided that we could make our proposed wedding date of August 1 as originally planned. We opted for six identical white wedding gowns. The tops were made without any hint of sleeves, rising above our shoulders. The U-shaped front showed a little cleavage, while the button up backs rose to our necks. Thus, even if we accidentally stepped on the bottom of our dresses, we would not risk pulling off our tops. Instead of a cone style, we chose a billowing style that used several petticoats. Of course, we wore our original Alexa high-heeled boots. Ania wouldn't let us wear anything but the best.

The morning of our weddings, Luisa, Sandra, Drina, Lona, and Lucinda got us six dressed and ready. We all learned a valuable lesson. All of us were working so hard to be completely independent that we entirely misunderstood the fact that all women needed the assistance of others to get into their fancy cone style dresses! "Oh don't be silly; none of us can get into these dresses without help!" Drina chided us.

Luisa then realized how we were overcompensating and pointed out, "We all have to help each other when we need to go to the bathroom while wearing these dresses. Haven't you noticed that we always go to the bathrooms in pairs?" We had not put it together this way, and I began to realized what we had been doing, overcompensating. Slightly embarrassed, I acknowledged our goof; Luisa smiled and understood. After much fussing, the women were satisfied with our looks. We looked in the mirrors and admired our appearances. Dita and I had our long, thick hair draped partly over the sides and front of our shoulders, hiding where our arms would have been. I looked at her and realized that Dita was perhaps the most gorgeous woman that I'd ever seen!

"I'm marrying the prettiest woman in the world," I whispered to her.

"No you're not. I am marrying the prettiest woman in the world," Dita countered. If the truth were said, all six of us looked beautiful and more importantly, we felt beautiful and special.

Lana's extended family and our four new friends comprised our wedding party. We six stood dwarfed in the magnificent cathedral. Its tall ceiling and huge stained glass windows exuded holiness in my mind. First, Lana, wearing her traditional purple priestess robes, formally anointed us as Holy Roses of the Universalist Church of the Three Holy Roses. Normally, women were given a golden rose broach that they could pin onto their blouses. In our case, the golden rose was attached to a long gold chain, which she carefully placed around our necks. Now we were officially sanctioned members of this church.

Lana then conducted our simple ceremony, beginning with Dita and me. "Bethany, do you take Dita to be your lawfully wedded partner from this day forward, in sickness and health. . ." I scarcely heard the words. Dita-Renzo was so beautiful. I was so happy that at last we could be together without hiding our love from the world. "I do," somehow came out of my mouth.

She repeated our vows with Dita, who at last said, "I do! I do! I do!"

"You may now kiss your bride," Lana formally proclaimed. Dita and I passionately kissed, while the group clapped.

"I formally declare for the entire world the union formed. I give you Mrs. Bethany Brozena Malina and Mrs. Dita Malina," Lana happily pronounced.

The whole ceremony was repeated for Dianna and Ania. At last, Lana declared proudly, "I give you Mrs. Dianna Anka West Po and Mrs. Ania Anka West Po." Again, they received a loud round of applause and cheers.

Then she joined Kali and Ilenakova, "I give you Mrs. Kali Kato da

Cassa and Mrs. Ilenakova da Cassa."

Gaily, everyone stately walked out of the Holy Chapel and into the large dining room, where the musicians played many slow dances and refreshments served. We had one large chocolate wedding cake with white frosting. (Dita's request.) Dita and I then had our first dance this lifetime. She came up close to me, pressing her body against mine, our heads rested on each other's shoulders. Dita whispered, "I've figured out how I can lead. Follow my head pressure. If I press on your cheek, we go that way. If my chin seems to be pulling you towards me, I'm backing up. If I'm pressing on you, you back up."

"Clever Dita!" I whispered back. After a short while, we both got the hang of how to feel the other's intent. After the first dance, our friends asked us how we were doing so well and Dita proudly explained what she had worked out. Soon we six danced as well as the other couples did. All six of us realized just how much we had missed dancing! We swore to start going to as many dances as we could.

After a few dances with our new spouses, the others began cutting in. Bale wanted to dance with me next. Thus, the time flew. Even the children wanted their turn. "Golly, Bethany, you dance really well. I didn't think you could, you know," Gianna whispered as she led me around the dance floor.

"You are good yourself, Gianna. I love to dance, so does Dita. If we get some musicians to come to our house to play for us, will you come over and dance with us?" I asked, knowing that any thirteen year old girl would just die for such an opportunity. She squeaked and exclaimed that she certainly would! I promised her that we would as soon as we all were settled in at our new home.

When it was time to dive into the cake, we had no choice but to allow the others to feed us our cake and hold cups to our lips. Even if we could remove our boots, with these dresses, we couldn't really use our feet in our accustomed way, too much dress was in the way. Just now, it didn't seem to matter, though.

Later, Enrico got the carriages ready and we said our goodbyes. Sandra said, "Watch how Arturo helps me step into the coach. I cannot get in safely without his assistance." She pulled up her cone hoop with one hand, while she took Arturo's arm to steady herself. Arturo then used one of his hands to lift up my dress, while steading me with his other hand firmly on my back. It worked well.

Ten minutes later, we pulled into our estate for our first night in our new home. The first thing we did was change out of these dresses into our nightgowns and then we six retired for the night. However, as Dita and I were about to slip between our satin sheets, Dianna and Ania came into our room.

Dianna whispered, "Dita, we are going to show you how it is done properly. You are going to experience what it is to be a woman, not a man."

"What do you mean?" she asked confused. "We can only kiss."

"We know that you don't have any experience having a woman's body. It's time that you learned," Dianna giggled. Sometime later, with the three of us doing our separate actions, Dita suddenly moaned and had a new understanding that she had never had before. Quietly, Dianna and Ania slipped out of our room and headed for Kali and Ilenakova's room. I knew what they were up to and grinned.

Dita whispered in my ear, "I'm so sorry, Bethany. I never had a clue about this as Renzo!" Now I knew what she meant.

"It didn't matter then, Dita. I just love you and want you." We kissed and kissed.

"Absolutely not!" Luisa exclaimed determinedly at breakfast the next morning. I'd just said that we all wanted to start going to all the dances again. "You must complete your training so that we know that you really can take care of yourself, should something happen, Bethany. There are limits on just how well we can protect your lives. Once we know precisely what you six can and cannot do, once we know that you are able to protect yourselves in basic ways, then we can go to all the dances that your heart desires."

"Don't fret, dear," Dita said coyly. "I want you to come down to the basement with me right now."

Crestfallen that we would not be going to dances right away, I dutifully followed her down stairs. "Da ta! Surprise, my love!" Dita proudly exclaimed. "I had a devil of a time keeping this a secret from you!"

There before me was a new torque ball court, modified as we had done it years ago when we were married. One wall had the two familiar horizontal lines, denoting a fair bounce if the ball bounced somewhere between them. She had several new balls waiting for our use. "Oh Dita! You remembered! We haven't played a good game in so long! Thank you!" I lunged at her and gave her a passionate kiss. Then, we challenged each other to our first game. As we started, everyone else, whom I discovered had been in on this surprise, came down to watch how it was played.

Wham. I knocked the ball onto the wall between the lines. Dita dashed after it and sent the ball flying back. The game was afoot! (Pun intended.) A half hour later, I won by a single point. Of course, Ilenakova wanted to try her foot with it, and Dita was very happy to show her how. Enrico and Arturo wanted to learn. An hour later, puffing, Enrico exclaimed, "Damn, Dita, you are darn good at this! It is good exercise and a valuable lesson in dexterity. I think that everyone should learn to play this game, especially your four friends. It'll help their dexterity a whole lot!"

"Oh no," Dianna feigned a protest.

"Honestly, it really is time that we begin your intensive training," Enrico announced.

We all moaned in mock protest. Although we knew we faced some grueling days ahead, the result would be worth it.

Chapter 24 Training

At first, I thought that the training would be that of endurance, dexterity, and control. At least the first few days seemed that way. Enrico had us all our running laps around our mansion grounds. Twice around was a mile, but he had us doing ten loops. At once, we saw that our heavy earrings had to go; besides, now they held no special significance here in Velona. While pretty, they continually got in our way. However, their heavy weight had enlarged our piercings, and Sandra inserted some of the gold disks and reworked the fastenings so that we could wear them whenever we desired.

The men raised a ladder to our roof. "Up and down, ladies," he announced. This was hard, but we used our chins for balance as we slowly climbed up to the rooftop. "Now you need to be able to do this quickly; you are all going like slugs!" he chided us. Ugh.

Balance I could see. Enrico has us walk along a raised, two-inch wide board for some fifty feet. Challenging, yes, it was; we all felt the distinct lack of arms on this exercise, as we wobbled to keep our balance. After a week of this, we got much better at it. Two weeks later, all of us were moving rapidly down the fifty feet.

I thought that the gymnastics were going to be more fun; somersaults ought to be doable. Wrong. While we started out that simple, Enrico had us really challenged. We had to run and then do a flip and somehow land on our feet. Racing towards him, when we got to his position we attempted to do a forward flip. If we were not going to make it, his arms caught our chests, and he helped us finish the flip. Arturo was there to catch us if we lost our feet on the landing. Repeatedly, we practiced this until we no longer needed either one of them.

His next exercise I thought was impossible! He'd tied a rope to a high branch in one of our stately trees and told us, "Climb to the top."

"What?" we protested in unison. He laughed and repeated his command.

"Look, use your feet to inch your way up, but use your necks to keep the top part of your bodies against the rope," he suggested.

Dita actually made it up to the top first; Ilenakova was not too far behind her. Me, I was dead last. I kept loosening my neck grip and flipping over upside down. Thankfully, Enrico was there to catch me each time. At last, I finally got the hang of it and touched the limb.

Three weeks into August, we six felt like a million. We were now doing all the exercises really well, getting compliments and encouragements from Enrico and Arturo. That's when he dropped the next bombshell on us, "Okay ladies, now we do all the exercises again, only blindfolded. No fair peeking!"

"What?" we screamed, "No way! That's not possible," I added. We began by running around the perimeter of our estate blindfolded. He gave us a solid tip, count your steps, and he allowed us one practice run to count them, before the blindfolds came out.

At least with the narrow board traversal, he led us to the board to get started right. More than once, we all fell off the beam, but Enrico and Arturo were right there catching us. What I found the most frightening was running blindfolded and then trying to do a forward flip. I could not see the ground to measure my landings.

Two weeks later, we had all mastered this, and I figured we must be about done. "Now ladies, I know that you all want to go to the dances and dress up and wear your high heels. So don your heels, and we do all these exercises in heels!" Masochist, we all called him, but he was right. We really needed to practice wearing heels and keeping our balance in all sorts of situations. If we were accidentally bumped on the dance floor, for example, we had no arms to grab a hold of our partner. At least we didn't have to do this blindfolded, I thought. Our vanity kept us from complaining this time, for we all wanted to wear our fancy heels to the dances, and we knew he was right.

After we got reasonably good, out came the blindfolds once more! Fortunately, we didn't have to try to do a running flip, primarily because one cannot really "run" in heels at all. However, his main goal for us was the narrow beam, feeling our way along it while wearing heels and unable to see. I realized again, he was being realistic. If the lights went out inside the dance hall at night, no one could see anything, and we would need a keen ability to maintain our balance while walking. While others could use their arms effectively in such situations, we would have to rely on our feet. I began appreciated how much thought Enrico had put behind our exercises.

Five weeks into our intensive training, I found Dita and Ilenakova near tears. I asked them what was wrong. Fighting back tears, Dita explained, "We need to be able to fight. We are Protectors. None of this is going to help us wield a sword or anything."

Ilenakova added, "We can't do a damned thing to fight back; we can now run away really well, like we are bloody cowards! I'll not run away. I'd rather stand there and let them chop my head off than look like a coward or a helpless thing."

My heart ached for them. Lenkova used to be one of the world's best defensive sword fighters, and Renzo had been highly skilled. Now they were, simply put, helpless. I couldn't think of a single word of encouragement. Instead, I called Enrico over and told them about what was going on with them, praying that he could give them some slight bit of hope somehow.

"Chins up. Dry your eyes. Renato Fuello, the monk of Monaco del Dio, is due here any day now. I hope that I have you all in good enough shape for him to take over," he said encouragingly.

"Yeh, like we are going to hold our swords in our teeth and fight that way," Ilenakova replied sarcastically.

"No, we hold the sword with our heads against our shoulders and fight that way," Dita added her gripe to the mix. It seemed impossible to me; swords were out.

"Dita, Ilenakova, if you end up having to fight that way, I will eat my hat!" Enrico chided. They managed a giggle. "Now come on, back to practicing."

Indeed, at suppertime, the bell rang at our gate. Enrico answered it, while the rest of us followed behind him. A short slender man wearing brown robes stood at our gate, holding the reins of a donkey. He had bowl-cut brown hair and eyes to match. He was homely at best, an unassuming personality. "Hello, is this the Brozena Malina estate?"

"Yes, Renato Fuello, I presume?" Enrico said, unlocking the gate. The short man nodded and entered. Arturo took his donkey and led it to our stables, rejoining us. Enrico did the many introductions, and I invited him to join us for supper. He seemed pleased, and we entered our large brownstone mansion.

One policy that we had adopted from our first day here was to share the domestic duties. With eight women staying here, each would cook our supper every eighth day. Each of us took a turn carrying the meal to the dining room and serving it. Each of us took a turn at the cleaning and the laundry. However, we all shared in the dishwashing. Admittedly, Sandra and Luisa did much of the meal advance preparations while we were training. Still, we insisted on doing the actual cooking. Tonight Dita had done the cooking, and it was my turn to serve.

"Have a seat, dinner's coming up, compliments of my wife, Dita," I announced. Enrico showed Renato where to sit, opposite our low side of the table. Using my yoke, I began slowly putting the dishes Dita had ready in the two baskets. True, I would need to make ten trips to the kitchen to get it all, but that's how it goes. Carefully, I positioned myself, lifted the baskets, and carried them to the table. By now, we all had enough practice to know just where to position them before sitting them down. I sat on the floor and raised a steaming bowl up to Enrico, who took it from me. Then, I got the next one and handed it to him. I got up, took the yoke across my shoulders once more, and headed back for the next batch. Nine more trips later, Dita and I finally took our places.

"Dig in everyone. I hope you like it," Dita said cheerily.

The monk said a fast prayer, "Thank you Lord for the food I am about to eat. I am alive one more day." As the bowls were passed around, Renato continually watched how well we managed. Enrico would hand me a bowl, for example, and I'd hold it in my feet, lowering it to our low table. Then, I helped myself to what I wanted and passed it on to Dita. Unfortunately, tonight, we had lamb, and we all needed our pieces cut up for us, which our four handy friends did for us. At least I thought Renato would be able to see that we were not entirely helpless.

When we finished and sat back drinking our tea, Renato said quietly, "Yes, adaption is the key." We six knew precisely what he meant and gave him a big smile.

"Tomorrow, you wish to learn to fight. Tell me why do you wish to fight?" he asked politely.

"I'm a Protector. I must protect and defend Bethany and the others," Dita replied without the slightest hesitation.

"To defend ourselves, naturally. I never run from a fight. I am no coward," Ilenakova added.

"Excellent. Then we may begin tomorrow," he replied, apparently satisfied that we had the right reasons for wanting to learn.

"Yes, sure. Are we to hold our swords in our mouths or with our heads against our shoulders?" Ilenakova asked, still bitter about the whole thing.

"Ah, I see that you wish to begin tonight. Eager are we. You must want to draw blood, yes?" he asked her.

"Well, no, I don't want to draw blood, just fight back. You know, defend myself and everyone else from the attackers who have swords," she explained. "Of course, if my blade strikes home, he will stop attacking us, but I'm not after his blood per se."

"Ah, that's better. Many more ways there are to defend than with a heavy sword. Far simpler they are. You are already equipped with them," he replied, rather cryptically I thought. What did he mean?

Seeing our baffled looks, he added, "Legs can be a lethal weapon. Tomorrow you shall see. Just now, I am tired. I have walked all the way here talking with my donkey. We got involved in a philosophical discussion about whether I should ride him or whether he should have a turn riding me. Then, I was here." We gave him a strange look. Enrico showed him to our spare bedroom and where the bath was. Then, en mass, we all did up the dishes; ten of us made short work of them.

The next morning, Renato began his training. The short little man said, "There are a number of very precise points on a human body where a blow can cause the person to be stunned, paralyzed for a time, or killed. These are precise spots. You must know them well. Allow me to demonstrate just one of them. Enrico, please draw your sword and face me." He did so, standing inches taller than the monk did and significantly more muscular. "Watch. I merely touch him so."

All that I saw was the little man touching Enrico on one shoulder spot. His sword arm dropped as if it was numb; his sword fell to the ground. "See, right amount of pressure on this precise spot, and he is disarmed. A larger amount and he will be unable to use his arm for a long period. This spot will not result in death. You see, Dita and Ilenakova, if you truly want to defend, there is no need of a weapon."

"Yes, but you have apparently not seen us well. We lack that appendage that you just used to touch him with," Ilenakova pointed out, just a little testily.

"Ah, again, Enrico, pick up your sword." He did so. Renato held his arms behind his back. As we watched, he swung his leg up and touched that spot and down went Enrico's arm and sword.

"How'd you do that?" Enrico asked, troubled by how easily he'd been disarmed.

"Mrs. Ilenakova, you do have legs. One could even use one's head if need be, but that is much more difficult," Renato said quietly. "In a real sword fight, the trick is to time it right so that your leg is not struck by the sword. Your first lesson is to learn these precise spots so well that you can find them blindfolded."

He had our full attention as well as the other four! He pointed out a dozen locations on his body. Then, he had each of us come up to him and use our toes to find them on his body. "I can tell by feel when you have the spot precisely." He then reversed the flow and touched those spots on each of us, well those that we had. Six of us were missing some, naturally. When he was precisely on a spot, I detected a sudden weakness emanating from that location. Amazingly enough, all ten of us realized that we could tell when someone was touching a given point correctly. We ten spent the rest of the day finding these locations on each other.

That's all that we did for the next three days! "You must be able to find these spots in an instant, not in two minutes, Mrs. Dita. Now speed it up." Renato continually pushed us all to do this faster and faster. Constantly changing partners only made matters more difficult, but valuable. Dita realized that she would need to be able to hit this spot on any attacker and worked harder than anyone else to be able to do this rapidly. Just when we thought we were getting good at it, he had our partners bend into a fighting stance, totally relocating the height and positions, to some extent.

For well more than a week, this is all that we did. Bring our toes up and touch whichever spot he suggested. "Now we go for speed and control," he announced. "As your partner closes on you, I will call out a spot for you to touch and which foot or arm to use. Speed and accuracy. Preciseness of touch, always, Dita. Enrico will close on you. Prepare yourself." He called out a spot and Dita reacted, but missed slightly the precise spot. "Good attempt, but you missed. This is a precision skill. We must work on precision first, and then comes speed."

Five days later, we had the precision finally down. He would call out a spot on someone closing on us and we'd touch it. Next, we did them all over again, working to get our speed up. "Speed is useless, if the touch is not precise!" He hounded us with this mantra repeatedly.

Three weeks after he'd arrived, we ten were doing great at this. Our speed, in my opinion, was good and we seldom missed. "Now we do these exercises all over again blindfolded," he announced the next day. We all groaned and saying this was impossible. At first, we were right! It was impossible. Renato never raised his voice, never got either angry or frustrated with us, though we were doing all three nearly constantly! Two more weeks passed and all of us were routinely hitting whatever spot he called out, while blindfolded.

At last, he announced, "Congratulations, you have passed the most difficult part of your training. The remainder is easy. Now we will work on the force of the touch: stun, paralyze, or kill. Three distinct amount of force is required. During his spare time these past weeks, he had constructed a number of dummies for us to practice actually hitting with our feet. Now all the dexterity and control that Enrico had worked on us so hard came into play. A week later, we had this down; he was right, this was drastically easier, the judging of the amount of force required.

"Now we will put you through a real test of your skills. Please do not paralyze or kill your opponents. Enrico and Arturo will actually be attacking you, but using wooden practice swords. Gentlemen, you are to actually try to fight these ladies, as if you were their enemies. Yes, it is very fair to give them as many bruises as you can inflict upon them. Be ruthless, be brutal, be their enemies. Ladies, your task is to defend yourselves as you told me that you wanted to be able to do. We will do just two of you at a time. Dita, Ilenakova, you face the men first. If you miss, you will be struck, and it will hurt, but not cause any permanent harm that a real sword would. Action, please."

"Damn, Enrico, that hurt!" Dita called out, limping on one leg. She'd missed and he hadn't. For several days, we six got fairly bruised up. I sported a dozen overlapping black and blue spots on my legs; this was not fun! Yet as the days passed, the men got fewer and fewer hits on us, until at last we stopped them every time. What a feeling we had when we six achieved this!

"Now, each of you will be facing two opponents at the same time," Renato announced.

I moaned, my legs were aching enough as it was. Dita called out, "All right!"

Ilenakova added, "Now we *are* getting somewhere!" Dianna and I moaned even louder.

Facing down two opponents who had swords in their hands and were attacking us was much more difficult. We had to judge carefully each person's movements, dodging when possible and striking when the opportunity arose. After a number of days, all six of us were reasonably well skilled at handling two opponents.

Renato was planning to stop here, but Dita and Ilenakova insisted that they had sometimes had to face three or four at the same time.

Thankfully, we four sat this one out, as Renato pressed Luisa and Sandra into service, though they were not very skilled at all with a sword. A few days and both were handling multiple attackers very well indeed.

"Now then do any of you wish to learn more specific types of attacks?" Renato asked. The four of us didn't, but naturally, Dita and Ilenakova both did. We watched while they were taught a powerful circle kick, using either leg and swinging either from the inside out or vice versa. Next, they were taught a flying kick, in which they launched their whole bodies at their opponent, kicking with both feet. Kali had used this one in her previous life and went back into the thick of it to relearn this move. It had once saved her life back then. The drawback of this maneuver was that it usually ended with our bodies falling hard on the ground, and it was awkward for us to rise easily. Maneuver of last resort this one became.

Just when I thought we were done, Renato said, "I understand that you women like to wear high heels. So now we do all this again while you are wearing them, please." Oh no, back to square one. That we needed terrific balance was soon discovered by us all. We had more spills than ever before. Yet, we did pick this up rapidly. I just hoped and prayed that he would not now blindfold us! Thankfully, he did not.

"Now it is time for your knife training. Please be careful and pay close attention. I do not want any of you cutting yourselves." He brought out a bunch of straw targets that would normally be used by archers. "Your passing goal is to be able to pitch four throwing daggers into the bull's-eye from a distance of five feet. Using your feet, you are not likely to be accurate at greater distances, nor will your force of blow be sufficiently powerful enough to cause damage at much greater distances." He gave us all a set of four beautifully balance throwing daggers, especially made for us! They were designed to be gripped between our toes, not with fingers.

Both Dita and Ilenakova really loved this! They threw themselves into learning this method with vigor. Even Kali went all out to learn this one. A byproduct of this knife training was that we all discovered that we could handle a knife, cutting our own meat. This, I greatly appreciated, as it increased our independence in normal life.

We then got a shock. "Now ladies, it is time that you learned to operate and fire a crossbow," Renato said in his familiar soft voice. "You will operate and fire from a sitting position."

"All right!" Dita exclaimed, feeling that proficiency with many weapons was beneficial.

While we were slow at reloading, we all quickly became good shots. It was actually one of the easiest skills that we learned. Finally, Renato said, "At last we come to the drawing of real blood. I know that Dita and Ilenakova really feel that at times they need to slice their opponents. Thus, I have some presents for all of you, and those two in particular." He presented each of us with a pair of leather leg bands, which would hold our four throwing daggers near our ankles. He had us each practice drawing them and then tossing them at the target until we were sufficiently proficient with this complex sequence.

Next, he gave Dita and Ilenakova a special pair of leather leg bands, which held their throwing daggers and had a trap release spring, which when activated extended a short dagger blade five inches below the base of their boots or feet. "These, you use when you are wearing boots. A tap trips the spring and the dagger extends to its position. Use a circle kick to slice with the dagger. Press here and it retracts."

The beaming looks on those two faces when they effectively sliced off the heads of the dummies that they were attacking was a joy to behold! Now both felt like real fighters once more, they could draw blood, if they needed to do so. Renato made two very elated women that day. "Thank you all for being such very good pupils. Now it is time for Renato to return to our monastery. The question still remains, will my donkey carry me or must I carry him." We packed him a large bag of food, gave him many hugs and thank you's, and watched him leading his donkey out of our gate and down the street, chatting away to the donkey. Strange man, I thought, but incredibly knowledgeable and an excellent teacher.

Suddenly, I realized that now we could go to dances, plays, and musical concerts! "Not just yet," Enrico shot us all down. "There is one more thing that must be done. I will let Linda know that you are ready. The Guardian, Chaucer, and Linda want to give you their gift of thanks that they promised you when you met them. Expect this to happen tonight. Now I think you've earned a good hot bath, ladies. Hop to it," he teased.

That night, Jes floated above me. *Usually, beings eventually face what is preventing them from doing this during therapy. However, I will undo it for you. Relax and face these things in your past, dearest Bethany.* A number of incidents discharged, incidents in which I doubted my own intuition that something was not right, that something bad was about to happen. In ignoring my hunches and feelings, I got killed, usually. Then, the basic incident came into view, where I had decided that I could no longer trust my instincts. When that one dissipated, he was finished, and I felt not only lighter, but well, somehow different.

In time, we six discovered that we just knew when danger as near us, when someone was about to attack us, even from an ambush situation. I now realized that our enemies would find it next to impossible to take us by total surprise anymore! Indeed, the Guardian had given us back a very powerful spiritual skill that we once had had.

The next morning we received news that Linda d'Grange had passed away. Her bank secretary came to inform us and tell us to report to the bank on Monday. She would begin training us on what was needed of us. High Priestess Lana West Po conducted her funeral, as per Linda's long standing wishes. Only a limited number of people who had known her well attended.

Her body was laid to rest in the catacombs beneath the Church of the Three Holy Roses in an elegant sarcophagus that had long awaited her body. It lay next to that of Chaucer d'Grange. We honored her memory, but we all knew just where she and Chaucer now were. Klara had given birth to twins, a boy and a girl, back in Wit, Dorota, where they now lived. For a time, Linda kept in touch with me to make sure that we had no questions about our new jobs.

While we now began to spend time at the Velona Banca del Dio each day, our training was not quite finished. Enrico insisted that we all learn to drive the carriage, though not in harnessing the horses to it. Now we all saw just why Enrico had us climbing ladders and ropes, these were just the skills that we needed to climb up into the driver's box, some five feet above the ground. Just as we were getting the hang of doing this, Dita sprung her surprise on me. Ilenakova also had a hand in it as well.

"This way, my love," Dita said coyly.

"Follow us, my fair Dianna; we have a surprise for you all," Ilenakova giggled. We followed them to the stables.

"Ta da! Bethany, I want you to meet your new horse!" Dita proudly exclaimed. She and Ilenakova had secretly been searching all over Velona for six of the finest horses that were best suited for our needs. I was very surprised at the type of horses she and Ilenakova had finally settled upon as ideal for we six! They came from the Northern Steppes! Short, furry horses, these were both hardy and swift, but were very much smaller than all other horses in Velona. However, they were used by and trained by the famous fighters of the Northern Steppes. Those fearsome fighters often galloped into battle with both of their hands holding bow and arrows or swords, controlling their horses with only their legs. Their saddles were more like pads to absorb the horse's sweat, quite unlike the hard leather Velona saddles or the high saddles that the armored knights used to ride. None took a bit; rather a hackamore was used if reins were ever needed.

"These are perfect for us. Easy to mount, they take their commands almost exclusively from our legs and body shifts, and we can saddle them ourselves, nothing to it. Well, not quite that easy. Ilenakova and I both have to work together to get the bridle on and the saddle cinch tightened. But we can do it, that's the point. Now we can ride whenever we want all by ourselves. These horses go fast too," Dita explained. I gave her a warm hug and passionate kiss. She'd done just what she had promised me she'd do when we were back in Dorota.

Now we also had to practice riding with our horses as well as driving the carriage. The next Saturday, we ten went out into the open countryside, and finally, Dita and I turned our horses loose, cantering into a full gallop, as fast as our spirited horses could run. The wind blew our long hair like yellow and black banners! Exhilaration, that's what she and I felt that day — that and freedom. I realized as we flew along, that no longer were we handicapped or helpless or dependent on others. We were truly free and incredibly happy. The others also realized this as well, with Dianna surprising us with, "Say, you know I can handle a knife now. Maybe I can continue what I started out to do this lifetime, figure out how our bodies really work." Amazing.

Chapter 25 Velona Banca del Dio

"Step right this way," the smartly dressed President of the Velona Banca del Dio said to we six women. He'd finished giving us a tour of the largest bank in Velona proper. "My wife, Sarah, is the Vice-president of Operations. She will be your primary contact person. This is her office. She will show you the ropes. We all will miss Linda, that's for sure."

A middle aged woman with blonde hair and hazel eyes looked up from her desk. She wore a blue dress billowed out by several petticoats, very like what we were wearing. Sandra was correct in her choice of bank business dress, I thought. We six closely matched what Sarah was wearing. "Hello, welcome to Banca del Dio. You must be Bethany."

I introduced Dita and the others. "If you will follow me, I will show you to your large office in the basement. Your office is totally secure. At night, this side door is the one that you will be using. Three guards are always posted here. We take security very seriously, naturally. Linda always did her work late at night. Will you be doing the same?" she asked, as seven sets of heels clicked on the stone floor leading to the steps to the basement.

"We aren't sure yet. Probably we need some time to get grooved in on everything," I said not willing to commit to a schedule quite yet." Sarah picked up the leading edge of her skirt and descended. Unfortunately, we couldn't duplicate her action and had to go much slower, being very careful of our balance and not being tripped up in our petticoats. Sarah noticed our cautious movements and apologized, "Oh, I'm sorry. Can you ladies manage the steps? I cannot imagine how terrible everything is for you poor things." She dumped unwanted sympathy on us. Dita gave me a dirty look, but now that we were appearing in public, I expected that we would receive no end of reactions.

We ignored her sentiments and followed her into our new office. The room was well lighted; twenty-five lanterns gave the spacious room a warm glow. The floor was carpeted, and six of our style low desks were arranged along one wall, two lanterns above each one. The purple carpet was soft and would take the chill off our feet while we worked with our toes. The other wall held numerous low drawers of files, clearly labeled. A set of incoming and out-going baskets were by the door.

"When you arrive, these baskets contain the latest documents and requests that you must monitor. If it says priority rush on it, then those must be handled first. Returning communications and dispatches go in the out-baskets. Someone will pick them up every hour during the daytime and first thing each morning. Always leave the lanterns on; the guards will handle lighting them and dousing them. If you have any questions, let me know. That pull-cord there by the door rings a bell at my desk. I will come down as soon as I can. I'll let you get to it then. Let me know if you need anything at all." She left us, and we did as she instructed. The door had a large deadbolt, which we could lock ourselves in securely, when working after hours.

Our job was three-fold. First, we needed to okay any large transfer of funds, double-checking if any real gold transfer was actually needed. Second, we needed to monitor the various bank presidents' requests for gold transfer to and from their banks. Whenever their gold on hand was too large or too small, depending on the size of the bank, naturally, they would request a physical monetary transfer from the reserves. If we Okayed it, the presidents would then schedule it.

Our third and most important job was to monitor these large transfers of funds. Often, Linda told us, these indicated some major action, such as a buildup of soldiers for battle, a pay off, and other nefarious dealings. Alert for these subtle clues, we ought to be able to figure out what plans others were making. Linda's cardinal rule was: follow the money trail; it leads to the action. We all quickly saw that Linda had to be a working genius to have handled all this work by herself and without her body, which lay sick in bed for nearly fifteen years!

Quickly, we six decided upon a breakdown of the workload. I took over the monitoring of all financial matters concerning Megalos. Dita handled those of Zargarb and Solamina. Dianna handled Velona and neighboring Barcella. Ilenakova handled the remainder of the Sea Princes and those of the Greenway. Kali watched over the huge accounts of Demokritos. Ania took over the rest of that southern continent, including Annelise and the remainder of the world.

Dianna suggested that we first deal with the priority ones and then the usual bank transfers. That took us an hour. Now came the real work. I found Linda's carefully logged journal of all Megalos transfers of funds. In date order, after each amount, she noted to whom it went, from where it came, and added notes after each. Some indicated that the funds ended up in the Church construction funds. I saw that we would need to follow the money trail. That is, after we logged a transaction, we would then have to keep an eye out for how the money was spent. Once we knew that, we would go back and add the notes opposite that transaction.

This familiarizing process consumed many hours. Kali commented, "Well, I now see how the new Emperor of Demokritos got his throne. Linda has noted who bribed whom. Clever, this is invaluable information!"

"Hey, the Church of Megalos has recently transferred five thousand gold to their main Velona church. This is way above their usual transfers. I cannot find any corresponding large transfers out. I wonder where it went?" I commented.

"Guess you ought to look at deposits into individual accounts," Dianna suggested. Ugh, that would take hours, I realized. Tedious work this banking accounting. Then, I hit pay dirt!

"Well, this is interesting. Commander Drakon Strate has become their new Supreme Prelate. They dumped the late Eros Maios' account into Drakon's account, forty-three thousand gold. That was back on Megalos. Now they've added another three thousand to his account, but it was done here in Velona. I see five other smaller deposits, all these add up to the five thousand that was transferred up here by the church. Twenty to one, Drakon and five of his henchmen are now somewhere in Velona! I wonder what they are doing here?"

"We should let mom know," Dianna replied. "This is not good. They must be here for some purpose and it can't be good!" I made a quick Mind Link to Lana West Po, telling her what I had discovered. She promised to step up their security. I felt her emotions; she was terrified that another of her children might suffer the same fate as Dianna had — namely kidnaped and tortured.

At the end of a long day, we six had caught up on all the necessary paperwork. I mentally contacted Enrico that we were ready to be picked up from the bank. The three guards nodded politely to us as we passed them. Damn, the door had a knob. "Excuse me, could you possibly open the door for us," I asked one of the guards.

He did so, giving us a sympathetic look, as if we were somehow pathetic. As we stood outside awaiting our carriage, I heard one of the guards whispering, "I don't see how those six can do anything. VP Sarah must just feel sorry for those helpless women and gave them something to do."

"Yes, probably so. There are an awful lot of those ignorant women around Velona today. Honestly, letting some religious nuts cut off your arms has got to be the dumbest thing I ever heard of."

I was fuming, but Enrico arrived and helped us climb aboard. We all were bothered by those comments and chatted about them all the way home. Tonight, the Po children were due to come over to play with Aunt Dianna and us, so we ate quickly. Right on time, several carriages arrived with the nine children, accompanied by the three wives.

Dianna got them all interested in a game of kick ball, while I chatted with Drina, Lona, and Lucinda. We arranged for Dianna's parents to dine with us on Monday nights; Drina and her family would come for Tuesday supper; Lona would bring hers by on Wednesday, and Lucinda and her family would dine with us on Thursday evenings. I felt that this would be good not only for Dianna, but for everyone else. They could get more comfortable being around us and see that we were going to be just fine.

On Friday nights, we began to go to the art events, either the musical concerts, a play, or a dance theater. On Saturday nights, it was dance hall night for us, our favorite night of the week. Sundays we stayed long in bed and usually went for horse rides in the afternoons. Yes, we were bound and determined to enjoy life.

As we were all saying goodnight to the children, I noticed a man in sky blue robes, watching our estate from the street. My newly kindled senses kicked in, as did the others. "Mano del Dio is watching us," Dita whispered, as the carriages began rolling out of our gate. Enrico locked up after them and watched the man slink into the shadows.

"Well, you can't go attacking someone who is merely watching you," Enrico commented.

Mornings, we took turns doing the shopping with either Sandra or Luisa. Darned if we didn't get an earful! Whenever we were just trying to be normal, as shopping in the open-air markets, some around us would make snide comments about us, taunt us from a distance, belittle us, or just plain make jokes about our "condition." I found this more and more disturbing. Dita came back on Wednesday morning in tears.

"Damn it, it hurts. They just keep on making fun of us, like we did this to ourselves," she sobbed. I consoled her, and then she realized that her body was more emotional than the male bodies that she was used to having. I left her pondering that mystery.

During the week, we spotted Mano del Dio men watching us. Some were now outside the bank when we entered, while others seemed to be watching when we left. Always we detected one of them watching our estate. At least, we didn't see them at the dances or the Laird Foundation events. There, they would look totally out of place in their sky blue robes.

I contacted Linda about them. *The Mano del Dio is constantly watching us. I am beginning to worry that they will try something.*

I was afraid of this. From Dianna's kidnaping, I was certain that they wanted some information. Now we know that they are after the Santi gold. I have some ideas, Bethany, but first, how is life now working out for you six. Honestly, how is it going for you?

We are getting by, but we are constantly the butt of humiliating jokes about our arms. It's starting to wear Dita down. Physically, we are okay. Well, sort of. I mean we are married and all that, but it is not quite the same. I think all of us realize that. Sandra and Luisa are now pregnant, we think. Dianna loves children, and we are having all of her nieces and nephews over once a week just to play. We need each other just to get by, but it's not the same as having a real husband.

I figured there might be difficulties. The Guardian believes strongly that you six need a backup plan, in case something happens to your bodies. If you and Renzo had your choice of your next bodies, I take it that you would prefer a female and Renzo, a male?

Absolutely. I had a devil of a time when it was the other way around. Dita is having an awful time of it, so I know she'd prefer a male. Why?

The Guardian is going to make something happen the way you would like for a change. I'm going to join us with the others. One second.

Dita, Ilenakova, Dianna, Ania, and Kali soon joined us. Linda explained that she was working on a backup plan so that we would have new bodies in case the assassins got to these.

Absolutely, a male body! That is, if Bethany is going to have a female one, Dita replied enthusiastically. Dianna and Ania chatted a bit and agreed that Dianna would have a female body next, while Ania would get a male one. Ania explained that she could do her political work far better as a male in these societies. Ilenakova opted for a male body and Kali chose to have a female one for Lenkova's sake. We all agreed that we wanted to be married properly to each other next time around. Linda chuckled.

Linda then joined Sandra, Arturo, Luisa, and Enrico with us. Apparently, she had already contacted them about the Guardian's plans for our future. *You bet we are ready to start our families,* Luisa exclaimed. *We've been holding off because we were so busy getting ready to support all of you. Now that all is going along well, both Sandra and I are quite ready.*

Linda explained the Guardian's plan for we ten. Essentially, the two women would begin to have children. These new baby bodies would be our new ones, tailored to meet our desires. *The Guardian guarantees you that this time, the births will be painless and that you will retain all your knowledge and skills that you now possess. If something should happen to your current bodies, Luisa will take over your positions at the main bank, guaranteeing continuity of our new base of power, information, and control. When you wish to resume these bank positions, you'll be welcomed, but you may have other choices when that time arrives.*

We thanked Linda and the four for doing this for us. I couldn't imagine having better parents and told them so. I know that they were pleased to hear this. I then asked Linda, *Do either you or the Guardian suspect something will happen to us? We know that the new Supreme Prelate of the Mano del Dio is now here in Velona. His henchmen have been spying on our daily lives. Are they planning something?*

There remains one loose end with the dissolution of the Santi del Dio. As you know, we accumulated a good deal of wealth. The idea that I disseminated was that the Santi dissolved because we ran out of funds building all those expensive fortresses and maintaining such a large army in peacetime. However, the Church of Jehosanity in Megalos is desperate for funds. I discussed the abduction of Dianna with the Guardian, and we believe that they still think that the funds are somewhere around Velona and that they want to steal it for themselves. I have been unable to get this idea out of their minds. Somehow, we must obtain closure on this last aspect of the Santi. It may well be my legacy to you to have to clean up this last detail that I was unable to do, Bethany. The others and I promised that we would somehow do this for her.

We chatted with Sandra and Luisa for some time about their willingness to become our parents. Both women were already pregnant and expecting in June; it was now late December 745. "How are we supposed to run two bodies at the same time?" Dita asked. "I mean, if these are still alive when the new ones are born, then won't we be controlling two at the same time?"

"No kidding, Dita. I've done just that! It was terribly confusing because I didn't realize what was going on at the time. Maybe it will be easier if we know about it," I replied. I related my experiences as Ket Bethany and Lizzy Ann. Everyone enjoyed hearing about it.

"Wait a second! What happens if these new bodies become adults and these bodies are still alive? That would be really weird!" Dita speculated.

"Somehow, I think that Linda is giving us a subtle hint that these are not long for this world," I said what was in the back of my mind. We all found this a sobering thought, but why else would the Guardian and Linda be working so hard to prepare new baby bodies for us this soon?

The next day at the bank, I began to wonder just what had happened to all the Santi wealth. Then, I realized that there ought to be an account for them and looked it up. Indeed, I found their account folder. The ledger balance read one gold piece. However, a sealed folder was also in their account fonder. Large red letters on its cover read: "Bethany, Dita, Dianna, Ilenakova, Ania, Kali: Do not open this folder at this time. The less you know, the safer you will be." How strange, I thought and did not open it. Well, I really didn't need to know about this right now anyway. Far too many other financial dealings demanded our attention in the present. None involved the defunct Santi organization.

As we were leaving, we received a note from High Priestess Lana West Po. "What does your mom want to see us about?" Dita asked Dianna.

"Dunno, must be important, since this is an official summons of hers. She sends these type notices when she wants someone to see her in her official monarch role. Something must be up, but I don't know what," Dianna replied.

Five minutes later, Enrico helped us climb out of our carriage before the main office of Lana West Po, where she conducted the running of Velona. Two business men were just leaving as we six walked up to the door. Darn, it had a doorknob, and we six stood for a moment staring at it, once again reminded of our unique position in this society. "Coming! Sorry about that," Enrico called out. His face showed that he felt awkward in not having recognized the situation sooner.

He let us in and we followed Dianna's lead. Six guards with long pole arms stood at attention just inside the door. One herald, wearing a very fancy twin tailed suit, announced our arrival. "Ladies Bethany, Dita, Dianna, Ania, Ilenakova, and Kali await your audience." We heard Lana's voice and he added, "Through this door." Then, he realized that we had no arms with which to open the doors and red faced, opened them for us. We walked in feeling somewhat ill at ease again.

We walked up a purple carpet to her throne. A number of tables and chairs filled the back of the room, a row of chairs faced her after those, and some twenty feet separated those from her throne. I figured most visitors would just stand before her, if the audience would be short. We six walked up to her. "Hi mom, we got your message. What's up?" Dianna said, discarding all pretenses of formality normally used before the ruling monarch of Velona.

"Come, let us sit as equals," Lana said, motioning us to the row of seats. Her elegant and regal purple robes fanned as she strode over to the chairs; we followed her.

"Honesty. I need you to answer me honestly, please. This is important," she began seriously. We promised her that we would be. "How has it been going for all of you as armless women in Velona? I don't mean within your estate. Truly, your father and I are most impressed with how well you all do manage. Out there in our society, how has it been going with you and the common folk of our city?"

"Humiliating, embarrassing," I began. "When we go shopping at the open-aired market for groceries, for example, we often find ourselves the brunt of jokes. Some ridicule us, call us names, poke fun at us, and call us stupid women. Some have even gone so far as to make jokes at our situation, teasing, and taunting us. Not good, I'm afraid. We are bearing it as well as we can. Is this what you mean?"

Dianna added, "Then, there are those that drown us in sympathy, 'oh you poor, poor things,' and all that crap. Sometimes, I'd like to crawl into a hole, but I hold my head up and continue doing what I must."

Lana sighed, "I thought as much. Bethany, was it like this when the Voyage of Exploration brought back so many women like yourselves to the Laird Foundation and the Santi?"

"No, it was a vastly different reaction back then. Yes, people were sympathetic to a fault, but they were also understanding and helpful — not like they are today. I suspect that much of the people's cynicism is due to the Elders of Dorota coming here, hypnotizing everyone, and convincing them to have women's arms removed. Three of us had ours removed the minute we were born — as if we had any choice. Dianna's were amputated just to save her life. Ilenakova and Kali, likewise, had little choice; their parents mostly forced it upon them and then abandoned them to their fates," I replied. "It is vastly different here this time. Why?"

"I thought as much. I have been reading mom and grandmother's journals of those times. Your opinion goes along with what they wrote. Yes, this time, our people are reacting very badly to it. We have a serious problem, which is why I called you here this late afternoon. In Velona — the city — we have now some fifteen hundred women, give or take a few, of all ages who are members of the Church of Jehosanity as women of the Eighth Degree. When these women are seen in public, they have maids and servants attending to their needs. They dress well and give the appearance of somehow being royalty. At least they are treated as such by all as if they were. The key here is that they appear to do absolutely nothing for themselves, always having others do everything for them."

"I've had the bank president check on a sample of these families. Indeed, all those families that he checked were indeed some of the wealthier families in Velona. Hence, they are able to afford such constant companions for their women. However, as you know, I accepted a goodly number of them into my church as Holy Roses, after the three founding members. You six are among them. At last count, there are one thousand three hundred thirty-five of them."

"With the exception of you six, they are not faring at all well. Again, I have been checking, and their families simply are unable to afford to hire constant care givers. These women and children are not adapting well at all. Many are losing weight from not eating right, dependent upon their husbands to get home from work, cook, and then feed them. The suicide rate among them has become alarming to say the least. We are averaging two deaths a day, mostly by drowning."

"Worse still, in my mind, are those husbands who have given up all hope of being able to support their wives and daughters. A day doesn't go by where our city guards are not called to some residence, find the father has murdered his wife and possibly daughters, and then killed himself."

"Wow! I had no idea this wasn't working out for them!" I exclaimed, shocked by her report. I could understand it, however. Without our extensive training, we would be just as helpless as these women were. Besides, I, too, longed for another body and to start over again.

"I've been in daily contact with the Laird Foundation, but in all honesty, they are now mostly artists and have little skill at providing the help and support that these women need just now. I do believe that they are more frustrated than I am. I thought about perhaps having the city or the church pay for a constant companion for each of these households, but then I have to consider the wishes of those who pay their taxes and tithes. Majority opinion is pretty much what you have said — that they made their own bed and now have to live in it."

"If I ignore their wishes and just do what my heart desires, I risk destabilizing the majority here in Velona. This gives the Church of Jehosanity a chance to grab more power than they already have, which I am loathed to do. So kids, I've asked you here to ask you if you have any bright ideas. I am in dire need of some clear thinking about now. I cannot just abandon them and allow more to take their own lives out of sheer desperation."

I sighed and decided to speak my mind before the others could. "You know, in many ways, if these families could move to Dorota, they would find life so much more tolerable there. At least the women would; the men might be a little bored with the lack of the arts and all that. Maybe if I could talk to them I might be able to convince a large percentage to move to Dorota. However, they are unlikely to be able to pay for their passage."

"If you can convince them to move, I will guarantee their free passage. I'll send a caravel fleet to Dorota, all expenses paid," Lana very quickly replied. "Do you think that you can convince them to do this? I mean, they would be abandoning their lives here, their relatives, and all that."

"They are abandoning their lives by killing themselves, so I think that leaving their other relatives might not be that important to them just now. If you can somehow get them together in one spot, I'll do my best to convince them to move, Lana," I offered my sincere help.

"Oh thank you! I will see what I can do. Perhaps I can get them to come to the church on Sunday afternoon. We can pack a thousand in the chapel easily. You can speak to them from my High Altar. That will lend more credence to your words, Bethany."

After a slight pause, she added, "There is another smaller problem, Bethany. We now have twenty orphaned girls ranging between three and sixteen years old. Other relatives, aunts and uncles, mainly, have adopted the boys. Even a few relatives who live in other towns have taken some of the girls. However, the many helpless girls are putting a terrible strain on our orphanages. Should we just move them to Dorota as well, whether they wish to go? If so, who will look after them when they arrive?"

"Damn, I ought to have anticipated that there would be orphaned girls," I replied bitterly. "Damn them all for having done this!" I took a deep breath. "Okay, I will talk with these girls too. Have them come after the meeting with the families, Lana."

"Thank you Bethany! I will do as you ask. May God guide your words. There, enough of this nasty business. Are we still on for dinner tonight at your place?" she asked greatly relieved.

"You bet mom. Six as usual. Tonight it's Luisa's turn to cook. See you and dad then," Dianna cheerily replied. We got up to leave, and as we got to the door, there were the abominable doorknobs barring our way once more. An embarrassed Lana rushed to open them for us. Dressed in our billowing dresses and Alexa heels, we could do little but wait, likewise embarrassed.

As we rode home, Dianna asked, "How are we going to convince them to move? I truthfully can give them my opinion about living there." I agreed with her. In fact, I got also got Dita and Ania to give their opinions as well. Perhaps after this long a time experiencing how life was really going for them in Velona, they would be ready for such a drastic change.

On Sunday afternoon, Lana, wearing her elegant purple High Priestess robes, opened the door for us to enter the High Altar with her. The church was packed with men and their wives. Lana gave a brief welcoming speech, introduced us, and turned the meeting over to us six. I was glad that we had dressed up for this meeting, lending more credence to our views. I stared out at the packed pews; more than a thousand were jammed in here. Per Lana's request, only the husband and wife of a family attended so that everyone could be present at one time. I sensed a wall of grief and apathy coming from the mass of men and women. I sighed and began.

I won't bore you with the speech. I told them about the four of us being raised in Dorota, having lived our eighteen years this way. Next, I related some of the humiliations, embarrassments, taunting, and jokes that we routinely experienced as we went abroad in the city. From their reactions, I knew they had also experienced this, perhaps far worse. I then outlined what life was like in Dorota, explaining how, for women like us, it was a perfect society. Further, I got them to begin to insist that they be given what had been promised to them, namely a holy life and a perfect society. I watched them rise from apathy and grief — their ruin in life now — on up to a demand for change. I had Dita, Dianna, and Ania relate their opinions and views of Dorota and life there for women like us and their husbands. Finally, I finally got them as a group up to hope and turned the meeting over to High Priestess Lana West Po, who told them that she would provide for all their expenses if they now wished to move to Dorota.

At this point in their lives, to the last man and women, they all wanted to move immediately! "Start packing! I'll have ships awaiting you at the docks in two weeks' time!" a very happy Lana ended enthusiastically. Everyone rose to leave, many thanking Lana and us for everything. Again, we were embarrassed, as we had to wait for Lana to open the door so that we could exit the High Altar area.

Our heels clicking on the stone floor of the long hallway, we followed Lana to her dining room, where she had a tea waiting for us. The orphans would arrive in an hour. She was so pleased with our work that she kept hugging us and thanking us, her biggest problem of the month was solved at last.

Next came the heart-wrenching meeting with the children, who had so little hope left at all. Their parents had died, usually by their own hands, leaving them to fend for themselves — a most hopeless situation. Since they were so few, Lana was going to have them all meet here in the dining room. I vetoed that one, "After all, they deserve our highest respect as well. We should have them meet in the church as well. Only you will have to open the door so we can get to the High Altar." She realized her gaffe and readily agreed.

I stared out at the twenty youngsters sitting in the front row of pews, where the wealthiest nobles usually sat during Sunday Services. This fact did not go unnoticed by the older girls. All wore extremely shabby dresses; some dangling sleeves were tied into a knot. Uniformly, their hair was dirty and snarled with tangles; their skin was in dire need of routine baths. I suspected that at the overworked orphanage, they were getting only minimal care.

After talking with them for an hour, fourteen also wanted to move to Dorota. Most of these fourteen were the older ones, many of which were also looking after younger sisters. The remaining six were between three and five years old and unable to fend for themselves.

"Okay, Lana, I want you to see that these fourteen all get a bath in your fancy bathroom; they are to get new clothes immediately, and I'll give them each a hundred gold pieces to help them with expenses until they get settled. Further, they are to be on the first caravel that sails to Dorota." The girls let out a war hoop, unable to contain their enthusiasm. In their eyes, their dismal lives had miraculously just turned around.

"What of these other young ones?" she asked.

"They are going to come and live with us!" I declared, much to the surprise of my friends.

"Great idea, Bethany!" Dianna exclaimed. "They will love it at our place."

I'd already Mind Linked with Enrico, Arturo, Luisa, and Sandra and got their permission to accept these six. I promised the four that I would hire a permanent tutor and maid to help them with daily life, until they could manage on their own. No way was I going to burden them with six more helpless women.

"These can be our kids," Dita whispered to me. I knew what she meant, as did the others.

Our carriage was jammed as we headed home with our six new children. Alessa was three years old with blonde hair and charming blue eyes. She took to me at once as if I were her mother, perhaps because of my long blonde hair. Black haired Bianca was four, and Dita could not resist her pleading black eyes. Cosima was the oldest at five, with brown hair and hazel eyes. She took to Dianna at once, chatting away about dresses and the fact that Dianna was a princess. Elena was four and had light brown hair and green eyes; she latched onto Ania. Fina was three with dark brown hair and brown, sad eyes. Ilenakova adopted her. Jemma was also four and had blonde hair, bordering on brown, with blue eyes. Kali took care of her.

First, we showed them around the huge estate and the many rooms. I explained that tomorrow we would get the three spare rooms all fixed up for them. They would be two to a room just as we were two to a room. I promised them that tomorrow we would go shopping and get them some good dresses and clothes too. First order of business, baths! Second came dinner. While we six took charge of giving them all a much needed bath and washed their hair, Luisa scrounged around for some clothes that we could use until we could get them proper ones tomorrow. Fortunately, she found some in the pile of old clothes that we had saved from the old brownstone estate.

Having children around us was heaven-sent; we all realized how much we missed having them around in our lives. Now we had shadows. Everywhere we went about the estate, our shadow was right there with us. I suspected that they were afraid that we would leave them or something similar.

That night, we each took ours with us to bed. I pulled down our sheets and covers. "Okay Alessa, in you go and scoot over so I can get in. Bianca, you climb in after me, and then we all make room for Dita." We four snuggled together, and I felt just wonderful, so did Dita, who leaned over Bianca to give me a warm kiss.

We spent considerable time with the children, showing them how to do things with their feet. The older ones caught on more quickly than the two three year olds. I hired Dino to be their teacher and tutor, determined to see that all six got a good education. Norma was hired to look after their needs while we were at work. As December ended, we were one large happy family, truly happy.

Chapter 26 Following the Money Trails

Cold January arrived — I say cold, but here next to the warm, blue waters of the Med Sea, I mean that the temperatures were in the low forties. We six were working at the bank, when I came across an interesting monetary transaction. "Hey Dianna, did you see a deposit in the Church of Jehosanity come in this week from their mother church on Megalos? I've got a transfer of funds amounting to ten thousand gold."

Dianna rummaged through the documents that she had not yet processed. Her foot soon held it up, "Yes, got it. Let's see it's made out to the Supreme Prelate Drakon. They have made the deposit. This one gets my red flag. Something is going on here."

"Okay, keep your eyes open for any withdrawals or transfers of a sizeable nature from that account, please," I asked, wondering what nefarious deals were being planned.

Two days later, Dianna got our attention. "Hey, about that ten thousand, Bethany, look, there is a transaction that just came in today's batch. That amount has been transferred to a Thad Owens. Who is he?"

We all shook our heads. "Okay, we must find out who this man is, gang." We asked some of those who worked here at the bank, but no one knew who he was, excepting that he had an account here. A teller said that he was an old man.

As we climbed onto our carriage for the ride home to supper and our girls, Dianna asked, "Enrico, can you please stop by mom's church for a minute? I need to ask her something." A few minutes later, while we all stayed in the carriage snuggling to stay warm in our cloaks, Dianna dashed inside, her heels echoing on the cold cobblestones.

"Well, maybe Lana or Sam might know, they are in their sixties," I sounded a hopeful note. "Gosh, it sure is chilly, but it beats the snow that we used to have in Dorota."

"True, but I always wanted to have a snowball fight with you, Bethany," Dita teased. I gave her a bump with my shoulder and she kissed me.

Dianna came hustling back, her face flushed. Enrico helped her step aboard and listened to what she had to say before climbing back into the driver's seat. "You'll never guess who Thad Owens is! He is a seventy-one year old, long retired Santi del Dio captain of the guards. He was stationed at Linda's brownstone mansion, providing security there. He probably knew everyone who worked there in the organization. Now why would the Mano del Dio be giving him ten thousand gold?"

Enrico drove us home, while we all began speculating all manner of wild things. None of these made any real sense at the time. Our carriage pulled up by our front door and, one by one, Enrico helped us down. As we six pushed open our front door, our six girls came running towards us. "Mommy is coming!" Alessa called out, as she came hustling up to me, pushing through my billowing dress to snuggle. My foot went out and around her, pushing her tightly to me.

"Mommy's home. Have you helped get our supper ready?" I asked her.

Bianca likewise ran up to Dita and pushed into her as well. So did our other four girls to their "mothers." Yes, the girls had now accepted that we were going to be their new mothers. Cosima, the eldest at five, had convinced the others to start calling us their mothers. Dianna was very pleased to have Cosima call her "mother." Each of us leaned over and gave a warm kiss to our little girls. Enrico and Arturo then undid our cloaks, hanging them in the hallway, while we headed into the warm dining room, following the girls' incessant chatter about what they had done this afternoon.

"Are Aunt Lucinda and Uncle Tom coming over, mommy?" asked Cosima. "I want to play with Tonia." She and Tonia were the same age. All the other children were older than she was.

"Yes, Cosima, they should be along in about a half hour. Come show mommy what you've been doing with your lessons," she asked. Of course, we all had to have a look see at what the four older girls had been doing. Dino had been teaching them their letters. Cosima proudly showed us her carefully drawn letters, which filled a page. Bianca, Jemma, and Elena had done theirs as well, but their letters were not as nicely formed as Cosima's were. Alessa and Fina had been learning to draw pictures with charcoals. I rather recognized our house in Alessa's rendering.

"Beautiful letters, Cosmia, you are writing beautiful letters," Dianna praised her.

She beamed, "I want to be as good as you are, mommy!"

Days passed. On Monday night when we played hosts for Lana and Sam, our dinner conversation drifted onto Thad Owens. "Say, that reminds me, kids. The captain of the City Guards informed me that Isabella Fucello was found murdered in her home this morning. Strange cause of death; we haven't ever seen anything quite like it."

"Can we examine the body?" I suggested, more out of curiosity than anything else. That phrase caught my attention. How could they not determine the cause of death? It would have to wait until morning. Cosima begged Grandpa Sam to tell her and the others another of his stories. He could not refuse those gorgeous hazel eyes and that pleading look on her face. Yes, the girls began calling them grandma and grandpa because they were Dianna's parents. I think that pleased Lana and Sam too.

The next day, we left for work earlier than normal, dropping by the undertaker's parlor, where the body of Isabella Fucello was being kept until the funeral later this afternoon. As promised, the captain of the City Guards was there to meet us and help us examine the body. "We've never seen anything quite like this," he said softly. From his attitude, he thought that showing us the body was about the stupidest thing that Lana had ever asked of him. Six armless, helpless women looking at a dead body — how could they know anything useful? I ignored his attitude, and we six gathered around to have a peek.

"See, something small and round entered here just above her left eye. You will notice that a substantial portion of her head is missing here at the back side," he pointed out, rolling her head over to reveal a massive wound.

"Damn!" Dita exclaimed.

"We've seen that before!" I added. "Back on Megalos before we came to Velona, one of the security men of Dorota was shot with one of their own new inventions called a gun. It is like a miniature cannonae that you hold it in your hand." I tried to explain, but found it a bit hard to do.

Dita continued her explanation, "It shoots a small lead ball out of a short barrel. It makes this kind of entrance wound and smashes out the backside. Yes, this woman was shot with one of those new inventions from Dorota. Sir, you ought to check if anyone heard a loud popping noise and, if you search the place where she was found, you ought to find what's left of that lead sphere."

Dianna added, "It might not be round anymore. I mean that after it hit the skull bones, it may have flattened out. Lead is awfully soft." The engineer in her was displaying itself once again. He promised to have a look and we left, heading to our jobs at the bank.

Later that afternoon, the very same captain visited us at the bank. Sarah brought him down to our room. "Excuse me, ladies. You have a visitor." In walked a solemn faced captain.

He held out a small piece of flattened lead in his hand. "You may be right about this miniature cannonae of yours. I found this on the floor not far from where her body was found. You must tell me all that you know about this new invention. Who has them? Where do they come from? How many are here in Velona? How can one defend against them?"

"All the Security Guards on Dorota carry them. That's where they were invented," I tried to start answering his questions. Dianna interrupted me.

"Excuse me, but I drew up a sketch here of what they look like, life-sized. This is what you are looking for; the guards always carried them in a leather holder strapped to their waists, at least the Security Guards on Dorota did," Dianna explained, handing her drawing to the captain with her foot.

She rattled on, "Now we know that the Mano del Dio killed three Security Guards back on Megalos and stole their guns and ammunition as well. My theory is that, if one gave one of these guns to any reputable engineer, he or she ought to be able to replicate its design, perhaps improving upon it in the process. I know that I certainly would do so. My money is on the Mano del Dio having begun to make and use guns in their assassination work."

"You drew this?" he asked, looking at the detailed engineering drawing, which she had done from her memories.

"Of course, it took me a while. I thought that you might find it useful to see what this new weapon actually looked like when you find it. Find the gun and you probably have found her murderer," she added.

"But how? I mean. . ." his voice trailed off. All six of us knew what he wasn't saying, that she had no hands with which to draw.

"We use our feet, silly," Dianna added. "We are not as helpless as you may think that we are."

I defused the embarrassing moment, "Say, Captain, do you know who this woman was? I mean did she have a job when she was younger? Was she an important noblewoman or something? Why kill an old lady?"

"Damn good question. None of us can fathom why anyone would want to murder an elderly woman. She used to work for the Santi del Dio, her daughter told me. That's about all I know. She was neither a noblewoman nor wealthy. This murder gets stranger by the hour. Excuse me. I've taken up enough of your time, thank you Princess Dianna for your excellent sketch." He bowed and left.

"Well, there's a connection," Ania spoke up. "She worked for the Santi del Dio. Yes! Now I remember her! Years ago, when I was doing my organization thing as we all setup the Santi, I put Isabella in charge of financial disbursements for the Santi at the brownstone mansion. She would go around paying our bills and giving our troops their weekly pay. Say, it's coming back, my old memories. Thad, I remember now, he was in charge of the small security group that escorted her around, whenever she carried gold coins to pay others."

"Ah ha! Suddenly the picture clears. The Church of Jehosanity on Megalos sends ten grand up here to Drakon, who then gives it to Thad. In return, I'll bet anything that Thad told them about Isabella. Now Isabella winds up dead, shot by the very same Mano del Dio," I put it all together.

Dita mused, "I wonder what they got out of Isabella before they killed her?"

"We ought to try and find out," I suggested. "I am going to send Enrico to visit this Thad Owens and find out what he can from there. I think I will ask Linda about Isabella. I concentrated and made contact with Enrico and sent him on our errand. Then I reached out a long way to find Linda.

Damn! I was right! They are still after the gold that they think we may have yet. Linda placed into my thoughts.

Could Isabella have told them anything that they might find useful? I found that folder on which you said not to open just now, by the way.

Linda gave a telepathic chuckle. *I knew you would find it, but you did it sooner than I expected. Yes, please do not open it until this matter with the Mano del Dio is handled terminally. Now about Isabella, let me think. No, she was strictly in charge of disbursements. She knew nothing about our income side or our treasury. I am sure that she lent credence to the facts that towards the end, we were spending large sums of gold maintaining everything. However, even if they find out where the Santi main treasury was located, they will find nothing there. Do be careful, Bethany; they may eventually come after you six! This is what the Guardian and I fear.*

We chatted a bit about how our girls were doing and then I broke the contact. Dita concluded, "Well, now I see what Linda meant by following the money trail. It clearly shows us what has happened in this case. Yet, it is not enough to have the guilty men arrested is it?" We all agreed that it wasn't, just by itself.

At supper, Enrico explained that Thad was mis-lead. A man claiming to have found some lost Santi funds visited him wanting to know if he recalled who handled the money for the Santi headquarters. He was given a "reward" of the ten thousand gold for his help in locating said people. She was the only person that he remembered who was still alive. Fortunately for us, Thad was never on the income side nor had he known where the Santi treasury was actually located. He did know of another man who used to ride protection on gold shipments that came from the treasury to the main headquarters. Abe Smith was the man's name, but he did not know whether or not he was still alive nor where he may be living. If Abe was living, he ought to be about seventy-five years old. Enrico said that Thad was grief stricken that he had been duped and that Isabella was dead because of his information.

"We had better locate and interview this Abe Smith fellow before the Mano del Dio gets to him! Ideas?" I asked everyone. None of us was familiar with the old Santi operations or personnel so we met the next day with Lana and Sam, enlisting their aid.

"Deal, we will see if we can locate this Abe Smith. However, this gun situation is extremely critical. Do you realize the magnitude of this invention, Bethany?" Lana asked. From the intense look on her face, I knew that she had heard about the murder by gun.

"Now men can kill from a distance," I replied flatly. "Gone are the old sword days when you had to face your opponent. Now you can just kill him from a distance."

"Right. The ramifications of this are enormous, Bethany. We must get our hands on some samples and then get our best minds working on duplicating them," Sam added.

"Improving them," Dianna broke in, adding her engineering viewpoint to the mix.

"Every country, king, ruler, and thug will want to get their hands on these as well. A whole new killing game has just been born on Tarra," Lana said angrily. "Now how do we protect ourselves against this threat? With swords, we developed armor; with cavalry, we developed fortifications, pikes, and cannonae. With cannonae, we have lost the use of the forts; they are pulverized in no time by those powerful blasts. About our only defense is fast cavalry who can charge them faster than their slow reloading times."

"Dear, counter batteries of cannonae also work," Sam added.

"Okay, I will contact Linda and get us some samples," I reluctantly volunteered.

The next day, Linda promised to get a shipment back with the caravels that were bringing the last of the Velona families to Dorota. Meanwhile, I decided to use the financial data that we had. "Gang, it is research time. I want to come up with estimates on just how many cannonae each country or ruler has purchased to date. From now on, we need to continually track this, along with the manufacture of guns."

We began searching through all the records, dating back to the invention of the cannonae during the Demokritos attack on Zargarb, when I was the Empress of Demokritos. From 702 to the present year of 746, all records pertaining to cannonae purchases had to be located from the piles of other transactions. Complicating matters was the simple fact that the bank did not exist back in 702. We estimated that in those earlier years, word of their invention probably spread slowly.

By the end of the third week of January, we had tabulated our results. Demokritos alone had purchased nearly five hundred cannonae, double anyone else, but then that country was many times larger than other countries. Velona had a hundred, as did Barcella and Zargarb. Other Sea Prince sectors had between fifty and a hundred. The ten kingdoms of the Greenway had between fifty and seventy-five each. Even the island of West Reach had some fifty cannonae. Worse, many hundreds more had been ordered, but not yet made or delivered.

I also discovered a new company on Megalos, the Helio Gun Company. Orders valued in the thousands of gold pieces were flowing in to them on a weekly basis, primarily from the Church of Jehosanity and the Senate who ruled the island nation. Only this week the first money transfer from Demokritos had been made to this company. I expected to see vast orders being placed in the near future from them. Either that or we would see new gun manufacturing companies opening up on Demokritos. No matter how we looked at the numbers, the situation looked dismal indeed. Man was rapidly gaining new and better ways to kill man.

In early February, Abe Smith was finally located. He'd retired to a small northern village. Unfortunately, Lana's guards had found him a few days too late. The report that we received was grim. The old man had seven fingers cut off, similar to what had been done to Dianna to get her to talk. A round bullet hole was visible in his forehead, right between his eyes. Dianna speculated that because not all his fingers were gone, he had finally broken from the pain.

"This means that the Mano del Dio now likely knows where the old Santi treasure was kept," Dianna explained to her mother and father. They had just broken the grim news to us on Monday evening when they came over for dinner.

"Well, we've been doing some snooping of our own, dear. Up by North Point, where the Santi used to have their main dock for their caravels, there is a cavern just at the edge of the small village. That's where they used to store their gold. These days, North Point has become mostly a fishing village, exporting dried fish, which they store in that very same cavern. If the Mano del Dio goes there, they are not going to find anything but smelly fish." She seemed relieved as she explained this to us.

"Well, checking that place out ought to slow them down some, mom," Dianna noted. "Besides by May you ought to have a shipment of guns from Dorota. Linda says that they are sending along a hundred of them and ten crates of ammunition. I'm afraid that I don't know if that is a lot of ammunition or not, mom."

"That is good news. Sam has arranged to put our best engineers on the gun project as soon as they arrive." She looked at Sam; something about the twinkle in her eyes alerted me that they had a surprise. Sam nodded, a big grin formed.

"Sam and I are officially retiring this Friday. Bale is taking over the leadership of Velona, while Lona will don the High Priestess robes. Dianna, if anything happens to Lona, you are to take over the High Priestess position. Now we can spend far more time with our grandchildren and relax. Honestly, running Velona has taken quite a lot out of us."

"Wow. Cool mom, dad. Hey, I don't know anything about being a priestess, mom," Dianna's face went from excitement to intense worry in a flash.

"Oh you shouldn't worry, dear. Nothing is likely to happen to Lona," Lana attempted to alleviate Dianna's sudden fears. "I know that your heart is with how things work, not on men's souls. That's why I have given that to Lona."

"Whew, for a second there, I was getting plenty worried. Besides, that job would be hard for me to do," Dianna added.

On March 1, a caravel from the Church of Jehosanity arrived from Megalos. A church representative deposited one hundred thousand gold into our bank under the Mano del Dio account! We let Bale know what had just happened, and he promised to keep an eye on them.

We speculated a good deal. What was this all about. Could this be a hit on we six? That's what we were most afraid of happening. For a week, we were on edge, watching our backs and being extra careful. Nothing happened at all, except for our paranoia.

At dinner on the next Tuesday, Bale reported that the Mano del Dio men were making many inquiries about buildings that would be suitable for schools. Apparently, the Church of Jehosanity was going to be starting up private schools for boy and for girls, separate schools, that is. "Keep up the good work, sis. It really helps us to know when to start looking for something. Without your clue that something was up, I might not have known about all this until much later. Linda sure did know what she was doing, setting this all up." We grinned, that she did.

During the winter and continuing into March, we six did routine therapy sessions on our little girls, beginning with Cosima, who was now six. Much to my amazement, I found children were not in what we adults would consider good shape, mentally! The operation was vivid in her mind and very ready to be handled, complete with screams of pain as she finally contacted the underlying physical trauma to her shoulders. I purposely kept the sessions on the short side, which worked out well. She tired easily.

Once this huge trauma was handled, her IQ soared. Tutor Dino was amazed at how fast she began learning, so were we proud mothers, for that matter. Of course, Cosima wanted more of this marvelous therapy, and I let Dianna take over for me. Our other children began begging for my therapy too. We obliged. During the next week, evenings we worked on handling our other girls' more recent shoulder traumas.

Little Alessa, who was now four, begged me for more, once we'd gotten her shoulders handled. Thus, for the next several weeks, all six of us worked on our little girls. I wondered what else could have possibly happened to these girls? After all, they were only between four and six years old. The expected tragic loss of their parents came up at once, followed by their births. After we handled these obvious ones, I was at a loss on what other possible traumas they might have had.

"Why don't we ask them if they have spotted something else that needs some therapy?" Dianna asked. I couldn't think of any reason not to do so, and off us six went with our girls. In hindsight, her idea was positively brilliant. These girls could see the masses of trauma in their minds and literally dove into them, once they were given the opportunity. To them, it seemed an exciting game to play.

The results were stellar with some unexpected realizations on all our parts! My little girl, Alessa used to be the famous Bonilla scout who knew every inch of the Seven Sea Princes. "Mommy, I was called Florencia Bugatti. I knew you a long time ago! I really liked you and wanted to be near you again. That's why I've been hanging around Velona. Mommy, please, please, please, you have to teach me how to ride again! You and everyone else rides, I must too!" All this from a four year old! I was shocked.

Bianca, Dita's five year old, realized that she used to be Janisseko Bottellio, a famous Sisterhood Fighter Group Leader for Bonilla. She, too, we had known, and she left Bonilla a long time ago to look for a new baby body here in Velona. Life had become too miserable there during the long occupation. She begged, "Mommy, you have to teach me how to fight somehow. I know I don't have any arms, but you don't either, and you can fight. You just have to teach me how to ride a horse as you do. You don't need arms to ride fast, so neither do I, please, mommy!"

Dianna's girl, Cosima, discovered her past identity as Sister Calli of Zargarb. She had been terrific at problem solving and unraveling mysteries. Indeed, she was famous because of her skills, so many years ago. She had heard of all the marvelous inventions being created in Velona and curiosity had driven her here for her next baby body. "Mommy, I want to solve more mysteries and invent things too, just as you do, please mommy."

Elena, who was now five and Ania's girl, discovered that she used to be Alicia Madriosa, the famous Zargarb Sisterhood High Council representative and most respected woman in that sector. She had the uncanny ability to moderate disputes, just like a Judger would. Ania promised to teach Alicia all that she knew.

Ilenakova's girl, Fina, who was four, discovered that she had been Alice Augato, the Fighter Group Leader of Pieta. Like Bianca, she began demanding that Ilenakova teach her how to ride a horse and to fight. "Mommy, you fight, and you don't have any arms, so I can too!" She said determinedly, planting both her little feet squarely on the floor. How could Ilenakova refuse?

Jemma, now five and Kali's girl, realized that she had known Kali before. Down in Demokritos, she had known her as Kallisto, the Kali assassin. Jemma had also been a scorned woman of the Eighth Degree and had learned the ways of the assassins, becoming independent and able to murder. She laughed and laughed as she discovered that for the past many years, she had been following Kali, trying to join up with her in another lifetime. Kali and Jemma just sat there and hugged each other for the longest time, tears coming from all four eyes.

I began to see that beings got attached to other beings, friendships or bonds of love and marriage, and that they often followed each other around, attempting to be close together in another lifetime. I wondered how true this pattern might be for others.

Tutor Dino was astounded with the girls after we finally finished their therapies. All six were many times brighter and eager to learn. "Honestly, Bethany, they are learning at a rate that is double the best that I have ever seen! Most remarkable girls, all six of them!"

As the weather warmed around March 1, Dita, Ilenakova, and I took our girls, Alessa, Bianca, and Fina out for their first horse ride. Of course, Enrico insisted on accompanying us as we rode north and east out of the Velona into the farming countryside.

I looked over at little Alessa, who was holding her wooden block between her teeth just as I was. She was so proud, so happy, so alive, that I nearly cried, seeing a little four year old riding tall, as if she was my friend Flo riding beside me as we had done a century ago!

An even more unexpected thing happened. One day, Alessa ran to fast and fell down, banging up her knee. While she was crying, Cosima ran up to her and said, "Alessa, close your eyes. Good. Now go through it. Tell me all about what is happening." I came running up and stopped short! Cosima was running our therapy on her little sister! Ten minutes later, Alessa was laughing, and the two got up and ran off to find the others. I noticed that her knee now showed almost no signs of having been badly scratched up; her wound healed remarkably in those ten minutes. Our girls now were routinely using therapy on themselves when needed!

This they continued to do by themselves, Cosima taking charge. Daily while we were away, the girls ran additional therapy sessions on themselves, squeezing them in during the breaks with their tutoring lessons.

When April arrived, both Luisa and Sandra were getting very big indeed, far more than one would expect at nearly seven months. Consequently, we six began taking over more of the chores for them. Yes, we even did the shopping for groceries at the open markets again. It had been nearly six months since we last made such ventures, having allowed Luisa and Sandra to handle it. They knew just how much all the taunting, teasing, and humiliation that we had received upset us. This time, there was far less of it, drastically so, I thought. I figured that with the thousands now gone and only the wealthy Women of the Eighth Degree around, the average person would have likely forgotten about them. This seemed to be the case. While we were often stared at, the merchants seemed kinder to our needs and methods of carrying produce and items with our baskets and yokes. Perhaps having our little girls along with us evoked a little more sympathy for us.

By May, the two women were huge, and our girls loved to put their feet against their bellies, feeling for movement of the babies. Indeed, the whole household grew more and more excited about the births. Drina, Lona, and Lucinda now checked up on Sandra and Luisa daily and we were to call them the instant that their labors began.

Finally, I decided to level with our girls and explain what may or may not happen here. "There are some bad, evil men out there who may try to kill all six of us. We do not want to leave you girls, so Sandra and Luisa are making new baby bodies for each of us. If these bodies are killed, we will have these new ones all ready for us. We will not leave you girls, but you might have to help them change our diapers for a while."

"I promise I will teach you to ride again, mommy," Alessa volunteered.

"Me too, mommy," Bianca added quickly. "But I don't want those bad men to hurt you."

Cosima broke in, "If they do, we will run therapy on you to help you recover from it, I promise I will!"

I was amazed at their reactions to all of this. They were not children in the usual sense, who I would have expected to cry and beg us not to die and all of that. Instead, here were six adults with little bodies! They knew that they were immortal spiritual beings, that they, too, had had many bodies and many lifetimes, and that what I was saying gave them complete confidence and assurance that we were not going to abandon them just because our current bodies might be killed. Amazing attitudes, I thought.

Chapter 27 Closure

In mid-May, I discovered another transfer of ten thousand gold from Megalos to the Mano del Dio Supreme Prelate Drakon, who was still here in Velona. Shortly after the funds were posted to his account, he transferred much of that into five other men's accounts. I began to have an eerie feeling about this.

We six solemnly discussed this on the way home that night. Dita ordered, "Okay, we take extra precautions starting now. No one goes out of the house alone. We stay in a bunch as much as possible." Ilenakova added some additional ideas.

When we got home, none of us expected the surprise awaiting our return, especially Dianna. "Mommy! Mommy! Come look. The blue light is on!" Cosima yelled extremely excited. She even tried pushing Dianna faster into the dining room. The last few days, Dianna had been showing off the old Grey Creature's blasters that she had found and put to good us during her lifetime as Enyo. Long ago they had used up all of their internal charges and now were totally dormant and useless. Hence, she thought it okay for Cosima to handle them and examine them.

They had left them sitting on the window ledge last night. The warm sun had shone down on them all day long. "See mommy! The blue light is on! Does that mean that these will now work again — like they did for you?" Cosima asked eagerly.

"Oh my goodness! Gang, look! They all have some charges in them again! How can that be? Kids, these are now very dangerous things to handle. If you turn on the button, an energy beam comes out and destroys or blasts whatever is in front of it. I used them to blast away the solid rocks so we could continue down that tunnel. Bethany, we have to put these someplace where it's safe."

"But mommy, how did they get more power again? Are they all charged up yet? Maybe we need to figure out how this happened," little Cosima chatted away all the ideas that she'd contemplated during the day while waiting for Dianna to return home.

Dianna forgot all about supper and all about the assassins. "Cosima, it must be the sun. That's the only thing that has changed. I kept them in a covered box all these years. We left them sitting on the window ledge, exposed to the sunlight. That has to be it. Come on; let's see how much they have already recharged. I wonder how they can recharge themselves? That is a good question to ask, Cosima."

Dianna sat down and picked one up very carefully, Cosima stood as close to her as possible, watching the device in her mother's feet. "See this line here says that it is half charged. If it gets to here, it is fully charged, as they were when I found them. Let's leave them in the sun another day and see if that does it. This is a very, very important thing that we've discovered, Cosima, very important. We now have seven blasters that are operational once more!"

The blasters became the sole topic of conversation for the rest of the night. The girls wanted to hear all of our stories about our harrowing escape through the underground river tunnels. Dianna was very happy to oblige them. Indeed, the next day, all seven were fully operational once more! I realized that these would be our main defense against Grey Creatures, if they ever showed up on Tarra again.

When Dita and I were finally alone in bed that night, she rolled over to face me. "Bethany, these Mano del Dio assassins — you realize that we might be able to take them out without getting us all killed in the process, don't you?"

"Dita, we probably can, but our objective is to provide closure on the Santi del Dio's gold reserves. As long as the Mano thinks it exists, they will continue to torture and assassinate innocent people in their ill-advised attempts to find it. Somehow, we must convince them that there is no more gold left. That is our true objective, Dita; convince them there is none left. Only then will they stop this madness and move on."

"I know love, but I've sworn to protect you. It will be hard for me not to do that. I love you so much, Bethany, but you are right, as always. Besides, I would rather have the opportunity to love you properly with a male body," she whispered. I just gave her a long, passionate kiss.

At breakfast the next morning, Cosima asked me, "Bethany, you are a Wid, so you must know the most of everyone, right?" I nodded. "Can we talk privately, please Bethany, it is important." Her pleading eyes I could not refuse, besides, I wondered what could be so terribly important to her. Dianna looked at me, wondering the same thing. After eating, Cosima and I went into my bedroom and she closed the door and slid the privacy bar shut. My curiosity rose even higher!

"First, I want to show you something," she said timidly. I sat down on our bed and watched as she slipped off her cotton dress. Naked, she walked up close to me and turned so that I could see her left shoulder. "Can you see it?" she asked excitedly, "there on my shoulder?" I stared at her shoulder. A tiny growth was plainly visible, no more than an inch long! Quickly, she pivoted placing her right shoulder in front of me. There was another similar growth on that shoulder as well.

"What is this? Maybe we need to get you to a doctor," I said, becoming very worried. Perhaps this was some aftereffect of her surgery; perhaps the doktor had somehow botched her amputations.

"What do they look like to you?" Cosima asked, sensing my worry. "I did something, but maybe I should not have done it."

"Let me have Sandra take a look at these growths, honey. She's a

Healer," I suggested. Cosima agreed. A minute later, a worried Sandra entered and began examining the small growths on her shoulders.

"Do they hurt, Cosima?" Sandra asked sympathetically. "When did you first notice these growths?"

"No, they itch a little. I did something yesterday, and I woke up all itchy this morning. They are supposed to be new arms growing," Cosima finally admitted timidly.

"What?" I jumped off the bed, startled beyond belief. Sandra's eyes opened wide and her mouth gaped, no sounds came out.

"I'm sorry. I'm sorry!" Cosima began crying.

"Dear, dear, there's nothing to be sorry about," Sandra put her arms around Cosima, comforting her. "You didn't do anything wrong. First, I need to really see what these growths look like. I'm going to fetch my bag. Be right back!"

"Cosima, this is incredible. What did you do?" I asked her, regaining some of my composure. Century-old memories of the Guardian restoring the lost hand of the Zargarb woman came back to me. It had been a holy miracle and widely known back then.

Before she could answer, Sandra came running in with her black bag. Of course, everyone else followed her curious about what was happening with Cosima, none more so than Dianna, her adopted mother. Sandra got out her magnifying glass and took a closer look. "This is the most amazing thing that I have ever seen in my life! Bethany, here you have to have a look!" She held the glass and I wiggled into a position to see the growth.

"Incredible! It does look like a tiny arm is growing out of her shoulder!" I exclaimed.

"Let me see!" insisted Dianna. "This is a miracle! Wow! Look at that! It is a tiny arm; you can see tiny fingers even! What a miracle! How is this possible?"

Cosima, her fears gone, beamed as only a six year old can smile. "Cool! It worked, just as I figured it would work! I'm going to have new arms, mommy!"

"How is this possible, Cosima? What did you do?" I asked completely shocked and mystified.

"Cool, Cosima!" Bianca exclaimed.

"We want new ones too," Alessa insisted.

Dianna helped Cosima put her dress back on and we all went into the dining room, where Cosima finally explained what she had done. Because of all the therapy sessions she had received, Cosima spotted something. "When I close my eyes, I can see my body's model of how it's supposed to be formed — you know, kind of like Dianna's engineering drawings. It is supposed to have arms, so I just gave that part of the model a little push yesterday. It's working, because now my body is growing some new arms so it can be formed as it was supposed to have been. I can see everyone else's models too. Can you see them too, Bethany? Do you know how these things work? I just gave mine a little push where the arms are supposed to be."

"Give mine a push too," begged Alessa.

"Me too," Bianca added, followed by the other four little girls.

"Er, no I don't, Cosima. I've never seen anything like it. I know. Can I Mind Join with you and have you show me what you are seeing?" I asked, my curiosity rising to an insatiable height. I just had to see what she did! So did Sandra and Dianna. A minute later, all of us, adults and children alike, were linked together mentally seeing what Cosima was seeing. She closed her eyes and concentrated.

There, see it? The bluish glow over my body. I pushed here and here. Cosima indicated the tops of her shoulders.

It's like an energy field around her body! Dianna exclaimed. *Now I see it, Cosima. Yes, it is like a blueprint or model for the body. Wow! Look, she can see all of ours as well! Look, there is where my arms used to be located! Incredible. Cosima, can you give mine a push as you did yours?* We watched fascinated as Cosima gave two gentle touches or pushed on the tops of Dianna's shoulders, where her arms used to have been located. *Wow! I feel energy of some kind — look; you can see energy flowing there now! Bethany, this must be our body's genetic blueprint. This must be how our body knows how to develop and create itself. It starts out as one tiny cell, which somehow multiplies and grows. So this must be the blueprint that it follows while it is developing in our wombs! What an incredible discovery, Cosima! Fantastic!*

As we watched, Cosima went from person to person, giving each armless shoulder's genetic blueprint one of her little pushes. As she did mine, I too felt the tiny electrical energy discharging in my shoulders. I dropped the Mind Link. "Cosima, you may have just performed a miracle!" I explained. "If this works, we all will be making new arms! Jes Amir, the Great Messiah and Guardian once did something like this to a woman in Zargarb, regrowing her lost right hand. Amazing!"

"How long will it take for us to have real arms?" Dianna asked eagerly.

Sandra, our Healer, had recovered from her shock. "Let's not be too hasty about this. While it does look like a miniature arm, time will tell if it does develop into useful, working arms. Don't get your hopes up too high just yet. After all, it takes nine months for a baby's arms to get maybe six or eight inches long when it is born. It may take several years for your arms to grow up to the point where they ought to be now."

"My shoulders itch," Dianna interrupted.

"Don't itch them! All of you, resist itching them. When someone has a wound, itching is a good sign of healing," Sandra cautioned all twelve of us. "This is just almost too incredible to believe, gang!"

"Say, if we are really growing new arms, shouldn't we drink a lot of milk or something to help our bodies build new bones in them?" I asked, thinking ahead of eventualities.

"Er, right, Bethany. If these arms continue to grow, we ought to make sure that each of you is getting the proper nutrition to help your bodies," our Healer replied.

"Say, won't we look a bit strange if it does take years to grow them?" Dita asked. "Here we are nearly full grown. What will we look like with arms and hands of a new born baby in say nine months?" I chuckled at the image she created in my mind; several others did likewise.

"If this works, I don't care what I look like as long as eventually I get my arms back," Ilenakova replied stoically. We spent the rest of the morning discussing this incredible discovery and its ramifications. Little Cosima was incredibly proud of her achievement.

Indeed, by the following morning, the other eleven of us now had tiny one-inch growths on our shoulders. Sandra carefully measured those on Cosima's shoulders and announced that they had grown a half an inch in one day. By the end of the week, there could be no doubts in anyone's mind that she and the rest of us were in the process of regrowing our lost arms! One look at the six inch appendages told all — miniature arms and hands, complete with tiny little fingers!

All of us realized that it would be a couple of years most likely before we had arms that we could really use. "But Bethany, how is this possible? Is Cosima performing some kind of religious miracle?" asked Ania, as she had Dianna measure the growth of her new tiny appendages a week later.

"It is not a religious miracle. I'm sure of that. I mentioned it to Linda and Chaucer and they know nothing about it. However, they asked Jes, the Guardian, about it and he said that the phenomenon is real, but that it is entirely a fleshly body thing, having nothing to do with we spiritual beings who inhabit our bodies," I replied.

"So it is really going to work then? We will eventually have new arms again?" Dita inquired, still uncertain about this whole thing.

"It appears so, Dita. I guess we just have to be patient and allow our arms to grow up and catch up with us," I answered the best I could.

"Can you see this energy field that Cosima sees?" asked Dianna, sipping her tea. Spread out before her were the numerous drawings of the fields that she had seen via the Mind Link with Cosima. "I've been looking myself, but so far I only see blackness when I close my eyes."

"Same here," Ania added.

"Er no, I still don't see it," I confessed.

"We do," Alessa broke in on our conversation. "Bianca and I can see ours too, but Fina, Elena, and Jemma can't," she added.

"This is vastly more interesting than dissecting bodies to figure out how they work," Dianna changed the topic. "If there is an energy field around our bodies, then it stands to reason that other energies can potentially interfere with it or cause other effects as well. Perhaps this field has something to do with the Elders and their voice tone that hypnotizes people. Say Cosima, were you affected by the Elder's voice when he mesmerized your parents?"

"Yes, I was in sort of a trance," she admitted sheepishly, as if she had done something wrong.

"Okay, Cosima, can you see any differences in the energy fields around Dita, Bethany, and yourself? Like something that might cause them not to have been effected by the Elder's hypnotizing voice tone?" Dianna asked curiously.

"No mommy, just that theirs is larger than mine because they are bigger than me now."

"Well, that kills that idea," Dianna grinned. "Still, I bet some energies will make a big impact on our bodies."

"You know this changes things drastically," Ilenakova brought up what was bothering her the most about this. "None of us are looking forward to living a long lifetime as we are now, armless. Honestly, I know that Kali and I are just barely able to do some of the things that Bethany, Dita, and Ania are able to do. Still, I have been watching you three for months now. Do you realized that even with all your gadgets and special ways that it takes you at least two to three times longer to do nearly any common ordinary task? Getting dressed is even longer. I know that I certainly don't want to spend my life this way; it's a total waste of our time."

She went on, "That's why I was so all for the plan of getting a new baby body soon and dumping this one. However, if these arms actually become normal arms — I mean the right size for us, then there is no real reason to dump this body and start over, is there?"

"Not really, Ilenakova," I replied. "Cosima, kids, it was my plan all along to get new baby bodies for you six once we got ours. You know, Sandra and Luisa might like to have more babies. No way was I going to leave you girls to have to grow up as we are now! While we can get by like this, it is not a fun way to live life, not even in Dorota, where the men look after you so kindly."

"Damn tough, if you ask me," Dita added.

"Mommy," Bianca volunteered, "do we *have* to use our feet to drink our milk and eat our cookies?"

"Huh?" Dita was taken by complete surprise. "You want me to hold your cookie, dear?"

"No mommy. Can we do it like this?" Bianca replied. As we watched, a cookie floated up off the tray and up to her mouth. She took a bite and the cookie floated down to the table. Her milk mug floated up to her mouth, and she took a sip. When mug was on the table again, she looked at Dita and said, "Like that. Can't we do it like that, mommy? It is so much easier to eat that way. Using our feet is so hard. Can we? Please?" she pleaded with Dita, whose mouth opened but no words came out.

"Incredible, Bianca!" I stepped in, "Wow. You can move things like Dita and I can. I didn't know that you could do that too! Yes, you certainly may eat like that anytime that you want, Bianca."

She beamed, figuring that she had somehow scored a major victory. "Can we do it that way too, mommy?" blurted out little Alessa.

I stared at her. "Er, sure, if you can do it." I didn't know what else to say. "It is a really hard thing to be able to do. I only know of a few people in the whole wide world that can move objects like that. Around here, it's just Dita and me. I don't know how to help someone else learn how to do it really."

"But we all know how to do it, mommy. Honestly we do. Cosima has been working with us all for a long time. See mommy." Alessa lifted up a cookie from the tray and floated it over to her mouth.

"Wow! All six of you can do this?" I asked flabbergasted. All six girls lifted a cookie off the tray at the same time and we adults grinned with immense pride. "Super job, Cosima, kids! You are doing something that only a handful of people on all Tarra can do!"

Sandra pointed out, "However, kids, you best be a bit cautious doing this out in the wide world. To the normal person, it looks like some kind of magic. They might become afraid of you and lash out at you. It's fine to do things this way around our house, but ask before you do it out there in the city. Okay?" They kids agreed.

Dita then spent an hour with the kids, seeing just how skilled they all were with using their spiritual being skills at lifting and moving objects. Dita had learned how to do this during her stay with the Guardian years ago, and as a Protector, she needed to know the kids' limitations with this skill. She soon discovered that they were very limited in the actual weight that they could lift. Her estimate was that they could lift no more weight than they could lift with their arms, had they had them. "You know, Bethany, I've been something of an idiot. I can use my skills to eat normally without using my feet as well, to say nothing of many other things."

"You ought to go ahead and use them, my love. I suspected that you were not using them out of respect for the rest of us five who cannot," I suggested. Dita had a sheepish grin on her face, which told me that I was not far from the truth. She agreed to experiment with the children's methods of eating in the future. We only decided one key thing, however, and that was to delay telling the extended West Po family about the growing arms until we were sure that they would really become useful, usable arms. No sense in getting their hopes up prematurely.

The next morning, we headed into work as usual, saying goodbye to everyone. All six of us knew, via our newly awakened inner sense, that today the Mano del Dio would be striking us, probably at work. At Dita's insistence and with Dianna's instructions, each of us carried a blaster in our dress pocket. The setting she insisted that we use was called "shield." I made sure that everyone knew what they had to do, especially the Judgers, who would be casting the needed illusions. By early afternoon, we had all the paperwork finished and were getting ready to leave, figuring that perhaps we had gotten the day incorrectly sensed or that they would be after us on our way home instead of the bank.

That's when I heard three faint popping sounds coming from above and beyond our subterranean vault. My new inner sense of knowing something bad was about to happen kicked in solidly. I looked at the others and saw that they too felt the same thing. "Spread out, make it harder for them. Ready your Judger illusions," I ordered, moving myself off to the right side of the room.

Suddenly, the door burst open, and six Mano del Dio men rushed in, holding their guns in their right hands. One was Supreme Prelate Drakon, who did all the talking and pointing. He quickly pointed to Ania, Dianna, Kali, and Ilenakova.

Dita called out, "Don't do this. The price that you will pay will be horrific!" She was angry, and rightly so.

Four small explosions echoed in the room, the sharp smell of sulfur filled my nostrils. I watched with a believable look of horror as a round hole appeared in their foreheads and their bodies slumped to the floor. While Drakon and another kept their guns pointed at Dita and me, the others began clumsily reloading their guns. Suddenly, I realized the big weakness of these guns, only one shot!

"Damn all of you to hell!" Dita screamed, but they ignored her.

"Okay, Bethany, we know that you are the leader of this bunch of pathetic women. We've put four out of their misery. You can save this gorgeous wife of yours and yourself. All you have to do is tell us the truth. Where is the Santi del Dio gold treasure hoard?"

"There isn't any left," I said, my voice struggling with emotion. Tears came down my cheeks, even though I tried to suppress them. Bang! I watched a hole appear in Dita's forehead and saw her slump to the ground as well! It was now all up to me.

Crying and looking as pathetic, and yet as convincing, as I could, I said, "We are in charge of all the old records here. We've gone over all the accounts. There is no Santi gold left. They over spent all their funds, building useless fortresses all over the world and manning up a huge army that did nothing but use up gold for pay. Thirty years ago, they went totally broke and could not borrow money from anyone. That's when Linda d'Grange dissolved the Santi. She had no money left to pay anyone, not even herself. I can show you Linda's account of the Santi that she left here when she died, if you want. She had only a single gold coin left in it. There just isn't any Santi gold around anymore. It was all spent thirty years ago, please, you have to believe me. There just isn't any gold of theirs around anywhere. If there were, the Santi would still be here and you wouldn't have been able to murder my five helpless friends."

Drakon pondered my words for a moment, and then said, "All right, show me her account."

I walked over to the filing drawer, sat down on my sloped back chair and began going through the folders. "Oh woman, you are totally pathetic! Move, I'll do it myself!" He shoved me out of the way, and I saw him pull her folder and look inside it. He cursed and then looked for a folder labeled Santi del Dio. He found it and looked at the last entry, a withdrawal done some thirty years ago. The account was stamped "Closed." I saw a look on his face that convinced me that he was at last satisfied.

"I guess you are right, Bethany. We'll be going now." He turned and walked to the door, followed by his men. He turned, pointed his gun at my head, and said, "Here, I'll put you out of your pathetic misery. I'm doing you a big favor." Bang!

Pain! Sharp, excruciating pain throbbed through my head, part of Kali's illusion. She was doing it all too well. I felt all control of my body relaxing, felt it slumping to the ground. Darkness. My body's eyes ceased functioning. I moved further out from its head, and my vision returned, all three hundred sixty degree vision that we beings innately possess. Much better. They were gone. I saw our six bodies lying there apparently dead, but saw five anxious beings looking at me.

Did they believe you? Dita asked.

I believe that they finally did. He saw both the Closed folder of the old Santi account and the single gold coin in Linda's account. I believe he now finally believes the story. Ladies, we've finished this job worth doing. I am certain that they will stop torturing and killing others in their search for Santi treasure. Well done all of you. Several protested that they hadn't done anything at all.

People shouting, people running — we heard voices as they came upon the fallen guards. "Okay, cancel the illusions. We'd better make this convincing." I got up and shoved the lock on the door into place, locking us six inside. Soon someone frantically pounded on the door, yelling if we were okay. "Go get Bale West Po immediately!" I yelled through the door.

The Judgers canceled their illusions, while Dianna speculated on the blasters. "Shield worked perfectly. See, there are the squashed lead bullets on the floor. I wish we had more of these things; they work great against these new guns."

"Okay, let's contact the others and our girls. We must let them know what has happened here," I whispered hastily. I made the large Mind Link.

I knew that Renzo and Lenkova could operate well as a free being, that is, as a being without a physical body. My therapy sessions with them in previous lives had helped them regain the skills to move around at will in the world. Enyo, Alexa, and Kallisto had limited abilities as free beings, however.

I found Sandra and Luisa were in the kitchen starting to put together supper. Suddenly both gasped and dropped their knives; they had been peeling potatoes. Both knew that we were here with them and suspected that the worst had happened. Instinctively, both very pregnant women sat down. I Mind Linked us all together, including Enrico and Arturo.

The job's done. I think that we have finally convinced the Mano del Dio that there is no more Santi del Dio treasure around. Our six bodies should have been quite dead. Guns. One shot to our foreheads, I explained. *The blasters worked perfectly. The Judgers' created a believable illusion for the Mano del Dio, who believed that they killed us all. We are all fine.*

Hey, I didn't even have a chance to get out of the way! Lenkova added. *These guns are almost unstoppable!*

Oh, thank god! Are you sure that you are all right? asked Luisa. I described what had happened, giving her and the others time to absorb the news.

Just then, Bale West Po arrived, pounding on our door here in the bank. I opened it and let him inside. Quickly, we related the attempted assassinations. "You see, they believed our illusions completely. If it had not been for the ingenuity of Dianna here and those old blasters of the Grey Creatures, you would have six more very dead bodies to bury."

"Thank god for those, Dianna. Brilliant indeed, sis!" he replied, very relieved that his little sister wasn't dead. Quickly his elation changed to anger; three guards were dead.

"Remember Bale. Take no action against the Mano del Dio until they are on their way back to Megalos. We must have the Supreme Prelate report to the Church of Jehosanity and their Pope Leo that there really is no Santi gold to be stolen. If you don't, this will never end. They'll be back killing others to find it."

"I know, but it is so hard. I want them to pay for what they have done here. Five people killed, to say nothing of the attempt on you six. That can't go unpunished," Bale replied. We talked more, giving him time to cool down.

At last, he agreed, but told me that he would never allow that man to set foot on Velona soil ever again. The next day, Bale sent word to us at breakfast time that Supreme Prelate Drakon and his five henchmen had set sail for Megalos hours after their assassination attempts. After they departed, Bale ordered wanted posters posted all over the docks. They showed a sketch of Drakon and contained along with his name: Wanted Dead or Alive. 10,000 gold coin reward.

Next, I let Linda know what had happened. She promised to Mind Link to us all later that night. Finally, we six headed home to explain to our girls what had happened. Dino ended their lessons early, because Enrico whispered what had happened to us to the girls' tutor. Enrico gathered all the girls into our front room, where the others were. We six hovered over our girls.

"Hi girls. It's really us. We are all okay; the assassins failed, thanks to the Grey Creature's blasters. Those bad men struck us today while we were at work. They tried to shoot us in the head with their guns. The shields of the blasters prevented their bullets from harming us. We are okay, but the assassins now believe that we are all six dead. We need to let them think that until they leave Velona."

Alessa said, "Mommy, did it hurt? When you got shot? Are you not now going to need the new baby bodies that Sandra and Luisa are making for you?"

"Yes, it hurt a little, but the shields stopped the lead bullet. It's too soon to say anything about the new baby bodies. Linda d'Grange will talk with us later tonight. I'll ask her about that, okay?"

Alessa grinned, "Okay, mommy. Close your eyes. I want you to tell me all about it."

Oh my god! I realized that little Alessa was going to run out my trauma! Immediately, the other five said pretty much the same thing to their moms! I relaxed and allowed her to run me through being shot. The dull pain in my forehead didn't erase, and little Alessa correctly asked me if there wasn't something earlier in time that was somehow similar.

I was staring at that grey mass that always obstructed my view of lifetimes before Uru days, when I was being Elizabeth Stanton. I spotted something and off Alessa went with it. Before I knew what was going on, I was re-experiencing an encounter with a Grey Creature, doing battle with it. However, it won by smashing in the side of my head with his fist. I remembered my last thoughts before that body died. "Now I can't see too well anymore!" I began laughing. No wonder my vision as a spiritual being had always been somewhat fuzzy and distorted all these centuries. As I looked around the room, everything was clear, far clearer than it had ever been before. I thanked Alessa, who sat grinning, proud of her accomplishment.

One by one, the others also blew off this recent slight pain trauma and thanked their little girl for their help. We all looked at the six proud little girls, sitting in a row on the couch. I couldn't have been prouder of them.

Alessa asked, "Mommy, will you still be tucking me in at night?"

"Yes, and I will still pick you up and give you hugs. See." I lifted her body up and gave it a hug. All the other girls stared with their mouths open. Alessa appeared to them as if she were somehow levitating all by herself. Dita then did the same thing to Bianca, who let out a squeal of joy and surprise. I knew that the other four could not lift things as a spiritual being, so Dita and I lifted their girls for them. Soon, we had six giggling, happy girls sitting on the couch.

"Mommy, I can see you," Alessa then said. "I can see all of you. I don't mean your bodies, but you." Indeed, all six could perceive us six. What a surprise. Here we were almost assassinated, and our girls were exhibiting incredible spiritual skills. Since there was still some time before supper, I decided to see if I could expand on their awareness of us. While I was the only true telepath here, so strong were the bonds between us, that I took a gamble. Soon, I had Dita making contact with Bianca herself without my assistance. I went down the line and got each of the others in mental contact with their little girl. In the days that followed, I continued to work with all of us adults and the girls on their special telepathic bond. As long as the girls were aware of our presence, this seemed to work, bringing mother and daughter closer together than ever before.

Right after dinner, the entire Po clan came by to see how everyone was holding up. Of course, Dianna's parents made a fuss over her; both were so worried that they had lost their youngest daughter. "It's a miracle that you were not killed today, along with the three security guards," Lana exclaimed, holding Dianna in a tight hug. "Are you sure that you are all right? Bale said that those alien devices somehow saved your lives."

"Right mom. They have a shield setting, which we used. It prevents bodily harm, though I do not know just yet how it works. I didn't get it figured out last lifetime either," Dianna replied.

Lona chuckled, "When Bale told me about the attack, I thought that I would be coming over here to work out your funeral arrangements with Luisa. Sure glad you figured those devices out, little sister."

"Hey, we all owe our lives to them," Dita added. "With a gun, there is not even time to react and get out of the way of the bullet. Incredibly fast action."

Again, I cautioned all of them not to tell anyone that we were still alive — at least not for a while yet. It would not do to have the Mano del Dio who still remained in Velona knowing that we six survived. Finally, satisfied that Dianna and the rest of us were okay, they all left. Since it was getting late, we tucked our girls into bed and gave them their goodnight kisses.

As we sat down in our living room, Linda contacted us, as promised, Mind Linking all of us together. *Well, this has certainly been an unexpected turn of events. We had all foreseen your deaths at the hands of these Mano del Dio men. Anyway, great thinking Dianna. Now then, I need to take you all to the bank and show you what you have been protecting. We will leave your bodies here on the couch, and I will make sure that you don't get lost or into trouble.* Dianna-Enyo, Ania-Alexa, and Kali-Kallisto found moving about the world without their bodies a difficult task, while Dita, Ilenakova, and I could do this easily, only now my vision was vastly improved thanks to little Alessa's therapy session.

While we watched, Linda lighted all the lanterns. *Now that is cool, Linda,* Dianna sent, most impressed with her skills. We seven were Mind

Linked together by Linda.

Now then, it is time that you all see the contents of that special folder. You need to see what it is that you have been protecting with your lives. Linda opened the drawer and retrieved that special folder, which was still sealed. She opened it and we six read what it said.

The Forza di Sicurezza, who protects our gold shipments, had a bank account balance of over one million gold! Our Forze Segrete or secret forces were subdivided into numerous accounts, one for every major country on Tarra. Most all contained a balance of at least one million gold, for a total of twenty-six million! Plus, there was a reserve fund consisting of another ten million in gold. We six were staggered at the totals we read on the pages!

Now do you see why it was so vital that the Mano del Dio believe that the Santi was broke, that there is no treasure? Linda asked. *There is more; look at the last page.* We did. It read, "In the event of an assassination attempt of Bethany Brozena Malina, a half million in gold will be deposited into her account." Similar lines said the same for my other five friends.

Linda explained that tomorrow the funds would be automatically transferred into our accounts. She gave each of us the account name to use and the corresponding secret password. Given these two facts, we could withdraw funds from any Banca del Dio anywhere in the world! In fact, when I added it to my account that Linda had set up for me when I was the Empress, I now had well over two million gold available. We all thanked her profusely. No longer would we have to worry financially; we would be free to pursue any needed course of action.

Now, for a time, you six must not continue to work here. It will destroy the illusion that you six are dead. Luisa wants to take over the job that you six were doing here, but she cannot do so, of course, until her babies are weaned. I believe that Renzo and Bethany have the skills to do it like I am doing now, but if you two prefer, I can either do it myself or find another to step in until Luisa is ready. Renzo and I agreed to give it a shot, promising to let her know if we could not quite manage all the fine motions needed to do all our work without using physical bodies. I'd never tried holding a quill and writing as a spiritual being before, just lifting trees and bodies, never anything this delicate and precise.

Now then, there is one final matter that I wish to do. We must deal with the Mano del Dio, who have become far too bold and brazen in their assassinations. Besides, they are the ones with the guns. I'm going down to Megalos and eliminate most of them, plus the five henchmen. The only Mano del Dio I want left alive is the Supreme Prelate, so he can deliver his message to Pope Leo. By wiping out this generation of these brutal assassins, this will give your new bodies time to grow up before they become as serious a threat to humanity as they are now. Believe me the Pope has more Mano del Dio than he has guards! This will be a very bloody affair. I will understand if you don't want to participate.

I cannot really do much, Dianna said. *Not without my body.* While Ania and Kali greatly wanted to participate, they too could do very little as pure spiritual beings. Hence, only we four would do this deed.

But what about the new baby bodies that we were supposed to get? Our new arms seem to be growing now, and we really won't need them. Dita asked the question that all six of us had been pondering but were reluctant to voice aloud.

I've talked this over with the Guardian and Chaucer. We are all in complete agreement. We want you six to take over these new baby bodies when they are born. For a time, you will be controlling two bodies each. Bethany, Dita, and Ilenakova should not have too many problems with it. We are of the opinion that not only can you manage it, but it will be spiritually beneficial to all of you. However, if you find that trying to run two at once is not feasible, especially Dianna, Ania, and Kali, contact me, and I will help you handle it. She left us pondering this unexpected turn of events.

After getting the other three safely back to their bodies at our estate, Linda led us off in search of the Mano del Dio. We headed down to Megalos and quickly spied the caravel carrying the Mano del Dio back there. It had only just set sail. Renzo, Lenkova, Linda, and I simply levitated the five sleeping men and dumped them into the Med Sea about six miles from the ship. When the Supreme Prelate rose in the morning, he would have a deep mystery to ponder!

From there, Linda took us on down to Megalos and the main Church of Jehosanity, where the Pope stayed in Constanza City. We found the barracks of the thousand plus assassins. It was full of various weapons designed solely for a quick, silent killing. I rather wanted to slay them with their own weapons, but Linda wanted it done another way.

Rip their head off of their bodies. I want lots of blood, Linda explained. I'd never before seen her this bloodthirsty! We complied. An hour later, it was done. Linda then used the blood to make a giant writing on the barracks wall, so huge that no one could miss it.

Her bloody message read: "Pope Leo. Stop assassinating men, women, and children around the world. Murder violates my law. If you ever continue this wanton practice of assassinating those who do not agree with you, I will return and do this to you and all your priests worldwide, ending your church forever. Lord Jehosa."

Yes, Linda actually had the audacity to sign it as Lord Jehosa, whom these people believed was the name of God! I laughed until I couldn't see straight. *Well, I am sick and tired of these people and their butchery in the name of holiness. I **will** have peace on Tarra,* Linda exclaimed. Yes, Linda was mad — angrier than I had ever seen her before. Yet, her anger was only there momentarily. *Now that's done. I have given you six time to get your* *new bodies grown, and the Guardian time to get his flock resettled. With any luck, we will be able to make real headway in freeing all spiritual beings on Tarra. We'd best get back now.*

When we returned, Linda left us. I related the grizzly scene of death that we left behind. The others roared with laughter when I told them about the message Linda had left for the pope. Then, Dianna asked, "Now what do we do? I mean how do we control two bodies at one time?"

Chapter 28 Now What Do We Do

The next morning, we kissed our little girls as they awoke and stayed close to them as they ate their breakfast, levitating their spoons and mugs. We could no longer go to work, not until the dust settled, so to speak. As I sat there watching little Alessa eat her breakfast, I realized fully that our girls were now no longer inside their heads at all, but were constantly several feet above and behind them.

This is an important fact. The entire Druwid movement depended upon able beings who were not plastered inside their heads. Indeed, many of the "magical feats" that we could perform, such as bringing down bolts of lightning, could only be learned and performed while outside one's body, never while plastered inside a head.

By now, all of us had our refresher courses from Enrico and the others. I explained my thoughts to everyone. "I am a Wid; Dita-Renzo and Lenkova are Protectors; Dianna-Enyo, a Planner; Alexa and Kallisto are Judgers. Have you noticed that our girls are now all outside their heads constantly? Why don't we see if we cannot train up our girls in the old Druwid tradition? They are certainly at the right ages to begin. What say you all? Game" Everyone was, besides, it gave us something to do in the immediate future.

While the girls continued to get their tutoring during the morning hours, we began to work with them in the afternoons and evenings. While they were busy with their tutor, I began working on getting Dita and the others to be able to use telepathy, at least in the limited sense with just their girl. If this would work out, I saw us all as having something worthwhile to do for the next five years while our new baby bodies grew up. Instead of just sitting around being bored, this gave us six a real purpose.

Late at night, Dita and I did try to do the banking, leaving our bodies asleep in bed. She had the skilled movements to deal with the chore, but I was useless except for lifting papers. Occasionally, when the volume of bank papers was too large, Linda stepped in to lend us a hand. After all, her new baby body was only months old.

Of course, our girls were thrilled to be learning how to do all the things that their mommies did, only now they had a name for it, Druwid skills. As always, we began with observing the obvious, a skill in which Cosima greatly excelled, far, far beyond that of the others. Indeed, I was shocked with her observations a few days later.

"Bethany, can we talk?" Cosima asked me one evening after we had finished the day's training.

"Certainly, sweetheart. What shall we talk about?" I asked, having no idea what she wanted.

"Well, I've listened to everyone's tales, talked to nearly everyone about this stuff, and made my own observations. If Alessa gets a cold, then often some of the rest of us catch it, right?" I nodded. "So colds are contagious somehow."

"Yes, a number of man's illnesses are contagious. Why?"

"Well, people do bad things to hurt others. I use my therapy to erase the trauma, but if I don't, isn't that trauma contagious too? I mean, like my dad, my real dad who died, and my mom who jumped into the Med Sea and died. When they have new bodies, won't dad and mom either have bad things going wrong with their arms or maybe they will go around hurting other people's arms? You know, a long time ago on Dorota, the mantis creatures ate all the women's arms. Once the bad insects were killed off, the people who remained already had many traumas from the mantis creatures, and they just continued cutting off women's arms — for centuries even. It just kept on going, like it was contagious just like a cold."

I was shocked — this from a young girl! "Yes, Cosima, yes. You are right! I see what you mean. You've made a vitally important observation! I've seen this kind of behavior repeatedly, now that you have called my attention to it. It happens right here in the Sea Princes as well."

She beamed and added, "But you stopped it from happening anymore in Dorota by erasing everyone's traumas. So in Dorota, from now on, no one will have bad things going on with their arms nor will anyone want to cut off anyone's arms any more, right?"

"Yes, Cosima, I do believe that you are right about that. We got to everyone there, millions of them. I doubt that anyone will have such urges to harm women in the future because of what the mantis creatures did to them so long ago."

"Good. But Bethany, what about the rest of the world? We've been studying the history of the Sea Princes and Velona. At the start of our history books, men treated women as if they were objects to be brutalized. The book said that they even cut out women's tongues if they spoke out of turn. That's when the Sisterhood of fighters came into being to help the women. Later on, the Church of Jehosanity continued doing bad things to women. We read about how they encased women's arms in iron bindings until their arms fell off. We've heard all about the many foreign women that you and the Santi rescued, mommy, Dianna-Enyo was one of them. They all had the mantis creatures eating off their arms or had bad men doing it to them."

"Yes, Cosima, all that is true. I see what you are getting to — we've never erased all those traumas here in the Sea Princes or other lands. Yes, we were able to erase thousands of women's traumas, but certainly not all of them. Not by any stretch of the imagination." I replied honestly.

"Maybe that's why so many people in Velona call us names and treat us so badly. They still have their own past traumas bothering them, and they are taking it out on us," Cosima theorized. "After all, we know that they cannot see their own images of the trauma and handle them by themselves. It takes our therapy to get those traumas even recalled let alone erased. Maybe that's why, don't you think?"

"You are probably quite right, dear. I hadn't thought about it, but sure. That is probably why they act as they do."

"Then, that means somehow, we need to give therapy to nearly every person in the world, don't we? That is, if we want to stop them from doing bad things to others," she observed.

"True, I think that the Guardian is trying to do something like that," I explained. "My job is to keep the people of Tarra mostly at peace until he can do it. Big wars just make a mess of things, making things vastly worse."

"Well, I am going to help by catching the bad men," Cosima declared. "Bethany, can I ask another thing?" I chuckled, wondering what new revelation she was about to bestow on me.

"When we run the therapies on each other, it seems like it follows a definite emotional pattern. Often, it begins with them in apathy, a near death emotion. Then they cry and get all griefy, and then they get fearful and scared sometimes. Anger usually follows that and then they get downright hostile and antagonistic about it all. We all know that you must keep going, Bethany; you taught us well. After that often they get bored with it and want to stop. We just keep going and then they become cheerful and laugh about it and the trauma is then gone. Does it always follow this pattern?"

"Yes, dear, as far as I can tell it always follows that pattern. Never stop until they laugh about it or are very cheerful. That has been my cardinal rule that I always follow."

"Well, we all thought so. What I want to know is does this also apply to whole groups of people, like countries? We've studied the other countries of Tarra. We think that Demokritos is in anger, while the many kingdoms of the Greenway are fearful or scared, as well as the jungle people of Wanakan. The horsemen of Vladimir, we think, are hostile or antagonistically inclined. But those of Annalise are mostly interested with a conservative outlook. Tashien and the people there we think are probably very apathetic. Dorota is in propitiation, well, it used to be so anyway, before your therapies. We just don't know hardly anything about the people of the Northern Steppes and the Axemen of Volksholm to say where we think they are at, except we know that they too are heavily into trying to control things and people. Megalos is probably in fear now, though they used to be antagonistic and then dropped down to anger."

"Bethany, I think she is on to something!" Dita butted in, having overheard part of our conversation, as did Dianna.

"Yes, Bethany, Cosima may have discovered something here," Dianna added. "It makes sense, you know. The Annalise people have never shown any hostility towards others at all; they seem a most conservative people.

She's on to something here. Dear, what about the Sea Princes? Where do you think they are at?" she asked curiously.

Smiling and sitting up straight, Cosima replied, "We aren't totally sure yet. We do know that the overriding consideration is that of control. It seems that many people in the Sea Princes are obsessed with controlling others and things. From our history lessons, that seems to be the most dominating facet, from the duality of the founding Sea Princes and their sharing ruling with the High Priests and Priestesses. However, Velona, Barcella, d'Grange, and Zargarb are now very different from the other four, particularly Bonilla and Vito, which we are convinced are in fear. Pieta and Solamina are also likely there as well, but we don't know enough about them."

"What about the other four?" Dianna asked, curious about what her girl thought of our own Velona.

"Well, we think that Fortress d'Grange is probably bored. Zargarb, Barcella, and us, Velona, are now probably at some kind of mild interest, a slightly conservative sort of emotional tone. We can't quite put a finger on it yet. It varies a bit," Cosima answered her mother.

"Fascinating observations, Cosima, just fascinating!" Dianna replied with a smile.

"Yes, but Bethany, what we want to know is this. If people display these emotional tones because of traumas that they have suffered in the past and which are now hidden from their conscious minds, do countries behave the same way? I mean, does this mean that most all the people of Demokritos have some kind of trauma, which is forcing them to be so angry all the time? It would seem so from what went on in Dorota, where everyone was in propitiation to women because of the traumas they all had suffered during the last couple of centuries. If they did, then maybe all you would have to do is to run therapy on everyone like you did in Dorota."

"What an ingenious idea, Cosima! I have no idea if this is true or not, but it certainly seems like it might just explain many things. I will relay your ideas to the Guardian, perhaps he might know," I volunteered.

"You know, dear, she is on to something important," Dita said to me. "With those in anger and antagonism, the targets of their hatred are plain and obvious for all to see. However, those in fear are the ones that you have to watch carefully, as they tend to strike covertly and sneakily."

"Interesting point, Dita. We'll keep an eye on that one with our banking data."

"Bethany, what could have happened to the millions of people in Tashien? It must have been really traumatic to force them all into such an apathy," Cosima speculated, hoping that I might have an answer.

"I don't know, dear. We know that the Grey Creatures were big on secretly controlling the populations under their control, doing their best to force spiritual beings solidly into their body's heads, and scrambling their memories. The mantis creatures were bent on creating their perfect slave societies, but where their lands bordered on those controlled by the Grey Creatures, they also fomented open hostility and wars as well. So the northern countries tend to be covertly hostile and fearful, while the southern ones that border us are likewise, but those isolated from us have their perfect propitiation societies. Neither of these fit what little I have seen in Tashien, which by the way has more people in it than any other country, including Demokritos. I too have often wondered what has happened to those people in the distant past to so drive them so emotionally low," I answered as best I could.

"Do you suppose that there might have been a third alien group on Tarra?" Dita speculated. "A group that controlled the totally isolated Tashien area? That would make sense, given everything else we know."

"Yes, but we have seen no signs of them anywhere outside of Tashien. When we were there in Tashien, we saw no signs of any aliens for that matter."

"Yes, but we didn't run any therapy sessions on them either. That's one of the big ways to find out, short of running into them, as we did here," Dita countered.

"If we run into any aliens, I have got seven blasters fully charged and ready to go," Dianna exclaimed enthusiastically. "Perhaps I need to get busy and invent more defenses." Her engineering mind kicked into gear at the thought that there might be further aliens on Tarra. I rolled my eyes in mock jest and we all laughed.

On June 12, 746, Sandra gave birth to triplets, two boys and a girl. Renzo, Len, and Enyo were their names. Two days later, Luisa gave birth to her triplets, two girls and a boy. Elizabeth Lilly, Kallisto Ann, and Alex were their names.

When Sandra's time came, I contacted Linda, who arrived instantly. Our girls were terribly excited and offering all kinds of aid. Drina, Lona, and Lucinda arrived shortly as well and insisted that the men leave the bedroom. "Warm water and blankets and towels, please," Drina asked and the six girls dashed off to comply. With Linda present working her magic, really just her powerful postulates, Sandra experienced no pain at all, mostly some slight discomfort.

A half hour later, the six girls returned, carrying the things with their new found levitation skills. Poor Cosima, the eldest at six, struggled to carry the heavy two buckets of warm water, just as she would have struggled had she her arms. Interesting detail, I thought. The others brought piles of blankets, wash cloths, and towels.

"I can see its head coming," Alessa called out.

Bianca stated emphatically, "That's my Dita-Renzo. He told me so. She's a boy now." The girls all giggled, who wanted to be a boy anyhow they thought.

Cosima began crying. "What's the matter dear?" asked Lona.

"I can't hold Enyo. See, here she comes now. I can't hold her!" she wailed. That put a damper on the spirits of the five women.

I took charge, "Sure you can, Cosima. You just have to hold her differently than does Drina here. I'll show you once Enyo is born, washed up, and covered. Trust me."

"Really, Bethany? I can? Okay, I will wait until you show me. Alessa, Bethany says that I can hold Enyo. She's going to show me how, and then I can show all of you how to do it too." Cosima was back to cheerfulness once again.

Later, once Sandra had delivered the three babies, her bed stripped and remade, the babies washed, diapered, and wrapped in blankets, Sandra laid down on her large bed. One by one, the three babies were laid beside her, Enyo on the outside. I had Cosima climb onto the bed and lay down beside Enyo, who looked up at Cosima. I moved her left leg around so it was on the other side of Enyo and had Cosima give Enyo a loving hug and kiss. Cosima grinned and chatted with Enyo. Naturally, the other five girls watched so see how it was done.

Luisa explained that they were not to try to lift the babies just yet, that their bodies would be very fragile for many months. However, they could help cuddle them and change their diapers. "You girls are now going to also be their helper mothers. Three at one time is going to be a whole lot for Sandra to handle, me too for that matter. So we are going to be depending on you six to help us out with the six babies. Mine are coming any day now too." They all promised and promised, very excited about the whole thing.

Days turned into weeks and into months. Linda was right, this time around, we six forgot nothing about who we were and what we knew. Our sole difficulty was getting used to manipulating our new little bodies and their muscles. The girls became an enormous help to the two mothers, handling our diapers and other needs. Day by day, the girls got better and better at handling the babies.

We continued to work them and drill them on the basics of our old Druwid religion and skills. I was almost alarmed at just how fast these girls seemed to grasp this extraordinary extra education that we were giving them! It was now June 747, a year later and dinner time. As usual, each girl was sitting next to one of us and feeding us, freeing up Sandra and Luisa from that messy task. Alessa brought up a spoon of mush to my mouth, which I gobbled greedily. The girls excelled at using their abilities to lift things without their arms.

Speaking of arms, all twelve of us definitely had arms, though right now, they looked awfully strange. Ours were about a foot and a half long and still fairly small in diameter. However, they were working as arms and hands! We could lift a cup and silverware, but because of their short length compared to the rest of our bodies, we didn't use them that much. Sandra estimated that another year or two and they would be nearly the right length for our body sizes.

Until now, we had been careful not to tell others about our arms being re-grown or having the kids use their lifting skills when others were around. However, seeing how well our arms were progressing, I finally decided to break the good news to the West Po clan.

The next night, when Lucinda and her family came around for supper, Cosima exclaimed, "Aunt Lucinda, look what I can do!" She lifted her milk glass, took a drink, and set it back down. Then, she used the spoon to give Enyo her first bite of supper. That certainly made for exciting table talk that evening. Suzana, Gerardo, and Tonia all wanted to know how Cosima was able to levitate and move things. They had quite a time explaining things that evening.

Next, I had Lucinda lower the top of Dianna's dress, revealing her small, but quite real arms. Poor Lucinda nearly fainted when she saw them! After all had seen Dianna's new arms, we then explained to them what Cosima had done. "We didn't want to say anything until we were sure that this was going to work. Yes, these new arms and hands are the real thing. They work fine, but Sandra estimates that they need at least another two years to finish growing enough for them to be really useful to us." The elation shown by Dianna's parents and extended family was beyond words. Most claimed this was a Holy Miracle, and we had a devil of a time convincing them otherwise.

I never will forget the first time that Dino said, "Okay girls, open your book to page ten and we will begin today's lesson," and six books floated up, opened themselves to the proper page, and sat there before their eyes, as if hanging in space. The shocked look on his face was classic! After that day, the girls began making their pencils do the writing, instead of their feet, claiming that it was much more comfortable this way and many times faster too.

By the time that we all had our fifth birthday, Number 42 Hampton Way was known as the House of the Precocious Witches! Indeed, to the outside world, the things that people saw when we were all outside playing appeared magical. How else do you explain a ball moving of its own accord up and to an armless girl only to be thrown as if by invisible hands towards the running mass of kids?

Enrico had made us swear to stop bringing down lightning bolts onto the metal fence wires atop the tall outer stone wall. Whenever it rained, the six girls practiced bringing down bolts onto the top of the fence, often melting the wire, which Enrico then had to replace. He always chuckled over it, but still, he got very tired of replacing the wire.

At our fifth year birthday party, Alessa and Fina were nine, Bianca, Elena, and Jemma were ten, Cosima was eleven, the eldest of us twelve children. We had wrapped up their Druwid training this past week. All twelve could use telepathy between each other and often did so. The six of them could handle and move objects as if they were using normal arms and hands; their detailed skills were vastly beyond anything that I could do or even Renzo, for that matter. Now all our arms had finally caught up to our body sizes, and we could use them like any normal person. Yes, the six were precocious. Even when they were out in the pubic eyes, they often tended to do things their way, by levitation.

Their Druwid skills tended to overlap a good deal, no longer falling into the usual seven categories that we had when we all received our training. Alessa was best described as a Protector-Horsewoman-Scout. She was in love with horses and begged us to help her raise and train horses. Bianca was basically a Protector-Planner, who liked to design things, usually pretty things. Her drawings of proposed buildings were a work of art; functional, yes, but also extremely aesthetic. Cosima did not fit the mold of the seven categories; she wanted to be a detective and solve problems and mysteries. She was a Planner with a very different use of the word planner. Elena and Jemma fit the closest to Judgers, taking after Alexa and Kallisto. Yet, both were fierce when it came to fighting. Fina was almost a pure Protector in nature, holding the closest to one of the seven categories.

What of us six adults? Our arms are now normal in size, and both Dita and Ilenakova have been working out daily, building up their muscles. Often, they take sword practice with Enrico. I cannot tell you how much better we all are! We have our lives back, all thanks to Cosima and her skills.

Until now, running two bodies at the same time has not been much of a problem for Dita, Ilenakova, or me. Dianna, Ania, and Kali, on the other hand, are not handling it at all well, becoming very confused more and more frequently now. Dita put her thumb on the situation rather well the other day. "It's like we have to span our attention across two bodies simultaneously." We three have been managing this rather well thus far; the other three are finding it terribly difficult, especially since our new bodies are now five years old and active.

When you combine their skills with ours and those of our parents, it was formidable: Sandra, Healer; Arturo, Loremaster; Luisa, Alex, and Kallisto, Judger; Enrico, Renzo and Len, Protectors; Enyo, Planner, and myself, Wid. We were a group of twenty-two powerhouses, albeit twelve of us were still children, little children at that. Still the potential that we represented was impressive, I thought.

At our fifth birthday party, I told them all, "You know, between Dorota and here, we all have done jobs well worth the doing!" I was very pleased with how things had turned out for all of us. The future looked bright to me.

Chapter 29 Kassandra Gavril

Born in 721, Kassandra Gavril was the daughter of Emperor Deimos and Empress Eirena Gavril of Demokritos, which is the second largest country in the world, population-wise, dwarfing Velona. She grew up hearing stories about the famous Empress Maren Elizabet, who according to the ancient prophesies, came from Annelise, a country east of Demokritos. Maren was a woman of the Eighth Degree and her exploits as Empress with Deimos were now legendary. In today's times, so many women of the Eighth Degree held her as their role model that nearly everywhere Kassandra went, she found herself continually exposed to Maren's fame.

Thus, as a young girl, she became fascinated with these Holy Women. She didn't know why. It seemed to her young mind that these women would be so completely helpless. Indeed, in and around her father's court, many noblewomen were of the Eighth Degree, and she often chatted with them. Repeatedly, she heard strange tales about Empress Maren. Yet, she could not understand how these women managed a life without arms. To her child eyes, they did seem happy, and their husbands did dote on them — that she easily saw.

However, her parents were totally against this religious action of the Church of Jehosanity and their Women of the Eight Degrees. For a time, her father even tried to destroy the Church, something that she just could not understand. To her and many others, these were the Holy Women; they had to be, given their situation in life. In fact, the laws of Demokritos were quite explicit regarding these women: any harm done to a Holy Woman was met with swift and terrible punishment! So much so, that the Holy Women could go as they pleased in Demokritos without fear of even a pickpocket bothering them.

Then, during her middle teens, that is during the 730's, two key events occurred that drastically altered the situation in this huge country. First, the Church of Jehosanity had spent a fortune building mammoth new churches, huge architectural marvels never seen before in Demokritos. Oh, the magnificent statues and the fabulous artwork, which now adorned their many churches, she and many others now found quite captivating, breathtaking. She began attending church regularly, discovering their angelic choirs, which sung such Holy Praises unto Lord Jehosa. Such music sent shivers down her spine every Sunday. That nearly everything that could be laced with pure gold trim was so done made no impact upon her. As the Emperor's daughter, she saw gold all the time, rather like water it was to her. No, the art, the music totally captivated her as a young, impressionable teenager.

Pope Leo's Grand Plan for the total expansion and reconstruction of the shattered Church of Jehosanity had begun to work all throughout Demokritos, as well as everywhere else that they now had these new churches. Indeed, Emperor Deimos had nearly destroyed the church, but when Leo was named Pope, he formulated his Grand Plan and now it bore fruit. Because the Church spent such vast sums of money on the construction and artwork, the local economies thrived, particularly the artists who greatly benefitted from this huge resurgence in demand for top quality art. By 735, the Church of Jehosanity had surpassed all expectations here in Demokritos.

The second event was the arrival of the Elders from a newly discovered giant island nation called Dorota. News of a "Perfect Society" spread throughout the Kingdoms bordering on the ocean. No one could imagine an entire society in which all women, old, young, even small girls, were of the Eighth Degree! Yet, these Elder missionaries spoke convincingly of their nation without even the minimalist of crimes. That anyone could walk anywhere in their country at any time without any fears of even the lowliest pickpockets was almost unbelievable. Yes, people began to pay attention to these Elders.

Soon, the Elders began giving special sermons, after which many who listened begged to join this new religious order. They had with them men called doktors, who performed the surgery on all the females in each family that chose to join their ever-growing flock. As time rolled on, these converts formed into small sub-communities, where these families began to live in the manner of Dorota Perfect Societies. By the late 730's, their numbers swelled to over nine thousand members. Unlike the Holy Women of the Eighth Degree of the Church of Jehosanity, who were all either independently wealthy or wives of wealthy noblemen, these new converts came from all walks of life, often the poorer strata. Rarely did they come from the wealthier zones.

Thus, by her late teens, Kassandra became exposed to Women of the Eighth Degree nearly everywhere she went. This only fueled her curiosity even more.

Demokritos has seven kingdoms, each with their own king and queen. Sitting directly above these were the Emperor and Empress. Four of the kingdoms bordered on the Great Ocean and were now masters of the shipping industry. Going north to southwestward, they were the kingdoms of Arolas, Penelopus, Thrace, and Alia. The three remaining kingdoms had no access to the sea, but their southern borders touched the permanent ice shelf that ran across the entire continent. These were the kingdoms of Thallyus, Theos, and Phindos. Emperor Deimos, who still fought the Church at every step, ruled from his palace in Kefall, Thrace, while the King of Thrace ruled from Axos, a hundred miles west of Kefall.

In the early days of the Church of Jehosanity, they had to fight the prevalent heathen religion of the Sun God, and they only had a few

Churches in a couple of Kingdoms. Now, in 735, worship of the Sun God had largely been abandoned everywhere. Great Churches of Jehosanity were in every one of the seven Kingdoms!

Residing across the ocean far to the north on the island of Megalos, Pope Leo had little choice but to appoint a Cardinal to oversee these Churches on Demokritos. Indeed, the Cardinal had to be very self-motivated, because a round trip communication with the Pope took nearly six months by sea. He chose an able man, one who totally supported his Grand Plan. Cardinal Drakon Erebos made his home in Kefall, Thrace. From here, he oversaw the entire Church of Jehosanity throughout all of Demokritos.

Pope Leo's plan demanded that he choose young men to be the new Cardinals, men of vision who would infuse life into his Grand Plan. He chose men who would take the initiative and make things happen. He'd had enough of the older Cardinals who fought change at every turn. Thus, he had appointed Cardinal Drakon Erebos to this highest of positions in Demokritos. He took over in 738 as an eighteen year old priest, the youngest Cardinal ever to have been appointed!

At the time of his appointment, several key events had happened of which he made good use. First, you must realize that Women of the Eight Degrees had long been a practice in this land. Originally, it had been invented as a means to keep husbands faithful to their wives. Because of the incredibly high divorce rate, this scheme came into existence, coupled with the hidden influence of the mantis creatures. During the time of the early reign of Emperor Deimos, the Santi del Dio had built strong fortresses along the coast. A bargain had been struck with the Church and their enemy, the Santi del Dio. The Santi had the best healers and surgeons in the world and they agreed to perform the necessary operations on the women who chose to become Women of the Eight Degrees.

With the fall the Santi organization, the skilled healers were given lucrative positions within the Church, again assisting and overseeing said operations. The practice of this mutilation of women, that is Women of the Eight Degrees, reached its lowest point of new participants during the early years of Emperor Deimos' reign. However, the practice continued, particularly among the very wealthy and after a few years, it began to grow once again. Cardinal Drakon often heard the confessions of the husbands of these women and more than once heard the real reason a husband had pressured his wife to do it: he wanted to both control her and to ensure her fidelity. From said women, he frequently heard of intense peer pressure to become such a highly respected woman. The legends of Empress Marin Elizabet only grew more wild and rampant around the kingdoms as the years went by fueling such fires, to say nothing of the impact of the Elders of Dorota.

Thus, one of the first actions Cardinal Drakon took was to have all

Women of the Eighth Degree members of each church sit in the front row, giving them a very high status indeed. He made sure of two things. One, these women would be called Holy Woman and given the highest respect in Church. Second, he ordered that comprehensive lists be kept of every Holy Woman of the Eighth Degree in all seven kingdoms. He instructed his many priests always to preach the idea that these were the Holiest of Holy Women. Thus by 740, these women were held in great respect all throughout the kingdoms of Demokritos, far greater than they had ever held in the past. Of course, as was his intention, this only fueled the desire for more women to join them. Quietly, Cardinal outlawed the lesser Holy Degrees, until by 740, the only surgery being performed was that of making a Woman of the Eighth Degree.

Still verbal battles raged between himself and his Church and Emperor Deimos and Empress Eirena. The latter two fought him and the Church in every possible situation. Thus, early in 739, Cardinal Drakon finally realized that the Emperor had to go! He spent an entire month drawing up plans for his idea of the ideal government for Demokritos, ideal in that his Church would be the true power behind the throne. Yet, nearly equal in power were the seven kings and queens of the kingdoms. Quickly, he realized that just a changing of Emperor and Empress was insufficient. No, if he wanted his Church to be the true power that it ought to be, he needed control of the seven kingdom's thrones as well! He spent an entire month working out how this might be accomplished.

Two events happened during that month that solidified his plan. In the kingdoms of Alia, on the coast, and landlocked Thallyus, the reigning Kings and Queens were aging rapidly and planned to give up their thrones soon. In Thallyus, the King desired to hand his throne to his son, Bakos Aristos, whose wife, Frona, was a Woman of the Eighth Degree. Cardinal Drakon saw his chance staring him in his face. With Frona as Queen of Thallyus, he had just the right person in the right place! He instructed his priests in Thallyus to lobby hard in support of Bakos becoming the next King of Thallyus. In 739, Kina Bakos and Queen Frona Aristos took their sacred pledges and their positions on the throne of Thallyus.

Down in coastal Alia, which had long been a hold out, seeking to prevent women from becoming of the Eighth Degree, he had his priests begin a massive drive to promote Spiro Stathis to the throne. Why? His wife, Melita, was a Woman of the Eighth Degree, and Spiro was an ardent supporter of the Church, having donated large sums of money to help them build and renovate their Churches in Alia. It was time to reward the faithful, Cardinal Drakon had said. Because of the massive push by the Church, Spiro became King of Alia in 740 and Melita, then twenty-two, became their Queen!

Cardinal Drakon now saw his own Grand Plan taking shape. The goal: every queen of Demokritos must be a Holy Woman of the Eighth

Degree, plus the Empress as well. When this was accomplished, he would have a powerful influence over the running of the entire country! He corrected himself: his Church would have that influence.

During that month, he tried to work out just how he could accomplish this with the Emperor and Empress situation. Traditionally, when an Emperor retired, he would give the throne to his eldest son, assuming that the Noble Houses of Kefall supported that. Emperor Deimos had no sons, only the one daughter. A bit of research later, Cardinal Drakon found that the daughter could also be given the throne, if she was married at the time! Brilliant, he said to himself, pulling on his short goatee as he often did when he was overly excited. Yet, this daughter, Kassandra, was not yet married. His priests reported to him that she was a dedicated follower of the Church. That was excellent, no hurdle to overcome there.

In January, Cardinal Drakon summoned a young man, Argos Aias to his private chambers. His Mano del Dio men had spent weeks searching for just the right man. Now their choice had come to meet him.

After exchanging pleasantries with the young nobleman, Cardinal Drakon said, "Argos, I have had my eye on you for some time now. You come from a wealthy family here in Thrace, you are very good looking, and you and your family have been loyal supporters of our Church."

"Yes, we are," Argos replied, still unable to fathom why the Cardinal had sought him out. Perhaps it was his flamboyant, playboy lifestyle. Was he about to be chastised for his actions?

"Now it has come to my attention that you have — well, I will be blunt with you, Argos. You have been having intercourse with women out of wedlock, something which the Church highly frowns upon, very unholy, son. As a nobleman, you are looked upon to set a good, moral example for others." He knew he had him right where he wanted him. The lad's face turned beet red, and he mumbled a bit and squirmed in the chair.

"How do you know that?" he asked at last, resigned to being ex-communicated from the church and bringing disgrace upon his parents.

"Lord Jehosa knows everything. He is everywhere, son. Haven't you paid any attention to your priests while in church?" The lad looked even more embarrassed and ill at ease, waiting for the axe to fall. Would his parents be forced to disown him? He'd be penniless! He would have to work! That thought scared him more than being ex-communicated. He could always change his name and go to a different kingdom's Church.

"Argos, Lord Jehosa can forgive our fleshly sins."

"What must I do?" Argos bravely asked, detecting a slight hope in the Cardinal's statement.

"Son, what I've said is just between you and me. It will always remain so if you and I can reach an agreement. I have some long range plans which you may help me attain and in so doing absolve yourself of these transgressions."

"Yes, I am always willing to help the Church." He thought that that sounded good.

"Argos, I want you to date the Emperor's daughter, Kassandra. I want you to have her fall in love with you, and I want you to marry her."

He knew that she was very pretty and available. It could be a lot worse. "The Emperor's daughter?" he asked.

"Yes, you may meet her at our Church here in Kefall. She attends every Sunday. Now after you are married, it is imperative that you convince her to become a Holy Woman of the Eighth Degree just as soon as possible. Yes, such women need constant assistants, but your family certainly can afford to hire appropriate servants for her. She must become such a Holy Woman as rapidly as possible."

"That's all you want me to do to atone for my sins?"

"Argos, is not becoming the Emperor of Demokritos sufficient for you?"

"What? Me, Emperor?" he asked shocked, though now that he had said it, such was obvious.

"Of course. The Church will back you all the way to becoming our Emperor, when Deimos retires, and will back you as Emperor, but *only* so long as Kassandra is a Holy Woman of the Eighth Degree. Remember this, son; she must be one of the Holy Women. If not, your sins will become known to the world. Do I make myself perfectly clear?"

"This is a threat, isn't it? Either I do this for you or I am ruined by the Church," he said slightly antagonistically. He suddenly realized that he was being blackmailed. However, this was a very nice blackmail — he as Emperor!

Cardinal Drakon did not respond to the lad's outburst. "Okay, we have a deal then," Argos agreed. The two men shook their hands, sealing the pact between them. That Sunday, Argos attended the Church which Kassandra attended, met her, and began a relationship with her.

In her defense, Kassandra found Argos to be handsome, polite, adventurous, intriguing, and a gentleman. He wooed her with flowers, discovered the things that she enjoyed and gave her more of the same. She enjoyed going to the theater, watching concerts, and plays. Thus, he took her to nearly everyone that played in Kefall or Axos. Against his steadfast determinism, she had no chance. She fell in love with his handsome young man.

Her parents could find nothing particularly wrong with Argos, except in his youth he had been a bit of a playboy around the city. He came from a fine, upstanding noble family. Emperor Deimos had little choice but to grant his permission for them to marry in 741. In fact, Cardinal Drakon presided over their wedding! This gave their wedding an enormous political boost, though it infuriated Emperor Deimos that his archenemy was performing the ceremony. He could do little but go along with it, especially since the

Cardinal often now spoke openly of the two of them mending their relationship.

The night after they were married and after making passionate love with her, Argos asked her, "My love, my dearest Kassandra, my flower of beauty, have you ever given any thought of becoming a Holy Woman of our Church, a woman like the famous Empress Marin Elizabet?"

She flushed; all her private thoughts of just such a thing for the last countless years flooded into her mind, causing her cheeks to heat up. "Yes, I have been fascinated with her. All the stories about her, why, I have them memorized. Yet, my love, if I did that, I would be so utterly helpless! I could not hold you tightly as I am now."

"Yes, I know that, but we can work that small thing out somehow. I would have to get you the very best of servants, I know that. With the large inheritance that I have, now that we are married, I can afford only the very best for you. I have talked to the priests who say that us doing this together — it binds us tightly together, for always. I always want to be here at your side. You are the only woman in the whole world for me. I want to shout it to the entire world. If you were a Holy Woman, why, that would scream out our love to the whole wide world. I do so love you, Kassandra."

"You wouldn't mind having to help me with absolutely everything?"

"How many times have you and I seen other husbands at the fancy inns feeding their Holy Women? I've seen you glancing at them often." Her face flushed once more. "Wouldn't you love to have me doing that and all things for you, my dearest, beloved Kassandra?" he poured it on heavy.

"Well, yes, I have often dreamed about it, wondering what it must be like. They always look so utterly happy, don't they?"

"Oh yes! Have you and I ever seen any of those couples who were not mad about each other? Yes, really, really happy I would say."

Timidly, yet hoping against all hope, she asked, "Are you really sure that you want me this way? You know that there is no way back if we do it? Besides, dad and mom will have a fit if I do this thing. They are so against it."

"I certainly don't know why they are against it! Yes, I am very sure about you, my flower, my dearest love! Think of the incredible fun we can have out there in the wide world showing everyone the utter depths of our love! Oh, do you think that your dad would try to harm me if we did it?" he added a little twist to his argument.

"Oh no! You are his son-in-law now. He just couldn't, though I know he would be very angry with us. I know dad. In a little while, his anger will go away, especially when he sees just how well we do with it."

"That's good to hear. Okay, then I am all for it, but I think you have to make the final decision. I think that's the way it's done."

Kassandra grinned, "Okay, then let's do it! When?"

"The sooner we do it, the sooner we can so enjoy it! I know it takes many weeks for a woman to heal, so the longer we dally, the longer it will be before I can take a gorgeous Holy Woman out to dine and to the plays."

"Well, we are supposed to be going on our honeymoon tomorrow," she hinted.

Argos explained, "Yes, my family has an estate on the outskirts of Axos. We could go there, get it done, and stay at the estate until you are healed. Then, we can return here and begin to enjoy ourselves to the fullest. What do you think?"

"Oh, that is perfect! When we return from our long honeymoon, I would be all healed up and just fine. There would be nothing that dad or mom could do but support us then. I love it. Oh, I will need all new dresses. You know how they wear their fancy, special dresses."

"Dear, we can pick out some of the finest in Axos beforehand or if you trust me, I can get them while you are recovering. We need to find some proper servants for you as well. I am getting terribly excited about all this!"

"Me too! Come here; let's do it again!" Kassandra pulled him back down on their bed once more.

The next morning, Argos sent word to Cardinal Drakon and asked him to arrange things for them in Axos. It had to be done in total secrecy. If the Emperor got wind of it, he would send an army to stop them. Argos cleverly bypassed having Emperor Deimos send along a large security force with them. He'd hired his own dozen bodyguards, which satisfied the Emperor, who was always concerned over the safety of his daughter.

On February 1, Kassandra had her surgery and spent six weeks recovering at the Aias rural estate. Beforehand, they were told that all Kassandra would really need was one personal assistant to help her with mundane, life things. After interviewing a number of young women, they settled on Selene, who was not pretty, but had a very kind, loving heart and who was sympathetic to the young couple. Selene then moved to the estate, a day before her surgery.

Kassandra woke. Her eyes burned. Mechanically, she raised her right hand to rub them. Nothing happened. She blinked and raised her left hand to rub them. Nothing happened. Suddenly, she became alert and looked at her shoulders one after the other. Tight bandages pressed against her armless shoulders! Now she remembered. She'd gone unconscious and the doctors had performed her surgery. She was now a Holy Woman of the Eighth Degree as she and Argos had planned! She was completely helpless; she panicked and screamed wildly!

Several people came running into the room, but Argos was the first one there. "It's okay, my love, it's okay! Congratulations! You did it! You are a Holy Woman now, just as we planned. The doctors say that it is perfectly normal for you to react and scream when you first waken. I am here now. I won't leave your side. You are the most beautiful woman in the whole world."

His soft, loving voice calmed Kassandra down. All became clear to her; the fuzziness left her mind sober at last. "I'm so helpless. Can you rub my eyes, please?" Argos did as she asked. He helped her sit up and held a glass of water so she could drink.

"It feels so utterly weird, Argos!" Kassandra tried to explain the intense feelings that were flooding through her mind.

"It must, dear. Remember what they said, take your time, and get used to it. Everything will be just fine, if we don't rush it. Remember, from now on, you must remember to ask us. Selene and I are right here for you, always."

Kassandra relaxed more; the pain was not as bad as she thought it might be. Perhaps it was dulled by something in the water that she drank. She realized that the doctors were right; this was going to be a very new experience and that she needed to stay relaxed and focused so she could learn how to cope with being the Holy Woman that she now was. Still, everything was so very different! How could she possibly manage life this way? Panic began seeping into her stomach once more. Argos began moving his hands over her body, gently rubbing her clear down to her legs. Oh, that felt so good. Slowly her panic subsided, and she remembered that, before hand, the doctors had instructed Argos on just how to rub her body when she had a panic attack. She smiled and gave him a passionate kiss.

Both Selene and Argos doted over her for the next few weeks. While she was recovering, Cardinal Drakon came to visit them, and he gave her his personal blessing, something that made an indelible impression on young Kassandra! Finally, the bandages were removed, and she could see the pinkish scars. The healers had done a good job. Her shoulders would look extremely pretty, no ugly, nasty scars. For this, she was grateful as she envisioned all the new dresses that she would soon be wearing, showing off her beautiful shoulders to the world.

One morning as Selene helped her to use the chamber pot and then got her dressed, Kassandra realized just how much she was now totally dependent upon Selene. "Selene, I am completely helpless now. I need you for almost everything! Are you being paid enough to help me all the time as you have been doing? I mean you have to spend so much of your time with me and all that."

"Yes, Argos is paying me a handsome amount, Kassandra. And besides, I like helping others. You are so very brave to become such a Holy Woman in the eyes of our Lord Jehosa. Perhaps one day, when I save up enough money, I too will be able to become a Holy Woman."

"I'd be lost without Argos, Selene. I think that you ought to find a good, kind husband too, before you become Holy like me. When you are ready to become most Holy too, I will do all that I can to assist you ever afterwards. I need you so much, Selene. One day, I may be able to repay you for your selfless help with me."

"Enough of such talk now. I am sworn to be your hands from now on. Come; see how you look in the mirror." Kassandra rose from the edge of her bed carefully, as she had learned to do. Without arms to help her catch her balance, she needed to be very cautious, especially since she insisted on wearing her high heels. She walked to the full-length mirror and looked at herself. Her green satin ball gown billowed out some four feet; the fine cloth draped perfectly over her large hoop, fastened at her waist. The matching bodice top was strapless, as was the preferred fashion for women like herself. It reached up to the top of her ample breasts, but no further. Thus, her shoulders were completely bare. Yet, there was enough cleavage showing to prick a man's interest, she thought. Selene fastened a matching green emerald necklace around her neck and then adjusted her long brown hair.

"Thanks, I do look presentable now. Nicely done, Selene. I think I ought to let my hair grow as long as it can, don't you?"

"Yes, ma'am. It would look very pretty indeed. You have such lovely hair. It is a pleasure to brush it out."

Pleased that Selene agreed with her, she said, "Well, I'm off to breakfast. Argos will take over now. You have the rest of the morning off." She walked carefully to the door and saw that it was closed. Automatically, she tried to open it with her non-existent arms before she felt that twinge of panic return. Even a closed door was a trap for her. Selene quickly opened the door for her. She nodded her thanks and walked proudly down the hall towards the dining room, where Argos promised to meet her.

By the time that they were to return to Kefall in April, Kassandra had a new wardrobe of very expensive dresses. She only wore the finest satin dresses that money could buy. Each dress billowed out some four feet around her, and her strapless tops always displayed her unique status as a Holy Woman of the Eighth Degree.

Upon their return to Kefall, as expected, the Emperor and Empress were visibly upset and angry when they met the young couple. However, their anger melted as they witnessed the love and devotion the couple visibly demonstrated to them. Actually, the young couple was doing just the actions that Cardinal Drakon had suggested to them when he had visited them in Axos. He'd said, "Such actions on your part will do much to put your parents at ease with your most Holy Action." They quickly found that his advice was accurate.

Indeed, for the next two years, life, though challenging for her, went as she had envisioned. Argos kept his word. Every evening, he took her to a fancy inn, and she always wore one of her many satin gowns. At least four evenings each week, they took in a play, a concert, or a dance. Every Sunday, they went to Church, and Kassandra proudly sat in the front row with all the other highly honored Holy Women. For these first two years, Argos and Selene worked very hard to see that she wanted for nothing at all. For

Kassandra, this was the best years of her life. She loved every minute of it. Argus doted over her and she enjoyed his constant attention.

Well, that was not wholly true. She and Argos wanted to start a family. Everyone else was and her parents fully expected that she would give them a grandchild, the sooner the better, her father teased her. However, after two years of constant attempts, she had not yet become pregnant. Slowly, this began to bother her.

One day after Selene had dressed her in her favorite green satin ball gown, she looked at herself in her mirror. Her long, soft brown hair now fell to the small of her back. Her light brownish face looked perfect, rather like the angels depicted in some of the art paintings in her Church she thought. Her blue eyes sparkled, her lips, thick and moist. "I do look beautiful, perfect, don't I?"

Selene, who looked almost homely, agreed wholeheartedly, "Yes, Kassandra, you are very beautiful and perfect."

"Yet, I am not perfect, Selene. Why can't I get pregnant? Everyone wants me to have a baby, even dad. Argos and I have tried almost every night for two years."

Selene chose her words carefully, "Kassandra, it might not be your fault. I've heard that sometimes men can have something wrong with them." A light went off in Kassandra's mind! Yes, she was perfect! It had to be Argus' fault, but how to find that out, she wondered. The seeds of an idea crept into her mind.

Chapter 30 Bliss Ends in 743

In very early January of 743, Cardinal Drakon received a coded letter from Pope Leo. Had it been intercepted, it would have seemed to be simply a note about religious doctrine. Carefully, he copied down all the capital letters and then read the real message:

It would be very beneficial to everyone, if at this time, the Emperor and Empress met with a fatal accident. You have my blessing and support.

Cardinal Drakon smiled. He'd kept the Pope abreast of developments here in Demokritos. Now, it was about to pay off. Quickly, he called his Mano del Dio Prelate into his office. The men spoke briefly. The next day, January 14, 743, Emperor Deimos and Empress Eirena were found dead in their bedroom in their palace. Their throats had been cut.

As the news spread throughout Kefall, Cardinal Drakon went at once to the grieving daughter, Kassandra, offering her his personal condolences and volunteering the Church's full support of her during her time of great personal tragedy. Shortly afterwards, he instructed his many priests to begin an all-out campaign of support for Argos and Kassandra to be allowed to inherit the throne of her parents. When it came time to make that decision, pubic support was so strong and intense, that those that chose had no choice but to allow it. On February 2, 743, Emperor Argos Aias and Empress Kassandra took their oaths of office as the leaders of Demokritos.

At once, Argos found himself to be the most powerful man in the entire country. He also discovered that he was very wealthy and that running the country did take quite a lot of time! Daily, he spent hours and hours with advisors, who began educating him on everything from their massive trading fleet of caravels to their armed forces, numbering in the hundreds of legions. He had to deal with the ever-constant skirmishes with the neighboring wild horsemen of Vladimir. He had to hold court to settle disputes and to deal with the ever-flowing stream of petitioners who sought an audience with the Emperor. Argos, fascinated with all this power, began to spend virtually all his time handling the business of the Emperor.

At first, Kassandra sat prettily on her throne beside Argos. Quickly, she discovered that he no longer paid attention to her. Within a few weeks, about the only time that he gave her the attention that she thought that she should have was late at night! Resentment took hold of her and slowly ignited into a raging inferno! Days went by where Selene was her only companion. Kassandra grew more and more dissatisfied and began to take action herself.

Purposely, she went to see her mentor, as she now referred to Cardinal Drakon. "Come in, my most Holy Woman, come in. It is so good to see you again. How is everything going for my Empress?" He acted his part.

"It's Argos. Ever since he became Emperor, he has been ignoring me almost totally! I am at a loss on what I can do. I dress perfectly. I look perfect, don't I?" she was near tears, he noted.

"Ah, yes, most perfect, my Empress. As beautiful as the Holy Angels themselves."

"What can I do? I am so utterly helpless like this. I never thought this could possibly happen to us. Is there something wrong with me?"

"Oh no, dear Empress. You are more than perfect! Why do you even think such thoughts?'

She decided to level with him. "I cannot get pregnant. We've tried so hard, but it never happens. Is there something wrong with me? Should I go to the doctors?"

"Lord Jehosa sometimes works in mysterious ways. I would not go to the doctors, for they might spread unseemly rumors about you. That would never do." He thought that now the time was right to sew the first seeds of doubt in her mind. "Perhaps it is best that you are not with *his* child at this time. Our Lord is very wise; do not doubt his great wisdom, Empress."

His child? She thought, what does he mean? Why not have Argos's child? Suddenly, she realized why. While their first two years of married life had been blissful and perfect, now that he had become Emperor and had the ultimate in power in Demokritos, he had abandoned her! Had he just been using her all this time to get himself appointed the Emperor? In a flash, she saw how this must be. She finally asked, "What must I do?"

Goals, she was asking for goals. He saw the seed of doubt blossom in her eyes and facial expression. Now to give her the proper goals, something that she could and ought to be doing. He replied, "Lord Jehosa recognizes that you, Kassandra Gavril Aias, are *the* most Holy Woman in Demokritos. As such, what would you do if you suspected that Argos was, shall we say hypothetically, unfaithful to you?"

"I'd have him, well I don't know, maybe drawn and quartered," she said antagonistically. She wanted to say have him killed, but refrained from so saying; he was her Cardinal and holy man.

"Precisely. Yet, our laws require what?"

"Oh I see. Proof. Yes, I should gather the proof that I need of his guilt."

"Exactly, Empress. One thing that you can do is to gather such proof secretly. Now if he actually is guilty," he continued, omitting guilty of what exactly, "ought he be our Emperor?"

"No, of course not," she retorted, thinking that was plainly obvious. He ought to be de-throned at the very least!

"Precisely. And who would then be running Demokritos?" he said slyly.

"Oh, I see. It would then fall on my shoulders to lead our people, as did my dad and mother."

"Exactly. And what do you need to know in order to do that for the betterment of all our people in the seven kingdoms?"

"I need to know all about everything that is going on. Yes, I see it clearly now. I must get myself into everything that he is doing. Find out everything that is going on, everything that is planned. Find out how everything works, since one day I might have to step in and run our country. Yes, that is a tall order. I feel so helpless to do all this. If I only had my arms back, it might be possible. But like this, I cannot even open a door or feed myself or even get dressed!"

"Of course you can do these things, my Holy Woman. You just need to start acquiring others to lend you their hands. You need to begin to have your own private staff, people that you can trust utterly with your life and secrets."

"Why, I am so sorry that I started to feel sorry for myself. It will not happen again. I am a perfect Holy Woman. Forgive me. Yes, I should have seen that for myself! Thank you."

"Now there are another two matters in which you may be of great aid, not only to yourself but also to the Church and other unfortunate women. This Dorota situation has completely collapsed, as you may have heard. So much for their 'Perfect Society.' Their Elders are now saying that it was all some terrible mistake. We have in all of Demokritos, precisely ten thousand five hundred sixty-three women of all ages that joined their pseudo-religion and have become like you, Holy Women. Yet, most of these are poor women, unable to support themselves or whose families are unable to afford them a proper servant. Many have taken their own lives out of desperation."

"I've heard those rumors. So it is true then? Oh, I can imagine how they must feel. When I awoke from my surgery, I felt so helpless. Without Selene and Argos attending my every need, I would have gone mad, I think. Oh, those poor women! How can I help them?"

"In two ways, Empress. First, our Church is accepting all those women who joined the Dorota cult back into our folds as Holy Women. We must show them our deep compassion for their sacrifice, even though they did it for the wrong reasons. Lord Jehosa's teachings demand that we help them regain lives as Holy Women. What can you do to help? Well, you need to acquire your own personal staff. Why not hire some of these most desperate women and even their husbands? Give them jobs within the Palace. If nothing else, the men can be your doormen. Perhaps you can find ways the women can be useful, such as message bearers or perhaps even waitresses. I am sure that you can find many things for these women to do. Pay them sufficiently so that they and their families may survive, and Lord Jehosa and all Demokritos will take note of your Holy Acts."

"Yes, I will do just that!"

"Good. Your Church has a complete list of those women in the direst of need. I will have someone send it back with you. Yet there are more of these needy women than you could employ. I beseech you to speak with the other Queens and have them do the same thing. Make this an official task of every ruling Queen. Eight of you can make the lives of so many worthwhile."

"Yes, that is a very wise action. I will so order it today!"

"Second, there is one other thing that you might consider doing to help so many in need. You have your Selene, but many have not the means to hire some kind soul to help them with their every need. In Megalos, they have redeemed many of the heathen black skin people of the Southlands, taking them on as their servants." He purposely avoided calling them slaves.

"These redeemed women work for the lowest possible wages, just enough for them to live. It is part of their redemption, you see. On Megalos, these women are known as Holy Helpers. Perhaps you could purchase many of these to assist you and other needy families. Of course, by purchase, I mean to help cover the cost of their training and transport here to Demokritos."

"Well, that is certainly something I can do immediately. After all, it takes months for them to get here from Megalos, if they left today. Say, I should get some of the very best of these Holy Helpers for our Palace and for the other Queens. Is it possible to get a hundred of these Holy Helpers?"

"I am sure that it can be arranged, as long as there are funds to support so many, say ten thousand?" he replied, hoping that this mention of a specific monetary amount would not upset her.

"Oh, I will do better than that! We are going to need many of these Holy Helpers. How about I send fifty thousand initially? I would desire say twenty of the very best Holy Helpers to assist me around the Palace and to assist the seven Queens. They ought to have some of the best as well."

"Thank you for your magnanimous generosity, Empress! Just transfer the funds to the mother Church on Megalos, and I will send your request by the next caravel north today! Bless you my child, God bless you!"

Her head swimming with plans and plots, Kassandra hardly noticed Cardinal Drakon opening the door for her and escorting her personally out and into her carriage, placing a large document with all the names and addresses of those women in dire need on the seat beside her. The driver asked, "Where to Empress? Palace?"

She came out of her deep thoughts, "No, to the Banca del Dio, please."

Later, she returned to the palace. Her driver helped her out of the carriage and handed her the document package before he realized his gaffe. She had no hands to take it from him. "Stick it on my shoulder, and I'll hold it with my head," she suggested. He did so. Kassandra then walked across the Palace grounds to their main entrance, where once more the elegant double doors barred her passage. "Damn!" she cursed and started kicking on the door. At last, an out of breath Selene came to her rescue, apologizing for not having seen her arrival sooner.

"No Selene, it's not your fault. I need my own personal staff here, if we are to live properly. That document you are holding contains the names of other unfortunate women who were deceived by those despicable Dorotan Elders. We are going to hire many of them to help us out around here, starting tomorrow morning. Now, fetch us some tea, and I have something to ask of you."

A bit later, Selene brought in their tea, poured two cups, and sat next to Kassandra so she could hold the cup for her Empress. "Thanks, Selene. Something is not right with Argos. I have a suspicion he's up to something. I need to find some people that I can trust with my life, some people who can be detectives and find out secret things about people. We must keep this a secret, just between you and me. Oh Selene, can you help me find such worthy people?" Kassandra was reduced to begging Selene. Everything depended upon her being able to find someone. Gratefully, she took a sip from her cup.

"I've noticed it too, Empress. I have two friends who might be perfect for you. Both are good fighters too. They know many things and are good at finding things out. Of course, they are in Axos, though."

"Well, send a carriage for them at once! Oh, thank you Selene! Thank you." She realized that it'd be a week before they got here. Nevertheless, Kassandra wanted to begin. With Selene's assistance, the two began to study the list that the Cardinal had given her. It was broken down by kingdoms and then by towns, so they focused only on Thrace and Kefall. Quickly, they saw the organization of the list. Each listing gave the name or names in the case of multiple women in a family and the occupation of the men, at least the last known occupation. Some names had already been crossed off; both women knew what that meant!

A bit later, Kassandra focused in on one family. "Let's start with this one. Go get the carriage ready and then help me get my crown on. I am acting in my official Empress duties. I'll see if I cannot get to my room myself."

Selene took their cups away and set off to make the arrangements. Kassandra, using her billowing dress, pushed the slightly ajar door open. Good old Selene, she thought, leaving it so I can manage. She was stopped again at the door to her own private chambers and once again simply had to wait for Selene to return.

A few minutes later, their carriage driver lifted her into the carriage and held a hand for Selene. Off they went down the cobblestone streets of Kefall. A quarter of an hour later, they pulled up at a rundown shack of a building, as far as Kassandra was concerned. Selene stepped out, supporting herself on the hand of their driver. Kassandra had no choice but to lean forward and allow him to lift her out. She couldn't lift her wide dress to see the steps of the carriage, much less keep her balance. She headed to the door, but realized that Selene would have to knock.

Inside a voice called out, "Come in. I can't open the door." Selene opened it and allowed the Empress to enter first, though she wondered if it might be better for her to go in first. Inside, they found a one room home, kitchen, table, and bed, all in one. Incredibly cheap housing.

"I'm looking for Cleo and Theo Mintah," Kassandra said, as he eyes adjusted to the dim light from a filthy oil lantern. The room had no windows. A woman, wearing what appeared to be rags, rose awkwardly. She was twenty-one at most, Kassandra thought, but in need of a bath and decent clothing.

"Are you — are you the Empress?" Cleo asked.

"Yes, you must be Cleo. How are you doing?" Kassandra thought that was about the lamest thing to ask! Clearly, she was in dire need and doing just awful.

"We are getting by, Empress," Cleo said meekly. What else could she say?

Kassandra decided to get right to the point. "Cleo, I am looking for some Holy Women such as you to come to my Palace and be part of my staff there. Your husband is a teamster?"

"Yes, he drives wagons. He has to come home at noon to help me. Why?"

"Well, I need a dependable carriage driver for my staff. Would you and Theo consider moving into my Palace and joining my staff? You both will be well-paid for your services."

Cleo was in the depths of depression. This sudden offer of salvation took her by surprise, though her priest continually told her and Theo to keep the faith. "Really?" a spark of hope kindled. "Theo is very good with horses. He works ever so hard." Then, she realized that the Empress had said that she was also needed and looked confused. "Me? What can I possibly do? Theo has to do everything for me now. I don't know why we ever listened to that Elder man!" She was now getting angry once again.

"Yes, he certainly deceived thousands of us, didn't he?" Kassandra tried to think of something appropriate to say. This was more awkward than she had at first imagined it would be.

"Damn him to the Eternal Fires of Hell!" she said antagonistically. "But what can I possibly do in your Palace, Empress? Surely, you need staff that is whole, not like we are."

"Oh come now, Cleo, you are as whole as I am. We just, well, we need to have help with so many things, don't we." Damn, she thought, this is much harder than I expected!

"But I can't be a waitress anymore. I used to be a waitress and carry trays of food and drink to the inn's tables. Now, I'm useless. How can we carry a tray, as we are? I told you that I'm useless to everyone."

"Well, maybe we could somehow fasten a tray to your waist. Then, you could carry food and drink to me and my guests and such. How about giving it a try?"

"I suppose I can. I simply must do something. Theo is at his wits end. Here he comes now." They heard another wagon pull up and the sounds of heavy work boots hitting the stones. After the shock of seeing the Empress in his home, Kassandra explained what she wanted them to do. Theo could not believe their good fortune! The Empress had them both agree to come to the Palace after their supper and they would get started.

All afternoon, Selene and Kassandra visited others on their list. By the time they headed back to the Palace, she'd gotten ten families to agree to come by this evening. Over diner, Argos asked, "Why are you bringing all these people here tonight?"

"I am filling up the Empress' staff. I need helpers too. We're going to have doormen, announcers, messengers, and servers, and I'll have my own carriage driver so I don't have to keep using yours. Besides, we'll be doing our part to help out these Holy Women."

His reply only convinced her that something was wrong. In a monotone, as if it was of no importance, he muttered, "Okay." He showed no further interest in what she was doing!

That evening was slightly chaotic, as Kassandra tried to organize her new help, making use of the individual skills that both the men and women had. One whole unused section of the palace she used to house these new families. She brought in three seamstresses and three tailors early the next day. All got new clothing. Two women, who had voices which carried well, she made her official Announcers. That is, when someone entered their throne room, these women would announce them. Three others she turned into her personal Messengers, who would deliver spoken messages that Kassandra dictated. Another three she used as Servers. She had a tray mounted to a band that tied around the woman's waist to hold the tray firmly up to her, and then from a neck collar, two straps anchored the two outside corners. While they could not bear heavy loads, they could certainly carry tea, snacks, papers, whatever Kassandra might need.

Some of the men who had few real skills other than common laborer, she made into her official Door Keepers. Their job was to stand by the doors and open them when a Holy Woman came or when important people came to see the Emperor or Empress. Some families had children and the boys she also used as Door Keepers, whenever possible. She gave Fetcher positions to the younger girls. She would tell one of them what or whom she needed, and the girls would run off to find it or them. These girls also were given small trays so that they could bring back smaller items, such as a document or quill and ink.

By the time the week had passed, her portion of the Palace was alive with people! All were grateful for such an opportunity to live once more. Kassandra had literally rescued them from their misery and given them new purpose. That they were also well paid, far beyond what anyone would expect, allowed them to begin to acquire things that they needed and bought their undying loyalty. As she sat on her throne, Kassandra now always had two Messengers and two Fetchers nearby. No longer did she have to wait on overworked Selene; she could ask one of these for assistance. However, she was most grateful for the new Doormen. Now the hundreds of doors within the palace were not a barrier or trap for her.

Since Argos paid so little attention to her, she began to dine with her staff, when the large group sat down to eat. She felt like they were now her family, so cordial, pleasant, and uplifting their chatting seemed to her. Boys and men fed their Holy Women, as did Selene. We are all in this together, she mused as she looked over her growing staff.

When Selene's friends arrived from Axos, Selene brought them into Kassandra's private meeting room. Here, with the doors closed, no one could overhear what was said. Selene introduced them. "This is Tanis and Thekla Chloris." Both were twenty-two and had been friends with Selene since childhood. They married when they were eighteen. Tanis was tall and had a fighter's physique, while Thekla was somewhat shorter. His hair was short and black, while hers was curly and auburn. Both had keen minds and sharp eyes that did not miss a thing. Kassandra decided that she liked both of them the moment that she saw them.

"I am in dire need of, shall we say, detectives?" Kassandra began her explanation. "From time to time, I desperately need some delicate matters looked into. You know, discover the truth of a matter. It must be done in secret. You only report to me, never to anyone else, especially not to Emperor Argos."

Tanis chuckled, "Discretion is our middle name. We've done a lot of detective work in the past. Thekla and I can handle ourselves in almost any situation. You should see some of her clever disguises! Why she even snuck into the Cardinal's study one time."

"Well, you are just who I need here. I want you to come work for me exclusively. You will have your own quarters here in the palace. As for pay, how about a hundred gold a week. Is that too little?" Kassandra had little knowledge of the price of things; her parents had always handed financial matters for her.

Thekla choked on her tea. "Empress! That is a king's sum!"

"Well, that's good then. Now I know that you will be loyal to me," she said what she was thinking and then realized that this was a social gaffe.

Tanis laughed! "Empress, that would be an understatement. Yes, money does often buy loyalty. We like to do what is right and just. If we accept your offer, and it is indeed a stupendous one at that, may we reserve the right to decline a job because we don't feel it is the right thing to be doing?"

"I'd think less of you if you didn't," Kassandra quickly recovered from her gaffe.

The two looked at each other, nodded, and Tanis said, "We are your private detectives. What is our first assignment? You must have wanted us for something right now, since your message said it was urgent that we come at once."

She grinned, "Yes, it is urgent. I am finding that this is terribly embarrassing for me to speak aloud to others. Okay, here goes. It's Argos, the Emperor. When we married and I became a Holy Woman, he doted over me and took me everywhere, helped me eat, everything. Since he's become the Emperor, he doesn't even notice me anymore. He rarely dines with me now. About the only time I see him is late at night when he comes to bed. Something is going on with him, and I want to know what. All the details please. Another thing, we've been trying to have a baby for over two years now. No matter what we do, I just don't get pregnant. Cardinal Drakon says that I am perfect, so it must be Argos somehow. Look into his past. I want to know all about his past. Maybe he had a childhood injury or something."

Thekla asked, "He hasn't hit you or anything like that, has he?"

"No, he just acts as if I don't really exist and am not important to him anymore. It might just be that he is swamped with work trying to run our country," Kassandra suggested one plausible reason for his behavior.

"Whew, that's something. I was worried that he might have roughed you up a bit. That would be criminal! We'll get right on it. Our stuff is down in Axos. When we know something, we'll report back and bring a wagon with our belongings."

"Excellent, say, do you need some expense money?" Selene gave them each a month's wage and a hundred for initial expenses. Thekla gave Kassandra a loving hug, which surprised her. Tanis followed his wife's lead and gave her a hug too.

They teased her, "We can't shake hands, so it will have to be hugs between us. Okay?" Kassandra grinned and agreed.

During the next month, Kassandra continued to hire more of the most desperate families on the Cardinal's list. She was pleased to have proper uniforms made for all her new employees. Nearly every door that she was likely ever to use now had a Doorman, dressed in a blue uniform. Even her carriage driver wore a fancy suit, looking very proper as he drove her about Kefall. Her various assistants also got working uniforms. Her Announcers wore blue elegant gowns, but flared out only two feet, not the four that hers did. Her Messengers wore green satin gowns of a similar pattern. Servers wore brown satin dresses, while the Fetchers wore pink satin, since most of the Fetchers were young girls. After a month here, every one of her personal staff was totally in love with their Empress!

After being on the job for a month, Tanis and Thekla returned one evening. Kassandra got them their room and allowed them to unload their wagon, before having them report to her. She was nervous. What would she hear? Still, she minded her manners and allowed them the courtesy of getting their possessions stowed. Around eight that night, the three and Selene met in her private study once more.

Thekla began, "Well, Empress, you were right to have us look into Argos for you."

"I knew it! He's up to something isn't he?" Kassandra interrupted, her fears flooding out of control.

"Well, we don't know everything yet," Tanis cautioned. "Let us make the presentation. We have acquired some supporting documents to prove our claims. It seems that two years before he met you, he was something of a playboy around town. You know, taking many women out for dinner and dancing. Well, we've discovered that he got a pretty barmaid pregnant back then, and she had his son. Did you know that?" Kassandra's shocked look told him that she hadn't.

He went on. "We tracked her back to the inn where she was living with her son. However, what we found most curious is that she up and moved to Levka, Alia, about the time that Argos met you. We then did a bit of questioning and found a man who saw Argos get a summons to meet with Cardinal Drakon about then as well. We've been unable to find out the purpose of said visit. We checked further and tracked her down in Levka. We've her statement in one of the documents there. According to her, one of the priests of the Church of Jehosanity came to her and offered her a new job working as a mayor's assistant in Levka. He gave her moving money and money for proper clothes and even made moving arrangements for her."

"He's not yet cheated on you," Thekla explained. "His immoral conduct came before he met you. However, if his actions were broadly known back then, why he'd of suffered some bad consequences, him being a nobleman's son. As far as we can tell, he's been the perfect gentleman up until he became Emperor. We will continue to monitor him, though."

Tanis added, "So, Empress, we suspect that the Church may have also found out about his conduct and took some kind of action that caused him to straighten out, so to speak. What that action is, we can only speculate at this time. Do you want us to try to find that out as well?"

"No." Kassandra replied automatically. She had great faith in Cardinal Drakon, but then, something changed her mind. "Yes, yes, please do so, if you can. Thank you very much. You are indeed the best! I am eternally thankful to have you in my employ! Now go get yourselves unpacked. Tomorrow, I will have the tailor and dressmaker visit you. I will see that you have proper court clothes. If anyone asks, you two are my Personal Assistants, while Selene is my Private Assistant." All three grinned.

After they left, tears swelled in her eyes, and Selene put her arms around her and let her cry on her shoulders. "Maybe there is something wrong with me after all," she wailed.

After a time, Selene whispered, "There is only one way to find out for sure." Kassandra knew what she meant. Only the how remained difficult to achieve without others finding out about it. Now she began pondering how she could do it safely.

A week later, a handsome young man came by the Palace to see if he could sell them some fancy bolts of satin. He'd heard about all the dresses being made and decided that he might be able to make a big sell for his father, a merchant who sold cloth. As he made his sales pitch, Argos could not have been less interested, and he finally excused himself and left. Kassandra made her decision.

After making a lengthy order, which only made the lad extremely pleased and happy. She added, "Say, will you follow me to my chambers, please? I want to show you the precise colors that these bolts need to be." He dutifully followed this beautiful woman, impressed with how aptly the Doormen opened the doors as she approached. Door after door, they passed, until they reached her bedroom. For a few minutes, she did show him the samples that she expected he would match. Then, she changed tact.

She moved close to him and began kissing him. Oh how she encouraged the lad, pressing her warm body against his. At last, the man yielded to temptation. Of course, she constantly flirted with him as he struggled to undress her. Sometime later, once the deed was done, right on time, Selene barged in on them, acting both shocked and surprised, hastily exiting. This was Kassandra's signal to move to stage two of her plan.

"Oh dear. We've been discovered! If you promise me that you will never, ever say anything about this to anyone, I will see that my Private Assistant does likewise."

"Oh, I promise, I promise!" the terrified lad pleaded with her.

"Good. Get dressed and leave quietly. Now a word to the wise, if I ever find out that you'd told anyone about our indiscretion here, I will see that the Emperor knows all about it. You know what he will do, don't you? Men are killed for far less." The sheer panic on his face told her that he'd never say a word about it. He quickly left.

Selene came in with a paper on which she had written down all the sordid details. "How did it go?" she asked as she took the key to their small safe from beneath Kassandra's dress and unlocked the safe. She put this document in it beside those that told of Argos' immoral conduct. After re-locking it, she fastened the key to Kassandra's undergarment once more.

"Perfect. He won't tell a soul. Now we should know something in maybe a month at the latest, right?" A month passed and Kassandra was definitely not pregnant. Kassandra became more and more frantic about her situation. During the course of the next eleven months, she tried this method eleven more times, all with different men, blackmailing them into silence. Her small safe was being filled with documents.

After that twelfth attempt also failed, Kassandra realized that something was wrong with her body, that she was indeed not perfect, as the Cardinal had said. Selene comforted her, "Empress, don't fret so. There are many women who would love to have your situation."

"Yes, but they would be common whores, now wouldn't they? No, I am doomed to having to have other people's children around me, if I want kids."

"Empress, you now don't have to worry. You can have any man you wish and not have to worry about becoming pregnant," Selene insisted.

"Selene! Don't you see that I no longer really like to be in bed with a man? They are just so crude and messy. I much prefer it when you pleasure me. You know how to do it right. I just wish I could somehow give you pleasure, my dear Selene."

Selene's heart skipped a beat. She'd just heard what she had been wanting to hear for so long. The Empress not only appreciated her, but also wanted to return the pleasure. "Empress, you can. I'll show you tonight!" Kassandra grinned.

Chapter 31 Carrying Out the Order in 743

In late March, Pope Leo received the orders from Cardinal Drakon. The sorely needed funds had already been credited to his account. Now he wrote out another transaction and sent for Rax, a dependable member of his Mano del Dio. Rax frequently traveled to the Southlands and was well experienced in the acquiring of new slave women or rather heathens who could readily be converted to Jehosanity. "We have received a request to acquire two dozen of the very best slave women to serve the Empress and Queens of Demokritos. Make darn sure that these are top-notched women. They also need another eighty regulars. I believe that they will be assisting the Women of the Eighth Degree with life chores. I have the money transfer here for you. Take the caravel and deliver them to our training facility here as soon as you can. This one rates top priority and make sure the two dozen are special. It's the royal courts, you know."

"You word is my command, Your Eminence. I shall procure the very best. Expect my return in a month." He bowed low and left with the money transfer. After visiting Banca del Dio, he took his small pack aboard the Roaring Wind and gave its captain his sailing orders.

As they began the ten-day sail, he thought about how best to fulfill the request. Normally slaves were usually taken from the vicinity of Sud, Southlands — taken from just north and east of there. Of late, the natives had moved further inland to get away from the slavers. Besides, the quality of slave taken here was not what his Pope desired. Rax decided to visit one who would know where to obtain the very best — a slaver called Raul, who was often found around Cape Hope, near the southwestern edge of the Southlands, now their destination.

Rax found Raul in a local bar roughhousing with other men of the trade. Raul was a heavyset man with solid muscles and bronze skin. His stubble face was long overdue for a shave. "Rax, my fine fellow! Hey over here, join me for a round. Haven't seen you for couple'o years. Whatsup?"

Rax joined him, downing a warm beer, before bringing up business. "I got a contract for you, real lucrative this one is. Interested?" Of course, Raul was and they got down to the details. After explaining what was needed, Raul pulled on his stubble with his fingers a minute.

"Real special, eh? Like really special?"

"Yes, for the Empress and Queens of Demokritos. I think they need to be halfway smart too," Rax emphasized. "What do you think? Can you get 'em for us soon?"

"Regular ones, I'll take ten a head. Now these special ones — they are going to cost you some. I know some real special ones, bit risky getting 'em, though. Cost ya triple," Raul replied, finishing off another beer and motioning for the barkeeper to send over another.

"Done, but I reserve the right to reject 'em if they are not what I think are going to be real special ones," Rax countered.

"Done. When ya want to leave?" Raul asked. They agreed first thing in the morning. Rax left to pack his things for a short overland expedition, while Raul downed another before heading out to round up his men.

In the morning, twenty rugged men, armed with bows and swords, mounted up. With them on several packhorses were their few supplies and of course leg irons. When they headed northeast instead of the usual northwest, Rax called out, "Hey, aren't we going the wrong way?" He pointed off to the right.

"Nah, you want 'em special, so special they be. I know just the ones, real special. You ain't seen nothin' like 'em. Risky to get 'em, but money's money. Here at the tip of the Southlands, the coastal mountain range was physical barrier to the vast jungles and savannahs of the Southlands. Once they climbed out of the last valley pass onto the semi-arid hills, Raul sent ten men off to the east, explaining the ten were going after the eighty normal ones Rax asked for.

Rax, Raul, and the other ten veered further to the northwest. Two days later, Raul pitched a base camp and sent out five scouts, all fanning out to the northwest of their location. Now he waited until they returned with news of the villages. A day later, the scouts returned. A half-day's ride would take them to a village, which had sufficient numbers of those that Raul sought.

Next day, Raul sent riders out searching for a herd of antelopes. Once found, they were to drive them close to the village they had selected. Meantime, Raul moved his remaining men into position and issued very clear orders. "This is the Utu Nation we are dealing with here, so stay alert. When the antelope run by, that will draw most all their men out, looking for fresh meat. Once they've left, we sneak in quietly and snatch the prettiest ones. No children and no older ladies. We want them as young women for the Empress. Two dozen. Drag them carefully out and get them over the hill here and start the leg chaining. Once we have them, we move out and don't stop for nothing!"

They waited out of sight of the village for several hours before they heard the hooves of the herd moving towards the village. Now they began to hear the excited shouts of the men rallying together to head off for the easy hunt. Raul timed it perfectly, from years of experience. In the men went. They saw six large huts that were fancier than all the others. Raul pointed to them and flashed hand signs. His men headed to the first three and ducked inside, while Rax and Raul kept a sharp lookout. Once, Raul had to shoot a brown skinned man, who had come back and saw the raiders. His arrow kept him from raising the alarm.

Shortly, the men came out, dragging a young woman in each arm.

Although the women were obviously protesting, they were helpless against such very strong men. As soon as they were pulled over the slight hill beyond the camp, another man clamped the leg irons on them, while the fetching men ran back for more.

Rax stared in total disbelief at these women! They were unlike any natives he had ever seen! Every one of them had brown skin, not black as usual. Each had layers of gold bands going from the bottoms of their necks to their chins. The chokers were so solid and tight, the women could not bend their necks at all. They were able to turn to look to the side, but they had to move their bodies to do so. All looked as if they had very long necks. That was not all. Both their top and bottom lips had been slit and large clay disks inserted into the openings, making them look rather like duckbills. To support the large disks, both the two top and bottom front teeth had been removed. Some of their disks were four inches around.

"Special enough for you?" Raul asked, seeing the staring Rax.

"Never seen anything like them before! As long as they are also intelligent, we are in business."

"Well, they're smart. These are the Utu Princesses, very special women. The Utu Nation prizes them above all things — like they are the mother of their nation, as best I can tell. Never lived among them, so I can't say for sure. Come on, we got our two dozen. Now comes the risky part."

"What do you mean? I thought this was the risky part."

"No way. I said these are Princesses. Once their men find out that we've taken some of their Princesses, they will be coming after us with blood in their eyes! We have to put some distance between us and them pronto or we will have a bloody fight on our hands." They made as much haste as they could.

Around noon, another of his riders drove another herd towards them, crossing their path and totally obliterating signs of their passage. Raul suggested that might slow them down for a while. "We'll be safe when we get to the coastal range. Doubt that they will head up into them or down on the coast side." To be on the safe side, Raul had one rider hang back. He would give them advance warning if the angry natives were getting too close to them.

As it turned out, they had a very narrow escape indeed. As they headed into the mountains, their rider came up with news that hundreds of them were getting close. Raul had one last trick. As they entered a very narrow valley, he had three men douse the stubby trees with all their lamp oil and then set fire to it. By the time that they headed downward towards the coast, the entire valley was in flames. By the time it died down, they'd be back at Cape Hope with the slaves loaded.

That was indeed the case. As they walked the new slaves through Cape Hope, the townsfolk stopped to stare at the strange women with their long necks and duckbilled lips. They were marched straight onto the caravel, and one end of their chain fastened to a 8X8 support beam. The next day, the other ten men came into Cape Hope from the east, leading a string of eighty black young women. At high tide, they set sail for Megalos.

Meanwhile back at the blazing fire barrier, King Otona stood and watched as his yelling warriors tried to find ways around the flames to continue their pursuit of those that has stolen their precious Princesses. Otona was angry. When it became apparent that they would lose days waiting for the fires to subside, he called a meeting.

"Long have we been told of the bronze slavers. Our Shinto neighbors have told us of this for years. Now it is time to put an end to this. I will send out runners across the whole Veld, even north of the volcano. Summon representatives of all nations here to me on the next full moon. It is time that we unite and drive these bronze slavers from our land forever." At once, several dozen runners took off in many different directions across the arid hilly Veld.

Ten days later, the caravel docked at the private dock of Constanza City. The slaves were offloaded and taken into the underground tunnels, a veritable maze beneath the enormous mother church complex above. They were taken to a special building, run by caring nuns of the Church. After the leg irons were removed, a doctor examined each young woman. Finding them all fit, he left them to the nuns. They were given a bath and then more properly dressed and fed.

For the next four months, the women were taught the language spoken on Megalos and Demokritos, the customs to be followed, and how to be a proper servant to a Holy Woman. Since there were a large number of these women on Megalos, many volunteered to serve as "models" on which these new servants could practice their skills. From dressing them to feeding them to brushing out their hair, these new women were taught everything that they had to know to become the arms of these Holy Women. Indeed, these volunteer models were well paid for their time and patience.

Once these slave women realized that they were supposed to be caring for the life needs of these armless women, a natural sympathy developed. They began to work hard to help their fellow women, even though they were bronze skinned. As they learned more of the language, it was explained to them that they were going to be very well treated and going to be a lifelong partner to an armless woman who desperately needed their assistance. This sympathetic bond was actually the key to such a rapid education and reorientation of these women.

By mid-August, the hundred plus women were loaded onto a caravel bound for the port city of Patri, Thrace. Late October, having had good sailing winds, the caravel docked and the women were loaded into numerous carriages and driven up to Kefall, arriving the first week of November.

Chapter 32 It Spreads

Beginning in the late summer of 743, Empress Kassandra began taking an active interest in the dealings of her husband and Emperor. Following the Cardinal's advice, she sat quietly on her throne while Emperor Argos held court, was briefed by his advisors, and carried out the business of running the country. Without being able to take notes, jot down key things for later reference, she had no choice but to hone her memory. As the months went by, she got better and better recalling the smaller details of transactions, messages, dispatches, and even advice given.

Argos also held more private meetings. These, too, she began to attend, once more sitting quietly in the back of the room, saying nothing, but listening intently to all that was said. Evenings, she often now dictated some key data which either Thekla or Selene would write down for her. What she found utterly amazing was that Emperor Argos hardly ever even noticed her presence!

At first, she was annoyed with his lack of attention. Soon, she realized that she no longer wanted his attention! She had her loving, dedicated staff now, along with two trusted detectives, and her affectionate Personal Assistant, Selene. Hence, she focused solely on the business of running Demokritos. By early fall, she realized that Argos was actually having to deal with many complex issues across many areas, including their economy and vast fleet of caravels.

Politically, four times a year, all the kings and queens came to Kefall for a weeklong conference with the Emperor and Empress. Now she understood why the Palace had this huge meeting room. The central large pair of thrones were for Argos and herself. The seven smaller pairs of thrones were for the seven kings and queens. Of course, there were numerous tables and chairs for all their associated advisors and such.

These quarterly meetings were held at the solstices and the equinoxes, though Argos did not call for his first one until the Spring Equinox in September. He needed the time to learn what he needed to do. By September, he felt knowledgeable enough that he could at last meet the various kings and deal with their interrelationships and needs. Their advisors explained that it was the Empress' task to see that their guests were properly housed, appropriate meals prepared, and most importantly arrange for their evening's entertainment. Note, this far south, the seasons are reversed. Spring begins in September, summer starts in December, fall begins in March, while winter starts typically in June.

The Palace already had a large staff that dealt with most of these issues. They had stayed on after her parents had been assassinated. For the first two, all that Kassandra had to do was to inform the Head Maid of the date of the Conference and inform the Head Chef, making any menu requests she might have. She sent off two of her Messengers to relay the date that the kings and queens were expected to come.

The Palace also had a pair of Overseers, a husband and wife team, Sethos and Penelope Alcmene. While he oversaw the overall physical operation of the large complex, she handled the domestic staff and similar things, such as seeing that the pantry was well stocked. Hence, all that Kassandra really had to do for the entertainment was to chat with Penelope.

"So when mom was going to entertain them all, what kind of events did she hold?" Kassandra asked. Penelope rattled off such things as dances, plays, and musical concerts.

"Okay, I like dancing, so let's plan an opening night dance and a closing night dance."

"Fine, but dear, you ought to also hold one in the middle of the week. Your mother always did."

"Okay, then all we need are two others, right? So let's have a play and a musical concert."

"I believe those will be appreciated."

"Can you arrange these for me?"

Penelope grinned. "Yes of course. Your mother always let me handle the details too. She would sometimes tell me the play that she wanted or the music, but she allowed me to orchestrate the details. Usually, they are all held in our giant ballroom."

"Thanks. Say are you getting paid enough for all that you do?" Kassandra suddenly realized just how much the everyday operation of this large Palace required of Sethos and Penelope.

She laughed and said that they were. Kassandra relaxed and returned to the main meeting. Now she could concentrate on her own personal agenda at the meeting. This would be the first time that the various kings and queens would be gathering here and meeting her, some for the first time. It was imperative that she be just perfect in all ways!

She had two new ball gowns made, both satin, one blue and one green. Each one, according to the suggestions of Penelope and her recollections of her mother at these affairs, had to billow out at least five feet from her. It was a very formal affair. Her primary goal with the queens was to have them see just how well these Holy Women and their families could work in her palace. Hence, she double-checked with each one, making sure that they were doing their assigned tasks just perfect. For the whole week, she darted around the palace. Her staff heard the words "Just perfect" so many times that they began to tease her about it.

She knew that after these queens saw how perfect her private staff actually was, then she could persuade them to follow in her footsteps and start hiring these Holy Women of Demokritos who were in dire need of a helping hand. No one worried about the wealthy Holy Women or those whose husbands were well off. Those could afford proper servants. It was these poor women who desperately needed assistance. Kassandra was determined to get these queens to lend a hand. If each one took on ten of the worst off families, that would be seventy families handled. Still, she realized this was only a start, but at least the very worst off would be salvaged.

This first meeting of the Council went "perfect." Queens Frona and Melita were Holy Women, like herself. Both immediately saw the great benefit of what Kassandra had done, particularly with the doormen! They too often felt trapped by a simple thing as a door. They marveled at how they could walk around the palace at will. As they approached a door, the neatly groomed Doorman or boy would elegantly open it for them. This they greatly appreciated.

By the end of the Council, Kassandra had gotten the other queens to agree to take ten of the worst off families, a total of seventy. She helped arrange to have the queens meet them, and she even paid these families' moving expenses. The queens took careful note of this — she'd made an impression on them. As Queen Frona was leaving for home, she gave Kassandra a compliment. "Empress, I do declare that you are as skillful as the great Empress Marin Elizabet was!" She had no way of knowing how greatly this pleased Kassandra!

As the ensuing days passed, she immersed herself in just how the country was run. Day by day, her knowledge grew. Still Argos ignored her. What he didn't know was that Tanis was keeping a close eye on his movements when he left the palace grounds. Still Tanis had nothing new to report to Kassandra.

In November, while sitting on her throne listening in on Argos and his advisors discussing the purchasing of thousands of guns, she realized that sitting here without arms to help her, her control over men who ran things was severely limited! She couldn't even push off unwanted advances, should some man make them of her, let alone fight back or fend them off. She began to wonder, if I become the sole ruler, how am I to keep these men in their place?

The only thing she had was her voice, her words. Then, she remembered how she had handled the dozen men that she had used to attempt to get pregnant. That night, she explained to Tanis and Thekla, "I need some leverage over these men, if I am to one day rule." Thus, she began her crusade to obtain "blackmail leverage" over all the key players who advised her husband. Later, this was expanded to include the dozen army generals. Then, her list included the most wealthy and influential people in each of the seven kingdoms. She soon had to add seven more private safes in her private quarters to hold all the "proof" that her detectives slowly dug up. Bit by bit, she began to have what she called her Aces up her sleeve, although she had no arms with which to have sleeves. Her logic was simple. If someone refused to do as she asked on a key, major issue, she would dig into her private safe and pull out the documents that would force him to do as she demanded. Alternatively, if someone tried to force her into doing something that she didn't want to do, she would use her documents to stop him. Curiously enough, at this time, she omitted all women from their detective work. She would later rectify her oversight!

She received word from the Church that her order of special assistants from Megalos had arrived in Patri and were on their way to Kefall. Immediately, she sent one of her Messengers to find Selene and had her also tell Selene that she'll be at the carriage waiting for her. Kassandra also sent a Messenger to ready her coach. She thought to herself, "My personal staff is working out perfectly." She then headed to the door of the large throne room, leaving the Emperor and his advisors in a heady discussion. None paid any attention to her leaving, except her Doorman, who smiled and perfectly anticipated her speed, opening the door gallantly for her. She gave him a nod and smile. She continued to admire her many doormen, as she walked down the halls, and eventually went outside onto the huge cobblestone courtyard.

A few minutes later, she and Selene were traveling through the streets of Kefall on their way to her Church to see Cardinal Drakon. When he heard that Empress Kassandra had come to see him, he stopped working on his planning sessions and headed to meet her in his study.

"Ah, I see my staff has gotten you seated. Forgive me. I was working when you arrived. How may I help my Holy Woman?" he poured on the charm.

"I received word that our assistants from Megalos have arrived in Patri and are on their way here to Kefall. Of course, I will use the two dozen special assistants for court use. I was wondering what would be the best use of the eighty other assistants. Although I was able to place seventy or so with the other queens, there are so many others on your lists. Ought I assign these eighty to the eighty worst cases — ones wholly unable to afford someone to assist them as I have Selene here?"

"Such a magnanimous gift would be a Holy Blessing for these unfortunate Holy Women. Yes, that would be most generous of you, my Empress. On behalf of all Demokritos, allow me to thank you very much." Her smile told him that he had pleased her, which was his intention. Selene went over the listings with the Cardinal, who had to scratch off several names of those who had forsaken everything and committed suicide.

"Might I ask that your priests and staff handle the distribution for me? I will have more than I can manage getting the two dozen special assistants handled. Of course, let me know how much these women's wages ought to be. I'll have Selene setup an automatic funds transfer for these eighty women's pay."

"Most generous of you, Empress. Yes, my staff will be very pleased to take these new assistants to those most worthy Holy Women. Again, thank you so very, very much."

Ah, I have him where I want him, Kassandra thought to herself. I'll get the credit in these family's eyes, but his staff will have to do the messy deliveries. She thanked him and rose to leave. Selene adroitly move her chair out of the way of her wide dress and opened the door for her, all in seemingly one continuous motion. Kassandra was able to make her exit gracefully in one flowing motion. She whispered a thank you to Selene as they walked to their coach. Selene grinned. Her employer and lover was very observant — yes, she dared use that word now, lover!

Back at her Palace, at diner with her large personal staff and their families, she counted thirty Holy Women in her employ now, of which ten were teens or young girls. "Tomorrow, Holy Women, I am very pleased to announce that our special, hand-picked assistants from Megalos will be arriving. We will have another two dozen sets of hands to help us out, though I will be sending a couple to Queens Frona and Melita to help them out as well. When they arrive tomorrow, I will send word to all of you Holy Women. It is my wish that we all meet them as they arrive. I'm sure that they will need some assistance in getting settled in here. My Messengers and Fetchers will be showing our special women around the palace, though I may accompany them as well. I do hope that these special women will be of great help to us all." The large group broke into a spontaneous round of cheering and applauding.

The next day, Kassandra insisted on wearing her fanciest green satin ball gown that billowed out some five feet before her. Carefully Selene adjusted her crown, double-checking that her Empress looked perfect, before Kassandra checked on her appearance in the mirror. "Perfect, as always, dear Selene! Come; let's head down to the main entrance."

One by one, her thirty women and girls arrived at the main entrance. Many complimented Kassandra on how beautiful she looked, which pleased her. Finally, the caravan of carriages pulled into the spacious courtyard, six of them. The group watched as the drivers stepped down, opened the doors, and helped the women down. Kassandra and her long line stepped forward to meet these special servants.

"Oh my!" Kassandra exclaimed as she got her first look at the women as they carefully stepped out of the coaches. All wore matching brown full dresses, their many petticoats fluffing their dresses out to perhaps two feet from them. Their faces were brown and circular. Uniformly all had black hair, straight and long draping to below their shoulders. None of this, however, was what was noticed. Rather their necks shone brilliant in the sun, reflecting off their gold neckbands, which gave the illusion that these women had extremely long necks! Even stranger, both of their lips had been slit and clay disks inserted in them, giving them the appearance of duckbills. The diameter of the disks ranged from three to four inches across, and they protruded straight out from their faces, held in place by their two missing front teeth, top and bottom. It was impossible to tell if they were smiling or not.

As the Utu Princesses climbed out of their coaches, they saw the wall of armless women and even some little girls. Their hearts went out to them immediately, knowing now that the nuns had not lied to them; they were going to help care for women who needed them. While they had been both trained and drilled on helping the armless women who came to the nun's facility, consensus among the Princesses was that this was some kind of nasty trick that was being played upon them. They only wanted to return to their homes, but all knew the reality of that! They were now across some vast waters, which they could not hope to cross on their own. Most expected that eventually the bronzed skin men would violate their sacred Holiness. As they now stared in awe at the line of needy women, they realized that they had not been lied to, and they didn't notice that these women were staring at themselves.

"Amazing, I do hope that they can understand us," Kassandra whispered to Selene. She took a step forward and addressed these most unusual looking women. "Welcome to the Emperor's Palace and Demokritos. I am Empresses Kassandra Aias, your boss. We are very pleased to have you join us. Can you understand what I am saying?" she decided to ask before she continued. She felt a bit of panic. What if they didn't understand what she was saying?

Several of the women nodded their heads slightly. It was impossible for them to really bow their heads or do much of a nod. Rather, they bent at their waists, which worked just as well. "Oh I am so grateful of that! Welcome, welcome, welcome. Each of you will have your own room and will be assisting us with many things, as you can plainly see. I will be paying your wages monthly, so that you can buy things that you might like. I will provide all your dresses, so you don't have to worry about that expense. I guess a better way to say this is that I will be providing you with your clothing, homes, and food. Now this is Selene; she is my second in command. If you can't find me, you can ask her for anything. You must forgive me. I have never seen women quite like you. Is it possible for you to speak and tell me your names? I would like to learn your names and meet each of you personally. I am so glad that you have come to help us here."

With the large disks combined with their missing teeth, the Princesses found speaking their own tongue nearly impossible. Thus, they had invented their own language used among themselves, consisting of sounds that they could make. However, they had been taught Kassandra's language well by the nuns and had been forced to attempt to speak it. Although they did try, many found themselves nearly impossible to be understood. Out of survival, they had elected the oldest of themselves to be their spokesperson. She was twenty-three, and now she stepped forward to face Kassandra, hoping that she could be understood somehow.

".ea.ing is .ardh .or us. I am .alled Udua," she spoke as clearly as she could, though her lips and disks did not move, just a slight opening and closing of her mouth. Kassandra thought that she understood her and moved her body close to give her a hug. Udua recognized her intention and put her arms around Kassandra. ".e .el. .ou," she added.

"You are called Udua, right. You will help us, right?" Kassandra said softly. Udua nodded, well bowed at her waist rather.

"Good. Good. I can mostly understand you. I am so curious about your neck and your mouth ornaments. You will have to tell me about these soon. Let me meet the others, Udua."

"I .ust s.eak .or .he.," she hastily added.

"You must speak for them?" Kassandra repeated making sure that she got what Udua was saying. She did her bowing nod once more. Inspiration struck. "Say, can you write our language a little?"

".es," was the reply.

"Good, then I will make arrangements for each of you to have paper and something to write with. You can keep them with you and when you need to say something, just write it out for us. Is that okay with you?" Kassandra hoped and prayed that it would be.

Again, Udua and several standing close to her who had overheard it did their bowing nods. It was impossible to tell any facial reactions of relief on their faces; their disks interfered with normal visual clues, as far as Kassandra was concerned. She went to each servant in turn and got their name, while Selene carefully wrote them down. Soon, it became obvious that their names were simple and pronounceable, even with the interference of these disks. Selene wrote down, Iua, Oua, Arra, Oda, and Ida. They were forced to use many vowels as these came across clearly, while most consonants were indistinguishable. Curious, thought Kassandra, why would anyone do this to their lips and necks? Well, she promised to find out. After all, this was precisely what everyone else would want to know the moment that they saw them!

After a lengthy tour, the women given their rooms and allowed some personal time to relax before dinner. At dinner, Argos, as did all the other men, noticed these newcomers. Kassandra merely stated that they were their new servants. Indeed, at diner, these women were polite and at once assisted the others. Udua sat beside Kassandra and fed her. She watched Udua carefully, but saw that she was very observant and anticipated her well, a very good sign. Later, Udua helped her undress for bed. Normally, Kassandra found getting into bed anything but graceful, an awkward falling, flopping action. To her surprise, Udua put her arms around her back and gently laid her down, making sure that her hair was above her head. Kassandra was impressed. So were the other women, she learned the next day. Within a week, Kassandra knew that these women were very smart, very intelligent, very polite, very observant, and very compassionate to the

Holy Women. Kassandra smiled. She had achieved a smashing success.

The first week in December and the start of summer, the representatives from the country of Annelise, which lay beyond that of the wild horsemen of Vladimir, arrived, bringing their yearly tax for the Emperor. As always, since the tax began in the days just prior to Maren Elizabet, they paid in raw jade. The Emperor and Empress sat on their throne as the representatives entered. Her Announcer called out clearly, "Hans Greb of Annelise." One man, immaculately dressed in what could almost be described as a tuxedo, pushed a cart laden with the jade. He moved swiftly toward the throne. Just as Argos was about to greet him, the Announcer called out, "Princess Maren Ditka."

All eyes returned to the huge double entrance doors, where the Doorman, assisted by the Announcer, held both doors open to their fullest extent. A young woman stood in the opening and began to move into the throne room. However, Kassandra's eyes stared at her in disbelief. Her gown was a rose satin, but it had to be at least fourteen feet in diameter where it rose just above the floor. Her bodice was low cut with no sleeves; rather the material formed short sleeves below her shoulders, as if someone had cut off the tops of the sleeves, allowing only a tiny bit of fabric to hold them to the bodice. Yet, Kassandra could not take her eyes off her waist. It was so utterly small, so tiny, which only added to the dramatic appeal of her gown.

Maren began walking towards the throne, but she moved extremely slowly, though Kassandra could hear the clicking sound of her heels on the stone floor. What she found utterly breathtaking was that the woman seemed to be floating across the room towards her! Her motion, her appearance, greatly impressed Kassandra, who had never seen anything so utterly graceful, poetry in motion, she thought. Still, it took over a minute for Maren to "float" up to the throne, where she curtsied and smiled.

"Welcome to Demokritos, Princess Maren Ditka. Your gown is just fabulous," Empress Kassandra spoke from her heart. "Come, sit beside me that I may examine your gown more closely." Selene and Udua extended their arms at their fullest taking a hold of the Princess's extended arms and helped her up and onto the smaller chair beside Kassandra's. Meanwhile, Argos chatted with Hans Greb about the jade.

"Oh, I am so very pleased to meet you at last Empress Kassandra Aias!" Maren gushed. She was nineteen and still very impressionable. Her enthusiasm was genuine. "I heard that you had become the Empress of Demokritos and I just had to come and meet you. You see, I am the granddaughter of King Hans and Queen Mia Ditka, who were the constant companions of the great Maren Elizabet herself. They've told me such stories about her. So when I heard the news about you, why, I just begged and pleaded for my parents to allow me to come and visit you. You do so look just like what I imagined Maren Elizabet would have looked like, sitting on your throne with your crown and all! You are positively beautiful,

Empress."

"Thank you, Princess," Kassandra was finally able to cut off her gushing chat. "I am truly impressed with your dress! I've never seen anything like it before. And your waist, how incredibly tiny!"

The young girl was very proud of her small waist. "I am now one inch from being the size of Maren Elizabet! I am down to a fifteen inch waist, though I know reducing it further is going to be very hard indeed, but that is my goal, to equal Maren's."

"I noticed that you walked slowly and so gracefully. To my eyes, it seemed as if you were an angel floating across the floor in your immense gown," Kassandra replied.

Maren smiled. "I know. It's partly these shoes and partly the dress and partly lots of practice. I'm glad that you noticed it. I've worked so hard to be able to glide, as we call it. Glide across the room is our motto back in Annelise."

"Incredible, Princess Maren, I am very impressed, so very like an angel. Say, would it be possible for me to get an outfit just like yours and have you teach me how to glide across the room?" Kassandra asked eagerly.

"Wow! What an honor, Empress! Yes, oh yes, it would be my greatest pleasure. Oh," she suddenly frowned, realizing one difficulty. "I've been wearing these corsets since I was ten. It takes years and years to get your waist down to fifteen inches. I'm sure my dressmaker can get you started on it, but she can tell us better. Even if yours isn't fifteen inches, it will look lots smaller than it does now, your majesty."

"That would be fine with me. I don't recall when I have been this excited over an outfit! Whatever your seamstress needs, I will see that she has it as fast as possible. I already have a large stock of satin bolts, so that should help. How soon could she begin? I don't want to impose on her really, but I just *have* to have an outfit like yours, Princess Maren. I too have heard all sorts of stories about Maren Elizabet. Please, dine with me and let us exchange stories, shall we?"

"Oh, I'd just love that. She is my idol," Princess Maren replied. "I'm even named after her."

"She is mine too," Kassandra whispered to her. "You must stay here at my palace for a time, before you return home. I insist."

Princess Maren got the attention of Hans. "Please fetch Elizabet. I want her to make a dress like mine for the Empress as soon as possible. And then get my maid to bring all my stuff here, please. We are going to stay here for a while." Hans smiled; he'd figured that his charge would end up enchanting the Empress. Princess Maren enchanted nearly everyone else, so why not her.

A few hours later, Empress Kassandra, Selene, Princess Marin, and Elizabet gathered in her private quarters. Elizabet wore a similar gown, though only ten feet in diameter. She also wore a tight corset, but Kassandra saw that her waist was not nearly as tiny as Marin's was. While Elizabet began her measuring, Kassandra asked curiously, "Do all the women in Annelise were such fine dresses and corsets?"

"Absolutely. One must be well dressed at all times. That is the motto that everyone in Annelise follows. I must admit that when the Princess told me to bring so many things and boots with us, I though it folly. Now I see that she has charmed you. Yes, I do believe that we have a pair of boots like Marin's that will fit you perfectly. I must warn you they do have really high heels, but we in Annelise are very experience in wearing them." She chatted on as she finished her measurements.

"Have you ever worn a tight corset before, Empress?" she asked.

"Well, no, not really. Why?"

"I will make yours a beginners. Did the Princess tell you that if you wish to reduce your waist, that you must wear the corset at all times, except when bathing?"

"Sorry, Empress. I didn't realize that you didn't know," the Princess hastily apologized.

They chatted a bit more before Elizabet explained. "Okay. I believe that we have with us enough for a starter package of corset, hose, and heels. We can get these on you and then put on your satin dress. While you will find the dress very loose around the waist, this will give you time to get used to the corset and to begin to learn to walk in these heels. The boots have re-enforced sides so that you cannot easily sprain your ankle. Still back home, everyone has a great deal of difficulty in learning to walk and to glide across the room in them. We have cleverly developed a learning method, which really does work wonders. Would you like to give that a try too, Empress?"

Several hours later, Kassandra sat on the edge of her bed, while Princess Marin and Elizabet finished getting the undergarments on her. "My, this corset is so tight! How do you breathe in it?" she asked. Princess Marin giggled and explained that she'd get used to it. Now, she stared at her new black boots, laced tightly up her caves nearly to her knees. They had explained that they needed to be tight for extra support. The heels were higher than anything the Empress had ever seen before. However, the explanation of the stockings, which were held up by the garters of the corset, intrigued her.

They were made from silk imported from Tashien and were very thin and expensive. While she knew nothing about that, she did know that they felt wonderful on her legs! Yet she worried a bit about the height of the heels. Would she be able to manage them? "Oh my!" she declared when she first tried to stand up in them. Both women caught her as she nearly fell while trying to walk around her room in them.

"Don't worry, Empress. Everyone who first wears these has made the same mistake that you just did. That's why we have invented our helper, our trainer," Elizabet consoled her. She then slid a tight fitting skirt up her legs, fastening it around her waist. "It is very tight all the way down, rather like hobbling a horse. This way, it is impossible for you to take a step that is too big, and you will naturally learn to glide this way." They then got her satin green ball gown back on her and tucked in the waist slightly. Indeed, her waist was at least four inches smaller now.

"There, all set. Now you are ready to begin to learn to walk in them and to glide across the room," Elizabet declared.

"Oh, I never thought about her having no arms," Princess Marin suddenly looked crestfallen. "I mean what we usually do now, Empress, is have two of us hold your hands with our arms extended so that the dresses don't mash together much. That way, we can support them as they learn to walk and glide. Oh dear, I'm so sorry that I forgot about that. Whatever will we do?"

"Well, perhaps just put a steading arm around my waist?" suggested Kassandra. They did, though their dresses bunched together tightly, hoops bending. "Oh my. Oh my!" she declared. "These are such tiny steps!"

"Keep your knees straight, don't bend them so," Princess Marin cautioned, as the lessons began in earnest. Soon, Selene took over for Elizabet, who began work on the many parts of the total outfit.

By suppertime, Kassandra was exhausted, but she felt she had made progress. All evening she and Princess Marin exchanged tales of the legendary Marin Elizabet. Each day, the Princess worked with Kassandra and by the end of the week, Kassandra was also gliding across the floor in her green satin ball gown. By the time that she had mastered the walk, Elizabet had finished the dress and its many components. Eagerly, the women dressed the Empress in her new satin gown, one that flared out seven feet before her, just like the one that the Princess wore. After many words of thanks and admiration for how well the dress looked on her, it was time for her to practice again.

That evening as Kassandra came to the dining room, she wore her new dress and proceeded to glide across the room, astonishing everyone. She received many accolades, praises, and comments. "Isn't this just incredible?" she exclaimed as she sat down to dine. "You know, Princess Marin, I would like to buy at least another seven of these dresses! Different colors, of course. Actually, wouldn't it be fantastic if all we women could wear such fine dresses?"

"You should work on your waistline first, before you have many more made," Princess Marin explained. "You see, as it gets smaller, the dresses won't fit right. I know. What if I come back in the fall and bring a whole bunch more with me?"

"Say, I have an even better idea," Kassandra interrupted her. "I know that your country has been paying their taxes in jade each year. Why don't we have you pay this year in complete outfits instead? Shoes, stockings, corsets, the whole works? Probably most should be starter outfits, right."

Unfortunately, these outfits were all hand-fitted and handmade for the individual person. Only the boots were standardized. Between them, they worked out a way to make it all work out. Because Kassandra swore that she would diligently wear her new corset all the time, Elizabet promised to return in the fall with a smaller one to help her reduce her waist further.

That night, Hans had a word with Princess Marin. "Look, Princess. We have been paying our taxes with these common ordinary worthless rocks. It hasn't cost us anything at all, save a little time to go out and collect them. These dresses and shoes — now they are going to be expensive. Your father might get very annoyed if not angry with you over this."

"Oh, I forgot, Hans, really I did. I'll fix it up. Besides, think of how much better the relations between our two countries will be if so many here adopt our fashions?" Hans didn't see her point at all, but allowed her to fix it, if she could.

The next day, Princess Marin explained to Kassandra, while they were alone, "You know that these dresses are very expensive. I would feel awful if we didn't pay our taxes in the jade that you need so badly. Honestly, Emperor Argos will have a fit if he doesn't get the jade, but gets only dresses instead. I have a better plan."

Kassandra agreed to her new idea. She would return in the early fall with more dresses for Kassandra, along with a newer corset. She'd send along a dozen seamstresses who would spend the rest of the year making outfits, returning with Hans after he brought the taxes by next December. Thus, Princess Marin was able to repair her economic blunder, and her father was very pleased with her diplomacy and wisdom, when she returned a week later.

What of Emperor Argos during all this time? When the Empress made her grand gliding appearance entering the throne room, Argos did notice her wide dress, but resumed his discussions with his advisors. Later, when they were alone again, Kyros, his eldest advisor, pointed out, "It is not my business particularly, Argos, but I have noticed that you've not paid much attention at all to Kassandra for months now. It looks like she is going to greater and greater extremes to get your attention. First, these strange looking brown servants and now this impossibly wide dress."

"I know, I know, Kyros. Let her. It is taking all I have to handle this Emperor business. Besides, we've given up on trying to have a child. There's something wrong with her. It's not me," Argos explained, but did not say how he knew that it was her and not him. Kyros wisely did not press that issue.

"Still, you probably ought to spend some time with her, if only for show. You don't want her to go to her Cardinal friend complaining that you are ignoring a Holy Woman. That could cause us big problems." What Kyros did not say was that the real reason Argos was having so much trouble dealing with running Demokritos was that he was about the dumbest lad he'd seen. Good looking, suave, but low on intelligence. Retirement looked better and better for Kyros!

"Oh, all right. I'll take her to a play tonight. Where's one of her Messengers? Hey, miss, over here." He got the attention of one of her Holy Women Messengers and had her deliver his offer to take her out to a play after diner.

"Dear, you must go," Selene admonished Kassandra, when she said that she didn't want to go to a play with Argos.

"The less I have to do with him, the better."

"But think about how it looks to other Holy Women. You must set a good example, dear. While I know that you'd much rather go with me, you should go with him this one time."

"Okay, okay, I will. Wait, should I try to wear this new dress? I've not practiced wearing it out in public. What if I stumble and fall? It would be so embarrassing."

"Wear your usual green dress. Elizabet showed me how to tuck it in so that the smaller waistline doesn't show much," Selene volunteered.

The evening didn't go well for either. She chose to wear her new high-heeled boots, which was a mistake. He continually hounded her with, "Can't you walk any faster than this?" Both were annoyed with each other. She mused over how different he was now. Before he was the Emperor, he was a real pleasure to be around, but not now. Now, they seldom slept in the same room.

On a different front in 744, another three hundred black women were stolen from their village huts in the wilds of the Veld. All around the edges of the Veld, Megalos miners used blacks as slave diggers, as they had for generations. Gold and gemstones in quantity came from these many mines, vital for the economy of Megalos. Without warning, waves of black men swarmed into the outlying small villages and even mining camps. Using spears and shields along with machetes, they butchered every person who did not flee and escape.

In response, Pope Leo suggested that the Senate in Galantas send out legions of Centurions to put down these raiders. By summer, the results were back. The five legions were lost to the savages! Hence, Pope Leo sent word to Cardinal Drakon to beseech Emperor Argos to send fifty legions to put down this rain of savage attacks.

Argos had an army of over a hundred legions at his command. His generals begged him to allow them to send the fifty legions so that they could get an opportunity to use their hundreds of cannonae that they had been purchasing for years. Now at last, they could blow up the enemy as they had been blown up during their ill-fated attack on Zargarb under Emperor Deimos so long ago. Argos signed the official document authorizing the attack.

For centuries, the wild horsemen from neighboring Vladimir had conducted raids into the kingdoms of Arolas and Penelopus. The nearly impassable mountain range of Katos separated the two countries. While Demokritos fielded the largest fleet of caravels in the world, the horsemen had only small fishing boats. Until now, Demokritos mostly ignored these raids. However, at the December Council, the kings of Arolas and Penelopus both beseeched him to do something about it.

Hence, in 744, Emperor Argos gave his generals permission to draw up plans to invade and conquer these wild horsemen and put an end to it. Of course, the generals insisted on making a full study of the assault and not much was actually accomplished early on.

Chapter 33 The Buildup

After the royal coronation in 743, Cardinal Drakon said to himself, "Three down, five to go!" Accordingly, he had his priests on the lookout for other candidates in the remaining Kingdoms, but it was nearly two years before he could take effective action. In 745, the King of Phindos succumbed to old age or so it was widely rumored. No one could prove otherwise, fortunately for the Church. The timing could not have been better, as the King's son was off on a long voyage to Velona when the King died.

Thus, Cardinal Drakon had his priests there in that kingdom launch a massive campaign in support of the late king's daughter and her husband to become the next rulers of Phindos. His priests effectively discredited the son, using his long voyage as a sure sign of "dereliction of responsibilities." While many in power favored waiting months for the son to return, eventually public pressure forced them to coronate King Dorieus and Queen Adonia Kadmos. At twenty-two, she, too, was a Holy Woman of the Eighth Degree.

A year later, following the Cardinal's orders, the Church backed another couple when the throne of Penelopus became vacant. That year, they coronated King Errikos and Queen Danae, who was only twenty-one, but was also a Holy Woman of the Eighth Degree.

The very next year, the Kingdom of Thrace also coronated a new couple. King Dimitrios and Queen Ariadne Diodros took the throne. She was barely twenty-one, the daughter of the late King and a Holy Woman herself. Once more, the king had died under mysterious circumstances. Some claimed that he had been poisoned, but most accepted the official findings from the doctor. He'd had heart failure. No one had detected the transfer of funds from Megalos to Cardinal Drakon and from the Cardinal to several other men, including two doctors. That the two doctors, the one attending to the late King of Phindos and the one attending the late King of Thrace, also mysteriously died went unnoticed.

Up in Megalos, it was May of 646. Pope Leo was sound asleep when a Palace guard pounded wildly on his door. "Your Eminence! Wake up! Something terrible has happened! Wake up!"

Leo jumped out of bed, throwing his purple robes over his partially clothed body and opened the door. One very frightened guard stood there, violently shaking. "What has happened?"

"Come with me! They are all dead! It's awful! The Mano quarters!" Seeing that he could get little useful information from the terrified man, he followed him around the palace to the Mano del Dio private living chambers, a vast barracks here in his giant complex in his Holy City of

Constanza. As he entered, he began to smell a distinctive odor. It was not yet dawn and the oil lamps still burned.

As he stepped inside the first bedroom, he saw fifty bodies lying in their beds. Their heads had been severed from their bodies. Blood covered the floor and bedding. He gasped and held his hand over his mouth. Hastily, he went from bedroom to bedroom. In each, the sight was the same, until he came to their largest bedroom, which held a hundred of his security men. The terrified guard pointed to the far wall. While the room was filled with corpses, Pope Leo saw the message written in blood on the wall. He stared dumfounded. The message read:

> Pope Leo. Stop assassinating men, women, and children around the world. Murder violates my law. If you ever continue this wanton practice of assassinating those who do not agree with you, I will return and do this to you and all of your priests worldwide, ending your church forever. Lord Jehosa.

He was silent for a long time. At last, the guard ventured, "Your Eminence. Is this really a message from our Lord Jehosa? What have we done to deserve such wrath?"

Instead of answering the direct question, Pope Leo asked, "Have you told of this to anyone else?"

"No, I came for you as soon as I saw it."

"You did wisely. Has other guards seen this and the dead?"

"No, Your Eminence. It is by chance that I came when I did. I was. . ." The Pope cut him off with a wave of his hand.

"My son. This is a hoax. Our enemies have snuck in here during the night and done this heinous deed. It shall not go unpunished, I so swear. I want you to go fetch a water bucket and mop and wipe that foulness off the wall. Once it is gone, go rouse the entire garrison. Be quick about it. I shall stay here until this blasphemy is removed from our Holy Walls. Go now and make all haste!"

While the guard was gone, Pope Leo carefully wrote down the exact message, word for word. Unfortunately, a Cardinal joined him. He'd discovered the guard and had been curious enough to follow him. As soon as he saw the carnage, he gasped and followed the guard to the Pope. As the Cardinal read the message on the wall, he wailed, "Woe be unto us. Forgive us, lord Jehosa, for we have sinned!"

"Oh stop that! This is a grim hoax, Cardinal. Pull yourself together, man. Some assassins have snuck into our complex this night and killed our Security men, our beloved Mano del Dio."

"But Your Eminence, how do you know that it is a hoax? That it is not a message from our dear Lord?"

"Simple. What language is the message written in?"

"Ours, Megalos," he answered, completely missing any point that the Pope had.

"Good. And what language has our Lord Jehosa spoken in all our most Holy Scriptures?"

"Ancient Arad. Oh, I see, it is not the Holy Language, so it is not really from our Lord and Savior after all. But then, who committed this foul and heinous crime?"

"That, my Cardinal, we must discover and take severe action against those perpetrators, our sworn enemies. Come, he has washed the blasphemy from the wall. Let us rouse everyone and begin to find out how this happened and see to the burial of our comrades."

Later that day, they laid to rest nearly eight hundred Mano del Dio men. Since there were none left here in Constanza City, Pope Leo had no alternative but to recall all the remaining Mano del Dio who were on assignments elsewhere. It was awful that his Supreme Prelate was still far in the north in Velona hunting down what might be left of the old Santi del Dio gold. He could have used his skills just now.

During the ensuing months and especially once the Supreme Prelate returned with the unequivocal news that there was no more Santi del Dio gold to be had, their investigations into the slaughter turned up little information about who was responsible. Many theories were examined. Who hated the Church so badly that they would do this extreme deed? Of course, at the top of their list was the Santi del Dio, but that was quickly discarded. They no longer even existed. Thirty years ago, they may well have done this, but now they were a group of the distant past. The Church had survived them.

After months of investigation, the only remaining viable possibility was Emperor Deimos of Demokritos. Exactly how he could have done this was a complete mystery, yet they had no other viable enemy on which to hang this horrid atrocity. Pope Leo retrieved a document from his personal secret vault and carried it to his office. He opened the sealed folder and retrieved the letter. Several years ago in late 742, he had sent this to Cardinal Drakon Erebos in Kefall, Demokritos. The letter was in code, but he had also kept his original message from which he'd created the letter. He reread what he had sent.

It would be very beneficial to everyone, if at this time, the Emperor and Empress met with a fatal accident. You have my blessing and support.

He pondered long into the night. Could the execution of his Mano del Dio have been a retaliation for his ordering the assassination of Emperor Deimos Gavril? This was the only remaining possibility, he thought. His men had ruled out all other wild ideas. Yet, now he had his chosen couple on the throne of Demokritos, and they were reasonably well under the control of the Church. Then, it struck him. It had to have been the action of old, hardline supporters of Deimos seeking revenge! Now he relaxed. While he could neither prove this nor speak of this to others, he felt renewed confidence. They had their revenge; now they would leave him alone and die of old age.

His next project was to find a large source of additional funds. By now, he had spent nearly all the Church's vast reserves on his massive Church expansion plan. While he still had enough funds in reserve, he knew that he needed to get his hands on a very significant amount within the next few years. It would not do to have the Church wind up in financial ruin. However, Pope Leo had faith. He knew that when the need was great, someone would step forward with the funds to keep the Church going.

Cardinal Drakon suffered his first setback of his Grand Plan, when in 750, the retiring King of Theos put his daughter and son-in-law on his throne, bypassing the Church. This wise king had seen the massive campaigns put on by the Church in the other Kingdoms. He simply bypassed all such nonsense, in his words. King Damon and Queen Athena Patra were subsequently coronated and became the new leaders of Theos. She was twenty-two and definitely not of the Eighth Degree.

While the Cardinal pondered his options for Theos, over in Arolas, the King of Arolas had an "accident." Both he and his wife drowned in the Pinos River, while on vacation. Once more, no one noticed the substantial transfer of funds, via the Banca del Dio. Quickly, the Cardinal stepped in and had the Church back heavily the King's son for the throne. In early January, King Hermos Pegasos and Queen Alekto, now barely twenty-one and of the Eighth Degree herself, were coronated in a lavish ceremony.

Only one remaining Queen stood between the Cardinal and his overall Grand Plan for Demokritos, Queen Athena of Theos. "Should the King and Queen meet with an accident?" asked his new Prelate Khristos Krates, a young man of twenty-three who had recently taken over from his predecessor, recently ordered back to Megalos. Cardinal Drakon had heard rumors of some vicious attack upon the Mano del Dio there, but could get no details from anyone. Pope Leo had totally hushed up the incident.

He wisely said, "No, there have been too many suspicious deaths in recent years. We would be pressing our luck. We must find another way to accomplish our goal down in Theos. Queen Athena cannot be persuaded. That I know. I've personally discussed the matter with her several times now. She will not listen to my valid reasons. She's adamant about not becoming a Holy Woman."

"Well, what about Damon, Your Holiness? Can we get to her through him?"

"That's what I am thinking. We need some leverage over him. See what you can dig up about his past. Perhaps he is hiding something that we could use."

"Your wish is my command, Your Holiness," Prelate Khristos Krates said and left on his new mission.

A month later, Cardinal Drakon sat in his official meeting room waiting for the arrival of the King of Theos, Damon Patra. He had a smug smile on his face. Shortly, his adept announced the arrival of King Damon. He rose to meet the twenty-six year old king, welcoming him cordially.

"Please, King Damon, have a seat."

King Damon disliked the Cardinal, who had twice now attempted to get his beautiful wife to have herself mutilated. In his mind, there was a veritable epidemic of this occurring all over Demokritos! Only he and his wife, of all the others kings and queens, had refused to join in with this despicable, wicked treatment of women. When he received this official summons from the Cardinal, he suspected that the Cardinal would attempt to persuade him to have it done. He had no idea what was about to happen.

"Thank you for coming on such short notice, King Damon. I know that you have your hands full running Theos. I will be brief. You are well aware that the Church, as well as most citizens of Theos, take a very hard view of married men having affairs with other women and fathering children out of wedlock. Such has ruined the careers of many a married man, in these times especially so. You would agree with me on this?"

"Yes, yes of course. Our leaders must be seen to be moral and upstanding models if they dare command the loyalty of those they represent. Why?"

"Well, something has come to my attention recently. I thought that I should first discuss it with you, before I took any action upon it." Cardinal Drakon paused judiciously, allowing the King to begin to worry. "You see, there is this young woman, a barmaid, very, very pretty, I'm told — it seems that two years ago, a certain King, probably under the influence of too much drink, took her to bed in secret. Now she has this boy child with the most remarkable eyes and face. I'm told that the child is a splitting image of his father."

As he spoke, he watched Damon's eyes and face closely. Suddenly, Damon could no longer confront him; his complexion began to redden slightly. Cardinal Drakon knew that he had him, so he said quietly, "That man has been positively identified by the young barmaid. She's identified you, King Damon, and I'm told that her son looks exactly like you, when you were a small child. Should I elaborate further?"

"No! Damn! Honestly, it was one slip, only one! She was pretty and, well, I fell victim to too much drink and human impulses. It won't happen again, Cardinal, I promise." Damon squirmed in his seat. This could destroy everything for which he had worked his whole life! It would irreparably hurt Athena, whom he loved dearly, to say nothing of his credibility as King of Theos.

"Well, King Damon, I do believe you — that you will not do such again, ever. Lord Jehosa knows that men sometimes commit great sins, but he has always given us a way to redeem ourselves."

"How can I redeem myself? I have tried to do the very best that I can not only as King but as husband and father of our two year old." Damon found himself grasping wildly on this thread of hope that there could be some way out of this mess, some redemption.

"If the world saw Queen Athena as a Holy Woman of the Eighth Degree and saw your continuing love and devotion to her until the day that she too passes away, then the world and Lord Jehosa would see that you have indeed redeemed yourself."

Damon looked aghast. The Cardinal continued, "Yet, I know only too well that she does not desire this. I will not ask you to make any attempt to persuade her to do this action, this most holy of actions. Fear not, we both know that would be utterly a waste of time."

"Yes, she is vehemently against such mutilations as she calls it. So how am I to redeem myself? I mean, if she were a Holy Woman, I could then prove my loyalty, my eternal love to her."

"There is a way, King Damon. It requires only one tiny action on your part, plus your lifetime of living proof of your love and fealty to Queen Athena. If you agree to this tiny action, then the Church will see that the entire problem vanishes forever. The barmaid and your son can be relocated to another Kingdom, where she can have a superior job, one which will allow her to raise your son properly."

"You guarantee that neither she nor my son would be harmed?"

"Oh absolutely, King Damon! I know of a mayor who is looking for a young woman to assist in his office work. She would be perfect for the job, which pays a good stipend indeed. She and your son could live well on the funds that she would earn, to say nothing of the vast increase in her social standing. Mayor's Assistants are important people in the smaller towns, as you well know, King. What say you? Shall we keep this matter entirely between you and I?"

"Yes, do I have your word that once I do this tiny action of which you speak that I shall never hear of this ever again? It would be ill advised for this topic to ever reappear again at some future date. I am not without connections myself."

Oh, the King was a shred man, the Cardinal observed. He cleverly avoided saying that he was being blackmailed. He wanted assurances that the next time the Cardinal wanted something from him, he would not use this against him a second time. Cardinal Drakon replied, "You have my sacred, solemn vow that I shall never, ever bring this matter up with you again, not unless you become unfaithful to Queen Athena again. If you betray her again, I will be forced to take further measures. You can understand my position, can't you?"

"Okay, I accept your word as the Cardinal. What must I do to make this go away and still provide for my unseen son?" King Damon sighed, resigned to do what the man asked. He had no choice, he thought.

"Tomorrow night, I want you to make up some excuse to have your palace guards be nowhere around Queen Athena's bedroom when she is asleep. You will see a man dressed all in black — yes an assassin. Call out her guards to give chase. Next morning, you would be advised to visit the Alexina Estate at the northern edge of Theolopolis. Normally, it is unoccupied at this time of year. She will be there and in need of your assistance. You may pretend that you have somehow discovered her abduction and have located where she was taken. After that, the entire world will be watching your marriage. I urge you, do not make the same mistake twice, King Damon."

"I give you my word that will be done. How will I sleep nights knowing what I have done to her?" Suddenly, Damon had a fit of conscience.

"Sir, you have *done* nothing to her. That is God's truth. In this matter of her abduction and treatment, you are blameless. You will indeed see an assassin outside her rooms. You will have done absolutely nothing *to* her, that I guarantee you. So relax, your secret is safe, and you have an excellent opportunity to redeem your soul, a chance that very few sinners have. You are blameless."

"Thank you," King Damon found himself saying, though he did not know why he was saying this. It was obvious that somehow his darling wife was about to become a Holy Woman of the Eighth Degree against her wishes. Well, he promised himself that he would do everything in his power to make it right with her. She would not lack for anything! A somber King rode his carriage the many miles back to his palace in Theolopolis. The next night after he returned, he did see a man dressed in black milling around outside Athena's suites as the Cardinal had said. At once, he sent her guards after what appeared to be an assassin in the night.

Chapter 34 Into Action Once Again

On January 1, 751, a rider pulled up outside Number 42 Hampton Way, now widely known as the House of the Precocious Witches! Yes, we kids were now five; we adults all healthy with our arms back to what they should be. I say we, because six of us were now trying to cope with running two bodies at the same time! I think that Dita-Renzo and I were probably doing the best with it, although we found ourselves constantly becoming confused by having double perceptions occurring at the same time. Our dear friends were, to be blunt, having an awful time of it.

These two sets of five year old triplets were supposed to be our replacement bodies. Linda and the Great Messiah or Guardian both thought that the Mano del Dio would kill our older bodies with their guns. Thanks to Dianna-Enyo that did not happen. Now we were faced with trying to cope with operating two different bodies at the same time, most confusing at best. Linda did say that the Guardian thought that we could handle it and that it would be spiritually beneficial for us. Okay, we were giving it our best shot.

Enrico let the rider inside and brought him into my cramped study. "I've a letter for one Enrico Angela. Sign please?" I didn't see any paper for him to sign and wondered what was up. Instead, I saw Enrico draw a circle in the air with his finger and then place two overlapping triangles inside it. The messenger nodded and gave him the oilskin wrapped package. He said, "If there is a reply, I will be at the docks on the Lucky Charm." He left and I asked Enrico what that was all about.

"It's the secret sign that we in the Forze Segrete use to identify each other. I ought to have drilled you in it before now. This is from Demokritos, Bethany," he replied.

"I thought that in each group there were only six members. Was he one of the six who traveled all the way up here? How did he know you? Is he part of your Forze Segrete group? I know that you said there were only four of you."

He grinned. "It is time that we fully indoctrinate you into the workings of the Forze Segrete. I can see that. No, whoever sent this first sent it up the line to the next group above them. One in their group sent it on up and so on. Eventually, it started back down the chain of command until it got to a member here in Velona or perhaps the fellow is from Demokritos itself. I didn't ask."

He opened the watertight container and found a sealed envelope inside. "Well, I'll be! It is addressed to you. Well, it's actually been forwarded to you from someone else." Enrico was so curious, that he opened the envelope only to find yet another envelope inside. However, its seal was broken. Attached to this second one was a short note.

I'm sending this to the very top. I think it warrants it. J. S.

"Well, whomever received this has sent it to the top, that's you, my dear. Can we read it together? I'm dying to know what it says!" I chuckled and agreed.

June 5, 750

Theolopolois, Theos

Help! This is Athena Patra, now Queen Athena. Damon and I have just been coronated here in Theos. Something terrible is going on across all of Demokritos, and I am now afraid for my life. I guess I should begin at the beginning. It all started with the assassination of Emperor Deimos and his wife. No one ever discovered who did it. The Church of Jehosanity, which I will hereafter refer to as simply the Church, heavily pushed for Argos and Kassandra Aias to take over. She is of the Eighth Degree. At the time, 743, the queens of Thallyus and Alia were also of the Eighth Degree. Many of us began to suspect something insidious was going on behind the scenes.

Our group kept a tight watch on things here in Theos. Until recently, all the action has been elsewhere. As you know, because of the Dorota mess, to say nothing of the Church and its widespread promotion of Holy Women of the Eighth Degree, there are thousands of such pitiful women here in Demokritos. It is an epidemic of horrible proportions! While we watched, over these last few years, primarily promoted by the Empress herself, all the seven kings and queens have taken on about thirty of these women and their families as palace workers. At least it does give them some means of support. From our investigations, these particular women were in the most desperate of ways before they came to work at the palaces. At first, we thought that perhaps this was simply a humanitarian action. Now it looks far more insidious than we first thought. Something is going on, but we have not yet been able to find out what.

In 745, the King of Phindos succumbed to old age. My group learned that his death was very suspicious. Our group closest to the royal family suggests that he may well have been poisoned. What really convinces us of that is that the group reported to us a year later the attending doctor had also died mysterious! Once more, the Church went all out to force them to coronate King Dorieus and Queen Adonia Kadmos, who is a Holy Woman of the Eighth Degree.

Not a year later, the king of Penelopus died. In front of a hundred witnesses, he slipped on the ice and cracked his head. His death may have just been fortuitous. Once more, the Church heavily backed the couple ultimately chosen to succeed him. King Errikos and Queen Danae Haimon. Again, she is of the Eighth Degree!

The next year, the King of Thrace died mysteriously. Again, our people closest to him suggest it was once more poison that was used, though no one could prove it. His doctor claimed his heart failed. Guess who launched a big campaign to support the couple chosen to succeed him? The Church. King Dimitrios and Queen Ariadne Diodros took the throne. Once again, she is of the Eighth Degree. We recently learned that the attending doctor has also died.

No sooner had all this happened when the King up in Arolas and his wife drowned in the Pinos River. Our group there swears that someone had sabotaged their boat. Once more, within days of their deaths, the Church was lobbying everyone for their choice of successor. In early January, they coronated King Hermos Pegasos and Queen Alekto. Again, she is of the Eighth Degree herself.

Here in Theolopolis, my dad, who like myself, is dead set against such mutilation of women, went ahead and unilaterally put Damon and me on the throne. That was a month ago now. He then retired. I've inherited and had to deal with having a personal staff of some thirty of these Eighth Degree women. Admittedly, these are fine women who try to do their very best, but they are useless, if the truth honestly be told.

Can you see the larger picture? The Empress and six of the seven queens are all the Eighth Degree. All those rulers who did not have such women on the throne have met their deaths, either natural or unnatural. I am now terrified for my own life! Damon has upped our security here at the palace in Theolopolis, but truthfully, I am scared that something awful will happen to us.

I am begging you to send me some help before it is too late! Please, I am begging you.

Queen Athena Patra
(Forze Segrete)

"Wow! We didn't know all of this," I exclaimed. "We've got to get down there fast, Enrico."

"Bethany, look at the date. She sent it six months ago! Damn, it took so long to filter up to us. She could be dead by now," he pointed out.

"What took six months? What was the message?" asked Dita, who now led everyone else into our large home. The kids, however, were still out playing ball. Dita wore a man's shirt, pants, and shoes. For the last three years now, she had taken to wearing only men's clothing and had several very fine suits, complete with twin tails and black top hat. She still kept her extremely long, thick black hair. I wouldn't let her cut it. Only if I asked her too would she wear her fancy ball gowns any longer. I stopped asking her to do that long ago.

I had everyone read the long letter from Queen Athena. "So when are we going, Bethany?" Dita asked as she finished reading it. I chuckled. I knew that she would insist on going.

"Very soon, dear, I think it best if only you and I go down there," I replied.

At once, Enrico, Luisa, Sandra, and Arturo began to protest, but Enrico's voice carried over the others. "Bethany, we are charged with protecting you! We can't let you go off into a highly dangerous situation!"

"Look everyone," I explained my reasoning, "even if Dita and I somehow have our bodies killed down there, we are still right here at the estate. Get it? Our bodies here are expendable. Yours are not and besides the kids still need all four of you. You are still guarding and protecting us here, get it?"

They did, although it was confusing. "Look, we ought to be able to contact other Forze Segrete folks down there if we need them and we can always send for all of you, if need be. Heck, we don't even need to use a Mind Link. I can just talk with my other Bethany body or Dita can with her Renzo body. Besides, I have a hunch that I am going to need some of you searching through all those bank records for clues. I need some of you up here, Dianna." She looked like she wanted to volunteer to go as well.

Of course, trying to keep Kali here was more problematical. In her previous life, she had been a resident of Demokritos and heavily involved in the underground movement there. Her knowledge of that country was vast. "Kali, I suspect that you too want to go, but I need you here going over the bank record of Demokritos. You have a good feel for the politics there. Perhaps you can make some vital discoveries that we can use somehow to rectify the mess down there. If we really need you, a caravel can have you there in three months or less." Kali sighed, knowing that I was right. She, of all of us, had the best chance of working out hidden conspiracies of Demokritos from the voluminous bank records.

"Okay, you win, Bethany. Now here is how the Forze Segrete hand signals work. If you are approaching someone whom you think may be one of us in another group, first you trace out a circle in the air. If the other person is one of us, he will duplicate the circle and add an enclosed triangle. You are then to inscribe another triangle upside down to the one they just drew. This way, both parties can confirm both are Forze Segrete."

Dita and I, along with the others, practiced the motions with Enrico monitoring us. "Just how many groups of Forze Segrete do we have in Demokritos?" I asked out of curiosity.

"One hundred that I know of at last count. However, they are pretty wide spread across the country. With seven kingdoms and the Emperor's palace, that is a lot of area to cover. Queen Athena has worked her way into a position of power. No one else has such a high position that I know of at this time," Enrico replied.

"Come on, let's get packing," Dita urged me. "Time's a'wasten!"

"What should we pack and take along?" I asked.

"Keep it simple," Dita replied. "My weapons, several changes of clothes. Honestly, we don't know what their dress customs are for sure. We can always buy new things that we need when we get there. It's mostly the long voyage to survive."

"She's right. I will transfer some expense funds for both of you to Patri," Kali replied. "Make for Patri, Thrace. That'll be the closest port. Take or buy a carriage and drive up to Kefall, where the main road into Theos ends. Follow that road up the Lonki Basin into Theos. From there, stay on it until you hit Theolopolis. It is impossible to get lost if you stay on those two main roads. There are many inns along the way. So be sure to pick up your funds in Patri. You could also transfer them on to Theolopolis if you wish. That might not be a bad idea, take what you need for immediate expenses and transfer the rest on ahead."

Dita and I headed into our room to pack. "If I take these dresses, I'll need several traveling trunks!" I exclaimed, looking at the volume even one dress occupied.

"Well, you could choose to wear pants like me. I think I can get enough into one large bag. If I absolutely have to have a dress down there, I'll just buy one. Besides, dear, how do we know that they wear cone dresses there?"

I stuffed several day dresses into a pack, along with a shirt and pants. It took me a little longer to get the miscellaneous items together. Hairbrushes were a necessity. When we were finally ready, we each had one large duffle bag stuffed. Dita also had a smaller bag filled with weapons. In the end, she decided to leave her longbow behind. "You know," she said as we took a final check of our things, "traveling this light, we could go by horseback. I suspect that would be lots faster than by carriage." I liked that idea.

We then said our goodbyes. Our little girls, now pretty much into their teens, said that they would really miss us. I pointed out that we really were not leaving them, that we were still right here with them. I pointed out my Bethany body and Dita's Lorenzo body. Everyone roared.

Enrico drove us to the docks and went aboard the Lucky Charm. He wanted to verify that all was actually on the up and up and to know when the caravel would sail. He was pleased to discover the ship was actually one of the Banca del Dio fleet. It's captain, Rodrigo, had just finished transferring a gold shipment and replied, "Aye, we can sail whenever you like. There is no return load this time. You women can have the main guest cabin. Of course, you'll have to put up with the fifty guards below decks." He gave a chuckle.

"Captain Rodrigo, it is vital that Dita and I get to Patri, Thrace, as soon as possible," I explained.

"Say, don't you work for the Banca del Dio here in Velona?" he asked.

I replied that we did. He then said that he would pull out all the stops to get us there as fast as possible. I didn't know that I had such pull! As we walked across the main deck to head down to our cabins, the crew eyed us and a few whistled. A long blonde haired woman with a long black haired woman made an unusual voyage for them, I suspected.

Entering the hallway to our cabins, we met the messenger who had delivered the message. Quickly, I made a circle and he replied adding a triangle. Dita then finished it off properly. He seemed greatly relieved, though he wasn't sure why two women were responding to the urgent letter. We decided to chat with him once we had stowed our things and were underway. Both of us wanted to watch the caravel set sail out of our beloved city of Velona.

Two hours later after Velona became a small dot on the horizon, we had him join us in our cramped cabin. His name was Kastor Gyros and he was from Patri. We pumped him for more information, which he readily provided. His detailed knowledge was limited to his own kingdom, Thrace. However, he pretty much substantiated everything that Queen Athena had told us in her letter.

Kastor certainly gave us a queer look when we introduced ourselves as Mrs. Dita and Bethany Brozena Malina. That we were a married couple surprised everyone onboard. However, Kastor was very helpful when it came to transportation and the long trip to Theolopolis. He agreed with Dita, "Yes, it is about six hundred miles from Patri to Theolopolis. If you go by carriage, it will take some twenty days. If you get good horses, ride from dawn to dusk, and don't stretch them, you can make it in around fifteen days."

"Perfect. That's for us," Dita exclaimed, excited about a long horse ride.

"In that case, I can map out for you how far to go each day so that you end up at an inn by dusk," Kastor volunteered.

"Now that is helpful," she declared. He smiled and promised to have it worked up by morning.

"Say, it is a three month voyage, Dita. I couldn't help but notice that you are packing many weapons. I assume that you know how to use them? Care for some practice sessions? Helps break the monotony." I thought that Kastor might also be curious about Dita, after all, she was just gorgeous with a superb figure to match her face.

"Sure you're on! I do need the practice. I am still a little weak and not quite up to speed as I ought to be," she admitted, though she dare not tell him why — that her arms had only recently regrown enough so that she could swing a sword again.

Captain Rodrigo, true to his word, continued to fly all the sail possible. Traveling light, we made excellent time on the run from Velona down to Patri, Demokritos. Only one unusual event occurred, I say unusual for me. Normally, a caravel would make a stop at one of the far Southland ports to take on fresh water and perishables. Captain Rodrigo explained that the black savages were on the warpath and that the combined armies of Megalos and Demokritos were battling them. Hence, no Southlands port was truly safe to utilize now. We stopped at a small Megalos western port to resupply. The usual ninety-day run was completed in just seventy-five days.

Ah, what do you do for that length of time cooped up on a small caravel with around sixty men, fifty of them fighters, and only three women, one being their portly cook? As soon as Kastor and Dita began practicing their sword fighting skills, many other of the ship's defense men wanted to have a round with her as well. She was a knockout and this, she admitted to me, she used to her advantage. Dita-Renzo needed all the sword practicing she could get and with so many men with varying styles and skills, she loved the challenging workouts.

During a break, while they were cooling down, Kastor asked, "Say, Dita, what do you think about all these guns that everyone is now using? It's making all our sword skills kind of obsolete, isn't it?" Over a dozen others overheard this and joined in the discussion.

About all Dita got to say was, "I really don't like them; they let you kill from a good distance. I like to face the man I'm fighting." After that, these Forza di Sicurezza men took up the argument. We found out that half of these men were armed with these new guns. While the army was buying at least half the guns made, guns were cheap enough that nearly anyone could buy one. Everyone's conclusion was that in another ten years, probably no one would be using a sword any longer.

They got off on a tangent, discussing the use of the cannonae. Some related stories of how the Emperor's legions were using them against the black savages of the Veld in the southern part of the Southlands. Others told of seeing some caravels of Velona being outfitted with cannone to be used either as shore bombardment devices or as anti-ship guns. Both Dita and I had seen firsthand the carnage these cannonae wreaked on the legions of Emperor Deimos during the battle of Zargarb, albeit I was the Empress and he was defending Zargarb from us at the time. Thus, while the Forza di Sicurezza men were enamored of these cannonae and guns, she and I were quite the opposite.

Dita surprised me on the second day out of Velona. She had brought along a torque ball and set up a court down in the cargo hold. Admittedly, it was a cramped space, but that made the game more challenging. Other men at first watched us battle it out and then soon asked to join it. Some challenged Dita's rules, wondering why she put in that second horizontal line. She didn't want to try to explain that she did it so that armless me and later armless she could play. Dita merely explained that it made the game more challenging.

For seventy days, the sounds of sword play or torque ball filled the cargo hold. We all found this passed the time far more quickly. When the lookout called out Patri ahead, I realized that we had the best voyage ever, far from utter boredom. Everyone headed on deck to watch the action, as the white marble city with its red tile roofs and grayish hills came into view.

Kastor said, "Look, when we land, let me take you to my home. My wife, Amynta, is one of us. She ought to know the latest news. I can send a rider to Theolopolis and let Queen Athena know that you are coming. Meanwhile, I'll arrange for some good horses for you. Do you want some of us to tag along and make sure that you get there safely? It would look better if you had a man traveling with you."

"Thanks. We'd like to meet Amynta, and good horses would be just what we need," Dita answered. "But look, you've been gone for about six months now. You should spend some time with Amynta. We can find others of the Forze Segrete along the way." He looked relieved and I knew Dita was right.

Memories came back to me as we docked in Patri. Many landmarks were still there, the Santi tower, for example, but so much had changed. The port had grown and now could handle twenty caravels at one time. An hour after we docked, the three of us arrived at Kastor's modest home on the edge of Patri.

When Amynta saw him, she shrieked and jumped into his arms. She had light brown hair, short, with blue eyes and a lovely smile. She was short and somewhat plump. Their two year old son sat in a baby chair where he could see everyone. Kastor had to give little Tas attention as well, picking him up and twirling him around, "Daddy's back now. Missed you, little Tas."

"Aren't you going to introduce your friends here," Amynta got his attention onto us two still standing in the doorway, watching the family reunion.

He flushed and said, "Sorry. Amynta, I've brought back the top Forze Segrete people. This is Mrs. Dita and Bethan Brozena Malina. They are married, you see."

"So very pleased to meet you! Such a light skin color. I didn't know that Velona folks were so tan. I mean we are bronze colored, but I thought Velona folks were pretty much white. I do say that you both look positively beautiful. Don't just stand there; come on in. Kastor, take their bags for them. Where are your manners?"

"We're fine, Amynta. You've a fine looking boy there," Dita countered.

"Amynta, can you believe that Dita here can whip me with swords? She's one heck of a sword woman. They are answering Queen Athena's plea for help. We are kind of in a hurry, so Amynta, why don't you bring them up to speed on all the latest news, while I go see if I can find two good horses.

They want to ride to Theolopolis starting at daybreak."

She agreed and he took off to make some arrangements. Amynta offered us tea and honey biscuits, along with some cheese. Once we were snacking, she began to explain what had happened during the last six months. It was awful. "Oh I think that you are too late for Queen Athena! Four months ago, they got to her!"

"What? She's been assassinated?" Dita cried out, nearly spilling her tea.

"Might as well have. No, she was abducted during the night, right from her own bedroom in her palace! So much for palace security! King Damon found her a day or so later at a summer country estate whose owners were gone for the winter. They had cut off her arms! Someone made her into a Holy Woman of the Eighth Degree! Her father, the former King of Theos, he was so angry that he had a heart attack and died! It's been awful, just awful. Now all our ruling women are these Holy Women. Helpless women, we call them. God help us. What is happening to Demokritos? So I'm afraid that you are too late. You might want to pack up and head back, dears. Not much more you can do here, I suppose. All I can say is that the rest of her Forze Segrete group — she was one of us, you know — they ought to be fired! How could her own group let this happen to her? Now she is worthless. It's a crying shame, I say."

"Damn, damn, damn," Dita cursed. "Say, was Damon pushing her to become one of these Holy Women?" she asked. I saw that she had a flash of insight on who might have been behind it.

"Oh no. Damon, like her, was publically against it. Damon has always been quite outspoken about doing such vicious crimes against our womenfolk. Maybe someone wanted to get back at him? Who knows? Probably will never know."

A while later, Kastor returned. "Okay, it's all set. You have my map. I have two top-notch horses out back. I took the liberty of sending one of our group on ahead of you to let Queen Athena know that you are coming. He ought to get there a day or so before you."

"Dear, they might not want to go now," Amynta scolded him. She explained to him what had happened. He looked devastated!

"It's all our fault! We took too long to get to Velona and get help!" he chided himself, rubbing his hands through his lowered head.

"No, it is not your fault," I declared flatly. "It is the fault of those who did this to her. We are still going to her as fast as we can. You have my word," I said solemnly, "that we will find those who did this and see that they are punished." This appeased both of them. Later, he took us to their large Banca del Dio, where we transferred funds to Theolopolis, withdrawing some to cover our expenses at inns along the way. Already the fall colors began to dot the landscape, while it was spring back home.

Early the next morning, Dita and I saddled up, stowing our bags securely behind our saddles. Dita, as usual, wore men's clothing and had tied her hair up in a bun beneath a cap. Except for her well-endowed bosom, she looked the part, well mostly. I wore pants and a blouse. We donned a pair of riding cloaks, mounted, and waved goodbye to our hosts.

"My, has Patri grown!" I commented, as it took us nearly a good hour to clear the city and finally hit the open road. Once free of traffic, Dita and I opened the horses up! Now we were living! The wind blew my long, blonde hair behind me like a pennant. For ten days, we rode like the wind, pushing the horses as hard as we possibly could, making sixty miles a day, on the average — twelve-hour days, mind you. For Dita and me, this was one of the happiest ten days that we shared together, although I do admit that we were very sore those first couple of nights.

Kastor had outlined our inns perfectly. At each one, we were able to make contact with a member of the Forze Segrete there. He or she saw to it that our horses were well cared for and that we got good service. Several insisted on covering our inn expenses, but they all wanted us to tell them whatever world news we had, particularly that of Velona.

Communication back home to our families was a bit weird. No, it was downright strange indeed. While Dita and I could have used telepathy, we didn't need to at all. Instead, when I wanted to chat with the others, I spoke using my five year old Bethany body. Likewise, Dita would chat with everyone using her five year old Lorenzo body. When others wanted to give us information, they merely told little Bethany or Lorenzo, which were us, of course. Confusing? I'll say, but it worked.

We learned that Ania (Alexa) had not been idle. She'd seen the demand for news and had just invented or rather started up a new project in Velona. She called it a Paper of News, in which she published on several pages all the latest things going on in and around Velona. A copy cost a copper and had already become a big hit there. However, the locals refused to call it a Paper of News. Instead, they began calling it the newspaper. Ah well, at least Ania was doing her thing. Politics and personal relations, governments and groups were her keen interests, as well as the latest fashions.

Around noon on our sixth day, we began gaining elevation as we rode up the spectacular Lonki Basin rim. Here was a steep cliff, which formed the natural boundary around the entire Kingdom of Thrace. The scenery was something out of a storybook, impressive indeed. Once we reached the top, we were now in Queen Athena's kingdom of Theos.

On March 28, 751, we finally entered the outskirts of Theolopolis, too late to save Queen Athena from being mutilated, but here to pick up the pieces anyway and prevent further tragedy. Once more, Kastor's map was invaluable. It was already dark and far too late to try to make the palace today. Instead, we followed his advice and stayed at his indicated inn.

We had just been served our late dinner around eight that night, when an older man and woman came up to our table. He discretely made a circle in the air. For a second I stared at him before I realized he was sending me the secret signal. I hastily duplicated his motion and added a triangle. He finished the signal and they sat down beside us.

"I am Morpheus Polopis, my wife, Zona. We are part of her Forze Segrete," he whispered. Dita introduced us to them. He then said, "Too many wandering eyes and ears. We should talk in your room later." Dita told him our number, and they left us, heading to the bar for a round of ale.

Dita and I continued eating. We were very hungry, not having had a proper meal since early breakfast. Around noon each day, we just had snacks while we rode on, unwilling to waste time on lunches at inns. A bit later, we headed on up to our room. Not long after, Morpheus and Zona knocked and Dita let them inside.

Morpheus was thirty, tall and lean, bronzed skinned. His black hair was not quite to his shoulders and he had a distinctive moustache. His eyes were penetrating, missing nothing. Zona was two years younger and four inches shorter, with dark brown, shoulder length hair, and dark blue eyes. Both carried short swords, but Dita spied the bulge of several throwing daggers concealed on Zona.

While we sized them up, they were doing likewise. As they looked at me, they saw a very blonde woman of twenty-three, whose thick, straight hair fell below her waist. They saw that I was tall and lean and had sharp, light blue eyes. Morpheus would have said that I was good looking. Dita was the same height, with thick, straight black hair that also fell below her waist. She had black eyes to match and was armed to the teeth with weapons. Yet, her clothes were distinctly male, but her large bosom gave her away, if her face and hair had not. Morpheus would have said that she was a knockout! Both of us had light brown skin color, vastly lighter than theirs.

For a moment, Morpheus was not sure who was in charge, glancing at Dita and then me. I broke the ice. "She's my wife. I am Bethany Brozena Malina and she is Dita Malina. We're from Velona. I guess you can say that we are the Forze Segrete top dogs. I am sorry that we didn't get Queen Athena's letter until the first of January. We left the day we got it and made all haste to get here as fast as possible."

"Looks like we were too late," Dita added.

Still marveling over our relationship, Morpheus asked, "So you are a dyke, Dita? I don't quite understand."

Dita flushed, "We are madly in love with each other. I am her Protector. She's the boss lady, so I wear the pants." She hoped this would satisfy their curiosity.

"Dear, that's their business," Zona chided him.

"Yes, but Dita will raise all kinds of questions if she goes around the court dressed as a man, love. That can't be useful," he replied.

"I can wear a dress when I have to," Dita replied, setting him at ease.

"We rode hard for ten days to get here from Patri. I figured that if we looked like a man and woman traveling together, we would be safer. We've transferred our funds to the Banca del Dio in Theolopolis. We came with few clothes, because we didn't know what clothes we ought to have to blend in down here and wanted to travel as light as possible. I guess we need to get outfitted properly tomorrow."

"Whew. I am relieved. Yes, that was very wise, Dita. Tomorrow, Zona can help get you new clothes. Then, we can take you to the palace. However, perhaps we should make some plans, first."

"Thanks, can you tell us what happened to Athena and what the current situation actually is? You are part of her Forze Segrete group, right?" I asked.

Zona took up the tale. "There were six of us, including Athena. Then, she got married, but we decided not to bring Damon into our group. Alexio didn't trust him. Alexio was killed. Oops, I'm getting ahead of myself. Alexio and his wife, Zoe Brosios, Barnabas and Xene Novia, Athena, Morpheus Polopis and me, made up our group. When she became our Queen, Barnabas became her carriage driver, while Xene became her handmaiden, but now she's her personal assistant. Alexio and Zoe didn't trust Damon from the start, and after she moved into the palace, those two took turns watching her bedroom from the distant streets during the night."

"The night it happened, Alexio was there. Zoe found him in the morning in a nearby alley. His throat had been cut. If only we could have heard what Alexio must have seen that night! Ah well, anyway, we concluded that someone drugged her and stole her out of the palace. Damon claims to have seen a black cloaked assassin fellow on the palace grounds and set her guards after the man. Yes, the guards did chase him; there is no doubt about that, but that must have been a diversion to allow them to sneak in and take her."

Damon went nuts the next day trying to find where they had taken her. Somehow, and we just can't figure this out, he discovered that she had been taken to a vacant summer estate on the edge of the city. He and his men went there and found her lying in bed. Her arms had been amputated! Someone had made her into one of those useless Holy Women of the Eighth Degree!" She spat on the floor in disgust. "Damon said that she was screaming in terror when he found her. She still does, according to Xene, who is constantly at her side now."

"How's she managing now?" I asked.

"Not well at all. According to Xene, she is terribly depressed, unhappy, and miserable. Who wouldn't be in her condition? Answer me that," Zona retorted. Obviously, she was totally against this Holy Woman aberration. "She missed the Fall Council in Kefall. Damon went; he had to go, but she said that she was not up to traveling yet. Damon and his advisors all reported that the Empress was very saddened to hear about Athena, and she sent three of her very special servant women to attend to her needs. Strange women, never seen anything like them before, really weird. You'll see. This Holy Woman thing is supposed to bring the loving couple closer, well it hasn't! Athena refuses to allow Damon into her bed anymore. According to Xene, she is horribly ashamed of how helpless she is and hardly allows him to kiss her now. Serves him right for allowing this to happen to his own wife!"

Morpheus added, "We've heard that the Empress herself is coming to visit Athena two weeks from now. Apparently, she thinks that she can help Athena to adjust. Guess we will have to see on that one."

"How do the members of your group communicate to each other?" inquired Dita. "Those two are in the palace, I take it."

"Yes, they live there with Athena now. Xene sleeps with her, swearing that she will not let any further harm come to her. Honestly, at this point, I think that Athena needs Xene just to be able to live," Morpheus replied. "Each day, Barnabas, their driver, comes to the inn just outside the palace for his evening round of ale and darts. He's been a fixture there for seven years now. Everyone expects him to drop by nightly and thinks nothing of it. One of the three of us is always there. We exchange messages with him, if there are any. There has been little to say since she was brought back from the estate, though. It's been mostly words about how badly she is doing."

Zona took up the discussion at this point. "I sent word to Athena yesterday that you two were arriving any day from Velona. I assumed that you would want to stay there with her, right?"

"Absolutely!" I replied, glad for her thoughtfulness. Zona was a bright woman and intuitive.

"Good. We needed a cover story for you that would not arouse suspicions. Via Barnabas, Athena is expecting two of her distant cousins from Velona to be coming to spend some time with her. I chose Velona, because not only we knew that's where you are from, but also because I figured you'd have an accent. I was right; anyone hearing you speak can tell that you are from Velona."

I grinned, "We're that bad?"

She grinned back, "Yes, but that is to be expected. What I didn't expect is that you both are not white skinned. So strange. I'd swear that you are from Dorota! But that cannot be; the women there are all missing their arms."

I flushed. I had not realized this detail, though I should have! I thought quickly, "Our father was from Velona and our mother from here, so our skin color is a mixture of them both. That is what we think, anyway."

"Ah, then that will fit with the cover story I made up," Zona said, very much relieved. "Zoe will meet with us in the morning and she and I will help you two get some acceptable court clothes. Once you are with Athena, she might have better suggestions for appropriate attire for her court, so we'll just keep it simple tomorrow."

"How has Zoe taken the murder of her husband?" Dita asked.

"Badly," Morpheus answered. "I know that she has spent untold hours trying to find clues to tell her who was behind it. Bright woman, Zoe. She has some evidence, but not enough to pin down whom just yet. She's convinced that it was one of the Church's Mano del Dio men that did it. None of us can figure out why. Alexio was not a threat to their Church in any way."

"How many of these Mano del Dio men are around?" asked Dita. She knew that we had killed a rather large number of them in Constanza City.

"Not that many, fortunately. We've never seen more than six at any one time here in Theolopolis, but usually only two. In Kefall where Cardinal Drakon Erebos lives, Zoe reports once seeing eight. It may well be that they travel around Demokritos a lot." Dita was relieved and I knew why. Though we chatted a bit longer, nothing more of significance turned up.

The next morning, we carried our bags down to the inn for breakfast. We spied Morpheus and Zona already having theirs and joined them. A young girl, perhaps a year younger than we, was dining with them. Zoe was as blonde as I was, but she wore hers very short, barely six inches long. She was short, but well-muscled, though her blue eyes still carried the sadness of the loss of her husband. Although Zoe had been briefed about us, nevertheless, she eyed us closely, particularly Dita, who still was dressed as a man, though her hair made any such notions evaporate in an instant; she wore it down this morning.

As we were about to leave, Dita asked, "Should I wear one of my swords or is it safe not to?"

Zoe gave her a double look, "How many swords do you have?"

"I came armed for a fight, but perhaps I am late. Been practicing a good deal with all the fighters on the caravel during our trip down here. I'm in pretty good shape now, if trouble comes."

"Impressive. Sometime, maybe we can have a round of practice," Zoe suggested. "I didn't quite take you for the fighter type — you know, such long hair and such a pretty face. I bet you have lots of guys coming on to you." Dita flushed.

"Unfortunately so, but I'm perfectly happily married to the love of my life, Bethany here. I pay them no mind," Dita attempted to talk her way out of this confusing situation. Zoe gave her and me a strange look.

Zona broke in, "Well, we should get you to a dress makers. Zoe thinks that we should just get you one dress. She says that Xene tells her that the ladies at court have fancy dresses, so maybe Athena can better tell you what you really need to get."

An hour later, Dita and I looked at each other in our new dresses. She wore a cardinal red satin gown, while mine was a rich blue satin gown. Identical styles, just different colors, our dresses fluffed out a few feet with several petticoats. "Well, I guess we look the part of distant cousins from Velona," Dita commented, "but I'd rather wear my suit."

I grinned, "I know, dear, just wait a while until we get back home." We headed outside, where Morpheus had rented us a carriage to take us to the palace. He'd already stowed our three duffle bags inside and he held his hand up, helping us climb inside.

He whispered, "Keep us posted via you know who. We are ready to help in any way possible." I thanked him and the driver rolled out onto the streets of Theolopolis. We gazed out the window at all the white marble. While the hills were darkish, these people were fanatical about their white marble buildings and statues. Unlike the open aired temple style buildings of Megalos, where heat was a killer, here, they used marble for even their outer walls, making the city shine brightly in the daytime. The many red tiled roofs contrasted along with numerous shrubs and climbing plants, to say nothing of the flowers. Here, they grew flowers from pots of all kinds, seeming inventing new ways to hang or support their pots. Many had special marble slabs protruding from just below their front windows. Uniformly, these were filled with growing plants of all types. The trees were just beginning to change into their fall hues.

Theolopolis was a city of about a million people, thus quite large. The paved streets thronged with people, pushcarts, vendors, wagons, and carriages, such as ours. It took us an hour finally to reach the center of the city, where their palace sprawled over a four city block square area, surrounded by a six foot marble wall, entirely overgrown with richly colored vines. At the gatehouse, two uniformed guards halted our carriage briefly. After checking on us, they motioned the driver to continue and we got our first look at the insides.

The king and queen lived in the largest of the marble structures, huge by our standards, and the carriage pulled up near its ornate entranceway. Here tall columns supported a vaulted roof over this grand entrance. We saw a Doorman and a young woman standing there. We got our first look at one of these Holy Women who had become employed at the various palaces around Demokritos. She wore a brown dress, and the moment she saw us, the Doorman opened the door and she entered hastily.

Our driver pulled up and soon opened our door and extended his hand to help us climb down. We took a few steps forward out of the way, and he proceeded to retrieve our bags, sitting the three near us. He nodded and climbed back onto his seat, and the carriage pulled away. Just then, the Doorman opened the door once more, and the young woman in the brown dress reappeared, leading another man and woman, who were smiling broadly and moved directly to where we were standing.

"Good morning. You must be Dita and Bethany Brozena Malina, right?" the woman began. She was perhaps twenty-four, with blonde, curly hair and blue eyes. Her oval face was cheerful, but she was slightly overweight. The man looked like a perfect gentleman, standing six inches taller than she. He had brown hair and matching eyes. What I found intriguing was that he looked non-descript in all ways. He was the kind of person that one would never ever notice in a group. He could hide in plain sight.

"Yes, I'm Dita, and this is my wife, Bethany."

"Welcome to Theos Palace. I am Xene Novia, Queen Athena's personal assistant, and this is my husband and the queen's personal carriage driver, Barnabas." We shook hands cordially.

"If you will allow me to fetch your bags, Xene will show you to your rooms," his mellow bass voice spoke politely, only adding to his image of a total gentleman.

"We need to know where and when it is safe to talk," I whispered to Xene.

"I know. Let me show you to your rooms," she said with a slight nod of her head, which I took to mean that she was aware of our needs. Quietly, as if he was not even there, Barnabas followed behind us. "That was one of the many doormen we have in the palace. They open the doors for those who cannot do it themselves, as you can understand. That was his wife there with him; she is one of the many Messengers we have in our employ. They deliver messages throughout the extensive palace complex. We were expecting you and were ready to meet you when she brought us word of your arrival. Other women like her are called Announcers, who will announce arrivals of our visitors. You will also see similar women with small trays fastened to their waists. These are her Fetchers, and they transport smaller things as needed, such as a pot of tea. At least, they are able to do something. As I understand it, these women and girls were victims of that terrible Dorota cult of the Elders. They and their families were very poor, and, when the cult thing fell through, they were left without hope and totally destitute, unlike those wealthier women who could afford a servant to assist them with everything. This is Empress Kassandra's way of showing humanitarian kindness by giving them a job that they can do and a place to live. Ah, here we are."

Just outside our door, a Doorman stood, but immediately opened the door for us as we approached and appeared as if we wanted to enter. Just as we were about to enter, a young girl — she couldn't have been over fourteen — came running up to Xene. She wore a brown dress, identical to the other girl at the entrance door. She too was a Holy Woman. "Xene, Queen Athena needs your help."

"Thanks Alexis. Tell her that her distant cousins have just arrived, and I will bring them to meet her in a few minutes."

"Okay!" the young girl replied cheerily and dashed off to relay the message to the queen.

We entered. After closing the door, Xene said, "We've only got a minute, so I'll talk fast. This is your private room, and it is safe to talk to anyone in here. That door back there leads to the large private bedroom of the queen herself. I took the liberty of giving you this adjoining room. The king no longer is allowed into her room. More about that later. Our room is on the other side of hers, but I often spend part of the night with her. She needs so much help. Across the hall is where her special brown-skinned Personal Helpers stay. Don't be too shocked when you see them. Looks can be deceiving. These women are very caring, very helpful, and very intelligent. Leave your bags for now; we'd best get to Athena quickly."

"Do we need to run?" asked Dita, growing concerned for Athena.

"No, she has those three special Personal Helpers with her. They can handle nearly everything that she may need physically. They even feed her. Come on; she probably wants something those women cannot do. Maybe it is something with the king or the preparations for the coming visit of the Empress herself." She chatted away as we walked down the halls to the queen's room, a throne room separate from both his private throne room and their formal, large throne room where they met visitors together. "You've heard that Empress Kassandra is coming?" We replied that we did.

Entering the Queen's Throne Room was like walking into a formal room on Dorota, so many women were armless here, shockingly so. Unlike Dorota where the women were able to do so many things themselves, here the women were helpless. No one had ever shown them that there were alternative ways of doing things for themselves. That was the way of the Women of the Eighth Degree, where their wealthy husbands provided servants to do everything for them. A Doorman opened the door for us as we approached and closed it after we entered. Another Doorman stood here beside the door on the inside.

We saw three women in the same style brown dress, Messengers, we presumed. Three others wore green dresses and had small trays tied to a band around their waists with two straps going from either front side of the trays up to their necks, supporting the tray. These, we assumed, were the Fetchers. A woman wearing a green dress stood right here by the door, and she politely asked our names. Then she spoke loudly and clearly, her voice carrying beautifully in this large room, "Mrs. Dita and Bethany Brozena Malina from Velona." Everyone stopped and looked at us.

Chapter 35 Queen Athena Patra

Which woman was Athena was obvious, the young woman sitting on the only throne in the room. She looked forlorn, morose, quite depressed indeed. She wore a billowing blue gown, which suited her complexion. Her shoulder length, wavy, blonde hair matched mine. Her eyes were a deeper blue than mine were. My height — she was twenty-three, the same as Dita and I. Her face was perfectly formed, and she was particularly beautiful, though in that department, many claimed that Dita had her beaten.

Rather what shocked both Dita and me the most was not the queen but her three Personal Helpers, as they were called. All three women were brown skinned, not black or bronze or tan, such as Dita and me. We'd never seen people of quite that skin color before. They wore brown dresses similar to those worn by all the other women here, except Xene and the queen herself. Rather what commanded our attention were their necks and lips. Golden coils were wrapped around their necks from their shoulders to the very bottom of their heads, as far up as they could go, making it seem that they had incredibly long necks. Both lips had been split lengthwise, cuts as wide as their mouths. Inside the opening, round clay disks were inserted and were about four inches in diameter, holding the thin rope-like remnants of their lips out in a circle slightly larger. In order to support the weight of the disks and to keep them from drooping downward, two front teeth, top and bottom, had been removed, giving the disks a firmer base of support. To say that these women looked strange was a total understatement of magnitude!

While we gaped and stared at them — yes, I admit I did stare at them, Dita too — the others in the room stared at us. Some thought that we came from Dorota and became alarmed that we might be here to seize them. They had nightmares now about the Elders and doktors of Dorota, who had deceived them into joining their perfect society cult and having their arms amputated. This feeling, I sensed immediately and quickly dispelled it.

"Welcome to my court," Athena said sadly. "Sorry I'm like this now. I can't do anything anymore. Come cousins. I haven't seen you since we were little girls." We approached her throne. At least, she still kept her wits about her; that was a start.

"Welcome cousin Athena," I said grandly. "It has been way too long. Gosh, how you have grown up! And so beautiful too. Why you were only this high when we last saw you." I indicated a small child with my hand. Turning to Xene as if explaining to her, but really, I was explaining to all the deceived women here, "Our mothers are her aunts you see, and they both married men from Velona. So we kind of turned out half bronze and half white, rather in the middle." Xene nodded, but the relief that I sensed from the other women was huge, and I chalked up a minor victory.

"Athena, dear, Dita and I are *so* glad that you have invited us to come and stay here at your palace with you." I began hamming it up, making it all believable. "Do show us around, please cousin?" I wanted to get Athena into a very private space and conversation as soon as possible.

"What did you need of me?" Xene asked, following my lead.

"Oh, someone said that the Empress loves green. Should we get new green drapes for the room in which she will be staying?" Athena finally remembered what had been asked of her. I suddenly realized that she probably was no longer making any decisions at all for herself! She was wallowing in self-pity, justifiably so, I thought.

"Say, that is a good idea, let's. Alekto, get word to the stewardess that we need this done, please." At once, one of the Messenger girls bolted to the door, the Doorman opening it for her.

"Queen Athena, why don't we adjourn to your private chambers and give you and your cousins a chance to chat? I'm sure that the official business can wait a while," Xene suggested. Athena mechanically rose, and Xene put her arm around her waist to steady her as she stepped down from her throne. Like a zombie, Athena followed Xene, with us two following behind them. Again, the Doorman politely opened the door for us, though he need not have.

A few minutes later, we entered her private suite of rooms. She sat down in a plush chair and made some slight attempt to talk to us. "I'm sorry I'm like this. I didn't want to be."

"That's okay, Athena. We came the very day that we got your letter. I'm so sorry that your message took so long to get to us at the top of the Forze Segrete. I can see that I need to make some changes in our lines of communications."

"I wish they had just put me out of my misery. What kind of a life can I have like this? They should have just put me out of my misery," Athena said in a hopeless apathy.

"Are you hungry, Athena?" I asked. Dita immediately knew where I was headed. She took Xene aside and whispered a lengthy explanation to her.

"No."

"Okay, then I want you to close your eyes. Good. Now let's see if you can contact the first moment when they kidnaped you from your room." She obeyed, and my first therapy session was off and running. Dita explained to Xene what may happen, that in the process, we might learn key details that might pin down who had done this to her. They sat quietly by the door, having asked the Doorman to wait outside.

Considering the depths of her apathy, I knew that it might take days to get her trauma erased. It was slow going at first just as I expected. "I'm so very tired for some reason. I fall onto my bed with my dress still on. Hands.

Hands pick me up. I'm moving somehow." After a long pause, she said, "I'm opening my eyes. My shoulders hurt. I try to move my arms to help me sit up. Nothing. I look at my shoulders and see these blood soaked bandages where my arms used to be. I screamed." Indeed, she let out a yell, but the room, fortunately muffled it. "I scream and scream, then Damon and his guards come busting into the room. He is shocked, and he carries me to his carriage and brings me home. That's all."

I thanked her and asked her to go through the whole event once more. Then, we took a break for lunch, which Xene fed to her, unwilling to allow her three Special Helpers to do it. Once we ate, I went right back to it. Around the tenth time through it, Xene began to pay close attention; Athena began recovering some key data that was said to her while she was unconscious.

"My late night tea is already in my room when I enter that night. I notice my window was open, but I didn't remember having opened it. After I drink my tea, I feel so very tired. I fall onto my bed. A man is lifting me up and carrying me out of my room. I try to wake up, but can't. A man says, 'I got her. Get going.' I'm in a carriage. I hear the horses and wheels. I'm moving somewhere. Now I'm being lifted onto a cold flat something. Someone is taking off my dress. I'm going to be raped, I think. Something is in my mouth. I have to swallow it. A voice says, "She's out cold. She can't hear or feel a thing anymore. I try to say that I can, but nothing works right."

"Pain! Pain shoots in my left shoulder. A voice says, 'there, that does it. Sew it up.' It feels like pin pricks around my shoulder. Pain! Pain shoots in my right shoulder. Now a voice says, "Well, that's that. Pity, we really should have put her out of her misery. What kind of a life can she have like this?" Another voice says, 'No, the Cardinal said that she must live. So make sure that you do a fine job of sewing her up.' Other voice says, 'Have a look. Perfect, wouldn't you say?' Other man agrees. I feel pressure on my shoulders. Oh, it's bandages; they put a lot of bandages on them. Man says, 'She'll sure have a pitiful life now.' Other man chuckles and says, 'Okay, she's stable. Time for us to leave. Damon is supposed to be here shortly. I heard footsteps. Then silence, total silence. Long time. I wake up. I see my shoulders and scream and scream. I hear men's voices and shouting. I hear running feet. Damon comes running into the room. He takes me home."

It was all that Dita could do to keep Xene from rushing out to find Barnabas and relay this incredible news! The Cardinal was the one behind this, and somehow Damon was involved in it too! By whispering to her that there might be even more discovered, Dita finally managed to get Xene to sit back down, as I put Athena back through it once more.

Twice more she went through it and then she opened her eyes. "Oh my god! They said that we really ought to have put her out of her misery. What kind of a life can she have like this! That isn't me. It's them!" She began laughing wildly, and I quietly ended the session; it was way past suppertime. "It's them! No wonder I don't want anything to do with Damon! He was somehow involved in it! I feel so light! What was that you did for me?"

Xene asked a Messenger woman to have our dinners brought up to the queen's room tonight. "I need to get all this to Barnabas before he leaves."

"Okay, but tell them not to do anything about it just yet. We need to find out more," Dita ordered. Xene left and soon the three strange Special Helpers arrived carrying large trays with food, drink — the china and silverware were for us. The Doorman again opened the door for these women who had their hands full.

"Come on in, Oda, set them anywhere. I'm eating with my cousins tonight," Athena said, then laughed again. "Oh, Dita, Bethany, these are my three Special Helpers that Empress Kassandra gave to me to help me with everything. She's called Iua, she's Oda, and she's Ida. They can't talk plainly, obviously because of their lip plates, but they are very bright and can write us messages instead."

They fixed plates for us three and then Ida sat beside Athena and began feeding her. Dita and I dug in, hungry as well. Naturally, I wanted to know all about these three special women, but now was not the time. Athena needed my full attention. We had not needed to look for earlier traumas, and I was a little concerned that she might relapse into an earlier one, if there was one. When we finished, the three left, and Athena asked her Messenger to have a pot of tea sent here. Her Messenger dashed off.

While we waited, Athena said, "The Empress had my dad take on thirty of these women and their families. They were all desperate, you know, near starvation and such. While we hated this whole business, dad took them on for humanitarian reasons. I'm glad that he did, now that I'm like this too. They are really helpful, when you can't do anything for yourself."

Soon the Doorman opened it again, and a Fetcher woman entered. Her tray held a teapot and three cups. Carefully, she came over towards us. Dita took them off her tray, and we three thanked the woman, who smiled. Dita poured our cups. "Forgive me, Bethany, I am afraid that you are going to have to help me drink it. If you'd rather not, and I can understand that, I can get Oda to help me."

"Nonsense." I held the cup so she could sip.

"It is just so awful, you know, being like this. I just can't do anything at all for myself. I just can't do anything." I noticed that her tone began to sag and got very alert. We chatted a bit longer, and she sighed, "I guess you need not have come. I just can't do anything for myself anymore."

I ask her to close her eyes and then if she saw images of an earlier trauma that was similar in nature to what she'd recently undergone. After a bit of fumbling, she replied, "I see a whitish picture." I was off once more. "Oh! They did this to me before! I am with a man. I think we are in love. Oh no, there I am walking into an operating room. I drink something and he says it will be all right and to relax. I did. Everything goes black. Oh! Pain! They are cutting me." She described the operation in detail this time. "Now they seem to be done. One says, 'There, done. She'll never be able to do anything for herself again.' Another voice says, "Yes, I know that she won't be able to do anything for herself. I've got servants for her now.' Oh!" Athena suddenly opened her eyes. "Oh!" She started laughing again.

"That was my husband talking. Duh. I never did do anything for myself after that. I hated being like that and swore I'd never do that to myself again. Duh. Now here I am again like that." She laughed and laughed.

Finally, she said, "Well, I don't suppose that I really can do much of anything like this now can it? I mean how?" She shrugged her shoulders. Suddenly, her face lit up. "Oh, those women on Dorota. I've heard that they do nearly everything for themselves. I wonder how they do it? Do you think that there is any way I could find out?"

Dita could not help but reply, although she was careful not to divulge too much. "Sure you can. We've met some and they do almost everything but heavy lifting. They use their feet and some told me about how their husbands built them special chairs and tables and kitchens and all sorts of things so that they could do their usual housework. We've heard lots about them up in Velona."

"Oh wonderful. One day, I just must figure that out. I don't want to always have others doing everything for me."

"Until we can arrange those kinds of things, Athena, you can still do many things to run your country. You are bright and know many things. You certainly can speak and issue orders to your staff and whomever to carry out your plans for Theos. You can make a good queen," I stated, trying to give her some doable ideas right now.

"Well, yes, you are right, of course. Dad taught me everything I need to know to run our kingdom properly. I don't need arms to do that and this is a big responsibility. Damn, what about King Damon? I don't trust him now at all! He had something to do with this."

"Well, play it cool for now. Let Dita and me see what evidence we can uncover. Pretend that you don't know his real involvement for a while, okay?" I suggested. She agreed.

Her change of attitude was remarkable. Everyone noticed it the next day. She was now cheerful and happy, though she continued to stay totally apart from Damon. Armed now with specific dates when these events occurred, I asked Kali back home to begin a thorough examination of all large money exchanges slightly before and after the date in question.

The third day of our stay, Athena asked me if it were possible for me to deliver my therapy to her other thirty women who were like herself. "Honestly, I feel so alive, so happy, I can hardly sit still."

"Have you been out and about your palace?" Dita asked.

"Well, no. I've just stayed indoors. Gosh, I'd love a walk and fresh air! It's autumn."

"Good, how about you taking a long walk and show us all around your complex here? As far as the other women, both Dita and I can do it, though as you have seen, it does take some time."

"Well, we have time now. Since the Cardinal was somehow involved and since now all of we queens and the Empress are of the Eighth Degree, I don't think I need to worry so much about being assassinated any longer."

"Probably true, but Dita and I need to find out why all this has occurred. Okay we will work with your women, but only after we get to see your beautiful palace here," I agreed. I was torn between my sincere desire to help all these other women and my desire to quickly discover what was really going on here in Demokritos. In hindsight, perhaps I ought to have delayed these other women's therapy sessions.

As we walked, Athena asked, "Dita, are you two really married? I mean like a real marriage, like unfortunately Damon and I are?"

"Sure, we are madly in love, and we had a beautiful wedding ceremony in the best church in Velona. Oh, I see what you mean. Most people just don't understand us. Kastor thinks I am a dyke."

"But how do you — well, in bed, I mean. It's not like Damon and I used to be. Damn that I ever fell for him anyway."

"No, we do things differently. We've adopted two girls so we have a family back home," Dita chatted on.

"But you are so gorgeous, Dita. You could have any man you wanted," she pressed her.

"I don't like men. I am in love with Bethany here," Dita finally admitted as much of the truth as she dared. In normal society, you just don't go around talking about having lived before. Fortunately, Athena accepted this explanation. The extensive walk and fresh air did wonders for her. She began seeing the world as a bright and wonderful place once more.

I decided to have a chat with one of her special Helper women. My curiosity swamped me. Before I tackled the thirty women, I wanted to know more about these most unusual women. Where did they come from? Okay, more importantly, why did they do that to their lips? And why were they stretching their necks, if that's what it was. It certainly greatly inhibited their movement, though already I'd seen that all three had nearly perfect posture.

With Athena's permission, Dita and I had a private chat in our room with the woman called Iua. She entered with a questioning look in her eyes. Did we really need her help? We had arms. "Hi Iua, come on in and have a seat. Athena said that we can ask you some questions about yourself. Is that all right with you?"

She nodded in her unique way. Her neck could bend only the smallest amount, so she bent at the waist, which gave us what appeared to be an affirmative nod. "Can you speak?"

".es," she replied. We couldn't decipher the first consonant, but the vowel and "s" sound were clear enough. Neither her lips nor large four-inch plates moved while she talked, well only slightly at best. They were pretty much fixed in place, forced solidly against her remaining teeth.

"Where do you come from?" I began, thinking this was as good a place to start as any. I didn't want to ask the obvious right away.

"U.u .a.ion," she said. Neither Dita nor I caught this one, though she repeated it twice more. Finally, she took out her small paper pad and pencil and wrote it for us. "Utu Nation."

"Do all the women in the Utu Nation have long necks and disks in their lips?" I asked.

"O. .o," she said, moving her head horizontally to the left and right, which we took meant no. She added, "O.ly .in.esses." this we just didn't get either. She again wrote it out for us. Only Princesses.

"Oh, I didn't realize that you are a Princess! Wow. I'm honored to meet you," I said nobly. Again, because of the tight, large disks, we could tell no real facial expression in a reaction to what I'd said. She was obviously unable to smile. Duh, I thought to myself.

"Why do you wear those lip plates? They must be terrible to wear," I finally asked what I really wanted to know.

"Se.y .em .o.e ..em," she said. Again, after two repeats, I had her write it, thankful that she somehow had learned to write Demokritos. Sexy. Men love them. We are very beautiful this way. She added a bit more than she had tried to say.

"And your neck gold bands? Same thing?" I asked.

Again, her head moved from side to side, indicating no. I asked her about them. This time she did not try to say it. She wrote: Not gold, brass coils. Long coil wrapped around neck many times so it is not loose. Neck coils show everyone in our nation that we are their Princesses. Princesses are the most honored women in our nation. We give new life to our people. We have many babies.

Dita interrupted my reading to say, "Bethany, I think those are tears. I think she is crying about something."

"Are you sad or upset about something?" I asked. She nodded, or rather bent her waist vigorously. Suddenly, I realized that she was sitting right in the middle of some terrible, tragic loss of some kind. She needed therapy too! But how? I couldn't have her write everything; that would never work. Then, I had an idea.

"You have seen how happy Athena has become haven't you?" She did her nod-bend again. "Well, I gave her my therapy and erased all of her pain and upset and trauma. Now she is much more alive. I would like to give you my therapy too so that you no longer feel so sad. Is that okay with you?" Again, she did her head-waist nod.

I explained what I was going to do. She said, ".o .an ..i.e ..a. .u.." She again wrote it: No can write that much.

"I know. That would not work. I have another way. I will join my mind to yours. You can think a thought and I will hear it. I can think a thought to you and you can hear me too. Shall we give it a try?" She did her head-waist nod and I concentrated and gently touched her mind.

Close your eyes. Good. Now I want you to go to the very beginning when you first had this loss. She did and I had her going through it, telling me what was happening.

We are in our long house, brushing our hair. A dozen of us Princesses live here in this house. Our door opens and a strong, big bronze man comes in and grabs my arm. He pulls me out of house. I try to say men are not allowed in House of Princesses, but he does not understand me. He drags me over the little rise and another man locks an iron chain on my leg. He leaves and another man brings Ida and chains her to me. In minutes, twenty-four of us Princesses are all chained together. They make us start running together or we fall down. We run and run. They ride horses.

I know that our men will be coming after them soon. It is a very bad crime in Utu Nation to harm or steal a Princess. Men are usually killed if they do it. I know these bad men are going to get killed soon now. We run all day. I see herd of antelope being driven back across the ground over which we just walked. I laugh, silly men. That will not stop Utu men. I still think that they are going to die for taking us. Next day, we climb into the mountains, where Utu never go. I know that will also not stop Utu men. I hear the sounds of Utu men getting closer now. Soon, these bad men will be killed and we can go home and have babies again. Now bad man lights a fire. Soon whole narrow valley is on fire. Tall flames. My heart sinks. Utu cannot get through the flames.

We are forced to walk again and soon we go down the mountains. I can see the ocean now. A big boat is there. We are led onto the boat and taken below. A man nails our chains to a large timber so we cannot escape ourselves. Boat starts rocking. It is moving. We are all terrified and scared. Many are sick and throw up. We are in the boat many days. They give us a bucket of water to drink and some food. It tastes bad, but we eat it anyway.

Now the boat stops and we are led on deck. What is this place? None of us knows. We see many bronze skin men and they lead us into a long, dark tunnel. I am afraid now. After a long while, I am lost. I know that I can never ever find my way back through this tunnel! We come out of the tunnel into a stone house. There are women there wearing black robes. We are unchained and these women are kind and lead us to a room with beds, tables, and chairs. We are washed, and they put strange clothes on us. They give us food and water.

Days and days, they teach us to understand their language and then to write it a little. Finally, when we can understand these kind women, they tell us that we can never go home and that we have to learn to help some needy women. I cry and cry and cry. We all cry. We all just want to go home to Utu.

Then, they bring in ten women. None have any arms! We are all shocked to see them. We feel very sorry for them. They cannot do anything to help themselves. The women teach us how to feed them and care for them. We already know how to brush their hair. We worked hard to learn how to put their fancy clothing on them. After a long time, we prove to them that we can take care of these poor women. We are then told that we are going to be taken to some very important women who have no arms and that our job is to care for them and to help them.

At last, I know that I am never going to be rescued or ever return to Utu. My old life has been stolen away from me. Yet, these women most desperately need our help. All of us agree that we would work hard and do our best to help these poor women.

Much grief came off during her lengthy pass through her tragic loss. I thanked her and had her go through it all once more. On the tenth pass, the grief did not lift and grew stronger. Accordingly, I asked her if there was something that happened earlier in time that was similar. At once, she saw the connection. A year before, she had a painful childbirth, which we went through, but the child was stillborn. For her, this was a tragic loss sitting on top of the birthing pain. After several passes through it, the pain erased, and she started laughing, though it sounded rather strange to our ears, the disks interfered again. *I decided I was not a fit mother to take care of children. That was stupid of me. My baby's body was missing some of its parts and could not live and grow into a man. Silly of me to decide that!* I ended the therapy session.

Her eyes were bright, though I had no way to tell if she were smiling. She seemed radiant, though. "..an. .ou," she said. I got that one and replied accordingly.

After she left, I told Dita, "Now I know why the black savages are on the warpath against those from Megalos. They've been in the slave trade for centuries now. This time, they stole the wrong women. I'll bet anything that the Utu men are on the warpath, trying to find where their Princess were taken." Dita shook my hand.

"How are we going to get them back to their home land?" she asked. I shrugged. I had no idea about that. These women were scattered all across the seven kingdoms and were really helping these Holy Women of the Eighth Degree.

The next day, as Dita and I were getting ready to start in on the many therapy session for Athena's staff, Iua came to me and asked, "..ease .i.e ..e.a.y .o Oda an. Ida." Again, I had to have her write it out for me. "Please give therapy to Oda and Ida." I told her that I would do that once I finished with the women for whom they were caring. Again, I could not tell if she was smiling or not, but she did her head-waist nod and left.

As Dita and I began working the first two older women, we rapidly discovered a horrible mess. Yes, they all had the underlying trauma and pain of their surgery, but that was totally covered up by the betrayal of the Elders, then being forsaken, and just dumped back into normal society, in which their husbands could not afford to have anyone be their servants. Fend for yourself while I try to earn enough for our supper was all too commonly heard. What a mess. What a tragedy for these women. Dita and I had to unravel the complex mess of pain, unconsciousness, loss, betrayals, and even near starvation, to say nothing of their emotional state of near apathy and death. It took us a whole week on each woman to get them finally straightened out and the root trauma erased!

By the time of the arrival of the Empress, we had only gotten four women handled, but they were now full of life, enthusiasm, and vigor. Naturally, the other women couldn't wait to get our therapy.

Chapter 36 The Visit of Empress Kassandra

On April 15, fifteen carriages pulled into the palace of Theos. Empress Kassandra had finally arrived. I knew this woman must like to control things, because she had sent a rider on ahead of her convoy of carriages to notify us of the precise minute that they would arrive. Consequently, many were standing outside the giant double doors of the main palace building.

King Damon stood beside his wife, Queen Athena, with Xene at her other side to assist her. Damon never volunteered to help her now unless she directly asked him, which she avoided at all costs. Dita and I stood beside Xene. On the other side of Damon, Iua, Oda, and Ida also stood, ready to help as needed. Additionally, many of the other women and their husbands and children also stood well back of this front group.

Once the lead carriage halted, the driver and the other man dismounted and opened the carriage door. Carefully, a woman appeared wearing an emerald green dress. She mostly fell out of the carriage into the arms of the driver, who caught her and gently sat her on the ground. She took small steps forward until her enormous dress was clear of the carriage. Her dress flared out sharply at her waist, spanning at least a circle fourteen feet in diameter around her. I recognized at once her tiny waistline and knew that she had to be wearing a tight-laced corset to get her waist that small.

Out stepped two other women, one wore a similar dress, but only ten feet across. Unlike the Empress, she had normal arms. She moved to one side of the Empress. Out stepped another of these special brown-skinned Helpers, which Iua had said would be Udua. I began to understand their names. Mostly they consisted of recognizable vowels and the limited consonants they could utter clearly. One by one, the other carriages began unloading as well.

Once Udua was at her other side, Empress Kassandra, head held high, began moving towards us. At once, I saw her amazing illusion. It appeared that both she and her companion were somehow floating or gliding across the cobblestones towards us. However, their speed of travel was so slow that Udua had constantly to compensate. Well, she moved with grace, I gave her that.

She came up to us and totally ignored King Damon. "Oh Queen Athena. You look so lovely. Why I don't recall ever having seen you this radiant! I had heard that you were, shall we say, depressed, but how wrong that certainly is! You look incredibly beautiful, Athena. You too, Damon."

"Welcome to Theos Palace, Empress," Queen Athena replied. She also saw that the Empress was not paying any attention to Damon. "We've got our best guest room ready for you. Our home is your home. I must say, your dress is amazing. You, too, look fabulous, Empress."

"Just Kassandra, dear. Let's not abide by such formalities. This is to be a visit between friendly women. Damon, no offence, but you may be excused. I've no official business with you or your advisors. This is purely a social visit with your charming queen."

Relieved, Damon said, "Very well, Empress. If you need anything, just send for me. It is a real honor to be able to entertain the Empress here at our palace. Good morning." He bowed and he headed back inside, followed by his advisors.

Another woman wearing the same style dress, only hers was blue, moved or rather glided up to the Empress. Both Dita and I saw at once that she was from Annelise, not Demokritos. "Allow me to introduce a very special guest. This is Princess Maren Ditka from Annelise! She is the granddaughter of King Hans and Queen Mia Ditka, who knew the famous Maren Elizabet!"

Recognition swept over me! When I was Maren Elizabet, Hans and Mia were my constant companions, helping be my arms! I could see a bit of each of them in her! I didn't hear all the welcome words that Athena gave her, but from her infectious smile, they pleased the young teen. I noticed that her waist was substantially smaller than Kassandra's.

Princess Maren bubbled, "Don't you just love this new dress of Empress Kassandra? And did you see the way that she just glides along now? She has the glide down perfectly. Such elegance, such grace!"

"Yes, very impressive, both of you. Please, why don't we show you to your suite of rooms and let you freshen up a bit, before we all chat in my private throne room," Athena played gracious host.

We entered the palace; the double doors were just barely wide enough to allow Kassandra to enter without bunching up her wide dress. We noticed that Kassandra, her Personal Assistant Selene, and Princess Maren moved at least half as fast as we, perhaps even slower. Kassandra make pleasant chat that the suite would be just fine. We left them to unpack and freshen up and headed to Athena's throne room, where she had added more soft chairs. She took a seat close to the throne, intending for Kassandra to occupy her throne. Wise move on her part, as Kassandra immediately headed for it when she was Announced as she entered about a half hour later.

After Kassandra sat down, Selene quickly adjusted the fall of her gown, before taking a seat next to Kassandra. Princess Maren sat next to Selene. "And who are these lovely young women beside you, Athena?" Kassandra asked.

"My cousins from Velona have come to spend some time with me, Kassandra. We haven't seen each other since we were children. I am so glad that they have come. Their presence has helped me recover. I've never felt happier in my whole life," Athena bubbled enthusiastically. Then, she realized that she forgot to introduce us, "This is Mrs. Dita and Bethany Brozena Malina. They are married, you see." Princess Maren's eyes did a double take. Empress Kassandra's eyebrows rose slightly.

"So very pleased to meet you, Bethany and Dita. Athena, you surround yourself with such beautiful women. At first, I thought that they were from that island place, Dorota, but then anyone can see that they have arms, and Dorota women are like us. I assume that one of their parents was a white Velonan?"

"Our fathers," I lied.

"Oh, I see. I do hope that your visit is not taxing Queen Athena too much. You see, she is still recovering from her tragic abduction and mistaken surgery. Athena, dear, has Damon figured out who abducted you yet?"

"No, I doubt that we ever will," Athena lied. She hoped and prayed that one day she could get the whole inside story.

"Tragic, yes, but I am so impressed with you, Athena. When I heard the news that you were too distressed to attend the Fall Council, I told the Emperor right then that I just had to make a personal visit with you and do my very best to help you adjust to a life as a Holy Woman. I know dear that you were totally against such, but now that you are one of us, I feel it is my duty to help you deal with it. I know how hard it is for you. Even though Argus and I both wanted me to become a Holy Woman and we had everything all worked out in advance, when I awoke from the surgery, I screamed too. It is most scary at the beginning," Kassandra chatted away. Dita and I both recognized cold ice behind her words!

"I must admit that I am very, very surprised to see you so, well, cheerful. From all the reports that I had, you were quite depressed. Such a dramatic change, Athena. It does you well."

She was probing for the reason. Athena sensed that, but she was not about to tell her about our therapy. She replied, "I owe my total recovery to my dear cousins from Velona. When they arrived two weeks ago, I was really in the dumps. I didn't even go out to welcome them! After being around them for two weeks, I am so utterly happy. My shoulders no longer ache either. I am planning to ask them to stay on and be my personal advisors, if they will. Both are so knowledgeable. And Dita is quite the sword woman. I could use more protection. I don't want what happened to me a few months ago to occur again! I am rapidly running out of body parts to lose!" Dita and I grinned at her jest, but the humor was lost on Kassandra. She was still absorbing the fact that Athena had the audacity to ask us to be her advisors and that Dita was a sword master.

"Is this true, Dita? Are you indeed a master of the sword? Dear me, what do they do with women up in Velona! Well, I do not expect that anyone will harm Athena further. After all, it is a very high crime to harm a Holy Woman of the Eighth Degree here in Demokritos. Men have been put to death for so doing. I'm sure that Athena will not need a sword master to protect her any longer. It is a shame that you didn't come here four months ago. Perhaps you could have prevented her abduction."

"I know. I would have protected my cousin here with my life," Dita readily admitted.

"Well, Bethany, I must thank you for having had such an amazing, almost unbelievable, effect on our Queen Athena here. Tell me, what is your secret for turning her from the depths of depression to such wonderful heights of enthusiasm," Kassandra pressured me.

"Oh, I have my ways with women," I said coyly, winking at Dita. I hope that she would get the wrong idea, that I somehow gave women pleasures. As she glanced at Dita, she again saw an amazingly pretty young woman and did get the wrong idea. Athena was nearly as pretty as Dita. That apparently satisfied her curiosity.

She changed the topic. "Say, do you realize that Princess Maren here and I both share the same idol? We discovered this on her first visit to Demokritos. Our idol is the famous Empress Marin Gavril, from Annelise!" She detected my sudden surprise. I couldn't mask it in time. This tidbit came as a sudden surprise to me. Damn, I had all sorts of trouble with that Maren body.

Athena came to my rescue, "Well, yes, Kassandra, you are now just like her in many ways. You are of the Eighth Degree just as she was and you are also Empress and you are wearing similar gowns, as I recall our history."

"Oh yes, yes. I am so very glad that you mentioned this fabulous gown. My outfit is the height of fashion in Annelise! You were not at the Fall Council, so I thought I had better have a talk with you about it. You see, dear, I have decided that all us women who meet in the main throne room must from now on wear such outfits as we three are wearing! Everyone must learn the art of gliding across the room. It is so elegant and refined. We in Demokritos must show the world that we are most refined women indeed. This includes our advisors and our assistants. However, our Special Helpers and the others, the Fetcher, Announcers, and Messengers are exempt. They are to continue wearing their usual color-coded dresses. That way, we can all know at once who is a Messenger and so on."

"Now I know that it is so very difficult to learn to wear these outfits. I certainly had a time of it, but Princess Maren has devised a method that speeds up our learning to glide with ease. I sent dress makers and a representative from Annelise back with the other six queens, so that come our Winter Session, they will all be suitably well dressed and can glide with ease about the palace."

"Mind you this is not a request, but an official Empress order. I don't mean to be harsh, Athena. I told the other queens exactly this as well. I don't want anyone of them or their advisors showing up at the Winter Council dressed in any other way, you see. I am trying to avoid any ill at that time.

I'm sure that you will want to learn to wear such absolutely stunning dresses and to glide like an angel across the dance floor."

"Mind you, don't wait to start learning. It does take quite a bit of time to get comfortable wearing these magnificent dresses and to walk in the heels and glide. I would urge you and your staff to start in as soon as possible. I know that the other queens already have a head start on you, but I am sure that with the proper dedication, you and your advisors will manage."

Princess Maren finally interrupted Kassandra. "She is going to have me stay with you and help you learn to wear our dresses and the proper way to walk! Isn't that just fabulous! I was so excited when she asked me if I would do it for you. I'll return to Kefall with you for the Winter Council. Don't worry. I'm a good teacher. Just ask Kassandra. I taught her and she now does just beautifully, don't you think so?"

"Yes, I was flabbergasted when I saw all three of you gliding up to us," Athena had to admit. "I've never seen anything so graceful before. I do hope that I can manage."

"Oh I am sure that you can," Kassandra replied. "You are like me now, and I learned rapidly. With Princess Maren's guidance, I am certain that you will all do just fine indeed. After all, we queens must be just perfect — set the very best example that we can for all the people that we represent. Don't you agree, Queen Athena?"

"Yes, we must all set an example for our people. You'll get no argument from me on that one!" Athena had to admit she had a point.

Kassandra went on. "Now the dresses ought to be made of satin. We all think that has the very best look and feel. The choice of color is up to the individual person. I only insist that none chose emerald green — that's the color of my dresses, as you can plainly see." Indeed, that was the color of her huge dress.

"Athena, I do believe that you would look perfect in a royal blue. What do you think?" Kassandra chatted away, unwilling to leave this topic.

Athena giggled. "Do I have to choose right now?"

"Well of course not. I've sent along quite a few different colors. There is enough in each bolt for one dress. What you don't use, please bring back with you when you come this summer. With Princess Maren are three dressmakers who can make your dresses. Just don't delay; it takes a lot of work to make one. Also, you will find a wide assortment of boot sizes. Our special boots that go with these dresses must be imported from Annelise. Since there is no time for you to do that, I've sent along a large bunch. Certainly, one will be the right size for you and your assistants. Again, just bring the rest back when you come."

"Also, when you do come, please bring along what your shoe sizes are and your dress measurements. The dressmakers will write this all down for you. You see, I will be sending in an order for more of these for us all later this winter. I'll be sending the order back with Princess Maren when she returns in early August. Mind you, there is no cost for you queens. It is my personal treat to each of you and your assistants. I so fell in love with these dresses and the gliding that I just have to spread the word about them to every woman. I know that I am giving you all rather expensive gifts here, but it pleases me."

Athena had to say, "Thank you very much, Kassandra. You are being very generous indeed. On behalf of my staff, thank you. Perhaps one day I can give you a worthy gift in return."

Kassandra beamed. "Perhaps one day you may. I am so glad we had this chat. I was prepared to stay as many days as needed to cheer you up. However, now I can see your kind cousins have done my work for me. I hope you don't mind if I leave for Kefall in the morning?"

"Oh no. I was hoping that you would stay for several days. Maybe take in a play or concert. Yet, I know that the Empress has many, many duties. I am so honored that you took your valuable time to come to visit me personally. Thank you ever so much, Kassandra. I will never forget it."

Kassandra smiled. "Well, that being settled, perhaps I can have a small tour of your palace here. We can talk more over dinner. I would like to chat more with your charming cousins as well."

Athena rose to begin the tour. "Oh dear me, Athena. Why don't you let one of your Messengers show me around? I think it best if the dressmakers get a start on their task, don't you? We can chat more at dinner."

Athena had no choice. She asked her Messenger to give the Empress a tour. Her two assistants went with her, while Princess Maren supervised her Annelise seamstresses. She said, "First, Queen Athena, who are you going to have at the Council with you?"

Shortly, Athena, Xene, Dita, and I found ourselves in Athena's private bedroom, along with the three seamstresses and Princess Maren. Already their coachmen had delivered a large number of boxes into the room for the women. First, they measured our feet and continued, jotting down our measurements. Next, they found the proper boots to fit our feet. We all gasped and stared at the height of those heels.

Princess Maren chatted gaily, "Yes, they take some getting used to wearing. Don't worry; you three will have a much easier time because we can all hold hands as you get used to walking in them. Athena will have the hardest time, I'm afraid. But look how well Empress Kassandra does in them. If she can walk gracefully in them and glide across the floor, so can you, Athena. I will help you all the way. Besides, everyone has a hard time when they first start. So we have worked out a way that makes the learning much, much easier. You will see. It looks harder than it really is. Now then, we have the right starter corsets for you and these fine silk stockings. They are very thin and very expensive. Kassandra just loves how they feel on her legs and feet. We import the silk from Tashien, you see. So what we will do is get you all into the corsets and hose, then get the boots properly tied, and then get our trainer skirt on and tied around your waist. You see, the problem everyone has at first is taking too large a step. The secret is to take very tiny steps. You will see."

While the seamstresses began working their initial magic on us, Princess Maren continued to chat away. "Now with the corsets, you absolutely must wear them all the time, except when you bathe. It is important to wear them even when you sleep, if you want your waist to become small. Now the legendary Empress Maren Elizabet had hers down to a mere fourteen inches! Isn't that just incredible? I've been working on mine since I was about twelve, but mine is still around fifteen inches. Now these starters will make a big initial reduction, but you are going to have to wear them all the time. When you come this winter, I will have new ones waiting for you because by then you will have smaller waists. You will see. It's like magic. Oh, as you can see, the boots fit very tightly. That's so you get more support, and they are re-enforced at the sides so you cannot sprain your ankles."

What had we all gotten ourselves in for? That thought we four held in common, as the women got us into their starter package, complete with the tight fitting hobble skirt, which she insisted would only allow us to take the proper sized steps in these boots. Once again, I felt the tight constriction of a corset, which I had thought I would never wear again, after my lifetime as Maren Elizabet. Once they had everything on us, they helped us back into our dresses, with the seamstresses taking in our waists, which were now about four inches smaller. A tuck here and a tuck there, they kept saying. At least, they were very efficient in their work.

We each chose our color of satin for the new dresses. Athena went with Kassandra's suggestion of the royal blue. Dita, becoming quite obstinate, chose bright cherry red. I chuckled over her choice. Xene chose a pale blue, aligning herself with her charge, Athena. I wanted the canary yellow, but it clashed so with my very blonde hair. As much as I liked the color, everyone shook their heads in dismay. In the end, I went with a sky blue, which blended better with my hair.

The seamstresses then told us that they would have our fancy dresses ready for us in a couple of weeks. Meantime, we were to practice walking as much as possible. Learn how to glide first before you don the wide dress was the best advice they had for us. By now, we four took their advice seriously.

First problem, stand up without falling down. Second problem, keep from fainting. Third problem, try to keep from falling down while taking one step. Poor Athena, she had the hardest time of all of us. Keeping her balance was challenging at best, while we continually held onto each other's hands. Princess Maren was constantly with Athena, for which I was thankful. In truth, the young girl did know what she was doing and soon had Athena walking on her own. Princess Maren, her gown temporarily off so we could see her boots, illustrated how to walk properly. Each of her steps were tiny, one boot just barely in front of the other. Slowly, we four started to catch on, though the hobble skirt enforced the lesson. No way could we take any larger of a step. After our knees began to give out, she allowed us all to recover.

"It is okay if you want to start complaining about how impossibly tight the corset is, how hard it is to walk and all that. Everyone starting out does. It's natural. So go right ahead. I don't mind it at all. I hear it all the time with new women. Yet, you just stick with it and in a couple of weeks, why, you will be gliding across the room as any elegant woman can! You must admit that we look just fabulous in these dresses, gliding along the ground as if we are floating. Such elegance, such refinement, such grace, such beauty. Why even Empress Maren Elizabet would be proud of you a month from now!"

I wanted to stuff my corset down her throat; perhaps that would shut her up! I was feeling awful once again. One glance at Dita and I knew she wanted to do far worse! Then, I opened my big mouth. "You know that your Maren Elizabet died during child birth because she had worn these tight corsets since she was a five year old girl? Her internal organs had been so shifted out of their natural positions that she ruptured, and internal bleeding caused her death."

That shut Princess Maren up, if only for a minute. She turned white as a sheet; her hands felt her corseted waist. Then, she brightened up. "No, I didn't. Perhaps that is why none of us is allowed to wear them until we are twelve! None of us Annelise women have had that happen to us, so that must have been the reason. No, I didn't know that. How do you know all about what happened to Empress Maren Elizabet?"

Dita looked at me as if to say, you idiot! Well, I felt like it anyway. "She moved to Velona after the great battle was over. Emperor Deimos returned here. We come from Velona, and her story is well known in our country. She got married to a wonderful man, but died right after her baby was born. The child lived, but her husband was very distraught and never remarried."

"Wow! I didn't know that, Bethany! Please, you must tell me all that you know about the great Empress Maren Elizabet! You must! You must! Please, please, please," she begged and begged.

I was feeling miserable, so I said, "I will only tell you about her if and when I feel comfortable in this total outfit, and I am able to walk well, and I am able to, as you say, glide across the floor. Only then." Okay, I was grouchy.

Athena heartily agreed with me and laughed. To my surprise, Princess Maren giggled too, and said, "Okay, Bethany. Deal. It will only be a few weeks after your dress is done. I will ask the seamstress to make yours first so we can get you there sooner. I can't wait to hear all about my idol!"

Shortly, Athena's three Special Helpers came. Apparently, one of the seamstresses sent for them. One explained, "We must carefully show these Helpers how they are to properly dress and undress Queen Athena." We three rose and slowly made our way into our room next door.

Once inside, Dita grumbled, "What you women go through is beyond me! I can't understand why a woman would torture herself like this!"

Xene looked confused, "But you are a woman, Dita."

"Not really. I'm a man," she replied, confusing Xene even more. She had just seen a few minutes ago that Dita's body really was female, a well-endowed one at that.

"Well, we are supposed to attract men's attention," Xene stated the usual idea, though she had already married and had not had to dress this dramatically.

"I only want Bethany's attention," Dita retorted. We all realized that we were just reacting to the overly tight corset, tight skirt, and impossible boots.

"Dita, if you can manage to glide over the floor in that cherry red dress, I promise you that I will go nuts over you!" That brought her out of her doldrums.

"Okay, dear. I will be holding you to that promise!" Both Xene and I chuckled. We had to try to make the best of this situation so we could support Athena. She needed us now more than ever, we three realized.

Later, the Empress and her staff joined Queen Athena and her staff for dinner. King Argos and his advisors were notably absent. I found that a tad unusual; apparently no one else did. With these tight corsets, we all ate far less than we normally did. Xene noticed it too. When we had finished, Empress Kassandra asked, "Dita, Bethany, would you accompany me on a stroll around this lovely palace grounds? Fall is such a lovely time; the fragrances are in the air once again. Oh no, Selene, I believe Dita and Bethany can look after anything I might need." Selene had risen with her; the homely woman sat back down. Did I detect a note of jealousy in Selene? I could not be sure.

As Dita and I, holding hands to keep our balance, moved to the door, we were only barely able to walk in these boots. Fortunately, our wobbling was hidden from view by our dresses, which also hid the tight hobble skirt worn underneath. On the other hand, the Empress glided across the room to the door, which made us look like klutzes. As usual, the Doorman open the doors for us as we approached. Most of the doors were far too small for Kassandra's dress to pass. The hoops beneath had to compress as she forced her dress through. "I am going to have all the doors at my palace in Kefall enlarged so that we can gracefully pass them," she explained.

Our steps, as I said, were tiny, with each step, one boot ended up just barely in front of the other boot. Many steps were required to traverse even the shortest distances. Dita and I continually had to think, "Slow!" I realized that it also required an attitude adjustment on our usual speed of motion. While our legs were really working, especially our knees, our overall progress was small. I also noticed that the skirt was forcing a swiveling motion of our hips. I wondered if that had anything to do with this smooth gliding that Kassandra and Maren were so keen on displaying. (Do I sound like I am complaining? Well, I am!)

Outside, the early evening air was cool. She was right; many delightful fragrances drifted into my senses. At last, Kassandra began talking, and fortunately, she slowed down her walk, but didn't totally stop. "I am so glad that both of you have accepted my expensive gifts of these wonderful Annelise fashions. I cannot thank you enough for what you have done for my beautiful Queen Athena. As I said before, I was so very concerned about her, you know. When we heard that she had been abducted and had the surgery performed, well I was just aghast. You know that she alone of the current queens was dead set against having it done, don't you?" We replied that we did.

"You can see why I was so very concerned for her well-being then — all the more so when Argus showed up at the council without her! Dear me, I swore right there that as soon as possible I would come to her myself and do all that I could to assist her in adapting and adjusting to her new, undesired role. You see, we are that — role models for the women of our country. Why even in our Church, we Holy Women are seated in the front rows, positions of great honor. The wealthiest must sit behind us, you see. But I digress. As I was saying, I'm so very pleased to see that I'm not needed here — that you two have done my work for me."

"By chance, can you tell me your secret? How did you get her out of her depression? I was told by Argos that she was depressed and moping around."

Dita sent me, *Watch it. I don't trust her!*

"Well, we helped her a lot just by talking with her about it. I had her tell me all about what happened," I naively explained. While this was not exactly the truth, it was not a direct lie. She accepted this.

"Well, again, I thank you so much for your outstanding kindness. I wish there was something more that I could do for you two women of Velona to show you my appreciation for your assistance with our Queen Athena, other than these new outfits. When you come to the Winter Council, if you need anything at all, my palace is your palace. I promise you I will see that you both are well supplied with appropriate new dresses to match your new waist sizes then. According to Maren, by then you four ought to be down to an eighteen-inch size, assuming you don't cheat and remove the corsets. I'm teasing," she added with a wry grin. "I'm sure that you won't. Athena must show our people she is still an elegant woman who can glide across the floor as well as anyone else. Will you be heading back to Velona after the Winter Council is finished?"

Ah, now we got to the real questions. I decided to be non-committal. "Not really, Empress Kassandra. You see, our dear friend Athena now needs us more than ever. We cannot just leave her in the lurch. No, we will stay as long as she has need of us, years if necessary. I'm sure that you would do the same for a dear friend of yours, right?" I pitched it back in her court.

"Why yes, yes of course. That is so extraordinarily kind of you. Athena is so fortunate to have two such dedicated cousins. I will make sure that you are given enough of these new dresses then, when you come this winter. Consider it my small contribution. After all, you must find it a bit expensive to travel so far from your home for so long."

She was alluding to finances. Dita answered, "Oh, money is not a problem. We are quite independent in that area."

"I see, that is good then. You will not be torn then between your desires to help Athena and coming up with funds on which to live. How are your knees holding up?"

"Badly. We are just barely able to walk in these," I replied honestly, hoping that they wouldn't give out altogether.

She smiled. "Yes, when I first began walking in these, I thought that at any moment my knees would fail utterly, and I'd flop onto the floor. Let us sit a spell on this bench before returning, shall we?" Honestly, a bench had never felt so good to us!

"May I ask some personal questions of you? I've no right to intrude, but dears, I am so curious."

"Okay, but if we might not want to answer," Dita replied.

"Of course. You were introduced as if you are a married couple. Mrs. Dita and Bethany Brozena Malina. Is this so?"

"Yes, we are legally married. I often wear the pants, so to speak," Dita answered truthfully, as this did not seem to be divulging anything relevant.

"Well, I would never have guessed, Dita. You are so pretty! Were you able to have a wedding?" she asked.

"Of course, our special day. We were married in a large church, not the church that you attend here, but one of ours in Velona. We each wore a beautiful white wedding dress. Our wedding cake was a bit different. You see, I love chocolate and so it was a chocolate cake." Dita chatted about insignificant details.

"Oh how wonderful! And you do not find others ridiculing you? I mean you must admit that yours is an unusual marriage, to say the least."

"You mean because we are both women?" Dita, slightly annoyed with her covertness, dropped the social pretenses.

"Well, yes," she was forced to say.

"We don't mind. Just recently, someone called me a dyke. Silly isn't it? We both believe that one should marry out of a deep love and respect for your mate, you see," Dita added.

I didn't quite anticipate her reply. "Oh I so totally agree. One should marry out of an abiding love, indeed so. I'm sure that when your cherry red dress is finished and you are able to glide in it, Bethany will be so proud of you. Just between us, Dita, when you come to the Winter Council, you will find that you are the prettiest woman there! Come, we should be heading back now. Think your knees will hold up?" she teased. Dita and I rose, holding tightly to each other's hand. Ever so slowly, we three headed back inside. I observed that our long walk consisted of one hundred feet here out of doors! Oh, this was going to take some adaption, some getting used to!

That evening when we retired to our room thankful that the day was done, Dita and I discovered that, constrained in our tight corsets, we could not easily undress ourselves. After helping each other take off our dresses, neither of us could bend enough to get to our own boots. Just then, Iua and Odu knocked and came in to help us. Iua wrote: We are supposed to help you undress and dress tomorrow. For once, I was glad for their help in untying the tight fitting boots.

Dita and I crawled into bed. "I don't think I can possibly sleep in this," she said. "Kassandra was sure pumping us for information. She is icy cold, don't you think?"

"Yes, I don't trust her. It feels like she may stab us in the back at any time. We must be alert around her."

At breakfast, Empress Kassandra told Athena, "Now when you come to the Winter Council, I want you to bring along your three Special Helpers and your thirty families of Holy Women. I want them to see the Royal Palace and give them a treat so few of our people get — a royal tour. I've asked all the other queens to bring theirs along as well. Besides, we will need much extra help, what with so many of us Holy Women around in one place. I insist that you bring all them along, dear."

Athena had no choice but to agree with the Empress. Later after she left, King Argos dropped by wanting to know what all the Empress had wanted. Athena told him the scant details and whom all she insisted travel to Kefall this summer. He looked annoyed that so many carriages would be needed. "Damn, we have to have a whole convoy! Okay, no crossing the Empress. I'll see to the details, Athena." He then left.

As promised, the Empress left the next morning after breakfast, leaving Princess Maren buzzing like a bee around us four women, especially Athena. Her three seamstresses began their lengthy sewing. Dita and I needed to get going on all the other women's traumas, but we had a buzzing bee in the way. Fortunately, Athena, who also wanted her women's traumas handled, took action. She insisted that Maren spend the day helping her adjust and learn to walk. Quietly, Dita and I slipped away to begin work on two more women.

Later that day, King Damon reported to Athena that the Winter Council would start on June 20 and run for a week. Considering the journey was some three hundred fifty miles by carriage, he insisted that we take as little time as possible on the journey. "You will spend long days in the carriage, dear. I want to get there in ten days at most. We leave on June 10, so you must be all packed by then." He left her to see to the myriad details of transporting her large staff.

Chapter 37 Time of Therapies and Practice

Thus, we had fifty-four days to both handle therapies and to learn to deal with these outfits. Maren worked out a schedule for us four, insisting that we walk several hours each day, gradually increasing the times. In two weeks, when the dresses would be finished, she had us scheduled to wear them for several hours each day, again while walking. Practice, practice, practice, she continually cheerily insisted. This also cut in on our therapy times.

Dita and I estimated that we would only be able to handle fifteen more women before we had to go to Kefall. We had thirty women and girls in need of the therapy, plus two more Special Helpers. I handled the two helpers first, since theirs were unlikely to take too long. By the time that we had to pack up and begin the long carriage ride, fifteen of her staff of Holy Women had their traumas erased. All had a new lease on life, vibrant and alive. Naturally, the other half wanted it as well, but they knew they'd have to wait awhile.

"How long must we wear these awful confining hobble training skirts?" I gripped to Princess Maren. I found them terribly restrictive and annoying.

"Until you no longer need them," she cheerily replied. Dita groaned. "Just keep practicing your walking. You are doing fine, although Athena is doing much better than you two are, and she has no arms to help her balance. You two just must spend more time walking, I insist."

Eventually, Princess Maren was bound to discover how Dita and I were spending the majority of our daytime hours. After two weeks of slower than Athena and Xene progress, she finally discovered what we were doing, giving them therapy sessions. Once we had finished four, all the other Holy Women on her staff were constantly chatting with these four. The attitude change, the vibrancy, the vitality, the cheerfulness shown by our first four "products" was impossible to miss.

"Just what are you to doing with these Women of the Eighth Degree?" Princess Maren insisted on knowing, while she was hovering over Dita and me, as we practiced our walking around the palace grounds. "You can't say that you are just talking with them! I've seen the four, and honestly, a blind man can see how you've helped them. So spill the beans, you two!"

"Can we stop and talk?" I asked, hoping for a respite.

"Not on your life! You two are way behind Athena and Xene. You simply have to catch up fast. Double time today. Now talk," she insisted. We groaned.

"Okay, how much do you really know about your idol, Empress

Maren Elizabet and what all she did for Women of the Eighth Degree?" I asked.

"Keep moving. It really isn't as hard as you two are making it out to be. Well, I do know that she had several close friends who were of the Eight Degree as she was. It is said that she took several of them along with her in a carriage when the Emperor went to war with the Sea Princes. Oh!" She suddenly exclaimed, having just recalled an key datum.

"Yes, my grandmother often told me that she did some special therapy on them. I see, yes, the results are similar to what I've seen here."

"Very good, Princess. Yes, Maren Elizabet did that. When she went to Velona, she taught others how to do her special therapy. Both Dita and I have picked it up from others. We are using that very same therapy on these Women of the Eighth Degree here. It salvages their lives, so to speak, by removing the traumas that they have suffered and endured."

"Wow! Super. Say, can I sit in on one of these sessions so I can see what happens?" she asked.

"Only if we can stop wearing these skirts," I tried to bargain with her.

"Ha, that won't work, Bethany. You need them. Here, I will show you." She squatted down and moved underneath my ball gown. I could feel her unbuttoning the huge number of buttons that held the skirt together at its hemline on up. She undid them all the way up to my mid thighs. "There, now let's see you walk," she challenged me.

I began to walk as I normally did, but took too large a step. Before I knew what was happening I lost my balance and landed awkwardly on the ground, quite embarrassed. She and Dita helped me back up. "See, you need it a while longer." She buttoned me back up. I shut up about the confining skirt.

I allowed her to sit in on the afternoon session, after getting the woman's permission for her to do so. Princess Maren got a real education really fast! The woman began running through her surgery, complete with screams and great pain. Poor Maren turned nearly green, but sat through the whole session. As suppertime approached, the trauma erased at last, and Maren saw the incredible release the woman had.

Later, Princes Maren confided in me, "You know, this is really awful, the amputation of women's arms! I always thought it was, well sort of the in thing to do. But the pain, oh my goodness. They've all suffered through that, haven't they? I don't think this Woman of the Eighth Degree thing is what everyone is making it out to be! I mean they look so beautiful and all that, so unusual, but honestly, between you and me, they are so helpless, really they are. If it wasn't for all the kindness shown by Kassandra, Athena, and all the other queens, why, these women would be in truly dire straits, wouldn't they?"

"You are quite right, Princess Maren. This is a terrible thing to do to a woman or to anyone. I'm glad that you see it as we do." I replied.

"I wonder how Empress Maren Elizabet managed? That must have been so terribly awful for her! You know, she is the only Annelise woman ever to have become a Woman of the Eighth Degree. How she must have suffered. Well, it just goes to show you that we Annelise are far, far, far more civilized that Demokritos! Say, do you know that Annelise has received a huge order from Velona for these outfits that you are getting? Why, they have ordered nearly a thousand of them. All are starter outfits, mind you. None will have such tiny waists as me, not for some time. So it looks like your Velona is about to join us as being the second country in the world to become totally civilized and proper. Isn't that something?"

Dita and I faked a moan, but in our minds it was a real moan! By the time that we got back home, the awful cone dresses were likely being replaced by outfits like these! Oh no!

"Now come on you two. Practice makes perfect. Your cherry red dress is about done, as is your sky blue one, Bethany. You both must be ready for the next phase when the dresses are ready. Let's walk more."

Data began coming in shortly after this. Kali reported that she had found where Empress Kassandra had transferred thirty thousand over to Cardinal Drakon, who had transferred it to Pope Leo, who had transferred three thousand to a man in Cape Hope. Obviously, this was her order for the slaves and what may have helped bring about the uprising there on the Veld. So far so good. She was now tracing a large sum of money that occurred around the time of Athena's abduction and surgery.

Barnabas met privately with us the next morning. "Zoe has had a breakthrough. She's been at this for months and it's now paying off. She found a young couple who were making out on the grounds of the estate where Athena was taken. They reported seeing a large wagon pull in there after dusk. Curious, they spied on them and saw two doctors and several nurses carrying what looked like medical bags and supplies inside. They then beat a hasty retreat. Zoe has got a good description of the two doctors and is going to try to track them down."

The next morning, Barnabas reported that Zoe had identified the two doctors. She wanted permission to kill them, which Athena did not give, not yet anyway. I relayed the names to Kali, hoping this would speed up her bank records correlations. It did. Two nights later, she reported some startling news!

I reported the news to Athena and our small group. "Guess how much it cost to have Athena abducted and her arms removed?" Several made some guesses. "Thirty thousand gold. It seems that Empress Kassandra sent that sum to Cardinal Drakon two weeks before your abduction, Athena. Shortly after that, the Cardinal transferred five thousand each to the two doctors that Zoe discovered. Another five went to the men who abducted you, Mano del Dio men. He kept the balance."

After a lot of cursing and swearing, including Athena's outburst, I explained that we really did not have evidence that would hold up in a legal proceeding. It was all just circumstantial evidence, unless the two doctors could be made to talk. "I knew that Empress Kassandra could not be trusted!" Dita declared.

"Kali says that in the years before this, there are some other transactions that are raising red flags in her mind. She's continuing to research it all and will report back," I explained.

"Should we have the others pick up these doctors?" asked quiet Barnabas.

"Not yet," Athena answered. "It is getting too close to our trip to Kefall. Once we are gone, there isn't any real way that we can hold them secretly all that time. We can deal with them when we get back. They aren't going anywhere, since their practice is here in Theos."

The next day, both Dita and my new dresses were finished. The seamstresses began dressing us up, while the three Special Helpers and the others watched and learned. We were both floored with how many parts the dress had. It looked as if it only had a bodice top and a huge skirt, but such was not the case. A large circular bun was tied around our lower waists before the huge hoop skirt was fastened. Slowly, article by article was added until at last the heavy satin outer skirt was finally in place. Both our dresses flared out twelve feet at the hemline, a few inches above the floor. We still wore the confining hobble skirt beneath all this.

A new problem had been added to our discomfort: we couldn't see anything closer to us than six feet before our dresses. "Look ahead and anticipate," Princess Maren instructed us, repeatedly, I might add. Later, Dita had to look in a large mirror to see how she now looked.

"Say, I do look sexy! I'm attracted to myself!" she exclaimed. I understood precisely what she meant, though the others took it at face value. That night, as promised, I bombarded her with my love.

Uneven ground and steps became our biggest hurdles now. Princess Maren was unrelenting in making us practice and practice. A few days later, it was Athena and Xene's turn to try out their dresses for the first time. Athena's was slightly worse than ours were, as it was fourteen feet across. "Well, we do look good," Athena admitted. "Honestly, Bethany, looking good is one of the few things that I can do well now." I understood what she meant, though I didn't agree with her. I knew that if I had lots of time, I could teach her how to be vastly more independent. One day, I hoped to do just that.

Mid-May, Kali relayed more news. "Bethany, I've detected a huge transfer from the Emperor's funds to Cardinal Drakon. One million this time. It must be something really big. Curious, there was a smaller one of fifty thousand made at the same time. You and Dita be careful down there. Something is stirring and it isn't going to be good!" I relayed the news to the others. Speculations began, all quite wild.

The next day, Princess Maren removed all our hobble skirts. When I asked her why now, she replied, "Haven't you noticed? For a couple days now, none of you have paid the slightest attention them. Just remember tiny steps or I will have to put them back on you!"

Freedom! We all were overly conscious those next couple of days. None of us wanted to be put back into that constraint. Now, Princess Maren drilled and drilled us on gliding, gliding, gliding. She explained, "Of course, we always need someone to help us get into these dresses. Arms don't matter. Now we also always need help with steps and when walking on rough, irregular surfaces. So let's practice both of these now. Remember, graceful as an angel."

Dita sent me in disgust, *Why don't we just pick up our bodies and actually float them over the ground? That's a whole lot less painful than this!* I gave her a quick, loving kiss.

When the time came to pack up and leave for the Summer Council, Princess Maren was quite pleased with all four of us. We all passed inspection. Dita also pointed out that none of us had yet tried to dance in these outfits. That we would have to leave to chance at the balls when we arrived in Kefall.

As soon as Kassandra returned to her palace in Kefall, she sent Tanis off on a vital mission. She paced her throne room impatiently for two days until he returned. Her Announcer spoke, "Tanis Chloris."

Demurely, she pivoted in place, giving her dress a slight circular motion. "Come, sit, and tell me what you've found out!" She moved as fast as she dared to her throne and carefully sat down. Selene adjusted the fall of her wide dress.

"I've both good and bad news. I was able to locate one of the Elders of Dorota who still resides here in Kefall. I described the two women to him along with their names, as you requested. He said that back on Dorota, there were two of their Holy Vessels who went by those names, and he said that the descriptions more or less fit them. He, unfortunately, had never met these women. Additionally, he pointed out that both of those women did eventually move on to Velona. After that, no one seems to have heard from them. However, the bad news is that there can be no doubt whatsoever that those two were of the Eighth Degree from birth. You said that both in Theolopolis most definitely had arms. The only conclusion is that this is an amazing coincidence, Your Majesty. Everyone knows that arms cannot be regrown. While there is an amazing similarity between these two pairs of women, they cannot be the same pair."

Kassandra sighed. "Well, it would have been much simpler if they had been from Dorota. I guess their stories must be accurate then. Amazing coincidences indeed. Okay, I have a message that I would like you to deliver for me. Please dine with us and then deliver it. You have done well, as always, Tanis."

The next day, Cardinal Drakon arrived at the palace. As he entered the door of her private chambers, her Announcer spoke clearly, "Cardinal Drakon Erebos."

"Oh do come in and have a seat, Your Holiness," Kassandra begged him. Selene double-checked the fall of her wide dress. Satisfied that her charge was perfect, she retired, taking the Announcer, Doorman, and the others with her, leaving them alone.

"You look lovely as ever, Holy Woman, my Empress Kassandra," he bowed and took a seat beside her. "I received your message that you had some urgent business with me. How may I help you?"

"As you know, I have just returned from Theos and visiting Queen Athena. As you also know, she did not attend the Winter Council. King Damon claimed that she was too depressed to attend and not adapting at all to becoming a Woman of the Eighth degree. I know that you were correct in suggesting that, since she was dead set against such, she would be most likely highly depressed afterwards. I went there to work with her and get her used to being one of us."

"However, when I arrived, she was, well, how shall I put this, she was a totally different woman. I saw no signs of any depression, rather far from it. She was alive, vibrant, enthusiastic, and readily adapting, even to these new outfits from Annelise! I managed to conceal my complete shock at such an incredible turn around. I know that Damon did not lie to us. I checked into his story while I was there. Indeed, she was a basket case until recently."

"Well, I am very glad to hear that Queen Athena is now doing so well. But I wonder, what caused such a change?" Cardinal Drakon asked what most interested him. "I admit that I am completely baffled by your report of Athena. I've never seen or heard of such a turnaround. More often those forced into it end up committing a great sin, suicide."

"Well, that's why I've asked you here. Apparently, shortly before I arrived in Theolopolis, two of her cousins arrived from Velona. They are a very strange pair of women, about her age. According to Bethany, all she did was have Athena talk about it. Now you and I both know that women often talk about what's happened to them, and it does little if anything really to help them. Just look at the many, many Holy Women that I and the queens have taken under our wings. They all have talked about their dire situations, but has it materially changed them? Not at all."

"Most intriguing. Tell me more about these two women, please," the Cardinal rubbed his chin. This was fascinating.

"At first, I would have sworn they came from Dorota. Their skin color matches people I've seen from there, a lightish brown. Both have exceptionally long hair, down below their waists, long, thick, and straight. Bethany is very blonde, while Dita's hair is black. Even more peculiar, they are officially a married couple, done in a lavish church ceremony somewhere in Velona, though they did not say which church. Dita is one of the most beautiful women I've seen. Now I had my assistant check up on them. According to the Elder of Dorota, two women match their descriptions almost to the letter. I thought that I had them! But no, the Elder swears that these two were Holy Vessels and most definitely were born without arms. Yet, I know Dita and Bethany have perfectly normal arms. So it must just be the most incredible coincidence."

"I know that this Dita and Bethany must have done something to Athena that they are not saying openly. Athena is a totally changed woman! While I was there, I observed that Athena now respects their point of view more highly than anyone else there, including her Personal Assistant Xene. They will be coming to the Winter Council with Athena as her advisors. I asked them when they were planning to return to their home in Velona. Here comes our little problem. They apparently have no plans to return, not for several years, until Athena has no more need of their advice."

"I see. These two women will be hard to control?"

"Yes, Dita claims to be a superb sword woman. From some of Athena's staff, I learned that she has a large collection of swords and weapons in her room with her at all times. If this is true, she could be a formidable opponent. Cardinal Drakon, I have given this considerable thought, especially in light of our plans. She and this Bethany may well give us trouble."

"How can I help?" Cardinal Drakon asked, knowing that he had Kassandra precisely where he wanted her. She played into his hands like putty.

"When they come for the Winter Council, it would be ideal if they had a similar experience to Athena's. Sooner the better, like the night that they arrive perhaps? Of course, remuneration is needed. Can it be handled? If so, how much?" Kassandra was quite blunt.

"I believe that this can be arranged. You are correct, it should be done soon, otherwise — well, unforeseen problems may arise. Are you ready with the funds for the Big Plan?"

"Yes, Your Holiness. I have instructed Selene to handle the transfer this morning after we are finished. This way, she can make two transfers."

"Excellent, Empress Kassandra. Excellent. Shall we say fifty thousand this time? If she is a master sword woman, the risk is greater."

"Perfect, as always, Your Holiness. If you like, you can accompany Selene now and verify the transfers yourself. The best time for the two would be arrival night. With seven kings, queens, and their whole staff arriving, there is always massive confusion that first evening, as everyone is getting settled."

"Excellent. It shall be done then. Oh, and our shipment has arrived. It shall be as we have planned." She nodded and the meeting ended. He and

Selene visited the Banca del Dio.

Chapter 38 Tragedy Strikes

Ten long days of utter boredom passed us by as we rode all day long in the carriages. King Damon and his advisors were intent on not wasting time while traveling. They kept our rest stops short and to the point. The winter temperatures were quite chilly, here near the end of June. Dressed in our heavy corset and gowns, we felt warm enough, a small benefit. All of us were rather grumpy at the end of each day.

Under better circumstances, Dita and I could have made use of this time by running more therapy sessions as we rolled along. Instead, we had to be content with Athena occasionally pointing out the sights that passed by our carriage. We four rode in one carriage, driven by Barnabas, of course. We did chat — speculate would be more accurate — about what devious plans were in the works. None of them sounded plausible. I pointed out, "Until we know their goals, we cannot anticipate their next move. Instead, we need to be able to minimize its damage when it occurs." While it sounded nice, Dita pointed out this was probably just a fanciful dream on our part.

We arrived in the early afternoon. Within a few hours, the other six kings, queens, and their staffs also arrived. In our case, Damon had brought along six of his advisors to help deal with the business side of the council. Of course, two dozen fighters rode along with us for protection. Counting ourselves, Queen Athena brought along, as Kassandra had ordered, eighty-one of us. Thirty Holy Women and girls and their families made up most of these. Also, Athena brought along their son, Anotolios, who Damon kept with him during the long ride. Once here at the palace, the nanny took over when Damon was busy.

I took pity on Kassandra's staff, which had to work feverously to organize this mass of incoming people and their many bags. Empress Kassandra was there before her enormous front doors to welcome each queen personally. As Barnabas lifted Athena down from the carriage, Kassandra began moving slowly towards us. He lifted his wife, Xene, down next, followed by Dita and me. No way in these dresses were we going to try getting down on our own.

"Oh Athena, you look so absolutely wonderful. Your glide is just perfect! Why Dita, you look simply stunning indeed! And your glide is perfect as well. I'm so pleased that you have so taken to these dresses! In a few days, the seamstresses will be fitting you all with a further waist reduction; they already had made three dresses for each of you. I do hope you like the colors that I've picked out for you. I've spent a small fortune on all of these dresses for you seven queens and your immediate staff."

"Oh, here comes Adonia now. If you will follow this woman here, she will lead you to your personal suites. I'm having all your staff located not too far from your quarters, the same with the other queens. That way, they will be right there to assist you. The Announcer will tell your staff when it is time for their turn to have a short tour. Tomorrow and in the days to come, they will get much longer and more detailed tours. Now, if you will excuse me, I must welcome Queen Adonia."

Kassandra glided across the cobblestone courtyard towards another large batch of carriages that had just pulled up. Dutifully, we glided after our guide. Athena already knew where her quarters would be, unless Kassandra decided to mix the queens up. Fortunately, she did not. "Ah, we will be in my usual suites here in Kefall. That's convenient. I know where everything is at," Athena stated, a bit more confident that all would work out for us.

As I looked around as much as I dared in these heels and dress, I saw only a vague resemblance of the palace that I had once lived in as Empress Maren Elizabet. Indeed, over these many years, so much renovation had occurred that it was barely recognizable. Queen Athena's suite was like a miniature palace of its own. She had a smaller version of a throne room, with her private quarters adjacent to it. On the other two sides, smaller rooms held her staff. Next to them was the throne room for the King and side rooms for him and his advisors. Adjoining Athena's private quarters were three smaller rooms, one for Dita and me, one for Xene and Barnabas, and one for the three Special Helpers. This way, someone could always be nearby to assist Athena.

While we watched, men carried in our many trunks and bags. Now we spent some time unpacking everything, made all the more difficult by our outfits. Athena could only look on and sympathize with us. She felt acutely helpless this afternoon. An Announcer came by to tell us that we four were expected to dine with the Emperor and Empress at six. At least Athena could lead us there, giving her a little something she could do. Always before, she would bustle about issuing orders to her helpers on what went where. I sensed this and asked her to jump in and keep on doing it. She brightened up when she realized that she didn't need arms to do what she had always done in the past. Soon, she forgot all about her situation; her organizational skills got a workout.

Around five thirty, we readied ourselves for the opening night's banquet. King Damon, carrying his son, put his arm around Athena and waited impatiently for the rest of us to fall in line. Xene and Barnabas followed the royal couple, while Dita and I were right behind them. His six advisors brought up the rear. Satisfied that we were ready, he began our procession. However, he continually tried to make us move faster than our tiny steps and glide motion would allow. Bit by bit, his annoyance rose, but he said nothing. Athena picked it up, though, and bore it as well as could be expected.

As we entered the huge dining room, trumpeters played and an Announcer called out "King Damon Patra, Queen Athena, Prince Anatolios!"

The fanfare lasted until a Messenger had led the king to our seats. Promptly, the trumpets announced the arrival of the others. The layout of the dining room for this occasion was thus. At the far end Emperor Argos and Empress Kassandra sat, along with their advisors. From their table, they faced all the others and could easily see everyone else.

In a giant semicircle around the Emperor's table were seven sets, one for each of the king's group. By virtue of the circular arrangement, we all could also see everyone else, though we faced the Emperor. Xene sat to the right of Athena; I sat to her left and Dita to my left. Barnabas was to the right of his wife. To Dita's left, King Damon sat, with his son next to him. His six advisors were to the left of him.

King Damon whispered to Dita, "Dita, you look ravishing!" She thanked him, but he continued to flirt with her. She sent, *Help! Damon's flirting with me! What do I do?*

I grinned and replied, *Start him talking about his son.* Soon, I heard Damon doing just that, how his son would one day be King of Theos and all that. During the long meal and music, poor Dita detected many, many male eyes watching her, staring at her. I spent my time surveying the other six queens and their advisors. Several had brought along their Special Helper to feed them. These women looked terribly out of place here, I thought.

Queen Frona Aristos of Thallyus was the oldest queen at forty. She was average size with short, curly brown hair and a pretty face to match. Queen Ariadne Diodros of Thrace was twenty-four. She was tall and had auburn hair parted, as did Dita and I did, down the middle of her head, dropping to below her shoulders. I caught a glance of her greenish eyes. She too was quite pretty, I thought.

Queen Adonia Kadmos of Phindos was twenty-eight with shoulder length red hair and enchantingly green eyes. I realized none of these queens was ugly; all were indeed quite pretty. The second oldest was Queen Melita Stathis of Alia, who was thirty-five, with curly black hair draped over her shoulders and matching eyes.

Queen Danae Haimon of Penelopus was twenty-five and had the shortest hair, a dark brown, cut in a pixie style. Queen Alekto Pegasos of Arolas was twenty-one, the youngest of the queens. She had darker blonde hair than mine, straight and long; hers fell to the small of her back, unlike Dita's and mine, which we continually had to avoid sitting upon.

Each had at least one child with them, but Ariadne had the most with three present. I was amazed at all the satin cloth that was in this room! Nearly every color of the rainbow was represented in many different shades. All we women were wearing these new Annelise outfits with the impossible boots to match. Well, I thought, Kassandra has us all here. I wonder what mischief she has planned?

After the music-accompanied meal, the Emperor rose and gave a long, boring welcoming speech. Then, Kassandra rose and gave her welcome address, outlining the many activities that she had planned for us. Only one I knew I wouldn't like — meeting with the seamstresses to be fitted with a tighter corset.

Kassandra also announced Princess Maren would be leaving us tomorrow to return home to Annelise. However, she added the Princess would return when they brought their yearly taxes in late December.

"On our last night, I have a very, very special festivity arranged for our entertainment. After dark, we will have a gigantic fireworks display accompanied by music and then dancing later on. The Emperor and I have imported twenty thousand worth of the finest fireworks available from Tashien. This will be most spectacular. I can't tell you how much I am looking forward to this gigantic display! Now enough of talk. I know that after such a long journey all of you are tired. So retire to your suites and rest up. I guarantee that you will have much to do beginning tomorrow!"

"Well, that is usual," Athena whispered to us. "She's right; after that long ride, I could do with a good night's sleep in a quality bed. So far, everything seems fine, Bethany. I've not detected anything unusual, excepting for the fancy fireworks display."

Back in Athena's private room, we chatted a bit. Princess Maren dropped by to say goodbye. "I will be back probably around the time that you meet here for the Summer Council. I do hope that you and Dita are still here! I've really enjoyed your company. Please come to Annelise one day." We gave the young girl a warm hug and she left. Her coach was to leave early in the morning.

Yawning, we all decided to retire for the night. Once in our room, our two Special Helpers arrived to help us out of these complex gowns and then the boots. After they left, Dita and I dove into the satin sheets of the bed with me passionately kissing the prettiest woman in the palace. It pleased Dita to have me spoiling her like this. Besides she had worn the cherry red dress today without a single complaint. I owed her a delightful time.

By now, our hair was messed up again, so we took turns brushing it out once more. At last, we laid down beside each other holding each other in our arms and fell asleep. As I drifted into sleep, there I was back home in Velona, kissing mom good night, as she tucked my five year old body into bed. All was well with the world.

In the middle of the night, I did not hear the slight hissing sound coming from our open window, which allowed a much needed air flow into our stuffy room. We were sleeping under a satin sheet and several blankets. Across the room, the fireplace crackled. Although I was sleeping peacefully, I began to dope off into a drugged sleep, but I was not aware of it.

Sunlight struck my face. I felt awful, slightly nauseous; my shoulders throbbed; my eyes seemed itchy and dry. I reached up to rub them, but nothing happened. Panic seized me. Blinking to get the sand out of my eyes, I leaned a little to look at my aching shoulders. I screamed! Gone were my arms. Bloody bandages held the surgeon's work tightly to my shoulders. Beside me on another table Dita, roused by my shriek, tried to get up and added her shriek to mine. For a minute, we both panicked and screamed our heads off. That released a whole lot of shock, surprise, and panic.

Dita looked at me and wailed, "Again, my love, I have failed to protect you! Damn! Damn! Damn! Here we are again, armless!"

"I can see that we are again in the pickle barrel, Dita. It's not your failure, love. I had no idea this was happening to us, did you sense anything?"

"No, I was asleep and here we are. Damn! Damn! Damn! Wait til I get my hands on whoever did this to us! I'll kill them!"

"Dear, you haven't any hands once more. How about just ripping their heads from their bodies?" I replied, trying to calm my own nerves with a touch of humor. "Pull your body up into a sitting position." We both did and looked around. "Where are we?"

"Dunno. I am too weak to stand just now," Dita replied.

Mommy! Mommy! What's wrong? It was my girl Alessa, who was now nine years old.

Mommy! Mommy! What's wrong? Simultaneously, Dita's girl, Bianca, who was ten, sent to here.

Alessa went on, *Little Bethany just shrieked waking us all up. So did Lorenzo. What's happened? Are you all right?* Having and running two bodies at the same time can be confusing. Apparently, our shock also reacted in our small child bodies back in Velona.

Quickly, I related what had happened, the little that I knew. We had gone to bed and had awakened in a strange place, and someone had operated on us, amputating our arms.

Okay, mommy. Close your eyes. Go to when it begins. Alessa was going to run a therapy session on me right now! Likewise, precocious Bianca was doing the same thing with Dita.

On my third time through the incident, I re-experienced the heavy pain of the surgery. Yes, I did scream, so did Dita. By the twentieth pass, I began laughing. With Alessa's aid, I had totally erased the entire trauma completely. There wasn't anything earlier. Now I had a clear picture of what had happened to us.

Someone had sent a knock out gas into our room through our open window. I heard four men climb in, felt their hands lifting my body up and with effort, sliding it out the window into other arms. I felt a long carriage ride, or perhaps it was a wagon. The voices said little that was recognizable. The wagon stopped and arms lifted my body once more. I was laid on something flat and cold, presumably the table on which I sat now. It was cold and hard. I detected two doctors and at least three, maybe four, nurses performing the surgery. At least, they didn't chat much, and they seemed to be highly skilled at this. My guess is that they had done it many times. I did catch the doctor's first names twice during the operation. The voices moved away, as if they were finished. I heard one say, "Athena will be notified in the morning where she can find them. They will probably sleep there until help comes." The other voice said, "Okay. Let's get out of here, before someone gets too nosy." I laid there for a long time before I woke up and screamed.

I heard Dita laughing and knew that Bianca had done well too. We both thanked our little girls. Now everyone began talking to us via little Bethany and Lorenzo. What a strange way to hold a conversation. Enrico wanted to send help to us immediately, Ilenakova insisted on coming straightaway. Kali, likewise.

"No gang. We can manage here. It is more important for you to trace the money. See if there is any way that you can find out what that million is for so that we can prevent it from happening. I'm now convinced that something awful is going to happen here at this Winter Council. If we do need you, we can let you know. After all, it is a three month voyage to get here. What will another day or so matter? Let's see how this plays out. Just let one of us know the second that you have any hunches about what the million is for — I bet ours was the fifty thousand. If so, the million must be one really bad happening, though right now, I have no idea what that might be." After more discussion, they agreed, and Kali and Ilenakova dashed off to the Banca del Dio to continue their work on the banking records. We desperately needed a clue if we were to stop this from happening, whatever it was going to be.

"How's your shoulders, dear?" Dita asked.

"Fine, the pain is completely gone. They are itching like mad. Yours?"

"Don't scratch them; they are healing. Same here. Bianca got rid of it all. I overheard them say that Athena would be notified where we are. I suppose someone will be coming to get us shortly," Dita tried to look on the bright side.

"I heard that too. I guess when we get back, we can have Cosima do her thing on our arms again and regrow them once more," I added hopefully.

"Well, it worked once. It ought to again," Dita added cheerfully. "I wish they'd hurry up. I am starving."

"I gotta pee. Well, I'm going to get up and try. Shit, I can't pull these panties down. Little help love?"

An hour passed and no one came. "Okay, let's go exploring and see what we can find," Dita declared at last, very impatient with the way things were going. We both got up and found our legs were still a bit weak, probably lost a lot of blood. We needed fluids and a meal soon. "Damn, in this corset, I'm not going to be able to bend enough to open this doorknob," she called out frustrated.

"Move out of your body and open it for us, or let me smash it down, dear," I replied. She had the finesse movements, while I could only move large, heavy things. The doorknob rotated and the door opened. We walked out of the room and found ourselves in an estate of some kind. No one was around. Much of the furniture was covered with sheets. We went from room to room, looking for the kitchen. At last we found it. Dita levitated two glasses, manipulated the cold water system, and then levitated the glass up so I could drink. When I was done, she did it for herself. Next, we continued our search for something they may have left behind that we could eat. For our efforts, all that we found was an unopened round block of cheese. Dita levitated a knife and plate. While I marveled at the skill she had over such small motions, she cut us out two large chunks of cheese, putting them on the plate opposite each other. I scooted two chairs over, and we sat down, leaned over, and began devouring the cheese greedily.

Just then, we heard a commotion, men were breaking in the front door. I heard Barnabas' voice calling out, "Bethany, Dita? Where are you?"

"We're in the kitchen," I yelled loudly. Shortly, he, Xene, and four other men, who we did not recognize, came rushing into the kitchen. They saw two women in their corsets and panties sitting at the table, heads together, eating furiously at two chunks of cheese.

"Oh my god! What happened to you two? Oh my god! Someone will pay for this!" yelled Barnabas, who suddenly lost his perfect gentleman's attitude. Xene simply screamed.

Dita, her mouth full of cheese, mumbled loudly, "You bet they will. Just wait until I get my hands on them. I'll kill them for what they've done to my Bethany."

"Are you all right?" Barnabas tried to regain some measure of coherency. The shock had overwhelmed him.

"Of course not! Two doctors cut off our arms!" Dita added. "Cut me another chunk of cheese, please. We're starving." He did as asked, while the four men quickly fanned out and searched the estate. "Just plop it down on the plate. You want more dear?" she asked me. I nodded and soon gobbled more cheese. I guess we looked rather funny, but we were very hungry. Then, we both were thirsty once more. Xene calmed down and handled helping us to another glass of water.

"Come on; let's get you back to the palace and safety," Xene said at last.

"Obviously, the palace is not a place of safety," Dita retorted, "but they've got food there." Xene managed a slight smile, though she fought hard to keep from bawling. Tears did trickle down her face.

Barnabas and another man picked us up and carried us out and into the waiting carriage. The other four had ridden horses, but Barnabas ordered one to drive the carriage. He insisted on sitting with Xene and us. As we began moving, he told us, "You were missed early this morning. Iua came to help you dress and found that you were missing and raised the alarm. The whole palace is outraged. Men were running everywhere trying to find you, hoping that you had simply gotten lost somewhere in that huge palace complex."

"Around nine in the morning, a messenger arrived at the palace saying that you two were safe and at the Mache estate. Athena is beside herself; she kept saying that this cannot be happening again. I think that she feared the worst, and she was right. Emperor Argos sent these four fighters, his very best, along with us to come to your rescue. Argos was livid with anger. Your abduction and mutilation right from his very own castle is casting a terrible blight on his credibility. He may never live this one down! Say, you two are doing remarkably well!"

Her voice suddenly very animated, Xene exclaimed, "Barnabas! You are right! You are — well, we expected to see you as invalids for a long time — recovering and all that! You are up and about and even feeding yourselves! How is this possible?"

I lied effectively, "We woke up some time ago and gave each other our therapy sessions. We've erased the trauma of the surgeries, but we are in need of real sustenance. Honestly, our shoulders don't hurt any longer, just awfully itchy."

"Well, that is a good sign of healing," Xene replied. "Well, now that I've seen it with my own eyes, I can say that your therapy thing really does work miracles. Do you realize that it was weeks and weeks before Athena was out of bed as we found you two? Incredible, Barnabas, just a miracle!"

"Oh, we heard the two doctor's first names," Dita remembered. She told them to Barnabas, who promised to get someone to see if they could be identified.

We rode in silence for a while. "Barnabas, are there contacts of ours here in Kefall?" he nodded. "Good. Contact them. I strongly suspect that the Empress or Emperor has paid the doctors fifty thousand to do this to us. What most concerns me is the other one million that was spent at the same time as the fifty. Something big is about to go down. We need to find out what before it is too late, as we were for us."

"Why would the Emperor want to do this to you, Bethany? He hardly pays any attention to Kassandra, Xene asked.

"I agree. I don't see a motive with him," I answered.

"But what has Kassandra got against you two? You are not queens or anything, just her temporary advisors," Xene added, mystified. "She seemed very impressed and taken with you two."

"I agree. I don't see a motive with her either. I'm just as baffled as everyone else is. I'm sure one day it will all become clear." I lied, well not lied, just tried to sound hopeful.

When we arrived at the palace, I saw guards everywhere. Two men carried Dita and me hastily inside, directly to our room lying us gently on our bed. They left and Athena, Xene, and others came in quickly.

"Oh no! It has happened again! Oh Dita, Bethany, I'm so, so sorry!" Athena wailed, losing her composure entirely. Xene put her arms around Athena to steady her. Now Kassandra entered with some others.

"I just heard! Oh Bethany! Dita! I'm so very sorry! This is just scandalous! Such a crime! Argos will spare nothing to find out who did this to you. Athena, you must let my doctor examine them. They may well be infected or worse."

Now crying, Athena nodded, her head buried in Xene's shoulder. The doctor began examining me, peeling back my bandage on my right shoulder. He gasped. "What's wrong, Beros?" Kassandra asked, her voice sounding terribly worried.

He peeled the left one and began looking at first one and then my other shoulder. "Whoever did this has done an excellent job. Very little scarring. The stitches are more than ready to come out."

"That's good, isn't it, Beros?" asked Kassandra.

"Absolutely. Let me examine the other young woman first." He went to Dita and very gingerly peeled back first one and then the other bandages. "Yes, your stitches are also ready to come out. There is no sign of any infections in either of them. They are healing very nicely indeed."

"So what's the matter?" asked Xene, still worried about his sudden gasp.

"Well, that's just it. I'm most puzzled. Their shoulders appear to have been healing for, oh, I'd say off hand about two weeks, maybe more. And you say this just happened last night, Empress?"

"Yes, they dined with us and retired for the night last night. This morning, they were missing," Kassandra replied. Now she had a very worried look on her face. "Doctor, what is going on here? Are they going to be all right or not?"

"Oh yes, they are already quite all right, healing nicely. I have no explanation for it. There have been some strange cases where a person has healed abnormally fast. I guess these two young women heal very quickly indeed. Most amazing. I will remove the stitches now."

Once that was done, he turned to leave. Kassandra asked, "Don't they need to be re-bandaged? I know I had bandages for weeks."

"No, they are doing fine. The air will do their shoulders much good." Kassandra gave us a very queer look.

She regained her composure. "Bethany, Dita, I am giving you Iou and Ida to be your very own personal assistants. They are very caring women and will be your hands from now on. This is the very least that I can do for you two. I've already given another two of mine to Athena. We all know how hard this initial adjustment is. We all will do everything in our power to help you both. If you need anything, please ask. Do you have any idea who did this to you? I want to have Argos go after those who did it and make them pay."

"No, not really. We went to bed and woke up in that strange place like we are," I replied, mostly honestly.

"Don't worry, Kassandra. Those who did this to us will pay, and pay most dearly," Dita threatened antagonistically.

I watched Kassandra closely. Oh, she was a cool woman. She didn't bat an eye when Dita made her threat.

"Oh, forgive me. The other queens wanted to come visit you," Kassandra said. "I will speak more with you both a bit later. Come, Athena, there is nothing you or I can do here now. Let's have some tea and make some plans to help your two advisors." Xene had to lead her, following after the Empress. The six other queens took this opportunity to glide in and offer their get-well wishes, sympathy, expressions of hope, and offers of assistance and understanding. We thanked them for their kindness.

Iou and Ida came in and covered us up with our sheet and blankets. Iou then opened the door and allowed some men inside. It was Emperor Argus and King Damon along with several uniformed army men, generals perhaps.

"On behalf of the entire country of Demokritos, please accept my humblest and sincerest apologies for what has happened to you. Never has such dreadful things happened here," Argos began. Dita wanted to add, "Except assassinations," but thought better of it. "This has cast a dark shadow of distrust upon our country. What Velona must think of us when you return! I promise you that I will leave no stone unturned to find out whoever did this to you and see that they are severely punished! Somehow, I must find a way to make amends for this great tragedy happening here in my very own palace. I know my wife has already given you two of her very able servants who will graciously attend to your personal needs. I will establish a trust fund for each of you. When you are ready to return to your homeland, the fund will disburse ten thousand each year for the rest of your lives. This way, up in Velona, you should not suffer want for anything. It is the very least I can do for you. Further, I know how you women love your fancy dresses. I have given my wife orders to see that her seamstresses make each of you a dozen of these fancy outfits, complete with everything that goes with them, boots and all. You forgive me if I don't know what all that entails," he grinned. He had no idea what it entailed, I thought to myself.

We thanked him for his thoughtfulness and he left. King Damon delayed, "You have no idea how much this has shaken him up. That this could happen right here in his own palace has really disturbed him! I've never seen him either this angry or this upset before. Let me offer my own sympathies. If you need anything at all, please let us know. I want you both to know I'm here to help you as well. I best be going. The Emperor is working with us to establish drastically higher security. Who knows who might be next?"

Finally, only Iou and Ida remained. We were nearly alone at last.

"Iou, can you get us some real food and drink? We are starving. Thank you." Again, I could not tell her reactions because of her large lip plates. However, both women's cheeks were wet. I knew that they had been crying. She waist-nodded and left.

"Well, I think that we can eliminate the Emperor. He's just given us a king's ransom, dear," Dita commented. "Say we live to be seventy-three, that's fifty times ten times two. Gosh, that's a million!"

"You have a point. We need to have Xene somehow verify that he has setup the trust fund for us. It must be Kassandra, but what has she got against us?"

"Dunno, but we darn well better find out before anything else happens," Dita growled. "Here we are again, my love."

"No kidding. Well, we'll make the best of it and continue. Ah, food!"

I was amazed at how well Iou and Ida did feeding us. Observant, these women anticipated our every need. Finally full at last, we asked them to get us dressed. Before they finished, two seamstresses appeared and cut off the frilly arm sleeves from our gowns. Now our dresses looked like Athena's. An hour later, dressed in our fancy wide Annelise gowns and tall heeled boots, we stood for the first time as Women of the Eighth Degree.

"Oh my, I guess we have been depending a lot on our arms for balance," I noted. "Slowly Dita, we take it very slowly!" We walked a little to get used to our new situation and then sat down in our easy chairs. I needed to think.

All signs pointed to the Empress concocting some huge plot. I was now almost completely convinced that the Church of Jehosanity was heavily involved, particularly this Cardinal Drakon. Whether she was merely buying some services from him or whether he played a more active role, I had not enough data to conclude. In fact, it could be the other way around. It could be the Cardinal was hatching some grand plan of his own and merely using the Empress. My head was swimming with possibilities, yet I knew that something major was soon to happen. I had one million reasons to suspect this.

We'd missed lunch, primarily because we'd eaten so much midmorning. By evening, we had enough strength back to gamble on our being able to join the others for supper. Yes, both Dita and I found walking now was a scary proposition, but we moved very slowly and deliberately. Our two Special Helpers always seemed to be around lending us a hand. Yes, the doormen we now greatly appreciated, as well as the Messengers. As we two entered the dining hall, many were already there. A spontaneous applause broke out from the men and boys, while the women simply cheered us. I think that they thought that we were being incredibly brave to be joining them less than a day from the operation.

During and after the meal, many came by to chat with us. Of course, everyone wanted to know what happened as well as to give us their love and support and sympathy. We could have done totally without the sympathy part. When the meal was done, everyone moved to the neighboring ballroom, where a group of twenty musicians began playing for their formal dance. Dita and I were still weak and decided that we shouldn't press our luck. We sat and listened to the music and watched the others dance.

The next day, the meetings began. We discovered that they had been canceled yesterday because of our abduction. Athena said that we didn't have to come and sit with her, but we insisted. All the kings and queens, along with the Emperor and Empress met in their large throne room. We advisors sat just behind our king or queen. The Emperor presented a detailed report of their economy, their current business dealings, and even a summary of how the skirmishes were going up in the Southlands. After he finished, one by one the kings presented additional information more specific to their kingdom's activities.

In the afternoon, the future planning sessions began. Here the advisors began to earn their pay. We quickly discovered that their planning was done in two stages. First, they worked on short-range planning, outlining actions to be done before the Spring Council meeting. Second, they then worked on long-range planning, goals which could take a year or longer to fulfill. Fairly soon, I discovered that the kings and Emperor had one set of goals, while the queens and Empress had entirely different things in mind that they wanted done.

One long-range goal came up fairly soon. A debate over the possibility of providing schools for all children under the age of fourteen became very lively. King Dorieus started it off by saying, "Now about our establishing schools for our children. As we know, the Church of Jehosanity has proposed constructing schools all over Demokritos. The goal is to provide an education for all our children. I think we're all in agreement here. This is a vital goal and a worthy goal. Yet, it is going to be a costly affair. Buildings are not cheap. Then, too we must consider the cost of hiring all the needed teachers. This will total into the millions. I say let's let the Church do it for us. Lots cheaper that way."

I whispered some advice to Athena; she grinned and spoke up. "Yes, cheaper. You get what you pay for. Do we really want all our children being educated by their priests? They would control what is taught and how. Why, in one generation, our children could well be taught all manner of things that we find deplorable. I say let us build our own schools, and man them with our own teachers and control what our children are taught." Many agreed with her and the discussion became even livelier. Nothing, however, was actually decided. Somehow, I wasn't surprised.

That evening, the Empress was hosting everyone at a nearby theater. She's hired an entire theatrical group to put on a special play for our entertainment. However, Athena advised Dita and me not to go. "Honestly, this will be a rough outing for us in these outfits. Lots of walking and stairs to negotiate." We certainly were not ready at all even to attempt such a challenge. Instead, she and I spent a good while just walking around the now heavily guarded palace courtyard. Yes, we were practicing. We certainly needed it now!

The next day was filled with dressmaking plans. Seamstresses came around to each queen's court. First action was to ascertain who was ready for a smaller corset. Empress Kassandra came along with her workers, encouraging everyone to take the next step in fashion. "Look at my waist! I'm down to eighteen inches now. If you consent, you will be matching mine!" Athena sighed; she was under too much peer pressure to decline. She was handled first. Once they had her new corset fully tightened, the woman measured it and pronounced eighteen inches. Everyone followed the lead of Kassandra and cheered her, and Athena managed a smile, though I knew that she felt very uncomfortable.

Soon Xene, Dita, and I had our old corsets removed and our new smaller ones put on and tightened. "Oh my! I can't breathe!" exclaimed Dita, very unused to such constriction. The other women giggled. I felt horribly constricted myself, but chose to grin and bear it, if only for Dita and Athena's sake. We could always discard these when we got back to Theolopolis. Kassandra then said, "You should keep your old corset and dresses, in case you become pregnant. You may wear these looser ones for a time, so they may be valuable in the future." I also thought that we could replace these tight ones with the old ones when we got Athena back home. Then we would at least have bearable ones.

With this handled, we found that Empress Kassandra had spoken truthfully. The dressmakers paraded out all new satin dresses for each of us, the exact same colors as we had, only with the modified waists. Soon, we four were admiring our new look in the mirrors. Yes, our waistlines did look dramatically smaller, equal to Kassandra's. "Don't we set a perfect example for our people, ladies?" she said.

However, she wasn't done with Dita and me. We each chose a dozen different colors, for the Emperor promised dozen new outfits, all satin, of course. Twelve identical sized pairs of these tight fitting, knee high, extremely high-heeled boots now lined either side of our bed. Kassandra insisted that all her seamstresses would be working on our dresses and that we would have them by the end of the council. I guessed that must have meant she had an army of seamstresses at her disposal!

As Kassandra was finishing up with us and about to move on to the next queen, I decided to ask her to do something for us. "Empress, I've heard you talk so much about your Church of Jehosanity here and how they honor women like us. I wonder if I could impose upon you to take Dita and me to visit your Church. Perhaps we could even meet Cardinal Drakon himself, if such a holy man ever meets with us women. Is this even possible?" I rather begged her.

"Oh, why, I would be delighted, Bethany. Certainly, we can go tomorrow right after breakfast! I'm sure Cardinal Drakon would love to meet visitors all the way from Velona. I would be honored to take you. Shall we say be ready at nine? How good of you to ask." She then glided out the door.

"I think that we should start practicing again," Queen Athena suggested. "I can barely breathe now. How about you? Our waists are sure striking, I'll give her that. I just am so out of breath!"

"No kidding, we are too," I confided. We spent the rest of the morning practicing. I suggested that we stroll outside where we could not be overheard.

Xene whispered, "Barnabas has reported that they have identified the two doctors." She gave me their names, and I silently relayed them to Kali, via my little Bethany body back in Velona. I was discovering more uses for attempting to run two bodies at the same time. Thus far, it was not too much of a problem, well yet anyway, because little Bethany wasn't doing much at all, merely playing.

"What do you hope to find out by meeting the Cardinal?" Athena asked. "He is heavily involved, right? Aren't you taking a big risk by seeing him?"

"It is a crime of magnitude to harm one of us," I replied. "I need to meet him and size him up. I just can't figure out this tangled web of intrigue. Who's doing what remains a mystery. Why have only women like us as queens? I don't see the point of it. Besides, don't your husbands really wield the power behind the thrones?"

"Well, yes they do. We are supposed to have an equal say, but of late, Kassandra has us all worrying more about these awful dresses and heels than the real business of running our kingdoms and country," Athena explained. "I don't see it either. Why have all us queens as mostly helpless queens? Are we not relegated to just looking pretty and fancy? Show piece objects? It is looking more and more like that is all that Kassandra has in mind for us."

Dita spoke up. "No, there is something deeper. She is cold and heartless. She is definitely up to something, though I admit I can't see any reason for putting us all through this torture. Do men really think we look good in these outfits?"

We three giggled. I answered her, "Yes they certainly do. Even King Damon tried to hit on you that first night, didn't he? Haven't you noticed all the men looking at us women at the dinner table?" Dita flushed and wished she'd kept her mouth shut.

Later that afternoon, Kali reported. She had traced the money to the doctors from the Cardinal, who got it from Kassandra. We ruled out Emperor Argos completely. Kali had verified that funds had been transferred to a bank in Tashien, probably for the fireworks, so she was on the up and up with that aspect. She also found a substantial transfer to several men that were not part of the Mano del Dio men. She gave us their names. I told Xene, Barnabas, and Athena, but they had never heard of these three fellows. He promised to set others to work finding these men tonight, when he could slip away to a pub. It was a little more difficult for him to slip away now that Argos had upped the security arrangements.

This evening, another dance was held, and Dita and I decided to try it. Oh how we both wished that we had arms to hold each other. Yet, we tried. Our giant hoops had to be forcibly pressed against each other so that we could touch our bodies together. Our old trick of using head pressure to guide came back quickly. We both discovered that we could only take the smallest of dance steps, however. And we ran out of breath rapidly and had to skip a dance to recover after one dance. Yet, we enjoyed ourselves.

On Thursday at breakfast, King Argos announced that in the late morning, he and the kings were going to inspect the warehouse where all of tomorrow night's fireworks would be set off. "Never has such a large collection of fireworks been assembled. This, we kings need to see! It will be a great outing. I am encouraging you fathers to bring along your sons, daughters too, if they wish. Join us and let's see this huge pile before they are set off tomorrow night. Since it requires a good deal of walking, I presume you women will wish to remain here at the palace. Fear not. I will have a strong security force with us. We should be back in a couple of hours with stories to tell!" Clearly, Emperor Argos was excited about this. Even Damon seemed excited and was taking Anatolios to see this amazing mountain of fireworks. Athena gave him a kiss and told him to have a good time. He was only two and probably wouldn't remember it. Still, I though it a nice gesture for these fathers to take their sons out to see something truly amazing.

At nine, Kassandra came to our door, and we were ready. Slowly, we three walked along the halls as her doormen open the doors wide to allow our wide dresses an easy passage. I swear that it seemed like it took forever to get out onto the cobblestone courtyard, where her personal carriage awaited us. Probably it was just me adjusting to once more being armless and so constrained. One by one, her coachman gently lifted us up and into the carriage. Selene came along just after we three had managed to sit and she hastily adjusted our dresses. "Sorry I am late. So many are going with the kings. Busy morning all around. Isn't it wonderful that the kids will get to see what these fireworks look like now and then get to see them set off tomorrow night?" She chatted away.

"I am just so amazed with how well you two have healed from your surgeries. You are like a miracle or something. Kassandra, you remember how long you were bedridden? Wasn't it several weeks before you were able to have the stitches removed?"

"Yes, painful memories, but I believe it was a little over two weeks. I wasn't out and about for what was it, about four weeks, Selene?" she replied, thinking back on her own surgery and eyeing us.

"Something like that. Honestly, these two women heal so very rapidly. I know the doctor said there are similar cases on record, so it must not be that unusual. Still, it must be rare. I am just so grateful that you are both doing so well. It is so tragic that this had to happen to you. I know that Queen Athena is just devastated over it and the Emperor is howling mad. Did you see him yesterday, Kassandra? He scolded his guardsmen! I've never heard him that angry over anything before."

'That's true, Argos doesn't rile easily. I'm sure that in time, he and his men will find those responsible. When they do, I sure would not want to be in their shoes," Kassandra added to Selene's words. "One day, you will have justice for what has been done to you. In the meantime, Dita and Bethany, my advice is try to make the best of it all. It can't be undone and life is within us today. We must just get on with it and do good things for our people and others. That's my philosophy: lead by setting a good example; always do what's best for our people. You know the women of Demokritos so look upon both the Empress and the queens as not only role models, but also to carry forward their wishes into the running of our great country. It just doesn't take arms to do that. We must inspire the women of Demokritos to achieve great heights, long denied to them by our men, who often waste the lives of our young men on their petty wars."

"Look at our previous Emperor Deimos Gavril. Why, he slaughtered so many legions in some land way up north! For what? Only to return home empty handed. I know that Princess Maren looks upon his original Empress as a role model — you know, the Empress Maren Elizabet. And I do too in many ways. You see, she was like we are, a Holy Woman, and yet she was instrumental in getting us out of that horrid war that Deimos got us into. Now she was a leader. If I can only be half the leader she was, why, Demokritos will rise to new heights."

"Yet, I must balance that with religious beliefs. Our people are only now coming to grips with true religion and true faith in God. I'm sure, Dita and Bethany, that you don't know that only a hundred years ago, our people here went around worshiping the sun god, the water god, the storm god, and all manner of non-existent things. Our sailors would pray to their supposed water deity and storm god to keep them safe while at sea. Today, so many of us see the utter folly in such nonsense. God has created us all, but then I am perhaps boring you young women with my rambling words," Kassandra finally ran down.

I had just learned more about Kassandra in these few minutes than all the time I'd known her! "Oh, do go on, Empress. I'm fascinated about hearing your governing philosophy." I wanted her to talk more about her relationship to the Church of Jehosanity and her position as Empress. "How about this latest topic on building schools for all your children. It certainly is going to be a costly thing to establish throughout all of Demokritos. Does the Church really plan to spend such a vast sum building their schools everywhere?"

She seemed eager to talk about this. "Why yes, I'm certain no matter what we decided to do, the Church is going to go ahead with their plans anyway. Personally, I would not want my children to be educated only in church-run schools. I feel it is very important for our children to get a wider, broader education. Certainly, our children must learn about our religion and God, but they also need to learn so many other more practical things, like how to build toilets and running water systems. Why, do you realize that we here in Demokritos had to import those from Velona? One of their very bright engineers, Enyo I believe was her name, invented these. We actually had to import them and have our people learn to copy them. Now that should not be. No offense against Velona, but why couldn't our people have been bright enough to invent such? Answer me that, if you can."

"We need to foster bright minds here and that can only be done by education. Besides that, Enyo was a woman, as I understand it. Am I right?" Kassandra asked.

"Yes, you are right. Enyo is a woman. Actually, she was like us, armless," I added. "She is very famous in Velona, having invented all manner of devices that have improved our lives."

"You don't say! I certainly didn't know that! I am truly amazed! Well, we women certainly can do great things! That only supports what I have been trying to tell you two. Please don't feel like your lives are now hopeless and useless. Oh, no. You and I and the others, we can and will do great things for our people. They look up to us to guide them. Oh, here we are. This is the largest church in Kefall. Isn't it spectacular?"

That was an understatement. One church occupied an entire block. It rose towering over all other nearby buildings. Ornate, entirely covered with white polished marble, it shone in the sunlight, like rays from God touching the earth. Gold leaf ornamentation trimmed the windows and beautifully carved mahogany doors, wide enough to allow passage of women wearing the Empress' wide dress. All the windows were huge. Their stained glass displayed all manner of holy images; I thought I recognized what must have been the Great Messiah's disciples.

"Oh, I should warn you two," Kassandra whispered to us, revealing a secret, "the Cardinal will do his best to get you to come to Sunday services."

Carefully, the coachman lifted us four women out of the carriage. He was strong and used to helping women down gracefully in our fancy outfits. A series of four steps led to these doors; even the steps were marble! Steps! Oh no. Dita and I were not ready for steps in these dresses and heels without arms to steady us. A slight panic swept over me. I remembered Princess Maren's advice, look ahead and judge your steps. I saw Dita having the same thoughts. I quickly discovered one benefit of these boots. The tiny steps helped me detect the edge of each step, and I found the going slightly easier than I expected, though I felt like I was doing this blind. My dress obscured all four steps as I neared the first one.

Selene and the coachman went first to get the doors open, he holding her hand, while she picked up her dress. I was following the Empress, and I saw she was having the identical problem that Dita and I had. She too moved very slowly, feeling for the steps with her feet. Well, if she could manage, so could we. I just hoped that I wouldn't take a fall; the marble was hard.

At the top, Kassandra paused to catch her breath. So did we; our eighteen inch waists made even this slight exertion a hassle. "There, the worst is over. I too still have to watch my steps on stairs. Come, there is so much artwork, so many things of great beauty inside that you cannot see them all in a month of Sundays!" Kassandra really did like her church; that was plain to us.

Inside, the main chapel was gargantuan; there are no other words to describe it. We'd never been inside one of their new churches before, and it dwarfed the Holy Rose Church in which we were married. Gold ornamentation and outlining covered everything. Enormous frescoes adorned the ceilings, which had to be at least a hundred feet over our heads. Dozens of marble statues lined either side of the room; plush carpeting covered the floor. Giant ten-foot paintings were perfectly aligned between the stained glass windows as we walked down the wide central isle. Kassandra's dress did not even touch the sides of the pews as we passed. To say that I was impressed would be an understatement. The Church of Jehosanity had certainly changed drastically from what I had seen of their earlier churches. If nothing else, the artisans of Kefall had certainly benefitted greatly from the building of this church.

"Oh you should hear the choir singing in here. I get goose bumps every time," Kassandra whispered enthusiastically. "Somehow, I do feel close to our Lord when I am in here. This way." She led us off to the right. Ahead a large double door led out of the main chapel. Again, Selene and the coachman held the doors open for us, as we entered the rectory. A long hallway with many side rooms lay before us. A robed priest walking down the hall saw us and beckoned us to follow him, leading us to the office of Cardinal Drakon Erebos.

His office, large and plush with many high quality pieces of furniture, smelled of polish. The Cardinal was young, I noted, half expecting to see an older man; perhaps he was thirty-three. He wore crimson robes, laced with much gold trim. His black hair was short with a red skullcap on top. He had a well-kept black moustache and a kindly looking face. As we entered, he rose from his desk and came around to greet us.

"Oh, Empress Kassandra, what a pleasant surprise. Do come in," he leaned over and gave her a welcoming hug. "Selene, so good to see you too."

He gave her a lesser hug, I noted, more like a perfunctory duty.

"Cardinal Drakon, I've brought the two young women from Velona who, as you have probably heard by now, were abducted from our palace, and turned into Women of the Eighth Degree. See how marvelously fast they have healed? This is Mrs. Dita and Bethany Brozena Malina from Velona."

"I am so very, very pleased to meet both of you at long last. The Empress has told me some about you. It is not often that we have such beautiful visitors from distant Velona." He gave both Dita and me a warm hug, as solid a hug as he gave Kassandra. "Please, have a seat. Can I get you anything to drink?"

"No thank you, we've just come from breakfast. Bethany did so want to see our magnificent church for herself. She's heard so much about it from me that she just had to see it and meet Your Holiness," Kassandra replied.

"So good of you to come, Dita, Bethany. First, let me express my sincerest apologies for the great tragedy that has befallen such lovely women of Velona. It is such a crime. I do hope the Emperor can apprehend those responsible. You see, here in Demokritos, becoming a Holy Woman of the Eighth Degree is the highest honor that a wife can do for her husband, binding them together in holy matrimony for life. It is a sacred, very special ceremony. Someone has greatly abused one of our most Holy Rituals by doing this to you. So I am so very sorry. Please, do not judge either our Church of our country by this despicable actions of some ruffians."

"Don't worry, Cardinal; we hold no such grudge against either your church or Demokritos," I replied honestly.

"Only the guilty culprits," Dita added. "When I get my hands on them, they will certainly pay dearly." The cardinal's eyebrows rose.

"You mean figuratively, yes, Dita. I understand. Anyone would feel the same way. Yet, if it is within your heart, you should forgive those who have sinned against you. Hold not onto hatred, for it corrupts your soul. I am intrigued with both of you. Empress Kassandra has told me that you both come from Velona. I ask because here in Demokritos, we have had the misfortune of having some religious zealots from a religious cult visiting our country. They came from an obscure island called Dorota, where their people have a skin color remarkably identical to yours."

"We've heard his before," I replied, needing to defuse this fast. "We are cousins of Queen Athena Patra. Our mothers came from Demokritos and married men in Velona. I guess that's why our skin is darker than those in Velona and lighter than here. What did these men from this Dorota do here?" I probed for his viewpoint.

"Wicked, wicked things. They claim in their nation, all women are born as Holy Women and that their women, who are as you three are, perform all normal things a woman with arms would do in life. They claim to have a perfect society, in which all women are highly respected, and there is virtually no crime. They came here to recruit our people into their cult and ways. Indeed, their Elders have a magic voice that so convinces men and women. I am so very sad to say that over the years so many of our wonderful people fell victim to their treasonous, vile words. When these people gave up everything in their lives to join, all their women had surgery to remove their arms. Despicable beyond words! They have taken one of our most holy rituals and turned it into such filth!"

"If that was not evil enough, they then said that it was all a big mistake! These poor women were then cast out into the world. Our church took compassion on these unfortunate souls, who were deceived, perhaps by the Devil himself. We have worked hard to find living arrangements, servants, and jobs for these women and their families. I am so sorry that we were not always in time; some committed the worst sin of all and took their own lives out of sheer depression and despair. I am so grateful for the Empress Kassandra here, who when she learned of their most desperate need, took thirty of these women and their entire families into her employ and got the other seven queens to do likewise. Because of their selfless devotion and kindness, nearly two hundred fifty of those in the most need have now been given new and productive lives. So you can see why we of the Church are so against these wicked men from Dorota."

"Yes, I certain can see that."

"In fact, I went further than that. Normally, women, such as the Empress here, who have become a Holy Woman out of love and respect for their husbands are held in the most highest of respect within our Church and country. I mandated that all the deceived women should also be so honored within our Church, and the Empress has kindly paralleled that within our country as well."

He went on, "So there is hope, Dita, Bethany. I do know that there are women such as you living in Velona. While some are Holy Women, such as Empress Kassandra here, most have come from the wicked Dorota Elders' actions. When you return to your Velona, contact the Church there. I will send word to the Cardinal in Velona to accept both of you into his flock as most highly respected Holy Women. This is the very least that I can do to make amends for the most brutal treatment that you have suffered here in Demokritos during your visit."

"Thank you, Cardinal," I said, biting my tongue. No way was I going to join their Church!

"Please, do not let this misfortune corrupt your hearts. As I continually tell Empress Kassandra, set a good example for all the other women of our world. They look to you for strength and guidance. In many ways, you are their role models. How can you not be so? When others look upon you, let them see strength, faith, kindness, love, compassion, and leadership. This you can give freely. Show them not bitterness, hatred, and despair."

"Oh we certainly will do that, Your Holiness. I've no bitterness in my heart or despair," I said quite truthfully. He was saying all the proper things that I might suggest; I could find little fault in his words, spoken with sincerity and compassion. I did not detect the icy coldness that I had with Kassandra. Yet, how could I tell who was using who? I already knew that somehow his very own Mano del Dio men were behind much of the treachery and assassinations in recent years.

"You mentioned leadership, Cardinal. Do your Holy Women occupy such positions of leadership within your Church? Are some ordained priests? I am sorry if I seem so ignorant of your church." I asked very leading questions of which I already knew the answers. I wanted to draw him out.

"I am afraid that our Lord Jehosa only allows men of pure hearts, chaste men, men who forsake even fleshly marriage, to become our priests. Long do they study and must discard worldly ways. We do have holy women who wish to contribute; we call them nuns. They often care for the sick and injured. Still, we try to do what little is allowed. In all our Churches, the Holy Women of the Eighth Degree are given the high honor of sitting in the front rows during Mass. No, by leadership I meant secular leadership, such as the Empress here or the many queens. Smaller towns need mayors to lead them and guide them. In Demokritos, there is no higher leader than our Empress. All eyes look to her. Only slightly less in importance are our seven queens. Even more eyes look to them for guidance in their lives. And so it continues on down to the smallest village who looks to their mayors and wives for guidance. At all levels, women can set good examples for the others to follow."

"A case in point, Empress Kassandra, seeing how cultured and civilized our neighboring state of Annelise is, has adopted their refined and fashionable dress. She has been instrumental in getting such wide spread among women of our country. I see that she has convinced both of you to join her in showing the world and other women how a cultured, civilized woman ought to dress. I am very impressed with your dresses, Bethany and Dita. Now other women, seeing you, will aspire to be equally well dressed. In time, our women will all take pride in their appearance."

"I see what you mean. But doesn't leadership cover more than just how we dress?" I baited him.

"Oh yes, yes, indeed yes. I merely used that as an immediate example at hand. Empress Kassandra and the seven queens have shown the country that we should accept these unfortunate families who were deceived by those from Dorota and lend them our help and support — not forsake them as foolish idiots and let them starve to death. I am so sad to say that that was precisely what the average person did — forsaking these unfortunate women and families, ridiculing them, and watching them starve or taking their own lives. Empress Kassandra and the queens, in setting a good example, are changing the way that our people now view these thousands of unfortunate families."

He was enjoying this conversation immensely, and he leaned over and said, "You know, sometimes, I think that women ought to be our leaders and not men. The Emperor is now fighting a war somewhere up north in a foreign land. I've heard that his generals are planning a large-scale attack on our next-door neighbors, the wild horsemen of Vladimir. Emperor Deimos led thousands of our young men to their deaths in an ill-advised, ill-fated attack on the Sea Princes. When this Dorota catastrophe struck, the Emperor did nothing at all to help the victims. I am so thankful that Empress Kassandra had the wisdom to intercede."

My viewpoint was still continually flopping about. At first, I thought that Kassandra was using the Cardinal and his Church. Now was the Cardinal using Kassandra? What a tangled web I had on my hands — well, figuratively anyway. I needed a way to sort out this mess. What could I ask that might shed more light on it?

Kaboom! I felt my chair vibrating from the enormous explosion that shook the entire building. Instantly, images of that volcano erupting as we fled from it, when we were out searching for the mantis creatures, and it had eaten my arms before we killed it, came vividly into my mind. Boom! Boom! Boom! Dozens of smaller explosions echoed around the city. Kassandra screamed loudly, quite startled.

"What in heaven's name was that?" Cardinal Drakon exclaimed, a look of shock on his face.

"Volcano, earthquake?" I suggested involuntarily.

Smaller explosions now started up, one after the other, sometimes several going off at once. Screeching, wailing sounds followed by booms filled the air with waves of noise. Now the noise became continuous and near deafening.

Dita was the first to work it out; she yelled above the cacophony, "Fireworks! It must be fireworks!"

"Oh dear lord! There must have been some horrible accident!" Cardinal Drakon suggested. Curious, no one knew anything at all, and he was suggesting an accident.

Kassandra shrieked, "Oh no! Our husbands are all there — the kids! Oh no! Selene, we must get there at once!" She rose to leave; we followed her lead.

"I will go there too, Empress. Perhaps everyone is safe and sound. I wouldn't worry so," Cardinal Drakon offered a positive idea.

Wearing these constricting outfits and an emergency do not mix, not remotely. We needed to make haste, but could only take the tiniest of carefully placed steps. Even the bit of rushing we attempted had all four of us gasping for breath by the time that we finally reached the main double doors and the four steps leading down to the waiting carriage. Seeing our plight, the coachman lifted the Empress and carried her down, over and into the coach. One by one, he did the same to the three of us, for which I was grateful, though still gasping to catch my breath. Already, I could see hundreds of people running down the street heading for the warehouse district.

Now our coach was rolling along, but soon he had to slow down. The streets were clogged with men, women, and children trying to see what was happening. The noise of fireworks exploding continued to fill the air with noise and flashes. As we got a bit closer, we could see a wall of flames and smoke rising in the distance. Something was on fire, and the fireworks seemed to be flying out of the inferno. My heart sank. I had a very bad feeling that I was witnessing that bad event that I had been trying to uncover and prevent.

At last, we could go no further. The street was packed with people staring at the conflagration. We didn't dare get out of the carriage; it was far too dangerous for us, what with these heels and wide dresses and the packed throng of people. At least our driver managed to get the carriage turned halfway around so that we could see the blaze. It was huge. We stared in disbelief.

Our carriage driver spotted a man on a horse pushing his way in our direction through the vast crowds in the street. As the man drew closer, I heard our driver waving and yelling to him. Now he nudged his horse our way. "Oh, that's one of Argos' guards," Kassandra wailed. "Over here, over here!"

The man finally got to us and dismounted. His face and neat uniform were covered in black soot. His eyes were crying, leaving cleaned streaks running down his otherwise blackened face. He was in shock and grief at the same time. "All gone! They're all gone!" he cried.

"Who's all gone? What happened? Where's Argos? Where are the kings and the kids?" Empress Kassandra demanded to know, using a sharp, piercing voice to try to get through to the guard.

"All of them! Gone! Big explosion! I can barely hear you. Yell louder. All gone!" Tears streamed down his face now like rain, washing soot down onto his uniform.

"What?" she shrieked loudly. "Who's gone? Gone where? Are they safe?" she yelled as loudly as she could. Both Dita and I already figured what had happened. We had a sick feeling in our stomachs.

"Argos, kings, kids — all inside — all killed. Explosion. Massive explosion. Walls crumbled. All gone!" he continued to cry.

"Driver, get us back to the palace," I took charge and yelled up to him. He responded, and ever so slowly, we began to move again. Kassandra sank back in her seat; she looked stunned and devastated, though she, like we, was still struggling to breathe.

As we moved along, she mumbled, "Dead? All dead?" Selene sat in stony silence, shocked.

I began wondering. Was Kassandra just putting on an act for us or was she genuinely shocked by this? The Cardinal made me suspicious by his rush to call it an accident, before he even knew what had happened. Of course, if he had a hand in causing it, he would know.

At last, Selene calmed down, as did Kassandra, who had finally caught her breath. Selene said, "Well good riddance to Argos, I say, Kassandra. You know how badly he treated you."

"I know, Selene, but the others — the kings, their kids! It's so horrible," Kassandra replied.

Suddenly curious, I asked, "Emperor Argos was treating Kassandra badly? Isn't that a crime here?"

Selene looked at Kassandra and vice versa. "Oh, I can admit it," Kassandra sighed. "Ever since he became Emperor, he's totally ignored me. We haven't shared the same bed in years. I know that he's fathered a child with some barmaid somewhere, but he hasn't hit me or denied me anything. He's always seen that I am well cared for — it's just that he isn't a husband or friend to me anymore, not for years."

Selene added, "I say good riddance to him!"

"Yes, but all the kings and kids?" Kassandra chided her.

"Well, maybe some of them were treating their queens just as bad, Empress. We should have made inquiries, you know," Selene replied.

Somehow, I felt as if this conversation had been carefully choreographed for our benefit. Why was this inside information only now reaching our ears? Was this an attempt to make less of this catastrophe?

Dita joined in, "Well, King Damon hasn't been the kind loving husband to Athena either."

"Oh, we didn't know that," Kassandra replied. I doubted that very much! "But her son! She loved and doted on her son. This is just too horrible!"

Dita became strangely silent. If indeed all the men had been killed in an explosion, who was going to take over control of this country? These women? Hardly, she thought, all they do is go around wearing these dresses and looking pretty. I bet there is going to be some big power play move. This she confided in me later when we were alone.

We pulled into the palace. As strong arms lifted us down, the queens and nearly everyone else came out to meet us, some moving rapidly, others such as Athena, very slowly. All looked pale and shocked. No one knew what had happened, only that the very earth had shaken with the violence of the explosion. They had recognized the fireworks effect and all feared the worst.

Selene whispered to Kassandra, but loud enough that we could hear her, "Kassandra, pull together. You must take charge now. Be the leader. Be strong for the queens." Kassandra did just that, slowly gliding once more across the cobblestones, moving towards the gathering crowd. Dita and I followed behind her, beginning our pitiful slow glide over to Athena. Good,

Xene was at her side.

Kassandra spoke loudly, "Everyone, may I have your attention." Only the distant exploding fireworks could be heard. "Apparently, there has been some kind of terrible accident at the warehouse where the fireworks are stored. Our guard here was nearby when the explosion occurred. He is covered in black soot. He says that all our men were inside when it happened. He says that they are all gone. Considering how massive that explosion was — it shook the very Church seats we were sitting in — I would not hold out hope for many survivors. The whole city is in the streets, and we could not get close enough to see. I am sure soon we will be given a full report by those that were there and somehow survived this horrible, tragic accident. We may have all lost our husbands and our children. I do not have words to express the loss that I feel. Yet, we must be brave and face the future, whatever that may be. We should pray for our husbands and children; perhaps somehow miraculously, they escaped the explosion. I will let everyone know the moment that I know anything for sure. Until then, we can only wait graciously and patiently and pray."

Athena fainted, but Xene caught her and kept her from hitting the ground. Other queens were having difficulty standing as well. The crowd began to return to their assigned posts, while Dita and I continued to make our way slowly over to Athena. Now Barnabas intervened and began carrying her inside; Xene could not keep up with him, and we had to be content to follow her slowly.

"Damn these heels anyway," Dita grumbled as we nearly fell over in our attempt at haste. Now we had to stop and catch our breaths as well. "Damn, damn, damn," she said between gasps.

When we finally got to her private room, she'd recovered and was lying on her bed, others hovering over her. She was crying. When she saw us enter, she called out, "Not little Anatolios, not him!"

Xene tried to comfort her, "Perhaps they are all right, Athena."

"You heard that explosion, too. I just know my little boy is gone." She continued to cry. Dita and I plopped into some other chairs too exhausted to do much but wait and see the outcome.

Around noon, the Captain of the Palace Guards returned, soot covered and hard of hearing. He gave the Empress and queens a full report. He was yelling, but thought he was talking softly. "Argos and the others had entered the warehouse and were examining the fireworks. We guards took up defensive positions around the building. The explosion was massive; walls collapsed. A number of guards were crushed by the falling debris. All of my men were thrown to the ground. We struggled to our feet when the flames burst out. I lost another five who were caught in the inferno. We saw no one get out of the building. Only an act of Lord Jehosa could anyone who was inside still be surviving. You must assume that they are all dead."

"But what happened to cause the explosion?" Kassandra yelled loud enough so he could hear.

He shrugged his shoulders. "No idea. No one was around that we saw."

Kassandra had all the queens and their advisors and Special Helpers join her in her throne room to hear this report. Quietly she suggested, "We should all remain here. Others may be coming with more information for us." Uniformly, all the queens were in grief and crying or sobbing silently, their assistants holding them and dabbing at the flowing tears. Kassandra, on the other hand, showed no signs of grief at all. Curious.

At irregular intervals, other guardsmen reported to their Empress. Each time the news was about the same. Some had been burned, and those she sent to the palace doctor. Around five, Cardinal Drakon himself arrived. His scarlet robes showed signs of soot and a few scorch marks. His face looked drawn and haggard.

Standing before the Empress and queens, he said, "It is with the heaviest of hearts that I have come here this late afternoon. I have just come from the warehouse, where I personally did what little I could. The fire is out now, but embers are still smoldering. While the rubble is still too hot for us to enter, alas, we have seen many bodies in the debris. I have talked with many who were there who survived. Never have I had to deliver devastating news such as this. I have not the words to describe it. My Empress, my queens, all those who went there today are gone. Our country has suffered the greatest loss of its leaders in the entire history of Demokritos."

He paused, while the women continued to cry, now harder than ever. "When the embers die down, I have asked that the remains be brought to our Church for burial. As they lived together and died together, it is fitting that they be buried together. The Church will erect a giant monument with all their names etched in the marble. I will let you know when the Church will conduct burial services for the fallen."

"I have asked the Captain of the City Guards to conduct a thorough investigation into the cause and if there was any foul play involved. However, it appears to have been just a tragic accident of some kind."

"Holy Women of Demokritos, I beseech you in your time of sorrow and grief, be brave, be strong. All of Demokritos will be watching you. Stand tall and proud. Give our people hope and strength to survive this monstrous calamity. As I get more news, I will personally come by and relay it to all of you. Thank you." He bowed to the eight and left.

The innocent voice of a ten year old girl Announcer broke the sounds of sobbing. "Dinner is ready." Many of us were hungry, and we urged the grieving widows to come with us and at least eat a little, if only to keep their strength up.

After supper, flowers began arriving at the palace. During the next two days, the outpouring of grief and sympathy from those in Kefall was a bit overwhelming. Wagon loads of flowers arrived nearly continuously over these two days. Thankfully, the staff of Kassandra took care of them for everyone.

After diner, Athena, Xene, Barnabas, Dita, and I met in her private room. Well, actually Iou, Ida, and Oda were also there, sitting quietly in a corner, ready to assist we three. I asked Iou if she could bring us some tea. A few minutes later, the duckbilled woman sat beside me, holding a cup so I could sip. By now, the shock had worn off Athena. While I knew that I needed to give these women therapy sessions to help them cope with this sudden and shocking loss, there were more important matters at hand.

Athena, who finally took a sip from her cup held by an insistent Oda, sighed, and said, "Well, I am not really grieving for Damon. You all know just how unfaithful he has been to me. He somehow had a hand in my getting like this," she shrugged her armless shoulders. "So there's no real loss there. It's just my little boy, my little Anatolios."

After telling them what we learned of Kassandra and Argos' relationship, Athena said, "Well, she won't be grieving much for him either. She's lucky that she didn't have any children perish with him. I guess our husbands got what they deserved, but how could something like this happen? It is all so wild and surreal. Something huge must have gone wrong. Did one of them light up a pipe and cause the explosion?"

"We will probably never know the answer to that one," Barnabas said quietly.

"Say," I had a sudden insight, "what about the other queens? How was their relationship with their husbands?"

Xene answered that a little. "I know that Frona and Melita are absolutely crushed! They've had a long and happy marriage. Frona has been with or rather was with Bakos twenty-one years. You remember, Athena, we went to their twentieth anniversary party last year. It is a good thing that their two children are married and not here. The others lost all their children except Adonia's girl and Melita's girl. Now I know for sure that Melita and Frona were very happy with their husbands, so their loss must run deep."

"Alekto, she's the youngest queen, she's only been married two years now. Imagine only being married two years and having given up your arms for him. She's probably just devastated too."

"I know," Athena spoke up, "I should visit Alekto, Adonia, Ariadne, and Adonia and pay them my respects. I ought to level with them about Damon too. It may help ease their overall grief. I will see if they had any suspicions about their husbands. Probably just Xene ought to accompany me."

The two left to make their rounds of the other widows. Iou continued to help me sip my tea, while I continued to ponder the situation.

However, Dita asked the key question. "Say, Barnabas, how goes the transition of power and thrones here? I mean, will they somehow choose a new Emperor and kings and all that? Will all these queens just move out and find a house somewhere — out of a job, so to speak?"

"Now that is an interesting question, Dita. If, say, the Emperor was killed, the Noble Houses of Demokritos would step in and name an heir to the throne. Often, it is the eldest son of the one who died. This last time, they chose to give it to the late Emperor's daughter, Kassandra. With the kings, it is done in a similar fashion, only it is the Noble Houses of just that kingdom who choose. Again, it usually goes to the eldest son, but far more often than with the Emperor, it can go to some other relative or even to a family who's never had a relative as king."

"But we've never had the loss of the Emperor and all the kings at one time, ever. Who knows what is going to happen? Worst-case scenario, the Noble Houses could elect new kings and Emperor. In that case, yes, our current queens would vacate their palaces, returning to a normal life as a noblewoman and Holy Woman. Bakos's son is old enough to be king of Thallyus. They could give the throne to Frona's son. Melita's surviving daughter is too young. Perhaps some of the queens may remarry and put their new husbands on the throne. Honestly, Dita, I have no idea how this will play out. A power struggle is certain, that I do know. Never has there been such a power vacuum in our country."

We continued chatting about the future power struggle. Sometime later Athena and Xene returned. She gave a full report. I noticed that by giving her something useful to do, her grief over the death of her son had subsided considerable.

"Well, Alekto is just devastated! She was coerced and pressured into becoming like us by her husband. You were right, Bethany, now she is terribly frightened about the prospect of living her life by herself without her arms. Honestly, I think that she is more afraid of that than she is grieving for her loss. Now, Danae is taking it better. When they were married some seven years ago, she kept her arms. However, Haimon kept pressuring her, and in 746, she finally agreed to do it. Now she is also frightened of a future without arms and no husband. Rightly so."

"I spent a lot of time with Ariadne; she's barely a year older than me and you. She's absolutely terrified, a real basket case right now. Dimitrios wooed her for two years and then proposed to her only after she was madly in love with him. When he proposed, he said that he could only be married to a Woman of the Eighth Degree or his dad would disown him. His parents have given large donations to the Church, you see. She was appalled and refused him, but he kept at her, until she at last gave in to his demand. Now she is terrified. She believes that soon Thrace will elect some other king, and she'll have to move out of the palace, but she has no place to move to, excepting back to her parents, which she doesn't want to do. I gave her a bit of support; I told her if that happened, she must come and live with me, wherever that ends up being."

"Adonia is a different story. She's been married eight years now. It was her idea to become like us to please her husband. For years now, she wishes that she could take that back. Instead of bringing them extremely closer together, it's had the opposite effect. He hasn't mistreated her, but he frequently slips out of their palace, and she knows that he's had three affairs with other women. She's got a country estate left to her by her father. She says that if Phindos elects a new king, she'll take her daughter and move to her estate. Of course, she asked me the thousand coin question: Would any man ever date her again? She means because she has no arms now. I had to be realistic and honest with her. It is highly doubtful that any of us would ever be able to find a new husband. After all, he'd be nuts to have one of us. We are so helpless and so completely dependent, that would turn any man off, now wouldn't it?"

"Don't be so harsh on yourself, Athena," Dita replied. "I'd marry Bethany arms or no arms."

"You did exceptionally well, Athena," I complimented her. "Now we can probably rule out someone murdering all the kings just because they were unfaithful to their Holy Women, such as Damon was. We've eliminated one theory, I do believe. I had considered that someone had killed them all to extract revenge on a collection of unfaithful husbands of Women of the Eighth Degree. I think we can now rule out revenge as a motive."

"But what possible motive could anyone have in murdering all the kings and so many innocent children?" Athena asked.

"If we knew that, we'd likely know who did it," Dita explained.

"Bethany, when this is over, can I beseech you to give your therapy to my fellow queens? I will pay you whatever you desire. I can see just how much this would help them," Athena asked.

"Of course, Athena. No charge. I'll do it when the time is right." I yawned; we all were tiring. What a day. A bit later, in our private room, Iou and Ida began undressing Dita and me. I hated to have to have them do this, but I had no choice in the matter. They did brush out our hair nicely and even helped us into bed so that we didn't have to mostly fall into it. I thanked them for their kindness as they left.

Chapter 39 Power Transition

The next morning, our many helpers began laying out our black outfits for us to wear for mourning. At nine, the Cardinal returned to the palace with news that the combined funeral would be held at three this afternoon. I asked for a private word with him before he left.

"How can I help you, most Holy Woman," he said kindly.

"About this combined funeral, is there a reason for this? Some queens were thinking of having their loved ones buried back in their own kingdoms," I explained, although I already suspected the real reason behind it. I was right.

"It must be done this way, Holy Woman. Their remains are almost impossible to distinguish. One can only tell child from adult. You can understand how truly sorry I am that we must do it this way," he said apologetically. I replied that I did and thanked him for not telling the grieving widows and mothers the reason. He gave me a big smile and hug, then left.

Our Special Helpers assisted us into our black satin gowns and boots. Then, they followed us to the dining room to feed us, before they went to eat themselves. I began to wonder why they always ate in private, never with us. I put that one on the back burner to find out. Not long afterwards, carriages began pulling up outside the palace, and slowly the queens and entourage began boarding. With we women and our outfits, this took considerable time. Likewise, when we arrived at the Cardinal's church, more time flew by as we disembarked and slowly moved to the front rows.

A half hour before the services were to begin, a large choir of men and women, many armless as well, entered and stood off to one side of the high altar. They began singing four part motets. Suddenly, I recognized these songs. "Dita, Chara wrote these! Remember her?" She did. They were using the music that she had written many years ago in Velona. I truly enjoyed hearing these motets once again. The musicians were perfectly in tune and on pitch. The reverberation within this enormous church greatly added to their sound. I understood why Kassandra said it sounded like angels singing. Now I began to understand the true motives behind these new Churches of Jehosanity.

In such huge spaces, the person was dwarfed and made to feel insignificant. God was dominant. Surrounded by all the riches of art and even gold, the House of God seemed to be heaven on earth. All this only solidified the Church's hold over its members. Devious, but clever. Thought went into all this, Pope Leo's thought, I realized.

I turned around only to see that the huge church was filled to beyond capacity. Even the long isle was filled with people coming to this historic funeral. I also noticed that all eyes were on us, we women in the front row! Kassandra was right; we were observed carefully, but then, who wouldn't want to get a firsthand view of your rulers?

Instead of the usual priest, Cardinal Drakon conducted the funeral personally, resplendent in his crimson robes, trimmed in gold. His words were designed to bring comfort to the widows. He eulogized each man with the choir singing a hymn between each eulogy. The service lasted for an hour. However, we had to wait nearly that long before the huge crowd left so we could move on to the actual burial site in the cemetery behind the church complex.

Because the ground was uneven out here, we all needed a strong arm around us so we could keep our balance. Once more, I was grateful for Iou, as Dita was for Ida. The saddest moment came when Alekto cried out, "I cannot even place a flower on his grave!" She broke down once more, though her personal assistant laid the rose on the burial mound for her. My heart went out to her.

We returned in time for supper. However, the Cardinal had left word with Kassandra that he wanted to speak to her and the queens after dinner. When Cardinal Drakon walked into the throne room, the Announcer said clearly, "Cardinal Drakon Erebos." He saw a sea of black satin. All of us were still wearing those dresses. He took a seat before the semi-circle of thrones and facing directly that of the Empress.

"Empress Kassandra, queens of Demokritos. Our country has just suffered the worst loss of top leadership in our history. I come to you this evening as both as a humble citizen of our great country and as the Cardinal of the Church of Jehosanity, the largest church in our country. I have not slept a wink since that fateful day, searching my soul for answers. As all of you are most likely acutely aware, the sudden accidental deaths of our top men and leaders has left an enormous political vacuum. From the past, we all know just how chaotic and sometimes vicious that power struggle can become to see who will become the next king or Emperor. Yet, this time that struggle may well be so huge, so enormous in scope, that our beloved country could well be plunged into a chaotic anarchy, bringing riots and ruin to our great country."

"This fear of the consequences of this unfortunate accident and great tragedy is what has kept me awake. As a citizen and as your highest religious leader, I come before you tonight to beg, nay plead on my knees if I must, to get you to consider what I am about to propose to you. I want more than anything else to avoid the chaotic aftermath. This can only be done with your help. My proposal to you is to stay on as our leaders. Yes, you, Kassandra are still our beloved Empress and ruler. You queens, you are still the queen of your kingdom. Stay on and demand and insist that you and you alone be allowed to continue to rule our nation!"

"I have supreme confidence that you women can and will rule

Demokritos fairly and justly. That you can do a superb job of it. Of that, I have not the slightest doubt! The kings' advisors live and can provide you with the same information and advice they gave the Emperor and kings. Only now, they will give it to you. You women, you run our country. You make all the decisions. You continue to rule and the political fallout, the chaos of succession will be completely avoided. Our country will remain strong, vigorous, and powerful."

As if on cue, Kassandra spoke up, "Cardinal Drakon. You know as well as I that the Noble Houses will begin to meet and try to appoint a new Emperor and kings. How can we do this that you ask?"

"Ah, I have searched the depths of my soul to answer this one. If you agree to continue to run our country and rule in place of your lost ones, then I am prepared to have the Church of Jehosanity back you fully, completely, and without any reservations. We will see that the Noble Houses give you the chance to prove that you can run our country and that you will do the kind of job that would make every citizen proud to call you their Empress, their queen. Yes, it will take some time for us to get to every Noble House and convince them to allow you to continue to reign. In time, I am confident that this can be done. Yet, it all hinges upon whether you, the most Holiest of Women in all Demokritos, will accept this heavy burden to rule our nation. I am begging you to accept this challenge. If you wish, I will get down on my knees and beg you."

Kassandra replied, "Your Holiness, that will not be necessary. I am the Empress, and I give you my word that I will continue to be your Empress and do my very best to be worthy of your trust and the trust of all our citizens. Queens, are you with me on this?" Here was the decisive moment that Kassandra had been waiting for — would they so agree. I saw her holding her breath. I bet if she had fingers, they would have been crossed.

Athena spoke first. "Yes, I will remain Queen of Theos and do my very best to rule." One by one, the other queens agreed as well.

Kassandra breathed a sigh of relief. "There is your answer, Your Holiness. Yet, I don't see how this can be done. If the queens return to their kingdoms, will not chaos follow them?"

"Thank you Empress, queens! Yes, Empress, you must give the Church time to deal with the Noble Houses. We will publish a broad statement tomorrow announcing that you are staying on to run our country. I will get started on the Noble Houses tomorrow as well. Yet, as we all know, that will take some time and some convincing. It is neither safe nor wise for the queens to return to their kingdom just yet, not until we get the agreement of all the Noble Houses."

Kassandra spoke up, "Then, we will follow your advice. Queens, you will stay here in the palace indefinitely. All of your advisors are here, so you can indeed perform your duties here, just as well as you could back in your own palace, perhaps better, since here we can all work together as needed.

We can lend each other our support, if not our hands. Plus, I will assume all the financial burden of your lengthy stay. Perhaps it will only be for a few months until this is settled." This, the queens found encouraging.

"Again, Empress, queens, I have not the words with which to thank you enough for taking on this extra burden in this time of your grief. I and my Church will get working at once on building support for your decision. If I can be of any further assistance to you, please let me know. I would like to invite all of you to come to our Sunday services and sit in your rightful places of honor. Thank you again. Good night."

After he left, Kassandra took charge. "Okay, queens, tomorrow we will have our work cut out for us. Let's meet here at nine and have the men's advisors begin to bring us up to speed on current actions. In the meantime, let's do this right. Let's get done the things that will really help our people and those in your kingdoms, shall we? Bring your ideas with you tomorrow, ladies. We are going to show our country that we women can effectively and justly run Demokritos!"

Back in Queen Athena's chambers, Fetchers brought us tea once more. Again, I had to have my Special Helper hold my cup. I was beginning to dislike having to be so dependent on so many others.

Athena commented, "Now that was totally unexpected and unforeseen! Imagine that. The Church backing us as being the rulers of Demokritos and not some men! It sure seemed like both the Cardinal and Kassandra knew what they were doing, while we queens were in the dark."

"Point well taken, Athena," I replied. "To me, it just seems way to improbable the way this is working out. It has been all way too much and way too fast. It is becoming more and more plain to me that all this has been planned well in advance."

"Queen Frona, Queen Melita, Queen Adonia, Queen Ariadne, Queen Danae, Queen Alekto," her ten year old armless Announcer called out. We turned and in they all came, accompanied only by their duckbilled Special Helpers.

Frona said quietly, "Athena, we all would like a private discussion with you and those that you trust with your life." Athena dismissed everyone except Xene, us, and the three Special Helpers. I realized these women chose to bring these Special Helpers because with their enormous lip plates, they were unable to speak much at all, even if they wanted to tell others what went on in here. They were being exceptionally careful, wisely so, I thought.

The seven queens sat together and Frona began, "Athena, what is going on really? Are those two serious about us actually running Demokritos? How are we to do that? We cannot even dress or feed ourselves. Now we are especially vulnerable; we are on our own and many of us feel exceptionally helpless! Will not some send assassins into our bedrooms? Perhaps it would be better just to have this all end now." She shrugged her armless shoulders.

"Other than shaking someone's hand and signing papers, I don't recall Damon needing his hands to rule," Athena chose her words carefully. "We all know some of the dumb things our kings did. Honestly, we only need to use our minds to rule. Sometimes I thought mine was far sharper than my husband's was. I know Argos was a real idiot, I hate to speak ill of the departed, but it's true. He was very, very slow to grasp things. If we use our minds, I think we can do a good job of it, though I know we're going to be challenged initially because our husbands kept many details from us that the advisors will now have to explain to us. I think that we can do it, especially if we all work together as a team."

She continued, "As far as the assassins go, we must depend upon Kassandra maintaining a high level of security here. In many ways, they are right. We will be safer here, where we are all in one place. I know I'm helpless but I'm not yet ready to die," she said defiantly.

I spoke up, "May I point out something?"

"Sure, Bethany. We are all so sorry about what happened to you and Dita. It's just awful. At least we had some wild reason to have it done, though most of us now wish we could take it back," Frona replied. I realized that as the eldest of the queens, she was acting as their spokeswoman.

"Just before you came, we were discussing what has happened. Don't you find that all this is happening way too fast? Doesn't the speech by the Cardinal and Kassandra seem like it was well rehearsed? They seemed to play off one another. It all seems too contrived to be a mere reaction to the disaster."

They agreed, made much their own observations, and admitted their own suspicions as well. I continued, "Dita and I have been for some time now trying to unravel this web of mystery, to lay bare the actual truth. We've gathered much incriminating data, but not facts yet, though we expect that in time, that will come too. There is no doubt in our minds that the Cardinal and his Church and the Empress Kassandra are somehow linked closely. Just how we are not yet sure. This evening's events has convinced us completely. It could be that this is all Kassandra's doing and that she is using the Cardinal and his Church. Or it could be that the Cardinal is pulling the strings with Kassandra as his puppet. We don't know which just yet, only that they are closely connected."

"Now what I find highly encouraging for your safety is that both the Cardinal and Kassandra want you here and as the rulers. I would have feared for your safety, as Frona has suggested, if this had not happened. That they both seem to be desirous of having you queens stay on and continue to rule, to me, that speaks volumes. I would hazard a good guess that this was the overall plan, though whose plan it was I am not yet certain. Thus, they have you where they want you. For now, my opinion is that you need not fear any assassinations."

"But what can they hope to gain by having such helpless women running our country?" asked Melita.

"Until I uncover more, Melita, I cannot say."

Alekto, the youngest woman here, spoke up, "Bethany, Dita, we are so miserable as we are. I'm truly sorry that they did it to you too. I just feel so helpless now that Hermos is gone. Do you really think that we pitiful women could actually do this?"

"Alekto, you are not pitiful, nor are you as helpless as you might think. Give it your best and see how it goes," I tried to comfort her and give her a little hope.

Frona spoke up again, "I'm the oldest and have been armless for the longest here. Yes, in private, we tell it like it is, armless, not the political and religious crap they feed us — Holy Women of the Eighth Degree. Anyway, we tell it like it is. I have told the others, and I feel I need to tell you and Dita this too. Yes, at the beginning I believe all women feel completely helpless. I found it so embarrassing to have to have someone dress me, help me go to the bathroom, and worst of all was having to be fed when dining. I found that horribly embarrassing for the longest time. Yet, as the years go by, I can honestly say it gets better. I'm still as helpless as I was that first day, but now I'm used to it and it doesn't bother me as it used to upset me. Alekto, you will feel better about yourself in time. So will you, Bethany and Dita. Give yourselves time to get used to it all."

She went on, "What you've said makes sense to me. I've never really trusted Kassandra all that much. Yet, if she and/or the Cardinal is behind this, it is imperative that we don't let on to them that we know!" On this, everyone totally agreed.

Frona then looked at me as if she were making up her mind about something. I smiled and she then said, "There is another matter that we wish to discuss with Bethany and Dita. Can we speak honestly and frankly here?"

"What you say will not leave this room," I solemnly promised. She seemed satisfied, but my curiosity rose.

"Cooped up in this palace, news travels fast, particularly between women." Everyone giggled. "Athena, some of us saw you shortly after your surgery. Some came to offer moral support in the months afterwards. Dear, we all know just how utterly depressed you were after your surgery. Some of us fully expected that you would likely take your own life. Here you come to the Winter Council, and we find that you are fully alive, very happy — that is, until this happened. You are vibrant and my gosh dear, your complexion is just radiant. The change is between night and day. We all noticed it and began making discrete inquiries." Now, I knew where this was going!

"If that was not enough, we all have accepted some thirty other women and girls like ourselves, armless, the ones who were in the worst situations in life, and given them jobs, funds, food, clothing, and a place to stay and for their families too. We all know perfectly well the atrocious mental state these women and girls are in, we see them every day, after all. Yet, here you come with yours and we find half of yours are also bright, alert, very much alive, exuberant, and full of life. You know how curious we women can be! We've discovered that Bethany and Dita did something to them and to you that brought about this miraculous change in their lives. Is this not true?" If she had arms, she would have placed them defiantly on her hips. I grinned.

"Yes, it is precisely so," I replied.

Before I could launch into an explanation, she demanded, "Well, Bethany and Dita, all of us want you to do it for us. We have agreed that we will pay any reasonable amount. Our staff too, all of we armless women. Please, you must do this for us, please," she was pleading now and I hastily cut her off. No need to beg.

"Frona, Dita and I have from the beginning intended to give anyone who wished it our therapy. The very minute that we arrived from Velona and discovered what they had done to Athena, we began her therapy sessions. While hers went swiftly, we found that those whom you have rescued have far greater traumas, including treason, betrayal, and ridicule. Before we came to this council, we were averaging about one week per woman and had only been able to get to half of hers. I had anticipated that we would be returning home shortly at which time we intended to continue until we had gotten them all, including the Special Helpers, who have their own traumas, different than yours."

"Now that Dita and I know the magnitude of the problem and now that we will be staying here for some months, we will get going on others soon. For now, I would like to keep Kassandra out of this. Please continue to keep this all a secret from her. If she is behind this tragedy and if she finds out about us and our therapy, she may well put an end to it or to us. The problem facing Dita and me now is that we really need to give each one of you our therapy sessions. However, you need to begin running the country, and we are also needed by Athena as her advisors. We cannot do so many things at one time."

"You have our word; we will keep it a secret from Kassandra. You can still do this therapy, now that you have no arms like us?" Frona asked.

"Hands are not needed at all. How about this idea. Kassandra will probably not hold you in session in the evenings. So starting tomorrow evening, we will both work on two of you. Once we have finished you six queens, we will continue with the many others who need it. Is this acceptable to you?"

"More than acceptable! Yet, how much do we owe you for this therapy?" Frona asked.

"I want not money, but rather to see you do a really good, honest job of running your country. That is worth all the gold and jade in your treasury to Dita and me."

"Thank you Bethany and Dita. Thank you. If I may suggest, could you take Alekto first? She is the most distressed of all of us," Frona asked.

"I had already decided she would be first. Dita will take Ariadne first. Both of you come to our private quarters right after dinner, assuming that Kassandra allows us the evenings free," I replied. "While I don't know why it is that you find yourselves suddenly in charge of your whole country, I do know that you seven can make a positive difference. I have faith in all of you to always do what is right and just, even if others do not, specifically Kassandra." All seven look quite proudly back at me. I could tell they were resolved to do just that.

Meekly, Ariadne, the long auburn haired queen, asked, "Dita, can I ask you a very personal question? Well, really all of us have been very curious about it."

"Sure thing," Dita replied, not knowing what the green-eyed young woman wanted to know.

"Are you really married to Bethany? Are you really like the man? Mrs. Dita and Bethany means the man comes first here," she asked. I saw that all the women were staring intently at Dita, eager to hear her answer.

"Yes, we are really married. We got married in a big church in Velona by the high priestess herself, and we both wore smashing white wedding gowns. And yes, I often wear the pants. Actually, I prefer wearing men's suits with the twin tails. I just hate wearing this Annelise outfit."

The women all giggled, but Ariadne looked confused still and asked, "But how can you do it in bed?"

Dita grinned, "We find ways. Honestly, my love for Bethany here spans lifetimes! We are madly in love still."

Ariadne giggled, "We all know. We can see it all the time. It must be incredible to have a love that strong. But now, I guess we will never know. After all, no one will even date us now, unless all they want is to become king."

Dita decided to liven it up a bit. "Ariadne, of the beautiful auburn hair and gorgeous green eyes, you'd better be careful. I might just come after you myself." She giggled and the others laughed. "Seriously, Ariadne, keep your eyes open. One day you might just meet the perfect guy. You too, Alekto. Just don't let him marry you just so he can get the throne."

Good going, dear. I sent her.

While we were having our meeting, Kassandra was holding one of her own. She summoned in the Captain of the Palace Guards for a meeting. "Just how many guards do we have?" she asked.

"One hundred, Empress."

"Not enough. Go fetch the generals please." Shortly, he returned with the three generals.

"Now then, I want to make myself *perfectly* clear. I *am* the Empress, and I am *now* running this palace and this country, along with the queens, that is. If you cannot take your orders from me, please resign *this* instant." None did.

"Good. Now then, what with all the nasty things that have happened around here, I want palace security quadrupled. We only have one hundred guards. Generals, find me another three legions. I want at least a legion on duty every hour of every day. We absolutely *must* protect the seven queens!"

"We can take them from the Kefall barracks, Empress. I'll have them operational by morning," one responded.

"Excellent, general. Now tomorrow, the queens and I will need a full and complete report on all our military forces, here and abroad. I believe that they will also want to know what your current orders and plans are and then the longer range plans. We will listen and learn, but we may well make some changes. Thank you gentlemen." They left.

She asked her Messenger to summon the Emperor's advisors next. The young girl grinned and ran off to deliver the message. A bit later, the six men entered the throne room of the Empress.

"Have a seat, gentlemen. I am still the Empress, and I am exercising my authority to rule this country. The queens are likewise going to rule their kingdoms. Starting tomorrow morning, we eight will be meeting daily to conduct the business of running Demokritos. Do I make myself perfectly clear? I and the queens are now in charge. Whether you know it or not, I have for years listened in on your conversations with Argos, so I am not wholly unfamiliar with what has and is happening and what must be done. However, tomorrow morning and every day after that, we eight will be meeting in the main throne room. At nine tomorrow, we will need a compete, total briefing of the current state of our country, the current plans that are being carried out, and what is being worked on for the longer range time frame. Expect that we will be making changes for the betterment of our people."

"The queens will need this overview as well. Later on, it can just be between you and me. I expect that the queens will also need time to be fully informed and briefed by their late king's advisors as well. We will do ours in the morning; they can do their local briefings in the afternoons for now until we eight are all up to speed. The only problem that I foresee will be the obligatory signature on official documents. How can this be handled, since I obviously cannot sign my name, nor can the queens?"

"Well, there is the Emperor's seal that is used to stamp the hot wax on the documents. He keeps it locked in his desk drawer. You can start by stamping the seal." He flushed, realizing she couldn't use the stamp either.

Another advisor suggested, "You could have your Personal Assistant, Selene, handle the stamping for you. In fact, she could sign it Selene for Empress Kassandra. That would make it official. I believe that the queens could do something similar, Empress."

"Perfect. Thanks. Do any of you foresee any problems with working with eight women? If so, I'd like to get them ironed out this evening," she stated.

"This is all highly unusual, but I can see that the government must continue to operate until the Noble Houses choose replacements," one replied.

"I aim to see that the Noble Houses do not choose replacements. I'm going to see that they fully support us eight women as our country's leaders." She watched their shocked reactions and knew she'd given them something to ponder tonight. They left whispering among themselves.

"Selene, have someone summon Jonas, Ikaros, and Horus. Yes, the top three key men from Kefall's Noble Houses. I need to see them in my private quarters. It is time that we begin to make use of what we have in our safe. Have them come about an hour apart. We don't want them to see each other here at the palace. Bring them in discretely."

Now Selene understood. She grinned, "This will be interesting, love. I'm on it." Meanwhile, Kassandra rose and glided to her door and headed to her private chambers. Selene returned, retrieved three packets, and arranged them in sequence according to when each man was to arrive. Now they waited.

Around eight, Jonas arrived, slightly put out by being summoned by the Empress at so late an hour. "Thank you for coming, Jonas. Now then, I will get straight to the point. I am now going to run Demokritos as I am still the Empress. The queens are still going to run their kingdoms. The Noble House will support us as the official rulers of our country, and you will exert your power to make that happen."

Oh, she was blunt, Jonas thought. "Is this some kind of joke, Empress? The Noble Houses will meet and elect a new Emperor, as will they a new set of kings. That is how it has always been done."

"Not this time. I and the queens are remaining in our positions, and you will fully support us."

He saw that she was not joking with him. "You can't be serious? Empress, you, well you are of the Eighth Degree." He dared play his high card with her, but he was careful not to insult her.

"I see that you require a bit more convincing. Selene, will you please hand that packet to Jonas." She did as she asked. Jonas looked at her, curious about this package. He opened it and began reading. As he read more and more of its pages, his face got redder and redder.

"Now then. If you fully support me and the queens in the Noble Houses, then this package will remain forever more in my safe. No one will know your dirty little secrets, like the five children you've fathered out of wedlock. Like the money you have embezzled from your company to spend on lavish vacations for your family and friends. If you do not do your part, this package will be sent to the Senate and the Judiciary. Your choice, Jonas. What will it be?"

"What guarantee do I have that you will not release it anyway?"

"None. But why would I want to destroy you when you are more useful to me as a very influential nobleman?"

"You leave me no choice. However," he grew very angry and clenched his fists, "I give you fair warning, Empress. If you ever try to use this against me again, I will send assassins. You have my pledge on that!"

"It's been a pleasure doing business with you, Jonas. Goodnight." He rose and left, most upset.

Twice more she and Selene repeated this action. Both men could not afford to have their dirty secrets revealed to the Senate or the public. Although extremely angry about her demands, they, too, had no choice but to agree to lobby hard for her with the other lesser influential Noble Houses.

As Selene finally began undressing her and getting themselves ready for bed, Kassandra pointed out, "See how long range, careful planning can work wonders for you?" Selene chuckled. Her Empress, her lover, was all that and much more. "Tomorrow night, we will do the same to three more."

"Can we count on the Cardinal? Will he keep his word?" Selene asked.

"We sent him another million yesterday. That should buy his cooperation fully. If not, we will have to get out his packet, won't we?" Selene laughed long and hard. Then she helped Kassandra lie down, and she crawled in beside her. Kassandra whispered, "See, it does not take arms to control men." Selene gave her a passionate kiss.

Bethany? Hi, it's me, Cosima. Mom and I have been working on your explosion. Did it really kill all their kings and Emperor? Cosima was chatting to me via my other body back in Velona. I had given them all the details and guesses and had them doing some research.

Hi, yes, I am afraid so.

Mom's saying hurry it up. Here goes. We started with your estimates on the dimensions of the warehouse and its construction. We assumed first that the cause was the fireworks. Dianna took apart some typical examples, and we measured the amount of powder in them. Using the cost that she said she paid for them, which Kali verifies as correct based on the bank transfers, I calculated the number of actual firecrackers present. Multiplying that times the amount in one gave us a rough total amount of powder. Next, we conducted some scale model simulations to see if we could reproduce the effects that you saw, felt, and heard. Results: not if all the firecrackers in the place went off at the same time could that have created such an explosion that demolished the sides of the building. However, based on the experiment, I made an estimate of what amount would have been needed to cause the effects that you and Dita felt and saw. Now that is a comparatively huge amount of the gunpowder. Based on my finding, Kali did some more searching and came up with an unusual purchase. Oh, she wants to tell you herself. Bye.

Good going, Cosima! Wow, I knew Cosima has a brilliant mind, but she is definitely becoming a detective, I thought, as Kali began talking to my little five year old Bethany body.

Hi, Kali here. Yes, their army routinely purchases gunpowder once a month from Helios Powders, located in Thal, Thallyus. They purchase ten thousand worth each time like clockwork. Then, a little over a month ago and in mid-month they purchased an additional fifteen thousand worth. Based on the going price, Cosima estimated the amount purchased. That total is close to her estimate on the amount of gunpowder required to bring down the warehouse. I believe that the perpetrators stole or were given the powder from the army, who then had to quickly replace it.

I thanked them for their brilliant work. Now we had a positive lead with which to follow up. Although it was getting late, I wanted to pass this on to Barnabas because I didn't know when I would get the chance tomorrow, what with all the planned meetings. I got as far as the door and stood there looking at the barrier. Damn! "Yoo-hoo? Is anyone out there?" I gave our door a slight kick. I heard a voice calling out and hastily a Doorman opened it.

"Excuse me. I know that it is late, but could you please send a Messenger to have Barnabas come here for a minute, please?"

"Yes, miss." He walked down the hall, and soon I heard a woman dashing off. "She'll bring him directly. Only one of us on duty at night, miss. Just holler out if you need something." I thanked him and waited inside my room. Dita had already fallen asleep. It had been a trying day. My feet still throbbed, but I couldn't rub them, and I sure wasn't going to wake someone to do it for me. Soon Barnabas came running; he had hastily thrown on a shirt; I must have awakened him.

"Sorry to bother you, but I've got information that I need passed along, and I don't know when tomorrow I will get the opportunity. I know the amount of gunpowder used in the explosion. I know where it came from and approximately the date it was acquired by our perpetrators." His eyes opened wide. I told him the date, the amount, and the basic fact that it was stolen or given from the army. The powder was used with their cannonae.

"Mrs. Bethany, I just don't know how you come up with all this key information! I will pass it along and set the hounds on the trail. We ought to be able to trace this! Well done indeed!" He returned to his room, and I slipped back into bed — rather I mostly fell into bed, no arms to lower my torso. I woke Dita, but told her to go back to sleep.

I lay there staring at the ceiling. I couldn't sleep; my mind was racing down theories. Someone had gotten a hold of a large quantity of gunpowder. That meant this was murder not an accident. Someone had very carefully planned this explosion. For a while, I tried to imagine ways that someone could have known the right time to set it off and how they may have done it. This was not fruitful except I concluded that someone must have been on the scene to know when all the targets were inside the building. Hence, I gave up this line of thought for now.

If it was murder, that meant it had to have been very carefully planned. All the kings and the Emperor would have to be gathered in one place, but not any of the women. The men all had different interests, and the attack caused minimal collateral casualties. Hence, sporting events, which might have had them all in attendance was out. I realized that few things would have guaranteed that all of them would have gone and gone together, I couldn't leave that out either. No matter how I turned it around in my mind, I always came back to the enormous firecracker event that was planned. The event was singular, a once in a lifetime event — a huge display by any standards. The Empress herself had thought this up, had purchased, and setup the fireworks event.

Did this mean that she planned the deaths of her husband and the seven kings and children? Had she intended all along to kill off the male ruling members? This seemed to fit the facts. However, in her defense, anyone else could have heard of the big event that she had planned and used it for their own purposes of killing off the male rulers. Still, how would these others know that all the males would choose to visit the warehouse, let alone when and all together? I tried to be fair, but I kept returning to the only viable line of reasoning, which was that the Empress had planned this murder all along. Chilling thought.

Yet, I knew that a million had been transferred from the Empress to Cardinal Drakon. That meant he had to be involved somehow. Had he been the one who arranged everything for her? Without arms, she would have had to have others arrange all the pieces. Why? Why would the Cardinal implement the Empress' murder plot? Why did he want all the male rulers slain? After all, we already suspected he and his Mano del Dio men of assassinating many other kings and even Emperor Deimos just to get these current kings, queens, Emperor, and Empress on the thrones. Why kill off the very men you handpicked to be the rulers? It made no sense to me.

So if the Cardinal was not part of the plot, then what was the million in gold for? As far as Kali could determine, most all of it was still in his account. Were there going to be further tragic accidents coming shortly? He promised to go to bat and lobby to keep the women on their thrones. Did he intend some accident to befall all of them? That made even less sense. Could there be something entirely different that was about to happen?

Someone was shaking me. I opened my eyes and stared up at Iou. She was gently waking me. ".i.e .o u.," she said. I gave her a blank look and she repeated it, and then pointed to the sun coming in our window.

"Oh. Time to get up," I said and she waist-nodded. I let her help me rise to a sitting position. One chamber pot later, she began getting me dressed. I got to choose the color of the dress today. For variety, I picked Dita's favorite color, cherry red.

"Wow Bethany, you look really sexy today. Hot lady!" Dita teased me. She wore her blue satin dress. Boots tied tightly to our feet and calves, we rose and moved slowly to the door, heading for the dining room.

I found time to brief Dita on my short conference last night, and she too thought the theft or gift of the powder would be traceable. "Wait! That means it was murder, not an accident!" she exclaimed. I smiled and knew that she would be running down the avenues of possibilities that I had last night. Perhaps she would spot something that I had missed.

When we filed into the main throne room where both the kings and queens met with the Emperor and Empress, we found Kassandra' staff had placed a goodly supply of paper and pencils at each queen's area and her own. Damn, I could no longer take notes! Neither could Dita. I hoped that Xene could deal with all the note taking. As we watched the queens arriving and seeing the paper supply, I sensed that they had the same reaction as I had. Shortly, Athena and Xene glided into the room and over to us. "Guess you are nominated to take the notes, Xene," I teased her. "I seem to have this slight problem with it." She chuckled.

Last to enter was Kassandra who made her grand entrance gliding perfectly over to her larger throne. After Selene adjusted the fall of her dress, she sat down and moved the papers over to herself. "Welcome queens and assistants. We are going to be bombarded with facts today. I do believe that the men's advisors will try to overwhelm us with facts in a vain attempt to show us that we cannot handle this job. Ladies, we are going to prove them wrong!"

"Here's how we are going to work this. In a minute, I will send for your usual advisors, the advisors to the queens. Once they are here, then I will send for the late Emperor's advisors along with the late king's male advisors. In the morning sessions, we will take up the empire's business affairs. After lunch, you will go to your own throne rooms and take up your kingdom's business affairs. I will not plan anything for the evenings, because I figure we all will need time to absorb the bombardment of facts. Ladies, let's show them that we can handle this! Are you ready?" The queens said that they were.

Kassandra sent one of her Messengers to fetch the waiting kingdom male advisors and those of the queens who were not already present. Once those had taken their seats behind their respective monarchs, she sent the Messenger out for the Emperor's male advisors, all six of them.

The male advisors did do exactly what Kassandra predicted. They fired off volley after volley of facts, figures, and current plans both foreign and domestic. By lunchtime, our heads were swimming in facts! I began to dread the long afternoon session! We let the men leave first because we would be walking far too slowly for their patience. A sea of gliding, wide, satin dresses sailed as slow as a snail down the halls and into the spacious dining room. Iou and Ida were already there waiting for us. Again, their faces were impossible to read; the four inch lip plates, top and bottom, obscured such. Iou began filling up my plate. I still felt embarrassed to have her sit there and feed me as if I was a baby. I sensed Dita, too, felt awkward about this, but what could we do just now? I promised myself that one day I would find a way to repay Iou and Ida for their extreme kindness.

The afternoon session went far better than the morning had. Athena's husband's advisors completely accepted her right to rule and tried very hard to make this transition as painless as possible. Later that evening, I learned that the others had faired similarly. Evidently, the only heavy opposition the queens would have was coming from the late Emperor's male advisors. Nevertheless, our heads were filled with even more facts, plans, figures, and such. I noted that all these were primarily concerning the present situation. Probably tomorrow, we'd be bombarded with the future plans that were being worked on when the men lost their lives in the gigantic explosion.

After we all ate supper in the dining room, when Dita and I rose to leave, both Ariadne and Alekto also rose. We four met by the door and Alekto asked, "Do I need to bring someone with arms with me?" I said no and the two queens followed behind us, all four gliding down the long hallways to our private room.

Once inside, I dismissed Iou and Ida, leaving just us four sitting comfortable on the wide plush chairs. I gave a short explanation on how the therapy worked and what was required of them. Then, off we went, diving into the traumas they had experienced. Of course, the recent loss of their husbands had their complete attention and that was contacted tonight as a first action.

I won't go into the details of what they encountered, only the results. When we ended for the night, the loss of their husbands had been handled. Their grief traumas were gone. Interestingly enough, Alekto discovered that in a previous lifetime, she had also become a Woman of the Eighth Degree for her husband, and he had betrayed her. Laughing wildly, she said, "No wonder I was so hesitant about doing this again!" This also gave me a clue that I had more than one surgery to erase starting tomorrow night.

Ariadne, likewise discovered that in a previous lifetime, she had been a Woman of the Sixth Degree, meaning that she had given up both her hands to show her love for her husband. All that lifetime, she had constantly worried about whether her husband was going to be there for her always. Even though they both lived into their sixties, this fear had been present nearly every day. The relief she felt when she discovered this was enormous. Dita also knew that she had at least two surgeries to erase ahead of her.

During the evening, Selene and Kassandra were busy once more. First, the late Emperor's business and financial advisor, Panos, arrived for the private meeting with the Empress. "Good evening, Panos. Well, you did your best to snow us with your facts and figures today. Impressive how you can just throw them out there so fast that poor Selene cannot write them all down. It is plainly obvious that you advisors are trying to sabotage our efforts to run the country. Now then, starting tomorrow morning, you are going to redo all that and work very diligently to see that we all understand everything. I know that Argos was an idiot. He had very little skill at this. You probably were often frustrated at his inability to grasp things. You will find that I am rather the opposite, as are the queens."

He sat there and looked a bit miffed. She continued, "You will do this and convince the other advisors to do likewise. Selene, will you show Panos the documents please?" Selene slid the packet over to him. As he read them, his face crimsoned. Anger lined his brow. His hands trembled.

"How did you come by these?" he lashed out at her.

"That is not your concern. Now then, if you cooperate and lend us the same full support that you gave my idiot husband, then these documents will remain forever in hiding. If not, well — need I say more?" she coyly added, very covertly. He had little choice but to agree with her and left.

Two hours later, Adonis, his army advisor, and Sethos, his shipping fleet advisor, had also agreed to her terms. Kassandra said to Selene, "Well, those three control the other three of his advisors, so I suspect that whole bunch of resistance is now handled. I'm sorry that you got writer's cramps today. I doubt that will ever happen again. I do wish that I could massage your hands for you, my love. I can at least kiss them." She did so, much to Selene's enjoyment.

Cardinal Drakon watched the inferno for a moment. Just after the explosion and the Empress left, he headed to the warehouse district to see for himself. After pausing to watch this spectacular fire, he moved in closer. His scarlet robes were recognized and ordinary people gave way to him. He was looking for confirmation. Ah, he spied the man he needed to see and pushed his way through the huge crowd towards the soot-faced man. As he drew close, the man merely said, "All," and then slipped off through the crowd in the opposite direction from the Cardinal. At once, he too reversed direction and began backing out of the crowd. Now he had urgent actions to take.

It took him longer to return to his church office than expected; half of Kefall jammed the streets to see this blaze. Entering the Church, he sent his adept assistant to fetch his men, while he entered his office and unlocked his desk. Two days ago, he had carefully written out the eight identical, lengthy orders to his head priests in the seven kingdoms and to Kefall. He laid the seven packets on his desk. Shortly, eight men in their sky blue robes slipped quietly into his room. One was his prelate, Khristos Krates. Damn, he thought to himself. I wish I had more Mano del Dio men. I wonder why they were all sent home but these eight?

"Your Holiness?" Khristos said softly, nudging the Cardinal from his personal thoughts.

"Ah yes, forgive me. I've been distracted with this most tragic event. Khristos, I am charging your seven men with the most critical of all missions. All events of the past have led us to this unique moment in time, a moment, which is unlikely ever to occur again, an historic moment, not only for Demokritos, but also for our Church. In the past, you have undertaken some highly dangerous missions for your Church and our Lord. While this mission has not the inherent personal danger for you, it represents extreme danger for the Church itself. I will explain what is happening so that you will have a clearer idea of this mission."

"Long have we worked to get the Empress and the seven queens to be Holy Women of our Church. We've accomplished that, as you know. Today, the Emperor and all seven kings have died in this tragic explosion and fire today. Now the Empress and the queens are temporarily the sole rulers of Demokritos. Thus, finally we enter the final phase of the Grand Plan. These Holy Women must remain our sole leaders." Several attempted to interrupt him, but he waved them off.

"Yes, I know that the Noble Houses will soon try to elect a whole new slate of rulers. We cannot and must not allow that to happen. This, then, is your mission, perhaps the most critical of them all. I am sending detailed instructions to the head priests in each of the seven kingdoms and here in Kefall. The Church will be lobbying the Noble Houses to allow our Holy Women to remain on their thrones and to rule. We will be asking that the Noble Houses give them the opportunity to prove that they can indeed run our country satisfactorily. The priests are being instructed to leave no stone unturned, to push and back this with the entire might that they possess. This must not fail! The Noble Houses must not be allowed to elect new rulers!"

"Of course, some of the Noble Houses will need more pressure than my priests can exert. That's where you come in, gentlemen. You may have wondered why I have been having you collect the information that you have over these past many years. Perhaps now you can see why. I want you to make full use of this damming material in any way you see fit to ensure that these Noble Houses all vote to allow our current Holy Women to continue to rule our country. This is so critical that you have the authority to see to it that accidents happen to those key Noble Houses who refuse all other attempts at persuasion. Return here only when your kingdom's Noble House has voted to allow their queen to continue her rule over that kingdom. Are we clear on this?"

The eight men smiled, they were. Now they saw the wisdom, the use of their hard labors of many years. Blackmail. Each picked up their packet and received a personal blessing from the Cardinal. Even though it was late afternoon, they galloped off out of Kefall going in seven different directions. The Prelate stayed a little longer; he was to handle Kefall and those who might offer the greatest pressure to elect a new Emperor.

"Prelate, I want you to being pressuring these Houses. The big three — delay a few days. We know that the Empress' spies have discovered much the same information on them as we. Let's see how she uses it. If in say three days, you do not hear that Jonus, Kapaneus, and Paeon are now supporting our Empress, then you may take action and make use of the information that you have gathered on them. The Kefall Houses dominate all the individual kingdom's Houses when it comes to the election of the Emperor. We get them backing Kassandra, and the others will fall in line."

"Your Holiness, what is the time line for completion countrywide?" Khristos asked.

"Because of the distance factor — Tinos, Penelopus being the furthest from here — I am allowing three months. By the time of the Spring Council, Empress Kassandra and the seven queens must have their mandate to continue ruling Demokritos. It will be impractical to keep them all confined here in Kefall any longer. Three months, Khristos, three months and our long labors will be over at last."

Khristos smiled, indeed, they had accomplished much in the last ten years. Still, he really didn't understand the Cardinal's Grand Plan. Initially, he saw the wisdom of getting their own men into these power positions. "Your Holiness, may I ask something that has been bothering me?"

"Of course, most worthy prelate," he replied in his most holy manner.

"Our Holy Women, the Empress and the queens — can they really run our country? They are so utterly helpless in so many ways. How will it be possible for them to do this? I am certain to be asked this many times by the nobles."

Cardinal Drakon had long known this would come up. In fact, within the documents now heading to the kingdoms contained his partial answer. He knew well that many would doubt that a woman, much less an armless one, could possibly be able to run the country or kingdom. Their objections had to be overcome with good reasoning or all would be for naught, although he could not reveal his main argument on their behalf.

"In its most fundamental meaning, leadership is the ability actually to control a group and by the giving of orders and the seeing that they are followed, to obtain further prosperity and expansion of the group. Women of Demokritos have long demonstrated this. Do we not give them total responsibility for the running of our own households and estates? Leadership does not require arms, rather it requires minds, thinking, intelligence, and of course, plans — good, solid plans for the future — plans that enable us to prosper and grow. During the past century, we have seen Emperors whose minds were less than desirable; some may call them idiots. Empress Kassandra and the current seven queens are not idiots, but in fact all are quite brilliant, with keen minds and a dedicated loyalty to our country and our people. Our Emperor and kings have always had many advisors who assisted in devising and putting together plans for the Emperor and kings. Some they chose to implement; others, they dismissed. It will be no different under the Empress and queens. Finally, you, the Noble Houses, have chosen them to be your Empress and queens. You owe it to them to give them an opportunity to show you and the country that they are up to the challenging task of running our great nation."

Khristos grinned, "Oh I get it. Really, the advisors are the real power behind them. They come up with the plans and such. All they have to do is okay the plans. I understand, Your Holiness."

Cardinal Drakon smiled as if this were so. He thought, this is why I'm the Cardinal and you're a mere Prelate. Of course, most believe the advisors are the real power! Often that is true; Argos was an idiot! What Khristos and everyone else will overlook is that these are *my* Holy Women of the Church of Jehosanity. It will be some of *my* plans that they ultimately see and push forward. The Church and I will now become the *real* power in Demokritos! I'm so close to total victory now! Perhaps three months and my control will be solidified.

He'd already proven that he had the control that he desired over Kassandra. He'd been successful in getting her to adopt the wearing of the very restricting dresses of Annelise, though when he had suggested it to her, he had not realized how difficult walking in their extremely high-heeled boots actually was. So much the better, as it had turned out. That he could get her to wear such restrictive clothing and get all the other queens to follow suit, convinced him of his control over her. Besides, he and most all other men enjoyed the beautiful figures that these women now displayed. Men constantly noticed them, some with greedy eyes.

As we all gathered in the Empress' throne room the next morning just before nine, Empress Kassandra, looking remarkably cheerful in her emerald, flowing, satin gown, sat waiting our arrival. "Good morning queens and assistants. I must apologize for the late Emperor's advisor's conduct yesterday morning. Indeed, they did attempt to overwhelm us with a myriad of dis-related information in an attempt to confuse us."

"Well, it worked," Athena called out, cheerfully. Others laughed.

Smiling, Kassandra continued, "I know. Poor Selene had writer's cramps. However, I have spoken to them, and you will find their conduct totally changed today. They will be starting over and making sure that we do understand the information. If they go too fast for you, please let me know, and I will slow them down."

"Gosh, Empress, whatever did you say to them?" Queen Frona asked, completely mystified.

Kassandra did not want to reveal the truth. Instead, she answered coyly, "I have my ways." She winked knowingly at Queen Frona, who was just as mystified. "Messenger, please have the king's advisors enter and then the Emperor's." Thus, it began once more. Indeed, the advisors completely changed their methods from yesterday's bombardment of facts.

We learned that the army now was three hundred legions strong. Fifty legions were off fighting in the Southlands. The remainder was preparing to assault our neighbor, Vladimir, the land of the horsemen. We received an accurate accounting of the Emperor's treasury and the yearly income and expenses for the last five years. Our country's fleet of caravels consisted of three hundred seventy, with a dozen more under construction. We had the largest merchant fleet in the world. I learned that each kingdom also had their own smaller armies, treasuries, and caravel fleets. Individual nobles had small merchant fleets of their own as well. The day, unlike yesterday, passed more smoothly.

That evening Dita and I continued with therapy sessions for Alekto and Ariadne. Now we hit the real physical traumas these women had endured. The best we could do in one evening was to take the edge off their surgeries, leaving them at a relatively flat point to be continued tomorrow night. While we both would have preferred to work them all day long, not just these shorter evenings, we had no other options. Both Dita and I found ourselves really becoming quite fond of these two queens.

After the session, Alekto said, "Bethany, I do so love your hair and Dita's too. Yours is so long! Mine only goes to my waist, but it has been getting a little lighter each year. Yours is so long. Do you suppose that mine will eventually get as blonde as yours is? Are you going to get yours cut shorter, like the other queens have? I mean now that you are like us? They say it is more easily managed, but I so love mine long."

"It's never been cut. I've always loved it long, and Dita has let hers grow for me because she knows how much I like it. I'll bean anyone who tries to cut it!" We both giggled.

"Can I tell you a secret?"

"Sure, Alekto."

"I've always dreamed of traveling in caravels and seeing the sights. I've heard such wonderful things about Velona. Is it really more advanced than here?" she asked. We chatted about Velona for quite some time, and Ariadne joined us when her session finished.

Ariadne then confided in us, "You know, Dita, I never really wanted to become Queen of Thrace in the first place. It was all Dimitrios' doing. It was his goal to become king, not mine. Now he's gone, and I'm stuck with it."

Alekto laughed, "Boy are we stuck with it! Being Queen of Arolas was the last thing I wanted to be! My folks were the previous king and queen. All my life, I hoped someone else would get the throne, especially after I got married. No luck at all. Ariadne, you think that one day you and I could sneak off to this Velona and leave all this behind us?"

Ariadne sighed, "We now have to think about our people, Alekto, and do what's best for them. Maybe if we can get others to take over for us we could go together one day."

I said nothing, but began to see that at least two of these queens really did not want this position. They were going along with the wishes of their Empress for the sake of the well-being of their kingdom and its people. Interesting. I wondered how many of the others felt the same way.

Chapter 40 Changes

The next few days, we were briefed on the future plans that were being currently worked on, both at the Emperor's level as well as the kingdom level. By the end of the first full week of meetings, all the advisors had had their say. We were fully briefed.

On the other hand, Barnabas came to me with a new problem. "Bethany, we are in trouble. Because the Empress has tightened security so much around here, I can no longer sneak off to the pub of an evening and make contact with other Forze Segrete members. We are locked in!"

That night, I thought about his problem, and suddenly, I remembered something. Long ago when I was here as Empress Maren Elizabet, I was in charge of the entire domestic staff and the running of the palace. In those days, we had a secret escape tunnel out of the palace, just in case of an emergency. I wondered if it was still there? True, the whole place had undergone extensive renovations, particularly with the addition of new devices, such as the toilets from Velona. It was located in the Emperor's throne room with another connection in the joint throne room. The Empress' throne room was a new addition since my days here so long ago. If it still existed, Barnabas could use it to come and go, but probably only late at night. Once more, I sent for Barnabas.

"I think there may be a secret emergency escape tunnel that you can use, if it still exists. The joint throne room has undergone the least renovations; let's try that one first. Do you think that it is possible for us to sneak in there tonight without being seen?" I asked him.

"Perhaps, but it will have to be after ten. The late shift comes on duty then. Only one Doorman and Messenger is on duty for each domestic wing and none for the rest of the palace. I can have Xene temporarily attract their attention and we can then slip out. I'm not sure how we slip back in though."

"I should go too," Dita insisted.

"No, I need you here. When we are ready to sneak back here, I'll let you know, and you can let Xene know and work out a distraction so we can return." She hated being out of the action, but I needed her assistance. We had to avoid detection.

Around eleven, Xene sent for the Doorman and the Messenger. Barnabas and I crept out of my room and stole quietly down the long hall. Silently, I cursed my boots, which made our progress seem excruciatingly slow! Finally, he opened a door, and we slipped into the deserted main hall. Here only an occasional lantern provided dim illumination. I whispered, "Damn these boots and corset! I'm a snail that can't breathe!"

"You are doing fine, Bethany. Stealth is more important than speed. Besides, you look like a royal queen yourself. Many men constantly watch you and Dita. Ah, here is the Emperor's throne room." He opened the door and we slipped inside. One tiny lamp provided the only light. Days ago, everything of value had been removed from this room and brought to the joint throne room where we met daily now.

"It was behind the throne. There," I tried to point. Suddenly realizing the fruitless of that, I explained in more detail as I slowly moved there. He'd gone ahead of me to begin looking. He was fumbling around when I finally got to the stone wall. Again, I became quite frustrated. If I still had my arms, it would have been a simple matter to operate the mechanism. Now I found myself having to explain everything in detail. I couldn't even point to the right stone block to push! Argh!

At last, he found it and we heard a soft grating sound as the section of the stone wall moved, leaving a dark hole — the old escape tunnel. He closed it, and quietly we began to make our return trip. As we approached our own hall, I let Dita know. Xene and she were in our room, supposedly now having a late snack. Xene quietly went to her room and summoned the two into her room, saying that Athena was finished. Meanwhile, he and I stole down the hall and into our room. I sank into a chair to catch my breath and ease my aching feet.

"How on earth did you know that there was that tunnel? How did you know how it operated?" Barnabas finally asked what he'd been silently forcing himself not to blurt out there in the Emperor's throne room. "That is incredibly useful!"

I certainly didn't want to tell him about my past life here. Duh. I twisted the truth around a little. "Well, I am the top Forze Segrete person. It's my business to know these things." He gaped at me. I explained where it came out and hoped that its exit was not blocked. He gave me a big hug and left to get a lantern and go exploring.

The next morning, Xene reported that he had been able to get out and to the pub. His other Forze Segrete members were getting very worried about the lack of contact with him. He reported that the doctors who amputated our arms had been positively located. They often performed this surgery for the Church. Now we knew that the Cardinal most likely was involved. The Forze Segrete was currently trying to find proof of said connection, interviewing people who might have seen someone meeting with the doctors beforehand to set it up. I felt progress was being made.

On Sunday, Kassandra allowed us to have the day off. She wanted to go to Church and invited us to go with her. However, the queens decided to hold a queen's-only meeting, which Kassandra readily accepted, figuring these women had much to digest and absorb from the hectic week of meetings. Really, the queens wanted to meet with us.

Around ten, long after Kassandra left, the seven queens met in Athena's private quarters, along with Xene, Dita, me, and nine of the Special Helpers, who were needed to assist us with our tea and anything else we might need. I could not make Xene responsible for handling nine of us all by herself.

Frona began, "Honestly, Bethany, it is truly a miracle! Just look at Alekto! She's so vibrant, so radiant, so alive! I've never see her so happy before. And Ariadne. Wow! I can't tell which of you queens is the most radiant!"

"Yes, we've finished with them. Both did really well," I replied.

"It was hard work but I feel so alive that I don't have words to express how I feel!" Alekto bubbled.

"I'm like I was as a little girl again," Ariadne added. "The world is so utterly bright to me! The flowers around here are fantastic."

I grinned, "Okay, Adonia and Danae, you are up next. With luck, Frona and Melita, we'll get you the following week." This pleased them immensely.

Frona then asked, "Bethany, Dita. Now that we have been privy to all the information our husbands had and have seen what's been going on around here, some of us have been putting together some of the political pieces. We've been comparing notes, so to speak. Most of us now suspect some dark political plot has been going on for the last ten years or so, maybe more. Since you are new to our country, let me explain what we mean. It may well have begun when Bakos and I were elected king and queen back in 739. Looking back on it, I now can see just how much the Church of Jehosanity in Thallyus backed Bakos for the position. I didn't think much of it at the time. Now, I'm of a different opinion."

"We all know that Emperor Deimos was assassinated. Again, it was the Church who lobbied heavily for Argos and Kassandra, though she being their daughter made her a likely choice anyway." She continued to rattle off the many other assassinations or deaths that seemed a bit unusual, such as the king and queen drowning in the river.

"Now here we are — all of us are of the Eighth Degree. Isn't this incredibly unlikely? The Empress and we queens — all armless, to be quite blunt and crass about it. Isn't it almost beyond all conceivable credibility that they would want *us* alone to rule our country? Well, we seven certainly think so. Bethany, something dark and sinister is going on here. Now, Athena here has suggested that you and Dita somehow know a whole lot more about what has been happening here that we do."

"We don't know how this can be so. You are obviously not from Demokritos, but from Velona. Yet, if you do have such knowledge, we queens beseech you to share that with us. We've come alone today. We will swear to keep everything you might say a secret, even from our closest advisors and assistants if you deem that necessary. Please, if you know anything, please tell us."

Listening to her and observing the faces of these women, I reached a decision. That they were alert, bright, and intelligent enough to have gotten this far warranted my confidence. I began, "Queens, you are precisely correct in your observations and conclusions. I tip my hat to you, well Dita's anyway. Back home, she used to wear a black top hat."

"At the moment, please do not ask us how we have managed to come by what I am about to tell you. Also know that our people are hard at world all over the world working on obtaining more proof and clues." I then told them all the facts that we had uncovered and all our speculations, including the details surrounding the deaths of their husbands and children.

"At this time, we cannot totally prove the involvement of either Kassandra or the Cardinal. I fully believe that in time, we will be able to connect them to these lower level men who carried out their orders. We still do not know the actual goal or goals of this mess. Is Kassandra behind all this and using the Cardinal and Church to achieve her ends or is the Cardinal behind this and using Kassandra? We just do not have enough information yet. But as I said at the start, we have people all over Tarra working on it. What we need it time to unravel it. I must apologize for not having worked out that they were planning to kill your husbands and children. I knew intuitively that something awful was about to happen. After all if Dita and I were worth fifty thousand, think what a million must buy."

While I was relating all this, I watched their reactions, which ranged from antagonism to downright anger. When I finished up, they had relaxed and were doing better. Frona spoke for the group. "Thank you, Bethany, Dita, for all that you have done on our behalf and for our country. While I know that we would die to know how it is that you know and have found all this out, we respect your request of anonymity. Perhaps one day it will be safe for you to tell us. Queens, it is clear to me that we have made the right decision: to stay on and attempt to fill the king's shoes. By staying on, we are preventing a political chaos that could have severe repercussions for our kingdoms and nation."

"I agree with Frona," Athena spoke up. "However, I am going to look very hard at anything that Kassandra wants us to approve or pass and even harder at anything the Church or Cardinal might desire!" The others wholeheartedly agreed.

"I think that you are being very wise indeed," I complimented them. "Perhaps we ought to hold these queens' meetings every Sunday morning. We can exchange information. Keep your eyes and ears open, ladies." We then adjourned for lunch, after which Dita and I began therapies on Adonia and Danae.

First thing on Monday, we all had a surprise. After we were all assembled and ready to go, an Announcer spoke the names of six noblemen. I had no idea who these men were. They walked up to the Empress on her throne and bowed. One spoke, "On behalf of the Noble Houses of Kefall, I wish to convey our complete and total support for you, Empress Kassandra. We have met and agree that you may assume the duties previously handled by Argos." She had a very smug look on her face, I noticed. Conclusion: she had something to do with their acceptance.

He turned to the queens, "While we cannot speak for your kingdom's Noble Houses, we will use what little leverage we have with them to have them support you as well." He then faced the Empress once more. "There is one thing that you must know, Empress. We will be monitoring your job performance. If we do not find that you are up to the task or are doing a poor job, we will elect a new Emperor." Kassandra acknowledged his veiled threat and they left.

The room buzzed with chat over this surprise development, but it was short lived. She called the meeting to order and we began once more. I wanted to ask Athena about the significance of this. Lunchtime would have to suffice.

"Now then, it is time for some changes," Kassandra began. "We've been going over the crime statistics, and we must give our people better protection. Where to get the additional men is the key. I have a proposal to solve that. Now we have all these legions training up to invade our neighbor, Vladimir. I asked why the other day. The answer I received was two-fold. One, they continually raid into the kingdoms of Arolas and Thallyus, where the barrier mountains are low enough to allow the horsemen passage. For centuries now, these two kingdoms have been asking for help with this problem. Two, we were told that we have deforested what little forest we have left in Demokritos, at least of the larger trees. We've used them up building all our extensive caravel fleet. Vladimir is ripe with forests with large diameter trees. Conquering that country will enable us to acquire more timber for shipbuilding. It is far too expensive to purchase them from the Southlands so the far north or to haul them so far overland from Thallyus and Theos, among others."

"Now these are the silliest reasons I can think of for us to go to war — a war over trees? Get real, gentlemen. You want our sons to spill their life's blood over some trees? I say no. There has to be a better way. I propose that we cancel all plans for that war. Instead, surely the horsemen of Vladimir desire something that we have. Honestly, our merchants and caravels bring in goods, some quite exotic, from all corners of the world. Surely, we have something that they could use in exchange for timbers. I propose that a trading delegation be sent at once to Vladimir and see what can be worked out."

"Further, I propose that we send twenty legions each to Arolas and Thallyus and station them in the areas where the horsemen have invaded in the past. Let's finally give these two kingdoms some support. That leaves hundreds of legions with nothing to do. I hate idle men. Thus, I also propose that we take these remaining legions, divide them equally between the seven kingdoms, and send them there. Their duties will be to provide a better police force to lower the crime rates in our kingdoms. This will meet with strong public approval and support for our queens as well."

"Now then, there are four proposals on the table. Discussion please."

Well, I thought that she was starting with a bang! Canceling the proposed war would sit well with the many mothers of Demokritos. Establishing more trading agreements and the acquiring of vast amounts of timber would greatly benefit the shipwrights, merchants, and associated nobles. More ships meant more money flowing into many pockets. The two kingdoms would definitely like the added protection from the horsemen's periodic invasions. What honest person wouldn't like a reduced crime rate? The only drawback would be the sheer number of the Empress' controlled legions within their kingdom.

Indeed, it was this last that drew the most discussion. Many were opposed to having so many of the Empress' troops within their kingdoms. All morning long, various advisors offered their opinions and counter proposals. By supper, an agreement had been reached at last. The legions would be sent to the kingdoms subject to several provisos. First, they would be under the leadership of that kingdom's generals. Second, after a six-month trial, each queen had the right to cancel it and send the legions home. Third, the Empress reserved the right to withdraw the legions at any time. She insisted that she have this power in case a national emergency arose.

The rest of the week held no surprises, just routine business actions passed or agreed with by the women. I found this aspect tedious and boring and looked forward to our evening therapy sessions. By the end of the week, we had finished Danae and Adonia. On the spy front, we now had sworn statements from three men and women who had seen the Cardinal make a visit to the two doctors, who had performed the surgery on us, just two weeks before it happened. It was not solid proof, just more circumstantial evidence.

The next week, after the routine business was handled, Kassandra announced, "Queens, I'd like to take up another idea of mine: schools for our children. In Dorota, we know that their government provides free schools for all their children from six to sixteen. We know that our Church is also proposing the establishment of schools here. Now while I certainly don't want to stand in the way of our Church, I do have reservations about priests doing all the teaching of our children, don't you?" she said with an icy overtone.

"I think that a general education for all of our children would be extremely popular with our citizens. Of course, our advisors have been clamoring about its cost. Honestly, can you put a gold value on a child's education? The benefits of having all of our people able to read and write, do arithmetic, know our history and customs — why the list is endless. So let's take this one step at a time. I propose we establish a national educational system here in Demokritos. Its purpose is to provide a good education to all of our children. Let's worry about the details if we are all in favor of doing it.

One step at a time, like we have to in our heels, ladies."

She called for a vote and it passed. Who could be opposed to education for children? Now they worked on the years the children would be in school. Six years old for beginners was agreed to immediately. The upper end took some arguments and debates to resolve. Some thought that sixteen was far too old for a person to be still in school. Others thought that it should end when they came of age at fourteen. Advisors pointed out that the fewer the years, the lower the cost. Eventually, they decided on eight years of schooling would be ideal, from six to their fourteenth birthday. That was the easy part. Now came the funding, the acquiring of buildings, supplies, and teachers.

This led immediately to: would each kingdom be responsible for the buildings and what was taught or would the Emperor-Empress be so responsible? If Kassandra ran the schools, all students in all kingdoms would receive similar educations. If each kingdom ran their own, differences in what was taught would invariably result. The queens liked the idea that they would be controlling what was taught, whereas the Empress wanted a uniform educational platform across the whole nation. If the kingdoms paid for the buildings or paid for the teachers, they wanted a say in what was taught. Besides, they disliked giving that much power to the Emperor-Empress. Yet, they liked the idea of Kassandra paying for everything. "Well, you can't have it both ways," Kassandra griped.

They then tabled that aspect and took up how it could be financed. Someone had to pay for the facilities and the salaries of the teachers. An advisor pointed out that there would also need to be some administrator to handle the bookkeeping and record keeping details. All this led to just how the two branches of their government were financed. I learned something here. At the countrywide level, that is at the Emperor-Empress level, income came from nation owned caravels, taxes from Annelise, and taxes from the seven kingdoms. At each kingdom level, income came from kingdom owned caravels and taxes of their citizens. It was a confusing mess.

Kassandra had the authority to demand higher payments from the kingdoms, but if she did, the kingdoms would have to increase the taxes they required of their citizens. For two days, this taxation issue was debated with no resolution in sight. I decided to toss my opinions into the fray.

"Look, perhaps we are going about this all wrong. Let's ignore the money issue for a moment. You want free schools and you want all children to be able to go there. Okay. Now you have rural children; how will they get to the school? You have small villages where one school would suffice. You have large cities where you need to have many schools scattered strategically around areas or districts. I don't care how you do it, but look, you are talking thousands of schools! Even if you have the funds, how can you suddenly go about such a mammoth project? It's not practical. How about doing this a step at a time?"

"Suppose you take the capital cities first. Let's say that you want no more than say five hundred children in any one school. You will need to divide that large city into school districts and build the needed schools and man them up with teachers and administrators. Once you have that city operational, then move on to the next large city and repeat it. If you have broken the city into districts, one way to finance them is to establish a new school tax. If I were a parent, I would readily agree to pay a bit more in taxes, if I knew that all of that new tax went solely to paying for the schooling of my children."

Well, they liked the first part, starting with one city and gradually expanding to others. However, my idea on the taxes drew more problems. Those in the poorer districts would be hard pressed to pay the new tax, while those in the wealthier districts could easily afford it. Another day passed.

At last, everyone agreed that some new tax must be levied to pay for the educational program. Finally, they decided the only way to do this fairly was to levy a new school tax on all citizens, much as the existing taxes were done. It amounted to another gold per person per year. An advisor estimated that they would then have roughly ten million to spend each year. Now they got going. Each kingdom would receive a seventh of the yearly sum. Next, they set to work on how to work out districts and how to build the schools in the first place. They set up advisors to get several model school plans designed and drawn, along with estimated costs. Other advisors would organize a countrywide search for existing teachers or those who might fill those needs. Others began working out just what would be taught and at what year of schooling. Now they began to make real headway.

I won't bother you with their myriad details, but by the Spring Council time, they had begun to implement the National Education Program. Ten schools were under construction in the seven capital cities plus Kefall. Within a year, these became operational. During the ensuing ten years, they continued to expand the program to the other larger cities and towns. To get to the smaller villages and rural areas would take a score of years. At least, I was pleased that they had begun, though it occupied everyone's attention all winter long.

The third week in July, Ariadne receive word from the Noble Houses of Thrace that they would back her as their sole leader. During the next few weeks, word came from the other kingdom's Noble Houses that they would support their queen as well.

By the time of the usual Spring Council meeting, Dita and I had handled another twenty women's traumas. All of Athena's women were finished, and we had a good start on Alekto's group. Kassandra was so busy with running the group that she didn't really notice what Dita and I were doing each night for the women.

During these weeks, Cardinal Drakon dropped by to check on the women leaders to see if they needed anything and if all was going well for them. Although we all kept a close eye on him, he did not attempt to sway anyone or even propose anything. It was like he was merely allowing the Empress and queens to deal with the running of their country. This again got us all speculating about who was using who and for what. I had expected that he would have tried to influence their work or make proposals. He did neither, just make sure they were succeeding.

Kali reported in early September that Kassandra had transferred another million to Cardinal Drakon two days after the explosion. However, thus far, it seemed to remain in his account. Kali also saw our big problem: time. The records of Demokritos transactions took nearly three months to arrive in Velona. She was just now getting the deals that had been made nearly three months ago! We needed faster knowledge.

After Kassandra announced that after the Spring Council, the queens could return home and continue running their own kingdoms, returning as a group at the usual quarterly times, the queens again met privately with us.

Frona suggested that the queens send a dispatch rider to us in Theolopolis with any significant news that might arise and vice versa. Everyone agreed to that. The queens definitely wanted to work more closely together. The thought of going home and being the only one in charge was a bit daunting to all seven. They realized that they had been working slavishly for three months, with no distractions at all. None of us had any outside life, not even time for a concert or play.

Frona also wanted to know how Dita and I would be able to run our therapy session on all the other women in their care. If we were down in Theolopolis and their women were so distant, how would we be able to do them? Athena solved that one by suggesting that Alekto send half of her remaining women who needed therapy home with us. On November 1, Alekto could sent the remainder to Theolopolis, while we would return those who had finished. We estimated that by the Yuletide holidays we would have finished all her staff. When we met at the Summer Council, we would begin on another kingdom's women.

As everyone began the long job of packing for the return trip, Ariadne and Alekto came to chat with Athena and us. The three queens decided that they wanted to take the last two weeks in December off and have a vacation from all this mess. They decided to meet on December 12 in Theolopolis, and we five could go off someplace quiet and simply relax and have fun. Athena agreed to set something up for us all. Thus, we five had something to look forward to besides a very heavy workload.

On our last day in Kefall and during the last hour of the daylong meeting, Empress Kassandra made another proposal. "Queens, there is another matter that I wish you to consider during the next quarter and be prepared to discuss it fully when we next meet. I am so proud of you for taking so well to these elegant, sophisticated, fashions from Annelise. We all look fantastic in these outfits! It is my wish that we can somehow share these with others in our country. I would like us to adopt some national program to encourage more women to wear such fine fashions. I know that these outfits are particularly expensive. The wealthier women could easily afford them, no problem there, but others would find them too expensive. Ponder how we could make such outfits more affordable or perhaps subsidize them for other women. Can you imagine walking down the streets of your city and seeing so many women looking as spectacular as we now look? Give this some though. We will discuss it when we next meet. Have a good holiday season." Inwardly, I groaned, Dita, too.

Athena followed the pattern that Damon had set on our long trip to her city. That is, we rode in the carriages for long hours, cutting the travel time to a minimum. On September 30, we rolled into her palace in Theolopolis at long last, safe and sound.

That same day, unknown to us, Cardinal Drakon posted his lengthy report to Pope Leo. He'd spent weeks carefully preparing it, rewriting it many times so that it was perfect. Part of the report read as follows.

Your Most Holy Eminence Pope Leo,

Here in Demokritos, the Church of Jehosanity has achieved something of enormous magnitude and importance. At this time, the country is now run solely by eight Holy Women of the Eighth Degree! Yes, the Empress Kassandra Aias and the seven queens are now the sole rulers of the country. The Noble Houses have all given their consent to allow these Holy Women actually to run the nation without any Emperor or kings.

I have monitored their work and can state unequivocally that they have so far taken actions that will endear them to their constituents. I am enclosing a synopsis of their work thus far that you may see that for yourself.

From now on, the Church of Jehosanity, by virtue of having only our Holy Women in sole control of the country, is in the position of subtly controlling the largest country in the world. Now finally Demokritos is in a position to forward your plans to the fullest.

I respectfully request that we discuss what legislation the Church desires to be passed at the Fall Council meeting. The Empress herself can handle some matters, but others will need the approval of the queens as well. Perhaps we should meet to discuss this further. It is inadvisable for me to travel to Megalos, as I do need to keep watch over our most Holy Women.

He continued for another three pages. Cardinal Drakon now had only one remaining potential problem: the two advisors from Velona who seemed to be somehow undermining his influence over these Holy Women. Exactly how eluded him. He'd gone along with the Empress' request because he assumed that as new Holy Women themselves, they'd join and bond with the others and even join the Church. None of that had transpired; both were fiercely independent. Somehow, he needed to find out more about these two most unusual women. No need to have them eliminated yet.

Chapter 41 Yuletide, 751

Queen Athena was welcomed when we returned. Her aging parents welcomed her and consoled her on the loss of her husband and baby. Many nobles came to both pay their respects but also complimented her on some of the changes that had been made during the long summer. The first few days were a bit chaotic for her staff. Soon, she was kept busy with a steady stream of petitioners, which the king had normally seen.

Zoe, Morpheus, and Zona had not been idle either. Zoe had broken into both doctor's offices and thoroughly searched their records. She discovered several notes from the Mano del Dio Prelate giving them the directions to follow. The notes suggested the request came from Cardinal Drakon, though his signature was not on these papers. Unfortunately, the notes absolved both doctors from any wrongdoing in their removal of Athena's arms. According to these notes, she had requested that it be done in secret and then gave the doctors their instructions to follow.

Additionally, the three had canvassed the area around which Zoe's husband body had been found the night when Athena was abducted. Three passers-by had seen a cloaked man moving toward Alexio that night. One claimed to have seen a bit of sky blue robes beneath the outer dark cloak, indicating a Mano del Dio assassin.

The three had also done additional legwork. Only one Mano del Dio man was frequently in Theolopolis. The Prelate himself came to the city only very rarely. They concluded that this Mano del Dio had to have been the one who killed Alexio. At least Zoe was now convinced of it. She begged us to apprehend the man. He was in the city visiting the priests of the Church, who had been lobbying heavily in favor of Athena staying on as their sole ruler.

Dita insisted that we apprehend him. "Look, dear, I can safely apprehend him, and I can get him to talk." She was insistent, and I knew that she was desperate to make up for having failed us when they abducted us in our sleep. Since we really needed more incriminating evidence and since I was now very worried about that second million transfer from Kassandra, I gave her the go ahead.

"What? Dita? But you — I mean, well you are helpless now," Zoe protested when she heard that Dita was coming with them and would do the apprehension.

Morpheus added solemnly, "Dita, I know that before you really could have helped, but you must accept the fact that you are now, well bluntly, useless. Without your arms, you cannot even defend yourself, let alone capture this extremely dangerous assassin. You would be a tremendous liability if we took you along with us. Perhaps you can question him after we snatch him and disarm him."

"Looks can be deceiving, Morpheus. Neither Bethany nor I want to endanger you three needlessly. These Mano fellows are nothing more than highly trained assassins in disguise. We know these fellows, Zoe. He'll take out all three of you before you can get him. These men are trained to fight even when their bodies are under intense pain. So we stick to my plan. You get me close to him, like a block away. Then, I will get him and disable him, while you remove his weapons and tie him up. We take him to the deserted warehouse that Zoe has and then I will question him and get him to tell us all. Now help me into the carriage and let's get going."

The three sighed, knowing this was very foolish. Morpheus lifted Dita up and into the carriage. Zoe and Zona climbed in and double-checked their many weapons. Morpheus climbed up and nudged the two horses into action. A half hour later, the carriage pulled up in a dark alley. Zoe whispered, "He usually is in that pub about this time every evening. Now what? Are you sure you know what you are doing, Dita?"

"Yes, get me out, please. Stay back here by the carriage until I bring him to you," Dita replied, breathing heavily. She was excited, but the constricting corset made breathing difficult. Morpheus lifted her down. Dita then glided along in the shadows until she came to the street, cursing every telltale click of her boots on the cobblestones. No one was around; she relaxed. From here she could see the pub's main entrance. The street was deserted and dark; only a sliver of a moon darted in and out of ghostly cumulus clouds. She waited.

Sometime later, she spied the man she wanted leaving the pub. No doubt about him, sky blue robes gave him away. Good, she thought, he's coming this way. Dita moved out of her body and positioned herself above his. Taking large forceful strides, he was headed towards the alley where her body stood in the shadows. Dita then struck. Well, more precisely, she lifted him up into the air and turned him upside down. Then, she moved him through the air to the alley and on down it to the carriage where the three waited. While the flailing man struggled mightily against the unseen force holding him, Dita glided along the alley to the carriage.

Zoe, Zona, and Morpheus stood spellbound, unable to grasp what was happening. The assassin was upside down in the air, as if being suspended by some kind of wires, rather like an inverted puppet. "Tie his hands first. I don't trust him at all," Dita ordered.

Morpheus was the first to recover from the shock. He quickly bound the man's wrists, then Dita lowered him so that his head touched the ground. Quickly, Zoe and Zona began stripping his many weapons, tossing aside his sword, three daggers, two throwing daggers, a knife, and several odd chunks of metal, which could be used to strike someone on the head. After the three searched him three times for additional weapons, Zoe said, "He's clean now."

"Open the carriage door, Morpheus; I'll get him inside. Tie his legs and make sure he cannot get free," Dita ordered. The three marveled at the assassin floating into the carriage and then being forcefully positioned properly in the seat. Morpheus jumped in and secured his legs and his arms even further. Zoe and Zona then climbed in and took seats beside him and directly opposite the man. Morpheus lifted Dita inside and quickly returned to the driver's bench. The carriage moved out of the alley.

"Let me go! You'll all pay dearly for this!" the man swore, but his eyes stared only at Dita, who wore her billowing red satin dress. In stark contrast, both Zona and Zoe were dressed in their fighting leather pants and tops, ready for combat. "I know you! You're Athena's cousin from Velona," the man finally connected with Dita.

"Yes, I am. And you are shortly going to tell us what we desire," Dita said softly, but firmly. She added, "You are one lucky assassin. You are not the ones who abducted my wife and me." He gave her a queer look and began reciting his holy mantra. Fifteen minutes later, the carriage entered the deserted warehouse. Morpheus closed the door and used the two carriage lanterns to light two more that hung from a central eight by eight wooden pillar. He then lifted Dita down, while Zoe and Zona forced the Mano del Dio man out, where Morpheus caught him and carried him to a rickety chair.

Dita glided up to him, annoyed at the loud sound of her heel clicks on the stone floor. So much for stealth, she thought to herself. Facing him, she repeated the facts that the three had uncovered about the assassination of Alexio and the abduction of Athena, during which the doctors had amputated her arms. He sat still like a marble statue while she spoke.

"Now then, what is your name?" Dita asked. He stoically refused to say a word. "Very well, have it your way. I admit that I am a little out of practice with this. Sorry if it hurts." She moved into his mind and forced his body to respond.

Fighting her all the way, he found his mouth speaking, "Sotiris Acteon." Zoe, as instructed, wrote that name down.

"Where you the one who killed that man standing just outside the palace grounds near Athena's rooms?" Dita asked. He clamped his mouth shut tightly. Dita took control of his body's motor controls and forced it out of him.

"Yes. He was in the way." Now the assassin intentionally bit off part of his tongue so that he could not reveal anything else. Zoe gasped.

"My god! What kind of beasts are these Mano del Dio anyway?" she cried out.

"Assassins," Dita replied quietly. "Now then, Sotiris, who ordered you to abduct Athena and who ordered the doctors to amputate her arms that night?" Blood gushed out of his mouth. She realized that further speech was unlikely. "Zoe, put the pencil in his hand. Good. Now Sotiris, you will write out the orders you were given and who gave them to you and on what date." What sounded like "No!" came from his mouth along with a mountain of gushing blood. Dita took tight control of his motor controls, just as the Guardian had taught her to do so many years ago when she, as Renzo then, had been with him in the Red Desert. As the three watched, the pencil began to write, albeit in a jerky, unsteady hand. When it finished, Dita relaxed her control of his body, and he instantly snapped the pencil into pieces.

Zoe read it aloud. Indeed, Cardinal Drakon has ordered him to arrange the sordid affair and had given him twenty thousand for his services. "This is damning proof!" she exclaimed, finally feeling vindicated and satisfied. This beast had slain her loving husband and had caused Athena to be violated and mutilated. He had to pay for this. She raised her sword to execute the man.

"Stay your hand, Zoe. You do not want his blood on your blade. He is mine to slay. I want you three to return to the carriage. I will join you shortly," Dita said.

"I want revenge! Dita; you can't hold my sword, but I'd gladly give it to you, if you could, though I want to do it for Alexio," Zoe cried out.

"I know you do, Zoe, but this way, none of you three will have his blood on your hands. You can swear to that. I will do it my way. You may watch, but it will be gory." Dita could have taken over their bodies and made them walk to the carriage, but she gave them the chance to decide to do it themselves. At last, hesitating all the way, the three backed to the carriage.

"Sotiris, for the crime of murder of Alexio and the abduction and mutilation of Queen Athena, you are hereby sentenced to death. Any last words?" Dita said softly. He spat out a wad of partially congealed blood, but it failed to reach Dita. "Very well." She took hold of his head and gave it a good twist. Neck bones snapped; he slumped over in the chair lifelessly. Dita returned to the carriage. "It is done. Lift up, please."

The three stared at her dumbfounded. At last, Morpheus lifted her back inside, and the two women climbed in after her. For a time as they rolled along the streets of Theolopolis, neither Zoe nor Zona said a word. At last, Zoe said, "Thank you. Alexio can now rest in peace. But Dita, how did you do all this? We saw you do nothing, yet his hands wrote, his voice spoke, his head twisted."

"To say nothing of seeing him floating along upside down," Zona added, now that Zoe began talking about these unearthly sights.

"Looks can be deceiving. I will tell you more when we meet with Athena in a short while," Dita replied. She just didn't want to have to do this twice, and she wanted me present when she told them. That way, I'd know what was said.

A half hour later, the four joined Athena, Xene, Barnabas, and me in the queen's private room. Although the Fetchers had brought us several pots of tea and some cookies, Athena dismissed all our Special Helpers, saying the others could help us. "Well?" Athena said excitedly. "What happened? How did it go?" She was dying to know, hating the fact that she could no longer be part of the action, not as a Woman of the Eighth Degree anyway.

"Dita must be some kind of goddess!" Zoe exclaimed. "Here, she made him write out his confession before she twisted his neck. Alexio has had his revenge!" Although she handed the paper to Athena, she just stared at it, a tear forming. Desperately, Athena wanted to take the paper and read, but she couldn't. Zoe realized her gaffe and quickly apologized. She read it aloud for her friend.

"So Cardinal Drakon did this to me!" Athena cried out, shaking her shoulders in lieu of her arms. "Death would be too good for him! That lying, two faced bastard!"

Zoe, Zona, and Morpheus then took turns telling Athena, their Forze Segrete member, all the details. "You are exaggerating, right?" Athena said in disbelief. All three swore that they were not fibbing.

Dita then spoke, "Looks can be deceiving. We are the top leaders of the Forze. We both have many spiritual abilities or skills. Lifting things and controlling other's bodies and minds is a specialty of mine, though I have not used it much before. It defies other's free will. This was really the first time I went all the way with it, because we needed a written confession. I admit that I failed utterly to protect my wife, Bethany, and me. My only defense is that I was asleep when they gassed us. We've paid dearly for my mistake. Love, do you want to explain this to them? You are much better at it than I."

I gave my usual speech about we are all immortal spiritual beings who inhabit these fleshly bodies for a time. At least Athena had some solid reality on this. In therapy, she'd discovered that she had previous lifetimes.

Dita then added, "We are not goddesses. We have our limitations too." She shrugged her shoulders to indicate such. "Can someone help me with a cookie, please?"

Zoe held one up for her, "But can't you just lift it up yourself?"

"Sure, but that would blow way too many people's minds, wouldn't it?" she replied. Now they all understood. They might try to hang us as evil witches or something.

"Can we use this to bring the Cardinal down now?" asked Athena.

"Not likely. If it was believed, we might be able to get him removed and sent back to Megalos," I replied. "Real justice is unlikely for this action. He could always claim that you or Damon begged him to do it. No, we need lots more evidence. Now if we can conclusively tie him to the murders of the Emperor and the kings, we'd have him," I replied. "We keep on trying to uncover more evidence of his guilt. However, I am still very worried about that second million transfer. We need to keep up our vigilance and stay alert." Everyone agreed.

Days passed by quickly. Dita and I now spent most of our time giving therapy sessions to the women that Alekto was supporting. Athena and her many advisors, men and women, were kept constantly busy with the myriad affairs of running Theos. By the time that third week of December came, Athena was more than ready for a vacation. I think what kept her going during early December was all her private planning for our vacation!

At last, Queens Alekto and Ariadne arrived with their small group of assistants and helpers. As the queens and we met in her private chambers, Alekto gushed, "I am *so* glad we decided to take a two week break! I have been *so* overworked! I haven't hardly had *any* time to myself since I got back to Naxos!"

"Same here," Ariadne added. "Continuous stream of people coming to see the queen. Well, they used to come to see the king. My poor assistants — all that writing they had to do. I sure do wish I could find someone to take over the throne for me."

"Me too, Ariadne, but how would we survive? I mean like we are and without husbands," Alekto added.

Athena decided to try to cheer them up, "Well, I've got a great vacation planned for us all! Down south of here by the Ice Sheet is the famous resort town of Trikala! It's a mini-city for vacationers. My folks have a small estate there. I used to live there until I was fourteen. You are all going to love this place! They have theaters, concert halls, dance auditoriums, to say nothing of spas and loads of other outdoor things. I used to go ice-skating there every day. They've indoor heated pools; the heat comes from somewhere underground. This time of year, it's pretty well packed with vacationers, like ourselves. We probably can catch a whole lot of popular plays and things, because all the actors and musicians love to gather there around now. It's a very popular spot."

She rattled excitedly on, "And no one is likely to recognize us there. We can just be ourselves for two whole weeks. No kingdom business, just relax and have fun. We'll be just some anonymous women down for a good time over Yuletide."

"Yes, but we had better leave our Special Helpers here, Athena. One look at them and anyone would know who we just had to be. They are so unusual looking, what with their enormous lip plates and neck rings. If we take them along, we will be recognized instantly, and there goes our private time," Ariadne pointed out.

"Yes, but we need them, don't we?" Alekto said rather dejectedly.

"Well, there are five of us who have to have a helper, so that means we need to bring along five others," Athena began working it out. "Xene and her husband Barnabas can come; she's my helper anyway, and he can be our carriage driver."

"Yes, but Athena, if we bring along another five, we'll need two carriages. Won't that look a little suspicious?" asked Ariadne. "I want no one to know who I am so I can just relax for a while."

"I gave all my other assistants but my Special Helpers the two weeks off to spend with their families. Ato is all that I brought with me," Alekto said a bit worried that she had goofed.

"Hey, I know," Athena had an idea. "We ought to also have some around us who can protect us, just in case something happens. I have three friends who could come with us. I know that they are not used to helping women like us, but Xene can show them the ropes, so to speak. It will be a bit awkward for us and for them, but then we can remain anonymous. If we take our Special Helpers, everyone will know that we must be queens, since everyone knows that the Empress gave those unusual women to us to help us get by."

"I don't mind helping you all get dressed and fed," Xene broke in. "I'm sure Barnabas would love to be an escort for you, helping you as needed."

Zoe, Zona, and Morpheus gladly agreed to go. In return for helping the women manage daily life, they would get a *free* vacation in *the* resort town of Theos! All three eagerly agreed.

We five now discussed what we would wear and take. At once, some unexpected, new problems arose for us five. Already Athena, Dita, and I found that walking in the snow with these terrifically high-heeled boots was very treacherous indeed. We had to have someone's arm constantly around us as we slipped frequently in the snow. Alekto suggested that we wear far more comfortable shoes. We five tried on our older shoes and found that we'd been wearing these heels too long without a break. Our lower leg muscles had altered, and we found it extremely painful to wear flats! While we all figured that in time we could gradually extend the now shortened muscles, we didn't have the time right now. More appropriate shoes were out.

Ariadne suggested that we leave these awful corsets behind, along with these huge dresses, although they would be useful in providing warmth way down on the Ice Sheet, where even in the summer, it was frigidly cold. However, we quickly realized that was also out. Our small waists would ease back to their original size, more or less, and when we returned, it would be impossible to get these smaller corsets tightened, and all our dresses wouldn't fit. We still had the original "starter" corsets, but only the one dress that fit us. When we returned to the Winter Council after our vacation, we'd catch heck from Kassandra. None of us wanted to draw her attention onto us right now. That might be deadly.

Athena had us try on some of her old dresses, but those also looked poorly and loose on us; our waists were so much smaller. With five sighs, we five resigned ourselves to wearing our current, wide, satin dresses. Well, that made our packing easier at least. Xene said that it also made dressing us uniform. Excitedly, we began packing. Morpheus and Barnabas acquired an oversized carriage that would sit us eight women, carry all our bags on its top, while the two men drove the four-horse team. On December 14, we began our vacation at the resort town of Trikala, some seventy miles nearly due south of Theolopolis at the edge of the permanent Ice Sheet that covered all the southern portion of the whole continent. The men decided to leave before dawn and make the journey in one very long day. We took along several chamber pots!

We arrived after dark at the block long Stavros estate, which still belonged to her parents. This large building and grounds had been her childhood home until she had moved to the capital city when her parents became the king and queen of Theos. Her parents still vacationed here, but mostly in the winter. Even though it was summer elsewhere, here it was cold and snow covered the ground. We five had to have a strong arm around our waists even to walk into the huge manor. However, an older servant couple had the fires going and a warm meal ready for us. Athena had sent them word a week before, and the elderly caretakers were ready for us.

Snow and frost covered the many windows; the fire crackled, filling the room with the aroma of pine. Our helpers removed our thick cloaks, and Xene quickly adjusted we three long haired ladies' hair. We sat down to a warm meal and handled the awkwardness of Zoe, Zona, Morpheus, and Barnabas, who did their best to feed us. It was general embarrassment all around. "Don't worry, by the time we head back, you'll all have the hang of it," I attempted to defuse the sinking spirits of the group. "If we are going to be anonymous, we can't have our Special Helpers."

Stuffed, we had a tour of the manor house. Athena showed us the bedrooms and her old room. There were not enough rooms for us all to have our own. The caretakers had the back bedroom. Athena and Alekto shared the bed in her bedroom. Dita and I shared a bedroom. Morpheus and Zona took another room. Xene and Barnabas, another. Ariadne and Zoe doubled up. We followed my advice and left all the bedroom doors open, that way we were not trapped inside and could call out for help if we needed it. Peaceful, restful sleep came over us all. It had been a very long time since we all slept so soundly. The stressful jobs that we had been doing had silently taken its toll on us all.

"Fourteen days of fun!" Athena exclaimed as we all ate a hot breakfast of bacon, eggs, and pancakes, following it with our usual tea. "First, we ought to take a stroll to the Ice Sheet. Everyone always takes that sight in first. There are all sorts of wintertime activities around there. It is perpetually winter here, you see. I used to ice skate every day when I was a little girl. You can go sledding or even skiing. I know that's all out for us, but honestly, the rest of you ought to go have some fun. We five can sit and watch you."

They helped put our heavy, warm cloaks around us and made sure they were securely fastened. "Hey, we don't need coats or warm mittens!" Athena pointed out. I smiled, that we didn't. The others bundled up in their coats and donned heavy mittens. "Off we go," she exclaimed rather excited about showing us all the sights of her childhood home.

"Outside, snow covered everything, a winter wonderland here in the middle of the summer! While we had a little snow in Velona, it was nothing compared to here, where it was deep and would remain. I was told that it was much thicker in wintertime. Now about as much of the snow that would melt had already done so. Smoke curled up from hundreds of chimneys. Sleighs occasionally passed us by on the streets, which were surprisingly crowded with bundled up folks, many, like us, on a Yuletide vacation. Our breaths sent white smoke clouds out before us. We all wore the local winter hats, compliments of Athena, who had thought of everything. Warm, fur bonnets covered our heads. Dita, Alekto, and I let our long hair fall down our backs and shoulders out from underneath our brown fur hats. The others had theirs tucked inside.

In these boots, simply put, we women could not have managed to walk without slipping and falling, whether or not we had arms! Our helpers had to hang onto our waists securely as we all slipped and slid along the snow-covered streets. Ahead, we saw the Ice Sheet, a bluish mass that stretched on south as far as the eye could see. Various sections were clearly marked off with stakes and fluttering banners. One area was for ice skating. Another was for skiing only. Yet another three were for those who wanted to play the unusual game they called Puck Battles. Ice skaters with sticks would try to hit a slippery wooden disk into the opponent's net. Already these three fields were taken with six teams having good games. I saw that another four groups were waiting their turn to get onto the ice.

At least fifty were out on the ice, skating around the large oval path. Young, old, kids, adults, the place was teaming with people out for a good time. At several booths, one could rent equipment, Athena pointed out. Three large pushcart vendors called out "Hot tea. Hot cocoa." She said that you could even get a light lunch from the vendors. Already several were in line to get steaming mugs to warm themselves up.

"Athena, this is perfect!" I complimented her.

"Over here," she tried to point out, but became instantly frustrated once more, as she couldn't point. "There are lots of benches where we can sit and watch all the action on the ice. Why don't you sit us there and go get some skates and try the ice?"

She wouldn't listen to the five's arguments that they didn't know how. "See those men and women in the yellow coats? Those are instructors. Just rent some skates and go over to them. They'll get you going. Really, it's easy, well sort of, but it's a whole lot of fun," Athena bubbled. Inwardly, I could tell she was really becoming depressed that she could no longer skate herself. I imagined her as a little girl coming out here to skate every day. I could sense her loss.

Laughing, the five headed off to try it, after making sure we were comfortable on the bench, our satin dresses bulging out from beneath the brown cloaks. We watched them and chatted and relaxed. Indeed, a while later, the five fumbled around on their skates, often falling down, often wobbling, but within a half hour, they were now moving around the large oval with the rest of them. Some young girls were doing all manner of fancy moves, spins, and even jumps. I watched fascinated, never having seen anything like this before.

Just then, a man in his mid-twenties walked up to us. He was tall, but well built, from the thickness of his coat sleeves. He had short brown hair tucked under his fur cap and sported a small moustache, an average looking young man from Demokritos, judging from his bronze skin. He had a curious expression on his face. "Athena? Athena Stavros? Excuse me miss, are you Athena Stavros, by chance?"

Athena, startled, looked up at the young man. "Oh my goodness. Andreas? Andreas, is that you?" she rose automatically, intending to throw her arms around him if he was. "Yes, I'm Athena."

He reached out to shake her hand, but saw no hand coming out from under her heavy cloak. These cloaks wrapped around us hiding our armless state from the casual eye. She was instantly embarrassed. "Sorry, I've no arms anymore, but it's me. Hug, may be, Andreas?" His startled look changed to sympathy. That was short lived. His original enthusiasm returned, and he threw his arms around her.

"Wow! I can't believe it's really you, Athena. You are all grown up now. Oh, I'm sorry, you must also be married, because of your arms," he said, his tone dropping from enthusiasm to concern.

"I can't believe it's you, Andreas! No, not any more. I was, but my husband was killed. Now it's just me and my friends here. Oh, forgive me. Gang, this is my childhood friend and pal, Andreas Myntas. We grew up here and played together nearly every day, that is, until I moved away to Theos. Andreas, these are my dear friends. They're like me. This is Alekto, Ariadne, Bethany, and Dita. Dita and Bethany are married and are visiting me from Velona."

"Wow. Most pleased to meet such beautiful women," he replied, giving each of us a warm, welcoming hug. "I'm sorry that I lost touch with you, Athena. Shortly after you left for Theos, I got a job on a caravel and went to sea. Now I own my own fleet — well three caravels at least. My ships sail the seas and trade with countries all over the world. I'm now living in Velona, that's where I've made the headquarters of Myntas Shipping anyway. Wow! After all these years, we cross paths again. Are you living here or on vacation like nearly everyone here?"

"Vacation. Two weeks of fun. How about you? The Ice Sheet is a long way from Velona."

"My folks passed away. I had to come back to help my younger brother settle their estate. I don't need the money, so I'm trying to sell everything I can and give it to Hermes, who could use it. I'm here for a couple weeks yet. You know how slowly legal things can go."

"Say, since you are single, how about us getting together — like old times? You remember when we snuck off and skated five miles out onto the Ice Sheet?"

Athena giggled, "Yes, I got scared that we were lost!" She explained what they had done when they were ten.

He then said, "You know, all the other kids that we used to hang out with around here are gone too, moved elsewhere. I have nothing to do until around four. Mind if I hand out with you five?" Athena scooted over to make room for him.

"Thanks, Athena. Say, you five can't be here on your own, can you? I mean, I really don't know anything about Women of the Eighth Degree. It's just, well, how can you manage, Athena?"

"No, we've got five friends out there skating away. They look after our needs. Honestly, yes, it's awful, being this way."

"Why? Why did you do it? Did your husband force you?" he asked most concerned, as well as curious.

"No, I was always dead set against it. You know that. I was abducted from my bedroom. They held something against my face with made me unconscious, and they took me away and did it. I awoke as I am now. Dita and Bethany were also abducted and knocked out, when they did it to them."

"Incredible! I always thought it was a special ceremony between a loving couple, at least that's what I've always heard. That must have been awful for you, Athena. And for you, Bethany and Dita. Who would want to do that to you? Why, that is just plain criminal, if you ask me. There's been a bit of that going on up in Velona — you know, with those strange fanatics from Dorota. Say, Dita, Bethany, you do look like women who come from Dorota, now that I think about it, light bronze-like skin color and all."

Athena quickly came to our rescue, explaining that we were cousins and that our fathers had been whites from Velona. He accept her explanation for now. "Hey, how about a cup of hot cocoa all around? Remember, Athena, how we used to always grab a cup after skating?"

"Oh, I'd love some, but," she said, suddenly realizing that she could no longer hold the cup — that he would have to hold it so she could sip.

"Oh, no problem. I may be a bit awkward, but ya got ta have hot chocolate!" He headed over to the vender.

"Damn! I should have said no," Athena whispered very annoyed with herself. "How's he going to handle all five of us? Damn. I'm sorry."

"Hey, I love chocolate! Don't be sorry," Dita exclaimed with a passion.

He brought back a whole pitcher, but only one mug. "I can't hold six mugs at once, and since you can't hold one, I figure we can all sip from one.

There's plenty, so drink up. Athena will tell you the best way is to slurp it, taking in a lot of air. You can really taste the chocolate better that way. Who cares about the noise; we're out here and there's no fancy court or anything around." He held it up so Athena could sip. At last, after he kept insisting, she demonstrated their special slurping method. A bit later, Dita tried it.

"Wow! It does taste better this way! More, more, more!"

"Don't hog it all, Dita," I teased her and everyone giggled.

"Hey, do you all have any dinner plans or plans for tonight?" he asked, while holding the mug for Alekto.

"Well," Athena hesitated.

"Ah, so you don't! I know you well, Athena!" She giggled and looked at her dress, remembering the fun times that they had had so many years ago. Or was it a lifetime ago?

"In that case, you and your other friends are all dining with me at the Black Sled Inn, say at six? There is this fabulous entertainment group playing at the theater here. The MBE Show it's called. They are famous in Velona anyway, and I just found out that they are on a big world tour, bringing their show to other countries, before returning to Velona. I've seen it twice now; it's impressive. I know. I'll get you all front row seats! How many of you are there?"

"But Andreas, you don't have to do this," Athena tried to protest.

"Of course, I don't, Athena. I want to do it. After all, we haven't seen each other in ten years! We can catch up on old times too. You can't say no. Ladies, don't let her say no, because you will be missing the greatest show on earth!"

"Well, all right, just this once," Athena agreed. Later, he returned the empty pot and mug.

"Say, how about us skating again, like old times?" he asked after he returned.

"But I can't skate like this?" she shrugged her shoulders; her cloak moved slightly, but he got the idea.

"Athena Stavros! You know that's a load of pig's crap! You were always showing off with me, skating all over with your hands fixed behind your back. I suspect you are out of practice; so am I for that matter. I'm not letting you get off that easily. Arms or no arms, we're going skating. Back with skates soon," he dashed off to fetch some, but quickly returned to ask her foot size.

"I'm not telling you that, so you can't get me skates!" Athena declared defiantly.

He left and returned with skates for himself and three other pairs. "One of these ought to fit." She tried to protest, but he ignored her. "Wow! What boots! Height of fashion, I assume?" he chatted as he removed her boots and put on her skates. She said that they were. "I got this style for you because it has a higher back heel than men's skates. I guess it is high enough. Okay, up you go, Athena." He lifted her up and put his arms around her waist, supporting her all the way.

"But I can't! I don't have any arms to catch my balance, Andreas! I'll fall down and hurt myself." He ignored that and move her over onto the ice. True to his word, he kept a firm grip around her waist, and they pushed off, she wiggling to keep her balance. We four held our breaths! Dita moved out of her body and over Athena, ready to grab her if she fell. She didn't. After several laps, her old skating skills began to come back to her. Soon, Andreas no longer needed to hold on to her, and she was skating well on her own, though he stayed right by her side. Our five friends saw Athena skating and came over to congratulate her, telling her this was total fun!

Sometime later, gasping for breath from the tight corset, Andreas carried her back, sat her down, and exchanged skates for her boots. When he was done, our five friends had finally had enough, but were more than curious about this strange man who was with Athena. After more introductions and explanations, Andreas said, "Hey, have you all been on the bobsled run? No? Athena! You are slipping! Come on, everyone, my treat, bobsled time."

"Wait, what exactly is this? I mean we five might not be able to do this thing?" I asked defensively.

"Can you sit?" Andreas teased. With our companion's arms around us, we headed off with him, while he explained. He was definitely unused to our slow speed. I was surprised at how quickly he adapted. On the other side of the town was bobsled hill. Here a long hillside sloped down from the edge of town. A booth rented the sleds, which carried five people at once, six if you crowded them in. We watch other groups as they climbed on board the sled and then went sailing down the long hill. At the end of the half-mile run, they dismounted and moved over to the side where a rope and stakes snaked up the hill. We watched as the folks huffed and puffed their way back up. Some of the fathers pulled the sled with their children in it. Well, our men were certainly going to have to pull us five back up!

Soon, Andreas returned with two sleds. He insisted on putting Athena at the front, with himself right behind her. He suggested that the armed people sit behind the armless ones to make sure they didn't fall off, though with the low sides, this seemed unlikely to me. A shove later and down the hill we went! Neither Dita nor I had ever experienced a bobsled run before, and we both loved it. The men didn't enjoy pulling us all back up, however. After three runs, they claimed that they were pooped, and we all headed back to Athena's for lunch, Andreas in tow.

After removing our cloaks and coats, our dresses now billowed out to their fullest and Andreas saw what Athena really looked like. "Do they still hurt? I mean your shoulders?" he asked her quietly. The two began a lengthy catch up on old time's chat, while we chatted about the morning.

Later, Andreas had to leave, but he said, "Well, you are already dressed up enough for the fancy inn and for the theater, Athena. See you all at six." Since our five companions were now thoroughly pooped, we all sat around the fireplace gabbing about this resort and of course, Andreas. The two queens wanted to know all about him.

At six, we arrived at the inn, a very fancy one. I was glad that we had worn these gowns. Everyone inside at the many tables was well dressed, though ours caught many an eye, both from men as well as women, eyeing our high fashion. After a delicious meal, we donned our cloaks and coats and were escorted a few streets over to the large theater. Actually, it contained a very large stage down front.

As promised, Andreas had reserved eleven seats for us in the front row, directly behind the orchestra pit. He, of course, sat beside Athena, the two still chatting like old friends. Slowly the theater filled up with people until the place was packed with over five hundred folks of all ages. A man went around damping out the many lanterns attached to the wall, and then the musicians entered and took their seats right in front of us. Finally, a well-dressed man, who was twenty-six, tall, thin, with light brown hair and a little goatee, walked out bowed, and spoke.

"Welcome one and all to the MBE Show, all the way from Velona, Sea Princes. We hope you like fine music and elegant dancing. Let the show begin." He stepped down into the musician's box and picked up a violin. He, we soon saw, was the music conductor as well as a violinist.

First, the musicians played a number of pieces for instruments alone. They were fantastic, and some were old folk tunes that Dita and I recognized instantly. Bard Tal, my son, used to play them, as did I. I saw a man pick up a bass flute and wondered. Yes, it was Lyneth's Lament! Soft and low the notes began, hinting at the great loss of her husband. Soon the notes doubled and the pitch rose overall, reflecting her inner turmoil and anger over her untimely loss. After a crescendo, the notes once more sank downward and slow as she accepted her fate, her loss. The audience gave them a standing ovation!

After more instrumental music, another nicely dressed man, who looked remarkably like the conductor, save his hair touched his shoulders and he had no goatee, perhaps twenty-two at most, led a group of singers onto the stage. The combined choir and musicians then played ten songs ranging from Chara's motets to lively Demokritos bar songs. Then, the singers moved back to the edge of the sides of the stage, and the young man walked off. Momentarily, he reappeared, leading ten women wearing our style formal ball gowns. That they too wore corsets beneath these distinctly Annelise fashions were obvious, if you had ever worn one.

Now both the singers and musicians played mostly elegant waltzes, and the man danced among the women who were also dancing for the audience. Dresses twirled, he held a woman's back, while she leaned perilously back, her long hair touching the floor. They put on a stellar performance of high fashion and dancing. The audience was thrilled, as were Dita and me; this was the style of dancing that we both loved!

Dita and I received quite a surprise. As they finished their last set, the male dancer turned to the audience and asked all those who wanted to join in with their dancing to stand up. Dita and I looked at each other and rose, along with a dozen other men and women, some older, some our age. "Come, don't be bashful, up on the stage with you," he called out, his face a giant smile. He saw our plight at once. While the other couples were coming down the aisles and going up the side stairs, he hopped down and lifted each of us gently up onto the stage!

One of the female dancers, dressed similar to us glided over to join us. "Will one of you long haired beauties care to dance with me?" he asked politely. I knew that Dita would prefer the woman companion, so I volunteered. As all the audience volunteers were moved into an artful position among his dancers, she put her arms around Dita and whispered, "Do you want me to lead?" Of course, Dita wanted to lead.

The young man put his arms around me and nodded to the violinist. With the choir joining in, the slow waltz began once more, and we began to dance. I marveled that he intuitively knew that I could only take tiny steps, but he twirled me around and even coached me into a deep back bend, while he held my back securely. I had a ball, so did Dita. When it finally ended, his arm around me, holding me securely, we pivoted to face the audience.

"Let's give all these wonderful volunteers a great hand! Thank you all for coming. Good night." The audience again gave a huge round of applause. After what seemed an eternity, the crowd finally began slowly filing out.

He carefully lifted me and handed me to the conductor who sat me gently before my seat. Then, a grinning Dita was lifted down beside me. The conductor whispered, "Ladies, please stay just where you are for one minute please." We grinned; we couldn't move anywhere anyway, not for quite a while. I guessed it would be at least five minutes for the many others to file out so that we could begin to walk back down the aisle.

"Dita, Bethany, you both danced beautifully!" Athena complimented us, while all the others added their accolades to hers. "You are so gutsy to go up there! I would have been just petrified!"

"No kidding!" Alekto added.

Just then, the two men came down from back stage carrying a handful of roses. "After each concert, we give out roses to some of the ladies up front. If you will allow me," he fastened a rose to each of us five women. "You are very special women. Thank you both for being so brave. Not many like yourselves would have done that. You dance exceptionally well. By the way, I'm Luigi Matteo and this is my older brother, Dario. It's our show, MBE — Matteo Brothers Entertainment. We're from Velona and this is our world tour. Are these your husbands?"

"Hi, wonderful show. I just love Lyneth's Lament! Oh, I'm Bethany

Brozena Malina and this is my wife, Dita Malina. We're from Velona ourselves, down here visiting. This is Athena, Alekto, and Ariadne; they've recently lost their husbands, and we are all here getting away from it all, vacation. These are our friends," I replied, introducing the five others as well.

"Wow, you actually know the name of that tune! Amazing. You know we are modeling our whole show off the famous Bard Tal and his group. You are the first person on this world tour that knew the name of that haunting song! And I must say," Luigi continued, "that you have certainly married a very beautiful woman." Dita smiled. He added, "So I take it you are members of that Jehosanity Church in Velona?"

"Oh no! We go to the Holy Rose Church," Dita corrected him.

"Wow! I am surprised. I mean aren't you five what they call down here — Dario, help me out."

The older gentleman spoke up, "Holy Women of the Eighth Degree, I believe. We don't quite know what that means, though, other than to say you have somehow lost your arms. Forgive our ignorance if we speak too bluntly, ladies."

"Say, our performance is done for tonight. Would you ladies and friends care to join us for a little refreshments at the inn next door? Our treat, if you please," Dario suggested.

"Yes, please do. It is rare indeed that we meet someone from our homeland, to say nothing of them being such beautiful women," Luigi added. "Perhaps you could educate us a bit about this degree thing. We've occasionally seen one or two like you in our audience, but never five in a row, and never has one volunteered to dance with us on stage. Please, take some refreshments with us."

"If you insist," I replied, eager to know more about these men and their fabulous show. While we were helped into our cloaks, the two brothers went backstage to fetch theirs. They returned accompanied with several of the women dancers who were wearing gowns similar to ours.

One asked, "Yours are from Annelise?" We said that was so and continued chatting.

Andreas put his arm around Athena and began assisting her down the aisle. Without the slightest hesitation, Luigi slipped his around Alekto, while Dario did the same with Ariadne. Barnabas held onto me, and Morpheus, Dita. I noticed that both the young men knew the proper pace to set, one that we could easily do in our boots.

Luigi commented, "I sense that you, too, are wearing the fancy boots. Some of our dancers wear them as well. So Dario and I are now experts at walking with you." He noticed that the other three women, who were dressed as we, put their arms around Zoe, Xene, and Zona for necessary support.

This was one of the inns that Athena wanted to bring us to see.

Elegance and ritzy best described this one. Plush carpeting, satin table cloths, ornate brass candle holders with multicolored candles at each table, waitresses in ball gowns, men in tails — all spoke of a high class inn. Evidently the waitresses all knew the Matteo brothers; they led us to a series of tables that had been pushed together to handle a large party. We certainly were that. I was intending to suggest that our friends intersperse themselves between each of we five women, but I did not get the chance. Oh, these brothers were smooth and efficient.

They pulled out the chairs for the women, unclasped and took their cloaks, and helped them sit. At once, they sat beside Ariadne and Alekto. Andreas followed their lead and sat beside them and Athena. Dita and I sat across from them, with Xene beside me to assist me, and Zoe, Dita. The three dancers sat across from our two men.

"Well, the drinks are on us tonight. They have an exquisite wine, a superb dark ale, a variety of teas, and the most delightful cocoa. What will you ladies prefer?" asked Dario. Amazing, the waitress had silently appeared just behind him! How did he know that she was there and ready to take our order?

"Cocoa please," Dita replied. I grinned, that figured. I chose tea. The queens decided on wine, partly I believe, so that the men would find it easier to assist them — less cup lifting. Our fellows chose the ale.

"You will have to forgive us," Luigi said to Alekto, "we've never sat beside women such as yourselves. You will have to give us some guidance with the wine."

"Just hold it to our lips so we can sip," Alekto replied. Her face flushed.

"You find it embarrassing?" Luigi correctly observed, surprising her.

"Yes, a little. I still do. I, we are not like normal people anymore. It wasn't supposed to be this way," she said, a bit relieved that it was now out in the open.

"Please, we do not know much about this land's strange custom," Dario added. "Although Dita and Bethany must come from Dorota. You have the light skin coloration, and we've heard that all the women there are born without any arms."

Athena spoke up, "Well, I was always dead set against this business, but I was abducted and knocked unconscious. They did it without my permission. Same with Dita and Bethany. They are from Velona down here visiting me. Like me, some men abducted them during the night and did it to them." Both men seemed aghast hearing that this was done to us without our consent.

"I suppose that we ought to explain how it is supposed to be," Ariadne continued. She began describing how it was supposed to be the ultimate in love and devotion to one's marital partner.

"But our husbands have recently died and here we are like this, without them to help us. We sometimes feel so helpless, so embarrassed. We'd give anything to be able to undo it, but that's impossible. Honestly, sometimes I feel so embarrassed about it, when I want to do something, and I simply have no way," Ariadne explained.

"Yes, I can understand how you must feel. Yet, you three are all still very young and you have your whole lives before you. Surely, you will find another who will love you deeply," Luigi replied in a very sincere manner. Neither brother had thus far shown any sympathy for us, deep concern, sincerity, and respect, but not that insidious sympathy that so many gushed our way.

Alekto answered, "You are only partially right, about our lives are ahead of us. However, here in Demokritos, it is rare indeed if one of us ever finds another husband. After all, Luigi, you have to look at us pragmatically. We are virtually helpless; we need help with nearly everything in life. What man in his right mind would want to marry a woman with such overwhelming needs as we have? Certainly not many at all. It is very rare for us to ever be able to remarry and then often it is not for love but just for survival, to have someone to care for our needs."

"Ah, dear Alekto, you should not be so harsh on yourself; you too, Ariadne!" Luigi replied. "You have your youth, you have your health, and you have your beauty, grace, and charm. All five of you have such a vibrant feel of life within you! Take it from us, Alekto, Ariadne, we have traveled widely through many countries now. It is so very rare that we meet women who are so very alive, such vitality you have within you! Yes, we meet women who are socially charming, who are breathtakingly beautiful, such as Dita Malina here. Yet, to find all these in one woman is as rare as a rose in the winter!" Alekto looked very pleased with his sincere compliment, as did Ariadne.

"Hey, all this has got me thinking," Dario spoke up. "You know, some years back now, some women from Dorota came to Velona and were helping some of our Velona women, who were deceived by their religious men and had their arms removed. As I recall, these Dorota women were able to do the most fantastic things with just their feet. Luigi, weren't they somehow associated with the Holy Rose Church? I seem to recall they were."

"I think so, maybe it was during Priestess Lana West Po's time, Dario. Yes, we heard all manner of things that these women were able to do. You know, feed themselves, cook meals, keep house — everything any woman does. I certainly have no idea how they could do these things," Luigi replied.

"You know, Alekto, Ariadne, if you can afford it, sometime you ought to consider coming up north to Velona and checking into this. Perhaps these women are still around and can give you some guidance. I can't imagine how awkward and embarrassing it must be for all of you," Dario said sincerely.

"We are still on a lengthy tour, but when we do get back to Velona, we can check on it for you and send you a letter with what we find out," Luigi volunteered.

"Thank you, that would be great," Alekto replied. "Just between us, I have always wanted to travel and see the world, especially Velona. I have heard such wonderful things about that city or is it a country?"

"Both. Velona is a country, but its capital city is also called Velona. We are from the city," Dario replied.

"I've been wanting to visit Velona as well," Ariadne added. "Maybe Alekto and I can one day take a trip and see it for ourselves."

Dita and I sat there figuratively biting our tongues. Oh, how we wanted to tell these women all about these things, but right now, we dared not. It would blow our cover. Too much was at stake. I swore that as soon as it was safe, I would have a very long talk with these women. I was becoming quite attached to these three.

For several hours, the brothers sat and chatted with us, particularly with Ariadne and Alekto. They told us of their travels, how they had put together their show, how it had slowly evolved. Little did we realize that the MBE Show was one of the most popular groups in Velona now. Raising our girls and our new baby bodies had taken up far too much of our time during the last five years. We were a little out of touch with the arts, mostly going to local dances. Suddenly, Morpheus realized how late it had become.

"Oh not to worry, we do not have a show tomorrow. It is our day off," Dario eased his worries.

"Say," Andreas volunteered, "tomorrow, why don't we all get together and have some more outdoor fun? Athena here went skating today and did really well. Why don't you two come and join us, since it's your day off. In the evening, I believe that there is a play going on over at the other theater. I'll check on it. If so, how about I treat everyone to a play? Don't know if it is any good though. What do you say, fellows? You can chat more with Dita and Bethany about Velona if nothing else."

Luigi looked at Alekto and asked, "Ma'am, would you mind my company tomorrow?"

"Of course not. Please do come."

"Ariadne, would you mind if I came with you tomorrow?" asked Dario, just as politely.

"Yes, do. You must come."

We thanked them for the wonderful evening and then headed the short way home. I nearly slipped three times, but Barnabas caught me each time. Darn boots anyway.

The next morning around nine, we met Andreas, Luigi, and Dario at the Ice Sheet area. As he did yesterday, Andreas fetched ice skates for Athena. Luigi and Dario followed him and took their cues from him, getting skates with higher heels. Although both women protested that they did not know how to skate and had no way to keep their balance, their protests were ignored. "Just look at Athena. She is skating nicely, as good as many others out there. So I won't take no from you," Luigi explained to Alekto. "I'll hold on to you always. Trust me." Dario did likewise with Ariadne.

Dita and I contented ourselves to sit and watch the three couples. Morpheus and Barnabas were extremely grateful for this. Neither had ever skated before yesterday and knew that they would be useless in helping us stand up, let alone skate. Eventually, Zoe, Zona, and Xene decided to try it again. "Please don't ask us," Morpheus begged me, as his wife awkwardly took her first spill on the ice. We giggled. "I had an awful time of it yesterday," he added.

Dita and I were very content to just sit, relax, and watch all of these people, some hundreds of them, out there having fun. It was very peaceful indeed. Only when lunchtime came did the three couples and the three women finally decide to hang up their skates and join us for something to eat. Our lunch turned into a three-hour chatting session, though Luigi chatted mostly with Alekto, while Dario talked with Ariadne, and Andreas, Athena. At last, we decided to go bob sledding once more, because now we had more men to pull us back up the hill.

For another two hours up and down we went, laughing and having the time of our lives. Fun, simple fun. Towards the end, Andreas and Athena became playful, more and more memories they'd shared came back to them. "Hey, remember when we had that big snowball fight?" he asked.

"Yes, but don't throw that ball at me now, Andreas! I can't move without falling down, and besides it's no fair now. I can't throw one back at you," she retorted playfully. He tossed one at her anyway. She laughed and nearly fell down; our boots were terribly slippery in the snow.

Later, we again dined in luxury, taking a long dinner break. Only as the time of the play approached did we finally end off and head over to the theater. The play was entertaining; we had nothing quite like this in Velona. The locals really seemed to enjoy it, though. It was around nine when we at last filed out of the theater.

"Say, Luigi, Dario, would you like to come over to our place for a while?" Alekto had finally gotten up the courage to ask him.

"Please, Dario," Ariadne added.

"You too, Andreas, you have to come. The place is the same as it's always been," Athena added. "We are staying at my parent's old estate. He and I grew up here together ages ago," she explained to the brothers. They didn't need any further encouragement.

Once there, the three women took the three on a brief tour of the rather large house, while the rest of us headed to the kitchen to whip up some snacks and brew some tea. Well, Dita and I watched and offered suggestions. Meanwhile, Morpheus and Barnabas began a dart tossing game. After everyone had their fill of snacks, I suggested that our two men give us a dart tossing demonstration. Cleverly, I got the rest of us into the playroom, leaving the three couples alone in the dining room. Okay, I decided to play cupid, of sorts. At least, we could give them some measure of privacy.

Dita said, "Well, I can play darts too."

"Oh no! No fair, Dita. You are supposed to throw them. No fair picking them up and sticking them in the bull's-eye," Morpheus teased.

Undaunted, Dita said, "Okay, you are on. Remove my right boot and someone has to balance me. I can't do it so well in these boots." A bit later, Dita picked up a dart between her toes and lopped it toward the dartboard. "Bit rusty," she explained as it stuck into the wood below the round board. A few more shots and she had the hang of it again. She had learned to throw daggers this way, but only from a few feet away. Now she gave the men a run for their money. The only way they could beat her at darts was to force her to throw from a distance that she couldn't manage. Either that or not help her balance on her one heel. We all got a kick out of them horsing around.

It was after eleven when the three men said their goodbyes. Athena and the others had promised to take in their show tomorrow night and if possible drop by to watch them practice in the afternoon. Once the men had gone, Athena giggled, "Andreas actually kissed me!"

"So did Dario! Passionately even," added an excited Ariadne.

"I nearly fainted when Luigi kissed me. Oh how I missed that," Alekto added. All three women were glowing.

After this, Athena's grand plans for things to do on our vacation went by the boards! We spent as much time in the company of Andreas, Luigi, and Dario as we possibly could — the three women begged us so. It was plain to the rest of us that these six were falling for each other. Only now that they were being so passionately kissed did Athena began to worry. None of the three men actually realized who the three women were, the queens of their kingdoms!

By the ninth day of our stay, Athena was feeling just awful about it. She cared deeply for Andreas and it was clear that he held deep feelings for her. Likewise, the budding romance with Ariadne and Alekto was unmistakable, and they too began to fret over this huge barrier. I decided that we ought to break our cover and let them know the truth. All three were convinced that this would end everything, but they felt that to continue as they were was unfair to the three young men. I invited the three over for late afternoon tea and brunch.

I decided to be the one to break the news, saving the queens the embarrassment. Once everyone was seated, I began, "Andreas, Luigi, Dario, I need to explain some things to you three. Actually, Athena, Alekto, and Ariadne are here incommunicado. They desperately needed a vacation from their recent work. Due to the unfortunate circumstances they were thrown into, they've had to do an enormous amount of serious work for months on end. They just had to get away and relax."

"Well, we can understand that. What kind of work were you doing? I don't want to pry. If you'd rather not say, that's okay. It's just, well I don't know what kind of work you could be possibly talking about," Andreas finally admitted. "I'm sorry if my words are too harsh, Athena. I just really don't understand what — well. . ."

Athena took pity on his fumbling. "Well, just what work can an armless woman do that would be so exhausting? It is okay just to say it, really. I mean we can't do anything about our lack of arms. It is always better to say what you mean. Yes, it can be awfully embarrassing to us, but we all would rather it be that way and be honest about it than try to be socially polite and dance around the truth."

I went on, "Their work has really been vital to Demokritos. I guess the best way to say this is just to come right out with it. Let me introduce to you Queen Athena Patra of Theos, Queen Alekto Pegasos of Arolas, and Queen Ariadne Diodros of Thrace."

"Oh my god! Athena? You are the queen here in Theos? I had no idea!" exclaimed Andreas. "Well, that's what I get for having been gone so darn long. Congratulations!"

"Wow! You are the Queen of Arolas? Wow!" exclaimed a very surprised Luigi.

Simultaneously, Dario declared, "Incredible, Ariadne, I mean Queen Ariadne! Very pleased to meet and know a real queen!"

"Dario! What idiots we are! Remember, we heard that last summer there was a horrible accident in Kefall that killed their Emperor and all their kings! Queens, please, we did not make the connection. I am so sorry for your tragic losses!" a shocked Luigi explained.

Athena took charge, "Please, please don't tell anyone. It will ruin our only time off. We have been so incredibly busy; they are allowing us to run our kingdoms and the whole country by ourselves. We need this brief time out." She sighed and added, "I am sorry that we may have led you on. It is okay with us if you now want to just go your separate ways and all that."

"Why would I want to do that?" Andreas asked. "I've had more fun, felt more alive these past few days with you, Athena, than I have in since I left Theos years ago. I know you've had fun with me too. I've seen it on your face. Oh," he had a sudden thought. "If you want me to go away and leave you alone, I will. Just say the word."

"Oh no! I didn't mean that! I've had more fun with you these past few days, Andreas. I just want you to know the truth about me. I sort of figured that now you would want to just take off, you know."

"Of course I don't, Athena. I am glad that you told me, though. It doesn't change the way I feel about you either." He gave her a playful wink.

Luigi looked at Alekto and said, "Alekto, I have been looking at you as a powerful, dynamic, vibrant woman. I am still right and I still meant everything I've said to you. You are the most impressive woman that I have ever met. Your secret is safe with us. I hope this does not mean that we cannot see each other anymore."

She blushed, "I was hoping that you'd still want to see me. Thanks."

"Same here, Ariadne. You've rather taken me off my feet these past few days. As Luigi says, we've never met such incredible women as you two. Please allow me to continue to see you as well."

"Are you sure? Me, armless me?" she teased, but was really not teasing, she was trying to be honest.

"Arms haven't anything to do with you, not unless you dwell solely on their absence. If you did, I wouldn't be here now," he replied. I sensed all three men were being honest and sincere, and I was relieved, for I sure didn't want these women hurt emotionally. Right now, they were particularly vulnerable.

"You know, men often make passes at me when I am on my throne. I've had six in the last couple of months, but they are just trying to use me so they can become king," Ariadne confessed.

"Well, you have no fear of that from me, Ariadne," Dario teased. "A. I didn't know you were royalty and B. I wouldn't be king if you paid me!"

Luigi laughed, "Me a king? Sorry, Alekto, no way. We're musicians and entertainers, not rulers. Oh! I hope this doesn't put a crashing stop on our budding friendship!"

Startled, she replied, "No way, Luigi! I really don't want to be a queen either, but I just don't know how I can stop being one right now. It is all so confusing."

"Same with Athena and me," Ariadne admitted. "We are all three rather forced into staying on as our kingdom's rulers. Bethany, can we tell them really what has been going on or is it too dangerous for them?"

"I think now it might be more dangerous for them if we didn't," I replied. "Okay, here's what's been going on in Demokritos." I spent an hour outlining the key events from the last ten years or so, including the suspected assassinations, "unusual accidents," abductions, and murders. I outlined our suspicions and presented some of our circumstantial evidence.

"I suspect that if anyone of these queens should remarry or perhaps even publically have a steady boyfriend, then that man might wind up in an alley with his throat slashed. We need more time to unravel this mess and bring the guilty parties to justice," I finished up.

Athena added, "So now you see. We three really want to get out of this. We don't want to be queen. Now Frona, she's been a queen the longest of any of us, and she likes it, but we know she hates also to have do the king's duties along with hers. Same with Melita, though I know she'd like to find a good man too. Adonia and Danae like being a queen but would rather just be a wife and mother. They were terribly devastated over the loss of their children in the explosion. We are in a fine mess, aren't we? So we three can understand it if you want to just say good night and depart. Honestly, if they find out that you might be interested in us, your lives may well be in danger."

Andreas exclaimed, "Athena! Why didn't you let me know that you were in such trouble long ago? Haven't we been friends forever? Okay, I know I've been out of the country for years, and I lost track of you, but we've run into each other again. I swear to you that I won't run out on you! Together, we can work it out. More heads are better, it's said." She didn't expect this and found herself wanting to hug him on the spot. Unable to do even that small gesture, she leaned over and rested her head on his shoulder; his arms slid around her shoulders, pulling her snug.

"I know," Luigi burst out. "Alekto, we can just take you with us when we leave Demokritos, smuggle you out of this country!"

Dario shook his head. "Don't be an idiot, little brother. She wouldn't do that; it would bring chaos to her kingdom and people. No, Luigi, that's the easy way out. We must help Alekto and Ariadne find the right way out. We need to devise a much better plan."

"He's right. Okay, Athena, we need to know your schedule, what cities you will be in and when. That way, we can arrange to be nearby to help out," Andreas kicked into his problem-solving mode, which had already made him a small fortune in the shipping industry. "Look, I am used to dealing with complex problems. How else can a man end up owning his own three caravels? Those are awfully expensive ships."

She explained that after our vacation was over, we had to go to Kefall for a week Summer Council. After that, we'd be returning to their respective palaces in the three capital cities, unfortunately widely scattered around the country. Of course, there was always the outside chance that the Empress would delay their return as she had all winter. I thought that a long delay such as we had experienced was unlikely, unless a large amount of new business had appeared. She might delay a week or two, but not three months.

"Okay, then the first thing that we must arrange is a safety net. That is, you three must always have a way to escape in an emergency. We'll work on that. Wherever you are at, Athena, you will know that I am nearby, ready to snatch you out of there. I'm sure that the bothers can also work something out for Alekto and Ariadne," Andreas explained. An interesting discussion began in earnest.

We were not the only people taking a Yuletide vacation. Prior to the holiday season, the leaders of the three most powerful Noble Houses in Kefall met privately. Jonas Sokrates, Ikaros Kadmos, and Horus Zarus met in the secure study of House Sokrates. All three men were in their late fifties and long used to wielding power. Jonas began, "Thank you for coming. I will be quite blunt. The times so dictate. I could not help notice that both of you had switched your support from desiring to elect a new Emperor to backing the Empress and the Church."

Antagonistically, Ikaros replied, "Well, so did you, Jonas. What of it?"

"We are the real power here, yet we three have given in to such a ludicrous request — having Women of the Eighth Degree running our nation. I admit that Kassandra approached me with some things that I would rather not have widely known. I suspect that she has done the same with you gentlemen. I know that you both went to see her, and after that meeting, you switched sides." Both men grumbled, but did not openly deny what Jonas said.

"Gentlemen, House Sokrates will not stand to be blackmailed, certainly not by such a helpless woman!"

"Yes, but we cannot openly defy her now, you know that, Jonas," Ikaros replied.

"She could meet with an accident," Horus suggested with an evil grin.

"Yes, but there is always a risk to that," Jonas countered. "Let us use that as a last resort. I have been asking myself for months now, why would the Empress desire total control of Demokritos? Why should that Church want to support having — let's face it, men — totally helpless women ruling our whole nation?"

"Say, like minds think alike," Horus broke in, "I've been pondering that one too."

"Same here," Ikaros added.

"I've found no earthly reason yet," Jonas continued. "My personnel and I have been over all the Empress' proclamations and decisions thus far and those of the queens. I will admit those have all been sound."

"I agree, but wouldn't that be what you would expect? I mean if you just took over control, wouldn't you want to pass measures sure to please your constituents? Make everyone feel that they made the right decision. After all, everyone only gave a hesitant approval to the Empress' proposal that they continue to run the country."

"Yes, the Empress is very shrewd. She's done exactly what I would have done, so far anyway. Popular opinion is now behind her and the queens," Jonas continued. "So now soon, I would expect them to start in on advancing the real agenda that they took over the thrones to pass."

Horus replied, "Well, if she is smart, she will only pass smaller things. If she tried to push through something major, such as new ways to elect emperors or kings, the damage to their credibility might be enough to reverse their popularity. We should look for creeping changes, right?"

"True. I'll be damned if I am going to stand for that though. I don't know about you, men, but I do not like to be blackmailed. If she did it once, she'll do it again. There goes our power down the drain. No, I simply cannot allow this to stand."

"I agree, Jonas. What are you suggesting?" asked Ikaros, a sneer on his face.

"I suspect many other Noble Houses in the kingdoms have also been blackmailed, though perhaps by the Church and not the Empress. My spies have seen the Church's men in blue traveling to the kingdoms. Not long after that, these men announced their support of the Empress and their queens. I believe that we are not alone in this at all. I propose that we three take a trip to these kingdoms and have private chat with the key Noble Houses in each. Let's organize a secret resistance movement against the Empress."

"I like it, but the queens are mere pawns in this. They lost their husbands and children. Kassandra is more or less holding them hostage. From all I can tell, the queens want to do what is best for their kingdoms," Ikaros defended the seven queens. "We should leave them out of our retribution."

"Agreed, but they obviously have to be replaced," Jonas consented. "What we need is a man who is popular, totally against this Church, and whom we can control as we see fit. He must also be strong and not easily intimidated, except by us."

"Who did you have in mind?" asked Horus, displaying an evil smile. He was enjoying this immensely.

"I am open to other suggestions, but currently my attention is on General Kreon Demon. He's very widely known throughout the land; he's battle hardened and despises the Church after what happened to his mother. You know that she died during their surgery to convert her into one of their Women of the Eighth Degree, don't you?" They nodded. "Women seem to think that he is handsome. He's obviously ambition oriented to have become a general at his young age of thirty."

"Yes, but he is still not married," countered Horus. "At least I don't think that he is."

"That is his only drawback. If we make him the proper offer, I believe that can be handled. Ambition out weights a wife," Jonas explained. The men laughed, that it did!

"If you agree on my choice, I will meet with him and set the ball rolling." Both backed his choice, indeed, General Kreon would have been their pick as well. "All right. Then we need to meet with the most influential of the Noble Houses of the kingdoms and clue them into our secret plans. They too should be working out replacement kings for their kingdoms. When the time is right, we go into action and sweep out the helpless and install our choices."

"Yes, but what about the Church and the Empress? Accident?" asked Ikaros.

"The time will be right when they have 'hanged' themselves. We can let the populace take care of them. Our hands will be clean, and our pathetic excuse for a woman will be handled, terminally." All three laughed.

"Okay, see if you agree on my choices here. For Thrace, we should see Acteon; Arolas, Agapios; Penelopus, it's Kyros; Alia, it'd be Nikias; Phindos,

Eros; Thallyus, Diabolos; and Theos, Linos. What do you think?" Jonas asked. They discussed these noblemen for a while and then agreed that these were the ones to visit over the holidays. Further, both men wanted to meet with the General when Jonas did. He agreed and set up the meeting for the next day.

"Ah, welcome General Kreon, we are so glad that you could come have a chat with us," Jonas welcomed the tall, handsome, well-muscled general into his private study. "Have a glass of fine wine with us?" The imposing figure accepted and sat across from the three men at the mahogany table. He noticed that every item in the room and its furnishings were the very best that money could buy.

"To what do I owe the pleasure of this meeting with the three most powerful noblemen in Kefall?" he asked, intending to let them know right off that he knew who they were and their significance.

"We will be forthright with you, General Kreon. You are aware of how our country and kingdoms are currently being run, are you not?"

"Yes, why on earth did you allow totally helpless women get such power? I was utterly appalled at your decision to back Empress Kassandra." Indeed, he had smashed a table in half when he had learned that these men were backing her to be sole ruler, dashing his chances of obtaining the throne himself. Perhaps now these men were coming to their senses, realizing their terrible mistake.

"Let us just say that for various reasons, we had little choice at the time," Jonas sidestepped this sensitive issue. He was not about to say they were blackmailed! "She does wield power of her own and right then was not the time to challenge her. After all, the public displayed great sympathy for her loss and that of their queens. Such a tragedy has never occurred before. For the sake of continuity and to avoid chaos, we thought it prudent to back her and the queens."

"However, we're confident that soon she will make huge blunders. In fact, we are very certain that will happen, only we're not sure just when that will be. However, when it does happen, we want to be united and prepared to immediately handle the vacancy. Of course, we must keep this secret until the time arrives for action. You know how the Empress has spies everywhere. We don't need her discovering our moves and then taking countermeasures."

"Of course, never give your enemies an opportunity to attack your flank. First rule on the battlefield," General Kreon replied. He definitely liked where this talk was heading.

"Now our choice for Emperor must work on the quiet to become fully prepared to take over on a moment's notice. He must be ready to lead in the crisis, using whatever force is necessary. In the meantime, we Noble Houses must become organized as well, so that when the time is right, we will be seen to be one hundred percent behind the new Emperor. Nothing can be left to chance. You understand what I am saying?"

General Kreon smiled; oh, did he ever understand this! He had not dreamed that they would be so forthright with him. "Certainly, ill is the general who leaves chance playing a role on his battlefield! That is not my way. I never leave anything up to chance. I've drilled that into my subordinates time and time again."

"Excellent, excellent. We have made our initial choice for this position. General Kreon, we would like to ask you to volunteer for the position of Emperor. You will certainly need our strong backing to succeed, of course."

Perfect! What a day! "Thank you gentlemen. I accept most graciously. Of course, I will need your backing." General Kreon wanted to jump and shout, but remained calm and collected. Time enough for celebrations later.

Jonas then said, "General, should we make all this come about, you will, of course, never forget how it was possible for you to ascend to the throne?"

Kreon realized that this was a covert way of saying that they would have agendas of their own that he would have to pass. Still, such was an infinitesimal price to pay to become Emperor of Demokritos. "One never forgets ones friends, gentlemen, never." All three men looked pleased and the general knew that he had satisfied them.

"Excellent, excellent. Now then General Kreon, there is one small complication that we must handle before all this can come to pass," Jonas now tackled the touchy issue. "Of course there must also be an Empress. You know how our people love their Empresses over the centuries."

General Kreon was afraid that this might come up. "I am aware of this. You know that I favor men, not women?" He tried to be discrete about his sexual leanings. He'd already had several male lovers, though none had lasted very long, unfortunately.

"Ah, yes, that explains much. Thank you for being so forthright with us. Yet, that problem remains. She must be seen as a virtuous, honest woman, one that our women can look up to and be proud of her." He was subtly telling the general not to marry a barmaid or such. "I know that this is a delicate subject. What would you think about us scouting out the perfect candidate for the Empress position?"

Relief swept over General Kreon, though he tried hard not to show it. "Yes, that would be optimal, I believe. If you left that choice up to me, what I might choose might not be agreeable to you fine gentlemen. Then, where would we be? No, I do believe that I should leave this delicate matter entirely up to you. I will abide by your choice. Fair enough?"

"Oh more than fair. Thank you very much, General. We will find the perfect candidate that will enhance your position as much as possible. We'll get back to you when we have found her. Now then, we should discuss some actions that we feel you ought to take in the meantime so that when the time comes, you are fully prepared to step into the position."

In early January 752, the three men met once again. They had returned from their "vacations" and compared notes. All seven of the nobles had welcomed their plan with open arms! That is, as long as their queens were not harmed or defamed. They promised secretly to set about the task of finding a new king and queen for their kingdom, coordinating their ascension with that of the new Emperor. "Gentlemen, the plan is now in motion. The ball is now in Kassandra's court. We must be ready to act the moment she fumbles the ball," Jonas stated. The three men toasted to their ultimate success.

Chapter 42 Summer Council, 751

Our vacation over and following a long carriage ride as well, we again moved into Athena's suites in the Empress's palace in Kefall for the Summer Council meeting, which was supposed to last a week, we hoped. Because of the short duration, Dita and I, in secret from Kassandra, gave our therapy sessions to the remaining Utu women, who were the Special Helpers for the remaining queens. How we could get to the remaining eight who assisted Kassandra was undetermined.

At nine that first morning, our large group assembled in the Empress' throne room, ready to tackle the larger scale business that impacted the whole country. We were surprised to see Cardinal Drakon as the first petitioner to address the court. I thought, here it comes.

"Let me be the first to welcome you Holy Women back from your kingdoms. I wanted to say that I personally thought that you all did a superb job this past winter. I came by today to make an inquiry. How did the past three months go for you in your capital cities?"

Queen Frona replied that we were uniformly accepted and that overall, all had gone well. The only problem really was the fact that too much local business got delayed for the three months that the queens had been here during the summer. Cardinal Drakon looked very pleased and complimented the queens. "Again, if there is anything that I can do to assist you or the Empress, please let me know. May you have a successful Summer Council." He left. Where was the bombshell, I wondered.

Next, the Announcer said, "Princess Maren from Annelise." Ah, taxes time again. A well-dressed man wheeled in the usual large load of jade. Additionally, several large crates were visible just outside the double doors.

"Empress Kassandra, so good to see you again!" the bubbly teenager bowed before her throne. She had glided perfectly across the room; her light pink satin ball gown, some fourteen feet in diameter at the floor, seeming to float across towards us.

"I'm very happy to have you visit with us once more, Princess Maren. Welcome indeed," Kassandra replied.

"Besides the usual jade, I've brought along some more outfits, compliments of my parents. You see, they were so impressed that you and all the queens were now wearing our elegant fashions that they insisted I bring some more for you and the queens. Oh, yes, I am supposed to see if clothing-trading arrangements between us can be arranged. We can deal with that stuff later. I can't wait to show you all the fine apparel that I've brought with me!"

"Oh thank you, Princess Maren! Please, be very sure to thank your parents for us. Queens, let's plan to spend this evening with Princess Maren.

We've just got to see what she has brought us!" They chatted a bit longer and Kassandra told a Messenger to get some staff to move the crates into her private meeting room. Princess Maren glided off to help them unpack the crates so she could make the proper presentations this evening.

Numerous business, financial, and army reports came next, consuming the morning session. In the afternoon session, various advisors reported on the progress of the army legion relocations to assist in making the cities safer, how the legions were doing on stopping raids from neighboring Vladimir, and on how the nationwide school planning was coming along. Uniformly all reports were acceptable, though there was some slight local resistance to so many legions of soldiers being deployed with the cities.

That evening after supper, we gathered in the Empress' private chambers, where the many crates had been opened. Princess Maren was very eager to begin. "Now, I didn't know how many of you would be ready for the next reduction step in your corsets, nor which step you would prefer to take next. It is really my fault on this, because I failed to go over all this with you properly before I left last time. Have you all been wearing your eighteen inch corsets all this time?" she asked, her face glowing with a youthful charm. We all had.

"Oh that is ever so encouraging. I had so hoped that you would all do so. Okay, then if you are ready for the next step, you must make a choice, though Empress Kassandra has already passed this one. At this point, you have two choices. First, you could go for the next step smaller, that is, seventeen inches. Second, you could stay at eighteen inches, but go for the three-inch waistband. You see, to really accent your tiny waists, you want your waist to be not only small, but also tall, rather like a wasp's body sections. Some try to go as small as possible and then work on the waistbands getting larger and larger to achieve the perfect look. Others prefer a more gradual approach, which would be to remain at eighteen inches, but increase the waistband from the bare half inch that it now is to three inches. Once used to that, then gradually shrink the waist, but always keeping the three inch band on further reductions."

"Now Kassandra has been wearing the three inch band with her eighteen incher, so she is ready for a seventeen inch, that is if she wants to do it," she looked at Kassandra eagerly.

"Oh you bet I do!" Kassandra replied.

Princess Maren smiled, "So since I goofed, I have brought you all both types. My dressmakers will make the small alterations on the new dresses, based on your choices. I've brought along all summer colors and styles. When I come back in the fall, I'll bring along the delightful fall styles with flowers, leaves, and birds on them."

"Can we just stay where we are currently at?" asked Queen Frona. She spoke for many of us. We knew that Kassandra would not permit us to take them off and wear our old dresses. However, this would at least be acceptable to continue as we were.

Kassandra gave her a frightful, icy, cold stare, "Of course not. Ladies, we are this country's rulers! Everyone is looking at us. We must be perfect in all ways. Elegant, refined, a model for all women of Demokritos to follow. Choose one or the other."

Diplomatically, Queen Ariadne asked, "Princess Maren, which would you recommend for us?"

"Oh that's easy. I would recommend going to the three-inch band, remaining at your eighteen inches. The new look will be amazing, very dramatic indeed, highly noticeable. It is more painful to reduce further and then try to expand the width," she gaily replied.

Three inch width waists it was all around. Later as the women fastened my new corset and drew it up tightly, I thought that my eyes were going to pop out of my head. Then, I was sure that I could no longer breathe! Cries of Oh! Can't breathe! Too tight! And many others echoed around the room as we all became even more constricted. Damn Kassandra anyway, I thought! Many shared my sentiments.

Next, Princess Maren handed out new dresses. "Bethany, I have a scarlet red satin dress for you so you can really please Dita!" It was quite red. She had a canary yellow satin gown for Dita so that she could please me. When she and I finally got to look at ourselves in our new dresses, I gasped. Now my tiny waist was very strikingly visible! "See, I told you so. You look absolutely stunning, doesn't she, Dita." Dita, struggling to breathe herself, gasped a yes.

Later back in Athena's quarters, we all found that now it was nearly impossible to bend any more; we were too tightly bound. We felt miserable and complained about it all evening long. Princess Maren had told us that now we ought to be eating six smaller meals a day, not three. I figured I might not be able to eat any! However, the next day, we discovered that Kassandra was even more miserable than we were. Hers was an inch smaller. Yet, she already implemented Princess Maren's advice. Thus, we had a light midmorning snack delivered to us, as well as a mid-afternoon snack. The kitchen staff was alerted to be ready to fill a late evening snack when the queens requested such.

At nine the next morning, I noticed that the male advisors were not present when Kassandra began the meeting. "Queens, this morning I want us to take up a new proposal of mine. Since we are the role models for all women of Demokritos and since we are setting the standard for elegance and fashion, I feel that we need to pass a law that requires all women with the means to begin wearing starter outfits from Annelise. Most certainly, when they are out in the public eye, they should be so attired. Shall we discuss my proposal?"

The queens uniformly wanted to say "Uggh! Argh!" and other

expletives, but they dare not. Queen Frona calmly pointed out that there were insufficient dresses in all of Demokritos to meet such a demand as she was intending. Kassandra pointed out that trading deals with Annelise could be worked out to provide many more outfits and that soon our seamstresses would be able to copy them here. The discussion raged for an hour, Kassandra defeating every objection the queens had.

At last, Kassandra seemed to compromise. "Okay. How about inserting a time qualifier, say by next Yuletide, all women who have the means to purchase these outfits do so and are required to wear them when in public places. That gives them a year to get outfitted."

Finally, this seemed to be the only detail on which Kassandra would compromise, and she got the queens' acceptance on her proposal. Next, came the trading agreement with Annelise. Kassandra had already worked this out; she was armed with the facts and figures. She must have spent months while we were away preparing all this. In return for five hundred complete outfits every quarter, Annelise received almost double their value in raw materials, such as wool and cotton. Annelise came out on top on this one, I mused. Princess Maren was summoned, and Selene signed the agreement for Kassandra, while Princess Maren did so for Annelise.

"I have to go now. I will be back for the fall session everyone. I'll bring you all new fall fashions! I know you'll love them. Don't worry, no more reductions until at least winter," she teased us. We all said goodbye. She meant well, but we were more miserable than ever before.

In our room that evening, Queen Athena griped, "You just don't go mandating to women what fashion they have to wear! It's natural for us to want to wear nice things and dresses similar to what is in fashion at the time. But we don't like to be ordered to wear a certain outfit. Mark my words, this proclamation of hers is not going to go over well at all!"

The next day we heard back from the initial steps to open up trading with Vladimir. At least this proved successful. Giant logs for various goods gave us a decided advantage in the deals. Already the ship construction industry began making expanded plans for more ships. All this would be good for our economy now and for the future. So far, things were going well.

That is, until the next day. Cardinal Drakon came to address the Council once more. This time, he did have some proposals for us to consider. His first request was to have an imperial proclamation to the effect that the Church of Jehosanity was the official religion of Demokritos. While we argued about it, there was little point in objecting to it. Already, this was about the only religion that remained. The old worship of the Sun God had all but vanished from the nation. His proclamation was mostly stating the obvious and his motion was passed. Selene wrote the document and signed it for Kassandra.

"Thank you for making this official. Next, as you well know, the Church, aided immensely by all of you, has been instrumental in providing needed assistance to the many women who were deceived by those evil Dorota Elders. At this time, I can report to all of you that we have been completely successful. There have been no further suicides by these unfortunate women since early last winter. All this has taken a toll on Church funds, as you might well imagine, providing support for so many Holy Women. Our Churches throughout Demokritos are simply the finest anywhere, something for which every citizen of our great nation can be proud, rightly so."

"Today, I come before you as the official representative of the Church of Jehosanity in Demokritos to ask, nay, to beg for your support. Our funds are nearly exhausted after providing for so many women and families in such dire need. In the past, we depended upon those wealthy men and women who wanted to help forward our Holy Ministrations to the needy of our land. In all honestly, I cannot keep going back to these same most holy people and ask for still more of their funds. They have already given most generously and far more than one would ever expect. Instead, since the Church is our official religion, I would like to propose that our government also donate a yearly tithe to the Church, perhaps ten percent of the countrywide net profits, as determined by the Empress. Such funds would come at a very needy time and can be used to further help all of our people in our great nation."

"Kassandra spoke first, "I absolutely want to throw my full and complete support behind his proposal. Our country must be seen to be supporting those organizations, which so help our people, especially those in need. However, we will, as usual, thoroughly study your most gracious proposal, Your Holiness."

"Thank you all so very much. There is one other small proposal that the Church wishes the Empress and queens to consider at this time. We are now the greatest trading nation of the world. Our fleets sail the world, visiting many barbaric and uncivilized portions of the world. It is our duty to Lord Jehosa to spread the Holy Word, the Holy Decalogue, to these heathens, that their precious souls can one day be saved, as yours, Holy Women, already have been saved. I wish that you would consider giving the Church an official mandate to spread the word of Lord Jehosa to the heathens of the world. Sponsor a caravel with our ministry aboard and send it to one of these barbaric lands, that we may begin God's Holy Work abroad. I will return when you summon me. Thank you, most Holy Women for your careful consideration of your Church's small requests." He bowed and left.

"Ten percent! Kassandra, that will never fly!" Queen Frona called out once he had left. Now the sparks began to fly! I noticed that Kassandra was still icy cold, covertly hostile to us all, now more so than before. I realized that finally she had seen the changes in the seven queens, the result of their therapy sessions. These queens were intelligent, vibrant, very much alive, and nearly always cheerful, except recently with our new corsets. The Empress had noticed them, and I detected she didn't like this at all.

Worse, during the arguments, which lasted all the rest of the day, frequently a queen would glance at me for support. It was unintentional on their part; they were genuinely unhappy with this turn of events, made all the more irritable by their painful, uncomfortable waists. More than once, Kassandra noticed them glancing over at me. By the time we ended for supper, I was sure that Kassandra now suspected that I had some part in all this open rebellion against her.

Just as we were about to break for dinner, Kassandra played her last argument. "As we break for food, consider this. You are all the Most Holiest of Women in our country. We are all living proof of the highest honor a woman may have: being of the Eighth Degree. It is up to us, we Holy Women, to assist our own Church in its hour of need. Do not forsake that which your Church has so holy bestowed upon you, this highest honor. Live up to our most Holy Status as Women of the Eighth Degree. It is only a small matter of earthly money. We will talk more in the morning."

After diner, the queens decided to hold their own meeting. "How can she honestly think that this will be accepted?" Queen Frona began their discussion, extremely irritable from her corset and irked that Kassandra would say what she had said about them. She had lovingly given unto her husband, and Kassandra had taken that from her. Their meeting was rather short. All agreed to vote no on those issues. They would begin to take a stand against their Empress.

The next morning, promptly at nine, Kassandra began the session. "With a good night's sleep, shall we now consider the Holy Cardinal's two proposals?" Kassandra began. None of us had a good night's sleep; the constant pressure and total uncomfortableness kept waking us up. "Now then about the tithes. I feel this is a very fair proposition. Is there more discussion?" No one said anything. Athena glanced at me and winked. "Then, all in favor say yes." Silence. Kassandra looked absolutely stunned, but only for a moment. "All against say no." Seven voices replied.

In an icy tone, Kassandra said, "No discussion, just a no vote. Is the percentage troubling you queens?" Her voice was like slicing razors.

Queen Frona spoke for them. "If the percentage were zero, we would vote for it."

"I see. Well, queens, you leave me no choice. If you won't compromise, then as Empress, I invoke Rule 49, which says that I have the right to pass any proclamation I desire over the wishes of the kings and queens. However, you then have the right to return to your kingdoms and conduct a vote count of all your citizens. If the majority votes no on this proclamation and more than half of the kingdoms so vote no, then the proclamation is nullified. This proclamation is so passed by me. Selene will draw it up and sign it for me. She will deliver seven copies to you for you to take back to your kingdoms so that you may conduct proper voting."

"Now then, is there discussion about the request for us to provide monetary support for a missionary caravel to spread the word of Lord Jehosa throughout the uncivilized world?"

"Yes, are we now doing just what those Elders from Dorota did? Aren't we making that very same mistake? Who are we to dictate to someone else what their religion ought to be?" Queen Frona asked.

Kassandra's icy stare cut into Frona, as if it were a dagger that would slay her. However, Kassandra's fake smile never left her face. "I take it that you are all voting no on this one?" Silence. "So be it. I declare this proposition passed under Rule 49. Selene will see that you have copies of this as well. Now then, let's move on to today's business."

The rest of the day was taken up with routine requests from merchants, nobles, and other court petitioners. Nothing was very critical or that important. Kassandra announced at the end of the day, "Tomorrow morning around ten, we will all gather before the palace's main doors for the official announcement of these two proclamations. You are expected to be there, but you will not be allowed to speak. Is this clear?" It was, and grumbling, we headed to dinner.

When we assembled the next morning just outside the door, a large crowd of people from Kefall had been assembled. This had "orchestrated event" all over it, at least to me. Standing tall in her huge emerald green ball gown, Empress Kassandra stood beside the scarlet robed Cardinal Drakon and Selene. The queens were told to form a line behind the three, while we advisors stood behind our queens. I estimated that over five hundred people had been assembled here this morning to hear the proclamations. Hopefully, this would be a short announcement.

Empress Kassandra began the announcement. "Ladies and gentlemen, it is with the greatest of pride that we are assembled here this morning to announce three formal proclamations that are long overdue. First, for a long time now, the Church of Jehosanity has been the only religion practiced in Demokritos. Hence Proclamation 1043: Be it hereby known that the Church of Jehosanity is the official church and religion of Demokritos. Here to accept this formal document is Cardinal Drakon Erebos." The crowd applauded as Selene handed him the parchment.

"Second, for quite some time now, the Church has been using its own funds to help out the thousands of our people who were deceived by the Elders of Dorota. Thousands of women and girls, even babies, lost their arms in this evil deception. Unlike our most Holy Ceremony of the Eighth Degree, these poor people were deceived with actions that are criminal in my opinion. As you know, I took upon myself the task of providing jobs, living arrangements, and food and clothing for thirty of those in the most need. Likewise, your seven queens each took on another thirty as well. Yet, though we have been successful, these represented only a tiny minority of the affected women. A few were women of wealth or whose families had wealth sufficient to provide for their care. Thousands were not. Again, the Church stepped in and provided assistance for those as well."

"Yet this has seriously drained their treasury, money donated by you to support their Holy Causes. Now Demokritos must step up and be counted. Proclamation 1044 states: In recognition of the Holy Works done by and to be done by the Church of Jehosanity in Demokritos, the nation shall donate one tenth of its net profits to the church as its fair and just tithe. These funds will enable the Church to continue to execute its humanitarian goals for all our people." Selene handed him another fancy parchment, while the crowd yelled and clapped loudly in support.

Cardinal Drakon spoke, "On behalf of the Church of Jehosanity, I accept this magnanimous and generous proclamation of the government's support of our Holy Works. You have standing before you visible proof of our Most Holiest of Women, your very own Empress Kassandra Aias and your queens. With these funds, your Church can continue to assist your fellow countrymen who are in need. Please, give a round of applause of thanks to Demokritos' Most Holiest of Women, your Women of the Eighth Degree standing here before you. Show them that you really do appreciate all of their hard work and efforts on your behalf." Once more, the crowd shouted and clapped loudly.

Empress Kassandra, thoroughly enjoying the massive attention bestowed upon her, continued. "Finally, Demokritos now has the largest caravel fleet in the world. Daily our fine merchants visit many foreign lands. Some of these lands are occupied by savages and heathens. To assist in bringing the word of our Lord Jehosa to these poor people, I give you Proclamation 1045. The national government of Demokritos shall finance one caravel for the Church of Jehosanity to use to visit these heathens and bring the word of Lord Jehosa to those so that their souls can be salvaged too. Yes, I know that this is a trifle — such a small donation on our part — but it is a start. If they are successful, I hope that we can increase our support for them. Perhaps one day, the entire world will recognize our one God, Lord Jehosa." Selene handed the parchment to the Cardinal who graciously accepted it.

He spoke once again. "Again, I am humbled by these, our Most Holiest of Women. Today, you have seen just how vital, how important Women of the Eighth Degree can be. These Holy Women are and rightly should be role models for women all throughout our great nation. If I may be allowed a brief word, I would like to take this opportunity to encourage all women who have the means to join with these Holy Women and become of the Eighth Degree. Unlike the deception and criminality of the Elders of Dorota, we here hold these women in the highest, Most Holiest of respect. Just look at what these eight Holy Women have accomplished in just a half of a year. If you have the financial means, I urge you, discuss it with your family and partake of our Holy Ceremony, become as these beautiful women — become also of the Eighth Degree, Thank you all for coming out here on such a fine summer day to help us celebrate these historic proclamations."

After the clapping subsided, the palace guards began ushering the folks out of the main gates, while we headed back inside. Selene told us to take the rest of the morning off, the meetings would resume after lunch. As we began disbursing to our private quarters, I spied the Cardinal following the Empress towards Kassandra's quarters. I wished that I could overhear what they were about to discuss. Dita decided to order some hot chocolate. I chose tea instead.

"Well, Empress, that went just perfectly, don't you think?" Cardinal Drakon said, when the two were quite alone in her private quarters.

"Yes, most impressive. Do you think that we need to issue a proclamation requiring more women who have the means to become as we?" she asked.

"Not at this time. Let us see how the word spreads on its own. If we do not see an increase, I will let you know. Your generosity has exceeded my humble expectations. Thank you, Kassandra."

She smiled, "Yes, I don't believe that the queens will be able to obtain sufficient votes to override my proclamations. If they do, I shall just reword it and make a new proclamation. Now then, we must discuss that matter I mentioned to you earlier — the two Velona advisors of Queen Athena — Dita and Bethany Brozena Malina. As you have seen, these two women continue to pose grave problems both for the Empress and for your Church. I have been unable to determine what evil magic spell that they have cast over all our queens. It has not affected me, but they have all succumbed to it. My special staff has also noticed that many of the queens' special staff has also become affected by the evil magic of these two women. As you know, the Empress has no such power or legal right to take actions against these two evil witches."

"Yes, that is the sole province of the Church, to cast out the heretics, the evil witches, the Daughters of Lucifer himself," he acknowledged.

"Then, you think that they may well be Daughters of Lucifer?" she asked most curious about his pronouncement. If so, this would explain much to her.

"Look what happened when we did as you desired, converted them into Women of the Eighth Degree. We both expected that they would then accept their new roles in society, join the Church, and be treated with the Highest of Honor, as you are, Empress. We expected that they would of necessity support you and your quality work. Yet, what did we see? The very day of their surgery, their wounds were healed and stitches removed! What should have taken many weeks, as you yourself know very well, happened in a day. How can this be explained unless they are Daughters of Lucifer himself. Did they accept their new roles? Did they join the Church and become Holy Women, held in the Highest of Respect? Did they begin to back your causes? No to all of these. Daughters of Lucifer can be the only explanation that remains."

"Then, we are doomed, Your Holiness," Kassandra replied, her icy tone gave way to dismay, a trace of fear in her voice.

"Not doomed, you have the might and power of the Church and Lord Jehosa on your side, Empress. I know that just now I may not have sufficient powers myself with which to deal with these Daughter of Lucifer. Therefore, I will beseech our Pope Leo for guidance and assistance in finding the proper way to handle them. Goodness, righteousness, virtue always triumphs in the end. Be patient and do not provoke them is the best advice that I can offer you. Give your Holy Men an opportunity to cast out these evil Daughters of Lucifer. Continue to use your authority as Empress to overrule these women as you have done today."

"Thank you *so* very much, Your Holiness! I am *so* relieved. Yes, one cannot expect an Empress to be able to deal with Daughters of Lucifer! I will see that the Church gets its 751 tithes later this week, after the Council is finished. Perhaps that will help you handle this unholy situation. Is there anything else that the Empress can do for the Church at this time?" she asked, sincerely meaning it. After all, Daughters of Lucifer were way, way beyond her powers, even her imagination.

"Well, Empress, Most Holiest of Women, we ought to put our heads together and see how together we can make our great country as god-fearing, as holy, as devout as we possibly can. You know, even though this Dorota situation turned out here to be a criminal disaster, there may yet be some good from that experience."

"How so? They completely blasphemed our most holiest of ceremonies," she asked, curious what possible good he could see in their conduct and actions.

"As you may have heard, these Elders from Dorota claimed that they had a perfect society, a society where everyone received an education, where everyone had a job, and were there was virtually no crime at all anywhere in the entire country," he began to carefully lead Kassandra.

"Well, I did hear something about that. Surely, they lied about that too. They claimed that their Eighth Degree women could do all normal things in life, such as feed, dress, and cook themselves. It has to be a complete fabrication." She, as just such a woman, knew it must be so, she depended utterly on Selene for everything.

"Of course, all is highly suspect with them. Yet, our Holy Pope Leo took it upon himself actually to visit Dorota and see for himself the truth of the matter. That was, of course, before they began claiming that it was all a big mistake." Here, the Cardinal very carefully chose his words, mindful of the Empress and her views. "Pope Leo did see a nearly perfect society there. Indeed, there were no local police forces, no security forces. Their banks did not even have a lock on its door, let alone guards inside. He has verified that there really is an extremely low, if any, crime rate on Dorota proper. He did see their schools and saw that boys and girls of all ages were being educated." He very carefully did not mention the state of their women. "He saw everyone going to church. Yes, he saw that these average citizens of Dorota were deeply religious, filled with a great faith in God, only they chose not to call him by his proper name, Lord Jehosa."

"All this has gotten me thinking, Empress. Is this not one of the highest goals of both the Empress and the Church — to have a nation without crime, where all people are deeply religious with an abiding faith in our Lord?"

"Yes, lofty goals to be sure, but wonderful to contemplate," she replied, uncertain where he was leading.

"Already, you have taken a solid first step, the establishing of public schools throughout our country. Yes, I know that it will take many years for it to be fully accomplished, yet you, my Holy Empress, have made it happen. You have launched it." Kassandra beamed with pride, yes she had!

"You have already answered the cries of your subjects for help in reducing crimes in our cities. Half of your army is now patrolling the streets of our larger cities and towns. Soon, I am sure that you will hear of a noticeable reduction in the crime rates. Yet, you and I may be able to do more to achieve our shared goals of a crime free nation of deeply religious citizens."

"How? Is there more that we can do?" she asked, still wondering where he was headed.

"I believe that we can take a two-fold approach to achieving such godlike goals, Empress. I have been observing how the thirty families, who were in the direst of conditions, are now doing under your care." For an instant, she began to worry; had she done enough for these women?

"If I had to describe the results that you have achieved with these Holy Women and their families, I would have to say that you have worked a Holy Miracle!" Her sudden fears evaporated; an even larger grin of satisfaction flashed instantly on her face, noted by the Cardinal. "I am sure that it is the same with those that you had the queens assist. Empress, these results have so impressed me!" She felt so light that she might levitate!

"Consider this image of our goals in action. All the women who have the means, whether themselves or via their husbands, are also Holy Women of the Eighth Degree, the highest honor the Church can bestow. In turn, they provide for those women who have not the means to provide for themselves if they were so themselves. These less fortunate women would be given highly paid jobs in the caring for the basic needs of these Holy Women, thus raising their own standard of living and that of their families."

"As you heard this morning, I again made a suggestion for more of these women who have the means to join you as a Holy Woman. Still, that would not be enough. Would we not also need to see every citizen of our great land attending services on Sunday? Indeed so."

"Can you envision the ultimate ideal scene now? All our people go to worship on Sundays. All women of means are Holy Women, who provide employment for the less fortunate of Demokritos. As I understand it, you are already in the process of having all women of means wearing most elegant of fashions as you always do. On Sundays, our priests would be able to guide our people down the path of righteousness, eliminating theft and criminal thoughts. Wouldn't then we come very close to a perfect society right here in Demokritos?"

Cardinal Drakon did not say the rest of his plan. Pope Leo had worked out why there was no crime in Dorota. Because their men had to work so very hard providing for their wives and families, they had no time left over for wanton drinking, gluttonous behavior, or criminal activities. They were constantly busy keeping their families surviving. Here, if the wealthy nobles and wealthier merchants were kept even busier, caring for the special needs of their wives and daughters, they would have less time for nefarious activities in which they seemed to indulge. By giving the poor citizens high paying jobs tending to the life needs of these wealthier women, they would be lifted from above the poverty level and have far fewer reasons to lie, cheat, steal, and pick pockets. Plus, every Sunday, his priests would have the opportunity to pound into their minds the moral values he saw that they so desperately needed. Thus, he would be able to control the lives of everyone in the country, guiding them on the path he saw fit. Oops, he quickly changed his thought. The Church would be guiding them. If he could pull this off here in Demokritos, he knew that he would become the next Pope! No doubt about that appointment. Pope Leo was aging rapidly. Soon, the Church would need a successor. Cardinal Drakon wanted that to be himself. However, time was not on his side. A few years at most he had left to complete his perfect society here in Demokritos. Thus, he was forced to move things along faster than he had originally planned. It had taken far too many years to get to the current ruler situation.

"Yes, yes, I can see it too, Your Holiness! A perfect society here in Demokritos *is* possible, isn't it?" She imagined all the noble women and wives of the wealthy merchants coming to her court, as they now did, but dressed as she and as she, of the Eighth Degree. No longer would they be stronger than she was. No, they would be as helpless as she was. This gave her a very warm, confident, consoling feeling. "I want to help, Your Holiness. I can at least make another formal proclamation that every citizen of Demokritos is obligated to go to church on Sundays. Yet, how would we be able to enforce this proclamation?" she asked.

"Oh, Empress! That would indeed be a start for us. How to enforce it? Well, let's hit them where it hurts, their pocketbook. Let us fine those who do not go to church a gold for every missed service — that is, missed by choice, not because of illness, injury, and such. Have the gold go directly to the Church. If that was part of the proclamation, it could be enforced by the legions that are now in the cities."

"Splendid idea, Cardinal, perfect. They intentionally skip church, and they donate to the church making the church even stronger. I like that!" She thought of her utter failures to get the queens and the Daughters of Lucifer to attend church with her. Well, the Daughters would now have to pay; she liked that idea immensely!

"Thank you Empress for your kind words. As far as the desire to have all women with the means partake of our Holy Ceremony, this has always been a personal relationship with their husbands and the Church. It would be unseemly if the Empress issued a proclamation so ordering them. Such would violate the entire basis of the Holy Ceremony. So I guess we must rely on our priests continually advocating it. It may take lifetimes to achieve our envisioned goal of a perfect society here in Demokritos," he sighed as if he found it utterly hopeless.

"Oh, you must have faith, Your Holiness," Kassandra played directly into his hands. He counted on her sympathy and willingness to help others in need. He'd put just the right degree of hopelessness in his voice. "I'm sure that we can find a way. While you are correct, I cannot issue a proclamation ordering someone to partake of our most Holy Ceremony, I can issue a proclamation that can help and help a lot! Suppose I issued a proclamation that said all women, who have the means, should partake the Holy Ceremony, and then hire a dozen less fortunate women to assist them with life activities. If such a woman does not wish to partake of the Holy Ceremony, she must send in a written petition to the Empress outlining why she should be exempt. There may be some extenuating circumstance that I cannot foresee that may well be valid. This way, I'm not ordering them, merely suggesting that they should or send me a petition saying why they want to avoid it. What do you think? Will this help us achieve our perfect society?"

Cardinal Drakon kneeled, "Oh most Holy Empress! This would be of monumental value in furthering our shared goals! I don't know what to say! I am so overwhelmed by your generosity, your wisdom, your intelligence. You are indeed our Most Holiest of Women!" His hands were clasped as if in prayer; his eyes looked as pleading and humbly as possible at hers as she sat on her throne. Her immense smile of satisfaction told him he's scored another victory.

"Consider it done. I will bring this up tomorrow. I suspect that the Daughters of Lucifer will corrupt the Holy Queens once again, but I will use my authority to make it so. Let them spend countless hours trying to repeal it. If the poorer citizens see that this will give them and their wives highly paying new jobs, the queens will find it impossible to get their votes against the proclamation."

"Oh thank you, thank you, Most Holy Empress, thank you," he poured out a seeming gratitude of great magnitude, re-enforcing her convictions. "You are indeed the best leader our country has ever had!" He gave her a departing hug and left, telling the patiently waiting Selene that she should enter now. It was all that the Cardinal could do to walk solemnly to his waiting carriage! He wanted to jump and shout for joy, to release his incredible victory to the world!

A half hour later, Cardinal Drakon summoned Prelate Khristos to his private study. "Any news about who murdered our man in Theos?"

"None, Your Holiness. It remains a mystery, unfortunately. I am sorry that I have failed you," he bowed humbly, having already sliced deep gashes in his waist, his pain washing himself clean of his utter failure. With his waistband of metal barbs now cutting deeply into those wounds, his pain, his penance was complete. He could stand before His Holiness once more.

"We now have the most important action ahead of us, one that eclipses all others. As you know, those two women of Velona who have become the advisors to Queen Athena have steadily become a problem to the Empress and to our Church. You have seen what happened with them after we made them of the Eighth Degree. In less than one day, their wounds healed, so much so that their stitches were removed later that same day. That was our first clue about just who these women really are. I have now finally identified them: Daughters of Lucifer!" The Prelate gasped; he was truly shocked by this revelation. He knew of the devil, Lucifer, from the teachings of the Church, but to have his own flesh and blood walking among them — this was revelatory to him!

The Cardinal went on with his litany of corruption offenses they had allegedly done with the seven queens and many of their staff. He needed to make sure that his Prelate fully understood the magnitude of problem that these women posed. "Prelate, it is with a hopeful heart that I give you this assignment, the most important one I have ever entrusted to you. You must find a way to keep these Daughters of Lucifer from further *speaking* their Unholy Words to the queens and others. Mind you, Prelate Khristos, these are Daughters of Lucifer. Their lips must be silenced, though I do not know how this may be done. I leave that entirely up to you. They are at the Summer Council now and will be returning with Queen Athena of Theos at its end in a few days. I wish I could give you better guidance about these Daughters of Lucifer, but I cannot. Perhaps you can find solace in our Holy Scriptures."

He bowed low, the pain excruciating. "In this matter, I shall not fail you, Your Holiness." He left, leaving a small pool of his blood on the carpet of the Cardinal. He spied it and sent for a servant to clean the spots before it dried.

In his own private, Spartan room, Prelate Khristos sighed,

"Daughters of Lucifer! I must be extremely careful." He spent an hour pouring over the Holy Book, reading every passage about the devil, Lucifer. The Devil was as immortal as Lord Jehosa; he and his spawn, akin to Lord Jehosa's Angels, could not be killed. Indeed, he feared for his own salvation if he dared try to kill one of these Daughters of Lucifer. His imagined wrath of Lucifer upon himself was terrible to behold! No, outright slaying was totally out of the question. Yet, their fleshly bodies could be harmed, witness the amputations. What did His Holiness require? He'd said that they needed to be silenced, so that their poisonous words could no longer corrupt the faithful, the Holy Women. Silenced, he focused on that aspect. Then, images of the Empress' Special Helpers came to mind. He grinned, "Yes, their appearance was strange indeed, but he dwelt upon the aspect that they could not speak and be understood. He'd seen them writing in order to communicate to Empress Kassandra. Ah! Here was his answer! Now for the means. He realized that he needed more information.

He donned his dark cloak, slipped out of the rectory, and headed across Kefall to the palace. A few minutes later, he was shown into the Empress' quarters. He told her what he needed, and Kassandra gave it to him, though she had no idea why he had such a strange request. Khristos met for an hour with Udua. The next day, Udua sent a small package to the Church for him.

Now Prelate Khristos began making his plans. Uppermost in his mind was his fear of Lucifer. He had to tread ever so carefully; his plan had to be foolproof. This was the most important, most dangerous mission he'd ever undertaken. Arranging the many assassinations and the explosion had been simple matters, get in, do it swiftly, get out. Here, here he was facing the power of Lucifer and his evil, wicked spawn! That these Daughters of Lucifer were obviously here on a mission somehow must play a key role in his plan. This was a vital detail, he knew instinctively. All his training screamed at him to make use of this fact; they were on a mission here on Tarra. Slowly, the plan took shape. At last, he began to make his many preparations. Once more, he deeply regretted that the Mano del Dio only had six remaining members. He could have used a hundred now.

Our lunch hour passed rapidly; all the queens and staff constantly argued about the morning's presentation. Queen Frona expressed what everyone thought, "Honestly, this will just not be tolerated by our people. At the Fall Council, I will return with Thallyus' total rejection of both those proclamations!" The other queens promised to do so as well. Ten percent was a staggering sum, all agreed. Many felt that it was not right for us to enforce and impose our religion on others.

At the afternoon's session, we received even larger shocks! None of us was expecting these. Kassandra, now full of self-confidence, took charge and declared, "Now, then, I have some more proclamations for us to take up." I will give her this, she orchestrated her presentation, her build up, perfectly, as if this as a formal debate. "I envision the future of Demokritos, an deeply religious country without any crime." She outlined her notions of such a society where even pickpockets were a thing of the past, where everyone worked for the good of their families and the country. On she went detailing what anyone might dream as a perfect society. When she had everyone in agreement that this was a desirable goal, and who wouldn't be, she laid the bombshell on us.

"To achieve this most worthy and lofty goal, I propose two proclamations. First, all citizens of Demokritos must attend Sunday services, unless they are ill, injured, or have a valid excuse. Those who do not shall be forced to pay a gold to the church for every Sunday they refuse to go. Our legions in the cities and towns can be in charge of seeing that this is enforced. Thus, our people will have the opportunity to hear the wisdom of Lord Jehosa and learn to follow his path of righteous conduct."

Queen Frona interrupted her, "You can't possibly expect to force people to attend religious services! That's unheard of!"

Kassandra totally ignored her, as if she had not spoken. "Second, we are going to help our Holy Church. We will issue a proclamation that says all women who have the means should partake of the Holy Ceremony of the Eighth Degree and then hire a dozen less fortunate women to assist them with life activities, thereby giving much better jobs and incomes to the poorer citizens of our country. They will be emulating what we eight have done with our staff. If such a woman does not wish to partake of the Holy Ceremony, she must send in a written petition to the Empress outlining why she should be exempt. There may be some extenuating circumstances that I cannot foresee that may well be valid. We are not ordering them. No one can order anyone to undergo our most Holy Ceremony. Rather we are merely suggesting that they should do this or send me a petition saying why they want to avoid it. Is there any discussion on these two proclamations?"

She fully expected the wild protests that the queens gave her. In her defense, Kassandra did her best to outline how these two proposals would help bring about a perfect society, if they were actually followed. She did have a very twisted sense of how this would benefit Demokritos. However, none of the queens bought her arguments in the slightest. No matter how she put it, she was ordering at least a third of the women of the nation to become helpless, armless women. She was perverting what had been a very personal bond between husband and wife into a state enforced action.

At the end of the afternoon, Empress Kassandra exercised her rights once more and formally made these two proclamations. Selene gave each of the queens, well their advisors really, copies of these two documents. Queen Frona had the last say, "Empress, I can guarantee you that when we return for the Fall Council, all the kingdoms will have voted to reject these proclamations of yours!" She was furious!

That evening, the seven queens held a private meeting to work out their coordinated plans to get these four proposals rejected by their kingdoms. Somehow, vote takers would have to visit every family in the kingdom, explain the proclamations, and obtain that family's vote. They had but three months to get this organized and executed, scant time indeed. Yet all seven were determined to make this their top priority.

In sharp contrast, the remaining days passed uneventfully. Routine business was dispatched rapidly. On January 5, 752, we again packed up and headed for home in Theolopolis, Theos. Already both the male and female advisors of the queens were working out their plans for the massive voting process. We pitied Queen Danae's task, because Penelopus was the largest of all the kingdoms, quadruple the size of Arolas or Alia. Still, Athena's task was huge. Theos and neighboring Thallyus were the second largest kingdoms, half the area of Penelopus. As our large caravan of carriages began rolling out of Kefall, the many advisors rode together, working on the best way to conduct the massive canvass. Such had not been done in over fifty years.

Chapter 43 It Is Our Decision

Once more, we faced a three hundred fifty mile carriage ride. As expected, Athena wished to get to Theolopolis as fast as possible. No one objected to her request that we leave long before dawn each day and stop well past dinnertime. By really pushing it, she hoped to cut the journey down to nine days, arriving at her palace on January 14. Our dozen carriages rolled along in a long line, accompanied by a dozen of her palace guards, riding along side. Mostly, they were along to ensure we met no difficulties; after all, it was a high crime in this country to harm a Holy Woman. We expected no trouble.

Near the end of the third day, we approached the long haul up the rim of the picturesque, Lonki Basin. Barren rocks thrust their mighty forms up from the gentle blanket of green that lay on the steep slopes of the rise. Our horses labored, their forth adding a white cloud before them. While Dita and I stared at the breathtaking beauty of the landscape, suddenly our inner senses activated. Extreme danger was at hand!

"Athena, there is big trouble coming our way very soon," Dita called out. Athena called out to her driver, Barnabas, who reined in the horses. At once, the other carriages behind our lead one halted as well. Her captain of the guards rode back to check with Queen Athena.

"Dita says that bad trouble is coming our way! Stay alert, captain!" she relayed urgently to him. By now, Athena never doubted anything that we two said. He ordered nine men to form a defensive position around her carriage, while he sent two men cantering on ahead up the steeply climbing road. From inside the carriage, we could not see anything, however. Yet, both Dita and I felt our inner warnings only increasing. The two cantering sets of hooves fell off into the distance. We held our breaths. Now the sounds of the two horses began growing louder.

"Hey, that's not a canter," Dita exclaimed. "That's a full out gallop!" Then, we heard the sounds of many, many horses galloping our way, thundering down from the high pass towards us. I envisioned our two riders as they encountered this mass, wheeling their lathered horses around, and doing an all-out gallop to return to us.

"What's going on?" Queen Athena demanded, growing afraid.

"Damn. Damn. Damn," Dita whispered. She'd moved out of her body to see for herself.

The captain barked orders for his men to draw their swords and rein in tightly around the queen's carriage. Suddenly, riders swarmed around our whole caravan. All wore dark masks to cover their faces. We could see many from our windows. Each held one of these new weapons, a gun, and they were pointed at the dozen guards, who had only their swords with which to defend their queen. Horses panted, froth flew around the area, but the thunder of hooves had ceased. A lone rider came closer, gun pointed at the captain. At last, the man spoke.

"If you do as I say, no one will get hurt. I want everyone to climb out of the carriages and the drivers and you guards to dismount. Now!" No one had any real choice but to obey. Barnabas complied, helping each of us out in turn, where we could now see the actual situation that we faced.

Should we start killing them? Dita sent. *We can get a whole lot of them.*

Let's see what they want, I sent back. *Maybe all they want to do is rob us.*

"There that is better. Okay, you two, yes you two from Velona, step this way." The man in charge definitely wanted Dita and me to step forward. I spied a carriage approaching from the distant top of the pass. I had an very bad feeling about this. "Good. See — no one is being foolish. We don't intend to kill anyone, but if anyone of you tries anything, we will not hesitate to shoot. Now then, you two, have your Special Helpers join you. We wouldn't want you to fall down or anything." Athena gave her okay to Iua and Ida to move up to our sides. Both women looked frightened, but complied.

"Now then, you two and your Special Helpers are going to come with us in yonder carriage when it gets here. If you do not voluntarily come with us, we will begin shooting your companions here. Do I make myself clear? You come with us and nobody gets hurt. Queen Athena, you have my word that we will not kill these four and we will return them to your palace in Theolopolis shortly after you get there, safe and sound, very much alive."

"You cannot do this!" Athena spoke up, suppressing her terror. "This is a high crime! These two are Holy Women!"

"You two. Decide, are you coming with us willingly or do we need to shoot some of these people first?" he said, ignoring Athena.

Dita and I both realized that against guns, we could not hope to take one hundred men down before many of us were shot or killed by the guns. *Damn! Damn! Double damn!* Dita sent. *I can get maybe ten at once, how about you?*

Yes, at least that many. But Dita, the ones we don't get can fire their guns before we can move on to them. That leaves maybe eighty of us being shot, maybe even us. We don't have a choice, not really. I realized that this abduction had been very, very carefully planned. We didn't dare fight back; we had to go with them. Our friends' lives depended on us obeying them.

"Okay, you leave us with little choice. We will do as you ask, but if you harm anyone here, you will pay dearly for that!" I replied.

"Bethany, you can't go with them!" Athena pleaded, though she too saw the futility of resisting. One hundred guns to a dozen guards with swords was not even a battle.

The carriage pulled up and a man opened the door. "Get aboard, your

Special Helpers can assist you," the masked leader ordered. We four complied and got into the waiting carriage. The driver shut the door and climbed back into his high seat. We felt the carriage moving and heard the masked leader talking once more.

"Do not try to follow us; we will shoot anyone who does on sight. I have promised you, Queen Athena that you will see these four shortly after you have returned to your palace in Theolopolis. They will be returned safe and very much alive. Do not do anything foolish. We will not hesitate to shoot to kill."

Now we were rolling past the other carriages, seeing the stunned faces of the other advisors and staff. Shortly, we could only see the beautiful countryside as the carriage headed back down the steep grade. Many horses followed us, surrounding the carriage. The masked man came along side. "Don't try anything stupid or we will first shoot those two helpers of yours and then you can fend for yourselves. We have a hundred guns on you all the way. Sit back and enjoy the ride."

Again, we had little choice. "Dita, we cannot risk getting Iua and Ida harmed. They are innocent in all this."

"I know. This gun thing is becoming an annoying problem. I'm going to see if I can think of a way to take all hundred out at one time. If I can, I'll let you know," Dita whispered to me.

A while later, she had an idea. "What if we could somehow whip up a blinding dust storm whirlwind that obscured all visibility? Then, we could pick them off fairly quickly." We remembered how the friends of the Guardian had whipped up sand storms over a century ago.

"That would work, but how do we whip up the dust?" I asked.

Before she could answer, the carriage came to a halt. The masked man opened the door. He handed a large tray of food and hot cocoa to Iua. "Here, it's past suppertime. We don't want to starve you women. Eat, it will be a long time before morning, and we can get you some breakfast." He closed the door and we began moving. Dita cursed, she forgot to ask him where we were being taken.

Dutifully, Iua and Ida began to feed us. Mechanically, we accepted their help, our minds working on how we could whip up all the dust around the road. Between bites, I suggested, "You know, I think I might be able to conjure up the dust obscuration. I would need time, so I would have to move way out ahead. . ." Damn! Drugged again! I drifted into a drugged stupor; the food had been doped. The last thing I recalled was hoping that Iua and Ida would catch on and not eat themselves.

"What should we do, Your Highness?" the captain asked as the large band of riders disappeared down the road following the lone carriage.

"Damn! Damn! Damn!" she exclaimed, then caught herself. "I'm beginning to sound just like Dita! Okay. We are still in Thrace. We don't dare go after them; we can only take their word that the four will not be harmed and will be returned to us in a few days. However, I aim to catch everyone of that sorry bunch and see that they are hanged for high crimes against Holy Women! Okay, wait an hour so they don't see you and then send one of your fastest riders to Axos and tell Queen Ariadne what has happened. Have her send out an army to track these vicious men down and hang them! Just don't let the rider interfere and get himself or them shot. I guess we ought to continue on our way."

He did as she asked and the caravan got rolling once more just as the sun began setting. Soon, they were in her kingdom and spent the night in more secure accommodations. She and her advisors speculated all evening about the what and why, but none had any real notion why these bandits wanted Dita and Bethany. It made no sense at all. It had been the queens themselves who had openly defied the Empress, not Dita or Bethany.

With sad, worried hearts, the group continued their long journey to their capital city of Theolopolis, arriving on schedule on the 14th of January. As they pulled into her palace grounds, Andreas, Luigi, and Dario came out to greet them. From the awful look on Athena's face, the three men knew that something was very, very wrong.

"Has Dita and Bethany got back?" she asked immediately.

"No, why?" asked Andreas. This was not quite the reception that he had planned.

I floated around in a drug mental mass, thick, black, gooey mental mass of some kind. My lips felt like they were on fire, perhaps an aftereffect of the drugged food. Sounds seemed disorienting as if coming from some distant place. Hammering. Metal. Impulses, pounding. No, pounding around some distant neck. Fluid, fluids in my throat. A gaging swallow. Was that me? It seemed miles distant from me. All went black and silent once more. I liked the silence, so peaceful.

Light. Was it dawn? Dull pain throbbed in my lips, along with a strange feeling in them. The swirling blackish mental masses began to move off. I heard voices some distance from me. I felt my body now; it was lying down. My eyes flickered and opened. The first thing I saw was a brownish clay disk about two and a half inches protruding before my nose with a strip what had been my upper lip going around it. Hence, the strange pressure feeling I had. No, there was another one just visible below that one. My lower lip had a disk in it too, about three inches across. Teeth! God, not my front teeth! I panicked, and my tongue felt them. Thank god! They were still there; they had not knocked out my teeth as Iua had. I tried to bend my neck and struggle to sit up, but my neck wouldn't move. I tried to turn my head to look for Dita. It only moved a tiny amount. I cried out, ".ita! .ita!" God, I couldn't even understand myself anymore.

At once, I saw the face of Iua leaning over me, her large lip plates near my face. Her arms slid under me and helped me up to a sitting position. ".etha..! .etha..!" I heard Dita's voice coming to the right of my bed. I tried to turn my head to see but it only rotated a little bit. I had to wiggle my body around to see her. Ida had helped her sit up and she was staring at me as I stared at her.

Both of Dita's lips had been sliced horizontally. Her upper lip was surrounding a brown clay disk about two and a half inches in diameter, while her slit lower lip surrounded one that was three inches across. Just as shocking, golden rings ran the length of our necks. They pressed hard against our shoulders and tightly against our heads, allowing only a small rotational movement of our heads and no other motions. Each ring appeared to be an inch wide. At least they looked pretty and shiny.

The men wearing the same masks and holding their guns, not on us, but on our two frightened helpers, walked over to us. "Ah, awake at last, Daughters of Lucifer. You have not been harmed. Now you can no longer corrupt our Holy Women with your devilry, your witchcraft, your lies, and deceit from Lucifer. You may talk, but no one will understand you just as they cannot understand your Special Helpers. Unlike them, you cannot write your words. Daughters of Lucifer, we have stopped you from your plans with our Holy Women."

"Now then, as long as you Daughters of Lucifer do not try anything foolish, we are going to put you back into your carriage and send you back to Queen Athena. Get up and don't try anything. There are a hundred guns around here, and they'd love to start blasting away." We took him at his word. Honestly, I was totally shocked and stunned. Iua had her arm around me, and she began leading me towards the door. I obeyed and allowed her to follow their commands. I was groggy and disoriented; Dita was as well. As we left the building, it was plain that we were in a town, but I could not turn my head to see much. A carriage was waiting, and its driver held the door open. Iua did her best to support me as I struggled to climb inside, very freaked by the total lack of movement of my neck. I sank heavily onto the seat cushion, my lips throbbing, my head still groggy, and my stomach growling. Dita fared little better, awkwardly getting in, unable to bend her head to duck or balance. She mostly fell back onto the seat opposite me. Our two helpers climbed in and were handed several baskets. I smelled warm food, bread at least.

As the driver shut the door and climbed aboard, a second man joined him. The masked man spoke again; I recognized his voice; he was the one who had spoken when we were abducted. "The driver and his assistant are local men who have been hired to drive you to the palace in Theolopolis and leave you there. They will be driving day and night. No stopping at inns along the way. There are chamber pots in there, and they will get you more food and drink periodically. Okay, get going." The driver clicked the horses into a walk, and the carriage began moving, leaving the men quickly behind us.

Iua and Ida opened the baskets and looked over the food, deciding what we should eat.

".rink. .rink," I attempted to say. Iua listened carefully and pointed to the water skin. I tried to nod, but had to mostly waist-nod, as I so often had seen these women do, made vastly harder by the tight corset. She carefully held the nozzle up to my mouth and allowed a little to flow. I got more than I could handle, swallowed greedily, but a lot came out, carrying semi-congealed blood. She took a cloth, soaked it, and began wiping the front part of my mouth, outside my teeth. I saw a good deal of blood residue on the cloth. She continued until my mouth was cleaned. Meanwhile, Ida did the same for Dita. Again, we attempted to drink.

I felt better now and slowly the two began to feed us bits of chicken, bread, carrots, and some dried apples to suck on. Once we seemed content, they helped themselves as well. I turned my body slightly so I could look out the window. The quaint countryside had replaced the colorful town buildings. The fresh air did wonders for my head, clearing out the residual grogginess.

At last, I again turned my body to the right so I could see Iua again. They'd finished, and I decided to ask them what had happened, and if they were mistreated. "What ha..e.ed to us? Are .ou oka.?" I finally manage to say clear enough for her to grasp. She waist-nodded and began to make writing motions, but she had no paper or pencil. Ida gestured that she did not either. They had taken them away from the women.

I Mind Linked Dita, Iua, and Ida with me. *There. What happened to us? Were you harmed or hurt? Just think your answers, Iua.* Well, first I had to get the two women over their shock of hearing me in their minds! It took a bit of an explanation, but they soon grasped telepathy, though now they thought of us as goddesses. It couldn't be helped.

You went asleep, so we did not eat what they gave us. We began to write to each other about what we should do. A man saw us and took them from us. We rode until it was very dark and came into that town. They took us inside and carried you onto to those beds. A man they called doctor came and showed us that he was going to give you both lip plates like us, and he asked us how it should be done. Ida showed him where to cut and how to put the right size disk in. Now you are Princess as we are. High honor for you, Bethany, Dita.

Then men came with gold brass rings. They are not like ours. Ours, we can remove, long spiral of brass that we wrap around our necks. We can unwrap them when we need to and get longer spirals when neck is longer and bands are too loose. Men put one ring around, use hot tool, and metal and hammer. Somehow, they pounded the two ends together. Then they put another ring, heat, and pound it around you. We do not know how to take them off you. We are sorry. Still, now you both are honored

Princesses, like us.

Yes, but we can't write what we want to say as you can, Dita pointed out the obvious. *We can't turn our heads either.*

Men make rings too tight. We try to tell them so, but they could not understand us. No paper to say it with, Ida explained. *But you can talk in our heads.*

Can we take the lip plates out? I asked.

Not for some days. Lips must heal. Disks help keep from bad bleeding. Still bleed some for a few days. Yours are small, so you don't need to remove teeth yet.

Thank goodness for that. When do we have to remove our teeth? Dita asked nervously.

Not for many months. When disks get too loose, make bigger disk. When disks get too heavy and flop down, then you can get teeth out which gives place to hold disks straight out properly. The bigger your plates, the more honor you will have, Iua explained. Maybe so in their culture, but now we were both freaks in our world.

When all healed, we take disks out at night when you sleep. Then you both can kiss. You will see how good it is. Very good kiss, very good, Iua added.

When we are alone, we take disks out so we can eat and drink better. When yours are healed, you can too. Princesses do not take them out when men are around. Never, Ida added.

When bands are too tight, you must turn body instead of your head, Iua continue her explanation. We'd already figured that one out.

Dita now changed the topic. *Did you hear any of the men saying what the name of the town was? Did any of the men say the names of any of the men?*

Once, Khristos name was used, Iua replied.

Isn't he Cardinal Drakon's head Mano del Dio man? Dita asked. I remembered hearing that he was the Prelate. *Well, now we know who is going to pay for doing this to us!*

You not want this high honor, being a Princess as we are? asked a confused Ida.

Thankfully, Dita thought before she replied. *It is a high honor among your people. That is good. Without arms, this is much more difficult for us.*

Oh yes, we see what you mean, Ida acknowledged.

Well, Dita, we'd better do our therapy on each other now. Maybe it will help get rid of the intense throbbing in my lips. I'll do you first. I dropped Iua and Ida from the Mind Link and began to run Dita back though our mess, beginning when she went unconscious after eating the tainted food.

Twice we needed to stop to eat a little more and to use the chamber pots. She finally began laughing, and I ended her therapy. We noticed it was very dark outside and must be quite late, though we had no idea of the time. Our two helpers were both asleep, their heads resting against the sides of the carriage. We joined them.

Daylight woke us up. Once more we ate, finishing off everything that was left. Now Dita ran therapy on me. It went well, mostly just routine actions. I'd never had anything similar done to me, so after about ten passes, I too was laughing. What we both uncovered was more or less what our two helpers had said. Instead of using the brass wire coils to make the neckbands, they somehow attempted to fuse the ends of a ring of brass together using heat and some metal and pounding, which made them not easily removable, certainly not by our two helpers. We were stuck like this for some time. Perhaps at the palace something could be done for us, I certainly hoped and prayed that it could!

Around midday, the carriage pulled into a town, which I recognized as having passed through before. We were definitely in Theos, which gave both of us some comfort. By turning our bodies, we could see that we were outside an inn. A short while later, the driver brought us two more baskets, brimming with food and more water skins. He kindly dumped the chamber pots. Once more, we began to move.

How many days were we there in that town? I asked Iua.

Three days. It took them a long time to get the rings on both of you.

I estimated that when we were stopped we were about six days from Theolopolis. Spending three days unconscious and now traveling non-stop, though not too fast for the horses, I estimated that we would get to the palace shortly after Athena and the others arrived. I sighed; at least she would not have long to fret over us once she got to her palace.

Dita came up with a good idea. *Love, we should practice our alphabet and see what sounds we can no longer make. That will give us a better idea of just how hard it will be for others to understand us. Ours are not as big as theirs are, so maybe it won't be as bad for us. Even if the disks are removed, our lips won't work to help form certain sounds.*

I thought that was a brilliant idea. We set to work to see what sounds just did not come out clearly any more. Vowels were still reasonably clear, which is why our Helpers chose the names that they did. The letters: B, F, M, N, P, V, and Y were undoable. Lips were vital in forming their sounds. The letter F was rather iffy as well. Some other combinations were not so clear as well. Overall, it could have been far worse. With our helpers, hardly anything but vowels were understandable, owing to their much larger disk sizes and lack of front teeth.

With that accomplished, we again stared out the window. Boredom began to set in — that and cramping from constantly sitting for three whole days and nights. By the second continuous day, Dita was getting very edgy. At last, she had an idea. *Bethany, I have been thinking. The Prelate works for the Cardinal. Since we are stuck here for days, I'm going to go pay the*

Cardinal a visit and see if I can find out anything. I'm going to spy on him. I promise you, my love, that before we leave Demokritos, I will kill that man! I urged her to be careful and not do anything foolish. She grinned, but I saw no sign of it, and she realized that she could no longer grin either and said, "Grr." As we rode along, I kept an eye on her body, but soon dozed off, as did our helpers.

Late that third night, she returned here. *Well, I didn't learn much really, but he does write things in a journal and has it stored in a secret place. Maybe one day that will be useful. I'm hungry again. I wish we had something besides water to drink. Guess none of us can speak clearly enough to ask the driver for some cocoa or tea.*

We ate once more and I noticed that we had entered a town again. Before long, I recognized that it was indeed Theolopolis! I let the others know and we four gazed out the windows. Soon we would be safe inside Athena's palace. Crap, then we would have to start dealing with our new tortures! Ah well, perhaps someone could get these neck rings off of us, that would be a start.

An hour passed before the carriage halted before the locked gates of the palace. I heard the driver chatting with the guards at the gate. Please let us inside, I thought to myself, as if that would somehow help. Relief! The carriage began moving once more, we passed through the gates. I heard men running. Once the carriage halted, the driver opened the door and said, "You are back at Queen Athena's palace. Please get out now." Our helpers needed no encouragement and climbed out. Next, Dita and I struggled to our feet and awkwardly got to the door. We mostly fell out, but both helpers worked together to catch us, but we definitely needed their arms around us to walk. Our legs seemed like butter; so did theirs for that matter. Perhaps we were supporting each other.

We walked up to the front doors. Just as the Doorman opened them wide for us in our huge dresses, Athena, Barnabas, Xene, Zoe, Morpheus, Andreas, Luigi, and Dario came rushing towards us. The shocked expressions on their faces told us just how freaky we now looked.

"Good God! What have they done to you?" exclaimed Athena. Others reacted similarly. "Are you hurt? I mean other than your lips and neck? Can you even speak now?" questions came rapid fire from the visibly shaken queen.

".ot .er. well," I replied. "Oka. .ostl.," I added.

The guards had already arrested the two men. I made contact with Athena. *Those men are innocent. They were just hired to bring us here. You should let them go. They treated us okay.*

Startled by me appearing in her mind, she blinked and then relayed my message to her guards. "Okay, time enough for talk later. We all have been worried sick about you four for almost a week! First, we get you out of those bloody, filthy dresses and into a hot tub. Then, you need a square meal and, I know Dita, hot chocolate." Athena took charge.

Before long, we found ourselves stripped and soaking in four hot tubs. A Fetcher arrived with four steaming mugs of cocoa and everyone discovered that we had another problem: how to sip the cocoa! Eventually, Oua wrote out the word spoon. At last, Xene and Zoe began using a spoon to put some into our mouths. Still, without lips, it soon became a messy proposition, as some invariable slipped between our teeth. This was rapidly becoming a nightmare.

Athena wisely explained to everyone, "Look, they have been through an ordeal. It is way past midnight. Let's let them get a good night's sleep. In the morning, we can hear all the details and make our plans for justice." I could have kissed her!

"Tha.k .ou! Tha.k .ou!" I tried to say, she understood and smiled. An hour later, our hair washed and now lightly brushed but still quite wet, many hands got us back into our corsets and nightgowns. Gently Iua and Ida helped us get into bed and laid down beside each other and snugly covered up. Soon the lights went out. Dita and I rolled on our sides and tried to hug each other, but our necks no longer allowed us our hug. Metal clanked upon metal. We tried to kiss each other but even that was intensely strange and we had to content ourselves to resting a leg over each other. Sleep quickly came over both of us.

The next morning, Iua and Ida came in to help us rise. First, they brushed out our hair and then dressed us. Iua put my cherry red dress on me so that I would please Dita, while Ida put Dita's canary yellow dress on her for similar reasons. I tried to smile, but that was fruitless. Nothing happened. At last, they had us look at our appearance in the mirror. Our long hair, they had carefully positioned so that it partially hid the golden rings, at least from all angles except from the front. Nothing could hide the two disks protruding from our lips. At least ours were small compared to theirs, small comfort. Very self-conscious, we headed off to breakfast.

We quickly saw just how terribly restrictive these neck rings were going to be. Unable to move our heads more than an inch or two in a rotation motion and wholly unable to move our heads in any other motion, forced us to constantly have to reposition our bodies to see off to the sides or to look at others not straight in front of us. Lacking arms, we had been dependent upon our heads to help keep our balance. Now even that was out. Our movements now had to be done with great care, especially in these new, tight corsets and impossible heeled boots. *Fashion is going to be the death of us,* Dita sent. I attempted a grin, but failed completely.

I tried not to notice everyone staring at Dita and myself, but realized that if I were in their shoes, I would be staring at us too. If nothing else, they needed to see just how bad our new condition was, if they were to be of any assistance to us at all. Sitting at the table, I discovered that I had perfect posture, unable to bend my neck enough even to see the plate before me.

Yet, Iua began to bring up spoons of the porridge to my mouth. I tried very hard not to slobber this time. Yet with only my teeth to keep the food inside, it was challenging. Fortunately, when it dribbled out a bit, it landed on my lower plate, which Iua carefully wiped with the napkin. Solid food went much better, especially the rolls and eggs.

When the tea came, it went even worse, with quite a bit trickling down onto my lip plate. If I could have moved my neck back, I could have used gravity to keep it inside. Ah well, what a new and embarrassing experience Dita and I had to learn to endure. Finally, I was full and now I had to give an account of what had happened.

"We ca.'t talk well," I began. "So.e sou.ds we ca.'t .ake." I repeated it twice before they all understood. I then made a massive Mind Link, shocking most of them. After explaining what was happening, that is I was using a telepathic link and that we could all hear each other if one just thought a thought, Dita and I began to relate what had happened.

The details finished, I then outlined the key information that we now had. *The man who did all the talking at the start was Prelate Khristos Krates, the Cardinal's right hand man, a Mano del Dio. What was interesting is that he constantly referred to Dita and me as Daughters of Lucifer. He seemed terribly frightened of us for some reason. I sensed that he was actually frightened of shooting us. Somehow, this seems to be important, though I do not know why.* The discussion over, I broke the huge link.

"Well, I have to get going. I am meeting with all the Noble Houses later this morning," Athena explained. "I sent word to them the instant we arrived yesterday afternoon, late. My advisors are still hashing out the best way to get the voting done. I expect that they will start implementing it this afternoon, though I don't see how we can get to everyone in just over two months. If you need anything, let me know and if I need anything, I'll let you know. I promise you that somehow I will get justice for both of you."

"Tha.k .ou," I replied. "A.dreas, what are .ou doi.g here? Luigi, Dario, too?" I sounded very funny, but a whole lot better than our Special Helpers. Their large lip plates made their speech almost impossible to grasp.

"I've decided to stay close to Athena from now on. I've vowed to protect her with my life," Andreas replied. "Besides, I have nothing better to do now. Got my parent's estate handled and time to kill."

"We've finished our tour in Trikala and were headed for their capital city anyway. We are supposed to put on a dozen shows here later this week. However, with what we've just heard from Athena, we are, frankly, quite disturbed and very worried for the safety of Ariadne and Alekto. Somehow, we'd like to protect them as Andreas is Athena," Dario explained. "Only we haven't figured out how we can do that yet. Still working on it. These new proclamations are scary."

"Oh, yes, we were supposed to tell you that a dozen women from

Queen Adonia will be arriving in a few days for your therapy," Andreas broke in, having just remembered it. "But will you even be able to do it? I mean since you can't talk well now?"

"We ca. sort o. talk," I replied. "Ca. a..o.e get these ri.gs o.. us?" They all looked baffled. *Can anyone see if someone can get these rings off our necks, please? That would help us a lot.*

All three men came over and began to see what the situation actually was. It didn't sound hopeful, though. Andreas commented, "Somehow the ends of these rings have each been fused together. You said you felt heat and pounding?"

".es."

"Well, I am not a metal worker, but it sounds like they intentionally fused the ends together. You said they stuck a metal rod behind them and pounded? That sure sounds like what blacksmiths do to fuse pieces of iron together. Man, these are so tight. There's no more wiggle room, is there? Okay, guys, let's go see if we can find us some metal workers who may be able to find a way of getting these off the women." All three left, but Dita and I had an awful sinking feeling that this was not going to happen anytime soon.

Well, that gives them something to do, but what are we going to do? Dita sent. I pivoted towards her and saw tears at last coming down her cheeks. For her, this was the final straw.

I leaned into her to give her our usual head hug, but we clanked our metal necks instead, which only added to her tears. *I can't take this anymore. Now we are really freaks!*

I know, love. Me too. Hang in there. At least, we are still alive and can work on getting justice for everyone. I need you, Dita. I need you now more than ever. She closed her eyes, and we sat there a while, our necks leaning on each other.

At last, since nearly everyone had left the dining room but us and our two Special Helpers, we got up and returned to our own room. Shortly after nine, one of the Messengers, a young teenager who had returned to life after our therapy, entered, "Bethany, Dita, there are two women at the gates asking for you both. One is heavily armed and the gate man is reluctant to let her inside."

Are you expecting anyone? Dita sent.

No. Let's go see, I sent back.

"We are co.i.g," I tried to say, but the girl figured we were coming because we rose from our chairs. We slowly and carefully followed her, as the doormen periodically opened the barrier doors for we three as we headed down the halls and corridors to the front. Outside, it was hot, but the sting to our senses brought us more into the present time. Eventually, we finally reached the main gates, where four guards now had gathered, eyeing the two strangers.

"Ile.ako.a! Dia..a!" I exclaimed, completely and totally shocked to see our two dear friends from home. Dita gave a squeal, but did not attempt to say anything, hearing how badly my words had come out. She didn't want to be even more embarrassed.

"Good god, Bethany, Dita! What's happened to you? This is worse than we expected! Some new kind of fashion? Or just joining your Utu friends?" Ilenakova exclaimed, rushing to me and hugging me, nearly causing me to lose my balance. I teetered but she held on to me. Dianna threw her arms around Dita and held her tightly as well.

The guard asked, "Is it safe to allow these two inside?"

".es! .es" I called out, praying that he would understand. He motioned for them to lead their horses inside, which they did. Before long, a stable hand took the horses from them, and they unloaded their saddlebags. Both looked healthy. Ilenakova was armed to the teeth, including a longbow. They wore their leather outfits and their faces were bright. While Dita and I both felt embarrassed by our current conditions, we felt overjoyed with their mere presence. It was such a relief to have them with us now.

Carrying their bags, Dianna said, "Lead on; it's positively melting out here. We've been sweating for weeks now!" Our Messenger led us back to our room. "Say, pretty cool, these doormen are really convenient. Do they always open the doors for you?"

"Oh yes, isn't it just perfect?" our teenage Messenger cheerily replied for us. "Here's their room. I will let the queen know that you have visitors, Bethany, Dita. I'm sure she will want to meet them, when she can get away. Bye."

"Co.e o. i.," I tried to say. Realizing that was pointless, I sent, *Come on in. Make yourselves at home. We have lots to say, but I guess we're going to have to do it this way. Obviously, we were abducted again. We were just returned late last night. I admit that I am really, really glad to have you two here, in spite of my orders not to come down to Demokritos.*

"We know, that's why we didn't tell you three months ago that we were on our way. But first things first," Ilenakova replied. "Dianna, have a look at them. Can you take off those neck rings? Those have to be horribly uncomfortable and terribly restrictive for you."

".o. Ca.'t get o..," I replied.

"Well, we'll have a look anyway. She's supposed to be an engineer and a healer," Ilenakova replied, taking her bow off her shoulder and unfastening her numerous swords and daggers.

Dianna gently pushed my hair off to one side and began inspecting the back of the rings. "Yes, I think that I can safely get these off of you, Bethany, you too, Dita. Now do you really want those lip disk things?"

".o! .o!" Dita called out. *No!* she decided to send to make sure Dianna understood.

Dianna grinned, "I didn't think so. I know you have those Utu helpers

— oh, here they come. Well, I think the best thing is to have you two lie down and let me examine your lips closely. Going to be my biggest challenge. I'm going to Mind Link with Sandra; she's the real Healer expert. I'm just a beginner." She helped us lie down and began to examine our lips closely.

Just then, the three men came in. "Oh, I'm sorry," Andreas blurted out. "We didn't know that you had company."

Ilenakova wisely chose to speak first, giving us a break. "Hi, we are their close friends from Velona. We heard about their troubles and came to lend them our hands. I am Ilenakova da Cassa. My wife, Mrs. Kali Kato da Cassa, is here in Demokritos as well. This is Dianna Anka West Po; her wife, Mrs. Ania Anka West Po, is also here in Demokritos. We've all come to lend our help." I realized that she was subtly letting these men know that both she and Dianna were married. Wow! Kali and Ania were also down here? Amazing, none of the four had followed my orders to stay put in Velona. Well, for once, I was very glad that they hadn't.

"Dianna's something of a doctor and an engineer. So while she's having a look at our friends, how about you fellows telling us who you are? Can someone please fill us in on what has been going on around here? Has this whole country gone nuts?" Ilenakova demanded to know.

"Andreas Myntas. I'm a longtime friend of Queen Athena's. With all the current trouble, I have decided to stay by her side to protect her. These men are also from Velona. Dario and Luigi Matteo, they are the owners of the MBE Show, a popular entertainment group down here on a tour. You see, we three rather ran into the queens while on vacation and well, we are trying to look after them. Does this seem confusing?" he asked, seeing that she was now rubbing her hands through her short, light brown hair, a rather exasperated look on her face.

Making matters even more confusing, Queen Athena, along with Barnabas, Xene, Zoe, Morpheus, and Zona now entered, slightly worried about us and these new strangers who had just shown up at the gates. "Are you all right?" asked Athena.

".es. .rie.ds .ro. .elo.a," I tried to say. *Friends from Velona. Tell them everything. I trust them with my life. We can't talk well enough to tell them everything,* I gave up and sent her.

"Bethany wants us to tell you everything and get you fully briefed. Honestly, that is going to take some doing. I'm meeting with some key people right now. How about we all sit down at lunch and spend as much time as needed," Queen Athena spoke decisively.

"Thanks, Dianna is a something of a healer and engineer. She's going to see if anything can be done for them in the meantime," Ilenakova replied. She took an immediate liking to this take-charge woman.

"Bethany," Andreas added, "we've checked around and the blacksmith doesn't think those rings can be busted loose without harming you. We promise to scour the city for someone who can do it."

I was going to try to say something, but Dianna spoke first, "Why don't you all leave us a while and let me see what I can do? You can help me by finding a wood chisel, a wooden mallet, and a pliers, please."

Everyone took the hint and left; the men went in search of the tools. I felt the presence of Sandra Mind Linking with Dianna, examining my lips. She carefully removed the disks, and I had immediate pressure relief. They were stretching the skin of my lips something awful. Of course, Iua would explain that was necessary to hold the disks horizontal and to get them to stretch the strips of lips so that I could get larger disks. I wanted no part of that!

We can do this, Bethany, Dita. There will be some pain; can you take it? It was Sandra!

Yes, do anything to fix our lips! Dita replied.

Okay. They are not yet fully healed. We are going to re-injure them and stitch them back together. There could well be some scaring involved; the gaps might not fully close, but it will be better than living with the lip plates, right? Sandra sent.

"Well, we need lots of boiling water and towels," Dianna declared.

Tell the Messenger. She's just outside the door. I sent.

For two hours, Dianna worked on our lips. I could tell that it was tedious work, and that Sandra was guiding her through the operation, step by step. I steeled myself from the low-level pain and the constant pinpricks, as she began sewing the fleshly lips back together. The insides hurt worse than the outsides, however. When she had me finished, she held a mirror so I could see my puffy lips. Many, many tiny stitches held the long cuts tightly together. Still traces of blood oozed out.

"Oh thank you! Dianna, Sandra! You are angels! I can talk, though it hurts some."

"Yes, it will for days to come. Your lips will be very sore and stiff. Try not to move them much," Dianna replied, beginning to work on Dita. The look in Dita's eyes as she saw my lips was uplifting. Her prayers had been answered.

Around eleven, she finished Dita, and Dianna held a mirror so she could see the results. "Thank you Dianna and Sandra! You have saved my life! That was horrible! Ouch, it does hurt a lot."

"Okay, now to see about these rings," Dianna replied, wiping the last traces of blood off her hands. She put the messy bowls and bloodied towels near the door, and picked up the tools.

"Now the secret is rather obvious. What they did was start with the bottom ring. I suspect they slid a metal rod of some kind down your neck to use as a backstop for their pounding. By placing a heated bar against the metal and by light pounding, they began to fuse the two ends together. Normally, this is done on an anvil with red hot metal. In that case, the fusion is almost as strong as the rest of the ring. However, here they improvised. The bonding, while strongest here on the bottom ring, gets progressively weaker the higher up the ring. At the very top, they probably found it very difficult to get the backstop metal bar in there. So as you can see, the metal is only slightly fused there. Well, I guess you can't really see that. Anyway, I am going to chisel it and see if I can break it loose. If so, I can bend and remove that band. Here we go."

By noon, Dita and I were free of the rings! We both hugged her tightly and repeatedly thanked her repeatedly. "You've released us from a living hell," Dita commented. Our little engineer looked very pleased with her accomplishments.

Since it was lunchtime, I hastily explained, "The others here don't know that we have been keeping you informed of everything. So let them explain things before you talk much. Honestly, I am so glad that you all disobeyed my orders. That was a living hell. Dita is right. Come on; we should head to the dining room."

"Wow. You do move slowly in those boots," Dianna commented as we joined others in the hall heading to eat. "I say, Bethany, your waist is spectacular; yours is too, Dita. So striking. You've rather mixed up your colors. Bethany, you look stunning in cherry red, and it goes beautifully with your very blonde hair. Same with you Dita; canary yellow goes great with your thick, long black hair, just beautiful both of you." She chatted all the way to the dining room.

The gasps, looks of shock and surprise, of wonderment from everyone when we walked in without the neck rings and with our lips looking like, well lips, though they were stitched up and quite puffy, was amazing. More than one commented, "It's a miracle!" Dianna was instantly elevated to a goddess position among these people, especially Athena. She insisted that the two sit near her. While our Special Helpers sat right beside us to feed us as usual, Queen Athena began the many introductions.

I detected a good deal of sadness coming from Iua and Ida. I Mind Linked to them quietly.

You do not want to be a Princess? This was their confusion and sadness. For them, we had become one of them, given the highest of honors with our lip plates. Now we had undone it. I carefully explained that we needed to be able to talk with everyone to help them and without hands to write our words, we just could not accept this honor now. *Maybe later you be Princess,* Iua finally accepted our decision, adding some hope for the future.

This turned out to be a very long lunch indeed. Queen Athena insisted that our two new friends be fully informed about all that had happened since Dita and I first arrived. Like a true leader, she made sure that everyone's contributions were fully explained, especially those within the Forze Segrete. Two hours later, we finally got to what Dita and I wanted to hear: why Ilenakova had decided to bring the four down here.

"The six of us are the top coordinators for the Forze Segrete and live in Velona. Bethany and Dita answered your call for help, ordering us to stay in Velona and assist from there," Ilenakova began.

"Say, can I ask a really dumb question?" Andreas interrupted. "If it's too personal, just say so. But Bethany and Dita are married. When we first met you, did I hear you correctly?"

"Yes, I married Kali Kato. Ania married Dianna. We six had our reasons. I just didn't want you fellows to get romantic ideas about us. Now then, where was I?" Ilenakova answered.

"But are all the top leaders — well, married like you six are?" Andreas looked a bit confused and slightly worried.

"Oh don't be silly. I only know of us six who have married women. We have our reasons, but I am not at liberty to divulge them. Yes, some of us do not particularly like men in that way." Andreas visibly relaxed. Now I understood his concern. Athena was in the Forze Segrete, and he was obviously in love with her. That she might marry another woman had been his fear.

"We've been following what has been going on down here. Kali has been instrumental in following the money trail. Obviously that first million was used to arrange the explosion and murder of the Emperor and your kings. We still have not been able to determine the ultimate intention of the second million that Kassandra sent to Cardinal Drakon. Frankly, that has bothered us considerably. Kali has Luisa monitoring the records in her place. As Kali said, we are at a distinct disadvantage because there is a three-month delay in getting the records from here up to Velona. She insisted that we ought to be down here to reduce that time delay."

"Well, Bethany, we resisted Kali's suggestion for a while. But then, Ania began correlating all the known happenings and, well you know her penchant for politics, she predicted that there was going to be a revolution down here, a violent one involving guns and all. That's when we decided that we'd best get down here in case you two needed rescuing. Looks like we got here none too soon."

"We were on our way from Patri when you relayed those four new proclamations of Kassandra's to us. Ania then nearly freaked out. According to her, all hell is going to break loose down here. That's when we changed our plans. We know how much you care for Queens Ariadne and Alekto. So Ania decided to try to get close to Ariadne, while Kali is off to try to get close to Alekto. Kali should be getting near Naxos and Alekto's palace tomorrow or the next day. Ania is having problems getting Ariadne to trust her fully. Perhaps you can get a hold of Ariadne soon."

"You all have done extremely well. Thank you, you have saved our lives," I complimented her and she smiled.

Queen Athena spoke up again, "Bethany, this gun situation — it's getting out of hand, isn't it? I mean, when they surrounded our carriages, they had a hundred guns pointing at us. If they had not had guns, I would have had our guards put up a fight."

"If they had not had those guns, Dita and I would have taken care of them as well," I added. "We've seen what they can do. One shot can blow a deadly hole through a person's head from many feet away. It happens so fast that there is nothing you can do about it."

"Yes, that's what I've heard. Now if the Cardinal's men have guns, who else has them?" she asked.

Ilenakova answered, "Ania and I have seen that many of the Empress' soldiers also have them. You know that they are now patrolling the streets of the larger cities? Who controls these men?"

"Well, Kassandra has dispatched them to the cities to help cut down on crime. She controls them, but indirectly. Her generals give the orders, but she orders them," Queen Athena answered. "I know that only a very few of my kingdom's soldiers have these guns. Most of the guns being manufactured are going to the Emperor's legions. My advisor can get you the figures."

"Well, I'm not so good at figures; maybe Bethany can go over them and get the information to Ania. She claims that everything is ripe for a very bloody revolution," Ilenakova replied. I could tell that she was very worried about the gun situation.

Dianna commented, "Golly, you all look so striking, so fashionable. Did your gowns come from Annelise? In Velona, Annelise gowns are now becoming all the rage. It used to be the more manageable cone shaped gowns, but since you two have been gone, gowns just like yours are popping up all over. They sure do accentuate your curves, and the satin fabric is really nice."

We women chatted about our things, while the queen's advisors went to get their summary sheets. Luigi and Dario began to whisper. At last, when I looked straight at them, both men flushed. Worry in his voice, Dario said, "We are concerned for the safety of Ariadne and Alekto. I mean Athena has all of you to help her, but they have hardly anyone. Our traveling group has forty members, whose safety is our main obligation. If this country is going to explode, we need to get them to safety, and yet at the same time, we want to help the two queens. Distance is becoming an awful barrier. Naxos, Arolas is about as far from here as Axos, Thrace. Our caravel is docked in Patri."

"How long would it take for your music company to get to Patri from here?" Dita asked.

"Our wagons go slow. We never needed speed before now. Three to four weeks. Why?" Dario asked, his voice showing more and more worry.

"Damn, their route takes them right through Kefall," Dita observed. "If trouble breaks out, they might wind up right in the middle of it."

"Yes, but in a couple months we are all going to be going to the Fall Council in Kefall," Athena noted.

"My best advice is to get your company to Patri and wait for you to get there. I am assuming that you both want to be with Ariadne and Alekto. By the way, I think that they have fallen for you brothers," I advised. "So don't let them down."

Athena added, "Luigi, if you wanted to go to Naxos and Alekto, the shortest way is to go to Kefall from here and then take the main road through Penelopus straight to Naxos. You can't get lost if you stay on the main road. If you went as fast as we did, leaving the inn before dawn and stopping late at night, you can get to Kefall in about nine to ten days. It's another fifteen days to Naxos. If you went the outer rim road from here to Naxos, it would take at least another week to get there."

"So slow! Okay, I'll go with our company to Kefall and then head to Naxos. With luck, I can be with her for maybe six weeks before she has to leave for Kefall and your council thing," Luigi decided.

"In that case, I'll continue on down to Axos from Kefall and join up with Ariadne. Surely, our company can go the short ways from Axos to Patri without us. Say, if anyone needs a ship out of here, ours has plenty of room," Dario offered.

"How many more people can yours accommodate?" Dita asked.

"At least fifty, unless there is a lot of baggage. Please, we would love to give anyone who needs it a lift. We'll go let our company know the plans." The two brothers left.

"Well, Dianna, Ilenakova, we should get you some rooms," Athena began, now that the news had been shared.

"We ought to stay with Bethany and Dita, to protect them," Ilenakova insisted.

"Okay, I will see that another bed is moved in there for you or will you require a bed each?" Athena didn't quite know how to handle women who were married to other women who were not here.

"We can double up," Dianna replied. "Say, we traveled very light. Our leathers don't quite fit in with your court. I can see that. Is there any way we can purchase some court dresses? I just love the shapely look you have. These Annelise fashions are quite something, aren't they?"

Athena replied, "Sure, Princess Marin has given us plenty. You should begin with what she calls the starter outfit. Any particular color you desire?"

"Any blue would be perfect! Thanks!" she said eagerly. I groaned, Dianna had no idea what she was about to be getting into, I thought.

Ilenakova wrestled with this and finally asked, "Queen Athena, would it be considered an affront for me to dress like a man in a fancy suit in the courts?"

"Well, probably it would, Ilenakova. I don't know of anyone who has done that in our courts. I think you would cause a big stir, if you know what I mean. People would certainly think less of you and probably haze you too. You'd stick out like a rotten apple," Athena replied honestly.

"Okay, then do you by chance have a brown outfit?" she asked.

Later in our room, our two Special Helpers began assisting Dianna and Ilenakova into their new starter outfits. When they finally got the corsets tied up, Dianna commented, "Oh my! This is tight, isn't it? I didn't realize it would be so uncomfortable."

"You'll get used to it," Dita offered. "We did, it takes a little time, still when it gets as small as ours," she was interrupted by Ilenakova.

"I can't breathe! This is torture! I can't bend!" Ilenkova gasped.

"Don't panic so. Take small breaths," I urged. "This summer, we all were mostly forced into far tighter ones. We're mostly used to them now."

"Tighter and with a wide band that chops you in to halves," Dita grumbled, though I know that she was mostly all right with it now.

"Oh my! These are much higher heels than the Alexa boots!" Dianna exclaimed a bit later as Iua finished tying her calf high boots tightly. She'd tried to stand up and could only do so by having her legs really bent at her knees.

"How can anyone walk in these?" Ilenakova griped, nearly falling down. Dita and I began relaying all the advice that Princess Maren had given us repeatedly for days. Since they were new to this outfit, our helper put the trainer skirts on them next, effectively hobbling them. "We can't walk in these skirts! They are too tight. Honestly."

"Well, you have to learn to take very tiny steps like we do," Dita explained, while our helpers tied on the waist buns and then the huge hoop skirt followed by the underskirt. At last, bodice and outer satin blue gown was fastened. Dianna ever so carefully moved to the mirror to have a look at her new fashionable look.

"Wow! I sure do have a striking figure! I wish Ania could see me. I bet she'd flip," Dianna gushed.

"But I can't bend enough to take my own boots off!" Ilenakova continued to complain. Soon she too admired her appearance in the mirror. "Well, I do look rather smashing don't I?"

Now we had to convince them to start practicing their walking. This gave we four something to do for the time being. Later, the advisor dropped off the estimates of the gun distribution in Theos as well as countrywide. None of us liked what we saw.

Chapter 44 The Voting Begins

"I will show them who is the Empress!" Kassandra declared defiantly. While she fully expected the queens would carry out their promise of obtaining a vote on her four proclamations, she did not expect the upheaval it was causing here in Kefall and in Axos. She had sent Tanis and Thekla out to infiltrate Queen Ariadne's vote counters. She wanted to see just how much of a threat to her rule this was becoming. Since Kefall and the Emperor's Palace was here in the middle of Thrace, Queen Ariadne's voting would be occurring long before the other kingdom's got theirs going.

The initial reports were inconclusive, in that the early results were coming out about evenly balanced between support of and against her proclamations. What was becoming more and more alarming were the reports of massive lobbying by people loyal to Ariadne and thus against her. According to Tanis, people were often seen in loud yelling matches, public debates, and all manner of unrest. That the priests were also working just as hard to convince voters of Thrace to back the Empress was irrelevant. It was obviously all the fault of the Ariadne rabble rousers. She'd sent a Messenger to find her the general in charge of her legions here in Kefall and in Axos.

Her pretty, armless teenager Announcer called out, "General Kletos." The fifty year old veteran general entered and bowed to his Empress. She nodded and suggested he have a seat.

"I am getting all manner of reports in from both Kefall and Axos that filthy rabble rousers are disrupting the public with their constant bickering against the proclamations. They are intimidating many voters who would rightfully wish to side with me. This lack of lawlessness cannot be tolerated any longer. Do you not have sufficient legions to arrest or shoot these lawbreakers?"

"Empress, we have not yet intervened because they have broken no laws. They have the right to a public gathering."

"That may be, but they are intimidating honest voters, and they must be stopped. I hereby give you the authority to use any level of force necessary to put an end to this fiasco in Kefall and Axos! Shoot them if necessary. Your men do have guns, do they not? We cannot and will not tolerate a few riffraff to undermine totally a lawful vote count. In fact, this may well begin occurring in the other kingdoms, once their vote counting gets underway. I shall issue direct written orders to all the generals. Selene, please take this down. I, Empress Kassandra Aias, do hereby authorize the use of any force necessary including guns to put an end to the public intimidation of voters by anti-Empress riffraff. I do not want to hear any more reports of such blatant public disturbances again." Selene signed Kassandra's name and put her official seal on the hot wax. She handed

General Kletos his copy.

He bowed, "I will see to it." He left and Selene dashed off six more copies and sent for a Messenger.

Across town from the palace, Jonas Sokrates was busily working out ways to raise more votes for Ariadne quietly. The Empress had gone too far this time. Ten percent of their net profits was outlandish. Who gave a damn about the savages of the world and this stupid church? Why bother wasting good money on supporting their missionary work? There was no profit in that, only losses.

"Dear, I need to talk with you about these proclamations of the Empress Kassandra. You know the vote counters will be soon coming. I believe that we ought to support the church. They have done so much good for those poor women who were so horrible deceived by those vile men from Dorota. Now the Empress has also decreed that we noble women begin wearing those enormous dresses from Annelise. They do make the women look very attractive, don't you think? And what about the decree that says I should partake of the Holy Ceremony of the Eighth Degree? Do you think that I should? I mean I would then be one of the Holy Women that are now so prominent in Church, and after all, even the Empress and all the queens have partaken of the Ceremony. Would it not help your community standing if I were too? What do you think? She says that when I do it, we are to take in a dozen of the poorer folks of Kefall and give them a good salary for handling my life needs. Of course, I would need such servants if I went ahead and did it, but what do you think, Jonas? I mean if I didn't, what could we possibly say in our petition for me to be exempt from the Holy Ceremony?"

Jonas didn't want to hear his wife's banter right now. She was pretty and could run his household effectively. However, he never interfered in her affairs nor allowed her to interfere in his. Just now, he found her continuous chatter annoying; he was busy. How to get rid of her quickly? "Dear, you know that I never tell you what to do. However, this time, I would really, really appreciate it if you would vote against this ten percent net profit tithe. If you do that, I will support you in whatever you decide."

"Well, okay then, dear. I will vote against the ten percent thing. But I do think that she is right, we need a better society, a perfect one. Crime is such a bad thing. I believe that I will do my part. Just think, dear, we will be supporting a dozen families raising them from abject poverty. That has to help the crime rate doesn't it? After all, aren't the poor the ones who commit all the crimes?" She continued to chatter away. He resisted the urge to tell her that it wasn't the poor who committed all the crimes. Indeed, the Empress was even guilty!

She left and decided to pay a visit to her two daughters-in-law. "Look Mache, we simply must get this Holy Ceremony done soon. I know that you have been against it. But you simply must change your mind. Think of your husband and my son! Do you really want the Empress and her guards coming to here and taking you away by force? Think of the irreparable damage you will be doing to his reputation, his standing in Kefall! Mache, if you continue to resist the Empress' proclamation, you are going to bring utter ruin down on your husband and your own son and daughter! For once in your life, Mache, think of your family and not yourself!" A bit later, Mache agreed. "Look we can do the Ceremony together on the same day. I'm going to see Theia now. I bet we three can do this together and lend our support to each other. I am so proud of you for doing the right thing for your husband and family." She gave her a big hug and left.

Later that day, she posted a message to the Church in Kefall, requesting a time to have the three of them to have the Holy Ceremony. She also asked for help in finding the needed three dozen families that they would be rescuing from poverty by their unselfish acts.

In another quarter of Kefall, Cardinal Drakon was busy meeting with his staff and doctors. He had ten doctors whom he used to perform the Holy Ceremony of the Eighth Degree. His pattern until now had been to rotate the ceremonies between each of the doctors. After all, they had their usual workload of sick and injured to attend. However, since the Empress' proclamation had become widely publicized around Kefall, he was being besieged with requests for the ceremony. Although he did not say so, he wanted to expedite each one so as not to give them time to change their minds. After all, each newly made Holy Woman added another family under his direct influence.

"I've called you here to discuss the handling of the many requests for the Holy Ceremony of the Eighth Degree. I know that in the past, I have sent perhaps one woman your way per month. Now I am afraid that I must ask more of you. So many women now wish to undertake this Most Sacred Holy Ceremony to bind their lives with that of their husbands, that I must ask you to be prepared to schedule as many as one per day for each of you. I am sure that this will only be a brief surge. Many have put it off because of Yuletide celebrations."

They discussed this and agreed that the Cardinal should send them a message at least a day ahead of the scheduled day he made with the woman. None seriously complained because the Church paid well for their services with their Holy Ceremony. In fact, their pay for one ceremony often exceeded their week's pay from the many others that they saw in their practice.

After the doctors left, Khristos, pale and somber, signaled the Cardinal, who flashed him a sign that meant to meet him in his private study. When the Cardinal entered, he found Khristos on his knees, begging forgiveness. "Rise, my Prelate. What has come over you?" he said and took his seat behind his large desk, which tended to make those visiting him seem smaller, while he seemed larger and more important.

"I have failed you utterly! I am a total disgrace and do not deserve to be your Prelate any longer," Khristos replied.

"What has happened, my holy son?"

"A rider has just returned from visiting the court in Theolopolis. He reports that the two Daughters of Lucifer have completely recovered. Their lips are as ours, and the encasing rings so carefully bonded together are gone. The Daughters of Lucifer once more speak their cunning, wicked lies. I have failed you utterly."

Cardinal Drakon thought this news over carefully. He had been given a full report on the abduction and silencing of the two women from Velona. Indeed, he had thought it was a brilliant idea to insert the lip plates, turning them into Special Helpers who could speak but not be understood. Brilliant idea — that coupled with neck rings that immobilized them further — rings whose joining ends had been fused so that they could not be removed — this should have handled the women without attempting to harm them. Yet, miraculously, they had undone the slicing of their lips? That was not possible, not for ordinary human beings, let alone the removal of fused metal rings. It merely firmed up his original diagnosis: Daughters of Lucifer.

"My son, you have not failed at all. You should rejoice! You have been able to capture these Daughters of Lucifer and so silence them. They speak but cannot be understood. You indeed were touched by the hand of Lord Jehosa to have thought of that brilliant scheme and to have been successful in its implementation. Remember, these are the Daughters of Lucifer and have powers beyond us mortals. Undoubtedly, they invoked the powers of their Dark Lord to undo your great Binding. You did right not to attempt to cut out their wicked tongues; they may have then lashed out at you and killed you on the spot."

"There is yet another thing that we may attempt to use to silence them. I have in my possession some historical relics from the early days of the Church, devices that proved ultimately effective on recalcitrant women who fought against the early founders of our Church. Again, these devices will not harm them, so you need not fear the wrath of Lucifer. Come, I will show you these relics. They are in the basement."

Greatly relieved, Khristos followed his spiritual leader into the basement. "Here they are. These metal helmets are fastened about the head of the woman and this oval ring is placed between their teeth forcing their mouths wide open. This bar connects to the helmet and is then locked into place. Now the woman can no longer speak but she can drink and eat liquefied food, since she cannot any longer move her teeth and mouth. Three locks fastened these in place. As I understand it, on those women deemed hopeless, molten lead was poured into the locks, making these then permanently attached to their heads for the rest of their lives."

"Here, take one of these rusty relics and see that two new replicas are made — made of the toughest iron, that they may not be broken. We will simply try to silence these Daughters of Lucifer once again. Shall we will give it another try?"

Khristos grinned, "Yes, this is utterly diabolical. With the gaps in the bindings, we could reattach the lip plate disks as well, further humiliating these Daughters of Lucifer. Could we not also modify them also to have metal eye patches locked into place so that they can no longer see as well? Perhaps even devise wooden plugs to be also locked into place such that they cannot hear much of anything? Lock them into total darkness from which they were spawn?"

Cardinal Drakon smiled. His Prelate was an exceptional man; he caught on to new ideas faster than any man he'd known. "Superb, Prelate. Once again, you have out thought even me! Brilliant beyond brilliant. Dead, blind, unable to speak, only able to consume liquids with their tongues, and with humiliating lip plates to set them apart as the true freaks that they are, positively brilliant. Harmed? Not at all, just rendered totally ineffective and non-operational in their Unholy Mission here in Demokritos!"

Mid-January, Queen Ariadne sat on her throne, alone with her thoughts. Oh how she wished she could just run off with Dario and leave this incredible mess behind her. A mess it was rapidly becoming. Her advisors got the vote counters hired and had begun the time consuming and tedious job of visiting every of age citizen of her kingdom to log their vote on each of the proclamations. Already, massive lobbying had begun. What she found most distressing today and why she was sitting alone on her throne, was the news that the issues were not falling either for or against the package of proclamations. Rather, some women were voting for the Holy Women proclamation, yet against the ten percent tithe proclamation. Indeed, it seemed her population was splitting their votes among them. Perhaps they were hedging their bets. Why wasn't everyone either for or against the whole group?

She sat alone so that her own utter helplessness could be intensely felt. How could any woman want this? She asked herself, but then realized that she had been pressured into having it done. Nevertheless, she had signed the document saying that she desired to become of the Eighth Degree. She had agreed to be completely helpless the rest of her life. Now here was a rash of other women seemingly desiring to be like her, and she felt powerless to alter the course of history moving past her. "They want to be like me, their queen. I am being their role model!" She now realized what might be partially responsible for helping these women choose to follow the proclamation.

How could she convince other women that she had made a horrible mistake? Was it even possible now? Perhaps it was too late. Everything was falling apart. Only this morning Bethany had somehow touched her mind to tell her that she and Dita had again been abducted and the horrors that they now bore. If this could happen to Bethany and Dita, the two most powerful people that she had ever known, she was doomed. Should she openly proclaim that she made a mistake and urge all women to veto this horrid proclamation? If she did, would the Church assassins come after her next? She was helpless to stop them. If Bethany and Dita could not, how could she?

Her Announcer came in and quietly said, "Mrs. Ania Anka West Po."

She sighed, "Very well, send her in along with the Doorman and my assistants, please." That darn woman again, she thought. "Back again!"

Ania, wearing her leathers and cloak, walked into the queen's throne room, ready to make another attempt to convince her to allow her into her confidence. Ariadne watched this short woman with brown hair and eyes enter. She still wore those practical clothes, she noted, and the woman's face was rather rounded. What she thought striking was her skin color; it was the same light brown as Bethany and Dita.

Just as Ania was about to make her third attempt to gain Queen Ariadne's confidence, Bethany made contact with Ania. *I'm going to chat with Ariadne.*

Good. I've just entered her throne room! Thanks, I've not made much progress with her.

Suddenly, Ariadne looked startled. Bethany was inside her head! *Hi, Ariadne. Bethany here. Dita and I are okay now. Some of our very dear friends have come down from Velona to help us in this crisis that we are all facing. One has gotten those rings off us and somehow sewn our lips back together, so we are okay. One of our friends is trying to get to you. She is Ania Anka West Po. She is my right arm back home. You should trust her with everything. Depend on her; she will protect you. Trust me; she is vastly more powerful than she looks, and she is brilliant with politics, which is what we all need right now.*

Okay! Wow! Thank you, I feel so helpless right now and in dire need of independent advice. She's right here right now. I'd better talk to her. Thanks. I am so relieved to hear that somehow you've overcome that horrible humiliating mess!

"Hi. Bethany says that I should trust you with my life. Is this true?"

Ania breathed a sigh of relief. "Yes, she has kept me up to date on the events here for the last year or so, but I am not sure what has been happening since your Summer Council."

"Fetcher, please bring us some tea and cookies please," Ariadne asked. "This will take us some time." For an hour, she related what she had been doing, primarily getting the vote count process going. She relayed what she and her staff had learned so far and about the sudden surge of women opting to partake of the Holy Ceremony.

Ania asked, "So, Ariadne, you've not said how you feel about being as you are, a woman without arms, if I may be so blunt about it."

"You may. I was foolish and I let my husband talk me into it. I wish more than anything that I could undo it and get my arms back. I am so utterly helpless like this. Sometimes I wish I could just die, though after Bethany's therapy, I no longer want to do that. I just want to get out of being queen somehow without hurting my people, who are depending on me to take a stand against the Empress. I really wish I could find a mate, someone to love me and that I can love too, but realistically, who'd want to marry a very helpless woman? What do you think I should do?"

"You have already taken a stand against this Holy Ceremony with the Empress. You should go very public with your opposition to having it done to women. Give some public speeches, talk to as many women's groups as you can, and tell them how it really is to be armless. Make it real to them; they may decide against it, and vote against the Empress as well. I will be with you all the way. There are quite a lot of things you can do. However, you are right. Once you take such a vocal stand, your life may be in danger. You must absolutely keep me around you at all times. Remember, I can use telepathy to contact Bethany or Dita. We can keep everyone informed almost instantly." That impressed Ariadne.

"Yes, but in that case, you can't wear what you have on now." Thus, Ania found herself having to wear similar constricting outfits as the rest of us.

In the ensuing several weeks, Ariadne followed every suggestion that Ania made. By early February, there were obvious signs that she was now being successful. The rate of women undergoing the ceremony had fallen off markedly, though still some ten women underwent the knives each week, down from almost five a day. People were openly debating their points of view in public sessions and over drinks in the pubs.

Early February, the sixty year old, white haired nobleman, Acteon Kadmos, head of the most influential and wealthiest Noble House in Thrace, came to have an audience with Queen Ariadne. Her Announcer called out, "Acteon Kadmos." The elderly noble, wearing his finest, most expensive suit, entered and walked determinedly up to the throne and bowed. "Your Majesty."

"Good morning, Acteon. We haven't spoken in quite some time. How can I help you?" she volunteered.

"Queen Ariadne, I wish to exchange some very private words with you. It is most urgent that we speak alone, in private." He seemed very intent on a private meeting. Since he was the most powerful and influential nobleman, she agreed.

"I must have Ania here with me to assist me. Anything that you can say to me, you can say before her. I trust her with my life. She will never betray either of us," Ariadne tried to alloy any fears he might have about this stranger being present.

"As you wish. May we speak both honestly and frankly, my queen?

The times that we now find ourselves are truly desperate," he asked.

"Of course. Honest and frank. What brings you to me this morning?"

"Many things have brought me here today. However, before I get into many of these, I am afraid I have to ask you a very personal question. Do not answer it lightly, for much is involved with it. Events are unfolding now all over Thrace and the country."

"All right, if I can answer it, I will." She had no idea what he wanted to know, and her face clearly showed that to him. He was an astute judge of people. For instance, he'd already sized up this new woman, Ania, she'd called her. She was bright, alert, sharp, and probably very politically savvy.

"Since the tragic accidental death of your loving husband and king and your young son, events beyond your control have placed you solely on our kingdom's throne. You have been doing the duties not only of a queen but also those of a king. I must say that at first, I was extremely skeptical that you could possible manage such a huge load. Yet, as I sit here before you today, my queen, I bow to you. You have done a magnificent job of running our kingdom and many, many of us are particularly pleased and proud of the way that you have been continually standing up against the insanities being proclaimed by the crazed Empress. For that, we all thank you very much."

Ariadne looked pleased. That the most influential man thought that she had done a good job of it meant something to her. He continued. "The question that I must ask you here at the beginning of our talk is this. Do you wish to continue being the queen of Thrace? Do you wish to remain on our throne in the future?"

"God! How I have wished that I could somehow just give it up and run away somewhere and be free of it! No, I don't wish to continue being your queen. However, I know that I have a responsibility to our people to continue representing them until — until well I don't know — when I can be replaced or something. It seems like we all want to be something that we never can be."

"Thank you for being forthright. I had so hoped that this would be the case. It is within my powers to grant you your wish, Ariadne. Events are moving rapidly forward across Demokritos, powerful events, events that will change everything. Because you have been the best queen that has ever sat on the throne of Thrace, I want to see that you are protected from this tidal wave that is soon to wash over our country and kingdom. The days of the reign of Empress Kassandra are rapidly coming to an end, a bloody end I'm afraid. When that end comes, I will see that you are moved to a place of complete safety. Simultaneously, a new king and queen with take over your throne, maintaining continuity of leadership."

"You have already picked her successor?" Ania asked astutely.

"Yes, when one knows that a hurricane will soon be blowing down your current house, a prudent man will construct a new one both out of its reach and in time to dwell in, once the hurricane passes."

"What about the other queens? They have been doing every bit as good a job as I have?" Ariadne asked, growing concerned about this doom and gloom talk. Yet, she too had been sensing that something was coming, just not what.

"As I am sitting here with you today, others of a like mind are speaking with the other queens. It is criminal on our part to have allowed you women, as helpless as you are, to shoulder the immense burdens of your entire kingdoms on your own shoulders alone. For that, I do beg your forgiveness. Until now, we saw not the hurricane coming. The others will be offered a way out, if they so choose. Our biggest concern is one of timing, but leave that up to us."

Ania decided to see just how much this man really knew or suspected. "I hope that this hurricane not only destroys the Empress but also the Cardinal of the Church of Jehosanity."

She observed his eyes jerk slightly and knew that there was much yet unspoken. "I am listening," he said softly.

"We have gathered much circumstantial evidence that Empress Kassandra paid over one million to Cardinal Drakon to arrange the explosion for the purpose of killing all the male rulers at one time, leaving the armless women the sole rulers. We also have similar evidence that the Church and Kassandra have been arranging the untimely deaths of previous kings so as to put some of the current ones on the thrones. Thus, we hope that the tidal wave, which comes, also impacts the Cardinal and his men," Ania said quietly, but with force and intention.

His eyes opened wide. "Proof? Oh, Queen Ariadne! Never have I been more impressed with your skills! This is far better than I had ever hoped for! My advice is gather the evidence together into one packet. When the hurricane hits, see to it that the Senate in Kefall receives that packet. Leave the rest to us. Then the tidal wave will wash all the vile corruption from our lands! I am deeply humbled by your wisdom and actions, my queen!"

They discussed more actions that could be taken to help swing more votes to their side and against the Empress. Two hours later, he left, far more hopeful than he had been when he entered. *Incredible woman, just incredible. Too bad that she is so helpless.*

The next day, Father Hypathos was announced; he was the priest who had performed her Holy Ceremony of the Eighth Degree. He too requested a very private meeting with Ariadne, who again insisted that Ania be there with her. The priest accepted this. "I have come to you today to ask you what has happened to you. Some three years ago, you greatly desired to become one of our Most Holy Women, forming a binding pledge of your undying love for your husband. Yet, now you are preaching that it is utter folly for women to partake of our most holiest of rituals. Indeed, you no longer even come to Sunday services. I am so very worried about your precious soul, my Ariadne. What has happened to so corrupt what was once so beautiful and pure?"

"Father Hypathos, several things have happened. First, I found out the real reason my husband so pressured me into having this done, and it was not a holy reason in the slightest. Second, I have had to live like this, completely helpless for three plus years now. A closed door is a total trap for me. I cannot feed myself or even use the chamber pot. I cannot get dressed or brush my hair. About all I can do is look pretty and walk and talk. Nearly everything else in life is denied me. Frankly, no woman should ever have to live this way; it is not living at all. Third, I have discovered that I am a soul; I do not possess one; I am it. Thus, I no longer believe in what you believe in. Yes, there is God, but I believe that your Church has perverted it to your own ends. As such, I cannot support your Church any longer."

"I do not blame you, Father Hypathos. I am sure that you believe what you have always preached. It is my responsibility. I signed those papers, so in effect, I did this to myself, and now I must live with it, Father. Sometime you ought to see what life is like without arms. Have someone tie yours up and see how impossible every normal action is. Sometimes, it is downright frightening to be this way. No woman should ever have to live this way."

"But you are given the highest honors within our Church. You have as many servants as you desire to help you with everything," he protested slightly, unable really to counter her statements.

"Father, that is precisely the point! I finally see it! Thank you for opening my own eyes! Yes, that is precisely why I am so rebelling. Help. Do you not want to help others? Is this not a basic drive in all human beings — to want and desire to help others? Of course it is! You said it yourself. I have all the servants I desire to help me with everything. Yes, my servants are very happy to help me. They work very hard to assist me with all things. Yet, what about me, Father? I also am a human being, and it is part of my nature to want to help others too. However, here I sit all day long every day of the year being constantly at every turn having to be helped by others and never given any real chance of helping someone else! I cannot even help someone who has fallen down or gotten a cut. I could not even put a bandage on my own son when he fell and cut his knee! All I could do was watch others do what I, as his mother, should have done."

"You and your Church should carefully re-evaluate this whole Eighth Degree thing and see the horrible damage that you are doing to the recipients, especially so with the idea of helping others." Father Hypathos looked both stunned and humbled. Truth had been driven home to this priest. He thanked her for her frankness, bowed, and left.

When he was gone, Ania complimented her, "Wow! Ariadne, that was positively brilliant. You are dead on, absolutely right about the help factor. I can now see why Bethany thinks so very highly of you! You are a most remarkable woman. As long as we are alone, I would like to share something with you. Women like yourself do not need to be so completely helpless. In Velona, we have many women like you who have learned new ways to feed themselves, dress themselves, cook meals, wash their clothes, and many more things. Perhaps when you are free of the responsibility of this throne, you will consider returning to Velona with us. I give you my word that I will make all that happen for you. You do not need to remain so completely helpless for much longer, though I will admit a doorknob can be quite a challenge."

"Really? Is this possible? I cannot imagine getting myself into this outfit!"

"Oops. Okay, no one can get into these outfits without help! I cannot even bend over to untie or tie these boots! Simple dresses can be managed, not these monsters."

Ariadne smiled, "We do look good in them don't we? I've never had such pronounced curves before. Dario certainly has noticed them," she blushed and then giggled.

February 10, Jonas Sokrates sent for General Kreon Demon once more. "Ah, I will be both swift and blunt. The time is rapidly descending upon us all. I would suggest that you find yourself in Thal, Thallyus very soon and with as large an army as you can safely take with you without raising suspicions. Perhaps another raid by the horsemen of Vladimir is imminent. You will know what to do when the time comes." The general grinned; he had thought that these wild proclamations might just be the signal that his time was near at hand.

"I will do so at once!" He bowed and left. Citing information from some recent merchants, he took twenty legions of cavalry with him to help defend the borders with Vladimir. The Empress herself signed off on his request. By the first week of March, he arrived in Thal. By then, the winds had begun blowing.

On February 21, 752, an aide came running into Ariadne's throne room, where she was meeting with several merchants who were trying to work out a trading agreement with the Vladimir representative. He didn't wait to be announced. "Queen Ariadne! It's happened! Fighting has just broken out in Central Square! The Empress' legions are shooting people! Bodies are lying everywhere!"

"Oh dear god! Call out our guards! Get my carriage ready. I've got to get there and stop this madness!" Ariadne cried out, suddenly feeling extremely helpless once again. Ania put her arm around her to steady both herself and the queen. Slowly they headed for the door. Others began rushing as well. By the time that they made it to the front entrance of her palace and the large cobblestone courtyard, her carriage was already waiting.

"Queen Ariadne, I urge you not to go. It could be very dangerous for you," the captain of her guards beseeched her.

"It's my people!" she replied. He saw the futility of further argument.

"Our men will surround your carriage," he said, bowed, and headed for his hundred men, who were already mounted. In the distance, gunshots could still be heard, faint popping sounds. Ania helped Ariadne into the carriage. Two of her assistants helped Ania manage for which she was grateful; she'd still not gotten the hang of these impossible Annelise outfits. Her trainer hobble skirt required that someone lift her up into the carriage. Soon the carriage began rolling out of her palace gates. Now the noise of the many horses' hooves upon the paved streets drowned out everything else.

"What can possibly be going on? Why would army soldiers shoot unarmed civilians? It doesn't make any sense," Ariadne asked, very near tears. She could not comprehend what was apparently happening, and she felt more vulnerable than ever. Besides she now found it hard to catch her breath; she'd moved much too quickly. These outfits had liabilities; emergencies were one, she realized.

Fifteen minutes later, her carriage and her hundred guards pulled into Central Square, a square block devoted to a bandstand where outdoor entertainment provided summer evening entertainment. Political rallies were often conducted here as well. Already the leaves had changed, and the ground was a patchwork quilt of many colors. Now the green and leaves were dotted with flows of red. If she had hands, Ariadne would have covered her mouth. Instead, she stared at the square from its southern edge. Bodies lay on the ground in a chaotic pattern, centered on the bandstand, red seeping in lines and flows from them. Standing in a tight military pattern was an entire legion of soldiers. The acrid stench of gunpowder smoke still hung in the air. The soldiers were reloading their weapons. In the distance, she could see many townsfolk running for their lives down the four streets and alleys that radiated from this city gathering place.

A general stood in front of the hundred men, issuing orders. Ariadne took a deep breath and headed for him, nearly slipping and falling, caught at the last instant by one of her male assistants. The other man caught Ania, who also slipped. Their boots were no match for the uneven, leaf-covered ground. "Allow me, your majesty," he said. His arm encircled her waist, and they slowly walked towards the general. The other assistant did the same with Ania, who whispered her thanks.

"General! What is the meaning of this? Why have you shot all these unarmed civilians? This is outright murder!" Ariadne cried out as soon as she was close enough.

"Sorry, Queen Ariadne. I am just following the Empress' orders to disperse riffraff crowd who continue to rail against our government and its proclamations. They were told that they had to leave before we opened fire on them," he replied formally, wishing that the queen had not come here so soon. Five more minutes and he and his men would have been nowhere to be seen.

"General, this is outright murder. Captain, place this general under arrest. The crime is murder. Many murders!" Ariadne ordered, her voice trembling, her legs nearly giving out, her breathing fighting against her tight corset.

"You have no authority to arrest me. I report only to the Empress, Your Majesty," the general pointed out.

Her captain hesitated. The general's men held one hundred guns. His men had but twenty between them. Ania sent a message to Ariadne, who then spoke once more. "General, I don't care if you report to Lord Jehosa himself! You have just murdered many unarmed civilians in my capital city. I am returning to my palace and issuing an order to mobilize the entire army of Thrace. There are over twenty legions within a day's ride, and many are at their barracks on the other side of Axos. Their orders will be to arrest you or to shoot you if you offer any resistance. If you wish to stay alive, I would recommend that you and your murdering soldiers here vacate Axos before my army arrives. If you ever set foot in Axos again, my soldiers will have orders to shoot you on sight. Do I make myself perfectly clear?"

"Yes Your Majesty," he replied. Ania noticed that he looked terribly pale and there was a slight tremor in his left leg.

Queen Ariadne turned and headed back to her carriage. "Hold me! I am fainting!" Her assistant deftly caught her and pretended that they were walking back, though he was mostly dragging her. He did not want the general to see that the queen had fainted. Ania and the other assistant followed behind, helping to hide the queen from the soldiers. She took a quick count of the bodies lying on the snowy ground. Thirty-five.

Once back inside the carriage, Ania got Ariadne conscious and helped her calm down. "Thirty-five bodies. We should get doctors there in case some are only wounded," Ania suggested. "We'll get on it as soon as we get her back to the palace."

"I can handle that, why don't you borrow one of the guard's horses and get the emergency people out there. You may be in time to save some of their lives," Ania insisted. He did as she asked. In fact, both men hopped out and headed off to take charge of the situation. A short while later, the carriage pulled into the palace courtyard. This time, their driver helped both of them down from the carriage. Her arms around Ariadne, Ania led her inside. Everyone quickly gathered in her throne room, dying to know what had happened.

While Ariadne recovered, Ania told everyone the gruesome details, what their queen had done, and ordered. When she had finished, Ariadne finally felt better, at least she was breathing regularly once more. "Okay. Advisors, Messengers. I need our kingdom's generals here as fast as they can get here. Get me those tally pages you did on the gun supplies, please. Messengers, bring tea and biscuits. We will have generals here soon. I need to send a dispatch to the Empress, so someone take this down."

Empress Kassandra Aias,

Today your general and one legion opened fire with their guns on a rightful assemblage of citizens of Axos in our Central Square around our public bandstand, where we usually hold our debates. They willfully murdered thirty-five Thrace citizens.

I request that you arrest that general and turn him over to Thrace where he will be tried on willful murder charges, and if found guilty, executed.

I have mobilized the entire army of Thrace. I have given them the orders to evict all legions belonging to the Empress from Thrace, excepting Kefall, of course.

If your legions resist, they will be summarily shot.

Queen Ariadne Diodros

"Okay, I know that we do not have an accurate count of the casualties. I know I have not yet given those orders, but write all that and then be prepared to make last minute changes as the data comes in," she explained.

"Your requested gun tallies," an advisor quietly presented her the sheets, holding them so that she could read them.

"Damn! Is it really this bad?" she asked. While she had an army of some thirty legions, that is around three thousand soldiers, barely one in five had one of these new guns. Nearly all the Empress' soldiers had guns. At the time, everyone thought that the best distribution of these new weapons should be with the soldiers most likely to go to war, the Emperor's troops, not the local kingdom's armies.

Shortly thereafter, her generals began arriving. She waited until all five were present. By now, they had heard all about what had happened. "Generals, you have all heard the news. The Empress' legions have opened fire on unarmed civilians in Central Square, murdering many with their guns. I want this ended. So I am ordering you to drive every national soldier out of Axos, to start with, that is, the legions controlled by the Empress. While I do not presume to know best how you ought to carry this order out that is what we need done. Ideas, generals?"

"We can succeed if we overwhelm them with our numbers. They travel and patrol in legion groups or smaller. If we divide into groups of at least five legions, they would likely yield to us and leave. That is except for one thing," a tall general suggested. "Guns. We are totally outgunned. They may challenge us because of this point."

"Yes, we've just reviewed the figures. I am sorry that we leaders made such a blunder, giving the newly made guns to the Emperor's soldiers instead of you. I am sorry for that. Is there anything that can be done about it?" Ariadne asked.

"Well, Queen Ariadne, there may be something that can be done," one general coyly suggested. "The Emperor has an armory on the south side of Axos where they store their guns and ammunition. If we raid it with sufficient forces, we might be able to capture many guns and certainly their ammunition. Without ammunition, their guns are worthless metal."

"Excellent. Do you men need signed orders from me to make it happen?" she asked. They did, and she dictated the orders; her assistant signed them for her and put her wax seal on them. Smiling and chatting among themselves, the generals left the throne room.

An aide to one of her assistants returned from the massacre site with news. Thirty were dead, but the doctors believed that five lives might be saved. She had that change made to her letter to the Empress, had her assistant sign, and seal it. A Messenger took it to the post rider to have it delivered. At last, her staff departed the throne room, leaving Ariadne and Ania alone with what was left of the tea and biscuits. Ania deftly held a cup so Ariadne could sip along with herself.

"You did extremely well under fire today, Ariadne. Impressive. Few could have stood your ground and delivered that fiery an ultimatum to the general."

"Yes, but I fainted. God, I was so scared! I was terrified that he would call my bluff, that he might even shoot us. I felt so completely helpless there. I couldn't walk in these boots on that slippery leaf strewn, uneven ground or could I even breathe. He could have just shot us right there, you know."

"Just so you know, he may have shot at us, but since I was there, the bullets would not have hit either us or your two men holding on to us. I can't tell you why just now. Perhaps one day, Bethany will allow me to more fully explain. As long as I am around you, in close proximity, no gun can harm either you or me. Trust me," Ania whispered. "I am also letting Bethany know what has happened here in Axos. She will let the other queens know too, and they can be prepared for similar crimes in their kingdoms. You've done very well indeed."

Ariadne stared at her in a combination of disbelief and total awe. Were Bethany and Ania some kind of goddesses? That the other queens would know was very comforting, but she realized that normally, it would be weeks before the far flung queens heard about it, not minutes.

Ania patted the Grey Creature device in her pocket. Dianna had insisted that they bring along one for each of them. She had the device set on field shield, according to Dianna's orders.

The next morning, Queen Ariadne sat on her throne, listening to the various reports that were now coming in about the attack. She'd just heard that indeed the doctors had saved the five wounded men and that they would recover. Her Announcer spoke, "Dario Matteo to see Queen Ariadne." Her heart leaped; her face flushed; she looked at the door and there he was, grinning at her.

"Everyone, take a break for a few minutes. I need to talk to Dario," she managed to keep her voice under control, though her heart was now racing. He'd come to her. He stepped aside as the dozen men and women filed out past him, many giving him a strange, curious look, wondering who this man from Velona was.

Once alone, she rose from her throne and walked towards him as fast as her heels would allow. Dario, arms wide open, rushed to her and threw them around her, picked her up, and twirled her around in circles. Sitting her down gently, she leaned over and passionately kissed him. He said, "Ariadne! How I have missed you! I love you, and I am not going to leave you until you can come away with me where it is safe. I just won't take no for an answer. I can't bear to be another minute without you! Will you marry me and come away with me? You must say yes. God, how I have missed you and worried about you for weeks! I just heard about how you were nearly shot by all those guns yesterday! I feared that I was but a day late and had lost the flower of my life!"

He paused slightly for a breath, and she took advantage of it, "Yes, if you will just calm your passions a moment. Yes, I love you too! I have missed you more than I can say. I have worked something out so that I will be able to responsibly give up the throne, and then yes, let's get away from all this, please. But are you really sure that you want me? I'm like this, you know." She shrugged her armless shoulders. "I'll always be a burden to you."

First, he kissed her again. "Dearest Ariadne, you have it all backwards. It is I that will be a burden for you! I'm afraid that you are going to have to keep up with me, and I am not going to let your lack of arms become your excuse for not keeping up, my love. Let me look at you. Are you sure that you were not hurt yesterday? Rumors are absolutely wild around the inn I stayed at last night."

It was at this moment that she fully realized that here was a man who was not going to be giving her that sticky, sickly sympathy over her physical condition that nearly everyone did! He had never say, "Oh you poor woman; let me help you." She had grown to detest that attitude that even her own assistants displayed towards her. "Honestly, I am fine. I just fainted from the overly tight corset and the incredible stress of the moment. I just had to handle that general for my people. Come. Sit down. Where's Luigi and your company?"

"Luigi is on his way to Naxos to rescue Queen Alekto, and the rest of the company is on its way from here to Patri, where our caravel awaits. The current plan is for us to head to Patri when the time is right. We can then sail around to pick up Luigi and Alekto. I am so glad that you are safe. What did happen yesterday?"

She signaled for Ania to enter and for some tea, before launching into a detailed account.

Chapter 45 March Madness

Queen Alekto arrived back home in Naxos, Arolas, in early February. She traveled to and from Kefall overland on the Great Rim Road, which encircled Demokritos, going from one kingdom's capital city to the next. She hated taking a caravel trip, which would cut the time by a third. Before her husband's murder, they had always gone by caravel, but now, as helpless as she was, she avoided ship travel. As her entourage pulled into her palace in Naxos, huge responsibilities rested solely on her young shoulders. She was only twenty-two, far too young to shoulder this much responsibility, she felt. Worse, she felt alone and extremely vulnerable and helpless, too, she admitted.

For over a week at Yuletide she had felt something that she had never thought that she would ever feel again, love. Luigi. That young man had kindled something deep within her that had long lay dormant. Not even her late husband had ignited it. Something in her early childhood made her totally alive and full of hope and promise, but in vain, she had long since been unable to recall exactly what that had been. Love was as close as she could come to touching it. But in those ten days with Luigi, that long buried feeling had ignited once more. Now, he was gone. For three weeks, she had ridden along in her carriage, putting mile upon mile from him. The closer she got to Naxos, the heavier the burden of her throne became.

The hideous, evil proclamations just had to be vetoed by Arolas. Somehow, she had to get that accomplished. She'd received quite a start when Bethany had made mental contact with her to tell her that she and Dita had been abducted again. The wicked things that these men had done to her two friends appalled her and made her feel the utter helplessness of her own body once more. That somehow miraculously they had recovered from the diabolical tortures inflicted upon them did cheer her up a little. What did cheer her up was Bethany's message that a Mrs. Kali Kato da Cassa was on her way to help and protect her. According to Bethany, she was to trust Kali with her life. Just who was this Kali, she wondered.

While her staff handled the unpacking and her advisors began implementing their plans for the massive vote count, Alekto sat on her throne, dealing with the steady stream of petitioners, merchants, and nobles pleading their petty cases. Petty, she thought, you are worrying about some unfair trading bargain, while the whole country is crumbling around you. No, I shouldn't blame them. It's just me. How can I miss one man so very much? I've only known him for ten days. Alekto! Put such nonsense out of your mind! You know that no man is ever going to want a hopelessly helpless woman such as yourself! She rejected a cup of tea one of her servants lifted to her lips. God, I have to be fed like a baby. I can't take this anymore. No one knows what it's like to be a freak like this, to have to lie all the time and say I am fine. No one knows what it's like behind these light blue eyes, the fear I know, the grief I feel, every hour of every day. No one knows what it's like to be me.

Her Announcer called out the name of the next petitioner; she sighed as her armless Announcer began to speak, but then she perked up. "Mrs. Kali Kato da Cassa." Alekto looked up at the woman wearing a traveling leather outfit, warm and comfortable. She had the usual bronze skin of one from Demokritos, she thought. The woman was tall, six feet at least; her legs looked powerful, though her arms appeared rather thin. Curly black hair draped to her shoulders, and her face was rather angelic, pretty, but not overly. She looked to be around twenty-five, three years older than she was. Yet, this woman's bearing, her eyes, her confront caught her attention at once. This Kali had a definite presence about herself as she walked confidently up to her throne and bowed.

Kali saw a dark blonde woman around twenty-two at most. Her long hair, parted in the middle, draped down her front to her waist, covering her shoulders, but it was the woman's light blue eyes that mirrored the queen. She knew instinctively that, while Bethany had erased the woman's trauma, she now was in a deep sadness. *Well, I've my work cut out for me. I can see that.*

"Hello, I am Kali Kato da Cassa. Queen Alekto, I am very pleased to meet you. Bethany has told me a lot about you. Has she contacted you about me?" Her deep voice carried in the room, but behind it came a sense of power, as one who is always in command, in control. Confidence seemed to emanate from her. Alekto took an instant liking to her. She began to perk up.

"Yes, I am very pleased to meet you as well. Sit down, please, have some tea if you like. Everyone, will you please give Kali and I a few minutes of privacy?" Quickly, her staff complied, though not without some glances at this newcomer.

Kali took off her cloak and asked, "Would you like some tea as well?" She poured herself a cup. "Need me to assist you with yours?" she asked.

"No, I am rather not interested in tea just now. Tell me about yourself. Are you from Thrace?" she made a wild guess here, based on her skin coloration.

"No, I was born on Megalos this time. I had a very bad run in with the Church of Jehosanity and that of Dorota. I moved to Velona as a teen. I am part of Bethany's group there. So is my wife, Ilenakova, a powerful fighter. She's with Bethany and Dita right now, protecting them. Looks like she got there a day late, though. Well, those two are now safe since Ilenakova is on the job. We never should have let those two come down here all by themselves."

"I've been analyzing the funds transfers between Empress Kassandra and Cardinal Drakon. If I had had the data sooner than three months late, I might have been able to alert everyone and maybe they could have avoid the murder of the Emperor and the kings and your husband. Well, I'm here now, Alekto. As long as you always keep me close to your side, no one can harm you, not even if they use their guns. You are very safe if you keep me close to you. Will you do that?"

"I don't understand how you can promise this, but right now, I feel, well, I feel really helpless. Horrible things are happening all around me, and it is on my shoulders to set them right. Honestly, I don't think that I can do it. It is all so very hard for me. I never wanted this in the first place, but I really don't have any choice in the matter, do I? Everyone is depending on me."

"Not if you value the people in your kingdom. Besides, if you didn't shoulder your responsibilities and help your people, I assure you that I would *not* be here this morning. Yes, right about now I assure you that we all feel helpless, and it has nothing to do with arms. Others have set things into motion, which we cannot stop, but we may alter their expected outcomes. If you and I work together, we may be able to thwart the Empress and the Cardinal."

"Bethany says that I should trust you with my life. I will do as you ask. Does this mean that you should sleep in my chambers with me?"

"I don't know what your current situation is, Alekto, but if you don't mind, that would be ideal. I can then guard you better. Do you have others sleeping with you? Those Utu women sure look unusual. I heard that they are your Special Helpers," Kali asked.

"I sleep alone. Oui tucks me in and is across the hall if I need anything. Always my husband took care of me, after I became like this. Since his death, I've been sleeping alone. Just now, I'd like some company, if you don't mind. Do you think someone will try to kill me during the night, like they did with Bethany and Dita?"

"I don't know, but I sure want to make sure that you remain safe."

"Okay. For appearances, you ought to wear something other than traveling leathers. Have you brought along other clothes?"

"Well, no, we left in a huge hurry, and none too soon it seems. I have what I have on; we figured we'd buy suitable dresses when we arrived. We are unsure what is appropriate in your courts down here."

"It depends. Most of my staff wears gowns as you probably have seen on your way here. However, Empress Kassandra has ordered we queens and our closest advisors to wear these latest fashions from Annelise. So if you don't want to have her take an instant dislike to you, you probably should get used to wearing them. They do take an inordinate amount of getting used to wearing. Princess Maren from Annelise has been giving us many very fine fashions. I have an old starter outfit that I don't wear anymore because my waist has gotten too small for it. I can help you learn to deal with it, if you like."

"No sense starting off on the wrong foot with the Empress. Okay, I will give it a go."

"Thank you. I appreciate your doing this for me. Kassandra can be scary at times. I ought to continue the meetings. I'll have Oui show you to my room and she can help you get into it. I'll drop by in an hour and help you master it and give you a tour of the palace. Then, we can have some lunch."

Kali took advantage of the bath in her room and then allowed the Utu woman to begin to dress her. She quickly found that although Oui could not speak understandably, she could write fairly well. However, she kept her questions to the minimum, hoping that Alekto would explain more. When the Doorman opened the door to allow Alekto to enter her chambers, Kali began asking. "This is so uncomfortable! How can you breathe? How can you stand in these tight, high-heeled boots? How do you ever manage even to walk in them? What's with this impossibly tight underskirt?"

Alekto giggled. "We all say those very same things when we first began to wear them. To quote Princess Maren, 'Practice, practice, practice.' She was right though. In a few weeks, you will hardly notice them all that much. You must always remember to take the tiniest of steps. That's what the tight underskirt is for; she calls it a learning training skirt. Once you no longer are bothered by it, you can take it off, as long as you don't go back to trying to take larger steps. Come on; put your arm around me for support, and let's go see the palace."

Ever so slowly, from Kali's view, they began moving towards the door. "Can I ask you something personal, Kali?"

"Sure."

"Are many women in Velona married to other women instead of men?"

Kali chuckled. "No, only us six. Bethany and Dita, Ania and Dianna, Ilenakova and me. I don't know of any others. I bet you were worried about that." The queen giggled, she was. "Well, we six have our reasons, and perhaps someday I will tell you. Sorry, I almost pulled you over! Gosh, this is hard."

That evening, Kali and Alekto allowed Oui to undress them. Kali was startled to discover that they would sleep in these tight corsets. When in Demokritos, do as they do, she reminded herself. She brushed out Alekto's hair and the two chatted for a long time. Alekto found talking with Kali so very easy, as if she was a lifelong friend.

"I know that I've done this to myself, you know. I did this to myself, no matter the extenuating circumstances. Only now, it is so very hard to live like this. I had no idea how awful it would wind up being. I am sorry that you have to do so much for me and that I can do so very little in return. That is one reason I am working so hard to make things right for my people here in Arolas. It doesn't truly make up for all that everyone has to do for me, but it is something."

"Sometimes I feel so low. Like today, just before you came. Honestly, no one knows what it's like to be me as I am now. Not really. Well, the thirty other women and girls that I hired on to work around here so that they can survive — they know. But normal people just don't."

"Can I let you in on a little clue, Alekto?" She nodded. "Some of us do understand, very, very well what it's like for you. I really, really do understand fully what it's like to be you as you are, Alekto. So do Bethany and the rest of us six. We totally understand. Maybe one day Bethany will allow me to tell you how it is that we six do know. Yet, Alekto, you don't have to live a helpless life, having everything done for you. In Velona, we can show you how you can indeed do darn near anything that you have a mind to do, except heavy lifting. Have you ever given any thought to perhaps traveling, say to Velona, when you no longer have to be queen here?"

"Yes, I've always wanted to travel, but Kali, something strange happened to me over Yuletide. We all took a vacation, Bethany, Dita, Athena, Ariadne, and I. We went incognito to a vacation spa and resort in southern Theos. I met this incredible man from Velona. Luigi Matteo, he's an entertainer. He and his brother put on just about the most fantastic music and dance show that I've ever heard of or seen anyway."

"Ah, Bethany told me about those brothers. Did you fall for him?"

"Well, yes, in a big way. I mean I only have known him for ten days, but those were the best ten days that I have ever had in my whole life! I know, I probably will never see him again. I think that he must have liked me too, though I don't know why he would ever want me, not when I am like this. That, I can accept. I mean if I am being totally honest and if I were a guy, I sure would not want someone like me, a totally dependent woman."

"Perhaps, you are being too hard on yourself, Alekto. I love Ilenakova for a large number of reasons; none is because of the way that she looks. We are like kindred souls in many ways."

"I would love to meet her. What I was trying to say is that something happened to me during those ten days! I sort of felt like there was something vital, really, really important buried deep inside me that suddenly came *back* to life when I was around Luigi. I felt it when I was a little girl, but it vanished as I grew up. Now, it's there again, but I can't quite see what it is. Kind of like a flower bud. If it can only continue, it will blossom into the most beautiful flower."

"Well, let's water the heck out of it, shall we? I'd love to see it blossom too! You know that you made an indelible impression on Luigi too. From what Bethany's said to me, he claims that he's madly in love with you. In fact, he's on his way here to be with you, while Dario is heading to Axos to be with Ariadne. He probably can't get here for a couple more weeks though. As I understand it, they are sending their company on to Patri, and they will join the others later on."

"Really? Luigi is coming here? He really does like me?" The news was like a glowing light coming from her light blue eyes, Kali observed. "Come on, we'd better get some sleep." She helped Alekto into bed and then crawled in with her.

"Thank you for coming here, Kali. I need your help," she whispered.

Just as her advisors got the proclamations on wide public display and the vote counters started on the lengthy task, Bethany made contact with both Kali and Alekto. *I have some alarming news from Axos and Queen Ariadne.* She gave them a lengthy description of what had happened there with the Empress' soldiers murdering the opposition people in Central Square.

The next day, Kali and Alekto made contingency plans, and then Alekto called all of her staff together along with all her kingdom's generals. Carefully, she relayed the news from Thrace. Angry curses filled the room, and per Kali's suggestion, she allowed them all to vent their feelings.

"Don't ask me how I know what has happened there yesterday. I just do. I am your queen. Now then, here is what we are going to do. I'll bet anything that the Empress' army here in Arolas will be doing similar shootings of our people, once they begin to hold public forums, that is. So let's take advantage of our prior knowledge. Generals, quietly pull all our legions back from the mountains. Let the Vladimir horsemen raid for a while if they want to do so. This is far more important. We know where the Empress' legions are located and their numbers. Arolas' soldiers have but a fifth of the guns of theirs. So generals, figure out how many of our legions you can put against their legions and be successful in running them out of the towns and cities. The very instant that they try shooting our people, I want you to raid the Emperor's ammunition depots scattered around the country. Confiscate all the guns there and all the ammunition. Distribute them to our kingdom's forces. When they make the first strike on our people, our citizens, I want your retribution to be both swift and decisive! Drive them out of Arolas. You have my permission to use whatever force you deem necessary to get the job done. Do you need written authority from me to do this, generals?"

They did. One of her assistants drew up the document. After she read it and Okayed it, the assistant signed it for her and put the official seal on it. The generals looked incredibly pleased with their queen. She was allowing them to take effective, decisive action on their own initiative, without telling them what specifically they had to do. Plus, everyone was impressed with her knowing about all this within a day of it happening in far distant Axos, Thrace, some eight hundred miles away. Speculation ran wild around the palace over how she came by this information. Two weeks later when riders came from Thrace bearing the same news, they were even more impressed.

The first week of March, Agapios Kednos requested a private

conference with Alekto. She explained hurriedly to Kali that he was the most powerful and influential nobleman in all Arolas. Agapios was fifty-nine, his brown hair greying, his blue eyes, still as piercing and intimidating as always. "I meant a private conversation, Alekto. Do you need her here with you?" he asked, somewhat annoyed that she had Kali with her. He'd never seen this other woman before.

"Yes, this is Kali and she is my arms and I trust her with my life. Anything you want to say to me, no matter what it is, you can say before her. To what do I owe the pleasure of this visit?" Alekto said politely. The last time he had come before her was to throw his support begrudgingly behind allowing her to remain on the throne and rule Arolas.

"So be it. Queen Alekto, I must admit that you have done a most remarkable job of running Arolas and standing up to Empress Kassandra. History will likely have you down as the best queen Arolas has ever had." She smiled, but highly doubted that. He's building me up for something; I wonder what he wants, she thought to herself.

"As you have so well pointed out to us all, Empress Kassandra has become something of a rogue leader. Her unilateral proclamations, bypassing our queens and their opinions and wishes, are going to cause severe repercussions all throughout Demokritos. I *strongly* believe that massive changes are coming to our nation and soon. Because of the brilliant and courageous way that you have ruled since the untimely death of your husband, I feel that I owe it to you to protect you from what's coming. However, in order for me to do that, I need to know one thing from you, Queen Alekto. When the upheaval comes, do you wish to remain our queen or would you prefer to step down?"

"I really get a choice?" she asked taken completely by surprise. "Yes, I'll step down the very instant that we have a suitable new king who will do a good job for Arolas, sir. Just say the word and I'm out of here!"

The surprised look on his face told both women that this was not what he had expected at all. "Well, then, that is even better, Alekto! Much better. Yes, already the Noble Houses wish to begin making their choice. I had come with some 'prepared marriages' to offer you, had you desired to remain our queen. Your decision allows us to make an even better choice for our new rulers. Thank you! The time for this change is not yet at hand. From what we've heard from Thrace, it may well be sooner than we all had thought. Honestly, murdering unarmed citizens for exercising their right to free public debate! The very nerve of that woman! Alekto, when the time is right, we will send word to you, and we will do everything in our power to get you away to a place of safety. When you hear the words, 'the hurricane comes,' that will be our signal to you. Be prepared to depart within minutes of receiving it."

"Thank you, Agapios. I will remember and be prepared. Until then, you may count on me to do my part in resisting the Empress' wicked proclamations," she replied. He chatted a bit longer and then left.

"I may be free of this yoke yet!" Alekto exclaimed to Kali, before she had Kali bring her staff back into her throne room.

Around this same time, Diabolos Andro paid a visit on Queen Frona of Thallyus, Thal. "Thank you for seeing me, your majesty." He, too, was the most powerful nobleman in all Thal, wealthiest too, it was rumored. "I must compliment you on your incredibly fine performance as our queen. I've heard about the stands that you have taken against her in her court this past summer."

"Yes, as the eldest of us queens, I felt it was my duty to bear the brunt of her backlash. I am sorry that we were unsuccessful in preventing her from taking her actions. Now we have this expensive voting facing us just to repeal her very wrong proclamations," Frona replied.

"Queen Frona, I will be frank with you. Many things in Demokritos are about to change for the better. Yet, it may well be seen more as a hurricane than a quiet change. I came to talk with you today about how that change may affect you. Key is your desire. Would you like to continue being in a ruling capacity or would you rather be done with being our queen and move on to other things?"

"Considering that I no longer trust rulers as I did in my youth, Diabolos, I would prefer to keep my hands somehow on the reigns of our nation, figuratively, I mean, since I lack them. Why do you ask? Am I to be replaced when the changes come?"

"We nobles feel that we owe you and thus want to do what is right by you when the time comes for change. Let me ask you another personal question. If you could be our Empress, would you accept an arranged marriage to a man who would likely never really love you as did your late husband and king? Don't misunderstand me, he would treat you with kindness and respect, just do not expect love."

"As Empress, I could do far more for our country, Diabolos. I am too old for love anyway. More children I cannot have. I've seen how the Empress can abuse the powers that we give her, and I would like to show our country how a real Empress works. She has disgraced her position. I would love to have the opportunity to bring honesty and integrity back to this highest throne. Yes, I would accept such a marriage so that I could be Empress. Are you offering me this choice?"

"I am indeed offering this proposition to you, Frona. Later this month, a general will be arriving in Thal. I will introduce you to him. He has already agreed to marry whomever we choose so that he can become Emperor. He is unmarried and that would pose a barrier on his being chosen. Do not reveal any of our conversation to anyone. We nobles are acting in total secrecy. Our lives depend on keeping our moves secret from the Empress and the Church. After you both meet, we will need to get you married at once, and at that time, we will name those chosen to be your successors here in Thallyus. No matter the chaos and confusion of the times, once you are married, you can depend upon him to keep you safe and alive during all that may come about."

"This is good news to my ears — that the days of Kassandra and the Cardinal are numbered. I will do this for my country. May I also ask a personal question? Why is it that I should not expect his love, if he does respect me and treats me with kindness?" Frona was intensely curious about this aspect. Such was terribly close to love in her mind.

"Promise not to breathe a word of this to others and I will tell you." She did, of course. "He loves other men, but has no current lover." Now she understood. In public, he would treat her as he should. It's just that — well, now she understood and accepted it. Her youthful beauty was gone, and she was armless; that she would have his respect and kindness was more than she could hope to have in a late life marriage.

"There is one other thing that I must ask you to do, now that you have agreed to become our next Empress. I need you to secretly pull our entire army from their current locations throughout Thallyus and have them scattered around Thal. Your new husband will be needing them when the hurricane hits." She promised to do so.

Bethany heard from the other queens as well. Danae and Adonia both agreed to give up their thrones, more than willing to return to a normal life outside the court. Queen Melita was more concerned for the well-being and safety of her fourteen year old daughter. She too decided to vacate her throne, on the condition that they bought her an estate on which she could live and where she and her daughter would be out of danger. Only she and Adonia still had living children; all the others had perished in the explosion that had killed their husbands.

This first week in March, Khristos came to see Cardinal Drakon in his private study. He carried a pair of large round objects covered with cloths. He removed the coverings. "There you have my revised designs, Your Holiness. See the lip plates are firmly bolted to the frame so that they and the lips surrounding them cannot move. These leather patches behind these steel bars will completely cover their eyes. The mouth ring assemblage is much as it was. I am afraid that disabling all hearing is more problematical. These leather patches will dampen down the sounds considerably but not block them entirely. I feel it is too risky actually to damage their ears. As you can see, eight locks and screws will need to be sealed to prevent this device from being removed. If we were at a blacksmiths, we could use molten iron, but since such a location is unlikely, I have found that tin or lead will do just as well. A small amount poured into the locking mechanisms or around the adjustment threads will prevent its removal."

"Brilliant, positively brilliant, Khristos! Diabolical even. Yes, we will not be harming these Daughters of Lucifer, so the Devil will have no cause to retaliate on us. Yet, these evil, wicked devil's spawn will definitely be unable to pervert anyone. Brilliant indeed. Now then, how will you be able to get their heads into these and when?" Cardinal Drakon asked.

"I have given that some thought. Undoubtedly, on their next trip to Kefall, they will be bringing along a large security force, so that we cannot waylay them as we did last time. We know already that the queens have greatly beefed up palace security. Certainly, Athena has done so. Hence, a nighttime snatch is out. I realize that you wish these Daughters of Lucifer to be unable to affect the coming Fall Council when it meets the last week of March. I will see to it that it is done before they arrive in Kefall. I shall not fail you this time, and the lip plates will remain on them as well!"

Cardinal Drakon gave a big hug of thanks to his Prelate. He thought that one day when he was Pope, he would reward Khristos with the position of Supreme Prelate of the Mano del Dio. Everything was now rolling right along towards his ultimate success. Hundreds of women had undergone the Holy Ceremony in just the past month alone, influential women at that. His power was growing rapidly. *All I have to do now is sit back and allow my ship to sail to victory!*

History claimed that March Madness began on March 4; however, many consider that it truly began back in February in Axos, Thrace. In every major city throughout Demokritos, legions under the control of generals loyal to the Empress began openly firing upon large gatherings whose members were talking against the proclamations of the Empress. Why? She began to get early reports on the voting results, though far from complete, she was losing out by a small percentage to the queens! Thus, she ordered her legions to put an end to the public condemnations of her proclamations. This they did most effectively by simply marching in and firing a barrage of a hundred bullets into the demonstrators.

The queen's forces immediately retaliated by bringing as many of their own legions as possible and counterfiring upon the legions of the Empress. By the second week in March, total chaos erupted in every kingdom! Citizens in support of the Empress began attacking the kingdom's soldiers, while citizens against the Empress began attacking the citizens who supported her, as well as also sabotaging the horses and equipment of the Empress' legions. Daily, people in the larger cities heard the sounds of gunfights scattered throughout their cities. By the third week in March, no merchant dared to open their street side shops for fear of being caught in the crossfire. Commerce came to a standstill that week. However, uniformly, the kingdom's armies slowly gained the upper hand. This was their home base, while the Empress' legions needed to be supplied to operate this far from their bases. By the end of the third week of March, the Empress' legions had been forced out of all the major cities throughout Demokritos. Now the battles were taken to the countryside.

Loss of life was high; casualties mounted daily, overwhelming the local capacity to tend to the wounded. No one was prepared for such injuries, which usually required exploratory surgery to attempt to locate the lead bullet inside the victim. No doctor had yet had experience in dealing with these kinds of wounds. Many died on the operating table, not from the initial gunshot, but from the exploratory work to find the bullet.

In all kingdoms, the queens replied upon their kingdom's generals to carry out protecting the cities and driving out the legions of the Empress. All they could do was hope and pray, appalled at the steadily rising combat tolls and the escalation of the fighting. The hurricane was definitely barreling inland.

On March 10, Luigi came riding hard into the palace at Naxos, having just narrowly bypassed a small skirmish. The gate men and the doormen were long ago notified to let Luigi Matteo in the moment he arrived. An armless teenaged Messenger met him at the door, giggled, and led him down the corridors, while doormen opened the doors as they approached. In the throne room, Alekto and Kali were going over yesterday's casualty figures, wondering what other actions the queen could take. Already she had set up emergency treatment centers around Naxos. Her Announcer called out, "Luigi Matteo."

Her heart skipped a beat, as she looked up from the papers Kali was holding before her. Suddenly, all her feelings and emotions from Yuletide came rushing in on her, drowning out the horrors of the current situation in Naxos. She wanted to run to him and throw her arms around him, but that was impossible for many reasons. "If you will all give me a private moment with Luigi, please? Take a well-deserved break, everyone." Several women smiled, but they all did as she asked.

"Hi there, Alekto! I'm here at last. You must be Kali. Bethany said that you would be here protecting my dearest love until I got her. Alekto, I know it is so sudden, and we've only known each other but ten days. Yet, it seems a lifetime to me! Every day that I was apart from you, my heart nearly burst. Alekto, I do love you so! I have come here to do everything that I can to win your hand in marriage! I want to marry you and spend the rest of my life with you." By now, he had finally reached her throne, where she had risen to greet him; her heart was pounding, and she was afraid that she might faint; her corset seemed like a prison for her emotions.

Instead, when he was close to her, pushing her wide hoop skirt towards her knees, she leaned forward and began passionately kissing him. She could think of no words to say. She felt like she had as a little child once again. He threw his arms around her and returned her embraces.

When they at last separated for a moment, Kali couldn't resist. "I am sorry that you came all this way to win her hand. As you can plainly see, she has none to win!" Alekto instantly realized that this was so! He would see this and now not want her. Panic struck her stomach. Luigi stared at Kali and then broke out laughing!

"Oh you devil!" he teased her, finally seeing the humor in his youthful, uncontrolled exuberance. "I'm going to have to get you for that one!" And he started to chase her, intent on tickling her or something, he wasn't sure. Both he and Kali were roaring with laughter, and Alekto's panic evaporated as suddenly as it had come. She giggled at their frolicking — all one sided, as Kali could barely move in the Annelise outfit.

"Okay, Alekto, I have come to ask for your body in marriage. How's that?" he said laughing hard. Now all three laughed at his altered statement.

"Seriously, Luigi," Alekto tried to keep a straight face. "You really want me, like I am, a really helpless woman who is going to require assistance with absolutely everything."

"Yes, yes, yes, a thousand times yes! However, if you call yourself a helpless woman just one more time, then I am going to have to tickle you until you faint in your corset! I'll hear no of such silliness. You are as you are. I am in love with you, not your body, though I have to admit, your curves are pretty attractive." Once more, the three laughed heartily.

"Don't you dare tickle me! I am very ticklish," she retorted.

"I know, that's my secret weapon," he teased. "Come here; I want to hold you forever!" Again, the embraced long and passionately.

She whispered in his ear, "I so hoped that you would come for me. I kept waiting and waiting, worried that you had gotten shot along the way."

"I very nearly did get shot today. It's crazy out there in the streets. Has the whole country gone nuts?" he asked.

"Ania was precisely correct. It has gone rather insane," Kali pointed out. "Ania had this predicted back last November, long before that Summer Council lit the spark. I don't know how she does it, but she sure can predict these things. One amazing woman."

"Say, Kali, can you sort of run things for me for a while? I want to take Luigi on a tour of the palace and show him my bedroom and things."

"Sure, Alekto. Go have some fun," Kali replied, wishing that Ilenakova was here. She missed having a good romp with her, especially at night.

Later that day, a dispatch rider from the Empress arrived announcing that the Fall Council would be delayed two weeks due to the current conflicts, which she hoped would be ended soon.

On March 15, General Kreon Demon finally rode into Thal, bringing with him some thirty legions of cavalry. They encamped on the outskirts of the city, while he rode on in to meet with Diabolos, as he had been ordered to by Jonas Sokrates of Kefall. Already, he had passed through cities where gunfights had broken out. Carefully, he had his men completely bypass the conflicts. His mission was to get this force to Thal by March 15, which he did.

"Ah, General Kreon at last. You've come none too soon. The hurricane is rapidly approaching. As you can see, our Queen Frona has maintained control of our city and has driven the Empress' legions far out of the area."

The two men shook hands. "Yes, we ran into fighting in other cities along the way, but I thought it was strangely quiet here in Thal. This must be a powerful queen to have so brought order so quickly," the general explained.

Diabolos replied, "Yes, she is that and more. As Jonas has probably told you, the last remaining barrier to your ascension to the throne of Demokritos is to marry so that you have an Empress."

"Yes, I am ready to meet that obligation. I just hope that she is not a pig." Both men chuckled.

"No, that she is not. She is many things, but not that. We have chosen her with extreme care. If you give her a chance, you will find her more than capable, general. Would you like to meet her now? Or would you rather bathe and freshen up first?" He chose the latter. That afternoon, Diabolos and General Kreon entered the palace in Thal.

As the Doorman opened the door to the throne room, the Announcer called out clearly, "Diabolos Amynta and General Kreon Demon."

Queen Frona looked up from the stacks of reports to see a handsome young man, not over thirty, very well built, good, solid muscles, and tall. He saw a petit curly brown haired woman who had turned forty; she still looked fair, but he could sense an air of authority, of command, about her. Diabolos introduced the two and left them alone to get acquainted.

"I am very much impressed with the order you have maintained around Thal. We've passed through many cities, and I'm afraid that lawlessness is rampant there, Queen Frona," he began to chat with her. He was uneasy being around a Holy Woman, though, and it showed.

I could do a whole lot worse, she thought. He is handsome and virile. If he respects me and is kind to me, I need not ask more of him. "Thank you, General. I do not stand for lawlessness. When it broke out here in Thal, I put an end to it in two days' time. How was your journey here?"

"Long and tiring. I know of your stands against the Empress and her proclamations. I find that most admirable. However, may I ask a question of you? You are one of their Holy Women, yet you have strongly opposed those proclamations that benefit your Church. I don't understand."

"Religion is a personal thing. I have come to discover that the Church I once belonged to is a fraud. While I regret the blind sacrifice that I made in my youth, it cannot be undone. Yet, I may convince others of such folly, and I may help others survive better. That's why I've taken on so many others who were deceived by the Elders of Dorota. I can see that you are not comfortable around me. I can understand that."

"Well, yes, I've never been around a Holy Woman before."

"Please, don't call me that. I hate it. I am far from holy. I am simply armless and always will be so. Yet, I will not be a bother to you as long as I have my various helpers to attend to those things I cannot perform."

"Agreed. Armless it will be. We will need to be visible together in public often. I must be seen and being, well you know, familiar with your unique needs. Is this possible?" he asked.

"Of course. As long as you are willing to learn what and how, I am willing to teach. I believe that with minimal effort on each of our parts, we can make this work to both of our advantages. I am no longer able to bear children, so you need not worry about that. If you desire children, I am sure that we can find an alternative way to make that happen."

"Excellent, Frona. What is it that you would have of me?"

"Respect and kindness," she replied honestly and forthrightly.

He grinned, "My respect you already have. Your fame precedes you. As for kindness, that I give freely, but I will need a whole lot of coaching on dealing with your unique needs."

"Thank you. That will be perfect. Just so that we both understand each other better right from the start, I have been told that you prefer to bed other men. Is this so? It is not a problem for me."

He flushed. She was forthright! "Yes, though I do not want such widely known, if you please. I will be discrete about it, and I will do as I can in your bed."

"More than acceptable, general. I suppose that we ought to get Diabolos and see what he has planned next for us. If you will put your arm around my waist, we shall go get him." He did so.

On March 16, they were married in a simple ceremony, attended only by her older married children.

The next day, Diabolos met with them privately. "Join your armies together and march towards Kefall, bring order as you go along. The Fall Council has been pushed back to the third week of April, so you have plenty of time to get there. For now, general, you are the King of Thallyus. However, that will be very short lived. Nothing should stand in your way with the combined armies at your command."

Now both Frona and Kreon began to see the overall plan. His long march back to Kefall would be restoring order along the way, and he would be able to march into Kefall with a large enough force to take over control of the palace and the throne, coup by force of arms, he concluded. He was only partially right.

Not yet, Bethany. The worst has yet to happen, Ania sent. *I know it is chaos in the streets, but here, Ariadne's soldiers are slowly putting an end to it. I predict that it will happen during the Fall Council, which has* wisely been postponed until the third week in April. *Trust me on this call, Bethany.*

Okay. I will. We are doing well here. Athena has gotten much of the uprising squelched and her forces have fanned out to other cities and towns now.

Ania stated, *Ariadne says that we need to leave for Kefall on the seventh in order to make the arrival on the fourteenth, the night before it begins. I guarantee you that she will not easily be able to return here. I'm advising her to bring along anything she wants to take with her when she becomes free of the throne. She will be going to Velona with Dario. You should have Athena and Alekto bring along anything that they want to keep as well. I don't believe that they will find it easy to return when it breaks loose. How soon will you be leaving Theolopolis?*

I sent, *Because of all the strife, she needs to allow two weeks travel time. She wisely insists on following your advice and is bringing along ten legions for protection. She doesn't want a repeat of last time. Neither does Dita or me! That was horrid. With so many men, travel will be slower. Alekto and Luigi have to leave the last week in March to get there on time. Same thing with Frona; those two have the furthest to travel. I believe that all the queens will travel heavily guarded this time.*

Ania added, *Good. Make sure Alekto brings everything she wants with her. I'm sure that it will be very difficult to get her back to Naxos quickly. I will be doing my best to make things relatively calm and safe here in Thrace by the time of the Fall Council in Kefall. Still, I expect all heck to break lose at that time. Probably that is when the Noble Houses will dethrone all the queens and install a new set of kings and queens, making the Fall Council a lame session whose decisions will be invalid. That's what I would do and, so far, they are following just what I had predicted they would do. This whole country has dropped from an angry tone to one of covert hostility under the current leadership, except for the queens. With all this chaos, it has dropped even lower into the fear zone. Expect that out of this will rise the new Emperor who will seize nearly total control and will be cheered on by the afraid populace. We'll have to deal with that later on, though.*

I replied, *Okay. It makes sense, but I don't see this new Emperor rising. I'll take your word for it; you've not been wrong yet. Let me know if you need anything. By the way, keep an eye out for Princess Maren of Annelise. She is due to come to the Fall Council and bring us all a new fall wardrobe. For heaven's sake, convince her to stay in Patri or just return home until this is ended. If she is harmed, Annelise will certainly raise even more problems.*

Ania declared, *Okay, you are very right on that point. I will see that she does. Ariadne says that she usually arrives a day ahead of time. Based on that and the travel time from Patri, I can determine when she will be arriving. However, she probably doesn't know that it's been postponed two weeks. Yikes, I'd better get hopping on this one right now!*

I broke the connection and set about making sure that Athena and Alekto knew what to expect and to bring all that they wanted to keep along with them to the council in Kefall. Andreas was a big help to Athena. He'd already had to deal with settling his parent's estate and had sound ideas of what she ought to consider doing before she left.

Cardinal Drakon read the reports coming in from his priests in all the kingdoms. What madness is going on, he wondered. Here in Kefall, all was totally calm and quiet as it always was. Apparently, elsewhere there were riots and soldiers shooting soldiers and soldiers shooting civilians. Even one of his priests was shot while trying to bring calm to a near riot in the port city of Preveza, Alia. Once more, he shuffled the large stack of reports and began re-reading them, hoping to find some clue as to what this was all about. Surely not the voting process — that was a simple matter of yes or no.

True, the number of women showing up for their Holy Ceremonies had dropped off to a mere trickle, but that was because travel was no longer safe, if the reports were true. No matter, soon order would be restored. He had faith in his queens, his Holy Women. They would not stand for such lawlessness.

At last, he gave up; the reports made no sense to him at all. He had the urge to go chat with the Empress, but quickly gave up that idea. It would be a big mistake for him to show her any sign of weakness! He had to be strong for her sake. He decided to do nothing, and let it all blow over. He carefully removed his journal from its hiding place and began to write this all down. Perhaps one day in the future, this would all be understood. Yes, time was the answer he needed.

"Well, I'm all packed, Bethany. Andreas was a huge help! I'm bringing along mostly my wardrobe and a few keepsakes. We've already transferred all my funds to the Banca del Dio in Patri."

"Yes, she certainly has a lot of clothes," Andreas teased her. "We have them on one wagon. When we get to Kefall, the wagon will go on to Patri and be loaded onto your caravel. All we need to do is make sure that we get there too!"

"Yes, that will be the challenge, Andreas. We also absolutely must bring along as many of the Special Helpers as we can. They are really princesses in their own country. Kassandra had no right to steal them from their nation. I've given my word that I'll take as many as possible back to their home," I replied.

"Do you have a plan on how we do all that yet?" he asked.

"Nope. We can't really do anything until the actual time is at hand and we know what the real circumstances will be. If we are really lucky, we can all climb into a carriage and ride to Patri," I answered. I was hoping and praying that it would be this easy, but if Ania were to be believed, it might be far wilder.

Already, Queen Alekto, Kali, and Luigi were on their way from Naxos. She had five legions of cavalry accompanying her, though few carried guns. She'd left the majority of the few guns available with the remainder of her army, which was still bringing order in Arolas. Like Athena, she had packed everything and was more than ready to sail to Velona with Luigi.

Just then, Kali made contact with me. *Bethany! Tell Dianna that they are working as she said they would. Our large group just passed through a minor skirmish area, where her forces were battling a legion of the Empress. A stray bullet came flying into her carriage and would have struck her in her shoulder. It was deflected, and she only has a small red mark to show where the bullet struck her. She's very spooked at this point, though Luigi is calming her down. How do I tell them how I stopped the bullet?*

Damn! Well, you can't tell them the truth about the Grey Creature's blaster. I don't know, maybe that spiritual beings can do many unusual things and that you are not perfect, which is why she has the bruise.

Okay, sounds plausible. More later.

"Gang, Alekto was hit by a stray bullet, but Kali prevented any injury. Damn, it will be dangerous just riding to Kefall!" I explained what happened to the others. Dita, Ilenakova, and Dianna understood fully. Dianna had set the four blasters to wide shield protecting an area of around ten feet from projectile type impacts. I had to use the pseudo explanation that I had suggested Kali use. This certainly put a damper on our excitement about leaving for Kefall.

Queen Athena began her last minute double checking, making sure that everything was set to go when nobleman Linos came to see her one last time. As usual, Athena kept Dita and me with her during this private meeting. "I came to see you off, Queen Athena. The hurricane will probably strike while you are at the Fall Council meeting. I was so hoping that it would have been sooner, while you were still here so that I could see that you were protected. Alas, it has not. Still, I have made arrangements for you in Kefall. When the time comes, nobleman Jonas Sokrates will send you word. I believe that he will be doing much the same for the other queens. Depend upon him to get you to a place of safety."

"Thank you, Linos. I will do all that I can to help our kingdom to the very last minute. We have the voting results with us, which will show our kingdom's nullification of some of her proclamations. I just don't see how they allowed some to pass."

"I know you will, Queen Athena. Truly, it is one big mess that we are in now. We must keep that ten percent tithe from happening; that is the worst one. Why they went for this Holy Woman proclamation, I surely do not know. I've heard that the Empress' legions have been beaten back nearly to the borders of Thrace. Be careful as you get to our border there. Please take no chances."

"We won't. I am leaving a qualified staff to help working on getting things back to normal here in Theos, but I don't understand why there is still some rioting and looting still going on in isolated areas," she replied.

"All this conflict between the two armed forces has spilled over among our people. There has long been a hidden antagonism between those favoring the Emperor and those favoring the Church of Jehosanity and still a third group that favors kingdom independence. I am afraid that all over Demokritos, these long suppressed antagonisms are now boiling over into the streets. The two warring armies have provided the catalyst. If the Empress' soldiers can shoot our civilians in the street, our people feel now is the time to strike back. Only they are striking out against those with whom they have long harbored grudges, not just with these murderous soldiers of Kassandra. Still, our kingdom's forces are working to restore order. I am sure that once the hurricane blows over, they will get everyone calmed down, and order restored. I had hoped that the winds would have come while you were yet here. Do stay alert for any word from Jonas."

"Thank you for everything, Linos. The advisors that I am leaving have all the data that the new rulers will need right away," she remembered to tell him.

"It is I who should be thanking you, Queen Athena. I best allow you to leave. I see that the others are getting impatient. Again, thank you. God be with you." He bowed and left.

"You'd think that with all this conflict the winds are already here," Athena exclaimed. "Whatever else can happen?"

I shrugged my shoulders. Probably Ania would have a very good guess, but she was in Axos. In a few weeks, we would be together, and very likely, she could give us a better appraisal. Dressed in our fancy dresses, we slowly moved down the halls to the main palace doors for the last time. I knew that we would not be coming back here again. Athena was very ready to leave this all behind her.

Five legions of Theos cavalry were to accompany us to Kefall, before most would be returning. However, Queen Athena did give the commanders permission to use some of the soldiers to help put down any trouble we might encounter along the way. These men were checking over their large packs strapped behind their saddles. Only one in five carried a gun, however. These men would have to endure field conditions for the next couple of weeks. There were not sufficient inns to house five hundred soldiers plus our large group. However, at least fifty of them would be on guard duty, watching over us as we slept at the various inns along the way.

By now, Ilenakova and Dianna had gotten used to wearing these elegant, but constricting, dresses from Annelise. In fact, Dianna was excited about having Ania see how she looked, and she dreamed about how Ania would look in hers. As we waited our turn to be lifted into our carriage, Dianna checked her blaster and Ilenakova's to make sure that they were fully charged. They were, and I felt more relaxed about all the gunfire that could still occasionally be heard. Now began another boring fourteen day carriage ride, the last one, I hoped.

We encountered some occasional skirmishes between rival groups in some of the smaller towns of Theos, but nothing like the larger battles. It certainly appeared as if the conflict was subsiding. Athena certainly hoped this was so. On our tenth day, we approached the border with Thrace and ran into trouble. Ahead of us were a hundred legions of the Empress' forces, on foot marching back to their base in Kefall. Of course, they were blocking the road, and they were well armed, unlike Athena's forces.

All four of us sensed danger was at hand. Ever since the Guardian had helped us unlock that spiritual skill, we intuitively knew when danger was near. The only times it had failed us was when we were asleep and knocked out by a sleeping gas of some kind. Now we were really in the hands of Athena's commanders, there was little we could do back here in the long column. Ilenakova stuck her neck out of the carriage to have a look and reported that respective field commanders were now meeting way up ahead of us. Still, we four continued to sense danger.

"If they won't let us pass, then what?" asked Athena. "What if they part allowing us to move past them and then they open fire on us as we pass them?"

"I'm sure your commanders are thinking of this, dear," Andreas attempted to calm her. "They won't make any agreements that will sacrifice your safety, I'm sure of that."

"What's taking them so long," Athena fidgeted. It seemed like we were just sitting here for hours now. At last, one of her commanders came back to report.

"They are going to issue orders to allow us to pass. We believe that it is safe to do so, Your Majesty. Sorry for the delay. Once we get past this barrier, I will send riders on ahead to make arrangements at another inn. This is costing us a half day delay."

Before long, we finally began moving once more and soon found ourselves looking at the faces of hundreds of marching soldiers as we very slowly moved past them. For an hour, we held our breaths that no one would get trigger-happy. No one was more relieved than Athena was, when finally open countryside appeared out the windows once more.

It was early fall and the view of the rolling grasslands, thin forests, and wild flowers was breathtaking, fall colors appeared everywhere. Soon, we all forgot about having been delayed for a half of a day. Only later on, did I finally realize that this delay had been arranged! Now the scenery changed dramatically, as we crested the rim of the Lonki Basin. Down we began descending into the kingdom of Thrace. Along here was where Dita and I had been abducted, and we were both just a little edgy as we passed by where we had been kidnaped. Our danger senses were quiet, and I felt relieved to see this area pass by us.

At dusk, we rolled into the first significant town across the border into Thrace, or the last town before the rim and the kingdom of Theos, take your pick. Suddenly, Dita and I became very alert! "Isn't this the town where we were taken to?" she asked, slightly nervously. I agreed and our mood turned somber, especially when the carriages pulled up before an inn, and we realized that we would be spending the night here.

A few minutes later, we had been lifted down and were escorted inside. As per the official arrangements, the inn was closed to all business except ours. The staff was pleased to see us and quickly began serving dinner for everyone. As usual, our Special Helpers handled feeding of us three, while Ilenakova kept a sharp eye out for trouble. None came, and later, Dianna took over while she ate hurriedly.

The room accommodations were somewhat cruder than the usual inns at which we stayed on our previous trips. Only two could fit in each small room. Andreas insisted that he sleep with Athena. "After all, we are soon going to be married, and I do need to learn how to care for my beautiful wife and her needs." We chuckled; they wanted some private time for passionate kissing, that was obvious.

Dita and I took the next room, and Ilenakova and Dianna the one next to ours. Other servants and staff had rooms further down the long dark hall. Athena's commander told her that, at all times, ten guards would be on duty watching various locations around the inn. He took her security seriously. Ilenakova took ours even more seriously. She brought part of their bedding into our room. Our Special Helpers had already finished undressing us, and now Dianna was brushing out our hair, when Ilenakova plopped the bedding down on the floor near our bed.

She explained, "One of us will be sleeping beside you all night. Dianna and I will take turns. One blaster will be protecting you three at all times, while one will be with whichever one of us is on guard duty. I will take the first watch, Dianna. I'll wake you when it's your turn."

"Thanks gang. Our sense of emanate danger doesn't work if we are asleep," I pointed out. Right now, I felt calm. Although we all wore our corsets, we had on our nightgowns. Before long, Dianna dosed the light, and we lay down to sleep. My body still felt like it was rolling along in the carriage, and I soon fell into a deep, relaxing sleep.

Outside our door, Ilenakova stood like a statue, her legs spread apart. She had tucked the blaster between her breasts out of sight. Her nightgown had no pockets, unfortunately. She did look a bit strange, though. She'd strapped her twin swords around her waist and fastened two daggers to each lower leg. She felt armed now. From time to time, one of the guards would walk the hall past her and nod, though they often gave her some stares, as they approached and covertly glanced back as they passed her.

Around midnight, she began to sense that danger was near at hand. All was very quiet, but she became instantly alert, a cat sensing the as yet unseen presence of a mouse. Silently, she drew one sword and then the other. She looked up and down the long dark hall but saw no one. She waited ready to pounce at the first sign of trouble, which she knew was close at hand. Nothing.

How long she stood there, she didn't reckon. Suddenly she detected motion out of the corner of her eye. She whirled and saw three masked men creeping around the far bend of the hallway at the other end of the hall from where she was standing. They stopped and stared at her, she, they. Then, the masked men quickly moved back around the corner. Ilenakova had to make a decision. Should she go after them and stop them? That would mean leaving her post and leave her three sleeping friends alone. No, she had to hold her position for now, she decided.

A bit later, one of the men reappeared suddenly, firing a heavy crossbow at her. She dodged and the quarrel missed her by inches, though it would have been deflected by the blaster had she not. She didn't depend on Dianna's mechanical contraptions, even if the Grey Creatures made them. The man had disappeared. Still, she refused to go after them. She debated whether to sound the alarm.

Just as she was about to start yelling for the other guards, another man appeared and threw a round object down the hall at her. Her inner danger sense screamed in her mind. At the last instant, she realized that this was a gas grenade, a glass ball containing a knock out gas. When it hit the floor, she would quickly be overcome. She reacted with a wild run down the hall after the men, holding her breath to avoid the fumes, which now rose from the remains of the ball after it smashed nearby where she had been standing. She rounded the bend cautiously and saw the three masked men on the stairs leading down to the main floor and the large dining area. Twang! Another quarrel just missed her. Inside, she could not launch a fireball or a lightning bolt; she felt a bit annoyed. Where were the guards anyway? Twang! Another came her way, she swung her sword and deflected it. If she could just get closer, she could easily dispatch them. She resisted the urge to chase them and was about to return to her post when a glass globe landed two steps below her, shattering and releasing its gas. She could not avoid a partial exposure this time. It had come from behind her. She whirled and saw a fourth man standing there, ready to toss another one at her. She felt herself losing consciousness, though she fought hard against it. She climbed the two steps and rounded the corner once more into the long, dark hall. Now she saw five more men, not the one. Her body slumped to the ground as her hands dropped their swords. Damn! Was her last thought before succumbing to the sleep gas.

Khristos smiled at his handy work, putting the next glass globe back into his bag very carefully. He motioned to the four men and then signaled the three below. Outside our door, Khristos now stood with two glass globes, one in each hand. He nodded and another slowly and quietly opened the door. He tossed the two spheres inside and heard them shatter on the floor, waking Dianna. "Is it my turn, Ilenak. . ." Khristos, holding his breath, peered inside, holding a lantern, which focused its light only in the forward direction. Dianna had fallen back down onto her bedding.

Khristos held up his hand and put up three fingers, then two, then one and brought his arm down sharply. His men began their well-rehearsed actions. Indeed, for a whole week, Khristos had had these four men and doctor practice their separate actions over and over and over until they could do them in their sleep. "Five minutes is all you have." This he constantly drilled into their minds. The five each had separate actions to perform in the right sequence, rapidly, and without any mistakes or fumbles. Timing was everything. He knew well that these Daughters of Lucifer would be heavily guarded this time. Five hundred cavalry was most significant if the alarm was sounded. They would be unable to escape on horseback. Instead, his plan called for abducting ten of the soldiers, knocking them out, and having his men don their uniforms, becoming a set of ten guards on duty, undetectable. Thus far, it had worked perfectly.

Ten guards lay bound and gagged in the blacksmith shop, where they had already melted the lead that they needed for the final step of the operation. Khristos stood outside the door, watching the hall and tracking the time. Inside, the doctor went first to one woman, holding a rag over her mouth and face, while counting to twenty. Then, he moved the rag over to the other woman and repeated it. With the women now unconscious, he retrieved his scalpel from his bag, sterilized the skin, and made his two precise cuts, amused that he had a precise scar line to follow. Once the first cut was done, he forced the clay disk into the opening, cut the lower lip cleanly, and inserted the large disk. Satisfied they fit properly, he moved on to the next woman, while the four men began working on the one he'd finished.

These four worked together, just as they had been trained, each one doing a precise action in sequence and with the right assistance of the others. Head lifted, metal case placed around the head, shut, leather eye patches in place, screws adjusted properly holding the eye patches firmly in place, mouth open, ring in, bolts fastened. Like precision clock makers, these four worked. By the time the doctor had finished and turned to leave, they had the first woman finished, adjusting the bolts that secured the center of the disks to the frame. They moved to the other woman. A fifth man now entered carrying a ladle of molten metal. He knew his job as well, and just a minute later, he had the right amount of molten metal placed at all the intended locations. He paused for a minute, while the four finally finished the second woman. Then, he repeated his actions on her metal frame. At last, he rose and left the ladle on the floor out of the way as he left.

Khristos, still holding the door open and tracking the time, nodded as the last man left. He looked inside and grinned, a perfect job indeed! Five minutes on the dot! Incredible. He blew out their lantern and closed the door quietly. Already his men had left, going back down the other stairs from where Ilenakova lay. Khristos turned and saw her.

Ilenakova continued to fight the effects of the sleeping gas. She knew that she had only gotten a small whiff of it, and she should be able to fight it off. She never gave up and succumbed to its effects. At last, she opened her eyes and saw the men going in and out of their room. She pushed up and got to a sitting position. With effort, she picked up one sword and then struggled mightily to get to her feet. She was not going to let anything bad happen to her dear friends! She saw the men leaving and her heart sank! Had they already done their dirty assassinations? Were Bethany and Dita already dead? If so, it was all her fault! One man remained, looking inside. He was the one who had gassed her. She could not run to catch him, yet she intended to stop him with every fiber of her being. Only one thing she could do. She leaned back and hurled her sword at him.

Khristos turned and saw Ilenakova barely able to stand, her arm following through on a throw. He saw the flash of rotating steel coming at him. His last sight was that of the tip of the blade mere inches from his forehead. Then came pain — pain beyond anything he had ever inflicted upon his body, pain he could not endure. Then darkness. His body slumped to the ground.

Staggering and using the wall for support, Ilenakova headed to our room. She opened our door and peered inside, fearing the worst, three slit throats. What she saw shocked her, and she gasped, nearly falling down. What to do now? Andreas. She struggled over the dead assassin's body and went to their door and knocked loudly, repeatedly, until at last, a sleepy Andreas opened the door.

"Oh my god! What happened?" he was suddenly awake.

"Help! They got to Bethany and Dita. Help! I'm gassed." She slumped to the floor and drifted in and out of consciousness once more, knowing that Andreas would take charge.

I felt like I was having a bad dream. Drug masses swirled around my mind. Voices, I heard shocked and scared voices, even weeping cries. What's happening?

Andreas lit several lanterns in our room and quickly checked on Dianna, who was unconscious, but otherwise unharmed. He looked at Dita and me and decided that our lives were not in imminent danger. He then began waking up the other staff, sending some off to fetch the guard commanders. One by one, our friends came into our room to check on us and reacted in many ways; all were shocked, and many wept.

Someone poured hot tea into Ilenakova, and she finally roused, jumping up, ready for action. Seeing three commanders standing by her, she relaxed. A dozen guards lined the hall. Staff and helpers were looking from their doors, all listening to what was going on, for some clues as to what had happened.

"They were guards, ten of them. I killed their leader," Ilenakova began. They insisted that she start at the beginning, which she then did, relating what had happened.

When she finished, one commander, who was examining Khristos, commented, "Say, this isn't one of our men. Look the uniform doesn't even fit him. He's got a bag of gas grenades, we don't ever carry those." The alarm was sounded, and the five hundred cavalrymen were quickly reviewed. Ten men were missing. Now it became clear to all. These assassins had taken out ten guards, dressed in their uniforms, and replaced the ten on duty. Thus, they had a free hand to do their dastardly work.

"How did you manage to drive your sword into his forehead?" one commander asked.

"I was down there just at the corner and I threw it at him. I was too weak to close or run after him. I had one chance, and I took it," she replied.

"My god, woman! That is an incredible throw! I don't know of anyone in my command that could throw a sword a hundred feet like a throwing dagger and hit the bull's-eye!"

"Like I said, I only had that one chance. I dare not miss. Who is he anyway?"

"I recognize him!" Athena said, her voice wavering. "That's Cardinal Drakon's Prelate Khristos!"

"Well, it looks like I got me an assassin after all," Ilenakova commented, "small victory for the devastating failure to protect Dita and Bethany. Have you seen what they've done to them? Can't we try to get that thing off them?"

Andreas said sadly and softly, "Not easily. They poured molten metal into the locks and over the threads of the screws. I tried; none will budge the slightest. It's just awful!"

"What do we do now?" Athena sobbed; she had been crying and still couldn't stop. She felt once more completely and utterly helpless; she had no idea how to help us.

"We've got to get Dianna awake," Ilenakova realized and spoke aloud. "She's a healer and an engineer. She will find a way to free them." She realized that she was probably the only one who was thinking clearly right now. "Clean up the glass shards, please. I'm going to see what I can do for Dianna. We need her awake now."

Stepping carefully to avoid the glass, she knelt down beside the unconscious woman. She concentrated and finally made contact. *Sandra! Sandra! Wake up! I need help right now. Please wake up!*

Ilenakova? I'm up. What's gone wrong?

We've been attacked. I failed utterly to protect them. They are now encased in some weird head contraptions, with rings forcing their mouths open; their lip plates are back in and fastened to the contraption; leather patches are over their eyes so they can't see. I don't think their eyes have been cutout. They and Dianna have been put to sleep somehow. I need to get Dianna awake so she can figure out how we can free them. How do I wake her?

Do you know how they were put to sleep?

No.

Do you see anything like a rag lying around? Something that they may have placed over their noses?

Well, yes, I got a rag here.

Smell it; tell me what it smells like.

She did her best to describe it to Sandra. *Okay. I think I know what was used. You need to get some very strong, black tea into her system. Careful that she doesn't choke on it. Let me know when she's awake.*

An hour later, coughing and spitting, a confused, dizzy Dianna finally woke up. Her head was spinning in and out of blackish drug masses. "What's happened? My head feels like a carriage ran over it."

"Dianna! We've been attacked again. I failed utterly. Come on. I need you to help Bethany and Dita. Up you come," Ilenakova picked her up and sat her on the edge of the bed.

"Oh my god!" Dianna suddenly came sharply into the present time, as she stared at her two unconscious friends.

Andreas said, "They used molten metal to make sure it cannot be undone. We found the ladle with more of it in it, but it's all hardened now. We must free them, but how?"

"Light. I need more light," she called out. Athena's staff was more than willing to comply and soon ten lanterns illuminated the room. "Damn! Damn! Damn!" she exclaimed as she examined every lock and screw thread on each of us.

"Can you free them?" Ilenakova asked quietly, very much afraid of her answer.

"Dunno, have you got a knife or dagger that you don't mind getting all nicked up?" Dianna asked. She handed her one from her leg sheath. Dianna began scratching at the hardened metal, but made almost no indentation in it. She then began scratching the steel framework.

"Damn! Damn! Damn! This was made to stay on their heads permanently! I can't believe that they use hardened iron, Ilenakova! It's as hard as your dagger! It'll take forever to cut through the metal frame. I might be able somehow to undo these screws, maybe given a lot of time. 'Course, I'm going to have to do that first. There is a sequence by which these were fastened together, and I will have to do that sequence in reverse before I can even try to get the head harness off them. Damn! Damn! Damn!"

"But can you do it?" Andreas asked.

"Well, given my complete workshop back home and a whole lot of time, yes. I can get them off of them. Anything can be done, if you have the right tools, time, and patience. In this circumstance, I lack the proper tools, a proper place to work, or time. We are in the middle of nowhere, and we have to get to the Fall Council. We just cannot stop and stay here for a month or however long it takes me. I don't even know it they have proper tools in this small town. I can probably find them in Kefall."

Sandra sent, *Okay, Dianna. Make doubly sure that their lips do not get infected. That is your number one concern for the next week. Keep them clean and as sterile as possible. If they get infected, we could lose both of them. Let them sleep off the drug. Be with them when they wake up, probably in the morning sometime. Keep them calm. Your second challenge will be to keep them properly nourished. Wake me anytime if there is even the slightest possibility of an infection starting. Keep a sharp eye out for blood poisoning and monitor their temperature at least six times a day. If it goes up, there well could be an infection starting up. That is our biggest fear, because with that head contraption, we can't get to the areas to treat it.*

The rest of the night, Dianna sat up with us. Pots of boiling water were periodically brought up. She sterilized some cloths and bathed our lips, removing the blood and keeping them clean with the water. By morning the bleeding had ceased, which she thought was a good sign.

Around ten the next morning, I awoke. I felt groggy and tried to open my eyes. I found that my eyelids wouldn't budge. My lips ached and felt funny, just like they had when they had sliced my lips and put those awful lip plates in them again. My mouth was wide open. I tried to close it, but my jaws wouldn't move. I felt strange, hard objects around my head and face. I screamed for help. I heard Dita scream even louder.

"I'm here, Bethany. It's Dianna. The assassins got you good this time. I'll help you sit up," the quite voice of Dianna reassured me, and although I could just barely hear her, I calmed down. "Okay, back out of your head and take a look at this mess you and Dita are in." I did as she asked and looked at what I was only feeling.

Oh my God! I sent her.

Damn! Damn! Damn! This is the very last straw! Dita sent, angrier that I had ever known her to be.

Ilenakova was crying, and she began to tell us how she had failed to protect us. After hearing all the details, both Dita and I convinced her that she had done an exemplary job of it. Dita and she then held a private chat. I was distinctly left out of it.

Dianna explained what Sandra had ordered her to do first. "We've got to figure out how to feed you nourishing food. It's going to have to be pretty well liquefied though. Let's get started, shall we?"

Fed by spoonful became the only way we could eat or drink. Even that was a struggle; just try swallowing with your mouth wide open sometime. Had we been stuck inside our heads, life would have been nearly impossible, blind and barely able to hear. Instead, both Dita and I remained outside our bodies, perceiving with our native spiritual perceptions, which were now far better than they ever had been since my little girl had ran out some traumas of mine several years back. At least this way, we could see well enough to move around and were not totally invalids. Since Dianna made no real attempts to free us, I had a sinking feeling that we would be trapped like this for some days. I made Dita promise to put her full attention on getting enough to eat and drink. We had to keep our strength up.

Fed and dressed, we were carried by strong arms out to the waiting carriage. As we began rolling once more, Athena said, "We are now almost a day behind schedule. I've asked them to go through the night tonight to make up the time. We'll stop for dinner, though. This is just about the worst thing I've ever seen — short of murder, that is. At least you are alive, and Dianna says that in time and with the right tools, she can get you both free. That's something; just be hopeful. I'll tell you what I am seeing as we go along. That'll help pass the time." I hadn't the heart to tell her that I could see fairly well, now that I took up a new position. I took the top of my head as my orientation point from which to view. Was I miserable? That's an understatement. I kept wishing their damn hurricane would hurry up and end all this.

Chapter 46 Fall Council, 752

We were the last to arrive in Kefall and the Empress' palace. Of course, Ania and Kali were there waiting for us. "Well, Bethany, I see that you have once again gotten yourself into a pickle barrel, even with our help," Kali teased me. My mouth forced wide open and with the disks holding my lips immobile, I couldn't even grin or retort back.

"Seriously, the queens are all here except Frona," Athena got us back on track. "I've sent my things on to Patri. So have Alekto and Ariadne. At least, we don't have to worry about that. I'm going to have someone right here with you, Bethany, and Dita twenty-four-seven. I know that you won't want to try to sit with us in the throne room, but Ania, Kali, Ilenakova, and Dianna have volunteered to take your places."

I sent to Ania, *I'll be there with you; my body is best left here. How about enlightening us on the supposed hurricane that's coming. I'm very much past wanting it to come.*

"Okay, everyone, Bethany has asked me to outline what I think is going to happen. This way you get to see how accurate my prediction is. First, I ought to give you the foundation upon what much of this depends. Demokritos, as a whole, used to be in anger. That was back in the days of Emperor Deimos and Empress Maren Elizabet, when he led that ill-fated attack on Zargarb. For some time now, the country has slipped even lower than such overt hostilities. During your reigns, the country has been operating in a covertly hostile manner, back stabbing and such. A hair below that is fear, which has been being demonstrated all over the country this past month — given all the fighting, riots, and shootings. People are afraid and lashing out right and left."

"People are now frightened and will be taking any opportunity to seize on a leader that offers some security. He will be more like a fascist dictator than an Emperor. He has yet to arise, that we know of, though I am sure that somewhere in Demokritos right at this very moment, he is already known to some. I predict that he will come from some distant portion of the country, sweeping like a tidal wave over the land to Kefall, where he will take the throne from Empress Kassandra by force of arms."

"But we have Noble Houses who pick the Emperor," Athena protested.

"You *had* Noble Houses, Athena. While I suspect that they have tried to have some choice in the next Emperor, I am afraid that it is now completely out of their hands, though they do not yet realize this. This palace is going to become besieged soon. While that is happening, this city is going to react the way your kingdom's cities have already reacted. Until now, they have been insulated from the strife and riots, primarily because it is the city of the Emperor and Empress. That will change when he sweeps in from the outside sometime within the next few days, I predict."

"That also means that the promises the nobles have given you — to get you all to safety when it comes, are pretty much wishful thinking. During the mad rush, they will be as powerless as everyone else will be. We ought to begin to work out our own way out of here."

Athena looked crushed, as did some others, "If the city is in complete chaos and the palace is being attacked, how can we possibly get out? Shouldn't we leave right now?"

Barnabas, tell them about the secret exit in the Emperor's throne room, I sent. He looked quite startled to hear me in his head.

"Excuse me, my ladies," he quietly interrupted them. "Bethany has asked me to tell you all that there is a secret exit in the wall in the unused Emperor's throne room. I have used it on occasion. We can escape that way."

"Ah, excellent. We have a way out. Now we need to work out transportation from there, which may prove tricky," Ania continued. "The main thing that still has me worried is once Kassandra discovers that her palace is besieged, it is highly likely that she will hold you queens as hostages to bargain with for her freedom. We must act before she tries that." Ania continued her explanation. She ended by asking each queen to compile a list of personnel of theirs who needed to be evacuated when the time came. She also needed to know who was to come with us back to Velona and who was to stay here in Demokritos.

I decided to work on the transportation. *Barnabas, don't the carriages sometimes need preventative maintenance?*

Yes, axles need greasing, leather works done, any number of things. Why?

Can you slowly begin to move as many carriages out of the palace under the guise of getting their maintenance done before the return trips?

I suppose so. Why?

We need to take them to some secure location. We need a place where they won't be seen by the average person and where we can get to them when we need them.

He pointed out, *That place of concealment might not be near where the exit of the tunnel is at,* but agreed to see what he could do. He and Ilenakova left us, as we continued to discuss our situation here in Queen Athena's private quarters.

Dianna suggested that she needed to care for us, and she and our Special Helpers moved us to our old room here. They had their arms around our waists and led our blind bodies along the hall and into our room. The two watched as Dianna again carefully examined our lips for signs of infection. She found none, thank goodness. I was starving and quite glad that she was again attempting to get some food in our systems. What an awful mess this was rapidly becoming. Our two helpers watched closely how Dianna fed us and wrote her a note saying that they understood how it was to be done now. She allowed them to take over while she supervised. I sensed that she was relieved that she was having some help with us. It seemed forever before I was finally full, after which, our helpers prepared us for bed.

Having little else to do, I began thinking ahead. I had promised these Utu women that I would somehow return them to their homeland. Yet, they had been kidnaped, brought here, and made to serve us for several years now. They ought to be at the very least compensated, but what did they consider valuable, other than returning to their home in the Southlands?

I reached out and made telepathic contact with Iua and asked her, *In your homeland, the Utu Nation, what do you consider to be really valuable?*

Cattle. She gave me a lengthy description of their life there. Both a man and a woman's wealth were measured in how many cattle they owned. I knew that Athena had been paying them reasonable wages, but I also knew that these women had never left the palace to buy anything with the funds. An idea struck me, and I resolved to see it through somehow. In so doing, I gradually fell asleep. All was darkness anyway for me now, as long as I was using my body to see anyway.

"Okay, Barnabas. The coast is clear. Let's get rolling," Ilenakova whispered. He got the horses going at a slow amble and left the palace gates. He'd already told the gatekeeper that he was taking the carriage to the blacksmith for some maintenance. They didn't bother to ask why he needed to go so late at night. It was now eleven pm.

All was very quiet at this time of night. Ilenakova crawled out from under the blanket. She'd changed into her leather pants and top, armed herself as usual, and had hidden on the floor of the carriage. Now she sat on the seat and kept an eye out for trouble. Unknown to me, Dita was there with her, considering herself perched on her shoulders.

So far so good. Now when we get there, look for the long building, not the Church proper. It is attached to it, Dita sent to her. A half hour later, Barnabas whispered, "Complex is on your right. I will make one pass around it first to give you the overview."

"Wow! It sure is a big church. Okay, I see the long building. Where are we going to enter it?"

Hang on. Let me go check it out, Dita sent. She left and moved into the building, enjoying this action without her body. Besides, her body was a frightful mess right now, best left lying in the bed. Dita was determined to get justice for what had been done to her and to me.

By the time that Barnabas had slowly driven completely around the huge church complex where the Cardinal stayed, Dita returned. *Got it. There are guards on all the entrance doors. See the fifth window from the street end of the building? I'll open it from the inside. You crawl in, and I'll lead you to the safe.*

"Barnabas, drive around for about a half hour and then meet us right here," Ilenakova whispered. He acknowledged her, and she quietly slipped out of the coach and blended into the shadows. After the carriage had moved around the corner, she hopped the low fence and moved like a hunter up to the designated window. Dita had gone on ahead of her, and from the inside, used her telekinetic skills to open the lock on the window and raise it for her. Grinning, Ilenakova slipped into the rectory.

Dita led her down a hall and into Cardinal Drakon's private study. Behind a fake set of books was a built-in wall safe. Dita spun the combination and opened the safe. *It's that black book,* she sent. Ilenakova snatched it and stuffed it into a small sack.

She hesitated and then grabbed several more items. *Okay. Close it now.* Dita did so and then replaced the fake books. Now she moved out ahead of Ilenakova, making sure that no one was around.

Hide, guard coming.

Ilenakova ducked under the Cardinal's large desk. Shortly, a dim lantern appeared as the door opened and a guard peered inside. She held her breath. A few seconds later, the light disappeared, and the guard continued making his rounds. Dita verified he was gone, before she got Ilenakova moving again. A few minutes later, she climbed back out of the window. Dita then closed it and locked it, before moving back onto Ilenakova's shoulder, very pleased with their clandestine action. They didn't have to wait long before Barnabas returned with the carriage. She slipped inside. "We got it! Mission accomplished. One Cardinal is going down!" she whispered.

"Excellent. I will head to the safe storage area now," he whispered back. A half hour later, he pulled up to a warehouse on the edge of Kefall. A man slipped out of the shadows and made a circle in the air with his hand. Barnabas did likewise and added a triangle inside it. The man duplicated that and added another triangle upside down from the other triangle. He quickly opened the door, and Barnabas drove the carriage inside, while the man shut the door the instant the rear of the carriage passed him.

"Lazarus," he introduced himself.

"Barbabas. Ilenakova." The three shook hands.

Lazarus said, "We got your message. I got here as soon as I could, but feared I was too late and had missed you."

"We had a little errand to take care of first. How many carriages can we store in here for just a couple of days?" he asked.

"I reckon that we can fit ten easily. What's this all about anyway?" Lazarus asked.

"We may need to make a secret escape in a short while. Can you trust this Jonas Sokrates nobleman?" Barnabas asked.

"Depends on what it is. If it is anything against Empress Kassandra and her legions, yes, he can be trusted about that. If it's money or business, I wouldn't trust him at all," Lazarus gave his opinion of the man.

Barnabas turned to Ilenakova, "Your call. Do we go with him as Bethany planned or do we use the Forze Segrete to deliver our packages?"

"Damn. Well, Bethany seemed sure of him. Coming from him, it should carry more authenticity. Let's gamble on him. If he lets us down, it will be the last thing he ever does. Dita will eliminate him," she replied.

"Okay. Lazarus, we need these two packages delivered to Jonas Sokrates first thing in the morning, sun up. Whatever you do, do not open them, or let anyone else open them before Jonas does. Lives depend upon this," Barnabas said, handing him the package containing all the evidence that we had gathered concerning the Empress and the Cardinal. The other contained the personal journal of Cardinal Drakon. Ilenakova did not give him the other objects that she had taken from his safe.

"Now we have a long walk back to the palace," he said quietly. "We must avoid the city guards, though. Too many questions would be asked and raised."

I'll keep watch over you, Dita sent to them both. Barnabas was still a little unsettled with Dita's thoughts appearing in his head, though he tried not to react to that. The two slipped out of the warehouse and began walking down the deserted street. It was one in the morning now. Dita did a superb job of warning them in time to duck into alleys to avoid the patrolling city guards.

After two hours of brisk walking, they arrived at a park not far from the palace walls. He led her to the stone mansion on the far side of the park. Making sure no one was around, he pressed on a stone, and a concealed door opened; a section of the wall pivoted. They slipped inside, and Ilenakova instantly cast her Blue Light, surprising Barnabas, who was feeling around for the lantern he'd left just inside. He closed the door and lit the lantern. "How did you do that?" he asked.

"A trick known to us six," she replied. "Honestly, Barnabas, it took us two hours of rapid walking to get here from the warehouse. The women move incredibly slowly, they'll never make it that distance. Besides, if the streets are filled with rioters, we'd never get past them; it's way too far."

"I know, but it's the safest place to stash a bunch of carriages. Besides, if the carriages were right here in the park, we'd never be able to get past the looters in them. Either way, we're toast. The palace is centrally located. If we can somehow get everyone to the warehouse, we can easily slip out of town. Come on; we best head on inside." The two began walking down the narrow escape tunnel, built at least a century or more ago.

"All these steps will be murder on the women," Ilenakova commented. They had to go down a steep flight, then along a tunnel, only to go up a steep flight before coming into a hall that led to the throne room's back wall. After Dita verified the room was empty, the two slipped out of the tunnel into the Emperor's throne room. Dita reported that there was a guard on duty just outside the room.

There, he's asleep now. Coast is clear, Dita sent to Ilenakova. She'd handled the guard.

She had to put three more to sleep before Barnabas reached his door, where Xene was anxiously awaiting him. Ilenakova quietly slipped into our room, where Dianna was sleeping beside us. Using only her Blue Light, she quickly undressed and lay down beside Dianna.

Frona found the journey towards Kefall both fascinating and shocking at the same time. With their joined armies and with the other legions of the Empress scattered all over Demokritos, nothing could stand in his way. Almost at once, Kreon sent out captains ahead of his main party announcing to each town, village, and city in their path, "Hear yea one and all. Our new Emperor Kreon Demon and his Empress Frona are coming to bring law and order back to all Demokritos. He will smash down the evil pretender Kassandra and the Noble Houses who have allowed her to bring our country to ruin. His mighty army is right behind us."

By the time that Emperor Kreon and Empress Frona arrived in that town, the whole town turned out to witness the event. Many cheers went up as he and Frona, sitting on top of a carriage, rolled by — he waving at the crowds. Occasionally, he'd punch his fist into the air, which only made the crowd yell all the louder. "See the popular support that we have, Frona? We no longer need or want the Noble Houses to back us. The people themselves back us." She just could not believe what she was seeing. More often than not, chants went up: Long live Emperor Kreon. Long live Empress Frona. This, of course, pleased her. She'd never before had such a welcome.

Often they encountered Imperial forces, under the control of Empress Kassandra. These, he handled easily with words. "I'm your new Emperor. You will swear your fealty to me now or surrender your weapons, uniform, and post. The Empress and I reward those loyal to us, but we smite down our enemies and all enemies that attempt to harm our beloved Demokritos! Even the Church of Jehosanity, if they stand against us. Join us now."

Uniformly, they swore their allegiance and joined his ever-growing army. By the end of March, he was at the border with Thrace, and his combined army had grown huge. They traveled slowly on purpose. He wanted news of his coming to be spread outward before him. It certainly was doing that now! As word came to a town, brief rioting broke out, with many taking their grievances with the current Empress out on those who had supported her. When he entered that town, he brought law and order with him, too late for many, however.

As promised, he was very kind to Frona, and he respected her opinions and judgments. He even went so far as to attempt to learn how to assist her with life needs, especially so when they retired to their rooms for the night. It would be unseemly for the Emperor not to be seen handling such with his wife, who commanded the respect of many who belonged to the Church. She was still, after all, a Holy Woman of the Eighth Degree. That he was so gentle and kind to her in the evenings touched her.

During the early days of April, the self-appointed Emperor Kreon continued his slow and calculated march towards Kefall. As he expected, he continued to gather forces in Thrace, though many of the Empress' legions had finally made it back to Kefall. Kreon knew well that the real battle would be in the Imperial city.

One night, a week away from Kefall, while they lay in the bed of an inn, he explained what lay ahead for them. His fingers gently pushed her hair aside, then ran gently down the side of her face, neck, and onto the side her breast. She'd already told him that the thing she missed the most was the loss of her own touch, and he'd responded. He understood. "In Kefall, half of the city is stanchly behind the Emperor or Empress, whoever that may be. Many others back the Cardinal and his Church. Still others have been steadily repressed over the years, but have had no outlet, no justice. Either the Empress or the Cardinal always wins in that city. Our coming will ignite a new hope, a new sense that the repressed will finally obtain the justice denied to them for generations now."

"Riots will break out as we approach the palace. Undoubtedly, we will have to take the palace by force of arms, deposing Kassandra. When that happens, you and I will be the very first Emperor and Empress who have taken the throne by their own means and not by being appointed by the Noble Houses. We will not have to put up with those nobles and their political agendas. We'll be the first ever to be free of them."

"On the other hand, if we cannot pull this off ourselves, then we can fall back on the agreement with Jonas Sokrates and his friends, who believe that they have chosen us to be their new leaders and will be putting us into office as it has always been. So Frona, either way, in a short while we will be the new rulers. We can't lose."

She replied, "Please, run your hands there again. I would prefer that we are independent of the nobleman. Too long has the courts had to follow their political games, mostly to the detriment of our people. We do represent change, don't we?"

"Yes, Frona, we certainly do. How's this?"

"God, that's good. I so miss such a simple thing."

Ilenakova slept in and was wakened by Dianna and our helpers attempting to feed us a liquid breakfast. I was really getting annoyed with our predicament. It took all my concentration to keep from choking. I heard gags from Dita and knew she was having as much trouble as I. At last, we were fed and now I felt our helpers dressing me.

"Come on, Ilenakova. Sleepyhead. You're going to be late. Do my boots please?" Dianna asked.

"You would be too, if you didn't get to bed until three in the morning," she grumbled.

"What?" she asked. While she put on Dianna's boots and laced them for her, Ilenakova explained to us four what she and Dita had done last night.

"So this morning, actually by now I hope, the Cardinal's journal and our documents incriminating both he and Kassandra should be in the hands of Jonas Sokrates. We'll soon see what comes of that."

"Very well done! Great idea, Dita!" Dianna exclaimed. Poor Dita wanted to reply but only made a gurgle sound. Damn those men anyway, I thought. With all the motions being made to dress us, none of which we were seeing, I concentrated on not falling down. Dita, likewise. We could concentrate and use telepathy later.

"Okay, Bethany, here's the plan. Ilenakova will be taking your places with Athena at the council in the throne room. I would, but I am going to have to keep an eye on you two continually, so I would miss too much. I'll wander around and be useful. Ania and Kali are with their queens. By the way, Ania is in love with the way I look in this dress. She's really turned on with my new look. She looks fabulous too. I can't wait until I get you out of this so you can see for yourself."

I think it is best if Dita and I stay in our room here. Trying to lead two blind, armless women around is going to be far too difficult to manage easily. Lord knows what would happen if we should fall down. However, I will float into the council and listen in with Ilenakova.

"Okay, good plan," Dianna replied aloud. "Oh, Xene says that Barnabas is working on getting us ten carriages. It is probably not enough, but it's a start."

Ilenakova skipped breakfast and joined Athena and Andreas, as they were making last minute adjustments to her dress. "Got a minute, Andreas," she asked.

"Sure, there you go my love. You look just perfect now; the dress is hanging properly. What's up, Ilenakova?" he asked cheerily as always.

"I came across these gems. Can you give me an estimate of their value?" she asked, handing him the ten stones she had confiscated from the Cardinal's safe.

"Wow! Some gems. Look at these, honey. Each one is worth about fifty grand, I'd say. I had to deal with my folk's collection when I closed their estate. That is a good guess anyway."

"Cool, Ilenakova, you've got a fortune in your hands," Athena exclaimed, admiring the large, pretty gemstones. She put them back in her pouch and slid the pouch down between her breasts for safekeeping.

Andreas, his arm around Athena, headed out the door, followed by Ilenakova. As they glided slowly along the hall, her other advisors came out and joined them.

While they filed into the Empress' throne room, the other queens and their advisors were gathering there as well. Noticeably absent were Frona and her staff. At nine sharp, Empress Kassandra in her emerald green, flaring gown came gliding expertly into the room, moving slowly over to her throne. Selene, her constant companion, followed behind her along with a number of her advisors. When she had taken her seat, everyone could see that she looked very different from the last time they had met here.

She had dark bags under her eyes. Her countenance was darker, her mood, more somber. Three months of dealing with the attacks and riots had begun to take their toll on her. That things could ever be out of her control was a foreign notion to her. Yet they had been.

"Welcome to our Fall Council. We have a tremendous amount of work to do this time. Has anyone heard from Princess Maren? She ought to have been here by now with our fall fashions?" No one said anything. Queen Ariadne had already met with the princess and told her what was happening. Princess Maren wisely chose to return home, leaving her large fall wardrobe gift with Ariadne, who now had it loaded onto our caravel in Patri. She, of course, said nothing about this to the Empress.

"Well, she is probably detained. I expect that she will join us later on. Now then, has anyone heard from Queen Frona or from Thallyus?" Again, no one had heard anything. "Well, she is late. I will not delay this council any longer. We have much that we must do. Our soldiers are being attacked by rabble-rousers and thugs, who are rioting in the streets, just terrible. Now we must put a complete and total stop to this madness."

"I propose we pull in all our Imperial forces from where they are stationed and have you donate your combined kingdom armies, placing them temporarily under our general's command. United, our mighty force can then be deployed into all major cities and towns, given the charge to keep the peace or else."

Queen Melita, now the senior queen present, spoke in reply. "Empress Kassandra, there is absolutely no chance that our kingdoms will ever donate their armies to the Imperial forces. That violates the very principles, which founded the empire. Each kingdom has its own army for good reasons. Not in a million years would they go for this. We might be able to work out some kind of joint operations, except that in our kingdoms, many of your generals are now wanted for the crimes of multiple murders of unarmed civilians."

Kassandra fumed. "So be it. I will just use my authority and so order it. You can all conduct your vote count later on," she said very nastily. Melita was now on her hit list.

"Next, Cardinal Drakon wishes to address our council. We will hear from him now," she spoke to her Messenger, who moved to the door, which the Doorman opened for her. Shortly, she returned with the scarlet clad man. Her Announcer spoke clearly, "Cardinal Drakon Erebos."

A smile on his face, he walked confidently into the throne room. While he had no idea of how the final vote count would turn out ultimately, he wanted to see how his chosen rulers were faring under the recent severe stress of the riots.

"Good morning Empress, queens. I'm so glad to see you all here in Kefall once more. You are all looking very fine indeed. Fall, I see, agrees with you." His eyes darted to Athena, and he noted that the two Daughters of Lucifer were absent. In their place, he saw what appeared to be a native from Demokritos. Ah, perfect!

"I wanted to drop by this morning to see if there is anything that I can do for you? The Church is always ready and willing to help. If you need supplies, medical facilities, anything to help in the aftermath of all this rioting, I am here to tell you that your Church is ready to assist you in any way possible."

Some queens thanked him politely. He commented, "Queen Athena, I see you have a new advisor. Did your cousins from Velona finally return home?"

This was more than Athena could stand. She stood, hoping her legs would not weaken. "You have a lot of gall standing there pretending that you know nothing about my cousins. You know very well that it was your Prelate Khristos who has most grievously harmed my advisors. He has paid for his savage treatment of them with his life. Soon, sir, you will meet that same fate. I will be issuing a formal proclamation leading to your arrest." She sat down, still fuming.

"My dear child. I most certainly do not know what it is that you are talking about. I do hope that your cousins are alive and well. My Prelate is his own man. What he sometimes does, I cannot be responsible for. Still, if others were involved with him, I will investigate completely and hand the guilty parties over to you for your trial. I will leave you lovely women now and let you return to your tasks. As soon as I know anything, Queen Athena, I will let you know. I know that you have your important vote count to handle."

He bowed and left. He looked slightly pale and more than a little upset. His well-ordered world had been shaken. Now he knew why Khristos had not returned, though his associates had, and they had reported their complete success. No matter, Khristos had died chaining the Daughters of Lucifer, no small feat. He would be highly honored for having accomplished that.

Kassandra barked, "Speaking of which, do you all have your vote counts ready?" The queens did. "Very well, let us take the rest of the morning off and let our advisors compute the final tallies."

"Well, that was a short session," Athena commented to Ilenakova.

"You certainly shook up the Cardinal. Something else has come up. I saw one of Kassandra's advisors get a note, and he whispered something in her ear while the Cardinal was talking. I wonder what news he brought? Shall we return to your chambers?" They and the other queens left, while their advisors met with the Empress' advisors and began the final tallies.

A half hour later, Cardinal Drakon entered his private study. He was angry now. Queen Athena was becoming more of a problem, but he decided that the best course of action was to round up a few of the men that Khristos had hired and turn them over to her. Perhaps she would be satisfied. He knew that nothing Khristos had done could be traced directly back to himself. That was the way of the Mano del Dio — to die protecting their holy men. He went to his safe, thinking that he should jot down what she had said to help him refresh his memory later on.

As the safe opened, Cardinal Drakon's heart nearly stopped. Gone! His precious journal outlining all the steps he'd taken to create his 'perfect society' was not there! Also, his secret stash of gems was missing. "I've been robbed!" Immediately, he summoned his guards and began questioning them about the robbery. None had seen anyone enter his study or the rectory. All swore that all had been a normal quiet night; there had been no break in, no broken windows, nothing.

At last convinced that his guards were telling him the truth, he dismissed them and sank into his chair. "I must have left it and the gems somewhere else, forgetting to put them away. That must be it." He got up and began searching. The more he looked, the more frantic he became. An hour later, he was exhausted; he'd turned his whole rectory upside down uncovering one lost gold coin for his troubles. His precious journal and gems had just vanished. As he sat panting for breath, an awful feeling began creeping into his mind.

Could it have been those Daughters of Lucifer? Indeed, he had not seen them today, but he hardly expected that Queen Athena would parade them into the throne room. After all, they were beyond helpless. Blind, hard of hearing, mouth forced open like some fish seeking food, lips stretched out with the lip plates of the savages, armless — why, it would be a miracle if they could even be led by others. No, she had wisely left them — deserted them most likely. Yet, it would have taken higher powers than mere man to have stolen away his journal and gems without raising any alarm whatsoever.

A higher power, that had to be it. Somehow, these Daughters of Lucifer had come in the night to take what was most precious from him! Revenge, that had to be the answer. He was fighting the Devil himself, and he felt ill prepared to do so. His Prelate was gone, obviously slain by these devil's spawn. "Well, no matter. I will just have to start a new journal. I can do a better job of relating how the pieces fell together. Yes, I shall do just that tonight." He finally relaxed and requested lunch in his study.

Across the city in the Senate President's office, Jonas Sokrates sat smugly watching the myriad expressions on President Sophos' face as he read the large stack of documents. Just wait until he reads the journal, he thought to himself. This was Jonas Sokrates' finest hour. He was not just the most powerful and influential noble in all of Kefall, but now all Demokritos! After this incident became public, his power would nearly be absolute!

"My god, Jonas! How did you ever acquire these documents? This is utterly incredible!" President Sophos exclaimed, excitedly.

"Read the journal. It gets even better," he said quietly, a broad smile appeared on his face.

A half hour later, President Sophos put the journal down. "This is utterly unbelievable. However, we have it in his own words. I will present this to the full Senate this afternoon. You may expect that we will have an arrest warrant issued for Cardinal Drakon and Empress Kassandra by nightfall. I would advise you to have your Noble Houses pick a new Emperor and Empress very quickly — like in a day or so, if you can possibly do so. The indictments will be issued this afternoon and will be served this evening. The charges against both will be at least high treason and murder, possibly much, much more. Thank you for the valuable service that you have done for your country, Jonas." He shook the nobleman's hand vigorously.

An hour later, he visited his fellow noblemen, telling them of the situation. Ikaros, Horus, and Jonas agreed that they should wait until two days after the two conspirators were arrested before making their announcement of the country's new Emperor and Empress. It would look too surprising for them to make the announcement sooner. Some might get the wrong idea that they somehow knew about this sooner.

Empress Kassandra glided to her private chambers. An advisor passed her a note saying that one of her generals had just returned to the palace with extremely urgent news, so urgent that she should temporarily halt the morning's meeting. Instead, she had them working on the vote tally, doing some useful work in her brief absence.

"General, so good to see you again," she smiled and floated over to her chair and bade him have a seat. Selene was right behind her, adjusting her dress so that it looked proper.

"Empress, I have the gravest of news to bring you, news that I simply do not understand. Advance promotion men have entered Kefall midmorning. They are going around proclaiming that we have a new self-appointed Emperor who will bring back law and order to Demokritos. They claim that your reign is over, and you are to be arrested for high crimes. They claim he brings with him a mighty army of followers, though I do not know how this can be. We've heard of no such army. Still, there is now a growing unrest about to explode in Kefall. There are those rabbles that are staunchly against your reign. Others are violently opposed to your Church. I believe it is these who are going to cause the trouble within the city."

"Is there any truth to this self-appointed Emperor? What does he call himself?" She asked, caring little about possible rioting.

"He calls himself Emperor Kreon Demon. Your Highness, we have a General Kreon in our services, a young thirty year old officer. I do not know if these two are the same. Yet, their names are the same. Perhaps we have a rogue officer on the loose."

"Where was this General stationed?"

"He was sent to Thal, Thallyus, we believe."

Kassandra began to get concerned. "Did they name his wife, the Empress?"

"Only by first name. Frona, I believe."

"Damn her! Queen Frona has become too big for her shoes! She openly defied me at the Summer Council. Now she has corrupted one of our own generals and has convinced him that he can take the palace and throne by force! Well, I'll show her a thing or two! General, recall all our legions into the palace. Prepare for a siege. We should consider that this is a major threat and deal with it with all possible force. I want that general's head on a pike, hers too! Seal this palace up tighter than a drum. No one gets in without my authority — once you have pulled our forces inside, of course. I will deal with the queens and their personnel myself. Enough of this high treason against the throne of Demokritos!"

He bowed and left. Selene looked terrified. "Kassandra, what does all this mean? I don't understand."

"Selene, I am scared too! Queen Frona has concocted some diabolical plot to take over my throne. She's seduced one of our younger generals and his having him bringing his army group here to try to storm the palace. Well, we have many legions around here. They will get here before he does and they will find us prepared for them."

"There will be fighting then?"

"I am afraid so, Selene. Our big concern now is what to do with the other queens."

"Perhaps, they do not know about Frona. None seemed to have any idea why she was not here this morning. I did not sense that they were lying to you, did you?" Selene asked.

Kassandra had to admit that she didn't. The only thing was Queen Melita's defiance, but that might have been related to the issue she'd laid on the queens about their armies. She knew well that she was intending to violate their founding principle of multiple armies. It was just that she had not had the time to show them why she wanted to do this and what wonderful good it would accomplish.

"We should meet with them and break this news to them. If they act shocked and surprised, we will know that they are not in on the plot. Still, they may favor Frona; she is a fellow queen. I think it best for their safety and our security to lock them in their wing of the palace. Ground them. That way they cannot spy for the enemy or get in the way of our defenders."

"Okay. I am still afraid, Kassandra. What about all those soldiers that came here with them? Where have they gone?" Selene asked, growing more and more uneasy. Her stomach began tensing up, knotting; she felt ill at ease, but tried to put on a brave face for her lover.

"Most have gone to the reserve army barracks on the north edge of town. Only a few are here in the palace. Selene, thank you for mentioning them. You kept me from making a mistake. Those guards should also be locked up! Heavens knows how much trouble they could cause moving around freely within the palace when it is under siege. Yes, I'll issue orders for all the queen's men to report to their queen's section of the palace. You see, Selene, one good aspect of the palace, is that their whole section can be cordoned off from the rest of the palace. There are only two entrances to their section: the one that opens onto the palace grounds and the one that connects to our section of the complex. We station strong forces at each spot, and they are locked in there."

"But won't they starve? I mean we all dine in the royal dining hall," she asked.

"Well, we will just have to have the cooking staff carry prepared meals over to them. I am sure that we won't be able to spare soldiers to guard them as they walk to and from the dining hall or stand around watching them eat. They'll just have to rough it like the rest of us. Come on; let's go begin relaying the orders to our staff before I resume the meeting." The two visited several groups before heading back into her throne room.

"There Bethany and Dita, you are all cleaned up," Dianna pronounced. "Just so you know, I've used this boiled water once more to clean your two lip wounds thoroughly. No signs of infection, and they are healing well. Sandra is right this time. If you get an infection, there is almost nothing that we can do to keep you alive. We just have to keep your lip wounds healing properly, period."

I gurgled an "Okay," which rather sounded like the word.

A Messenger entered and said, "The council meeting is going to resume now." The Holy Woman turned and left; the Doorman shut the door after her.

"Well, it's back to business," Ilenakova said, rising from her bed, where she had been dozing. She was still tired from her late night adventure. "See you all in a while for lunch." Slowly, she glided to the door and left to join Athena and the others.

As the various groups merged in the long hallway, Ania signaled Ilenakova and Kali, who hung back waiting for Ania to glide up to them. "Gang, I feel tensions building. Stay very alert for trouble. Can't you feel it?"

"Well, not really," Ilenakova replied sleepily.

"It's an emotion coming from all around us, almost a fear," Ania pointed out.

"Hey, yes, I can sense it too," Kali said rather surprise that she felt something. "It's almost like the collective emotion of many people, right?"

"Right, the hurricane is almost upon us. I'll bet anything. Come on; we're falling behind. God, we sure can't hurry in these fancy outfits!" Ania commented slightly annoyed.

"Yes, but doesn't Kali look fantastic in hers? It's all I can do to keep my hands off her," Ilenakova teased. Kali blushed.

"I know, Dianna looks really sexy in hers," Ania admitted. "She looks good in blue satin." The friends filed into the large throne room of the Empress and took their seats with their respective queens.

At the same time, Andreas, Dario, and Luigi returned to our room. "Dianna, we've searched all over, and this is the best that we can find," Andreas explained. He gave her two small metal saws, while Luigi handed her two pliers. They had stolen them from the only workshop they could find.

"Well, they are better than nothing, thanks guys," Dianna replied, wishing for the hundredth time that she was in her own workshop at home where she had proper tools.

"Say, something is up, Dianna. The main grounds are full of soldiers. We saw some of the Empress' soldiers rounding up some of the queen's soldiers from their barracks. I hope they are not going to harm them," Luigi commented.

"Well, we'll know soon enough. Right now, our task is to attempt to get this off them. Let's try the saws first. Here, I'll show you guys what we'll try first. Bethany, Dita, we are going to try to saw off the bolt holding one of the leather eye patches down. Let us know if we are hurting your eye too much while we saw. Like this, cut here on the inside of the frame. Be very careful that you don't go too far down with the blade or you'll cut their cheeks. Don't put much pressure on it or you'll hurt their eyes. Easy does it, let the saw do the work." I felt her sawing on my right eye. Weird feeling. It didn't sound like any real progress though, not like a saw cutting through wood.

Andreas took the other saw and began work on Dita's right eye bolt. "Are you sure this is going to work?" he asked after a few minutes of sawing.

"Yes, it will take us some time. Luigi and Dario can spell us when our fingers and arms tire. Patience," Dianna advised. I wasn't listening; I was sitting on Ilenakova's shoulder at the council meeting.

"Our council is back in session. Are the vote counts finished?" Kassandra asked. I could tell that she now had very little interest in the results. Something else had her attention.

"Yes," her top advisor reported clearly, so there could be no misunderstanding. "Votes from Thallyus are not present and thereby are voided. The ten percent tithe proclamation has been vetoed by the kingdoms and is hereby stricken. The support of one caravel for missionary work has been vetoed by the kingdoms and is hereby stricken. The proclamation that all women of means should be well dressed in gowns from Annelise when in public has passed. The proclamation declaring the official religion of Demokritos shall be Jehosanity has passed. The proclamation that all citizens must go to church on Sundays or be fined has been vetoed and is hereby stricken. The proclamation that all women with the means should partake of the Holy Ceremony of the Eighth Degree has passed by the narrowest of margins." He sat down. Many gasped at the passage of the last one. Athena actually broke down and cried.

Fierce lobbying by the Church got that one through, Bethany. Ania sent to me. *I hope the next rulers cancel it or there will be hell to pay down here in the future.*

"Now then, an emergency situation has arisen here in Kefall. It seems that Queen Frona has become a traitor to all Demokritos. She has somehow corrupted one of our fine young generals, Kreon Demon. She has him convinced that he can be a self-appointed Emperor of Demokritos and she, the Empress! They have marched her army and his down to Kefall from Thallyus and are expected to besiege this very palace in a vain and futile attempt to take the throne of Demokritos by force of arms! Already, there are widespread reports coming into the palace of looting and rioting out ahead of their army's arrival. I have declared a State of Emergency here in Kefall. All our Imperial legions are, as we speak, being summoned here to the defense of this palace. This rogue general will not succeed, and I will have the head of this traitorous Frona on a pike by morning."

"Until then, because of this emergency, I have ordered the remaining kingdom soldiers that you have here within the palace to go at once to your section of the palace, there to guard and protect all you queens. As a further precaution, I am ordering your whole section of the palace to be locked down. No one will be allowed in or out without my direct orders. Your safety is of paramount importance to me. While in my palace, I am responsible for your well-being. With all the fighting about to take place, along with the slaughtering of these rebels, I do not want you to have to witness such or become accidentally injured during the fighting. I will send Messengers from time to time to keep you fully informed. Meals will be delivered to your wing."

Queen Melita asked, "Empress Kassandra. This is a total surprise. How could Queen Frona do these things? Have any of you heard from her these past three months? Are we in any real danger, Empress?"

No one had heard anything from Queen Frona; that was quickly established, much to the relief of Kassandra. She now felt confident that the queens were just as surprised about this as she had been which meant that she did not have to fear them as well. "As long as you stay in your section you should be safe. I have sent all your soldiers who remained here at the palace to your areas. They should be sufficient to keep you all safe. I will have my soldiers guarding the two entrances to your section of the palace. As long as you all stay in your section, I don't believe that any harm will come to you. This should all be over in a day or so, went I hang this upstart of a general and behead Frona for her treasonous acts against our whole country. I suspend our council. Meeting is adjourned," she declared formally.

Everyone was talking at once, as we all headed back to our section of the palace. Once the last of us entered, the palace guards shut the door and bolted it. Queen Melita's men placed an iron bar across the doors on our side, preventing attackers from breaking in easily. Athena called out, "Queens, to my chambers."

Sitting on Ilenakova's shoulders, I could see that the six queens were starting to panic, and I asked Ania to help. Ania said, "Okay, the hurricane that has been predicted has finally arrived. She has locked down the palace, so do not expect your noblemen to be able to get to you, Melita, Adonia, and Danae. However, Bethany has been working on plans for just such an event. Since Bethany is indisposed right now, I'm acting as her spokeswoman. If you follow us, we will get you all rescued somehow. The first thing we need to do is to remain calm and make our plans. Each of you, please have your advisors count how many guards you have remaining. Let me know the numbers. You should post half at each entrance to this section of the palace."

"Go through your things and pack only what is irreplaceable and most valuable to you and your staff. We will probably have to go on foot from here, so we have to be able to carry those things with us. Above all, remain calm."

Melita asked, "Surely we will be safe in here. If Frona is behind this, I'm sure that Frona means us no harm."

Ania answered, "I'm sure that she doesn't want any harm to come to you queens or your staff. However, when the two armies are fighting it out, hand-to-hand here inside the palace, all of us could well become collateral damage. No, what you should fear is not Frona, but Kassandra. If she becomes seriously threatened, she will undoubtedly hold you as hostages to attempt to buy her freedom. Either that or take you down with her as a last act."

Melita asked, "Could we somehow send a message to our kingdom's armies? Could they come to rescue us?"

"She has the palace locked down. I'm sure she'll not allow you to send a dispatch rider to fetch your armies. Remember, it's been your armies that have been fighting her soldiers the last couple of months out in the kingdoms. Melita, Adonia, Danae, Bethany will somehow get you three to the safety of your armies. Athena, Alekto, and Ariadne will order their armies to join with yours and help guarantee your safe evacuation and return to your kingdoms."

"But what about those three?" asked Melita.

"They are coming with us to Velona. All three have had enough of Demokritos. Bethany has also promised to return your Special Helpers back to their own land and people. Okay, ladies, let's get things organized. When the time to leave comes, we may have to go in a hurry," Ania ended and came to see how I was holding up and to report.

"Any progress, Dianna?" Currently, Luigi and Dario were doing the sawing.

"Slow but sure. In time, I will have their sight restored. That's the first and easiest step," she replied. Ania nodded and then gave us a report on the events so far.

I explained to Ania, *Excellent Ania. Our first action must be to get a message somehow to the queen's forces. We need them to obtain some carriages for them and to be ready to depart the moment we can get their queens and staff to them.*

"We could send someone out through the secret escape tunnel, though once they surround the palace, that park area is likely to be filled with soldiers," she advised. "We don't know just how soon Kreon's army will arrive so we don't dare do it right now. His army might arrive just as they are trying to pick them up and who knows what might happen."

No, we wait a while longer. Now isn't the time to evacuate. You are right. Thanks for substituting for me, Ania. This is utter hell. God, I hope they can get me out of this soon!

Just then, one of Athena's armless Messengers entered and said, "Queen Danae wants to speak with you, Ania or Bethany."

"Send her in, thanks," Ania replied.

Danae glided into our room, her dark brown pixie style short hair matching her satin gown perfectly. "Oh dear god! I had no idea it was this bad!" she exclaimed very shocked at the contraptions on our heads. Luigi and Dario looked up from their sawing and took a break, their fingers aching.

"Yes, this was Cardinal Drakon's handiwork," Ania said flatly. You needed to talk to us? Bethany can hear if you speak loudly."

"Well, I wanted to say that it is possible for me to get a message to my general where they are camped on the north edge of Kefall. He ordered me to bring along a couple of carrier pigeons in case of trouble. I guess this is trouble. I can send them to him, but he can't return my messages, though. Will this be helpful?"

"Danae, I could kiss you!" Ania exclaimed, exuberant over the news. Danae flushed; she knew that we six women were married, and perhaps Ania meant that she would kiss her. "Yes, that is the answer. Just now,

Bethany and I were trying to figure out how to get word to your armies and have them acquire carriages for you three queens and staff. Actually, you also need to take the staff of Athena, Alekto, and Ariadne with you as well. How lengthy a message can the bird carry?" The two began working out the wording. Unfortunately, it had to be kept short. An hour later, an advisor of Danae's affixed the message to the pigeon's foot and let it go out her window.

I relaxed; rescue of the many other innocents was in the works. Just how I was going to get the rest of us out and to safety remained in doubt still. Ania, all doom and gloom, believed that circumstances might prevent our leaving with them. I hoped not, it would be far easier if we could.

Chapter 47 The Hurricane Comes

By late afternoon, we began hearing sporadic gunfire in the distance. Well, Dita and I could not; our ears muffled much sound. Dario encouraged me by saying, "Bethany, I'm halfway through the bolt. Hang in there." What else could I do?

I imagined the queens' armies were taking action now. However, Dita, bored to death, went to check on them. *I can see them lining up carriages now. Looks like the message got through to them.*

Where are you?

About a hundred feet above their large encampments. There are thousands of them. Each kingdom's soldiers wear a different colored uniform. Pretty cool. Okay, coming back now.

Dinner was brought into the complex by a large number of soldiers, who handed the many trays to the queens' guards and quickly bolted the doors. Soon, Dianna was once more attempting to feed us. Honestly, I hated this part, unable to eat properly. Once we finished, she again used her sterilized water to wash off our lip wounds very carefully. The throbbing pain was gone now, leaving behind a strange stretching sensation in my lips. Once more, the men resumed their sawing.

When the dishes and trays were ready to be picked up, Empress Kassandra paid a surprise visit to us. The Announcer, an armless fourteen year old girl, spoke clearly, "Empress Kassandra." I tried to look, before I realized that was a silly action to take, merely reflexive.

"Oh dear god. I had no idea. Who did this to you, Bethany? Oh, she can't talk, can she," Kassandra exclaimed as she entered. Her muted voice did sound as if she was genuinely shocked to see us like this.

Ania answered her. "This is what your illustrious Cardinal Drakon does to women. His Prelate Khristos did this to them while they were en route here. Ilenakova killed Khristos, but he and his men had already done this to them."

"Why? Why would he do this? They are Holy Women too. I don't understand. Can you get those awful things off of them?" she asked.

"We're trying, we're trying," Dario replied, somewhat disgusted. His fingers were aching.

"Well, do your best. I came to see how they were doing. Also, word has come that this rebel general has entered Kefall and will be storming the palace very soon. Please make sure that everyone stays put. I am responsible for your safety. Let me know when you get them free of that," she said and left to inform the queens.

"I believe that she was genuinely shocked to see you like this, Bethany and Dita," Ania said. Soon her voice was drowned out by the sawing noise.

Sometime later, I felt a sudden release of pressure over my right eye. Dianna carefully pulled the leather contraption off, and suddenly I could see once more out of that eye. My vision was partially blocked by a band of metal, which ran right across my face, centered on my eyes. I gurgled, "Hurray!" but it sounded mostly like noise. Shortly, Dita gurgled too; she could see out of her right eye at last.

"Sorry, I am pooped out," Dario explained. "I'll work on the other one tomorrow, Bethany."

Thanks! I sent him, and he looked very surprised to hear my voice inside his head.

"Well, it's started," Ilenakova called out. She had put a chair up to our window and was listening to the noises from outside the palace. "I can hear lots of horses and men. Lots of gunfire is getting closer."

Across town at the largest Church of Jehosanity in Kefall, Cardinal Drakon was just finishing his dinner. One of his aides came into his room, but was pushed aside by the green uniformed Captain of Kefall City Police. Six other policemen were right behind him. All seven held drawn guns, now pointed at the Cardinal. "What is the meaning of this," he stated using his most humble priestly tone. "How may I help you?" His stomach lurched.

"Cardinal Drakon Erebos, you are under arrest for high treason against Demokritos and the murder of the Emperor, seven kings, and their children. The Senate has ordered your arrest and speedy trial. You will come with us now. If you resist, we have orders to shoot to kill."

He tried to protest that this was all some big mistake. Seven guns convinced him to rise and follow them. His hands were tied behind his back, and he was put into a carriage. During the drive to the Senate building, they passed a number of rioters burning down several buildings belonging to some noblemen. Chaos was raining down all around him. If only Khristos was alive, he thought to himself.

He was helped out of the carriage and led into the Senate Legal Office, where the President of the Senate sat waiting him. Sitting on the table was his own journal! His heart skipped a beat. He sunk into the chair before the President.

The President picked up his journal and waived it in the air. "This, coupled with the evidence collected by Queen Athena Patra and her cousins from Velona will have you convicted of these crimes within minutes tomorrow. Hanging is far too lenient a punishment for such vicious crimes. Your trial commences at nine tomorrow. By ten, you will be hanging from the gallows. I have sent the Kefall City Police to arrest Empress Kassandra on similar charges. It may well be that you will have company as you hang in public for all to see. Do you have any last words to say to me? I will not have any further words with you after this."

Cardinal Drakon's emotions ran wild. He wanted to protest his innocence, but realized his own words in the journal did condemn him. Fear rushed through him. One question burned in his mind, "How? How did you get my journal?" His voice sounded strange to his own ears.

"This was acquired by the women from Velona who are currently advisors for Queen Athena Patra," the President answered him.

Cardinal Drakon's body sank deep into the chair; all his muscles collapsed. This was all the doing of the Daughters of Lucifer! Even though Khristos had silenced them perfectly this last time, still they were devil's spawn. He imagined these devils somehow robbing him during the night. His men would be powerless against them, as was he. If only there was some way that he could get a message to Pope Leo warning him of these Daughters of Lucifer! Powerless, he could think of no way this could be accomplished. He sank into the depths of utter apathy. The police had to lift him out of the chair and drag him to his cell.

At the morning's trial, he continued to sit like a lifeless lump of flesh, saying nothing, answering nothing. What could he say? The Daughters of Lucifer were vastly more powerful than any human being was. This was Lord Jehosa's will. Somehow, he'd failed him. He paid no attention at all to the Senators and their trial or the evidence presented. He did not even hear the sentence as it was spoken clearly by the court.

He came to his senses as he was dragged atop a hastily built wooden platform, where a rope and noose hung in the bright spring morning sun. A large crowd of people stood and stared. A few yelled "traitor," while others begged for his release and forgiveness. He felt the rope around his neck and a voice called out, "Any last words?"

Yes, he had to get a message to his Pope. "Someone tell Pope Leo that the Daughters of Lucifer have come to Tarra! Warn him, I beg of you!" He felt the floor go out from under him and he fell.

Around seven the previous night, shortly after the arrest of the Cardinal, Emperor Kreon and Empress Frona finally arrived near the palace. Riding atop their carriage, he waved to the throngs that had crowded the streets to welcome him. In other parts of the city, rioting was running rampant; many were seeking revenge for decades of what they believed were crimes committed against them by the Emperor, Church, and/or the nobles of Kefall. However, wherever the new Emperor's forces went, the rioting and looting, shooting and killings ended. His was the magic touch, the hope for a better day, better justice.

Kreon explained to Frona, "Our forces have now surrounded the palace. In the morning, we will send word to Kassandra to surrender. Until then, no one goes in or out. Perhaps, she will surrender to us and avoid a blood bath."

"What about the queens, dear? They are inside and innocent. We must ensure their safety," Frona insisted, very worried about her peers inside, locked up by this vile woman.

"I have given strict orders to the army. They are not to be harmed in any way. Our forces will avoid attacking that section of the palace. They will be totally safe as long as they don't join with Kassandra."

"There is no chance of that, Kreon. None at all. I am just afraid for them, that's all."

"Come on, our inn room is waiting for us. Perhaps tomorrow night you may sleep in a bed more fitting my Empress," he replied respectfully. She smiled.

"Emperor, a captain of the City Police wishes to enter the palace," a guard broke in on their conversation. "I have told him that no one is being allowed in or out. He is most insistent. I brought him here to speak with you."

"Excellent. Bring him forth," Kreon said, amused.

"Sir," the captain said as he stepped forward, "I have an arrest warrant issued by the Senate for the arrest of Empress Kassandra. The charges are high treason and murder. I have been ordered by the Senate to present these charges to the Empress, to arrest her, and take her to a cell in the Senate Legal Department to await trial in the morning."

Kreon laughed. "Do you honestly think that you and your half dozen men are going to be allowed inside the palace? Can you defeat the Imperial army she has inside protecting her?" The captain looked confused. All this was very true. "I will allow you to be escorted to the palace gates and protected while you deliver your message to Kassandra. However, we both know that she will not walk out of her palace. Tomorrow I will capture the palace and Kassandra. Once I am finished with her, you may have her for your trial. Acceptable, captain?" It was.

A few minutes later, the captain stood before the palace gates, surrounded by a hundred soldiers. He called out that he had a message for Kassandra. After waiting a while, he then read off the charges against her and asked that she surrender herself to him for trial in the morning. Again, he waited for a time. Hearing nothing in reply, he then left, returned to the Senate, and reported to the President.

Indeed, Kassandra heard the message. A Messenger came to tell her that someone at the gate requested her, and she had come, albeit slowly in her confining outfit. She and Selene had heard the accusation and request. She spat on the ground and returned to her quarters.

"What do we do now?" asked a terrified Selene. "Why would they arrest us?"

"No matter. Once we defeat this rebel general, I will order my army to eliminate those stupid Senators as traitors as well. It will be all right, Selene. You will see. Come, let us try and get some sleep. The battle won't start until the morning, I'm sure."

One of Danae's guards at the door also heard the message. He quickly relayed it to all the queens and their staff. "Well, let's get some sleep," Ania advised. "Nothing will happen until morning." She was right.

Boom! I was startled awake. Even though the leather ear patches dampened most sounds, I heard that explosion. The assault on the palace had begun. I could barely hear the sounds of gunfire, though from the many alarmed faces I could see with my one eye, the sounds were terrifying to the others, especially the queens and the other Holy Women, who I knew felt utterly helpless.

After getting dressed, Andreas and Dario began sawing once more, while we all waited for someone to bring our breakfast. Gunfire from inside and outside became a constant background. Finally, around ten, our guards brought in breakfast. The cooking staff was overwhelmed by having to feed so many men, who were now defending the palace walls.

Athena dropped in to say that everyone was fully packed and ready to go the moment I gave the order. She looked terrified, and Andreas held her tightly for a while, telling her it would be all right. Alekto and Ariadne came to be with Dario and Luigi too. They took a break from sawing to comfort them, while Dianna and Ilenakova continued with the sawing.

Dianna explained, "Bethany, I don't want to remove the ear leathers until we make more progress on the lips and mouth. Those earpieces hold this contraption firm. I am afraid that if we get them off, the thing will be loose and damage your mouth or lips." I didn't find this very encouraging.

Around noon, the noise suddenly stopped. Everyone had a rather shocked look on their faces. Silence, pure silence. "What's going on?" Athena asked what everyone wanted to know. For some reason, they all seemed to be holding their breath, as if the gunfire would start up if they dared to breathe.

Ilenakova dashed to the main doors that led to the palace grounds near the main gate. She put her ear to the door to listen. Dita and I moved out of the vicinity of our bodies and over to the main palace gates. We both saw the carnage. Some of the soldiers were carrying the wounded back to the stables, where the two palace doctors, covered in blood, were frantically trying to save lives. To the right of the gates, others were piling up the bodies of the dead, having no other place to put them. We saw Empress Kassandra and Selene gliding across the grounds to the gates. Selene was carefully directing her around the bodies still lying where they had fallen.

"I am here. What do you want, traitor? Surrender now, and I will spare your life," Kassandra spoke loudly through the thick, iron re-enforced gates. Her voice had a distinct tremor in it. Fear, she was in fear, I noted.

Outside, the self-appointed Emperor Kreon spoke clearly and loudly. "Empress Kassandra, I have called a halt to the attack that we may speak. By now, you must realize that your position is completely hopeless. It is only a matter of time before my forces break in and capture the palace."

"We will never surrender the palace. You are the traitor," Kassandra replied, unable to think of anything better to say.

"Is this your choice then? To allow my army to completely destroy all your soldiers, your advisors, your staff?" Kreon asked, taking a different approach.

"We will destroy you," she replied defiantly.

I heard Frona's voice whispering to him. So Frona was indeed with him! His voice tone changed abruptly. "Empress Kassandra. You have many innocent lives inside your palace. The six queens and their advisors and staff are innocent of our conflict. Both you and I are responsible for their safety. Before we battle it out and more lives are lost, could not you and I come to some kind of agreement to allow some or all of those innocent queens to depart the palace to a place of safety? Neither of us can afford to have these queens harmed in any way. They are, after all, Holy Women of the Eighth Degree. There is no higher crime in Demokritos than causing harm to them. What say you and I agree to allow them safe passage out of our conflict?"

Selene whispered to Kassandra, who then replied, "Will you give me some time to consider this? I agree; they should not be harmed."

"Yes, I will give you such time as you need. Send for me when you are ready to discuss this further. I am pleased that you also take their safety so importantly," Kreon replied. Selene and Kassandra headed back to her section of the palace, accompanied by two of her generals.

Ilenakova raced back to us, as Dita and I moved back behind our heads once more. She related what she had just heard to everyone. I was glad that I didn't have to do it telepathically to so many people. Quickly, the queens relayed it to their staff.

Ania theorized, "This may be the chance that we've been waiting for to get the others out of here and to their carriages. I suspect that Kassandra will come for a parley with us. I would be shocked if she released all of us. I'm sure that her generals are telling her that we can be useful hostages.

If that happens, see if you can get the others released while we all stay behind as her hostages, I sent to Ania. She nodded.

Why wasn't I surprised to hear the Announcer call out, "Empress Kassandra," a short while later? Damn, Ania was good!

She and Selene, who looked positively pale, entered. The six queens were with us. "The rebel general has asked that I release some of you. We both do not want to see any harm come to you. I have discussed this with my generals. They point out that if we run into difficulties, we may be able to use you as bargaining pawns. I know this sounds awful to you, but I must do what I have to do to defeat this traitor to the country. You can understand this I'm sure. I've decided to let some of you go as a show of good faith."

"Thank you for your extreme kindness, Empress Kassandra," Ania spoke for the entire group. No way was she leaving this one up to chance. "Athena, Alekto, and Ariadne wish to remain behind, along with us and their Special Helpers. We beg you to allow their advisors and staff to leave with the other queens. This way, you will still hold half of the queens, but have drastically fewer mouths to feed."

"You three would do this?" Empress Kassandra asked rather surprised. Ania knew that she had been coached on how to proceed when all the queens insisted on being allowed to leave. That half volunteered to remain thus took her by surprise.

"Yes," Athena spoke up. "We would. We know that you will not allow harm to come to us, but we are so worried about our advisors and staff, even our few remaining guards. Please, allow even our guards to accompany them. Then, you will only have a few of us, and you won't need hardly any of your soldiers to watch over us anymore."

Kassandra liked this idea. Three queens, two assistants unable to do anything, with only four others and three men to help them, this she liked. "I will accept your suggestion, Queen Athena. You are truly a wise queen. I look forward to continuing our relationship as soon as I can put an end to this rebel general."

Ania then asked, "Empress Kassandra, since we will now be so few, could you possibly spare some more of your Special Helpers? We can use their help with these five, two of whom need constant assistance with everything."

"Yes, that would be reasonable of me. I will send them along when the exchange is made. Please tell them to prepare. I will send a guard to get them when it is time." Ania thanked her, and she and Selene left.

"Okay, spread the word; have everyone get their things together. When you get outside, ask them to send a message to your forces to bring your carriages and pick you all up," Ania explained hastily.

Danae came over to me and said, "We will all be praying that you get out safely too. Words cannot thank you enough for all that you and your friends have done for us." She leaned over, and we touched bodies, the best hug that she could manage. Adonia and Melita also thanked us and said that they would do what they could to get us out too. Melita promised Athena, Ariadne, and Alekto that they would get their staff safely back into their kingdoms. It was a tearful departure for them. They felt awful that we were being left behind.

Barnabas and Xene begged to stay with Athena; she was part of their Forze Segrete. Via Ania, I convinced them that they really did need to return to Theos and be our eyes and ears there. They and Athena wept as they said their farewells.

About a half hour later, the guards unlocked the main doors. Slowly the large group filed out and was escorted to the gates. Dita and I were both hovering above the gates, ready to take very drastic action if anyone tried to harm these people. *I'll fireball the lot of them and rip their heads off if they harm these women and men,* Dita sent angrily. I knew that she would too!

Emperor Kreon and Empress Frona welcomed them, and she personally walked with them down the street away from the battlefield. Dita and I decided to stick around until we saw them safely off in the carriages. It took an hour, but soon we did see a long line of carriages approaching. We were very relieved indeed. A bit later, the carriages left the area completely, on their way to join up with the kingdom's soldiers at the north edge of Kefall. At last, she and I returned to the vicinity of our bodies, where the men were still sawing away. I reported to Ania what we'd seen, and she relayed it to the queens.

With my one eye, I looked at our much smaller group. All told, we numbered my six, the three queens, their three boyfriends, and sixteen of the twenty-four Special Helpers, less the four who were with Frona and four with Kassandra. These we could not get to if we had wanted to. I had Ania explain to the newly arrived Special Helpers that we would be taking them back to their homeland when we left here. This pleased all of those women immensely. One wrote on her pad: What about our other four?

Have her tell you where they are at when we are ready to leave, and we will somehow get them too, I sent to Ania. Now it was waiting time once more. Around three, our lunch was brought to us and shortly after that, the gunfire began once more.

After Dianna and Ilenakova finished feeding us and Dianna had once more used the last of her sterilized water to wipe down our lips, Ania said, "Bethany, I would expect that they will attempt to breech the gates this evening. Kreon needs a swift end to the siege. Every day that he fails, he will lose enormous amounts of his momentum. He cannot afford to drag this out for days and days. If I were him, I would attempt to enter under the cover of darkness. Of course, that makes it very dangerous for us; collateral damage is very likely when scared men cannot see well what they are shooting. We ought to be prepared to make our exit tonight. If we time it when they do break the gates, everyone's attention will be focused there, not the rear where the Emperor's throne room is located."

I gurgled an "Okay."

We huddled in my room, listening to the sounds of constant gunfire and the continuous sawing on our next bolt. The three men's hands were sore and aching, so Dianna and Ilenakova relieved them and continued the lengthy sawing process, made even more difficult now because both saw blades were completely worn down.

Andreas had just lighted the lanterns when I suddenly felt the pressure against my left eye vanish. Then, light! I could see again out of both eyes. Dita too. Everyone cheered the group of sawers for a job well done. Yes, it was weird trying to look ahead with a half-inch metal bar right across the eyes, but I could see well at last. Dita and I would not be such a horrible burden on the others now. I felt very much relieved at last.

Now we waited for supper to arrive. It didn't. We consumed the last of our water and continued to wait it out. Still the battle raged on outside of our section of the palace.

Around eight, the firing subsided and then ended. Ania said this was likely to be considered by the defenders as the end for today. However, she told us to expect an explosion or something that would smash the gates down. We double-checked that everything was packed and ready to go. The three men carried everything for all of us in three large sacks. Neither were heavy, just hairbrushes and other personal items. If we had to, the three sacks could be abandoned.

Like silent statues, we sat in my room waiting for the inevitable. Stomachs growling, we waited. Boom! The explosion shook the very floor of the room, jarring us all. The Special Helpers let out unintelligible screams of shock. The three men put their arms around the queens for support.

"Okay, up and at it," Ania called out. "We will go down to the end of the halls where the exit into the Empress' section is at. Ilenakova is our leader. Follow her."

Dianna put her arms around me, while Ania did the same with Dita. Kali took up the position of rear guard. Slowly, we left our room; the hallways were deserted. No one had even lit the lanterns along the way. This slowed us down a bit, as they felt their way along. We could hear wild yelling, screaming, and of course loud gunshots. These were totally muffled for Dita and me though. At last, we halted. Ilenakova was at the door. On our side, the barrier bar had not been put back in place after our soldiers had left. However, the barrier bar had been laid across the doors on the other side.

Dita, we need your assistance, I sent. She moved to the other side, lifted the bar, and opened the doors, much to the utter amazement of everyone. I sent, *Ania, we get everyone safely inside the escape tunnel. Then, we go after the other four Special Helpers.* Ania whispered the plan to the others. Slowly we began to move down the next set of halls. A guard suddenly appeared in front of Ilenakova. Ania fired off her spell, and the guard dropped to the floor asleep, astonishing the group. We moved on.

Three more times, Ania needed to use her special skills at convincing another that they needed to fall asleep. I held my breath as we passed by the private quarters of Kassandra and then her throne room. At last, we entered the darkened Emperor's throne room. Once Kali closed the door, Ilenakova cast her Blue Light, and we five followed suit. Again, the others gasped. We had enough light to see, and quickly she pushed open the sliding stone entrance, revealing the pitch-black escape tunnel. Two lanterns were just inside. These she lit and passed to the men.

Via Ania, I explained the next step. Ilenakova and Kali were going to go bring the other four Utu women to us here. Dita would float along with them to help as needed. While they were off doing that, the others were to move down the dark passage and assist the women in safely getting down the long stairs to the bottom, far underground. The men would need to carry Dita's body because she would be off with the other two. Once they got the four found, they would join us. With that settled, we went into action.

Yes, in these outfits and especially me with this darn contraption on my head, we women had a most challenging time descending the long stairs. It was very cool down here, downright chilly. Quite a lot of time was needed to get us all safely down. By the time that we all were safely at the bottom and ready to head on along the tunnel, the others joined us.

"No problems. She led us to their room, and we found the four scared to death, huddling in a corner. Had to only kill two guards," Ilenakova replied, "Kali got one of them. Damn, going down these stairs is murder in this dress and heels. I should have changed into my leathers!"

A bit later, she muttered, "The next time we plan on making a secret escape, let's not wear such clothes! We are snails in these boots, and these wide dresses are awful to deal with!"

Try doing it without arms, I teased her. She chuckled.

"At least it is quiet down here," Athena tried to sound a more helpful note.

It must have been closer to eleven when we reached the halfway point along the tunnel. Here a side tunnel connected. Rusted iron bars blocked all passage that way. An awful stench came from it. As Kali, bringing up the rear, passed it, she called out, "Hey Bethany. I recognize this side tunnel. It is part of the storm drain system." I didn't think much of her observation at the time. A while later, we stopped. Ahead lay the step stairs up to the outside secret entrance.

"Gang, I'm pooped. My feet are killing me," Dianna complained. Can we take a little break?"

"Yes, I'll go and check on our exit point," Ilenakova volunteered, though I knew her feet were also aching.

About a half hour, Ilenakova reappeared at the top of the steps. Dita lifted her up and gently brought her down, once more surprising everyone. "Thanks, Dita. My knees are taking a beating in these heels. Okay, we have a big problem," she began to explain. "Half of the army is camped right where this escape tunnel leads. No chance at all that we can safely get out there. There is still some gunfire around that area too."

Kali asked, "Is it supposed to rain?" No one knew that at all. "Well, there is another way we can get out. Actually, I think that I can get us all the way across the city to near the warehouse where Ilenakova left the carriages for us."

"How?" Ania asked, echoing what everyone wanted to know.

"Through the storm drains. As long as it doesn't rain, we should be safe. We used to use these to get around unseen," she explained. We knew what she meant. In a previous lifetime, she was part of a secret organization that got justice for mistreated Women of the Eight Degrees. Yes, she had been an assassin.

Lead on, Kali. Brilliant. You've again saved our butts, I sent her.

She grinned, "Bethany says lead on. Back to the rusty bars, everyone." A few minutes later, we arrived back at the smelly tunnel. I latched onto the grate and broke it loose from its mounting, once more shocking many with us. I heard lots of "How'd they do that?" coming from the others.

"Okay, it will be tricky walking, but I'll knock down the spider webs as I go. Ilenakova will follow me and get any that I miss. Slow and easy does it. We have a very long walk ahead of us. We'll keep our Blue Lights up too," Kali advised us. Off we went into the noxious smelling tunnel. Soon, however, our noses no longer sensed it.

There were many junctions along the route. Often Kali would have us wait, while she checked down several, making sure that she chose the right one to follow. Time dragged on, and we were tiring rapidly. Kali knew that as well, and finally, she led us to a special junction, which had a long stone platform against the side wall. Here was a main junction.

"We can stop here and get some sleep, though we are going to have to sleep sitting up," she explained. The men helped us women up, and our feet and knees greatly appreciated the respite, though our stomachs growled for food. While the queens laid their heads on their fiancés, Dita and I clanked our heads together and soon I drifted into a deep sleep. I thought that I heard Kali whispering to Ilenakova just before I fell asleep.

Daylight woke us up! We were under a street cover where the rainwaters would fall into these storm drains. Both Kali and Ilenakova were now wearing their leathers. "Wake up sleepyheads. Breakfast is served," Kali teased us.

As she and Ilenakova passed around bread, cheese, and some water, Kali explained that they had climbed out of the storm drain and acquired us a bit of food. Everyone greedily devoured the food, while thanking them profusely. Dita and I, however, had to wait while Dianna managed to turn our bread into a mush that we could swallow. We nearly choked on the tiny pieces of cheese however. This at least quenched our hunger and thirst. With some daylight illuminating the tunnels, our going was easier.

Then, it was night once more, and all of us were very hungry and thirsty. Kali kept encouraging us on, though our legs and knees were nearly wiped out. Our rest breaks came more and more frequently. "Just a little further," she encouraged us.

"You don't have to do this in your heels anymore," Dianna complained. Both were carrying very large sacks with their dresses in them. I gurgled my agreement, while Dita gurgled a laugh. She was right though. Finally, she stopped, had Dita lift the grating above our heads, and then lift her up and out. She gave a hand signal, and one by one, Dita lifted the rest of us up and out, much to the shock and surprise of nearly everyone. Grate back in place, Ilenakova led us down a deserted alley. It had to be the middle of the night, but we had no way to tell for sure. She slid open the warehouse door, and we slipped inside.

There were ten carriages waiting for us. While the men, Ilenakova, and Kali began hitching the horses up, the rest began searching the place for any scraps of food. We found a water barrel though and at least had a long drink with Dita and me struggling to get it down. We only needed five carriages now. Three carriages carried six of the Utu women each, while two more rode with Dita, me, Dianna, and Ania. Andreas, Luigi, Dario, Ilenakova, and Kali became our drivers. Though it was the middle of the night, we headed out onto the road anyway, more than anxious to leave Kefall behind us as soon as possible.

Chapter 48 Fallout

Boom! The giant explosion shook the very foundations of the Empress' private quarters, sending a wave of fear through Kassandra and Selene. She'd decided to coordinate their defenses from her throne room. Not that she actually did any coordination — not more than telling her generals to defend the palace and kill the rebel general Kreon. Periodically, military aides had been reporting on various aspects, mostly the dead and casualty counts.

"What was that?" asked Selene terrified. All of this loud noise and gunfire had shaken her nerves. This explosion turned fear into terror.

"I — I don't know," Kassandra replied, visibly shaken herself. "Perhaps someone will come and tell us soon." She'd already told her various staff members to go hide in their rooms. If she needed anything, she'd send Selene for them.

Selene, her arms tightly around Kassandra, now shivered with every gunshot, which seemed to be an awful lot louder than before. An icy fear began to seep into Kassandra's mind and stomach. The noise of the battle grew even louder, and an aide, bleeding from a shoulder wound, rushed into the throne room.

"Your Highness, the gates have been breached. The enemy is flooding inside. We cannot hold them back much longer. You must hide somewhere." He turned and raced out the door.

This cannot be happening, Kassandra thought. "How could this happen?" She sat dumbfounded on her throne. Quickly, Selene raced to the doors and locked them, but realized if they breeched the massive gates, this mere door would not protect them at all.

"Kassandra, we must hide or flee or something. We must save ourselves! Come on; where can we hide? Where can we go?" Selene was in a complete panic.

Hide? Go? The Empress? This should not be happening. Her mind, her thoughts turned upside down. Go? At last, that registered. "Selene, press the secret door block. Quickly."

Behind her throne, during the extensive remodeling, an escape tunnel had been installed. Selene did as she asked and a section of the wall opened, revealing the dark blackness of the tunnel. Selene pushed her way through, her wide hoop bent as she squeezed through. A lantern hung on the wall. Her hands were shaking so badly that it took five tries before she was able to light it. "Okay, come on."

Now Kassandra pushed herself through the opening, fighting against her fifteen foot in diameter hoop skirt. Selene gave the door a shove and the stone door slid back into place. The two stared off into the darkness. "Where does it come out?" she asked.

"Dunno."

"Okay, follow me. Stay right behind me. Oh, there are all these spider webs in here. Icky." Selene began batting at them with the lantern, which only broke them, many now clinging to her skin. She panicked and nearly dropped the lantern. At last, her fear began to drive her onward, sounds of the throne room door being smashed could dimly be heard. Now she ignored the webs, which grabbed at her face, hands, and hair, and pushed forward into the darkness. Kassandra followed right behind her.

It was obvious the passage had not been used in years. Ahead, she saw a thick layer of dust unmarred by any footsteps. She took a little encouragement from that. Then she came upon steep steps going down further underground. "Careful, dear, lots of steps going down." The passage was too narrow for her to walk side by side with Kassandra, not with both of their wide hoop skirts in the way. Very slowly, she began to descend taking one step at a time. Behind her, Kassandra fought back her panic. She could not even see the steps. Selene's dress and hers completely hid them. In their extreme heels, the going was even more treacherous. Both women descended primarily by feel, very slowly and cautiously.

After what seemed an eternity to Kassandra, they reached the bottom. Here the air was quite chilly, and her shoulders grew uncomfortably cold, but there was nothing she or Selene could do about it, except continue. On they walked as more and more spider webs accumulated on them. Occasionally, Selene would feel creepy things crawling up her arms. She sat the lantern down and wildly thrashed them off her and tried to remove some of the webs. She prayed that they were not crawling around in her hair.

Two eternities later, Selene called out, "More stairs going up this time. I think we are getting somewhere." By the time they reached the top, both women thought that their knees would fail them. They gasped for breath, constricted so by their tight, wide banded corsets, an inch tighter than those worn by the queens. "Let's rest," Selene gasped.

More time passed. Now rested, the two continued their walk through the spider webbed tunnel until finally it ended in another wall. "Now what?" Selene asked. The two women stared at the wall. Selene spied a small iron lever. "Maybe this will open it." She tried to pull it but the lever was rusty and stuck. She sat the lantern on the floor and used both hands, throwing the full weight of her body down on the lever. At last, it creaked and moved downward. A section of the wall opened and Kassandra pushed herself through the narrow exit. Selene was right behind her. However, the second that Selene was out, the door shut, leaving the two standing outside in the dark of the night. Their lantern continued to burn inside the tunnel.

"Where are we?" Kassandra whispered. Both women strained to see anything that looked familiar. They were in an alleyway, but little else could be seen. Gunfire sounded not too far from them. "Let's try this way,"

Kassandra suggested. The two moved slowly down the alley to the street. They had no idea that it was now one in the morning or where they were — some four blocks from the palace.

As they began walking down the street, Selene moved beside Kassandra and put her arm around her to steady both of them. By now, their feet and knees were aching from their exertion. Their progress was indeed slow. "If only we wore normal boots," Selene whispered.

"What are we going to do now? Where are we going to go?" Kassandra asked, the stark reality of their dire predicament hit her hard. She was lost, set adrift in life with no one to cling to but dear Selene. That she was now totally and utterly dependent upon her lover became sharply real to Kassandra. Gone were the servants who had always tended her needs, came when called, assisted her with everything. All that she had known all her life was gone — utterly gone. Only Selene remained.

"I had a girl friend of mine once, before I came to the palace to work with you. We can go there. She can give us some food and a place to sleep until we can figure out something," Selene suggested.

"Okay. That sounds good, love."

"Yes, but I don't know where I am now or how to get there," Selene whispered back. She was so scared that she was once more shaking. That Kassandra was now just as frightened, maybe more so, didn't help matters. They walked on slowly down the street for some time.

All of a sudden, two men slipped out of the shadows. "Well, looky here. What have we found — two noble ladies out for a stroll, eh. Well, hand over your money pouches," one man demanded.

"We don't have any," Selene replied. Kassandra panicked again. They had left everything behind in their mad dash to escape. Oh, if only they had planned for this. Brought along money, gems. Arranged for a carriage to meet them, if, if, if, she thought. She felt rough hands feeling her, looking for a concealed pouch.

"Damn, they ain't got any. Well, those are mighty fine dresses you are wearing. I bet those will fetch a fine price. Take them off, and we'll spare your lives," the other man said.

Nervously, Selene began to take hers off, piece by piece. Finally, she was down to only her corset, hose, and boots. "Leave'em. Those ain't worth much. Now do your friend here." While Selene did as he asked, the other man began grabbing all her clothes into a large bundle.

When she finished undressing Kassandra, the first man said, "Now get going before we change our minds and have some fun with you." Shaking visibly, both women continued to walk on down the street. "Man, that one's so ugly, I wouldn't do her if ya paid me to."

"Ya, and who wants one with no arms. No fun in that. Come on; these'll fetch a hundred or more."

Humiliated, disgraced, and shivering from the cold fall night, the two women continued walking. A number of blocks later, two groups of men came running down the street, firing guns back and forth at each other. Suddenly, Kassandra felt Selene jerk violently, her hand, which was tightly around her waist, slipped loose. Selene dropped to the ground. Instinctively, Kassandra dropped to her knees. "Selene! Selene! What's wrong?" Now waves of panic swept over her. She had never felt more naked and helpless in her life. Using her head, she managed to roll Selene over. Blood seeped out from her chest, soaking her corset. "Selene! Selene!" She was powerless to do anything to help her lover.

Gasping, blood coming from her lips, Selene whispered, "I love you."

"I love you too. Please don't die. Get up, get up!" Selene didn't respond; she didn't move. Kassandra looked at her chest and realized that she was no longer breathing. She was dead. Kassandra began bawling, grief stricken. She realized she'd just lost the only person in the entire world who had actually loved her, cared deeply for her. She now knew that she also loved Selene, but it was too late to tell her so.

Worse, Kassandra was now totally alone, totally helpless, totally unable to do anything but walk! Even if she rose and walked, then what? She couldn't even feed herself. She had nowhere to go now that Selene was gone. No one to look after her. For the first time, she realized just how totally complete was her helplessness. She sank into an apathy and laid her head on Selene's body. At last, Kassandra just gave up. She'd lie here until she too died.

The men's footsteps grew louder, and they soon dashed past her and the fallen Selene and didn't stop, but took another shot at their pursuers. Now more footsteps approached. She didn't notice. She was dead to the world. The footsteps stopped beside the two women. She did not see that they were the City Police, who had been chasing down some looters. "Damn, looks like they shot one of these women. Here, miss, let me help you up." Kind, gentle hands pried Kassandra's body up off Selene.

A voice said, "She's dead. We'll send the wagon around. Looks like they were robbed too. Who are you miss?" Kassandra stood staring at Selene and did not answer. One shone his lantern light on her face. "My god! It's the Empress Kassandra! What luck! Half of the city is out combing the streets looking for her. We'll get a promotion out of finding her! Go get the wagon. I'll hold her." Kassandra stood silently, staring at Selene oblivious to all else.

Later, a wagon came; the man lifted her aboard, and the two of them lifted the corpse onto the wagon as well. Kassandra again stared at the lifeless body as the wagon rolled through the nighttime streets of Kefall. They halted at the Senate Justice Department's Jail. One man lifted her off the wagon and carried her bodily inside. Other men verified their catch, and he carried her to a cell, sat her on the hard wooden bench, and locked the door.

Oblivious to the cold, oblivious to the world, Kassandra sat there motionless, a complete apathy. Life was gone for her. The morning came, though she hardly recognized it. Men came and took her before the President who read off the charges, which she didn't hear. Her trial, she also ignored. Her sentence became a hot topic of debate.

"The Emperor wants her executed," one said.

"We can't do that! She's a Holy Woman of the Eighth Degree. It is against our law to kill her."

"Damn. You are right. What in the blazes are we going to do with her?"

"Lock her up and throw away the key," another suggested. That was finally the punishment they adopted. Strong arms carried her far underground. Someone threw a feed sack-style, crude dress over her. They pushed her into a cell ten feet by ten feet, windowless, with stone walls, and one entrance door. At the bottom of the door was a five-inch opening, where food and water could be slid into the cell. The door was locked, and someone poured molten lead into the lock. "There, now no one can be tempted to open this door. When she dies, then we will break the lock." He called out to her, "Food will be slid under the door twice a day." Then, silence. Utter and complete silence. High on the wall a soot covered lantern cast the dimmest light possible into the cell.

She sat on the bench staring at the floor. Time passed. Now thirst and hunger brought her attention to her surroundings. She heard the sound of something sliding on the floor. She could barely see anything; the cell was nearly pitch-black, but she could smell the food. She moved over to where the tray was at and stepped on it. How can I even eat, she wondered. She dropped to her knees and groped with her head and mouth, finally finding the food. She ate like a pig might, getting food all over her face. She was force to lick the water from the bowl like an animal. Later, she paced around her cell and banged into a bunk. She laid down, but could not figure out how to get under the covers. Kassandra began to cry once more, not over her loss of Selene, but because she now knew what it *really* meant to be a Woman of the Eighth Degree — the true reality of what it meant, and it was not anything that she had ever thought it was before. Now all she could do was wait for death to come. Maybe there was a God. Maybe he would take pity on her and allow her to join up with Selene once more. Oh, if she could only have that one single wish.

Emperor Kreon accepted the surrender of the remaining palace forces. An all-out search began for Kassandra, but neither she nor her assistant, Selene, were found anywhere in the palace. Frustrated, his only assumption was that they had somehow snuck out during the confusion of the break in. Further confusing him was the missing three queens, who were supposed to be here within the palace as well. His men could find no trace of them anywhere, and he finally began to assume that they had never been here when the assault had started. Perhaps they had been visiting friends elsewhere in Kefall and had not actually been inside. He regretted not having detained the others who he had allowed to rejoin their forces and leave for home. At last, he told Frona, "They must not have been here. Probably they were indeed visiting someone in Kefall when the palace was locked up and could not get back in after that."

"Have you searched everywhere?" she asked. He ordered a thorough search and an accounting of all the dead bodies, as they were removed. A day later, he answered her question. They were simply not here.

Meantime, Frona brought Kassandra's staff into her new throne room and told them, "You now have a new Empress to serve. You already know me. A far as your jobs and pay are concerned, nothing has changed at all. Once we get this mess cleaned up, all will be back to normal." The relief that shown on their faces told her that they would indeed be very loyal to her now. Nowhere else could they earn such pay and have such good living conditions.

That settled, she asked if they had seen the three missing queens. Indeed, several had seen them, but after the battle began, no one had, but then they were mostly confined to their private quarters. Frona began to believe now that somehow the three queens had evacuated with the others, probably disguised as one of the many armless servants. This she told to Kreon, who finally had an explanation that he felt was right. They had escaped from Kassandra by disguising themselves. Certainly, that was something he might do under the circumstances. He passed this along to the nobles who asked. In time, if they got a report from Thrace, for example, wondering where their queen was at, then he would have to worry. Such reports never came.

By the third day of his reign, the palace had been cleaned up. Work was begun on the repair of the destroyed main gates. He also learned that the Senate President had arrested, tried, and hanged Cardinal Drakon. Also, the City Police had found Kassandra wandering half naked in the city streets in the middle of the night. She too had been tried and convicted. He learned that she had been sentenced to life in prison. He regretted that he had not been able to apprehend her, though Frona told him just how terrible her punishment would be for a Woman of the Eighth Degree. He realized that death would have been too easy a way out for her and was content with the decision.

His main concern was now restoring law and order to Kefall. By the end of the week, even this had been accomplished. He had ignored the requests from the Noble Houses to meet with him but finally consented once his grip on the throne was totally secure. The three men left his presence shocked. In no uncertain terms, Emperor Kreon explained that he was the ruler and that he did not need their approval or consent. They realized that somehow the control of the Emperor and Empress had been wrestled from their hands. Hence, their shock.

At the end of the week, he received news that Thrace had appointed a new king and queen. He sent word for them to visit him at their leisure. In the days following, the other kingdoms also sent word that new kings and queens had been appointed there as well. He sent word for them to visit as well. He unilaterally decided to hold council meetings only in the spring and fall. He needed little from the kings. From now on, they would be minor dignitaries in his grand scheme of things. He controlled it all. That a little over ten thousand men and women had died directly or indirectly during the past three months as he took over the throne meant nothing to him. He had achieved something never done before in Demokritos. He was a self-appointed Emperor, owing allegiance to no one but himself and Frona, whom he soon found to be indispensable. His respect for her keen leadership skills only grew as the days went by.

His first legally binding rulings came in response to Frona's request. He cancelled the proclamation that women partake of the Holy Ceremony. He cancelled the ten percent tithe to the church as well as the support of their missionary efforts. He cancelled the proclamation that everyone had to go to church on Sunday, but he let stand the proclamation that Jehosanity was the official religion of the country. Frona won that small compromise for her Church. He also let stand the proclamation that women of means dress well when in public, which pleased Frona. Thus, the reign of Emperor Kreon Demon and Empress Frona began in April of 752.

Chapter 49 Escape

It was pitch black as our five carriages rolled out of the warehouse at the western edge of Kefall sometime in the wee hours of the morning. Andreas, Luigi, Dario, Ilenakova, and Kali drove steadily through the night and near dawn, entered a small town. Ania explained the obvious to us all. "Look, we cannot let people see either the Utu women or Dita and Bethany. That would give us away instantly as being from the Imperial palace. You are somehow going to have to fetch food and water and bring it to us in the carriages. Probably the best idea is to get the food and then move on down the road to some secluded location where we can stop and eat and stretch in secret."

"Undoubtedly, already there is a new king on Ariadne's throne. If they discover that we are running off with the Utu women, that might force them to take action against us. We cannot take such a chance. Once we are safely past Axos and on the home stretch to Patri, we might be able to lighten up."

"But then, we are nearly there," Ariadne pointed out. "We might as well just continue in secret all the way. I can hold off on a bath and a real bed for a week. How about the rest of you?" We all agreed to rough it. Hence, the five headed to the inn as it opened to grab a stockpile of food and water, enough to last us until the evening.

An hour after sunup, they pulled the carriages off the main road, hidden from view by a hill and some trees. Here we stretched our legs and ate our first solid meal in quite a while, well, all except Dita and me. Poor Dianna had an awful time trying to make a swallowable mush out of our meals for us. We had it rough, trying not to choke as we ate it. She now had no access to sterile water and insisted that they take time to boil some for her to take along in our carriage. She hovered over us like our mothers might have if we were ill.

Finally, around ten, we were back on the road. Dianna commented, "Our drivers are going to get awfully fatigued. None of us has had much sleep. Ania and I can also take turns driving."

Can we bunch up more and eliminate one carriage? Perhaps squeeze eight Utu each in two carriages? Then, we would need only four drivers, with three to take over in relief, I sent to Ania.

Dita sent, *I can drive in a pinch. It will look a bit weird, seeing no body holding the reins, probably best if I drive when it's dark. I have been slack in helping out.*

At our noon stretch break, Ania spoke to the Utu women, who agreed. Honestly, they were so happy that they were somehow going home that they would agree to anything we asked of them. The others though this a good plan; already they were falling asleep. We made the adjustments, and

Andreas now drove the empty carriage, which he then sold in the next town for more supplies.

After we ate our dinner at dusk just outside another small village, we decided to let everyone get some sleep. They were all extremely tired. Dita and I volunteered to stand watch. We let our bodies doze along with the others, while we two sat on top of the carriage keeping an eye out for trouble. None came.

Refreshed, the next day went well, with driver rotation every few hours to keep them all alert and rested. A couple days later, we approached the capital city of Thrace, Axos, where Ariadne had been queen. When they returned from getting our breakfast from an inn, Andreas relayed the news that indeed Thrace had a new king and queen. Because of all the riots and looting, the king had tightened security countrywide. The word was out: find our ex-queen. Apparently, the noblemen were still trying to find Ariadne, who right now didn't want to be found.

"We can go around the whole city on country roads, but that will delay us a whole day," she said. None of us wanted that kind of a delay. Once past Axos, we would be on our ships in two more days, free of this whole mess.

"I know. Kali and I will cast appropriate illusions on everyone if we get stopped," Ania explained. "Look, Ariadne, Kali and I can make the Utu appear to be normal women and you can look like a simple servant. They won't even see these metal contraptions on Bethany and Dita. Trust me." That settled it; we headed on into Axos.

At the edge of the city, we ran into a dozen soldiers guarding the road and searching all vehicles, especially wagons and carriages. As we pulled up, there were five ahead of us, and the soldiers were searching them one by one. Ania and Kali began casting their Druwid spells. By the time that we pulled up, they had finished. Kali also planted the suggestions in the men's minds. She whispered, "Okay, move on; nothing in here."

To Athena's surprise, the men repeated those very words, and Andreas moved on down the road. Kali and Ania repeated this thrice more, and soon we found ourselves rolling into the largest city of Thrace. By afternoon, we finally had gotten through the crowded streets and were headed out onto the open road, when once more we met a similar roadblock. Again, the two cast their spells, and a short while later, we left them behind us.

Ania finally relaxed. It should be smooth riding until Patri. She now had an opportunity to chat at length with me. "You know, Bethany, you have been extremely lucky in all this. If you think about it, first you and Dita were abducted and had your arms cut off. They could have killed you both, but they didn't, just making you into Eighth Degree women. Then they abducted you both again and slit your lips, inserting lip plates and those neckbands, emulating the Utu princesses. Again, they could just as easily have killed you both. Then, once more you were abducted, well attacked might be better. Again, they went to an awful lot of trouble to encase you in these monstrosities as well as the lip plates. I say an *awful* lot of trouble. As Dianna can verify, those head contraptions had to be specially made and probably at great expense. Yet, they could have far more readily just killed you both."

We kept being gassed and knocked out, I sent, *so we couldn't really do much about it. But I do see your point. Why not just kill us?*

"Well, that is what I have been wondering for weeks now. Why? Why go to these extreme lengths, when it would have been far easier, simpler, and certainly cheaper just to kill you two? Now from the bank records that Kali researched, we know that it was Kassandra who paid the Cardinal to have your arms removed. Why did she do that? Why not just kill you?" Ania asked.

"Well, they rather annoyed her," Athena answered for me. "They appeared out of nowhere as my advisors, and together we began causing her trouble. Perhaps she just wanted them out of the way and figured making them like me would cause them to freak out or something."

"Makes sense. If you two were actually assassinated, that would raise all manner of questions, especially since so many assassinations had already been done by the Cardinal," Ania theorized. "That would make sense. Kassandra needed you two out of the picture to better control Athena here. She couldn't risk more assassinations, especially foreigners. What better way than to make you as helpless as possible? Makes diabolic sense. Then, when you continued to be with Athena and continued to cause problems for her, she had to take more actions. Actually, all that therapy you did — she must have discovered that was going on. I'll bet that is what threw her for a loop. Here you two were not stopped but continued to help the women; I bet she became afraid of you. She couldn't have you assassinated now; you were now of the Eighth Degree. Killing you would have been the highest crime in the country! I bet that really ticked her off!" Ania felt that she probably had Kassandra's thinking pinned down now.

"I bet that she got the idea from the Utu women, who cannot really speak, but only write. Since you can't write, no hands, she figured that turning you into Utu princesses would effectively silence both of you. Of course, when that failed, she probably became exceedingly desperate, especially since in her mind you seemed to be the driving force behind all resistance to her dominating of the queens."

I don't know. We really upset the Cardinal sometime before they attacked us the third time. Perhaps he took this on himself to silence us. We could tell for sure from the recent bank transactions when we get back. If there was another fifty thousand transferred from her to him, then your theory is likely. If no funds were transferred, then my theory holds more water.

"Then, there is another thing to consider. We kept finding entries referring to you and Dita as Daughters of Lucifer. What does that mean?" Ania asked.

"Oh, I know that," Athena replied. "In the Church teachings, the archenemy of Lord Jehosa, or God, is the devil, whose name is Lucifer. Daughters of Lucifer refer to what they call devil's spawn. That is, children spawned by the unholy mating of Lucifer and a human woman. They believe that these unholy children are possessed of great supernatural powers, given to them by Lucifer, probably because they inherited them from him."

"Well, now this all makes far more sense, Bethany. You and Dita really need to watch this more carefully. Look, both you and she did many, shall we say, strange and unusual things, starting with having your stitches removed hours after extensive surgery to remove your arms. While we all know that is simply a usual and expected byproduct of your therapy, they don't! That must have seemed terribly shocking to them, explainable only by your being Daughters of Lucifer. If you had been associated heavily with their church, they might have equally decided that you were angels or something, coming from Lord Jehosa himself."

"They saw the miracles you worked on the queens. Just look how alive, alert, how cheerful, how full of vitality and life these three queens here are now, once their traumas were erased. Again, unexplainable phenomenon from the Cardinal's point of view. Undoubtedly, you and Dita did other unexplainable things."

"I see what you mean. We have all seen all of you do so many unbelievable things these last few days. Blue Lights, controlling men's minds, talking in our heads, on and on," Athena blurted out.

"She's right. You and Dita have used your native spiritual abilities out in the open among people to whom this appears supernatural. They have no explanation for its happening. We all know that someone will invent an explanation, if there is not one readily available. It's the nature of man to have to have some kind of explanation for the unbelievable that happens. In this case down here in Demokritos, you blew the Cardinal's mind, and he sought out the only explanation that fit into his world view — Daughters of Lucifer. Now, he could not outright have you slain because first, you were now Holy Women of the Eighth Degree and second, you were Daughters of Lucifer. If he killed such daughters, he would bring down the wrath of Lucifer upon his whole church, destroying it. He could not afford to do that. So he had to shut you up. I'd say the man was terribly inventive, Bethany; you two are really shut up at the moment!"

I gurgled and banged her with my foot. She giggled and went on, "So you see, even though we are powerful spiritual beings, we cannot operate alone in this world effectively. Together, we do far better. Second, we bring down disaster on our heads when we overtly use such powers that others cannot understand or grasp. In short, Bethany and Dita, I hope that you two have learned a valuable lesson for the future. There, I'm done."

Again, I gurgled, leaned over, and pressed my body against hers, the best hug I could manage now. *Thank you, Ania. You are precisely correct once again. We've been rather fools haven't we?*

"Yes, you two have been rather foolish, but it is a good thing that you have us as friends."

"Is it possible for others to learn how to do these things? I mean like me?" asked Athena, now very curious. She felt like she had just been privy to powerful beings' most private thoughts.

"Sure, Athena, but it takes getting a whole lot more therapy sessions and years and years of study. If you have the time and desire, when we get back to Velona, we can see what we can do," Ania replied. "First, we are going to have to teach you how to do things for yourself — you, Alekto, and Ariadne. Once that is done, we can move on to many other things. There is a whole world of possibilities waiting for you, Athena. Only you can walk the path of your desires."

"Say, what's going to happen to my country now? We got rid of two bad leaders. I don't quite see what anger and covert hostilities had to do with it," Athena asked what she'd been wondering about since this whole mess happened.

"You can experience a lot of different emotions yourself. Enthusiasm and cheerfulness are tops. When you fall away from that, you get conservative and bored and then one can fall down to antagonism, lashing out at others. Often that results in your receiving some form of pain, such as getting hurt or someone hitting you. If one continues downward, you end up angry with people, things, and life. If your anger is blocked or you succumb further, you become afraid of overtly striking back, too many bad consequences for you, so you then do it in a covert manner. If you are pressed a little harder, fear comes in to haunt you. If you drop even further down, you begin to feel like you have to propitiate to the opponent to gain any way of getting their approval or consent. If all that fails too, one ends up in grief, loss. If the loss is too severe for you to handle or cope with, apathy results. If one keeps on sinking, death follows. We all experience these emotions in life."

"When we suffer a traumatic event, we slide down these emotions. How far we drop depends on the trauma severity, you see," Ania explained.

"Yes, that is very real to me. When I got my therapy from Bethany, I was like in the pits, near apathy about it all. God, they took my arms without my consent and left me helpless like this for the rest of my life! But I remember now, as I got the therapy, I got scared, then angry, and then the massive pain hit me. After that lessened, I was very bitchy about the whole thing. Bethany kept me at it and then I began laughing and none of it really bothers me anymore, except that I get so frustrated having to live like this," Athena explained how it was with herself.

"Right. Now if you take a whole group of people, like your country, all together as a mass, the group will also display the average emotion too. If the majority of the people are angry, the group then acts as a person would when angry," Ania explained.

"Oh, I get it. When I got mad because I could do something anymore, I kicked my chair over. Duh, lot a good it did to do that, kind of like the wrong target," she added sheepishly.

"Right. Now the point is, if you observe the group, you can be aware of the overall emotion of the group. Knowing that, you can then predict how the group will act and react. Emperor Deimos ruled when Demokritos as a whole was mostly angry. He and his army lashed out at the world, attacking Zargarb Sector of the Sea Princes. Duh, he was soundly defeated. After that, I predicted that the overall emotional level of Demokritos would drop a bit further."

"Well, you have now lived through a period where the rulers were being covertly hostile, stabbing others in the back, so to speak. Kidnaping others and cutting off their arms while they were knocked out, all the subterfuge between Kassandra and the Cardinal, including the murders of the Emperor and kings — all were done sneaky, behind the scenes, instead of outright attacks," Ania pointed out.

"I tried to warn Bethany and Dita to be exceedingly careful around these types people, because they will backstab you when you least expect it. When all six of us were together, our joint actions made it harder for them to accomplish that. My own opinion of the current mess is that now the country has gone fascist. Emperor Kreon no longer answers to anyone but himself. Plus, he's going to be very popular with the people. The power of the individual kings and queens will be drastically less than it was when you were on the throne. If he wants to make a new proclamation, the people will support it, even if the kings do not. You now have a dictator on the throne."

"Power tends often to corrupt, but in this special case, you have Frona also sharing the power. She may tend to moderate his power; at least I believe that will happen. I think that actually emotions as a whole may have dropped down to one of propitiation as a means of controlling others and getting one's way. If you give a guy enough presents, eventually he will feel obligated to do as you ask."

"Grim isn't it?" Athena asked. "Well, in some ways, it's safer maybe that way, instead of all the fighting and backstabbing. How do you know all this stuff?"

"Years and years of study and observation," Ania replied. "Actually, I've been learning and studying these things for several lifetimes now. I'm interested in the study of large groups, politics, interactions, things like that. Love the stuff, but not many do, though. Kali does also; she and I love this stuff. It is our specialty. Bethany, she knows more about more things than any of us do, but Kali and I know more about groups and politics than she or any of the rest of us. Now Dita and Ilenakova, they know more about fighting and related things than the rest of us. Dianna knows more about the healing arts and engineering than any of us. Oops, I am supposed to relieve Ilenakova. Bet she's tired of driving."

Riding in the carriage was not conducive to fine sawing. Dianna didn't want to risk accidentally harming us. Thus, we rode along looking at the scenery and being terribly bored and stiff from so much constant sitting. We welcomed the brief respites when we pulled over to eat and stretch. Two long days later, we crested a hill and finally saw the large port city of Patri!

Here two caravels were awaiting our arrival. One was owned by the Matteo brothers and carried their entertainment company and all their personnel, costumes, and musical equipment. The other was our caravel belonging to the Banca del Dio. I wanted us to ride straight through the city to the docks, get aboard, and sail away as fast as possible. Maybe then, they could get this damnable contraption off Dita and me. However, the carriages halted.

Ilenakova came to our door. "We can see that there is an even larger checkpoint just outside the city. I have a bad feeling about this. We're going to move the carriages over behind those boulders and hide you. Then, Andreas and I are going to go on ahead and check it out before we try to head through them with the four carriages. Stay alert everyone." I gurgled an okay.

After an eternity, from my anxious point of view at least, they returned. "Well it's a good thing that we checked on it," Andreas began excitedly, with some worry in his voice.

"They are on the lookout for the Utu women. The Empress has sent out word that these women are missing. They are also looking for the three queens. Even worse, the Harbor Master has halted all shipping from leaving port until their inspectors come aboard and check everything out," Ilenakova replied. "There are fifty men ahead doing the searching. Can you Judgers handle that many at one time?"

"Er, not that many," Ania admitted.

"Hey, they are on the lookout for a convoy of carriages too, at least four or more traveling together. I think someone is guessing that we are going as a group or someone got wise to us in the many towns we've passed through," Andreas added.

"Ariadne, could we try to sneak in from some other direction or perhaps head to the shore and walk along the beach to the docks?" Ilenakova asked, trying to visualize other means of getting us into the city and to our caravels.

"Not easily. Patri is in a big rocky basin. It will be hard to go around to another side of the city from here. The beaches beyond the docks are very rocky and almost impassable on foot," she answered grimly, becoming more worried by the minute, as were many of the rest of us.

"Say, we've got long boats for emergencies," Dario suggested. "We could have our boats ferry us from the land out to our boats. If we did it at night, we might get away undetected. Is there a convenient spot where we could take the carriages close to the ocean and not too far from the ships?"

"Good idea, but the best place is five miles up the coast," Ariadne replied. "Patri's expansion has been severely limited by the surrounding coastline. We've been planning a new port about ten miles further north of Patri. Work is supposed to begin on it this summer."

"Well, isn't this a fine mess!" Ilenakova declared, putting both her hands on her hips. "We've come all this way and can see our destination from the ridge line but we can't get there!"

What about entering late at night? I sent to Ilenakova.

"Good idea, Bethany. What about our going in there in the middle of the night? Likely to be far fewer guards at the checkpoint," she asked the others. This seemed to be our best chance; however, it would mean no food or water for the rest of the day. Ugh.

What a long day it seemed. We sat, waited, and dozed. We grumbled and complained. Time dragged on like a heavy weight. At sunset, we became more hopeful, but we still had at least another five hours to wait. I was asleep when the carriages finally began to roll once more.

We calculated right. As we pulled in at the checkpoint, only five guards were on duty. Ania and Kali created the appropriate illusions, and we were allowed to pass. "A load of very tired tourists," she had the guards repeat several times. Well, we were sort of tourists, sort of.

Around three in the morning, we finally pulled up at the docks. Our two ships were docked at the extreme end of the docks, away from the normal traffic, because neither ship was taking on or off loading cargo. To have these berths cost the captains ten gold a day — rather expensive waiting charges. The darkness gave us the added benefit of being able to sneak everyone aboard without raising any suspicions.

Initially, Ariadne and Alekto went onto the Matteo Brothers caravel, though we would later transfer them over to our ship to help them learn new ways of caring for their needs. Initially, we wanted them to enjoy their boyfriends and to begin to learn the language spoken in Velona. Everyone else boarded our Banca del Dio ship. Normally, the ship carried fifty security guards, but because Dianna expected them to be a rather long time on Demokritos, all but five hopped onto other Blanca ships as they docked during the last months. The crew of seven and five guards remained to secure the ship. Thus, we had plenty of cabin space for everyone.

Since we couldn't sail until high tide around noon the next day, Dianna suggested that she and Andreas, along with the security guards pay a visit to Patri in the morning shopping for the tools she would need to free us. On board, they had a full carpentry shop, but hardly anything for metalworking.

Our first action on getting aboard was to sleep! In the morning, we women had to make a decision about our clothing. All of us wanted out of these confining dresses and boots. However, Ania pointed out, "You know, after getting used to these corsets, we do look smashing in our dresses and they are rapidly becoming *the* thing in Velona. It would be a shame to take them off and then not be able to get back into them and our fancy dresses. Besides, just look at the sheer number of fancy dresses that Princess Maren left us! I vote that we leave our corsets on, but that we wear our usual comfy clothes and shoes."

"I do love how terrific you look in yours," Dianna grinned. "Let's!"

"As long as I don't have to fight, I will go along," Ilenakova added as a precautionary note. Kali gave her a big hug. A bit later, we were all dressed in our usual leathers, with Dita and I wearing soft moccasins that we could easily remove to use our feet for things, just as soon as these contraptions were removed. We all felt a whole lot better now.

While Ilenakova struggled to feed us, and we struggled to swallow without choking, Dianna and Andreas left to do some shopping. The guards accompanied them as a safety precaution. They returned around eleven with several bags of tools — quite a lot of saw blades, I noticed.

As noon approached, I heard a loud argument coming from topside. The others headed up to see what was happening. Dita and I dared not show our heads, so we left our bodies and floated up to see for ourselves.

The portly harbor master was arguing with the captain. "No, you simply cannot set sail at high tide today. You have to wait for permission, and they won't be able to get to you until at least four this afternoon," he declared antagonistically.

"Look, high tide is about now. We can't wait until four; the tide will be out by then. Tell them to get organized. Time is money in the shipping business."

"Too bad. You've been parked here for months. What's another day or two?" he bantered back.

"We've got our sailing orders and that's that. They can do whatever they need to do in the next ten minutes, then we are sailing," our captain argued back.

"That's impossible. You set sail, and the Dragon will blow you out of the water!"

"Are you threatening us?" our captain yelled back. The harbor master stomped off the gangplank in a huff.

"Well, they insist on a full, complete inspection before we can sail. Won't happen before four, and we'll be stuck here another day," he explained to Ilenakova. "Your call, but I don't think that they would dare shoot us with their cannonae."

"Idiots. If they shoot at us, they will regret it!" Ilenakova stomped her foot on the deck. "Set sail."

"Aye, aye." The captain barked his orders. On the Matteo caravel, their captain followed suit. Mooring lines were dropped, and ever so slowly, the two big ships began to glide away from the dock. Meanwhile, Ilenakova, Dianna, Kali, and Ania all stood at the railing, keeping a sharp eye on the Dragon, a modified caravel with six cannonae sticking out amidships on either side. We would have to sail right past her, as she was anchored far out in the harbor waters.

Twenty slow minutes passed as the two caravels inched out of the port, pivoted, and got into position to lower the main sails. Just then, We heard two distant explosions, and saw two blasts of flames puffing out from the cannonae pointed our way. "Damn! They really are firing upon us!" our captain yelled. Two great splashes rose up across our bow, sending spray onto the foredeck, soaking one crew member, who cursed.

At once, Ilenakova cast her Protector spell, Push. She sent a large wave of water smashing into the side of the Dragon, which rolled heavily in response, tipping thirty degrees to port. "You wanna fight it out?" she yelled at the distant gun ship. Of course, they couldn't hear her.

Boom! Boom! Boom! Three more salvos fired at us! As the first splashed even closer to our bow, I became worried. The second nearly hit us! Dita, angry as usual, moved and shoved the third flying ball out of the way so it landed harmlessly before our bow.

That does it! Ilenakova, give another Push. Bethany, you and I grab hold its main mast. When the push hits, let's pull it over, she sent to us.

Ilenakova cast another of her Push spells. When the wave rolled onto the side of the ship, Dita and I pulled on its top mast. Oops, we pulled too hard. The Dragon rolled over onto its side. Men began jumping overboard. *That'll teach them to mess with us!* Dita sent.

Our captain and crew, as well as those on the other caravel, stared awestruck. "How did you do that? Freak wave or something?" the captain asked Ilenakova.

"Taught them not to mess with us, that's all. Let's get out of here," she replied. He issued more orders and the crew dropped all the sails. A few minutes later and both ships picked up speed rapidly, leaving the floundering, sinking Dragon far behind us.

We were on the Little Lady and our captain was Cesare Rino. The Matteo Brothers ship was called the Matteo Express, captained by Drago Ettore. Both were seasoned captains in their late thirties. Cesare's wife, Elda, was the ship's cook.

We eight occupied the four passenger cabins, while our twenty Utu women paired up into ten of the below deck cabins usually occupied by the security men. Now that we were finally underway, we congregated in the galley, where Elda made a big fuss over our predicament, promising to make a healthy mush for us to eat. Dianna gave us a thorough examination, found no infections, and declared that the wounds were mostly healed. That was something anyway. Now she and Ilenakova began to work on us with their new saws, while Ania and Kali worked with Athena and Andreas.

While he spoke acceptable Velona dialect, he wanted a brush up. Athena needed to learn our language from the basics onward. Plus, Ania began to show her how to do simple things for herself, beginning with feeding herself. Unfortunately, they all quickly discovered that her corset was interfering. Regrettably, she had them remove it for now. At supper that evening, one incredibly proud person fed herself, well mostly. Athena was beginning to regain her own self-respect.

Meanwhile, everyone took turns sawing away on us two. That night, the top bolts were cut and our top lip plates were free. By the next night, our bottom plates were freed. This was a necessary step in the undoing process, Dianna explained, but it really didn't help us much at all. So our lip plates could move a little now. The rings still forced our mouths wide open.

The next day, Dianna told us that she would be working on the bars that held the rings securely in our mouths. Yes! Two more long days of tedious, careful sawing passed before finally the rings could be removed. Oh, how sore our jaws were, but what a relief finally to be able to close our mouths! Now we could at least eat properly, if not drink from cups. The annoying lip plates interfered with that.

Dita now explained, "Okay that was the easy part. The hard part will be to get these contraptions off. Based on how the others went, I'd estimate that we will need about two weeks of sawing."

"Arghhhh!" Dita yelled loudly.

"Well, Dita, we are dealing with fired iron here, very hard stuff. They make swords out of this stuff. Look, see here, we need to saw through here and here and here. Then it should swing open on the hinges on the other side," she explained, pointing out the spots on my headpiece for Dita.

What about me just pulling it apart? Nothing is really in the way, Dita asked.

"Well, if you concentrated a pull here and here against here and here, it might bust them open, but honestly, you'd have to have super strong muscles to do that."

Well, I don't aim to be another two weeks caged like this! I'm going to try it.

Be careful, Dita. You might hurt yourself, I cautioned her.

She moved out of her body and latched on to the stress points Dianna indicated. She began to exert her pulling force, gradually bit by bit increasing it. We watched, Dianna very closely. After a few minutes, we could see the metal bending. Suddenly, the contraption flew open and fell onto the floor!

".eh! .es!" Dita exclaimed. *I'll get you free now, love.*

I felt her pulling on mine. I would have kept my fingers crossed if I had any. I held my breath; don't know why I did it though. I felt a violent jerk, and my encasement flew open, falling to the floor as well. I was finally free!

".eh! Wa. to go! Tha.k .ou!" I yelled free at last.

"Dia..a, what a.out these disks?" Dita asked, barely understandable.

Dianna carefully removed our lip plates. I felt a relief of pressure from my two lips, naturally. The fleshy pair of lips now hung down several inches, flopping about our chins and dangling below them. We both could see that the wounds had fully healed. I had a bad feeling about this.

Dianna sighed. "Well, the good news is that they are fully healed. No chance of infection anymore, completely healed up very nicely. Er, the bad news is now I can't just stitch them back together anymore. I mean I can stitch them but they won't grow back together, since the halves have fully healed up. Like stitching two fingers together, it won't accomplish anything."

".ou .ea. we are goi.g to .e like this alwa.s?" Dita wailed, sort of understandably.

"Well, when we get home, maybe Sandra will have some ideas of how to fix your lips. It's beyond my skills. I am truly sorry, Bethany, Dita," Dianna looked terribly upset that she couldn't do anything more for us.

My Special Helper came up to us and wrote extensively on her pad, "Take out disks when eat. Leave in until go to bed so don't catch on stick and rip. Rip is very bad. Worst thing can happen."

I nodded that I understood. She wrote more, "If disks get loose and drop down, make larger disks. Larger disks get too heavy, knock out front two teeth."

Dita moaned when she read that. Loose or not, neither of us were going to remove our teeth! We thanked her for her advice, and she looked pleased that she could help us again.

We tried speaking with the lip plates out to see if we could be more understandable. Not really was the result. We now lacked lips where they ought to be. Certain vowel and consonant sounds were just impossible to make. Plus, we both quickly realized that she was right. If we went around with our lips hanging down loose, we ran a high risk of their catching on something and tearing them, leaving us with dangling strings instead. Begrudgingly, we allowed Dianna to put our disks back into place once more. We looked like duckbills; we might as well get used to it, at least until Sandra could have a look at us.

Chapter 50 The Utu

Two months of sailing lay ahead of us, before we would reach the Southlands. Now free of the contraption, I began to work out how we could return the Utu princesses safely to their homes. The problem was complicated because of the war going on across the Southlands. Finally, the natives had rebelled against the Megalos slave traders. Waves of these warriors raided the gem mines, gold mines, and smaller villages, which Megalos men operated.

In response to these butchering raids, Megalos sent in legions of Centurions and legions from Demokritos. Now, however, the soldiers from Demokritos had been recalled, leaving the Southlands a no-man's land. Adding to the complexity was my desire to reward these selfless women with a small herd of cattle each, something highly prized in their nation.

Where could we safely dock? Where could we get between one and two thousand cattle? How could the cattle be transported to their homes? Where actually were their homes? How could we avoid the hostilities taking place there? Yes, I had some difficult problems, which needed answers.

I borrowed a map of the Southlands from our captain. Of course, it was a sailor's map, showing the coastline and ports. Most of the inland area was blank space. I showed it to Iua and the other Utu women and asked them, "Ca. .ou show .e where .our ho.es are at o. the .a.?" I had to repeat it several times. Iua wrote on her pad if I could write it, duh, no hands. I didn't let that stop me. I sat down, picked up her pencil in my toes, put her pad on the floor with my other foot, and wrote out, "Can you show me where your homes are at on the map?" Of course, my antics brought smiles and giggles from the women.

Athena looked at me with a shocked look on her face. "You can write with your feet?"

".es, I'll show .ou how," I replied. Iua shook her head no. None of the women had any sense of the larger geography of their land. I didn't let that stop me. I had another idea. I brought the captain in on this. He was familiar with all the coastal ports. I had the women describe the port from which they had first boarded their first ship. After many pages of notes and questions, he determined that they had set sail from Cape Hope.

That was the breakthrough we needed. They described their journey from their homes to that port. The captain and I did a bit of dead reckoning as he called it, and we now knew that their homes were located about twenty-five miles into the Veld northwest of the Coastal Range behind the port, a region relatively inaccessible.

Armed with this data, I contacted Sandra and asked her to make inquiries about where on the southern Veld we could buy a thousand or two head of cattle and how we might be able to move them to the Utu nation. It took them a week to find out. She contacted me, and I gave her the go ahead to set it all up.

There was a rancher, Stephanos Straton, who raised cattle on the Veld close in on the Coastal Range. He shipped cows back to Megalos quarterly, using the port of Cape Hope. She sent a Banca del Dio representative there to arrange the cattle deal. We were nearly halfway to the Southlands, and the timing could not have been better. They would arrange the deal about a week ahead of our arrival. The problem for us would be the war that was going on all across the Veld. I figured I'd worry about that when we got there.

In the meantime, we had the responsibility of educating three women on how to become independent, namely Athena, Alekto, and Ariadne. On a calm day, we moved the two over to our ship and Dita and I began showing the three how to do things. Athena proudly demonstrated feeding herself. That impressed Ariadne and Alekto immensely and the three threw themselves wholeheartedly into the challenge of learning new ways. Dita and I also needed the practice ourselves. We had been depending on our new arms for some years now and had to limber up and remember just how it was that we did certain things. Combine all this with continuing language lessons and now writing lessons, and we five kept very active for the long weeks at sea.

For Dita and me, our biggest hurdle came in trying to figure out a reasonable way that we could drink from a cup without making a complete dribbling mess of it. Without lips and only teeth, the fluids continually dripped out. At last, we gave up and just used a spoon.

Finally, on July 1, 742, we made landfall, and a day later found Cape Hope and sailed into its small docks. Half of the town had been burned to the ground! The raiders had come more than once. Two thirds of the population had been either killed or had fled for other places. It was more of a ghost town. The docks could handle three ships at one time. However, only the Lucky Lady docked. The Matteo Brothers anchored just off shore to wait for us.

Also docked was another of the Banca del Dio ships. As soon as we docked, Desi Ercole hailed us. We joined him on his ship. Ilenakova did the introductions, though he and all the many crew and guards stared at Dita and me. They just couldn't pry their eyes off our faces. Kindly, he didn't ask about us, thankfully. I had no idea of how to explain our lip plates to others yet.

"Yes, the cattle deal has been completed. He charged at least twice what they are worth, mind you, but Sandra said to get them at any price. I've a map that shows how to find his ranch. However, you are going to need a guide, someone who knows the inland Veld. He'll get you in and get you out. I've found one who knows the area well; unfortunately, he is a slaver and is not to be trusted, but he's the only one around who is familiar with the indicated area. It is a remote area that you are heading for, you see. His name is Raul. When you are ready, I'll take you to meet him. Oh, here is the cattle contract to verify that you are the purchasers." He handed the document to Ilenakova.

We found Raul in the last remaining bar in Cape Hope. He was currently arm wrestling with another brute of a man. Raul was a heavyset man with solid muscles and bronze skin. His stubble face was long overdue for a shave. He won the match and sauntered over to us. He stared at Dita and me, "Well, you remind me of some slaves I fetched a number of years back, but you ain't Utu though. Name's Raul. Guide you anywhere in the Veld."

Ilenakova introduced us all. "We got ourselves a little problem, Raul. Those women you kidnaped, well, now you get to help us return them to their homes."

"Whatever you say, though it's mighty strange that you'd be want'n to return them. Rax was very specific, says he needs two dozen very special women. Well, business is business, especially these days. Get'n slaves out'o here is now far too risky. Black savages everywhere are on the warpath. Hit Cape Hope here twice now. Most folks left. You want 'em back home, Raul's your man. Going to cost you plenty, though, highly risky venturing onto the Veld these days. Are you plan'en on take'n an army there with you?"

"No, six of us women and the Utu women, that's all, and you, of course," Ilenakova replied.

"You nuts lady? You's just gon'a get yer'selves stabbed with a spear is all and me too!"

"No chance of that. We can take care of ourselves; you just guide us where we need to," she replied.

"Suicide trip, that's what this is, going to cost you plenty," he protested, balking at the offered deal. I suspected why. He was probably the most wanted man in the area by the Utu's and many other tribes. Still, we needed a guide, and he was our only choice. I gave Ilenakova the okay.

"Will this make it worth your risk?" she tossed one of the fifty grand diamonds onto the table.

I thought that his eyes might actually bulge out of their sockets! He held it, felt it, and kissed it. "Damn fine gem. You ladies have a deal. I'll get you all there and back. I take no responsibility for your safety at all. I keep this as advance payment. When do we leave?" Raul replied. I could almost read his mind. With this one gem, I can retire and live like a nobleman!

"Is tomorrow okay with you?"

"Yes, indeed," he grinned. They discussed what else would be needed. He planned to bring along a horse for each of us and make the slaves walk. We vetoed this as we realized that they probably didn't know how to ride. Besides Dita and I now would have difficulty holding the reins because of the lip plates. Instead we bargained for two wagons to carry us; he would drive one and Ilenakova, the other. He would provide the provisions.

She then told him that we would first be going to Stephanos Straton's ranch to pick up a herd of cattle. This worked out better, he said, since the wagons could get to his ranch from here more easily.

The Utu women were very happy to know that tomorrow they would begin their homeward journey. I could tell from their eyes; they couldn't smile, of course.

In the morning, our bunch headed ashore to find Raul. He was ready with the wagons. We six wore our leathers, though it was very hot out, the dead of summer. After they helped Dita and me onto the wagon, the twenty Utu women climbed on board. Off we went, but not before a wild scene, in which the women recognized one of the men who had abducted them, Raul. They made big noise, until Ania told them that we were making him take them back home.

We headed northeastward, and Iua wrote that this was the wrong direction. Ania explained to them that we had to pick up their new herd of cattle first. "Each of you will get around sixty cows." This brought a lot of strange clicking and chattering sounds, which I suddenly realized was their own private language! While they could not speak normally with these large lip plates, they, nevertheless, had developed their own language consisting of sounds that they could make. I regretted that I had not discovered this before. I could have learned it by now and thus spoken with them more readily.

As we rolled along, the heat was oppressive. The Utu women, still wearing their gowns from the court in Demokritos, began taking them off and tearing them up. As we watched, they proceeded to turn the remnants into their own native style wrap-arounds. They were naked from the waist up, and the wrap-around only fell to their knees. The also removed their shoes as well. They were going home and wanted to look properly dressed!

The trail wound its way up the Coastal Range and was scenic, but hot. The second day, we left the mountains and reached the level ground of the vast savannah, the Veld. Around noon, we rolled into a giant, sprawling farmstead. Many hands were visible, all armed to the teeth with weapons. Cows were everywhere.

Stephanos looked like what I imagined a rancher might. Tall, thin, wiry, he vigorously shook hands with the four, "Welcome to my ranch. I have the cattle rounded up for you." He was fiercely independent — he had to be to be out here in the middle of a vast, largely uninhabited savannah. He offered us lunch, but we wanted to get going as soon as possible. He led us to the large holding field where over a thousand cows were milling around, anxious to get out once more.

Once we explained that these were their cattle and were now trying to figure out how to move them, they jumped out of the wagons dashed around looking for small sticks. As they then moved in among the herd, Iou came up to me and wrote out, "We are ready to drive them home. Which way?"

"Okay, Raul, lead on; they will be driving the cattle after us," Ilenakova called out. By now Stephanos and a dozen men stood watching the unfolding spectacle; some were laughing. Raul climbed aboard and rolled off westward. We watched, as these women, making all sorts of cackling noises, got the cows moving, quickly dividing them up into bunches. Each woman managed her group, we quickly discovered. By choice, Ilenakova kept our wagon in the very rear of the herd. "Rear guard," she called out. We waved goodbye to the amazed ranchers, well not Dita or I, of course.

The heat on the savannah was almost unbearable. Soon, our leathers were soaked, and Dianna exclaimed, "I'm going native!" she stripped off her clothes completely and rigged up a piece of their dresses as a wrap around too. "Much cooler. Try it"

"Oh do you look sexy," Ania teased her. Soon she too went native. Before long, we all were "native." Well, Raul would get a good look, that's for sure. Ilenakova kept her leathers on, primarily because she had all manner of weapons on her as well as the gemstones tucked safely in her bosom. She was driving, albeit at a slow walk.

At camp that night, Raul's eyes roamed from woman to woman, eyeing us greedily. He was mightily amused, that's for sure. "Two more days," he informed us.

The next day, we saw nothing but scattered trees fighting for survival, tall, sparse grasses, and occasional wildlife. Not another single soul did we see. Dianna and Ilenakova had white skin, the rest of us light brown to bronze. Dianna began to sunburn badly and finally was forced to find ways to shade herself. "Told you that was not a good idea," Ilenakova called out. She continued to sweat it out in her leathers.

The second day passed identically. One could easily get hopelessly lost out here, I realized. There were so few landmarks to use as your anchor points. Yet, Raul continued, as if he knew precisely where he was heading. We rolled slowly along, the women cackling and switching the cows on before them.

Suddenly, as if out of nowhere, a dozen brown skin men rose. We six had our inner alarms fire, signaling that danger was at hand, but we were at the back of the line. The Utu warriors all had spears and shields. So sudden was their appearance, that Raul had no time to react. Six spears hit him before he had drawn his gun to fire. Up ahead we could see the trouble now. All six of us were standing in the wagon trying to see ahead.

Our women began making loud noises, and the warriors spread out, looking very surprised to see them and the cattle. By the time that we pulled up next to the other wagon, the twenty women were dancing around the surprised men, chatting away in their own language. They looked at us and were even more confused. Two looked similar to their own princesses. Now I wondered if the men and women could even communicate with each other. If not, we might be in big trouble.

Certainly, they were uneasy with us six and made motions with their spears that we should get down out of the wagon. We complied. Several came up to Dita and me and touched our skin, which was a very different color than theirs. At last, they made up their minds and motioned for everyone to follow them. Two began leading the wagons, while the Utu women ran back and got their cattle moving once more. Ilenakova, as she walked past the body of Raul, snatched our diamond back. "He'll not need this anymore. I guess he really was a wanted man out here."

Late that afternoon, I saw smoke curls and knew that we must be close to their village. Soon, hundreds of men with spears swarmed around us, but did not actually threaten us, only intimidated us. We walked along as if we belonged here. Nothing like displaying a little confidence. Soon, we entered their village. Many huts sprawled across the landscape. We saw many women and children playing, but they all stopped to stare at us and the cows. At the far end of the village, we spied a number of women come out to see what was going on too. Ah, these women also wore lip plates! These must be more of their princesses, we assumed.

At last, we stopped before one hut, and a tall, thin man with brown skin stepped out. Everyone became silent, and he walked up to us. The twenty princesses quickly came forward and began their usual cackling noise, really their language. He raised his hand and they shut up. He looked closely at Iou and then said, "Iou?" She waist-nodded. A big grin flashed instantly across his face. Rapidly he went down the line of women calling out their names. Each waist-nodded in response. Now he gave each woman a big, warm hug. His smile was huge. He spoke something, but we could not understand his language, but his arm swept over the huge herd of cows, now grazing on the tall grasses, quite contented. Each of the women again waist-nodded.

Iou looked at me and then him and came to me. She no longer had her pad; she knelt down and wrote in the dirt, "Otona, leader, king."

We all repeated his name and waist-bowed, though we need not have; we were not wearing the restrictive neck coils. He grinned. Now Iou began to try to explain all this to him. Slowly, I realized that he could not understand her cackle speech; she could no longer speak their language. Instead, she drew pictures and he spoke. This strange conversation went on for at least a half hour before she finally thought that he understood at last. She wrote for us, "He knows you rescued us and gave us cows. You will be highly honored. Feast tonight. War is over now. Princesses are home."

That was a surprise; we'd just ended a war. Iou led us into the village, while our other Special Helpers personally escorted each of us into their village. We were led to the huts of the princesses. Here we were introduced to the many other princesses. I was shocked to see that the oldest of these women had a top lip plate that was a foot across! Her bottom plate was slightly larger. Many of the older women had plates almost as big. They all cackled among themselves and hugged each of our returned Utu princesses.

While the women were celebrating, others prepared the evenings feast for us all. Iou wrote in the dirt, "Otona wants if you four want lip plates too." That was easily answered. She then wrote, "Otona wants to make Bethany and Dita proper princesses. We put neck rings on you now. You can take off when you want. Big honor if you do this." We consented; at least we could remove them! Dianna watched carefully as the princesses gathered around us and began two wrap the long spiral brass around our necks. Ugh. When they were done, Dita and I realized that these were nowhere near as bad as the solid rings that the Mano del Dio had forced us to wear. We still had some head movement, unlike before. Still they were heavy.

As dusk fell, we shared their feast. Men played music and danced for us. In all, we were accepted as dear friends of the Utu Nation. Later, we were allowed to sleep with those that we had brought back. In the morning, they replenished our water bags.

Iou brought us a present from the many princesses. She wrote, "Princesses give you these disks. When yours get loose, use next size larger. You will now have high honor when you return to your home. We all thank you." She handed us a large sack filled with the disks. We bowed in their fashion, and she hugged us.

Ilenakova asked her, "Our guide was killed. We do not know the way home to Cape Hope, where our boat waits for us." Iou ran off to find Otona. After a few minutes of confused discussion, she finally got him to understand. He nodded and spoke. She came back to us and wrote, "Otona sends six warriors. Guide to mountain pass. Two days."

As we prepared to climb into our wagon, all the princesses came to say goodbye and hugged each one of us. At last, Ilenakova lifted Dita and me into the wagon, and we got rolling once more. Two long, hot days later, we arrived at the Coastal Mountains and the pass, which began the long descent into Cape Hope. Here, the six warriors left us; they said something, but we could not understand it.

After we were about halfway down, Ilenakova called back to us, "Do you all want to go through Cape Hope dressed as you are or not?" She was teasing us. A bit later, she stopped, and we changed back into our leathers. They undid the neck spirals as well. By evening, we walked back onto our caravel, ready to set sail for home, Velona.

In our quarters, Dita and I examined the gift of the disks. "Oh .y! I do.'t wa.t to ha.e to wear those!" exclaimed Dita with a panic-stricken look. Four were around a foot in diameter!

"I thi.k we are screwed," I finally admitted to her and myself. Our lips had healed up; the two sections were now wholly separate. After all, fingers don't suddenly grow together, or toes. We both looked at each other and then leaned into each other, resting our heads on the other's shoulders, comfortingly.

During the night, we set sail once more, though we missed the event and woke up at sea once more. At least now, we could watch the coastline of the Southlands off our starboard bow. We continued to practice doing everything with our feet and helping Athena, Ariadne, and Alekto learn as well. A strong comradery developed between the five of us, as one would expect. Their grasp of our language improved steadily as well, and everyone now spoke Velona dialect only, reverting to Demokritos only when they misunderstood something. At least when we arrived, they would be able to speak and understand our basic language.

Dianna very carefully went over our long ago discovery that four of us living close together was an optimum arrangement. They realized now how this was so, as Ariadne took a turn brushing out Alekto's long dark blonde hair. I began to wonder if perhaps somehow we five should live close together. Obviously, Ariadne and Alekto would soon marry the Matteo brothers and probably want to live with them. At least the two of them working together could get by. Joining forces with them was not too likely. Athena and Andreas would also marry soon, and he had a shipping business and his own home. She, we worried about the most. Living alone as we are is very tough, whereas two can more easily manage things, with four being an optimum number.

On the other hand, Cosima had been able to somehow do something to the energy field around our bodies causing them to generate our missing hands and arms. While it had taken nearly five years to re-grow them properly, it had worked. Would it work again? Could Cosima work her miracle on us a second time? Could she work it on our three new friends? If it would, we'd only have to endure this for five years at most. This then was the pivotal factor I concluded.

That evening, I relaxed and contacted Cosima. *Hi. Bethany here. You've heard that Dita and I managed to lose our arms again, haven't you?*

She laughed, *Yes, you two just can't seem to keep them attached to your bodies.* She giggled again.

Can you do it to us again? What you did to start our bodies making new arms, I asked.

Have you noticed them growing yet? she asked.

No, why?

Well, I did it again to both of you several times now, since we heard that you lost them again. I was hoping that you'd tell me that they were re-growing already. You don't see any sign of them at all? She sounded concerned.

Wow. Cosima, I'm proud of you for doing that for us all on your own. No, no signs at all, not on me and not on Dita. This isn't good, is it?

No, I don't know why they haven't started yet. Maybe because you are fully grown now. When you get back I will try again. How soon will you be here?

Thanks. About four more weeks. Maybe around the first of August. I miss all of you.

We miss you too. Do you really have duckbill lips? That must be really strange.

Unfortunately we both do now. It is going to be horribly embarrassing for us, and we don't speak very well like this.

We love you all the same, Bethany. We all miss you and Dita a whole lot.

We miss you all too. Thanks. Bye.

Well, that was disheartening, to say the very least. Perhaps Dita and I are going to have to pay the price this time. I related what I'd learned.

"This is .ot good, is it?" she said.

Chapter 51 Miracle Aboard Ship

A few days out from Cape Hope, the Matteo brothers wanted to come aboard to chat and one morning when the winds were low, the transfer was made. After a round of passionate kissing with their girlfriends, Dario asked if we could all have a long talk about the future and their fiancés. Andreas wanted in on the talk as well. We six and the six of them headed to the galley, while our cook rustled up some tea and biscuits for us all.

Dario began, "Bethany, we wish to get married right away, just as soon as we possibly can. We were all thinking that perhaps you could arrange it so that we could all marry at the same time in the Church of the Holy Rose in Velona. We know that they honor women like ours, not condemning them. We owe them the chance to start out by having others respecting them and not thinking less of them because they once gave up their arms. Is this possible?"

Dianna spoke up before I could. "Oh certainly! My sister, Lona West Po Benez, is the High Priestess of the Universalist Church of the Three Holy Roses. I'm sure that she would love to perform your ceremonies. My mom did it for us six, but she and dad retired. I'm sure that first she will want to make you three women blessed as honored Holy Roses of the church. Mom did it for us," she stopped short, almost revealing too much, that we had been Holy Roses!

Fortunately, Andreas broke in rather excitedly, "Your mom was the leader of Velona! Now I get it! Wow, I didn't put it together before. Gang, her mother used to be the monarch of Velona! Now the duties are divided between her brother and sister. Bale runs the fiscal part, and Lona handles the religious sector. Cool, Dianna. We are with real Velona royalty here!" That diverted the talk for a few minutes.

Suddenly, Andreas opened his eyes wide, and I knew that he finally had put it all together. Our cover was blown! "Wait a minute! Dianna — now I remember! You — you were like Athena! Weren't you abducted by the Mano del Dio and taken to Dorota and tortured and lost your arms? I remember hearing about that. You came back with — oh my god, these are the ones! But you have arms? There were six of you that came back — you were all armless. I know I am not dreaming this up! You are them, aren't you?"

"What's he talking about?" Luigi asked, confused.

Dario interrupted, "Hey, I recall hearing about that too! They returned armless! High Priestess Lana West Po's daughter, Dianna, came back to Velona along with three from Dorota and two from Megalos. The six were armless, now I remember. You have to be them, but how?" Now Dario looked confused. Athena, Alekto, and Ariadne looked first at Andreas, then

Dianna, then Dario, then all six of us, just as confused as their boyfriends.

Well, it was bound to happen. Eventually, one of them would recognize who we six actually were. We might as well tell them about us now. I really wanted to explain about us to them all.

".es, .ou are right. That's us," I tried to say, but realized that I had better let someone else explain it all to them. "A.ia, Dia..a, will .ou tell the. all a.out us, .lease?"

"I suppose that we had better — now that the beans are out of the pouch," Ania grinned. "Where to begin? Well, it all started when the Guardian asked Bethany to go to Dorota to see if we had missed finding more of the mantis creatures. Er, that won't do will it?" She looked at the still confused faces?

"Who is this Guardian? More mantis creatures? What are they?" Andreas asked for the five others as well as himself.

"Golly, this is harder than I thought. Okay, we are spiritual beings, immortal, and we've had lots of bodies — lifetimes here on Tarra," Ania tried again. "A long time ago, Bethany was the wife of the Great Messiah, Jes Amir, who this whole Church of Jehosanity has totally perverted and altered from what really happened way back then." The three Demokritos women gasped. "Yes, nearly everything that your crazy church preaches about their Great Messiah is a total fabrication and/or alteration. Anyway, when Jes died, he went on a crusade to help free all us spiritual beings from total dependence upon our fleshly bodies. He's now called the Guardian, and he is about the most powerful being that I know."

"After Bethany lost her empress' body," Ania continued.

"Wait, what empress body?" Athena interrupted.

"Oh, she was Maren Elizabet, your one time empress, Athena, before Deimos married Eirena. She died in childbirth leaving Dita, well he was Renzo then, to have to raise their child. Anyway," she was interrupted again.

"You — you were Empress Maren Elizabet?" Athena exclaimed, her eyes wide opened. Alekto and Ariadne simply gasped. "Now it begins to make sense — how you knew so much about everything and the palace and the secret escape tunnel!"

"Wow! Oh!" interrupted Alekto, her sudden wild excitement changed to wonderment as her thoughts caught up with her realizations. "You were like us, armless. Well no wonder you could do so well!"

".es," I replied, wishing I could smile.

"Anyway, as I was saying, the Guardian and others discovered that all the women on this newly discovered island of Dorota were armless. Everyone thought that there must be more mantis creatures still on Tarra," Ania continued, until she realized that they didn't know about the mantis creatures. She backed up once more and gave them an explanation of the mantis creatures, what they did, and how we had been systematically eliminating them here on Tarra.

Four hours later with lunch in the middle of all this, Ania and Dianna finally finished their long explanations. Next, Kali told them about our rescuing some little girls who had lost their arms to the Elders of Dorota here in Velona and that we had adopted them. She explained how we had worked our therapies on them and that they had become somewhat precocious, highly talented, very able spiritual beings. Little Cosima had made some startling discoveries about our fleshly bodies and had managed to trick ours into re-growing our lost arms.

"Well, it took five years for them to come back," Ilenakova interrupted. "Mine are only now back to the strength that they should be at. That's how come I was able to toss my sword a hundred feet into Khristos' head, thank goodness."

I decided to let them know about Cosima's attempts with Dita and me. "Cosi.a has bee. tr.ing to get Dita a.d .y ar.s to re-grow. .othi.g has ha..e.ed .et. It .ay .e that our .odies are .ow .ull. grow. a.d her tech.ique wo.'t work o. us .ow. She'll try it agai. whe. we get back. I. it works, do .ou wa.t to gi.e it a tr. too a.d see i. .our ar.s will re-grow too?" I gave up and sent telepathically to everyone. *Cosima has been trying to get Dita and my arms to re-grow. Nothing has happened yet. It may be that our bodies are now fully grown and her technique won't work on us now. She'll try it again when we get back. If it works, do you want to try it too and see if your arms will re-grow too?* These lip plates were really beginning to annoy me!

Of course, all three were ecstatic about such a miracle! For another long while, they chatted about such a miracle and how it would turn their lives around. In the meantime, they really did want to learn how they could manage life things on their own as we used to do and that Dita and I now had to do so once more. The three men wanted to know if it would be possible somehow for their three fiancés to live either with us or close to us.

Just then, Linda and the Guardian made contact with me. *Hi, Linda here. The Guardian wants to know if this is a good time for us to come and have a long chat with you and everyone, including the three queens that you have rescued.*

Sure, Andreas finally figured out who we really are and we've been sitting here for hours telling them about us. Right now, we are all trying to figure out ways for us armless ones to dwell together, so we can help each other. I am hoping that Cosima can do her magic on us again, though so far she's not been able to convince our bodies to re-grow arms again. We think it's because our bodies are now fully grown. Perhaps that has something to do with it.

"E.er.o.e, the Guardia. a.d Li.da wa.t to talk with us. This ought to .e i.teresti.g," I said.

Suddenly, the ghostly images of Linda and Jes appeared here in the galley. Even our cook dropped everything and stared at the miraculous sight. Their bodies seemed real enough, but a bit thin, with a slight yellowish glow around them.

Jes spoke, "My dear Bethany, you've managed to pull off another miraculous feat. Had the Church of Jehosanity managed to retain control over the rulers of Demokritos, millions of souls would have been in dire jeopardy of dropping further in tone and vitality. All Tarra would have suffered enormously. I wanted you to know that I am sending a number of the Givers of the Holy Gift to Demokritos. They will work behind the scenes to provide necessary therapy to the thousands of women who have lost their arms to the Church's misguided Holy Ceremony. In time, I will see that all who desire therapy gets it."

"Tha.k .ou!" I replied. The three queens echoed my thanks as well.

Athena, though totally in awe, added, "The therapy that Bethany gave us has given us a totally new vitality on life. We three are so more alive than we have ever been, even if we are doomed to have to live like this. For all other women like us in our country, please accept my sincere appreciation and thanks." She still held on to her queen's attitude, I noted.

"Thank you, Queen Athena," the Guardian acknowledged her. "I am aware of what Cosima has discovered. Yes, these fleshly human bodies are capable of repairing an enormous amount of damage while in the womb and even during body growth. One day Cosima may learn even more of the spiritual powers that we all innately possess, but which so many have forgotten about or have hidden them from view. I wish to lend some assistance to you five, who have been so instrumental in freeing Demokritos from the clutches of the Church of Jehosanity."

"Because your bodies are fully grown, Cosima's method will fail. However, there is another way. If you will allow me?" he asked.

"Sure," I replied, glad that the word was say-able.

He leaned over me and touched my shoulders. I felt a warmth, a soothing feeling, I felt warmth in my arms and hands. My fingers tingled. What? I looked down and I saw two arms at my sides! Everyone else saw them appear as well! A dozen gasps resounded around the galley. I raised my new arms and hands and just stared at them. "Tha.k .ou!" I exclaimed, totally shocked. I knew that Jes had done this to others centuries ago. I sighed a huge sigh of relief.

Now Dita was making similar exclamations. I turned to her and saw her staring at her new arms, just like her old ones! Athena let out a shriek as her old arms suddenly reappeared. Likewise, Ariadne and Alekto! What was our first action with our new arms? Dita and I threw ours around ourselves and hugged each other tightly. Likewise, Athena hugged Andreas; Alekto, Luigi; and Ariadne, Dario! The men had tears flowing down their faces, so great was their surprise, joy, and emotions. We had witnessed five absolute miracles, as far as we were concerned!

The Guardian then spoke once more, "One day, Bethany, you will realize that this is really not a miracle, but commonplace, a mere trifle of what your true potential actually is. However, I admit that I have an ulterior motive here. In a while, I will have another dangerous mission for you and Dita and your friends to tackle. You will be better able to handle it if you have your arms back." I began to wonder what was in store for us next.

Meanwhile, he chose to face and address the three queens. "Alekto, during your therapy sessions, something precious has been awakened within you. I would like to encourage you to pursue that to its fullest. Mankind will forever be grateful that you did so." She flushed, how did he know that?

"I promise that I will," she said very softly, still totally at a loss for words. She knew that she must be in the presence of God's son.

"Ariadne, you have tasted of greatness and your heart desires to create more. I also urge you to pursue doing just that. Again, the entire world will benefit from it for generations to come."

"I will," she squeaked. How did he know her most private thought and desire? She had not even spoken of it to Dario yet!

"And you, Athena, your mind has been opened, as you know. Like a child who first sees how a thing works and cannot ever stop working out how other things operate, so shall you be now. I urge you to continue to fulfill your thirst for knowledge, and you will find what you have been searching for, and many others will ultimately benefit from it."

"Yes, I promise that I'll not squander or waste this godly gift that you have given me," Athena finally found her voice. How did he know that she now had an unquenchable thirst to know?

"We've taken up enough of your time now. In a few years, we will return asking once more, my dear Bethany Madelyn Amir, for your help."

"We'll .e readi., Jes. Let us k.ow whe.," I replied. He gave me a hug, and the two ghostly forms vanished. For a moment, we all stared spellbound. Then, everyone began yelling, cheering, and dancing wildly around the galley! We five had just received what we considered a true miracle, a renewed lease on life!

"He's real! The son of God is real!" Ariadne said as she danced around the tables, unable to contain her happiness. Exuberance, yes, that and incredible relief might best describe our intense feelings. We felt like we might explode.

Dita took hold of me and suddenly looked annoyed, "Da..! I forgot to ask hi. a.out these li. .lates! Da..! Da..! Da..!" I laughed, we were so in awe over getting our arms back, we forgot these stupid lip plates!

"Well, .a..e Sa.dra ca. do so.ethi.g a.out the.," I replied.

"This is surely a holy miracle!" Luigi interrupted us. "This changes everything! Now my dear Alekto is whole again, and we don't have to intrude on you and your family for help! Thank you, Bethany. We owe you more than we can ever repay you. If you ever need anything that we can do to help you, say the word!" Alekto, Ariadne, and Dario echoed his

642

sentiments. They decided to transfer back to their caravel and get out of our hair. They did promise to keep our secrets safe, however.

"Bethany, the Guardian says that I must continue my thirst for knowledge. Would it be possible for me to come to your home during the daytime when Andreas is at work and learn all that I can? Would you and your friends be willing to teach me things? There is so much that I crave to know now. Like he said, it is an unquenchable thirst that I have now," Athena begged.

".es. O. course .ou .a. co.e! We'd .e ha... — glad to teach .ou!" I replied. She gave me a big hug.

Andreas now shook my hand, grinning broadly. "I'm the first to shake your new hand," he teased. "I want you to know that we will always be here for you — all of you! You need something, give a holler." I gave him a hug.

The two lovers then headed up on deck to be alone. Ania commented, "Athena is out of her head most always now. I bet I can make her into one fine Judger!"

".o! I will .ake her i.to a Wid!" I teased.

".o! .rotector," Dita teased back.

"Oh no, you are all wrong, I'll make her into a Healer and Engineer like me," Dianna joked, playfully and gave us all a hug. Then, she added, "Seriously, what are we going to do about your lip plates?" I shrugged. I had no idea and began to think about how Dita and I could deal with the embarrassment when we were in public.

With our arms back, things quickly returned to mostly normal for us all. Now Dita and I could deal with our duckbills as needed; others did not have to feed us any longer. We did spend considerable time alone trying to figure out a way that we could live with these without being totally humiliated all the time. As the days passed and we drew closer to Velona, Dita and I both noticed that our lip plates were hanging lower and lower, drooping downward. About four days from Velona, they were more like hanging straight down.

We both were in tears as we finally got out the sack of disks that the Utu women had given us. The original disks literally would not stay on us, and we had no choice but to move up in size to the next larger set, which stretched them out horizontally once more. Our top plates now were three inches in diameter, while our lower ones were three and a half inches across. After we both got them in, we looked at each other. Now they were sticking out straight once more, but our skin-lips again felt stretched tight! We hugged each other tightly.

A bit later, Ania commented, "Well, that does look lots better, you two. I guess that you can always say that this is the very latest in fashion. After all, if we can wear these extremely high heeled boots, wasp-waist corsets, and gargantuan hoop skirts and call that high fashion, then surely, you can call your lip piercings high fashion as well. If you want to do that, we will all back you up."

As Velona drew closer, this was the only avenue left for us to avoid horrible embarrassment and humiliation when we were out in the public arena. Dita suggested that we wear our Annelise outfits there as well to further back up our claim to high fashion. I agreed as long as she wore the canary yellow satin dress, but I ended up agreeing to wear the cherry red one for her.

Chapter 52 Back Home in Velona

On August 10, 752, Velona appeared as a small dot on the horizon. Andreas brought Athena on deck so she could catch her first glimpse of her new homeland. We all joined them. For the next hour, the huge city slowly grew before our eyes. Andreas was the first to point out the Holy Rose Church and, begrudgingly that of Jehosanity. We women were wearing our fancy Annelise outfits, ready to meet our families and friends, looking like we were indeed in the height of fashion. Even Ilenakova agreed to don hers, a detail that Kali loved, having pummeled her with passionate kisses as an added incentive.

As we began the last glide into the docks, I counted over a dozen caravels either loading or unloading. Athena had never seen a port quite as large as ours. On the other caravel, neither had Ariadne seen as large a port as Velona was, nearly double the size of her Patri. Alekto commented that her port of Andros was as large as this, however. Now I spied our welcoming party!

Everyone had shown up to meet us, our entire large families. All began waving as they spied us on the deck. We waved back. Once the gangplank went out, we began our very careful descent to the docks. Navigating the three-foot wide path in a dress the flared out six feet in front of us coupled with the impossibly high-heeled boots was challenging. None of us fell into the water, thankfully.

Gracefully, although far too slow for our family, we all glided perfectly toward their outstretched arms. A long round of hugging and chat ensued, with many comments about how Dita and I looked. Then came the introductions to Andreas and Athena along with Luigi and Alekto and Dario and Ariadne.

Sandra and Arturo Bastiana, now both twenty-eight, introduced their now seven year old triplets: Renzo, Enyo, and Len. Luisa and Enrico Angela, also twenty-eight now, introduced their seven year old triplets: Elizabeth Lilly, Kallisto Ann, and Alex.

"Oh! Now I get it!" Athena finally grasped the dual bodies. "Dita has Renzo here and Bethany has Elizabeth, Dianna has Enyo and Ania has Alex. Cool. Kali has Kallisto and Ilenakova, you're Len. Got it! Pretty cool, this time you have it all worked out right." Everyone roared; we did indeed.

"And these are our little girls," Ilenakova introduced our girls. "This is Fina, ten, she's my little one. This is Kali's, Jemma, she's eleven now. Alessa, ten, is Bethany's girl, while eleven year old Bianca here is Dita's. Cosima is the eldest as you can see, she's twelve and is Dianna's girl, and Elena is eleven and is Ania's. We've quite a group here."

Cosima spoke up, "Yes, now that I am twelve, Dianna is going to let me start wearing the fancy dresses that you are all wearing! You all look absolutely beautify! Why do you walk so slowly? Oh, mom, I'm now a junior Velona Detective. Bale finally appointed me. Honestly, after I've solved five cases that his detectives couldn't, he'd better have! When I am fourteen, then I can be an official Detective."

"Mom, can I get my lips pierced like yours?" Bianca asked. "Yours looks so neat. Did it hurt a lot?"

".o!" Dita replied.

"Oh, I can? Wonderful! When," Bianca asked excitedly, misunderstanding Dita.

No! No! No! A frustrated Dita sent. Bianca's face soured momentarily.

Sandra interrupted the now constant chatting of our young girls long enough to say, "We've a carriage for each of you fellows. I know that you are anxious to show your fiancés around. Please, drop by our place 42 Hampton Way tomorrow around five. We've planned a large welcome home dinner for everyone. You six simply must attend. We are all dying to meet you and hear about everything, especially the girls. We won't take no for an answer. Dress informally, please. With this many kids running around, we seldom dress formal. Oh yes, Dianna's extended family will be there too, so you can ask the High Priestess about your weddings."

The six agreed and gave everyone a hug before they headed off to their carriages. The large staff of the MBE had now gotten off their caravel and waved to us as they headed for more carriages. We then headed for ours, our girls chatting madly, with Bianca and Alessa begging to have their lips pierced so that they could look as unique and great as we did. Arturo and Enrico already had arranged for our many bags and crates of Annelise fall outfits donated to us from Princess Maren to be delivered to our estate later today. Already crews were beginning to unload them. "How many fancy dresses did you bring back, mommy?" Alessa insisted on knowing. "Can't I at least try some on? After all, I am now ten years old and almost eleven."

Bianca, not to be left out, peppered Dita, "Mom, I ought to be allowed to wear some too, since I am almost twelve, well, eleven and a half, but that's close enough isn't it? Cosima gets all the fun just because she's twelve."

".es, .ou ca. try the. o.," Dita gave in, ".ut, .ou'll .e sorr.!"

"Mom, you talk funny," Bianca added, "but you look really great! Please, can I get mine done too?" Dita and I both began to laugh.

At the same time, my little Elizabeth body said excitedly, "Now Renzo, we can run and play again; they are back!"

"Cool! I sure haven't liked sitting around for so long. Mom kept saying that we would distract ourselves," Renzo added. I looked at Dita and we chuckled again. We'd forgotten all about this bit of added confusion.

Evidently, Sandra and Luisa had been keeping our other bodies quiet while we were gone, so as not to distract us.

Three days later, the three young couples were married by High Priestess Lona West Po Benez in a lavish ceremony attended by our huge family and many of the men's families and their production company. For their honeymoon, the three decided the smartest move was to take their brides on a tour of the sector, showing them the sights and allowing them to become familiar with their new country.

As things finally quieted down, Sandra took Dita and me aside to begin to see if there was anything that she could possibly do for our lips. She commented, "Already they have stretched way beyond their original size, which is not good at all. Worst case scenario, I could remove the lip loops, but then you would look strange without lips. You would be noticeably disfigured. Your teeth would always be showing and it certainly won't help your speech any, but you would not have to wear the disks. Or we could just leave the disks out and hope for the best, but that also looks strange, seeing those two large loops of lips dangling down in front of your mouths. You'd have to be careful not to catch them on things, but no disks."

".ut we'd still look like .reaks!" Dita protested, hope sinking.

".e'd .ot ha.ve to lose our teeth," I consoled her.

"One thing I could try is to carefully re-cut along the inner, now healed edges, and then try to sew them back together. Because of the stretching, it might not look right at all and the scarring will be extremely noticeable, I'm afraid. Plus, it might not work," Sandra concluded.

She added, "Perhaps the best thing would be to leave the disks out except when you have to go out in public. That way, the stretching would be minimized and large disks would not be needed for a long time, perhaps."

"I like the re-cut," Dita said.

"Don't forget, Dita, this is all just a wild guess on my part. Nothing like this has ever been tried before. With any surgery, there is always a great risk of infections. Here it could well prove fatal, so close to your head. Plus, there is no real guarantee that it will even work," Sandra cautioned.

"Let's lea.e the disks out exce.t whe. i. .u.lic, Dita, a.d see how it goes. The. wo.'t stretch .ore that wa. I. it does.'t work out, we try surgery," I suggested. Begrudgingly, she agreed for now.

Now we fell into a normal life pattern finally. Athena came by daily to study with us. Yes, she began official Druwid training, but also she and Cosima spent time together. Cosima began working her therapy sessions on Athena and carefully training her on how to do it to others. It seemed that there was nothing that Athena was not interested in learning!

On Friday nights, we all dressed up in our Annelise outfits and went to the Laird Foundation arts events; some were plays, some were music concerts, and some were art shows. However, we all opted to wear Alexia boots instead of the much higher heeled Annelise boots. Because we had so many outfits in so many sizes, we allowed our girls to also dress up in them as well. Since they were not fully grown yet, many of the tighter corsets fit them, whereas they would be torture for we adults to wear. Yes, we allowed them to wear Alexia boots as well. All six really felt quite grown up and extremely proud, when we all went out dressed to the hilt. We even dolled up our seven year old triplets as well, but not in such extreme fashions.

On Saturday nights, we all went to dances, where music and fine dancing prevailed. Often, Andreas and Athena would join us. Sunday afternoons was family time, when we took them horseback riding, on picnics, or just playing in the parks. After three months, Dita and I felt far less worried about our unusual appearance in public, looking like duck bills. Most just thought that we were going a bit overboard on fashion, thankfully.

As the Yuletide time approached, Dario and Luigi invited us to attend the grand opening of their new theater. They'd pooled their funds, with major contributions from Alekto and Ariadne, to purchase a much larger building and renovated it to be *the* theater in Velona. Elegance was their byword: plush red carpeting, fancy brass lanterns, which burned the very latest invention of gaslights, finely polished wood, and seating to match. Actually, the best seats in the house were in either the two balconies or the front row. Here they seats were wide enough for our billowing dresses.

Neither brother would give us a clue about what the grand opening show contained. They kept saying that it would be exceptional and that we all had to dress to the hilt for it, since we would be in the front row, taking up the center twenty-two seats. "Bethany and Dita must sit in the exact center of the front row. Our wives insist upon this," Dario had said. With so many women and girls to get dressed up, as usual we began in the early afternoon. The show was at six. At last with all hairs brushed out, dresses adjusted for the tenth time, the impatient boys' hair combed, we at last climbed into our many carriages.

Arriving, as we stepped out of the carriages, well dressed doormen offered all the ladies a hand stepping down. Once inside, equally formally attired ushers led us down to our very comfortable seats, and they insisted that Dita and I take particular seats. We were facing the curtained stage, about five feet above it. There was an empty orchestra pit below us. As we chatted and waited, neither Dita nor I really cared whether others were staring at our duckbills or not. Our attention was on the grandeur of this new hall, which held seven hundred people at one time. By six, the entire place was packed. We saw many other women dressed as we were in Annelise outfits sitting high above us to our left and right in the balconies.

The lights dimmed and Dario, wearing a fancy tuxedo walked out on the stage, to a polite round of applause. "Good evening ladies and gentlemen, girls and boys. Tonight is a very special night, very special indeed. We are premiering two brand new works for your entertainment. There will be a twenty minute intermission between the two works, so that the stage can be adjusted. At this time, MBE is proud to turn the baton of our orchestra over to Alekto Matteo who will conduct the largest orchestra ever assembled in her brand new work called Symphony Number 1, entitled Romance. It consists of four separate movements. Please withhold your applause until the fourth movement is finished so that you may experience the full range of the symphony. Ladies and gentlemen, let's welcome to the stage composer and conductor, Alekto and her Symphony Number 1!"

While the audience began applauding appropriately, Alekto glided onto the stage, wearing a light blue, satin Annelise dress. Her dark blonde hair draped over her shoulders and fell below her waist. The curtain pulled back revealing a sixty piece orchestra. Her baton rose, and then she made a sharp downward gesture; the music began. A loud driving rhythm began on the lower instruments and drums; gradually their theme was picked up by the violas, then the violins and finally the woodwinds. Such a sound we'd never heard before. So compelling was the music that I could not keep from tapping with the beat. When she finally finished the first movement, the audience broke into a thunderous applause, instead of waiting for the whole piece to be finished. She had to turn and face the audience several times, bowing and accepting their appreciation before she could continue.

In stark contrast, the second movement depicted a springtime pastorale. So moving was the theme, so realistic the melody and sound, so moving, that at times, I alternated between having shivers all over my body to tears trickling down my cheeks. When she finished, the applause was utterly deafening. Folks began shouting, "Repeat! Repeat! Repeat!" Soon the whole theater echoed with that chant. She had no choice by to replay the second movement. The third movement was an orchestrated set of variations on Lyneth's Lament. I cried throughout it; I couldn't help myself; her music just pulled the emotions out of me!

The rousing fourth movement again brought the house down, forcing her to have to repeat it once more. When she finished, she received a standing, thunderous ovation, which didn't die down for five minutes! It took the intervention of Mario to finally quiet them down, announcing a twenty minute intermission. Not long after that, Alekto, grinning broadly, glided out to us.

"That was the .ost i.credi.le thi.g that I ha.e e.er heard!" I exclaimed.

She beamed, "Here, I have an autographed copy of the score. I have dedicated it to you and Dita." She handed us a thick package of musical score pages. "It is starting to come out of me now; the flower is beginning to open up. I owe everything to both of you." We chatted a bit, before others began coming up to her and complimenting her wildly.

Twenty minutes flew by quickly. Before we knew it, Dario was back on stage once more. "Ladies and gentlemen, if you will all take your seats, we will present the second half of this premier concert. It is with extreme pleasure that MBE is now introducing a new art form to you this evening. It is called opera. It combines an exciting story line, musicians, singers, and dancers — all to tell you the tale. Please welcome Ariadne Matteo's first opera, The Beggar in Disguise done in three acts. Let's give her a big hand, as she will conduct the singers and dancers in this premier performance of her work, while I conduct the musicians." I now noticed that the pit had filled up during intermission.

Ariadne walked out onto the stage, her long auburn hair flowing behind her. She wore a pink satin Annelise dress and glided into her position off to one side. Now the curtains parted to reveal a highly decorated stage. One side looked like a palace of some kind, while the other side appeared to be a street within a town. Quietly, the singers dressed in all manner of costumes walked on stage and took their initial places. Ariadne turned to Dario and gave a slight nod, he brought his baton down, and the lively overture began, a catchy tune that the audience immediately began to enjoy. Ariadne, now no longer the focus of anyone, raised her arms and began conducting the singers.

Lucinda, a princess, was pining for her lover, Adolfo. A bit later, Adolfo was on the streets, hearing some gossip about his love, Lucinda. The fellows were teasing him that she might not be faithful to him. He concocted a plot to disguise himself as a beggar and see if he could get her to betray Adolfo. Later on, her handmaiden got wind of the plot and told her about it. And so the convoluted, but highly entertaining plot began to play out. The songs, the music were enchanting, plus the singers sung the talk, instead of a play in which they would have merely spoken the words. More than once, the audience demanded a repeat of a particularly memorable aria or tune.

When the opera finally ended, with Lucinda and Adolfo embracing and proclaiming their undying love for each other, the house once again broke into a thunderous applause, another standing ovation. Because of the huge crowd, we remained seated until many had filed out to the giant lot where the many carriages had been parked. A bubbling Ariadne, escorted by Dario, glided over to us, while we chatted about these two incredible works.

"Hi. Hope you liked it. I too dedicated my first opera to both of you. Here's an autographed copy for you," she explained. "Alekto and I are both hard at work on our next ones."

"I told you that these women were incredible, didn't I, when we first met down by the Ice Sheet," Dario said proudly. "They have invented entirely new musical forms. The crowd absolutely loved it. We've never had such a reception before. Plus, tonight, we grossed over a thousand for three hours work."

"Dear, untold hours of rehearsal time, not just three," she corrected him.

"Yes, yes, but we give three performances a week at a grand each! We can afford even more lavish costumes and sets. We've hit the big time as showmen, but the real winners are our two incredible wives! Can you believe all this from them in only three months' time?"

Indeed, these two new art forms were the talk of Velona the next day. They played to sold out houses for months and months. Hundreds of years afterwards, these two composers are still perhaps the most famous in the music world. Alekto's twenty-one symphonies are studied by every would-be composer and conductor. Ariadne's twenty operas are still performed today, centuries later. Yes, we never missed a premier of their new works. Never had we heard such music, such singing. Often, we returned to hear it all over once more. A year later, the MBE moved into an even larger theater, which would hold nearly a thousand at one time and even this was woefully insufficient to meet the demand for performances.

The Guardian was quite right about these two women. Their combined works helped elevate societies worldwide. We knew that we had done a job well worth the doing.

The End.

Other Books by Vic Broquard

The Return of the Wizards: Twelve Companions – The Making of Wizards (fantasy)